SKELETONS

IN

THE

CLOSET

SKELETONS IN THE CLOSET

Barbara Ann Sterr

SKELETONS IN THE CLOSET
Copyright © 1998 by Barbara Ann Sterr

All rights reserved. No part of this publication may be reproduced, stored in a retrieval system, or transmitted, in any form or by any means, mechanical, photocopying, electronic, recording, or otherwise, without written permission.

Manufactured in the United States of America.

ISBN: 0-9664702-0-6

Library of Congress Catalog Card Number: 98-090450

This is a work of fiction. The characters, incidents, and conversations are products of the author's imagination and have no relation to any person or event in real life. Any resemblance to actual persons or events is entirely coincidental.

Copyright permission and / or purchase information can be obtained through E-MAIL skeletonsinthecloset@juno.com

This book is dedicated to my beloved husband,

Kenneth

who has encouraged me in my endeavors.

Also, to the treasures of our life together, our children,

Kevin

Tim

Troy

Roxanne

Christy

Contents

Chapter 1: Departure	1
Chapter 2: Mysterious Person	33
Chapter 3: Deadly Disease	53
Chapter 4: Seduction	98
Chapter 5: Scheme and Betrayal	154
Chapter 6: Fiery Death	212
Chapter 7: Dreaded Secret From the Past	259
Chapter 8: Illegitimate Child	310
Chapter 9: The Rape	332
Chapter 10: The Deception	394
Chapter 11: The Suicide	452
Chapter 12: The Abortion	481
Chapter 13: Child Abusers and Bootleggers	516
Chapter 14: Deadly Accident	560
Chapter 15: The Explosion	587
Chapter 16: Meddling Sister	630
Chapter 17: Terrifying Stranger	664
Chapter 18: Attempted Murder	690
Chapter 19: Evil Brother	735
Chapter 20: Last Wish Before Death	759
Chapter 21: Sinister Memories	778

Chapter 1
****
Departure

The shrill cry of a rooster woke Della Aslen from her deep sleep. She opened her dark-brown eyes and looked about the room as she rested for a few more minutes in the comfort of the soft, warm feather bed.

The bedroom was small and tidy. It was furnished with crude pine furniture. Opposite the double bed, which she lay in, was a chest of drawers with a mirror hanging over it. Next to the only window in the room, a crib stood.

Della slowly pushed the multicolored patchwork quilt off herself, crawled out of bed, stood up, and stretched. Quietly, she walked to the window draped in white sheer curtains and pulled up the dark-green shade.

As she looked out the window, rays of early morning light began to filter over the rounded, forested mountains. The pyramid-shaped pine and spruce, clothe in their darkest green dress, nodded in the mild breeze. At the base of the mountains, a few young trees sprinkled the blanket of green that covered the meadow. Fluffy big white clouds, which looked like heaps of cotton, scattered the immense blue sky.

At the edge of the meadow, a gray, weather-beaten barn stood in solitude. A clear, blue stream rippled lazily past the side of the barn and snaked around several ancient oak trees that stood like columns near its lily-dotted edge. As the green tree leaves danced in the breeze, Della could see several dull-colored birds with long tails and slender beaks resting among the branches. She was going to miss all that.

Sadden by the thought, Della turned from the window and looked at her two-year-old Otto sleeping so snug in his crib. Soft, blonde curls outlined his small face. His pink fat checks moved ever so slightly as he occasionally sucked his small thumb between his rosy lips. Della gently replaced the part of the soft embroidered blanket that had moved off his small rounded shoulders.

She tiptoed over to the feather bed where her husband Phillip had his face buried in a white pillow. Della shook his strong, broad shoulders.

Slowly, the head of massive black hair turned around. Phillip looked at Della with his bronze-colored face and stretched his tall body under the covers. Beneath his well-trimmed black mustache was a soft smile.

"Good morning," said Della as she bent over and kissed him.

Phillip sat up, grabbed her hand and gently kissed it. "I love you," he said. He tossed off the quilt and sat at the edge of the bed for a few minutes as he gazed out the window.

Della took off her blue nightgown and put on her long-sleeved, floor-length purple dress which fit snugly at her tiny waist. She buttoned the white buttons on the bodice with her small fingers and then straightened the white collar. After brushing her long dark-brown hair, she tied it neatly together behind her head with a white ribbon. She folded her nightgown neatly and placed it inside the open pine trunk, which was setting beside the front of the bed.

Phillip, clothe in his underwear, got off the edge of the bed and walked to the back of the bed where Della had neatly hung his clothes the night before. He put the white shirt, dark trousers, and vest over his muscular body. Grabbing his gold pocket watch off the doily that garnished the chest of drawers, he checked the time. He fastened the watch to his vest, then tucked it into a small vest pocket. After putting on his ascot, he sat on the bed that Della had just finished making to put his shoes on.

Della grabbed the doorknob and waited until Phillip was ready to leave before she opened the door. As she opened the door and they entered the kitchen, they could feel the warmth of the fire in the fireplace and smell the aroma of the coffee cooking beside the flame.

The kitchen was a fairly large room. A long wooden table, with benches, set in the middle of the room. The wall, opposite the bedroom door, was lined with a fieldstone fireplace and a sink which drained outside. Next to the sink was a large wooden water barrel from which they dipped water. The wall between the fireplace and bedroom was lined with a three-foot high stack of dry wood.

The crude kitchen door opened. A small, gray-haired woman, whose body was bent from years of hard work, walked in. In her one crippled hand, she had a basket filled with a small block of cheese and several big white eggs. When she saw Della and Phillip, a smile crossed her wrinkled, pale face.

"Good morning, Della--Philip, are you excited about today?" she asked.

"I'm excited and saddened. I'm going to miss you and Papa," said Della as she grabbed the black iron kettle hanging over the sink. She dipped it into the water barrel until it was half full of water and then put the kettle next to the coffeepot on the fireplace crane.

The old woman took the eggs out of the wicker basket and put them into the kettle.

Della went over to the other side of the room. Beside the bedroom door stood a roughly made credenza. Della opened the credenza's doors and took out several of the stacked stoneware plates and set them on the table.

Phillip grabbed his jacket, went out the door, and walked down the unevenly worn wooden steps. As he walked the dirt path to the barn, his shoes occasionally touched the grass that was heavy with dew. The songs of the cuckoo, lark, and thrush filled the quiet crisp morning air. When he got to the barn door, he took a deep breath and admired the beautiful scenery for a few minutes. He wondered if there could ever be a place as beautiful as this where he was going.

The wooden peg in the iron hasp had been removed from the barn door, so Phillip pulled on the hasp to open one of the doors on its rusty hinges.

Inside the barn a skinny man, with a shiny balded crown and gray hair on the back and sides of his head, sat on a three-legged wooden stool. The old man was sitting next to a brown cow's slender back legs and hand milking her. "Sh-sh-sh-sh" was the rhythmic sound the milk made as it hit the metal pail.

"Good morning, Pa," said Phillip as he walked past the two small cone-shaped piles of hay setting on the dirt floor. He stopped next to where his father was sitting.

"Good morning, Phillip," his father replied. Next to the cow were two, three-foot high rectangular stalls. Inside one stall was a black horse with white markings. The horse had short, heavily feathered legs and a long, coarse black mane and tail. In the other stall there was a brown horse with short, black feathered legs and a black mane and tail.

Hanging from the dusty wooden barn rafters were two single-rein bridles. Phillip reached up and took the bridles down. With the bridles in his hand, he went over to the stalls. He patted the horses' rumps so they would move over and allow him into the stalls. Once inside the stalls, he bridled the horses and led them out to the front of the barn. There he hitched the horses to the farm wagon, which was setting in the barn opposite the stalls. Phillip opened the other front barn door. He climbed up onto the wagon, sat on the wooden seat, grabbed the reins, and signaled the horses to move forward. Once the wagon was outside, he signaled the horses over to the stream where they drank the cool, spring water. Phillip jumped from the wagon, secured the horses to a tree, and then went back into the barn to see if his father needed any help.

His father had just finished milking the cow. Beside the stall was a metal milk can from which Phillip removed the cover and into which his father poured half of the milk. After putting the cover back on the can, Phillip carried the can out to the stream where he submerged it in the cool water. He secured the can so it could not tip over or perhaps roll down the stream with the current.

His father closed the barn door as Phillip walked over to the horses, took hold of the bridle, and led the horses to the front of the house. His father, carrying the pail of milk in his hand, walked with him. Both knew this would probably be the last time that they'd walk the path from the barn to the house together. As they looked at each other, they knew each other's thoughts. Phillip secured the horses then put his arm on his father's shoulders as they walked up the steps.

Meanwhile, inside the house, Della was in the bedroom finishing packing things into the trunk.

From the bottom of the dresser drawer, Della pulled out a

beautiful, winter-white crocheted bedspread. Della slowly rubbed her hands over the soft, neatly folded bedspread.

As she looked at the bedspread, her mind began to wander into the past. She could see her bedridden mother, sitting and resting her back on several pillows. Her white hair was pulled neatly back into a bun. Lying beside her on the bed was a ball of yarn. In her small dainty hand was a large crochet hook. Sometimes she'd crochet all day and far into the darkness of the night. Next to the bed was a small dresser on which set a tattered Bible and a gas lamp, which flickered in the darkness of the room. Two days after finishing the bedspread for Della, her mother had died. She deeply missed that dear sweet woman. Della caressed the bedspread to her heart. Tears filled her dark-brown eyes and rolled down her brunet complexion.

"Mama." The sound brought Della back to the present. Otto was standing in his crib, hanging onto the rail, and shaking the crib back and forth.

Della quickly stroked the tears from her eyes and wiped her sniffing nose.

"I'm coming, sweetheart," said Della. She put the bedspread into the trunk, walked over to Otto, and lifted him out of the bed. Gently, she kissed and hugged him before she placed him on the coarse wood floor.

Otto's little feet started to toddle toward the open bedroom door. Della quickly grabbed him and put him on the feather bed. She took off his pajamas and grabbed his clothes that were neatly hung on the back of his crib. Over his short, fat legs she put white tights and dark breeches. A white shirt and dark jacket covered the top part of his body. After combing his fine hair, she set him on the floor, and he toddled up to the threshold of the bedroom door.

Della folded the pajamas neatly and put them into the trunk. She closed the trunk, put the hasps down tight, and locked them with a padlock. The key for the padlock was on a metal chain, which she put around her neck and tucked inside her dress.

As he stood in the threshold, Otto watched his grandmother. She was putting square pieces of fat pork, slices of bread, a jar of honey, and boiled eggs on the table.

Della gently picked up Otto, walked into the kitchen, and set him on one of the long wooden benches that stood at the kitchen table.

"Well, good morning, my sweet little one," Otto's grandmother said as she smiled. She put her wrinkled hand around the bottom of his dimpled chin and kissed his pink cheek while she hugged him.

"I have something for you," she said. She took a cooked egg, removed its hard shell, and placed the peeled egg on the plate in front of Otto. Then she untied her russet apron and put it around his neck so he would not soil his traveling clothes.

The kitchen door opened and Philip came in with his father. His father gave the milk pail to Phillip's mother who filled Otto's glass with milk.

Phillip and his father went over to the water barrel, put some water into the sink, and cleaned themselves before they sat at the table.

Della took the coffeepot out of the fireplace and filled the cups with steaming black coffee. After the prayer, there was silence at the table while they ate. In their mind, everyone was imprinting the memory of their last few hours together and cherishing every moment.

After breakfast Della washed the dishes while Phillip's mother dried and stacked the dishes inside the credenza. When they had finished, Phillip's mother sat at the table as Della continued to tidy up the kitchen.

Otto sat on a colored braided rug in front of the sink. As he sat, he played with a miniature iron fire wagon, driving it back and forth over the floor and rug.

Phillip swung his legs over the bench, got up, and walked over to the credenza. He opened one of the drawers and took out a newspaper and a piece of paper. He sat down again on the bench next to his father and placed the pieces of paper in front of them.

"It took me some time to figure this timetable out for the train. But once I figured it out, it was easy to understand. According to this, our train leaves the station for Bremen in about three hours," Phillip said as he looked up at the pendulum clock setting on the fireplace's wooden mantle. "It's seven o'clock now. So by ten o'clock we should be on our way."

Phillip put the timetable aside and opened up the newspaper. After turning a couple of pages, he pointed to a section of a page.

"According to this ad, I have to stop at this place, the American Consul in Bremen. The Consul will give me directions and names of people who can help me find a place to purchase. It is very important that I don't lose this ad," Phillip said. He tore the page with the ad on it out of the paper, folded it neatly, and put it into the inside pocket of his jacket.

Phillip rose from the table and walked over to the water barrel. He moved it slightly. As he knelt on the floor, he removed a small section of a floor board revealing a hole. A little wooden box was inside the hole. After picking up the box, he sat by the table again. He opened the box and pulled out the money that was inside.

"According to the ad, a boat ticket should only cost us this much," said Phillip as he counted out a certain amount and set it on a pile. "Just in case we can't get a ticket right away and have to stay in Bremen, we better put this much aside to hold us over," Phillip said as he counted out a certain amount of money and put it on a separate pile.

"And this I'll carry in my pocket to use as we travel for food and lodging," Phillip said as he counted out a few extra marks and put them into the pocket inside his jacket. He took off his shoes, took the money from the two piles, equally divided it, folded the money, and placed it inside his shoes. He put his shoes on.

"I don't think we will need these few marks. So I'll leave them for you and Ma," Phillip told his father. He put the marks inside the box and then put the box back into the hole in the floor.

Della, who had finished tiding up, went into the bedroom and put on her purple cape and bonnet. She took her purple drawstring purse off the dresser and put a roll of yarn and a crochet hook into the purse. Also setting on the dresser was a small, dark, wide-rimmed hat. Della grabbed the hat, went into the kitchen, and put the hat over Otto's curly hair as he played with his toy.

"Otto," said the grandmother as she put her arms out in front of her motioning Otto to come to her. Otto got up with his toy in his hand, walked over to her, and sat on her lap.

Phillip looked at the clock again. "Well, I think it is time to go." He rose from the table and went into the bedroom. A few minutes later he came out carrying the trunk. Phillip's father got up and opened the door for Phillip. They both went outside. Phillip lifted the trunk onto the back of the wagon. Then he climbed up and pushed the trunk up to the back of the wagon's front seat.

Della and Otto came down the steps and stood beside the back of the wagon.

Phillip jumped off the wagon. He lifted Della onto the back of the wagon. Once on the wagon, she walked over to the trunk and sat on it.

Phillip took Otto's hand, and they walked to the front of the wagon. Phillip helped his father climb onto the seat and then handed Otto up to his father. His father grabbed Otto and put him in the middle of the seat.

"Ma, are you coming?" called Phillip.

Soon the figure of the old woman appeared in the doorway. A white bonnet covered her neatly combed gray hair and a white crocheted shawl hung over her drooping bony shoulders. In her hand she had a small package.

She closed the door and walked slowly down the steps. Phillip went to help her walk down the last few steps. With his arm in hers, they walked to the back of the wagon, and Phillip lifted her onto it. Slowly, she walked over to the trunk and sat on it next to Della.

"Here is some cheese in case you get hungry on your trip and you can't stop to get food," Phillip's mother said as she handed Della the block of cheese wrapped in unbleached cheesecloth. The cheese was aged; it had an overbearing smell.

"Thank you," Della said as she took the cheese and placed it inside her purse.

Phillip walked around to the front side of the wagon, climbed onto the seat, and sat next to Otto. Taking hold of the reins, he signaled the horses to move.

Della had a feeling of loss and sadness as the wagon slowly moved down the winding road, and the farm became smaller in size until it finally disappeared. She tried to hold back the sentimental tears, but some managed to roll down her cheeks. Nothing would ever be the same. There was so much that she'd miss. She turned slightly away from Phillip's mother and slowly wiped the tears off her cheeks.

As the horses pounded the rough dirt road, dust would fly about their hoofs and the spoked wooden wagon wheels. The wagon moved along in a bumpy manner. Occasionally, the wagon wheels would hit a big rut in the road, and the wagon would suddenly jolt almost knocking Della and Phillip's mother off the trunk.

The wagon traveled through the rolling green hills, past neighbors' houses and barns. It soon passed a small, white clapboard church with six stained-glass windows. The church was nestled among tall green pines and blue spruce trees. It had a tall, white steeple that rose far above the sloping, wooden-shingled roof.

Della's mind again returned to the past. Memories of her wedding day three years ago flashed through her mind. It was a beautiful sunny day in June. Della was dressed in white from head to toe and had a bouquet of garden-cut daisies in her hand. Standing beside her was her father, a tall, dark handsome man. They were waiting at the bottom of the church steps for her sister Clara and Charles, Clara's husband. Before long, Clara and Charles arrived in their farm wagon. Clara, a bit chunky and short, was Della's maid of honor. She was dressed in a sky-blue dress with puffed sleeves that tapered to the wrist. Charles was dressed in a dark suit, tie, and white shirt. He was Phillip's best man. Phillip's parents had only two children. Phillip was the only one alive. His older brother, Franz, had died thirteen years before their wedding in the Franco-Prussian War. The other person deeply missed at Della's wedding was her mother. She had died a year before their wedding on Della's eighteenth birthday. They had a small wedding. There were only a few neighbors sitting in the carved church pews when Della entered with her arm wrapped around her father's arm. Della remembered how beautiful the altar had looked that day. Vases full of red, yellow, pink, and white flowers arrayed the wooden altar that was draped in a long, white linen cloth. The most beautiful thing about the altar was the carving of the last supper in the front panel of the altar. An old, hand-carved wooden cross hung above the altar and looked down at them as they knelt and said their vows. With their eyes, they promised that they would love each other forever and ever and ever.

After the church service, the few relatives and neighbors who had been in church held a joyous celebration at Phillip's parents' house.

The surprising wedding present of one thousand marks from

Phillip's parents on that day made this venture, which they were now embarking on, possible.

They were going to buy a farm in the area with that money. However, one Sunday a German Catholic priest, who had visited America, spoke at their church. After hearing him tell about the marvelous opportunities in America, Della and Phillip decided that was what they wanted to use the money for. However, by then Della was pregnant and not feeling well. Therefore, they decided to wait until the baby was born and old enough to travel. Time passed swiftly, and what they had talked about so much was finally a reality.

The church slowly disappeared out of sight. Graceful white birch trees growing among the green pines crowded near the edge of the road. As the wagon rattled over an old beam bridge made of wood and slabs of stone, Della turned to Phillip's mother.

"Why don't you and Pa join us in America after we are settled?" asked Della. "We will send you the money for the trip and you could live with us."

The loving old woman looked at Della, smiled, and gently touched Della's hand.

"That is very nice of you, but I was born and lived all sixty-three years of my life here. My parents and Phillip's brother are buried here. My friends are here. This is home, a familiar and comfortable place. America is a new and strange place. I dread the thought of dying in a strange place so far away from people and things that I've known all my life. When I die, I want to die in a familiar place. It is fine for you young people to go. You have a whole life ahead of you, but my life is almost over. Perhaps you think I am an old foolish woman, but a familiar place makes the thought of death less frightening and more peaceful," the old woman sweetly explained.

"Well, if you ever change your mind, you know Pa and you will always be welcomed," replied Della as she hugged the little adorable woman whom she had grown to love so dearly.

Before long they were traveling down the narrow, cobblestone streets of Bayreuth. As they slowly passed the large three and four-story white buildings setting close together, Della remembered the music festival that Phillip and she had attended last year in July. People from all over Europe had crowded the streets that day. The loud "hustle and bustle" noise of the street filled the air. Della remembered grasping Phillip's hand so she would not get separated and lost within the crowds.

The streets were different today, only the "clip-clap" of the horses' hoofs on the cobblestone and sweet laughter of children playing echoed in the still air of the morning.

On one side of the cobblestone street there were several small girls. They had neat braids tied with brilliant ribbons and wore clean faded long dresses. They were singing nursery rhymes as they jumped rope with a piece of gray clothesline.

Shortly, thereafter, the wagon passed several boys of different sizes. They were busy playing marbles. A few of the boys had faded knee-patched trousers. Other boys had worn-out shoes and holes in the elbows of their dirty plaid shirts.

The wagon stopped in front of a little red building enclosed in a large platform. Above an open door the word DEPOT was printed and painted in big white letters. People with black trunks and brown bags were sitting on the red wooden benches that were on the platform.

Phillip jumped off the wagon. "Wait here," he said.

He walked inside the open door and disappeared.

Inside the building more people with luggage were sitting on benches. Opposite the door, which he had just entered, was the ticket window. Phillip walked over and looked inside. A uniformed man was working at a paper-cluttered desk.

"I'd like to buy three tickets for Bremen," Phillip said.

The uniformed man turned around in his black swivel chair. His dark, beady eyes looked over the wire rimmed glasses, which rested on his protruding large nose. He looked at Phillip and asked, "What do you want?"

"Tickets, three of them," replied Phillip.

The man raised his stout body from the chair and walked up to the ticket window. He searched through items behind the window for a few minutes then he placed three tickets on the window counter.

Phillip looked up at the price chart hanging above the man's desk. He reached into his jacket's inside pocket and pulled out some money. He counted out the right amount and pushed the money toward the man's hand. The man took the money and said, "Thank you."

As he put the money into the register, he asked Phillip, "Do you have luggage?"

"Yes, a small trunk," replied Phillip.

"Well, if it fits, you can put the trunk under the seat that you will sit on in the train. If it doesn't fit under the seat, ask the conductor what you should do with it," the man said. He turned away from Phillip, sat at his desk, and continued his work.

Phillip looked at the tickets, put them into the inside pocket of his jacket, and walked out the door.

When he returned to the wagon he said, "Well, I guess this is good-bye."

Phillip's mother moved and sat on the seat where Phillip had been sitting. Sadly she hugged and kissed little Otto for the last time.

Phillip reached for the boy, grabbed him, and set him on the ground beside the wagon.

Affectionately and with watery eyes, Della embraced and kissed Phillip's mother and father. Phillip helped Della down from the wagon. Then he climbed onto the back of the wagon to get the trunk. Before he picked up the trunk, he hugged his mother and shook his father's hand not wanting to let go. "Good-bye," Phillip said with a lump in his throat. He unloaded the trunk and carried it up the two steps onto the platform. Della took Otto's small hand and followed Phillip. From the top of the platform, they waved and watched as the two old people in the wagon slowly disappeared down the twisted street. There was a feeling of loss.

They walked behind the red building where they would be boarding the train. There was no place to sit. All the benches were occupied. So Phillip put the trunk down; Della and he sat on it. Phillip held Otto on his lap.

Quietly, they sat and watched a tall brakeman as he signaled the engineer to move the locomotive and tender. Slowly, the enormous, black locomotive and tender, filled with a large heap of coal, moved backwards. The engineer had his head stuck out of the open window in the locomotive. He watched the brakeman's signals as he backed the locomotive. Soon the couplers of the tender and yellow wooden passengers' car met with a CLANK. Behind the yellow passengers' car was a red wooden passenger car, several brown wooden box cars, and a red caboose.

The brakeman shouted, "Okay," to the engineer.

The engineer rang the bell, located on the top of the locomotive, and started to back the train up to the depot's platform.

The loud CLANKING of the bell scared Otto and he started to cry. Della took him from Phillip and tried to soothe him.

The train came closer and finally stopped at the platform. Otto stopped crying, and they boarded the yellow car.

Inside the train there was a narrow center aisle, which ran lengthwise with rows of crosswise black leather seats on each side.

Della carried Otto, and Phillip awkwardly carried the trunk through the aisle until they came to an empty seat. Phillip lifted the top of the seat and put the trunk inside the hollowed boxed bottom of the seat. Then he put the seat back in place and sat on it. In the opposite seat, facing Phillip, Della and Otto sat. The straight-back seats were very uncomfortable. Soon all the seats on the train were occupied. A short timid man with a pug nose sat next to Phillip. His hands were clutching a small black case, which he had placed on his bony thighs.

The whistle blew, the bell clanked, and the train jerked as it started down the track. Shortly, thereafter, a pudgy uniformed man with a large head came down the aisle. He took everyone's ticket and tore it in half. Half of the ticket he gave back. The other half he kept in his hand.

As the train "clickity-clacked" along, it swayed, shook, and rattled. Huge clouds of black soot from the soft coal thundered out of the locomotive's large cylinder smokestack. The soot came through the open, dirty fingerprinted, glass windows and soiled their clothes. Occasionally, Otto choked on the smoke, and the smoky smell made Della nauseated.

The train rumbled through green rustic valleys scattered with small farm houses and barns. It passed brown, black, and white cows grazing in emerald pastures.

The locomotive's loud noise would often frighten the deer that were lying near the edge of a dense green forest. The frightened deer in their shiny red coat would quickly jump to their slender legs and gracefully dart with their white tail erect into the forest, out of sight.

As the train traveled, Della and Phillip enjoyed and marveled at the beautiful, breathtaking scenery.

Little Otto played with his miniature iron fire wagon.

"Mama, look at me," he would say as he drove the toy on the back of the seat, on the seat, and on Della's lap.

When Della would look at him and smile, he would smile and laugh excitingly.

Daylight was slowly being stolen away by the velvety-black of the night. Everyone's eyelids were getting heavy with sleep; their stomachs were beginning to growl. It had been more than twelve hours since they had eaten. Della opened the purse, which she had in her hand, and took out the block of cheese.

"Would you like a piece?" she asked the timid man.

A smile crossed his young, clean shaved face and he replied, "No, thank you."

Della broke the cheese into three pieces and gave Phillip and Otto their piece. Otto, who usually was a slow and picky eater, had his piece devoured before Della even started eating.

Della broke a piece off her piece and gave it to Otto. Before long he had that piece devoured also.

When everyone had finished, they got out of their seats and stood in the aisle. Being quite stiff from seating so long, they stretched a bit.

Della held Otto securely as she braced herself against the swaying of the railroad car by hanging onto the top of the seat.

Phillip and the timid man took the facing seats and extended them into a berth. Phillip and the timid man would sleep there tonight. Above their berth, Phillip pulled down a concealed folding berth. Della and Otto would sleep there.

An uneasy, uncomfortable, and restless sleep haunted them all night. Before the first light of day approached, most everyone in the passengers' car was awake, sitting in their seats, and looking out the windows.

Sometimes as the train passed through the low rounded mountains separated by green valleys and plateaus, a medieval Gothic castle, perched on the mountain top, would look down at them.

Occasionally, they would pass a sparkling stream. Sometimes a solitary young boy or an old farmer would be sitting on the stream's edge fishing.

As they traveled, the terrain of the land was gradually becoming flat with low-lying areas. Plants with hollow or pithy stems like cattails and reeds rose above the low-growing green treeless grass areas. Some of the low-lying land had ponds filled and choked with spongy plant remains.

The train seemed to be losing some of its tremendous speed. A forest filled with pyramid-shaped green pine and spruce, tall columnar poplars, and white barked alders started to gradually appear.

As the train slowed more, they passed the forest and a town started to appear. Large, white three and four-story houses stood in view, one house crowded right next to the other. Some were decorated with dark wood and others had dark shutters.

Finally, the train came to a jolting stop in front of a quaint red depot. The timid man and the other passengers took their luggage and slowly pushed through the railroad car door.

Phillip and his family remained in their seats until the train was partially empty. When they got up from the seats, their bodies were stiff again.

Phillip stretched before attempting to lift and carry the trunk toward the door.

Near the door stood the pudgy ticket collector. With a friendly smile, he was bidding everyone "good-bye."

As Phillip lugged the trunk down the aisle toward the man, he asked, "Do you know a place where we could spend the night and eat?"

"Eric's is the only hotel in town." The man pointed out the train window. "You see the green vine-covered building with the sign extending from the building into the street?"

Phillip looked in the direction the man was pointing. He could see the large rectangular sign with the white letters ERIC painted on a green background.

"Ya, I see it," replied Phillip.

"Well, that's the place," said the man. "Have a good night."

"Thank you," said Phillip. He went out the door, down the steps, onto the depot's worn, wide-boarded platform.

Della followed Phillip with Otto who was clutching her hand. As she passed the pudgy man, she smiled and bid him a friendly "good-bye."

When Della was out on the platform, she tried to wipe the soot off their clothes with her hands. But as she wiped, the soot smeared on the clothes and they looked worst. Realizing what was happening, she stopped. She took Otto's hand, held it securely in her hand, and followed Phillip as he began to walk toward the edge of the platform.

As they stepped off the depot's shaded platform, the greeting midday sun fell upon their weary faces. Slowly and tiredly, they walked down the narrow cobblestone street toward Eric's.

Finally, they were in front of Eric's. As Della pushed open the dark heavy door, she was stunned at the sight inside the dimly lit, spacious room.

"My God! This is a tavern. I can't stay here," Della remarked.

"If this is the only place that has food and a room, I'm afraid we'll have to stay here," replied Phillip.

As they entered and closed the door, Della disgustingly looked around.

In one dark corner, a shaggy red-bearded sailor was sprawled on the unswept floor.

In the opposite corner, an untidy dressed sailor was drooping over a round, wooden table cluttered with empty steins.

Opposite the door they just had entered, a long dark wooden bar stood. At one end of the bar near the wall, a scar-faced sailor spit into a filthy dark spittoon.

At the other end of the bar, next to the wooden stairs, a burly man with bushy eyebrows stood behind the bar. When he saw Phillip approach the bar, he asked, "What can I do for you?" The man took a few of the empty steins off the sticky bar and placed them under the bar, out of sight.

"Do you have any rooms?" asked Phillip.

"Sure do," he answered and turned partially around. On the wall behind him, next to the large cracked mirror, part of a spike stuck out of the rough pine wall. There were several keys hanging on the spike. The man grabbed the first key. It had a white three on it. He handed it to Della. "Room three, at the top of the stairs," he said.

Seeing the repulsive look on Della's face he politely added, "I am sorry about the appearance of this room, lady. But the poor sailors are at sea for two sometimes three weeks. When they do dock at a port, the captain only lets them come to the tavern one night to 'wet their whistle.' So I'm kind of lenient with them and let them enjoy the few hours of free time that they have."

Della gave him a quick little smile. Lifting the bottom of her dress slightly off the floor, she and Otto followed Phillip up the steep, narrow wooden steps. At the top of the stairs, a white three was painted on the center upper part of a dark door.

"Well, this must be the room," Della said as she let go of Otto's hand and unlocked the door.

As she entered, Della was surprised at the cleanliness of the small one-bedded room. Phillip closed the door, put the trunk down, sat on it, and rested for a few minutes.

Opposite the door, between two windows, was a washstand topped with a white basin, pitcher, and neatly folded towel.

Phillip walked over to the washstand and poured some water from the pitcher into the basin. Even though the water was warm from setting awhile, it felt refreshing when he washed his face with it. Using the towel, he dried his face. He looked in the small mirror hanging above the washstand and straightened his ascot.

As he moved away and sat at the edge of the bed, Della washed her face and Otto's. Otto climbed onto the dark-green bedspread and rested his head on the fluffy, white pillow. Della gently pulled the bedspread out from under his small body and covered him with the bedspread up to his shoulders. His heavy eyelids closed, and he fell fast asleep. Della kissed his forehead tenderly and sat on the bed next to Phillip.

"I'm going to find the American Consul and see what he can arrange for us. I hope we can leave soon. The less money we spend waiting. The more we'll have to buy land with when we get to America," said Phillip.

He took off one of the shoes in which he had hidden the money, took out the folded money, and placed it on the bed. Grabbing into his inside jacket pocket, he took out the folded page of newspaper containing the ad. He unfolded it and examined it once more.

"According to the ad, I will probably need this much for tickets. But to be on the safe side, I'll take a little more just in case the tickets cost more," Phillip said as he counted out the money onto a pile. He folded the money from the pile and put it into the pocket located inside his jacket. The remainder of the money he returned to the inside of his shoe.

Pulling out his pocket watch, he looked at it and said to Della, "It's one o'clock now. When I come back, we'll go and eat supper. As long as Otto is sleeping, why don't you rest until I come back."

He kissed Della, rose from the bed, and went out the door.

After he closed the door, Della took her shoes off, folded back the bedspread, and laid her tired body beside Otto.

Once downstairs, Phillip asked the burly man, "Where is the American Consul?"

"Just a few buildings down the street. It's not far from here," answered the man.

"Thank you," replied Phillip as he headed for the door. As he touched the doorknob, he turned and asked, "Do you serve supper?"

"Sure do, right in the dining room there." The man pointed to the closed double doors next to the bottom of the stairs.

"Good." Phillip approvingly nodded his head and went out the door.

Phillip had only gone a few feet when a young boy with a loaf of bread came running down the street. The boy was running so fast that he never seen Phillip. With one sudden blow, he knocked Phillip on his rump.

"Ouch," said Phillip as he rubbed his sore rump.

Just as he was getting up, a tall skinny man with a white apron came running down the street.

"Come back here, you little good-for-nothing thief," the man shouted as he shook his fist in the air after the boy.

Phillip stood up, dusted his trousers off, and watched the yelling man come toward him. When the man was close to Phillip, he stopped. Panting heavily and trying to get his breath, he looked scornfully at Phillip and said, "That little thief--he is not going--to get away this time--." The angry man shook his fist again in the direction where the boy had now disappeared. The man turned abruptly and walked back down the street stamping his feet angrily and scorning under his breath.

Phillip shrugged his shoulders and continued to walk down the street. Soon he came to a building that had green vines growing around the windows. On one of the windows, printed in red and white lettering, were the words, AMERICAN CONSUL.

"This is the place," Phillip said to himself.

As he opened the white door, a small bell rang. Opposite the door was an oblong counter cluttered with stacks of paper. Behind the counter, a man was reading a big black book that was setting on a desk laden with books of all sizes and colors. Above the desk was a huge gray and white map with the words UNITED STATES OF AMERICA printed in big black letters over the gray part of the map. Next to the map was a ticket price list for the ships.

As Phillip walked toward the varnished pine counter, a six-foot, strongly built man turned around and rose from the pine swivel chair. The man had a full black beard and was extremely neat in appearance.

"Can I help you?" he asked in a tranquil manner as he approached the counter.

Phillip reached inside his jacket, into the pocket, and pulled out the folded newspaper page. He unfolded the page and laid it on the counter.

"According to this ad, you help people make arrangements to go to America?" Phillip said in a questionable manner.

"Yes, I can," replied the man. From below the counter he pulled out a big pile of messy stacked papers and placed them on the counter.

"When would you like to go?" he asked.

"As soon as possible," answered Phillip.

The papers rustled as the man paged through them. Suddenly, he stopped and pulled out a long, yellow sheet of paper.

"A family of six has decided not to leave tomorrow on the *U.S. Eastern.* So there are six empty places on the ship. If you take their places, you would leave early tomorrow morning around seven o'clock," the man told Phillip.

"That would be fine," replied Phillip with an air of happiness. "I'll need three tickets."

As the man wrote out the three tickets, Phillip looked at the price chart. He took his money out of his pocket and counted out the correct amount. He placed it on the counter and grabbed the tickets. After examining the three small white tickets, he put them and the remaining money into his pocket.

"Sign the names here." The man placed the yellow sheet of paper in front of Phillip. It had hundreds of names written on neat little lines. The man gave Phillip a pencil and pointed to the six empty lines. Phillip signed his name on one line, Della's on another, and Otto's name on the third line.

When Phillip was done, the man took the sheet. "You will leave tomorrow at seven o'clock on the *U.S. Eastern*. The ship is at the dock at the end of this street." The man pointed in the opposite direction that Phillip had come. "Is there anything else?" asked the man.

"Ya, where do I go when I get to America?" asked Phillip.

"We have a Commissioner of Immigrants in New York where you will be docking," the man said as he pulled out a small map and a pencil. "You will dock here." He made a small circle with the pencil. "Follow these street names." He drew a line with the pencil past several names and then drew a circle. "Right here is the commissioner's office." He handed Phillip the map. Phillip looked at it, folded it, and put it into his pocket.

"The commissioner will make all the arrangements for wherever you would like to go," explained the man.

"I'd like to go where I could farm and where there are people who speak German," said Phillip.

"Well, some German's from around here settled in Wisconsin. The land is fairly good for farming once it is cleared. You can get up to one hundred and sixty acres free if you homestead it. In order to homestead the land you must first file a declaration of intention, a statement saying that you intend to become a citizen of America. Then you must live on the land for five years. All you have to pay is the filing fee. If the land was lived on before, you can't homestead it. Then you may have to pay $1.25 an acre. The Wisconsin Central Railroad also has land for sale. You think about what I told you. You can decide when you get to America. The Commissioner of

Immigrants is there to help you and protect you from swindlers. So I'd suggest you see him first," said the man as he handed Phillip the map.

"Thank you," said Phillip as he took the map, folded it, and put it into his pocket.

"Good luck," said the man as he shook Phillip's hand and smiled at him.

When Phillip was outside, he stood in front of the door for a few minutes. His blue eyes began to sparkle. A smile of excitement crossed his face. He could not wait to tell Della that everything was ready for them to leave. Hurriedly, he walked down the street. Soon he was in front of Eric's. As he opened the door, the barroom seemed a different place. The sun's bright rays where flowing into the open window and gliding across the clean swept floor and washed tables. The room was empty except for a round, plump, short lady behind the bar. Her gray hair was neatly braided behind her head. As she washed the bar, the flabby skin of her arm shook. When she saw Phillip, a merry smile crossed her double-chinned face and her blue eyes glistened.

"Hi, nice day isn't it!" she exclaimed.

"Ya, it is," Phillip replied cheerfully. He could smell the aroma of sauerkraut cooking. The double dining room doors were open. As he peered quickly into the room, he could see several sailors sitting at tables and eating. As he headed for the stairs, Phillip stopped and asked, "What are you serving today?"

"Boiled potatoes with jackets, brown crusted bread, frankfurters, and sauerkraut," replied the woman with a smile.

"Could you please set a table for me, my wife, and son?" asked Phillip.

"Sure can," replied the woman.

"We'll be right down," Phillip stated as he hurried up the stairs two steps at a time.

When he entered the room, Della and Otto were standing looking out one of the windows. Della turned and smiled. "Did you get everything taken care of?"

"Ya, I did. We leave tomorrow morning at seven o'clock. Let's go downstairs and eat. I'm starved," said Phillip.

Della took Otto's hand, and they went downstairs to eat supper.

It felt so good to sit down and enjoy a warm meal. This was the first time Della ever had someone else serve her a meal. She felt like a "queen."

Before going upstairs after supper, Phillip stopped at the bar and asked the woman, "Could you please wake us up at five o'clock tomorrow morning?"

"Sure can," replied the woman as she filled a stein of beer and gave it to an elderly man standing at the bar.

Phillip and his family went to their room and retired for the night.

****

At the other end of town, near the dock, the small one-roomed carpenter shop of Hans Duren was getting dark.

Outside, the bright warm sun was slowly setting behind the forest. Its warmth and light were slowly disappearing from the room.

Hans, sitting on a wooden stool, stopped carving on the music box that he held in his broad hands. He looked up and out the twelve-pane back window.

As the sun set over the forest, the fluffy white clouds with their flat bases and rounded tops appeared purple, orange, and yellow in the sky.

The green pine trees stood straight and proud with their pyramid-shaped crowns and branches arranged in tiers. The brown cones, at the tip of the green spruces' branches, bent the ends of the branches downward. Among the green branches of the pine and spruce stood the white bark of the alder and the smooth gray bark of the beech.

Gazing at the forest brought back memories to Hans. Soon the chambers of his mind took him back twenty years when he was a pug nose boy of ten. In the vividness of his memory, he could see his jovial father--a tall, dark, wide shouldered man--chopping down the enormous pine with his axe. After the tree was down, he and his father would dig a hole and plant a small tree to take the place of the one that they had chopped down.

On hot autumn days, when they had almost finished their work, his little sister, Theresa, would come out. She'd bring them cold chocolate milk and fresh baked oatmeal cookies. On her small face she would wear a proud smile. As she walked, her blonde locks of hair would dance above her shoulders. Those were happy, carefree days of his youth that were full of pleasant memories.

The contented, reminiscing smile on Hans's glowing face was soon replaced by a saddened pale stare. His mind was now haunted by another memory and tears began to fill his dark-brown eyes. It was an autumn day, and the tree that his father had just chopped was ready to fall.

Suddenly, their mother came out of the kitchen door yelling hysterically, "Theresa--Theresa!"

Hans and his father looked in the direction that she was pointing. There in the path of the falling tree was Theresa. Their father ran to get Theresa out of the way. He snatched her up with lightning speed. As he was running with her in his arms, he tripped and fell on top of Theresa. The enormous tree came down with a thunderous sound and smashed their father's skull. His body had protected Theresa from the tree, but she had cut her face on a sharp stone as she fell. The cut left a grotesque scar that extended from her right cheekbone to her jaw.

Their mother always worried that no one would ever marry Theresa because of the scar. But her worries were needless, Theresa grew into a kind, generous, loving young lady. At the age of sixteen, she had married the banker's handsome son. A year later they immigrated to America.

Theresa always wrote letters to Hans after she had left Germany. Hans enjoyed reading about how prosperously they were doing and how extremely beautiful their new home in Wisconsin was. But suddenly, five years ago, the letters from Theresa ceased. Nevertheless, Hans continued writing to her. Every time the steamship that carried the mail docked, he'd check the mail for a letter from her. There never was one, and Hans finally concluded the inevitable had happened. Theresa and her husband must have died.

Five days ago when the ship docked, Hans purchased his ticket for America. He decided to go to Wisconsin and make a new home for himself and his family. If America was like Theresa described, it must indeed be the land of beauty and opportunity. In any event, Hans was soon to find out. He decided to settle in Wisconsin because Theresa had written that there was an abundance of unclaimed forest land.

A sudden sound broke the stillness of the room and startled Hans out of his deep thoughts. The sound came from the varnished oak cuckoo clock hanging above his workbench. Hans looked up at the clock.

"Cuckoo--cuckoo--cuckoo--cuckoo--cuckoo," a little wooden bird said and then it slid back inside the little door, which was located near the top of the clock, out of sight.

It was five o'clock. Hans reached for the small, hinged, wooden box that was setting in the middle of his oblong workbench. He opened the metal latch and lifted the wooden lid up. Hans placed the carving knife, which he had in his hand, into the box next to the other neatly arranged carving tools.

He rubbed the small wood shavings off the smooth, delicate music box that he held in his other hand. Admiringly, he looked at the music box. Finally, his surprise present for Lena was finished. Carefully, he placed it into the carving toolbox and closed the lid, securing the latch tightly.

After rising from the stool, he brushed the wood shavings off his gray trousers. He grabbed the bright greenish broom setting next to the workbench. He swept the wood shavings that scattered the uneven boarded floor out the back door.

Glancing around the shop, he checked to see if everything was in order. The workbench was clear of everything except his wooden carving toolbox. Opposite the workbench, setting near the other wall, the fire in the black potbellied stove was extinguished. The small pile of dry unused wood was stacked neatly up against the wall near the stove. Hans nodded his head as if to say to himself, "everything is neat and exactly where it belongs."

Between the front door and the front twelve-pane window, a hook protruded from the wall. On the hook hung a gray, knee-length, double-breasted dress coat. Hans grabbed the coat and the gray hat, which rested on the coat as it hung. He put the coat over his broad shoulders and tall body. It fit snug at his trim waist and had a flared skirt. As he put the gray hat on his dark wavy black hair, he reached up with his right hand and grabbed a small bronze key off the door's framework. He walked to the back of the shop and locked the back door. As he walked past the workbench toward the front door, he grabbed his wooden carving toolbox. He opened the front door, turned around, looked at his shop for the last time, and then went out the door. Once outside the shop, he locked the door and checked its locked condition by turning the knob. On each side of the front window was a dark wooden shutter. Hans covered the glass window with the shutters.

As he looked toward the river Weser, the last beam of sunlight made the sky-blue water sparkle like diamonds. In the dock stood a huge, gloomy, dark-gray, steel steamboat. Rising far above the ship was a tall, slender white pole. Near the top of the pole, a flag--with six white stripes, seven red stripes, and thirty-eight white stars in a blue field--fluttered softly in the gentle breeze.

On the weather deck, the deck crew was busy loading cargo with the masts and booms. A tall, slim uniformed man was standing in a partially enclosed space at the middle of the ship. He was watching and supervising the work of about twenty men.

Hans turned away from the ship and started to walk down the narrow cobblestone street. He walked the streets in solitude. Everyone was in their home eating supper. That is what Hans should have been doing at this time of day, but he was a little late.

As he walked along the twisted sixteenth-century streets lined with gabled buildings, he hummed a merry tune.

Empty white wooden flower boxes hung from the windows of the three and sometimes four-story buildings. A month from now, the boxes would be glowing with dazzling red, yellow, and pink flowers.

The silence of the street was soon broken with the laughter of children. The laughter became louder as he walked on. As he turned the corner, he stopped suddenly. He was astonished at what he saw.

In front of the white fifteenth-century town hall was a square, gray, wooden frame set upon a gray platform. The frame had four rounded openings that were now locked in place. In the top two openings were two skinny, dirty hands with bitten off fingernails. In the two bottom openings were two feet covered with shoes that had holey soles. Behind the frame was a wooden stool. On the stool sat a small, dirty faced, ten-year-old boy with disheveled, mousy brown hair. A tattered green plaid shirt was draped over his bony shoulders. Around his skinny waist, a piece of yellow twine held up his baggy, short, black trousers. Hans recognized the boy. It was Pete, the orphan.

Walking around the frame that locked Pete's wrists and ankles in place were two mindless, rowdy boys. They were jeering and pelting Pete with small stones. They would throw the stones as hard as they could at Pete. When he yelled "ouch," they would laugh at him.

Hans shook his head and a scowl crossed his merry face. Angrily he shouted, "What's the matter with you two fools? He is being punished enough by being in that hideous and uncomfortable thing. Get out of here before the authorities and I have you two put in there."

The two boys dropped the stones. Terrified, they ran past Hans as quickly as they could.

Hans watched until they disappeared around the corner. Then Hans turned and looked at Pete. Hans shook his head back and forth and gave a sigh. "You got yourself into a mess this time, Pete. Oslo finally caught you stealing his bread, huh."

Pete nodded. "Ya, I guess so. Well, it's not so bad being in here at least my stomach is full and doesn't hurt. Being in here is not going to stop me from stealing from Oslo. When I'm hungry, I'll do the same thing over again."

Hans showed his disapproval on his face. "I've told you that when you are hungry you should go to my house. My Lena would give you something to eat."

"I don't take charity, and I don't want to owe anyone--anything--ever," Pete sternly replied.

"Well, you steal from Oslo, don't you think you'll owe him something, someday?" asked Hans.

"Not that old crook, he owes me. He stole that bakery from my father," snapped Pete. His voice and eyes were full of hate and anger.

"It seems to me that you are the one being punished, not Oslo," remarked Hans.

"No, you are wrong about that Mr. Hans. Every time I steal a loaf of bread that is one less loaf he can sell and losing that money is more painful to him than losing an arm," replied Pete.

"I'm not going to argue with you, Pete. If you are going to be in that thing all night, I can bring some blankets and cover you after supper. These May nights are quite chilly sometimes," said Hans.

Pete glanced up at the clock built into the tower of the town hall.

"No thanks, Mr. Hans, they are letting me out of here in about an hour," replied Pete.

"You are welcome to spend the night at our house, if you wish," offered Hans.

"No, I don't think so. I've got a nice cozy spot on top of Mr. Hassel's straw pile in the livery," answered Pete.

"Well, good night then, Pete," said Hans.

"Good night, Mr. Hans," replied Pete.

Hans turned and continued walking down the street. Finally, he came to the end of the gabled buildings. The next several houses were graced with small green lawns and outlined with white picket fences.

The third house in the row was Hans's. It was a two-story, white house with four, front, twelve-pane white windows. Each window had a pair of black shutters and a black flower box hanging from it. The first story windows aligned with the second story windows. A large, carved, wooden black door was centered between the two first story windows.

In front of the house, beside the cobblestone sidewalk and enclosed in the picket fence, a tall shady linden stood waving its green leaves gently in the soft breeze. On the lower branch of the tree, an empty swing that was made of gray rope swayed.

As Hans walked up the two wooden front house steps, he could smell the aroma of fresh baked bread. He opened the door, stepped in, and took a deep breath.

"Ah, that smells good, Lena," Hans said as he closed the door.

Hans placed his toolbox on a small table, which stood next to the door in front of the window.

Lena, a very small woman with plump hips, was standing in front of a rectangular black cast-iron stove. She was stirring a stew in her cast-iron Dutch oven. When she heard Hans, she turned her head of straw-colored hair around and looked at him. A sparkle filled her blue eyes and a glistening smile crossed her smooth, fair face.

"Did you get everything done that you wanted to get done?" asked Lena. She turned around, seasoned the stew, and took the bread out of the oven.

"Ya," replied Hans as he took off his coat and hat. He hung them on the oak clothes tree, which was standing beside the door.

The room felt warm and had a coziness about it. On the left side of the room, centered in the middle of the wall, was a carved china cabinet. The varnished oak hutch top had a cabinet with two full-length wooden shelves. On the shelves, behind double-glass doors, were Lena's Dresden china dishes standing upright. The dishes had lovely soft colors and delicate designs of roses on them. The buffet base had four drawers that were the length of the cabinet.

On the right side of the room, an open stairway, with a wooden railing and turned spindles, extended the length of the wall.

Across the room next to the stove was a closed bedroom door. Next to the door was a small white sink.

In front of the sink, rosy-cheeked eight-year-old Anna was sitting on a small braided rug. She had white ribbons tied at the end of her dark-brown braided hair. Her small chubby hands were dressing her dark-haired china doll. When she saw her father, her dark-brown eyes sparkled. She ran to him and gave him a big hug.

In the middle of the tidy room, setting on a large braided rug, was a round varnished oak table with a hefty oak pedestal that was carved in the shape of a massive ball and claw. Around the table were four chairs with carved backs, turned spindles, and legs. On one of the chairs sat twelve-year-old Ludwig. His large hands were fastening a cotton line to a long bamboo fishing pole. Lying on the floor, beside his large feet, was a lead weight, steel hook, and a cork. When he heard Hans, he looked up with his twinkling blue eyes. "Hi, Dad! Can you help me with the fishing pole?" he asked.

Anna and Hans walked over to the table. Hans pulled two chairs away from the table. Anna sat on one chair while Hans sat on the other chair next to Ludwig.

"Sure can help you," replied Hans as he messed Ludwig's blonde hair with his hand.

"Oh Dad, don't do that," Ludwig said as he pulled his head back and straightened his hair with his hand.

Anna rested her elbows on the table and held her chin in the palm of her hands. Attentively, she watched Hans and Ludwig.

While Hans and Ludwig were busy with the fishing pole, Lena set the table with food, dishes, and silverware.

When the table was set, they put the fishing things next to the clothes tree and sat at the table. Soon they were all sitting down to a tasty beef stew, warm brown crusted bread, and cinnamon flavored applesauce.

After supper Lena washed the dishes, while Anna dried them and placed them inside the china cabinet.

While Anna and Lena were doing dishes, Hans cleaned a section of the table and then sat back in his chair at the table.

Ludwig rose from his chair and went over to the china cabinet. He opened the bottom drawer and pulled out a small brown box. Ludwig returned to the table with the box and sat across from Hans at the table.

Hans took the box out of Ludwig's hand and opened it. He poured out twenty-eight small, flat, oblong dominoes. After turning them face down, he shuffled them. Soon the nightly domino game was on between Hans and Ludwig.

After Lena and Anna had finished dishes and tidying up the kitchen, they sat at the table and watched until the first game was finished. Anna sat next to her father and Lena sat opposite Anna, next to Ludwig. When the second game started, everyone was playing. Sounds of laughter and excitement filled the room.

While they were playing, Hans looked up and said to Lena, "I've got the shop clean and tidy. All you have to do is sell it. When you have the shop, house, and the forty acres of woods sold, you and the children come and join me in America. When everything is sold, you wait here until you hear from me. I don't know exactly where I am going to settle in Wisconsin. If I find a place for us quickly, you can come right away. But if I don't have a place, it would probably be best if you waited here until I did. Until I find a place, I'll be moving around. You may not find me."

"I hope everything goes well so we can join you soon," said Lena.

"I hope so too," said Hans as he reached across the table and touched Lena's smooth, slender hand.

"Domino!" shouted Ludwig.

"Oh, you are too good for me. You always win," Hans said as he smiled at Ludwig.

Ludwig counted the dots on the other dominoes. "I score thirty-seven points!" he exclaimed with excitement.

"So you do," said Lena smilingly. "I think it's time for bed."

They all looked at the square pendulum clock hanging above the white enamel sink.

"Guess so, it's nine o'clock already," said Ludwig as he pushed himself away from the table and rose from the chair. "Good night, Ma--Pa--Anna." He went up the stairs.

"Good night, Son," replied Hans and Lena.

"Good night, Ludwig," said Anna.

"Come on, Anna, I'll tuck you in," said Lena. As she rose from her chair, she gently touched Anna's hand.

Anna got up from her chair and kissed her father on the cheek. "Good night, Daddy, I love you." Anna and her mother went up the stairs.

Hans watched them until they disappeared up the stairs. He gathered up the dominoes and stacked them neatly into the brown box. After putting them inside the bottom drawer of the china cabinet, he locked the front door with the small key, which was lying on the top of the door's framework.

He glanced toward the stairs. When he saw Lena was nowhere in sight, he took the music box out of the toolbox. Quickly, he walked into the bedroom and put the music box inside the top drawer of his seven-drawer dresser.

The bedroom was small and dark. Opposite the door was a bed with a high wooden headboard. It was covered with a colorful quilt and oblong rugs lay on each side of the bed. Next to the door was Hans's seven-drawer dresser. Against the right wall of the room stood Lena's one-drawer vanity and chair. Centered against the left wall was a wooden chair.

Hans lit the oil lamp that was centered on top of his dresser. He walked over to the chair, sat down, and took off his shoes.

Soon he heard Lena's small feet coming down the wooden stairs. She turned the flame out in the lamp that was setting in the middle of the kitchen table. As she came into the bedroom and closed the door, Hans looked up and smiled at her.

Lena sat in front of the vanity and looked in the large mirror, which hung above it. She took her straw-colored hair out of the bun and brushed her hair until it glistened.

Hans quietly walked over to the dresser and took out the music box. As he turned to look at Lena, he hid it behind his back. Slowly, he walked toward her.

She looked in the mirror and smiled at him as she brushed her long hair.

Hans took the music box out from behind his back and placed it in front of her on the vanity.

Lena's face lit up when she saw it. She picked it up and rubbed her hands over it.

The music box was sanded so smooth. It had four beautifully carved little legs. Centered on the top were two carved lovers holding hands. At one side of the box a small key stuck out. When Lena turned the key, the box played "Brahm's Lullaby" and the two lovers went around as if dancing.

"Oh, Hans, it is so beautiful!" Lena said as she looked up at him with a smile that made her eyes sparkle.

"I made this so even though we are hundreds of miles apart you will always think of me when you see it and know that I love you very much," Hans said.

"Oh, Hans, I love you so much. I could never forget you." She reached up and rubbed her soft palm along his smooth shaved face. "I do love you." She rose from the chair and kissed him tenderly.

Hans took the music box out of her hand and placed it on the vanity. He lifted her up into his arms and carried her over to the bed. He laid her in the bed and then he lay next to her.

As he held her warm body in his arms, he lightly stroked her soft hair and gently kissed her moist pink lips. They stayed in each other's warm, loving arms until the early morning hours. Sometimes they made love. Sometimes they'd just lie quietly in each other's arms and only their heartbeats could be heard in the silence of the night.

As the oil lamp gradually flickered out, they fell asleep caressing each other.

****

Before the sun kissed the early morning dew on the rooftops, the Aslens, Durens, and other immigrants were hustling and bustling about getting ready for the trip.

By the time the sleeping chimneys greeted the day with their gray smoke, the streets of Bremen were crowded with noisy people.

When the shrill loud whistle of the steamboat blew, the last of the immigrants boarded the ship.

As the ship moved away from the dock, immigrants on the deck waved farewell to their dear ones left behind on the dock.

Lena, dressed in her prettiest sky-blue dress, stood with tears on her pink cheeks. She clutched the music box to her heart as the ship departed.

Ludwig and Anna were standing beside her. With tears in their eyes, they waved a good-bye to their father.

The farther up the river the ship cruised, the smaller the people standing on the dock became until they finally vanished from view.

As the ship traveled out to the North Sea, the trim, half-timbered towns tucked beneath castle-crested cliffs and green terraced vineyards slowly disappeared from view.

The blue sea seemed to touch the blue sky.

A feeling of loss and emptiness settled in the hearts of Phillip, Della, and Hans.

They were leaving the security of a life they'd always known for a life of--what? The unknown was frightening.

There is an old saying about things being "greener on the other side of the fence." Are things really better somewhere else? Or perhaps is what we leave behind for "betterment sake" the best that we can ever have. If the place we go to isn't better, then we say to our self, "someday we'll go back." But do we ever get that chance? There is always a reason why we don't go back. Maybe we don't have the money or we don't have the time. So we live with the thoughts of how things might have been, and we die with the way things really are. Once we turn a page in life, we can never go back. There is no time machine to take us back and live our lives in a particular time. Time moves on and so does life.

The decision a person makes affects everyone that they come in contact with, even if it is for a mere second. For it is in that mere second, a person enters someone else's space in time. So it will be for the Aslens and Hans Duren. Their decision to leave Germany will affect the lives of people they meet in America, and the people they leave behind.

Chapter 2
****
Mysterious Person

As the ship docked in New York, a blanket of dense fog hid the city from view. Only foghorns and large brown barrels that cluttered the wharf greeted the ship of immigrants.

As the Aslens left the ship, Della was carrying Otto in her arms, and Phillip was still lugging around the trunk.

When they came to the end of the wharf, Phillip stopped and set the trunk down. He reached into his jacket and pulled out the map that the man at the Consul had given him. He studied it for a few minutes then gave it to Della.

"We'll keep on walking until we come to the street that the man circled on the map. Otto can walk by himself while you compare the street names on the map with the streets we pass," said Phillip.

"Okay," said Della. She put Otto down. In her one hand, she held his hand; in her other hand, she held the map.

The three of them walked down the street and soon disappeared into the fog.

Hans Duren was one of the last immigrants to leave the ship. As he was walking along the wharf, he suddenly stopped, remained very quiet, and listened very closely. He thought he had heard someone calling his name.

"Well, that's ridiculous! I must be hearing things. No one here knows my name," Hans thought aloud.

Shrugging his shoulders, he walked on with his toolbox in his hand. After a few steps, he heard the sound again. He stopped and looked toward the barrels. The sound seemed to be coming from behind them. He listened again.

"Mr. Hans, Mr. Hans." A soft whisper floated through the air.

"Oh, that can't be! There is only one person who called me that," Hans said to himself as he walked closer to the barrels and looked behind them. A surprised look covered his face.

"My God, what are you doing here?" Hans exclaimed shockingly.

"Is it clear for me to come out?" asked the voice in a soft whisper.

Hans looked up and down the wharf. The thick fog had hidden the ship and the street. Hans could see no one, and no one could see him.

"Ya, it is clear but you better not stay around here too long. You are sure to get caught, and I heard that they are not too nice to stowaways," Hans said as he grabbed Pete's hand, and they hurried off the wharf and down the street.

"You are lucky it is foggy. No one can see very far. How on earth did you get on the ship anyway?" asked Hans as they walked along.

"After they let me out of that thing, I went down to the dock, snuck abroad, and hid in the galley," Pete bragged.

Hans shook his head, sighed, and said, "I don't know about you Pete. What are you going to do now?"

"Well, I heard that they hire anyone to work in the factories that they have here," said Pete.

"Oh ya, they hire anyone who can walk, but they don't treat a person very nicely. A kid like you who doesn't have anyone to look out for him will really be abused. They will probably make you work all day and half the night too," said Hans.

"Well, I'm not used to being treated like a king, Mr. Hans." Pete chuckled.

"I think, you better come with me," said Hans as he put his arm around Pete's shoulders.

"I don't want any charity, Mr. Hans. I can work hard and long if I have to, and I have to. I intend to be a rich man someday, and I'm going to go back and show them all, especially Oslo," said Pete scornfully.

"Well, first you have to survive. I don't think you'll be able to do that by yourself, not right away in this strange place. I don't even know how I'm going to survive yet, and I'm a grown-up. However, I do have an idea. If it works, we both can survive and maybe even become rich," said Hans.

"Well, I suppose, I could give your way a try. But if it doesn't work," said Pete, "I'm going my own way and doing my own thing."

"Fair enough," said Hans as he extended his arm, and they shook hands.

As they walked in the fog their clothes became damp and their bodies chilled. The sound of their footsteps on the large square-cut stones that made up the deserted, foggy street echoed in the air.

The farther they went from the wharf, the thinner the fog became. Slowly, the midday sun began to peek through the grayish roll-like clouds that covered the sky. As the sound of the foghorns faded, the sound of pounding horses' hoofs and rumbling wagon wheels filled the air of the bustling street.

Soon Hans and Pete came to a street that was crowded with a long line of people. Some people had trunks; others had suitcases. Hans and Pete stopped and looked down the line. They recognized a few of the people. Some had been on the ship with them. As they looked farther down the line, they could see everyone was lined up and waiting to go into the Commissioner of Immigration office.

Since Hans was also looking for this place, they took a place at the end of the line.

A man in front of Hans turned around and extended his arm for a handshake.

"Hi, my name is Phillip Aslen," he said.

As Hans shook Phillip's hand he replied, "My name is Hans Duren and this is my friend, Pete Hof."

"Hi," said Pete as he took his hand out of his holey pocket and shook Phillip's hand.

Sitting on the trunk in front of Phillip were Della and Otto. When they heard Phillip talking, they turned around out of curiosity.

Phillip turned and pointed his hand at Della and Otto. "This is my wife, Della, and son, Otto."

Della smiled, nodded, and said, "Hi."

As they waited in line, they talked about their life and relatives who still lived in Germany.

The rays of daylight were beginning to disappear as Phillip Aslen and Hans Duren finished their business at the commissioner's office. By the time they left the office, their future was almost entirely arranged.

The Aslens had purchased tickets for the town of Beechwood. The commissioner had told them that there was plenty of land available there for farming. Most of the land had already been homesteaded; as a result, Phillip would have to pay for the land that he wanted. Some of the people who previously settled there were selling their farms so they could homestead other land. Therefore, Phillip could have his choice of several farms. Beechwood had a bank and deed's office that would help him.

Hans wanted to purchase a ticket for Dry Springs but was unable to. The railroad did not go that far. So Hans bought a ticket for himself and Pete for as far as the train would go. From there Hans planned to take a stagecoach or whatever type of transportation was available to Dry Springs.

After they left the office, they ate and spent a comfortable night in a nearby hotel.

The next morning the sun was just awaking as the train left the chilly air of the depot. The passengers' car was crowded with quiet people peering out the windows at the new sights that they would probably never see again.

The gray streets and crowded houses of the city soon disappeared and were replaced by sights of small rural farms and green pastures. Sometimes the train passed a farmer who was turning over the earth's green blanket and revealing its brown undercover.

Occasionally, the train's brakes would screech and the train would come to a jerky stop at some crude little town with dirt streets and boarded walks. Some people would get off, and the train would get emptier.

After several of these stops, the distance between towns became greater. The wilderness soon became more prevalent. Vast green virgin woods stocked with an abundance of wild life skirted the sides of the train. Gradually, the farms and then a town would appear only to disappear again and be replaced by woods.

Shortly after the Aslens left the train at Beechwood, the train entered another "tunnel of greenery." A tall, dark-haired man with a Vandyke beard came into the passengers' car. As he stood in front of the door, he shouted above the noise of the train, "We're going to spend the night at this next stop and leave about midday tomorrow.

The tender has to be filled with water." He then turned and limped out the door on his crippled leg.

As the train slowed, Hans looked around the passengers' car. In one seat sat a quiet, white-haired man with a tall, black cylindrical silk hat. He possessed an "air of distinction" and was elegantly dressed in a black suit, vest, and tie.

In another seat, across the aisle from Hans and Pete, sat two boisterous strong muscled men. They had boarded the train a few stops back. Ever since they were on the train, Hans had leaned one ear toward them. Occasionally, he laughed to himself as he overheard the unbelievable tales that they told each other of their great physical bravery and ability.

One of the men had a shaggy, red beard and was dressed in a torn, red plaid shirt. Dirty suspenders held up his dark staggered pants, which showed his holey gray stockings.

The other man had a French-Canadian accent, which he used to spice up his adventurous tales. He was dressed in an old fringed buckskin and heavy woolen pants. A soiled hat, with a crumpled rim, covered part of his shoulder-length dark hair.

The train soon stopped and everyone got off.

As Hans stepped outside the train onto the wooden depot platform, he was amazed at the sight.

Flanking the railroad's right of way, for as far as the eye could see, was a cool shady woods filled with great stands of gleaming white pine. Mixed with the pine were tall oaks with broad crowns of lustrous green leaves and maple trees with dense green foliage and short trunks.

Adjacent the depot was an enormous water tower for the train. Hans looked around, but he could not see the source of the water supply.

Across the track a Greek Revival style inn, with white clapboards and second story fan-shaped windows, stood. It was quietly nestled in the breathtaking greenery.

Hans and Pete followed the others up the three porch-length steps into the inn. As they entered the doorway, they were greeted by an open staircase. For a moment, they watched as the quiet man in black walked slowly up the stairs and lightly slid his hand, filled with brown age spots, along the dust free varnished oak railing.

To the right of Hans was a spacious sunlit room. Setting in the middle of the room was an oblong table covered with a white oilcloth and surrounded by eight dark chairs.

In the center of an outside wall, between two windows, sat a round oak table with two chairs, a checkerboard, and checkers. The engineer and conductor sat down and started a game.

In the middle of the other outside wall, there was a black pot-bellied stove. Beside the stove, two "captain's chairs" stood.

The two boisterous men, still talking about their great feats, walked over to the "captain's chairs." As they walked, they scratched the varnished oak flooring with the calks on their leather boots.

Suddenly, the door to the left of Hans opened. He backed away from the door into the room. As a small, fragile woman wearing a pleasant smile walked through the doorway, the air in the room became filled with a sweet lilac smell. Glistening locks of carrot red hair cascaded over her shoulders. She was dressed in a bright green dress that was trimmed with a collar of white Irish lace. Her green eyes twinkled as she greeted them with her head held in a dignified manner.

"Hello, gentlemen," she said.

The engineer looked up from his checker game and replied in a gravelly voice, "Hi, Kate."

The conductor, too busy to look up, said, "Hello, Miss O'Leary," as he moved his checker on the board.

"As soon as you give me payment for the room, you may go up and take one," she said as she stood at the bottom of the stairs with her palm extended slightly. "There is a basin and a full pitcher of water in the room. Dinner will be served in a half-hour. If you wish to sit at my table, you will kindly wash up and shave." She graciously smiled.

She looked at the two boisterous men's boots as they approached her. "Please take those boots with calks off outside," she said in a commanding tone.

The two men did as she said, placed their room fee in the palm of her hand and proceeded upstairs.

"Here is my room fee and this is for my friend, Pete." Hans

motioned to Pete as he took the money from his wallet to pay her.

"Thank you," she said and then disappeared into her room.

At the top of the stairs, a well-lit hallway extended to the left and to the right. The two men, the engineer, and conductor took the four rooms to the left of the stairs.

The man in black was coming out of the room next to the right of the stairs. Pete took the room opposite him.

Hans walked over to one of the doors at the end of the hall and turned the knob. The door seemed locked. Hans tried again.

"That's the cook's room. You'll have to take the other room," said the man in black as he closed his door and went downstairs.

Hans, carrying his toolbox, went into the room next to Pete.

After supper the engineer and the conductor continued their quiet game of checkers. The man in black disappeared into his room, and the two boisterous men sat quietly on the porch steps enjoying leisure puffs on their pipes.

Hans and Pete went for a walk. Hans was curious as to where they got the water for the tower.

"There must be a water source some place near here; otherwise, they would not have made this a water stop," Hans commented as he walked along.

As they walked behind the inn, near the edge of the woods, Hans stopped suddenly and motioned Pete to be still.

In the silence of the early evening, Hans heard a rumbling, thunderous sound coming from inside the woods. They followed the faint trail which led into the woods. As they approached and entered the woods, the sound became louder.

It was damp inside the dusky woods. They became chilly and shivered as they followed the twisted path around thorny bushes and enormous trees. The path soon ended on the weedy bank of a rapid flowing stream. The crystal clear stream cut through the dense part of the woods and tumbled over water polished stones.

They stopped and examined the pristine surroundings.

"This would be perfect," Hans thought aloud as he nodded his head. "Ya, this would be perfect."

"Did you say something, Mr. Hans?" asked Pete.

"What--oh, it's nothing," said Hans.

"Come on, let's go back to the inn," Hans said excitedly. Hurriedly, they walked back to the inn.

As they opened the door to the inn, they found the room empty except for Kate. She was tidying up the room and looked up when she heard Hans and Pete storming into the doorway.

"Is something the matter?" Kate asked.

"No," said Hans as he closed the door. His face was glowing with a look of enthusiasm.

"Can a person homestead or purchase the woods around here?" asked Hans.

"No, you can't homestead it. Someone already owns it," replied Kate as she straightened a chair near the table.

The gleam started to disappear from Hans's face as he asked, "Do you know who owns the woods?"

"Yes, I own it," replied Kate.

A surprised look came across Hans's face. He had never heard of a woman having ownership of anything.

"Why do you want to know?" asked Kate.

"Well, I'd like to buy the woods," replied Hans.

"You would?" replied Kate in a questionable tone.

"Ya, I would. Would you consider selling it?" asked Hans.

Kate finished arranging the chairs around the table and walked over to Hans. She put her hands on her slender hips and asked, "Well, how much would you pay me, and how much would you want to buy?"

"How much of what you own would you sell?" asked Hans. The gleam of hope came back into his eyes.

"I own two hundred acres of woods on this side of the railroad track. My land ends on the other side of the stream, which is behind my woods. If you wanted to, you could buy my land up to there. Then part of the stream would be on your land," replied Kate.

"Ya, I would like that," stated Hans.

Kate folded her arms. A serious look came across her face as she pressed her small pink lips together.

"You're positive. You want to buy some of this woods from me?" asked Kate.

"Ya, I am," replied Hans.

"Very well, you wait here. I'll be right back," Kate said as she turned, lifted her long dress off the floor, and went up the stairs.

Hans and Pete looked at each other in bewilderment as they stood at the bottom of the stairs.

A few minutes later Kate came down the stairs. Following her, with his briefcase in his hand, was the man in black. When they were both at the bottom of the stairs, Kate introduced the man, "This is Judge Horatio Emery. He knows all about the legal aspects of buying and selling property."

"Hello," said the judge in a dignified manner as he shook Hans's hand.

"Hello, Judge Emery. I'm Hans Duren and this is my friend, Pete Hof," Hans said as he shook hands and motioned to Pete.

Kate then opened the door to her room and motioned the judge, Hans, and Pete inside. The room was elaborately furnished with Early Victorian furniture that was hand carved and had a lustrous mahogany finish. The furniture sat on an oriental beige rug decorated with brown flower patterns. The rug covered most of the oak flooring.

Pete was amazed at the wall-length bookcase and went immediately over to it. He had never seen so many books.

The judge sat on a red velvet chair near a writing table. He put his briefcase on the table, opened it, and took out several pieces of blank white paper.

Hans sat in the citrus green "gentlemen's chair" that Kate had offered him. Once in the chair, Hans looked around the room. It was so elegant!

Kate walked to the mahogany console table topped with white marble. She grabbed a decanter filled with a brownish liquid and filled one of the several decorative lead crystal wine glasses, which were setting on the table. She handed the filled glass to the judge.

"Thank you, Kate," said the judge as he took the glass and drank it half empty.

"Would you like some sherry, Hans?" asked Kate.

"No, thank you," replied Hans.

Kate poured herself a glassful, took a sip, and sat on the other red velvet side chair next to the writing table.

"Now what is this about selling some land, Kate?" the judge asked as he pulled a pair of wire rim glasses out of his pocket and put them on his face.

"I want to sell all the woods from the inn down to where my land ends. All I want to keep are the woods around the inn that extends from the railroad's right of way to the other side of the stream where my land ends," stated Kate.

"That only leaves you twenty acres of land," said the judge astonishingly. "You're going to sell this stranger all the rest of the land! Your dad worked so hard and long for that land. He gave his blood and sweat working for the railroad so he could buy it. You better think about this a little more, Kate. I knew your dad like a brother, and I know that he wouldn't want you to sell this woods."

"I've thought about nothing else ever since Dad died last year. I know that he wouldn't want me to sell the woods, but I don't want it. I can't do anything with it. I have a hard time keeping the inn operating. It's a good thing that the train only stops here three times a week. If it would stop more, I couldn't handle all the work. Even with the cook helping me, it would be too much. Dad had a dream about the woods and the inn, but he died before he could do anything about his dream. I can't fulfill his dream for him. I have my own dreams," stated Kate.

"Okay, if that's what you want. I'll draw up the necessary legal papers for you. When I come back this way next week, you both can read the papers. If they're what you want, then you both can sign them," the judge said as he started writing on the white sheet of paper that he had taken out of his briefcase. Suddenly, he stopped writing, turned to Hans, and asked, "Do you have any money?"

"No," replied Hans.

"Well, how do you expect to pay for the land?" asked the judge.

"I thought I'd pay Miss O'Leary so much out of what I made on the land until I had it paid for," said Hans.

"Oh, a land contract. I'll write one up," the judge said. He turned around and wrote on the paper again.

"There is a lean-to behind the inn. It's full of my dad's lumber tools, if you would like to use them, you may," offered Kate.

"Thank you," said Hans. "I sure could use them. All I brought with me were my carving tools."

Mysterious Person 43

Hans turned to Pete who was now standing beside his chair. "All we need now is a draft horse," he said.

The judge stopped writing and turned around. "I could get you one and bring it along on the train when I come next week," offered the judge.

"That would be fine," said Hans.

"You can pay me back with four cords of firewood. I have a house to keep warm too," said the judge.

Hans nodded his head.

"You and Pete can have free room and board if you keep me supplied with all the firewood I need. The cook and I find that job quite hard and difficult," said Kate.

"What do you say, Pete?" asked Hans.

"After tasting the cook's dinner tonight, we'd be foolish not to accept the offer," said Pete.

The judge chuckled and said, "You're right about that. The cook here makes the best meals that I've ever tasted."

The judge put the paper into his briefcase. "I'm going to retire for the night," he said as he closed the briefcase and rose from the chair. Carrying the briefcase, he went out the door and up the stairs.

As Hans rose from the chair he said to Pete, "You're my right-hand man from now on. I think tomorrow we start making a sawmill on the stream."

"Ya, Mr. Hans," Pete said enthusiastically. He went out the room and ran up the steps two at a time.

Kate finished writing something on a small piece of paper and handed it to Hans. "This piece of paper states what I intend to sell you. It should be sufficient until we sign the legal papers next week."

"That will be fine," Hans said as he took the paper and looked at it.

"Good night, Miss O'Leary," said Hans. He folded the paper, put it into his pocket, and went out the door.

"Good night, Mr. Duren," said Kate as she closed the door behind him.

When Hans reached the top of the stairs, the door at the end of the hallway closed. Hans could hear the key turn in the lock and see the light of the room beneath the door.

"That cook is a strange person. She--or maybe he--keeps pretty well hidden. Really strange!" Hans thought aloud as he entered his room and retired for the night.

Early the next morning, the rhythmic tears of a saw against the trunk of a tree, a striking axe, and the piercing ring of an iron sledge on a metal wedge were the sounds that filled the air.

Hans and Pete worked extremely hard all morning. Their stomachs began to growl, but they still worked on. Their ears were perked up waiting for the sound of the dinner bell.

Finally, the welcomed sound filled the air. They dropped their axes and scurried to the inn.

The railroad track was empty. The train and other passengers had departed after breakfast.

As they opened the door, the smell of crisp brown chicken filled their nostrils and made their stomachs growl more. They flew up the stairs like a streak of lightning, washed up, and came down as fast as they had gone up the stairs. The mashed potatoes and gravy were steaming as they sat at the table that was set for three.

Hans looked at Kate, who was sitting across the table from him and Pete. He asked, "Where is the cook? I was looking forward to meeting the person who cooks so well."

"The cook is a very shy person who doesn't bother anyone and doesn't want to be bothered either," Kate explained kindly. "How are you coming on your project?" asked Kate.

"I figure by early autumn we should have the sawmill finished down by the stream. We'll probably spend all autumn and winter clearing some of the trees off the land. Then when spring comes, we'll saw the lumber, air-dry it, and then ship by the railroad whatever we don't need and sell it," replied Hans as he continued eating.

"Why doesn't the cook like people?" asked Pete as he filled his empty plate with a second helping of food.

"I didn't say the cook doesn't like people. I said the cook likes privacy," explained Kate. She took the pitcher of milk and filled Pete's empty glass.

"Thanks," said Pete as he continued to gobble his food.

"What do you get out of working for Hans?" asked Kate.

"I get one-fourth of everything Mr. Hans makes," replied Pete as he washed his food down with a glass of milk.

"Well, now that's a very fair beginning for a young lad like you," said Kate as she smiled at Pete.

After dinner Hans and Pete went outside and started walking toward the path. While they were walking Pete asked, "What are you going to do with all these woods?"

"I'm going to clear the land of most of the trees and sell the cleared land in forty acre parcels. I'll use some of the lumber to build houses on the parcels and sell the lumber I don't need. After enough people settle, I'll clear the woods near the inn and build a little town," said Hans. Hans stopped, turned around, and looked at the inn. As he turned, he caught a glimpse of someone looking out one of the upstairs windows. When the person seen Hans turn and look at the inn, the person pulled the curtain back over the window.

"That window is in the cook's room. Why is the cook spying on us?" Hans thought aloud.

He turned to Pete and said, "I'm going to own that inn and the rest of the woods someday, too."

"You think so, Mr. Hans?" said Pete.

"Ya, I know I'm going to. If this place was run right, it could be a regular gold mine," Hans said as he turned and walked down the path.

"Did you write Mrs. Hans yet and tell her about this place?" asked Pete.

"No, not yet. When I get time, I will," replied Hans.

"What about going to Dry Springs?" asked Pete.

"I was going to Dry Springs because my sister said there were a lot of woods around there. I've bought some woods here. So I don't have to go any farther. As for my sister who lived there, I think she's dead. I haven't heard anything from her for five years. However, to satisfy my curiosity, I plan on going there as soon as I get settled here," replied Hans.

With the moonlight showing the way, they came back to the inn. As they approached the inn, they saw the silhouette of a person walking from the small barn toward the inn's back door. As they came closer, they could see the person was wearing a dark dress and a scarf. Part of the scarf was wrapped around the person's face hiding everything except the eyes. When the woman seen Hans and Pete, she hurried into the kitchen door.

"That must be the cook," said Pete as they continued walking.

"Ya, at least we know the cook is a woman. Come on, let's go in the kitchen door, too. Why walk all the way around the inn to go in the front door when the back door is closer," said Hans.

They walked up the back porch to the door. Hans turned the doorknob. The door was locked.

"Well, there's one thing you can say about that cook, she likes her doors locked," said Hans disgustingly.

They walked around to the front of the inn. As they entered the door, they caught a glimpse of a black dress disappearing around the corner at the top of the stairs.

When they reached the top of the stairs, they heard the key turn in the cook's door. From beneath the door, they saw a light go on.

Pete and Hans looked at each other in bewilderment and shrugged their shoulders. They bid each other "good night" and went into their rooms.

Their drained bodies felt relief as they rested in their beds. As their eyelids became heavy and closed, their ears became numb to the night sounds around them. They plunged into a tight sleep that lasted until the early morning rays came through the window and kissed their eyelids.

Their days ahead would be long and filled with plenty of hard, difficult work. They would catch more and more mere glimpses of the cook and their curiosity of her would grow. Kate would mystify them more by changing the subject when they became too inquisitive of her.

****

Farther down the track, near the town of Beechwood, the Aslens were riding on the seat of a farm wagon. Two bay Morgans were pulling the wagon on a dirt road filled with deep, dried mud holes. Lying in the back of the wagon was a bed, a trunk, and food supplies. Tied to and walking behind the wagon was a Holstein.

After passing some dense woods that crowded to the roadside, Phillip stopped the wagon. Standing in front of them in the middle of the flat acreage was a dilapidated barn and a one room log cabin.

Mysterious Person

They climbed down from the wagon and looked at the buildings and the acreage. In one field several rows of bent unpicked cornstalks were still standing from last year's planting. In another field a chilled cast-iron moldboard plow stood in solitude amid turned over sod that was spotted with new growths of green.

"Oh, Phillip, this place is ugly!" cried Della. Tears began to fill her eyes and trickle down her cheeks.

"I know it's not the prettiest place around. However, it was the cheapest one that was available, and we need a place to live," Phillip said as he looked at the land. "The land is good and that's what will make a living for us. We can't live off a house. I promise you, Della. When the farm is paid for, I'll build you the best house anyone has ever seen."

"Everyone is laughing at us for buying this run-down place." Della sobbed. "When I was in the store this morning buying food supplies, the storekeeper asked me what place we purchased. When I told him, I heard two women behind me snickering. Oh, I wish we had never left home." Della began to sniffle. She pulled a handkerchief out of the pocket on her dress and wiped her nose.

"Oh, my dear Della," Phillip said as he embraced her to his chest and stroked her hair. "It doesn't matter what you start out with. It's what you end up with that's important." He lifted her chin and smiled at her. "We'll have the best someday."

Della returned Phillip's smile. He wiped the tears from her face, kissed her, and lifted her into his arms. "And now, my dear, I'll carry you across the threshold," he said.

Della put her arms around his neck. "Oh, Phillip, I love you." She kissed him on the cheek.

"Well, I should hope so," said Phillip.

When they were inside the house, Phillip put her down on the puncheon cabin floor. He then went out the door to get Otto who was standing beside the wagon.

While Phillip was outside, Della looked around the musty room. The rays of sunlight shining through the only window in the cabin showed the accumulated dust on the abandoned table and chairs. Orb spider webs filled the opened, double-door hutch that stood beside the film-covered window.

"Aah!" Della screamed as she saw an enormous black rat run over the ash-covered andirons into the small pile of firewood setting against the wall.

"What's the matter?" Phillip asked as he came running into the cabin carrying Otto.

"Oh, I saw a rat!" Della replied frantically holding her hand over her chest.

Phillip put Otto down and commented, "If you only seen one rat in this place, you're lucky."

As Otto was about to touch the table with his hand, Della grabbed it gently. In a soft voice she said, "Otto, please, don't touch that, it's filthy." She held his small hand in hers. "Come along with me."

"Where are you going?" asked Phillip.

Della grabbed an old wooden pail, setting near the hutch, with her other hand. "I'm going to the pond to get some water so I can clean this place and make something to eat," replied Della.

"Ya, I think I'll make the barn ready for the animals. When we looked at the place the other day, I saw some hay and straw in the loft. I'll leave the wagon set in front of the cabin until the cabin is clean enough to unload the bed and supplies. I better unhitch the animals and put them in the shade near the pond. It's going to be hot today," stated Phillip.

"That sounds like a good idea," said Della. She kissed Phillip as she and Otto went out the door hand in hand.

"Bye-bye-Daddy," said Otto waving his little hand as they walked toward the pond.

The pond was surrounded on three sides by a dense woods. The other side, which faced the cabin, was bordered by a few scattered trees. Della could see the reflections of the trees in the tranquil water as she dipped the pail into it. After pulling the pail out of the water, she examined it.

"Boy! Are we lucky, Otto, no holes." Della chuckled as she grabbed Otto's hand and headed back to the cabin.

On the way back they met Phillip, who was leading the horses and the cow to the pond. Near the edge of the pond were two box elders. Their large extended leafy arms shaded part of the pond and the long green grass from the early morning sun like an umbrella. Phillip tied the horses to one tree and the cow to the other. He left enough slack in the ropes so they could drink from the pond.

As he headed toward the barn, he stopped at the wagon and took his newly purchased hammer and box of nails out from under the wagon seat. He hummed under his breath as he walked down to the barn. As he opened the rotten unlatched barn door, it fell off its rust-corroded hinges. Phillip quickly looked back at the cabin. Della was nowhere in sight. Thank goodness Della didn't see that, Phillip thought to himself.

Phillip knew "his Della" was a very loving and sensitive woman who became quite upset about little things. Things Phillip often considered and knew to be unimportant would upset and worry Della. If she had seen the door fall off, Phillip knew that she would have become terribly upset. She would have worried if it could be fixed and what else was going to fall apart.

After fixing the door, Phillip boarded up the dangerous, rotten holes in the loft and fixed the stalls for the animals. He nailed some of the boards, which had fallen off because the nails had rusted away, back onto the barn. After sweeping out the barn, he put hay into the troughs and straw into the stalls for bedding.

Della spent the day cleaning out the fireplace and stacking the wood neatly beside it. She washed the window, the walls, and scrubbed the floor on her hands and knees. When Otto became cranky, she fed him, washed him, and dressed him in clean clothes that she had in the trunk. She peeled and sliced potatoes, which she mixed with salt pork to make a hash. After putting the hash into a cooking kettle, she placed the kettle on the fireplace crane to cook for supper.

As the dimness of the departing day filled the cabin, Della lit the gas lamp that was setting in the middle of the scoured and now neatly set table. She pulled out one of the four chairs and sat by the table waiting for Phillip.

As she waited, she looked over at their bed, which Phillip had placed near the fireplace. She smiled to herself as she watched "her little Otto" sleeping so snugly under the warm covers of the bed. He was breathing so sweetly and evenly. His one little hand clutched the miniature fire engine lying beside him. The other hand, with the fingers clenched into the palm, was up by his mouth where his small red thumb was resting in his mouth.

A warm, fresh breeze was slowly flowing into the open cabin door. The flame in the fireplace was diminishing and the andirons were being covered with gray-white hot ashes.

"I better get Phillip. The hash and coffee are going to get cold if he doesn't come in now," Della thought aloud.

As she rose from her chair, a tall figure stood in the doorway blocking the beams of moonlight. A salty, sweaty smell filled the room. It was Phillip. He had finished working in the barn and was ravenously hungry. His dirty face was streaked with lines of sweat.

"Hi, honey," he said as he sat at the table with his unwashed hands.

After supper they sat quietly at the table with their hands around their steaming cups of coffee. As they sipped their coffee, they looked about the room and tumbled visions of the future in their minds.

As Della set down her empty cup, a depressed look came across her face.

Phillip reached his callused hand across the table and touched Della's red, rough hands.

"Don't look so upset, honey. We can have anything we want if we're willing to work for it. Our dreams will come true. We just have to work so they do," said Phillip.

"I know," said Della in a tired and depressed tone. "Our dreams just seem so far out of reach." Della raised her eyebrows. "Impossible is more like it."

"Nothing is impossible. It just takes time and a lot of work. Someday this is going to be the best farm in all of Beechwood, and you're going to have the best house around," Phillip said as he rubbed her hand softly.

"Ya, sure," Della replied doubtfully. "Until then we'll be 'the laughing stock' of the town." Tears started to moisten her eyes.

"Don't let those women in town bother and upset you. They probably didn't always have everything so nice either. They just forgot or don't want to remember how they started," Phillip said comfortingly as he patted her hand and gently squeezed it.

Still holding her hand, he turned his head around in the direction of the door.

"That June air is warming tonight. I really sweated working out in the barn today. It must have been a hundred degrees in the sun." He turned his head around and looked at Della. "All the dust that flew around when I swept the barn just clung to my sweaty body. I really feel sticky and dirty."

"According to the old thermometer hanging near the window," Della said as she motioned toward the window with her head. "It was ninety degrees at noon."

"I'm going to the pond and take a bath. The water should be nice and cool. You come with me?" asked Phillip.

"No, I don't think so. I better not leave Otto alone," Della said hesitatingly.

"The pond is only a little way from the cabin. If he calls, you'll hear him." Phillip looked at the fireplace. "The fire is out. He can't burn himself. Come on," Phillip said as he got up still holding her hand.

As he smiled and motioned toward the door with his head, he raised his bushy eyebrows as if to say, "you know what else we can do. I love you so much."

"Well, I suppose, I could take a bath too. I sweated a lot today also, working in this grimy place. The cool water would feel good," said Della.

She got up, untied her soiled apron, and put it on her chair. She took the lighted gas lamp and put it on the fireplace mantle where Otto could not reach it if he happened to wake up. They took their shoes off and placed them beside their bed. Once outside, Della closed the door.

Slowly, hand in hand, they walked in the shimmering moonlight down to the quiescent pond. The stars sparkled like diamonds in the black velvet sky and the warm gentle breeze caressed their faces. The soft cushion of cool green grass gave their tired feet relief as they walked. Hundreds of blinking fireflies spotted the moonlit fields and woods as the male cricket sang his chirping song.

The glowing moonbeams danced on the water as Phillip and Della's nude bodies glided hand in hand through the refreshing cool water. When they were waist-high in the pond, they stopped. Phillip cupped his hands and filled them with water. He moved his water-filled hands up and down Della's lily white arms and smooth shoulders. Carefully, he untied the ribbon that fastened her hair behind her head and spread her hair over her shoulders. Gently, he pulled her toward himself and caressed her warm body. She lovingly embraced him and rested her head on his shoulders. Phillip kissed her shoulders, neck, and lifted her face up to his.

"I love you." He kissed her. "I love you so much." He kissed her again. "I love you--I love you--I love you--"

The beginning of the next day was the beginning of a whole different world for Della and Phillip. They were on their own now. Phillip's parents were no longer around to help with things. It was just Della and Phillip--alone against the world.

As the days faded into months, they worked side by side, planting and harvesting their crops.

Della made no excuse for herself and worked just as hard as Phillip. She eventually accepted the crude building as her "home." Perhaps it wasn't what other people had, but it was enough for her. It was her home now, a place filled with the richness and warmth of love. A home filled with the laughter of a child that was made from love. Della came to realize a house doesn't make a home any more than a heart can make one love.

Chapter 3
****
Deadly Disease

The white curtains danced across the black cast-iron hand pump and sink as the brisk breeze floated into the open window. The cheerful song of the robin came in with the breeze and filled the silence of the room. A slender, well-manicured hand was covering a packed, brown wickerwork basket with a checkered red and white cloth.

A gentle voice interrupted the robin's lyrics. "Are you coming with us today, Pete?"

"No, not today, Kate," replied Pete who was sitting on a chair near the table. He was bent over shining his black shoes.

"Do you like the shoes I gave you for your birthday yesterday?" asked Kate.

Pete stopped shining his shoes and looked up at Kate. "I sure do," he replied, and a big smile crossed his freshly shaved face. "After eighteen years I finally got a pair of Sunday shoes. I never knew a person could own two pairs of shoes at the same time. They feel a lot different from those big leather boots that I always wear at the sawmill. Thanks a lot, Kate." Pete rose from the chair and kissed her pink cheek. "You're the closest to a mother that I've ever had."

"Ah, that's very nice of you to think that way about me, but don't ever call me 'Mom' in public. I'm only twenty-nine, and I think you'd raise a few eyebrows," said Kate as she laughed a bit.

"Ya, I know what you mean," replied Pete as he handed Kate the shoe shine brush.

"Besides, if I didn't buy you a Sunday pair of shoes, you'd run around in those leather boots all the time. You're just too tight to buy yourself another pair." She laughed as she put the shoe shine brush into the cupboard drawer.

A serious look suddenly crossed her face. "I hope you aren't making a mistake by using all your hard earned money to buy stocks in that electric company. That electric company man, who stopped here a few years ago, could have been handing you a 'line' just to get your money."

"No, I don't think so," Pete said confidently. "Electricity is the thing of the future. It's coming. It's just a matter of time before it gets here. If you had seen in New York, what I saw when we stayed in that hotel that one night, you'd believe what I'm saying. The streets were lit up with electric bulbs. It was a fantastic sight, Kate!"

"My dear Pete," Kate said doubtfully as she shook her head, "all you've got to show for eight years of hard work are those pieces of paper that you keep locked in that strongbox of yours."

"Those pieces of paper are certificates of stock and prove my share in the company. It's preferred stock. So if the company goes out of business, I'll have first claim on the assets left after debts are paid. But they won't go out of business, and someday my stock will be premium. I'll make a lot of money from them," Pete explained reassuringly to Kate.

Touching his shoulders with her hand, Kate said, "I hope so, Pete. I really hope so."

Pete smiled at Kate, held her hand, and said, "Don't worry about me, Kate. I've been taking care of myself for a long time. I know how to survive." He walked over to the sink and pumped himself a glass of water.

Kate pushed his chair under the table, rested her hands on the back of the chair, and said, "I saw you talking to Betsy Cork after church today again. Is that where you might be going with those shiny shoes?"

Pete put the empty glass into the sink and replied, "Yup, Betsy invited me over for Sunday dinner at her house to celebrate my birthday." Pete walked past Kate over to the oak hall tree and looked in the plate glass mirror. He fussed with his black tie and then said, "This black suit and vest Hans gave me for my birthday really makes me look different, doesn't it?" He turned around and looked at Kate who had followed him to the hall tree and stood watching him.

Kate put her hands on his tall, broad shoulders and said, "You look like a million bucks." She gave him a big hug.

She backed away, took his hands in hers, and said, "I'm going to miss not seeing you and Hans fish like you always do after our Sunday picnics. Of course, I won't miss cleaning the fish." Kate laughed.

Pete laughed and then said, "Well, there is always next Sunday. I won't get invited to Betsy's for a while. Her father doesn't like me because I'm not 'refined' like Todd Bester."

"Oh, Todd Bester," Kate replied disgustingly. "If he's a 'refined' twenty-year-old man, I don't want to meet another 'refined' man. He says the most disgusting things that I've ever heard. If he acts the way he talks, I wouldn't let my seventeen-year-old daughter anywhere near him. In fact, my one meeting with him decided me against another meeting."

"Well, Mr. Cork is pushing Betsy his way," said Pete. "He even arranged for Todd to take her home last month after the church dance. Betsy didn't like that at all. She can't stand his arrogant ways, and she seems really afraid of him for some reason."

Kate raised her eyebrows, folded her arms, and said, "Mr. Cork would do well to keep his pretty daughter away from that blonde Casanova."

Pete pulled out his marred pocket watch and looked at it. "Well, I better be going. See you later." He went through the dining area door and out the front door. Kate heard him whistle as he walked onto the porch and down the steps.

Kate shook her head and smiled to herself. "Ah, young love," she thought aloud.

She took the basket off the table, rested it on her forearm, and walked into the dining area. She stood at the bottom of the stairs and called up, "I'm ready, Hans."

Hans appeared at the top of the stairs, his dark-brown eyes sparkled as he said, "So am I." Hans looked so handsome as he walked down the stairs in his brown suit, vest, and tie. His round face was shaved, his black wavy hair was neatly combed, and he smelled of a fine cologne. When he reached the bottom of the stairs, he took

Kate's hand in his hand and out the door they went onto the porch.

While on the porch, Kate paused standing near one of the white porch pillars. "This place has really changed," Kate said as she looked at the small town which now stood near the railroad track where her woods used to be.

Enclosed in a white picket fence were Mr. Cork's grocery store, house, and three oaks of antiquity. Kate smiled to herself as she thought, a tree for each of his children.

A short distance from Mr. Cork's place, several great pines stood as sentinels around the bank and Mr. Bester's house.

Across the street a massive oak, with its broad crown, shaded Dr. Gibb's house and the post office.

The playground, which was located around the little red schoolhouse, was scattered with plenty of broad oaks just right for playing tag and hide-and-seek.

Maple trees, painted with autumn's splashes of red and yellow, lined the dirt road that led to a little white church. The church stood on a null, which overlooked the town below.

As Kate looked in the distance, she could see the small farms with their five and ten acres of woods scattered upon the open land.

Her eyes wandered toward the stream where Hans's sawmill and carpenter shop stood. The large waterwheel whirled with the flow of the rapid stream. Kate nodded her head as she looked at the sawmill and said, "You have done quite well financially, my dear Hans. You have paid me everything that you owed me in less than eight years. You have a lot of money in Mr. Bester's bank. Why you're a rich man, Hans Duren. What are you going to do with all that money?" Kate asked as she turned and looked at him.

"I'm going to buy that," Hans said. He pointed to the woods on the other side of the railroad track.

"Why you don't even know who owns that woods," Kate said surprisingly.

"I'll find out. I almost have enough money to buy it outright. When I do, I'll give the person an offer they can't refuse," said Hans.

"And when you have the woods, then what, Hans?" asked Kate.

"I'll build a mansion that will be the revival of the castles of Germany," Hans answered with a most satisfying grin on his face as he looked at the woods that he knew would be his someday.

"Come on, my mansion builder," Kate said as she tugged him down the porch steps after her. Hand in hand they walked behind the inn and disappeared into Kate's woods.

As the fallen autumn leaves of maple and oak crushed beneath their feet, Kate said, "I'm going to miss these picnics when winter comes."

"Ya, I will too," replied Hans as he smiled at her. His smile soon vanished; he became serious in tone. "You've lived around here a long time, haven't you, Kate?"

"Yes, I was born here. That's why my dad bought this land and built the inn. He couldn't travel with the railroad crew anymore because he had a family who needed him at home. My mother's health failed terribly after I was born. She died when I was seven. Since then, it was always just my dad and I," Kate said as she walked along kicking the leaves with her feet. "You would have liked my dad, Hans. You did with the woods what he had dreamed of doing but was unable to."

"If you've lived here all your life, you must know who owns the woods then," said Hans.

"Oh, yes, I know who owns it," replied Kate.

"Who?" asked Hans.

"There really isn't any need for you to know because the person isn't going to sell it," said Kate.

"Well, how do you know?" Hans asked suspiciously.

"I just know," replied Kate as she stopped under one of the tall oak trees that stood on the bank of the stream. "Well, here we are at our picnic spot," Kate said as she set the basket down.

Hans and Kate sat on the long matted grass, which was dotted with white petaled daises tinged with pink, and ate their lunch.

After lunch Kate rose and sat at the edge of the green, grassy stream bank that was beautifully decorated with the gray, silky catkins of the pussy willow.

Hans sat under a tree with his back against its course, gray bark and his arms wrapped around his knees. Scattered around the trees, amid the tall green grass, were the swaying tall flowering stems of bright blue chicory and loose yellow clusters of goldenrod.

As the soft breeze blended with the peaceful spirit of the trees and the thrushes fluttered about making their piercing, chirping sounds, Hans watched Kate as she tossed little, brown oval-shaped acorns into the rapid stream.

Watching her sit, aglow with beauty and warmth, caused a deep flaming desire within his heart for her, as he thought. How he would love to feel her soft body touch his. How he needed her and wanted her to fulfill his burning need. Could he have her only on her terms, or could he persuade her to do things his way? Were her terms so impossible? If that was the only way he could have her, why not accept her terms and let her have her way. He just knew that he had to have her. He couldn't control his desires for her any longer.

As Kate tossed the acorns into the stream and watched them sink out of sight, she remembered what she had told Hans the other night when he came to her room burning with desire for her. As she remembered, she thought. Was it perhaps a little archaic what she had told him? Was it right denying him the most natural human desire? But that was the way she had been raised. That is what the nuns had taught her at the Catholic boarding school where her father had sent her every year. She could not spend ten years of her life with nuns without some of their teachings affecting her attitudes. Did she scare Hans away from her? Would he never want to even kiss her again? Oh, she could not stand it if he would never hold her or kiss her again. Was she terribly wrong when she set up terms for their relationship? Terms he could not accept.

Suddenly, she was startled by a hand touching her hand. She looked up from the stream. It was Hans who had touched her hand as he sat beside her. Looking at him, she smiled.

"I love you, Kate," he whispered. He held her close and gently rubbed his fingers through her soft, fresh smelling hair. He pressed his moist lips against hers as he pulled her closer to his body.

Kate returned his kisses and embraces. She seemed to--M-E-L-T-- in his strong arms as she thought maybe the most important thing in the world was to be loved and held by Hans. Nothing else really seemed to matter now, when he held her and kissed her.

As they laid their bodies side by side in the soft grass, Hans began to kiss her passionately. Slowly, his strong hand began opening the dainty pearl buttons, one by one, on the bodice of her black dress. He started to breathe heavy over her body as he pushed his hand inside her opened bodice.

Suddenly, Kate pushed him away and sprang to her feet.

"No, Hans!" she shouted as she quickly buttoned her bodice.

Hans sat up and grabbed her hand. "Please, Kate, I love you." Hans pleaded with his eyes that were burning with desire.

"I can't, Hans. I'm sorry," she said softly as she pulled her hand away and turned toward the stream. "I can't go through with it this way. If you really love me and want me, you know the only way you can have me."

There was a moment of silence. Soon Kate felt hands around her waist and warm breathing down her neck.

"Okay, Kate, we'll do it your way," Hans said as he kissed the back of her neck.

Kate turned around and put her arms around his neck. "Are you sure, Hans?" she asked.

"Ya, I'm sure," replied Hans as he looked at her sparkling green eyes and smiled.

"Oh, I love you, Hans," Kate said ecstatically as she hugged and kissed him. "I love you."

As they stood beside the stream, amid the long green grass and yellow goldenrod, they kissed and held each other in their arms. A radiant smile covered Kate's face as she held Hans close to her. As Hans held Kate, his smile disappeared and was replaced by a serious, worried look.

****

As Pete held the Cork's white front house door open, a petite, shapely figure with locks of dark-brown hair, a slender nose, and glimmering blue eyes, came out the door in a bright pink dress trimmed with a white collar and cuffs.

"You really look pretty today, Betsy," said Pete.

Betsy smiled at him and said in a sweet voice, "Why, thank you, Pete."

Pete closed the door as they walked over to the edge of the railing-less porch. He took his suit jacket and neatly laid it near the edge of the porch between two white porch pillars. At Pete's motion,

Betsy sat on his jacket and he sat beside her. As they talked, they dangled their feet over Mrs. Cork's flower bed that burst with colorful chrysanthemums and whose strong scent filled the warm air.

"Last spring when my dad told us that we were moving from Chicago to start a new grocery store in a quiet little town in Wisconsin, I cried my eyes red. I didn't want to leave all my friends and move in the boondocks, but now I'm glad that we moved here. Because if we wouldn't have moved, I would have never met you," said Betsy as she reached over and touched Pete's hand that rested on his one leg.

"I'm glad you came, too," Pete said as he smiled at her and gently squeezed her hand.

"There's one thing that I can't understand. My dad said that you've lived here a long time. But I never even knew you existed until I saw you in church with Kate this summer. Where were you all last year? How come I never saw you?" asked Betsy.

"This summer is the first summer that Hans and I haven't worked all the time. For the last seven years, we worked every day out of the year from sunrise to sunset. Even when the weather was terrible in winter, we'd go down to the sawmill or Hans's carpenter shop and make furniture inside. I'm glad that he's got his land paid for so we don't have to work all the time, and I can see you more often. Being able to see you every Sunday morning after church and sometimes in the afternoon, gives me something to look forward to," explained Pete.

"Why did you work so hard?" asked Betsy.

Pete shrugged his shoulders. "Well, until now, I didn't have anything else to do. Besides, Hans paid me well, and I don't want to be owing to him for taking me in when I came over here. I don't like to owe anyone," explained Pete.

A puzzled look crossed Betsy's face. "You mean you came here with Hans, not your family?" Betsy asked.

"I don't have a family," Pete said and paused for a few seconds. "Well, that's not exactly true. There's a man who's supposed to be my uncle," Pete replied disgustingly.

"What do you mean, 'supposed to be your uncle'?" Betsy asked bewilderingly.

"Oh, how I hate that man," Pete said angrily. "If it wouldn't be for him, my parents would be alive." Pete angrily slammed his fist on the porch.

"I'm sorry, Pete. I didn't mean to upset you," Betsy said consolingly.

"After all these years that man still gets to me." Pete rose from where he had been sitting, walked to the other side of the porch, and stood near a white pillar. He put his one arm around the pillar and rested his head against it.

Betsy rose and walked over to him. She put her arms around his waist and rested the side of her head on his back. "I'm really sorry, Pete," she said softly. "Maybe it would help if you just let go and let everything out. I'm willing to listen and help if you need me."

Pete turned around and held her smooth hands in his. "Maybe you're right. I should get everything out. I've had this bottled up in me for years. Ever since I can remember." He put his arms around her shoulder. They walked to where his jacket was, and he picked it up. They walked down the porch steps, which were opposite the front door, and walked under the cool shade of a tall oak that stood in the fenced yard. Pete put his jacket on the grass and they sat on it.

"My grandfather used to own a big bakery in Bremen," Pete said as he looked at the grass and pulled out a few green blades. "My father and his brother, Oslo, worked in the bakery for him. Everything was going fine until my grandfather fell down some stairs and broke his hip. He then came to stay with us so my mother could take care of him." A smile crossed Pete's face as he said, "I still can remember coming home from my first day of school and sitting on his lap as he gave me a ride through the house on his wheelchair." The smile disappeared as Pete stared into infinite space. "My grandfather was old and his hip didn't heal right, so he had to stay in the wheelchair indefinitely. After Christmas that year, my mother became pregnant and bedridden. She was terribly sick and could no longer take care of my grandfather. So Oslo and his wife took my grandfather. About two months later, my grandfather died and then everything changed. My mother became sicker and unpaid doctor bills mounted. One hot summer night while I was asleep, a scream from my mother's room woke me. I could hear a woman soothing my mother and telling my father to hurry and get the doctor. While my father was gone, the agonizing screams of my mother filled the house. I sat in my room with my hands on my ears to stop the screams that tore at my heart and made my eyes weep. Soon I heard the house door open and my father walk across the wooden floor to the bedroom. A little while later everything was quiet except for the sound of my father sobbing. It made me cry more to hear him. I heard him explain to the woman how he had met the doctor coming out of his house on the way to treat Oslo's wife for a cold. My father told of how he had pleaded with the doctor to come, but the doctor said that he couldn't afford to spend any more of his time with people who didn't pay their bills. He pushed my father aside as he climbed into his brougham and ordered his servant to take him to Oslo's."

"I sympathize with you, Pete, but I don't see how it's Oslo's fault. I think that it's the doctor's fault. He's the one who didn't come," replied Betsy as she wiped the tears from her eyes.

"He didn't come because my father didn't have any money and that was Oslo's fault," Pete said defensively.

"I don't understand why your father didn't have any money. I thought he worked in the bakery?" Betsy asked in a puzzling manner.

"Not after my grandfather died he didn't." Pete turned to Betsy and explained, "You see my grandfather said that he had put in his will that when he died the bakery would be made into a partnership between my father and Oslo. But while he was at Oslo's house, he changed his will and gave everything to Oslo. My father was left paying the funeral expenses."

"Oh, your poor father," Betsy said sympathetically as she gently squeezed his hand.

"That's not all Oslo did," replied Pete. "After he had the bakery, he decided that he couldn't afford to keep my father as a worker. Oslo and his wife decided to do the work themselves and fired my father. He tired to get work all over the town but was unable to. After my mother died, he just fell to pieces. He blamed himself for her death and started drinking heavily."

With tear-filled eyes, Betsy sat and listened as she held Pete's hand.

"One morning," Pete continued, "when I was eight, I woke up, and my father wasn't lying drunk on the floor with an empty bottle of booze in his hand like he usually was. So I walked down the streets looking in the alleys for him. When I reached the dock, I saw a large crowd had gathered near the edge of it. Among the crowd, I saw Oslo, with his long, snooping nose. One of the individuals next to Oslo said, 'That's your brother.' Oslo stretched his neck to see over some of the crowd and said, 'Ya, that's the drunken bum.' Boy, I could have strangled Oslo for saying those words. Instead, I ran home. I didn't want to see my father that way. I heard he was drunk, fell into the river, and drown," said Pete. He could shed no more tears. He had shed enough so many times before that the story made him numb with no feelings of sadness. Only feelings of hate still remained and became stronger as the feelings of sadness had disappeared.

"Did Oslo take care of you then?" asked Betsy.

"No, he wouldn't even let me work for something to eat," Pete said scornfully.

"How did you live?" Betsy was concerned.

"I just did," replied Pete. He didn't want Betsy to know that he had been a thief. He was ashamed of that. Not because he hurt Oslo, but because he knew that she would consider it a bad thing. Pete didn't want Betsy to think badly of him. Besides that was all in the past, it didn't have anything to do with now. Let the past in the past, why let a skeleton out of the closet. He was an honest man now. He had worked hard for everything he had.

"Oh, my poor Pete," Betsy said in a soft, sympathetic voice as she gently shook her head and rubbed her hand down the sides of his hair and face.

"Oh, don't feel sorry for me, Betsy," replied Pete. "I learnt something from all that. I don't plan to ever get married until I have enough money to support myself, my wife, and any children I might have. I don't ever want to have to rely on anyone like my father relied on my grandfather. Until I can be my own man and take care of myself financially, I don't intend to take on the responsibility of taking care of anyone else. I don't want a child of mine to grow up the way I did. If Hans wouldn't have taken me with him, who knows what my life would be like now."

A disappointed look crossed Betsy's face as she said, "If you wait until you think you have enough money, you may never get married."

"Well, then I'll never get married," Pete replied casually.

"Well, you're pretty well set financially now, aren't you?" asked Betsy. She was hoping he'd say "yes" because she cared for him dearly. She didn't particularly like the idea of waiting too long to get married. Besides Pete, Todd Bester was the only boy around who was about her age. If she had a choice, she'd want to marry Pete. Betsy also knew that if Pete waited too long to ask her to marry him, her father would push Todd Bester her way more than he had been.

"Nope, not yet," replied Pete.

Betsy held back the disappointment of the answer. She smiled at Pete, and said, "Well, guess that's settled."

There was a moment of silence as they both sat casually tearing off the tops of grass blades and tossing them into the breeze.

"Say, why don't you come to the inn with me after church next Sunday? You can come along on our usual Sunday picnic," said Pete. "That's if the weather is nice."

Betsy made a frown. "No, I don't think my dad will let me go," she said in a disappointing tone.

"Well, why don't we ask him. All he can say is 'no,' " replied Pete.

"Ya, you're right. All he can say is 'no,' and he probably will," replied Betsy dishearteningly.

Just as Pete started to get up, Betsy grabbed his hand. "Let's stay out here awhile. I like talking to you," Betsy said as she looked up at him and smiled.

Smiling back at her, he said, "That sounds fine to me." Pete sat down again.

While Betsy and Pete sat under the tree talking, Mr. Cork was watching them through the sheer living room curtain. "That boy isn't right for our Betsy," said Mr. Cork. He shook his head and took a few gulps from the brown bottle of beer that he held in his hand.

Mrs. Cork, sitting in a rocker across the room near a cold, black potbellied stove and a basket full of white balls of yarn, looked up from her knitting at Mr. Cork. She rolled her eyes upward and moved her head sideways as if to say, "for God's sake leave the boy alone." However, Mrs. Cork knew that she shouldn't say anything defensive about someone Mr. Cork didn't like. So she just quietly thought her share, kept on knitting, and listened to him talk. Sometimes, when she'd stop knitting to look at him, she'd stroke her gray hair that was pulled neatly into a bun or finger the buttons on her calico dress.

"Now, Todd Bester, he'd make a fine husband for our Betsy," Mr. Cork said as he motioned with the beer bottle in the direction of the Bester house. He took a few more gulps out of the bottle and then examined the contents. Seeing it was empty, he put the bottle on the round table, which stood in front of the window and was decorated with several family pictures.

Holding his black trousers up over his predominant belly was a pair of wide white suspenders, which he extended slightly from his body as he held them in his fist. While holding his suspenders and slowly rocking back and forth on his feet he said, "Ya, Todd Bester he'd be just right for our Betsy. He's got a good education and is a teller in the bank. Someday when his dad retires, he'll probably become president of the bank. As the town gets bigger, the bank gets bigger. The bigger the bank gets, the more important its president becomes." Mr. Cork's face became radiant as he talked on. "Why if Betsy married Todd, she'd be the most prominent--not to mention the richest lady in town."

He turned away from the window and looked at Mrs. Cork, who was busily moving knitting needles back and forth in her short, fat hands. "Well, what do you think, Ma?" he asked.

"I think we should let Betsy choose the person that she wants to marry. Working in a bank doesn't necessarily mean a person has money," replied Mrs. Cork as she knitted on, never even looking up.

Mr. Cork didn't exactly like her slight contradictory reply and frowned a bit.

"Well, don't you think that he'd be a nice catch?" he snapped at her.

Knowing that he was upset by her reply, she softly said, "Whatever you think, my dear. You're the head of the house." Carefully, she put her knitting into the basket and rose her plump body from the rocker.

"I think I'll start supper now," Mrs. Cork said as she grabbed her apron, which was neatly folded and hanging on one of the rocking chair arms.

"It's getting dark. I'm calling Betsy in. I don't trust a boy like that with my daughter if I can't see him," said Mr. Cork as he walked toward the door.

"What do you mean by that?" asked Mrs. Cork softly as she tied her apron strings behind her back.

Touching the doorknob, Mr. Cork turned and said to his wife, "Oh, look at the environment that boy is around. That Miss O'Leary and Hans Duren living under the same roof for all those years. Don't tell me they haven't been to bed together more than once. Morals like that are sure to rub off on the boy. Who knows maybe he's even been in bed with Kate a couple of times."

Mrs. Cork rolled her eyes again as she turned toward the kitchen door. She disapproved greatly of what he had said but was not about to let him know and start an argument. She opened the kitchen door and disappeared inside the kitchen.

Mr. Cork opened the door. As he stood in the doorway, he shouted, "Betsy, it's time to come in."

"Okay, Dad," Betsy called back.

Pete rose and pulled Betsy up. She looked toward the house. Her father had shut the door and gone back inside the house.

Betsy took Pete's hand and ran with him to the side of the house that extended from the edge of the porch. No one in the house could see them. Betsy pulled Pete close, she stood on her tiptoes and gave him a long kiss.

"Well, how did you like that?" asked Betsy with her arms around his neck.

"Come on, I better get you in the house before your dad comes out here," said Pete.

"Oh, just one more kiss, Pete," begged Betsy as she reached up to kiss him again.

"No, come on now," Pete said as he grabbed her hands off his neck and pulled her up the porch steps to the front door.

Just as Pete started to grab for the doorknob, the door opened. Mr. Cork was standing in the doorway.

Pete and Betsy looked at each other as they thought. Boy, that was a close one! We made it just in time.

"Come on in, Pete," said Betsy as she started to pull him into the house in front of Mr. Cork, who was looking sternly at Pete.

"No, I better be going," Pete said as he pulled away from Betsy's hand. Pete could see and feel Mr. Cork's resentment.

As Mrs. Cork came through the kitchen doorway, wiping her hands on her apron, she looked at Pete and smiled.

"Hi, Pete," she said in her soft voice.

"Thank you for the delicious dinner, Mrs. Cork," Pete said gratefully.

"You're welcome to stay for supper, Pete," she said.

Pete, seeing the displeased look Mr. Cork gave her, replied, "No, thank you, Mrs. Cork. Kate probably has something for me."

"Ya, I bet she does," mumbled Mr. Cork with a smirk.

Mrs. Cork turned her piercing blue eyes in Mr. Cork's direction and gave him a long disgusting look.

"Good night, Betsy," said Pete timidly as he turned to go out onto the porch.

"Wait, Pete!" shouted Betsy.

Pete turned slowly around and looked at Betsy.

"Dad, can I go to the inn after church next Sunday and then go on a picnic with Pete, Kate, and Hans?" Betsy asked enthusiastically.

"No," her father sternly replied. "Todd Bester is coming for dinner," he paused, turned to Pete, rose his bushy red eyebrows, "and supper," he added.

Betsy's smile faded.

Mrs. Cork's eyes popped wide open. Mr. Cork had really surprised her. That was the first time she had heard Todd was coming. In her heart she knew why Mr. Cork had said that. It was to hurt Pete and keep him away from Betsy. She glanced at Pete. From the gloomy look on his tanned face, she could see that Mr. Cork had succeeded in hurting him. Mrs. Cork sighed and gave Mr. Cork a disapproving look as she looked away from the snickering look on his bearded face.

Mrs. Cork smiled at Pete. "Good night, Pete," she said softly as she stole away into the kitchen.

"Good night, Pete," Mr. Cork said authoritatively as he held the door open for Pete to leave.

Pete could take a hint. With his ego shattered, he timidly left the house. As he paused for a few minutes on the porch, he could hear Betsy and her father.

"Dad, you didn't have to be so mean to Pete," Betsy said.

"He's not right for you, Betsy," said Mr. Cork.

"You don't even know him, Dad," replied Betsy.

"I don't want to argue. Your ma has supper done. Now let's go and eat," Mr. Cork commanded.

Depressed, Pete walked down the porch steps as he pulled out his pocket watch. "It's seven o'clock," Pete thought aloud. "I'm an hour late for supper. Oh, who cares! I'm not hungry anyway. Mr. Cork spoiled my appetite."

Slowly, in the subdued light of the twilight, he walked in a sulky mood back to the inn. Thin gray clouds crept across the full white moon that stood alone in the starless sky. The continuous rumbling of the stream filled the loneliness of the twilight. As he walked in the lazy breeze, he kicked a stone that lay on the worn path to the inn.

The inn was dark except for the yellow beams of light that filtered out through the open windows in Kate's room.

When he reached the inn, he sat on the last porch step, picked up the stone, and slowly tossed it back and forth in his hands.

"Oh, why get so upset," thought Pete aloud. "I don't need Mr. Cork. I'm not ready to get married anyway. Maybe by the time I am ready, Mr. Cork will have changed his mind about me. If he hasn't, who cares. I don't need him. Maybe I won't even care for Betsy by the time that I'm ready for marriage. Times change--people change."

Voices, which came from the inside of Kate's room, interrupted his consoling, rationalizing thoughts.

"Oh, Kate, you look lovely," said a gravelly voice.

"Good thing you decided today. Tomorrow we leave to see my parents, and we'll be gone for a month. You'd have to travel over to Beechwood," another voice said, which sounded like Pastor Clark.

"Did Kate invite him and his wife, Martha, to supper again? Strange! She didn't mention it to me," Pete thought aloud.

"Well, a certain person didn't want to wait. And as long as you and the judge were here together, we thought this would be the perfect time." Pete recognized Kate's voice.

"Oh, I don't blame you for not wanting to wait," said the gravelly voice as he chuckled. "If I would be younger, I tell you. I would never have waited as long as you did, Hans. I would have made my move right away. The first time I seen Kate--I would have made her mine."

After that remark, laughter filled the air and Pete heard the ringing chime of glasses touching.

"May you always be happy," said the gravelly voice.

"Thanks for letting me wear your dress and for the beautiful bouquet, Martha." He heard Kate say.

"I'm glad the dress fit you. The dahlias really make a beautiful bouquet. My flower bed is just a mass of color this year," replied the voice.

"Hey, come in here, Pete," yelled a voice.

Pete turned his head in the direction of the voice and looked up. There, leaning out the open window in Kate's room and motioning with his hand for Pete to come inside was Charlie, the conductor.

"What's going on in there?" asked Pete as he tossed the stone aside.

"A celebration!" he replied. "Come in and join us."

After the conductor pulled his dark head of hair back into the room, Pete got up and entered the inn.

Just as he entered the doorway to Kate's room, the conductor limped over to him and handed him a glass of sherry.

While the conductor stood beside him near the doorway, Pete looked about the room.

Kate, holding a brilliant bouquet in her white-gloved hands, was standing in front of the bookcase talking busily with Martha. Kate looked like an angel aglow in pure white and quiet innocence.

Seeing Kate dressed like that confused Pete. A bewildered look crossed his face.

"Hi, Pete," said the gravelly voiced engineer as he approached Pete carrying a glass of sherry in his hand.

"Good to see you again," said Pastor Clark who was following the engineer.

"Say, what is going on here?" asked Pete.

"Kate and Hans got married a little while ago," answered Pastor Clark as he sipped some more of his sherry.

Pete's jaw fell, his head perked up, and his eyes stood wide open when he heard that. "Kate and Hans are married?" asked Pete in an unbelievable tone.

"They sure are," replied the pastor as he took another sip of his sherry. "I performed the ceremony, and the judge supplied the legal papers."

"I wonder what those people up North are going to do after the judge retires next year?" said the conductor.

"Ya, he's the only judge that goes up North to those lumberjack towns. When he comes to a town, he's busy day and night writing up divorces, performing marriages, and writing land contracts. You name it. He does it," said the engineer.

Pete faintly heard what they were saying as he stared at Hans, who was standing next to the writing table talking to the judge. A frown crossed his brow as he wondered what on earth Hans was thinking about when he married Kate. Surely, he couldn't have forgotten about Lena--had he? Did Lena die? If she did, why didn't he mention it to him? The thoughts rolled over and over in his mind.

"Well, what do you think about that, Pete?" asked the gravelly voiced engineer.

Pete, still a little bit dazed and incoherent, looked at the engineer.

"Sorry, I didn't hear what you said," replied Pete.

"We're talking about the judge moving to Boston," said the engineer.

"Oh, is that where he is going when he retires?" asked Pete. As he drank some of his sherry, Pete's eyes strayed over to Hans.

"Yupe," replied the conductor. "I bet Kate will really miss him. He's been like a dad to her ever since her dad died."

"Kate wanted him to retire here. She even offered to give him a piece of land to build on," said the engineer, "but I guess he and his wife want to live near their daughter who lives in Boston."

"Ya, ever since I've known Kate, the judge always seemed to watch out for her," said Pete.

"Well, now that'll be Hans's job," said the pastor as he finished his sherry and set the empty glass on the oval mahogany table setting near the door.

"Think so?" said Pete, a bit leery as he glanced at Hans.

"I guess Martha and I will be leaving now," said the pastor.

Pete followed the pastor over to where Martha and Kate were talking.

As Kate smiled radiantly at Pete, he embraced her and said, "Congratulations, Kate."

"Thanks, Pete. I'm so happy." She looked at Hans. "I love him so much." Glancing back, she looked at the bouquet in her hand. "Aren't the flowers beautiful? Martha picked them for me from her garden."

Pete smiled. "You're the one that's beautiful, Kate."

"Oh." Kate blushed. "You're a flatterer."

"No, Kate, it's not flattery," replied Pete sincerely. "It's the truth." He touched her hand. "Excuse me, Kate. I want to talk to Hans." With that, he walked over to Hans and the judge.

"Good evening, Judge Emery--Hans," said Pete.

"Hi, Pete, my boy," the judge said as he put his hand on Pete's shoulder. "Well, aren't you going to congratulate the groom?"

"Oh--ya--congratulations, Hans," said Pete. "A little quick--this marriage," he raised an eyebrow, "wasn't it?"

"It's the way Kate and I wanted it," replied Hans. He was nervous and afraid like a man dismantling a bomb. A wrong word from Pete would be like a wrong move and everything could explode.

"Ya, I bet it was," replied Pete.

A puzzled look crossed the judge's face, and he could feel a strange and unusual strain between the two. He could see Hans was uncomfortable around Pete now, and that Pete had a strange, hostile attitude toward the marriage. The judge surely thought Pete would be happier than anyone else because of the fondness he knew that Pete felt for Hans and Kate. The sudden change in attitude was indeed strange. The judge looked at his empty glass. Oh, well maybe he had too much to drink and was reading more into what Pete said than there really was. He pulled out his pocket watch. It was eight-thirty. Time to leave, he thought.

"Well, I think I'm going to kiss the bride again and then retire for the night. See you tomorrow," the judge said to Hans and Pete as he set his empty glass on the writing table. He walked over to Kate who was still talking to the pastor and his wife, Martha.

While he held Kate's one hand, he gently patted it with his other hand and looked into her face with a smile. "I hope this marriage keeps those beautiful green eyes as radiant and as happy as they are now. I hope that they'll never be dampened by tears of regret."

Kate smiled. "Oh, don't worry, they won't be." She embraced him and kissed his cheek.

"See you tomorrow morning, Kate. Good night, Pastor Clark--Martha," said the judge. He went out the door and ascended the stairs.

"Just what are you up to now, Hans," Pete whispered in a highly suspicious tone.

"What do you mean?" Hans asked. The innocence of his question was betrayed by the look of guilt that covered his face.

"You know exactly what I mean." Pete's face was full of anger. The very idea of Hans acting as if he was a dumb jackass who didn't know what he was talking about. That he was that dumb and didn't know about Lena. That he was so dumb that he didn't know it was against the law to have two wives. My God! He wasn't the smartest person, but he wasn't the dumbest either. It angered him tremendously to have Hans imply that idea.

Hans looked over at Kate who was saying a good-bye to the pastor and Martha. "Let's go somewhere and talk about this," Hans said as he grabbed Pete's arm.

"Ya, we better before Kate comes over here," Pete said as he looked over at Kate.

They went into the dining area and then into the kitchen. Behind the closed door and in the shadowy darkness of the still room, they talked.

"How could you marry Kate? You already have a wife," said Pete.

"That really isn't any of your business--now is it, Pete? I don't bud into your business, and you don't have any right to bud into mine," replied Hans in a justifying manner.

"Well, I care about Kate and that makes it my business," Pete replied defensively.

"I care for Kate, too. I don't intent to do anything to hurt her," Hans replied reassuringly.

"Well, now that's really funny. How do you think she is going to feel when she finds out about Lena, huh?" asked Pete.

"She doesn't ever have to know. I haven't heard from Lena in over a year. For eight years I've been a faithful husband, but I have human needs too. I can't wait forever. Lena should have sold our property by now. Maybe she's found someone else also," Hans said defensively.

"There are plenty of girls in Beechwood at the tavern who would be more than happy to help you through your human needs," Pete replied sarcastically.

"I wouldn't go near those sluts with a ten-foot pole. I would just be another paying customer to them. I couldn't make love to someone who didn't even care enough about me to even ask my name. I need someone who wants me and someone who can love me in more ways than just satisfying my sexual needs. I couldn't live in the empty vacuum of a slut's so-called love," said Hans.

"Kate has a right to know, Hans," said Pete.

"Well, I could say the same about you. Maybe we should tell everyone what 'good, honest, hardworking Pete' was like in Germany," remarked Hans.

This upset Pete because it was important to him what people thought of him. He knew the good reputation, which he had built here, would mean nothing if people found out that he was a thief in Germany. "Once a thief, always a thief," that old saying was even known here. That was the second time today that he regretted what he had done in Germany. It seemed as if he was paying more for it than Oslo did. It didn't really seem fair. Oslo was the "bad guy," but he was being punished for trying to survive. People just didn't seem to understand the circumstances of things. If only he would have thought farther ahead, instead of from day to day. He never realized then how important being known as an honest person would be to him. It's a small world, and there is always someone who knows something about a person. A person can do a thousand good things, but people only seem to remember the one bad thing a person does. People are so "funny." They seem to thrive on hearing the worst of a person. Somehow, it seems more interesting than the good. For Hans, to throw that in his face was shocking!

"You know my Achilles' heel," Pete said as he raised his eyebrow. "Don't you? And you have no intention of ever letting me forget, do you?"

"Achilles' heel! My! My! You're really getting educated from all those books of Kate's that you read," Hans replied sarcastically.

"You should try reading them sometime. At least no one gets hurt by my actions," replied Pete.

"We all have an Achilles' heel, Pete," said Hans. "You keep my secret, and I'll keep yours."

"Huh! I really don't have a choice, do I?" said Pete.

"No, not if you want to keep your past in the past," replied Hans.

"I'll be watching you real close, Hans," warned Pete. "If I think Kate is going to get hurt more than I would if people knew about my past, I'm telling. I know for sure the judge wouldn't think kindly of this situation."

"I could care less about the judge," replied Hans. "He won't be coming around here too much longer anyhow."

Pete was shocked at that reply.

"You sound almost glad to get rid of him. Why? I thought you liked him," said Pete.

"With some people it pays to act as if you do," replied Hans.

"Is that what you're doing with Kate, acting?" asked Pete.

"No, I really have feelings for Kate," replied Hans.

"Well, I always thought that when a person gets married, you have more than 'feelings' for a person. You should love the person," said Pete.

"Oh, I love Kate," said Hans.

Somehow Hans didn't sound very reassuring. Pete didn't know if he should believe him or not. Hans seemed to be changing, and Pete didn't like the new Hans very much. It seemed like the more money he made, the more shrewd and less thoughtful he became.

"I don't know why you're making such a fuss, Pete," said Hans. "Lena is in Germany, and Kate is here. They'll probably never meet."

Suddenly, the kitchen door opened and a lighted gas lamp came into the doorway and into the room. It was the cook. When she saw them, she scurried back out the door, shutting the door behind her.

"Wait!" said Hans as he hurriedly walked toward the closed door. By the time he opened the door and looked outside, she had vanished.

Hans shook his head. "Even after all these years, she sparks my curiosity. That scarf on her face hides everything except her eyes."

"Ever since we came here, we've been trying to find out about her. She obviously likes her privacy and wants to be left alone. So why don't we leave her alone," said Pete. "I'm not curious about her anymore. I don't care what she does. I've got my own life."

"Boy, we don't agree on anything anymore, do we?" said Hans.

"No, I guess not." With that statement, Pete walked out the door into the dining area.

Hans followed him and thought to himself, he didn't need Pete for anything, anymore. He almost had everything he wanted. However, it would be wise to keep Pete around, just to keep an eye on him.

As Pete went up the stairs, Hans went into Kate's room where Kate was talking to the conductor.

Kate greeted him as he entered the room, "Hans, the conductor was looking for you." She put her arm around Hans's waist as he stood next to her.

"Looking for me! Why?" Hans looked puzzled as he looked at the conductor. Then he became suddenly nervous and tense. He felt a lump in his throat. Did the conductor know about Lena?

"You were asking about a town called Dry Springs a few years ago, weren't you?" the conductor asked.

"Ya, you told me that you never heard of it," replied Hans. He felt a moment of relief, he relaxed, and put his arm around Kate's slender waist.

"Well, I met a guy on the train the other day who used to live there," said the conductor.

"Oh, ya, where is it?" asked Hans eagerly.

"It doesn't exist anymore. It used to be a small town up North. It was built in a valley surrounded by hills that were covered with woods. The lumberjacks came and cleared the hills of all the woods. After the trees were all gone, there was nothing to absorb the water from the spring thaws and rains. So every spring the town was flooded. I guess the people just got sick and tired of the floods and left. The man said the town has been deserted for at least fourteen to fifteen years," explained the conductor.

"Well, that still doesn't explain why my sister and her husband seemed to have vanished from the face of the earth," said Hans.

"Oh, I asked the man about her. Her name was Theresa Merts, right?" asked the conductor.

"Ya," Hans replied. He was eager again.

"The man said he knew her and her husband. He said that they moved along with the rest of the townspeople, but he didn't know where. I'm sorry I can't help you more," the conductor said sincerely.

"Well, thanks for asking for me and letting me know," Hans said disappointingly.

The conductor pulled out his pocket watch and examined the time. "It's time I leave you newlyweds alone. Good night."

"Good night." Kate smiled.

"Good night," said Hans as he closed the door behind him. As he leaned against the door, a pleasing grin crossed his face and his eyes gleamed. At last Kate was his--to hold--to make love to.

"Are you ready for bed?" he asked as he looked between the slightly opened bedroom door at the neatly made bed that waited for him and Kate.

"Yes," replied Kate.

He reached out and touched her hand. He turned out the gas lamp and led her into the bedroom.

****

Shuffling down a rural gravel road, in the warm afternoon sun, was a small boy dressed in dark, ankle-lengthened trousers. In his one hand he held the end of a leather strap. The leather strap was slung over his one shoulder and held tight several books, which rested on his back. Gently, the soft breeze tossed his blonde curls about his head.

At the edge of a driveway, the boy stopped. On each side of the entrance to the driveway stood a tall rectangular brick pillar. Extending from the top of one pillar to the top of the other was a wooden arch. Painted on the arch in bold black letters was the name ASLEN. The boy stood silent as his blue eyes roamed over the vast acreage, which stretched in front of him. His eyes rested on a blue pond that was now graced with a few dabbling ducks.

A sadness crossed his light-colored face as he thought. He wished he didn't have to go to school on these nice warm autumn days. It would be so much fun to stay home and help his father on the farm. Then when the work was done, they would wash the dust from work off with a nice afternoon swim in the cool pond. A smile crossed his face as he thought about the fun that his father and he had this summer cooling off in the pond after a hard day's work.

Today would have been a nice day for an afternoon swim. Sadness appeared again. He supposed that they wouldn't get another nice day like this until summer came again. Darn it! He had wasted a perfectly beautiful day sitting and sweating in an old red schoolhouse.

He shuffled under the arch and up the brick driveway toward the white, classic Revival style house.

He passed the surrey and horses, which stood in front of the house, went up the steps onto the portico, and into one of the double doors.

"I'm home, Ma," he shouted as he laid the leather strap with books on the bottom step of the open stairway.

"I'm in the kitchen, Otto," called a voice.

He walked down the bright foyer, opened the door to the left of him and went inside the room.

A dainty, well-groomed woman, who was peeling potatoes at the sink, greeted him with a big smile and merry dark eyes.

"How was school today?" she asked as she finished peeling the potatoes.

He shrugged his shoulders. "Oh, it was okay--I guess. I'd rather stay home and help you and Dad on the farm." He sat on a chair by the table and reached for the stoneware cookie jar, which centered the shining clean table.

Hearing the click of the cookie jar, she turned around. "Only two cookies, Otto, we will be eating supper soon."

"A gosh, Ma, I'm starved. Walking all the way home from school made me hungry." He grabbed out two cookies, put the top back on the jar and pushed it back to the middle of the table.

"Ya, I know how it goes. When supper comes you'll be too full of cookies to eat what's good for you."

She washed the potatoes, put them into a kettle, wiped her hands on her apron, and put the kettle on the hot stove.

"Do I have to go to school tomorrow, Ma?" asked Otto disgustingly as he finished one of his cookies.

Gently, she touched his shoulder. "Yes, you do. What you've got up here," she pointed to his head, "no one can ever take away from you."

"Oh, I'm just going to be a farmer. I don't see why I have to go to school." He started to munch on the other cookie.

She grabbed a small, blue-colored glass off the wooden shelf, which hung on the wall next to the single basin white enamel sink.

On the sink stood a white stoneware pitcher covered with beads of condensation. She grabbed the pitcher, poured some of its milk into the glass, set the glass next to Otto, and said, "A farmer should know how to read and write. He should try and be as well educated as anyone else. Then no one can take advantage of him. You're in fourth grade now, and it won't be long before you'll be out of school."

"I wish I'd be out already." He finished his cookie and grabbed his glass of milk.

"Oh, my dear Otto, you have such a tough life." She chuckled and ruffled his hair.

"The milk is really cold tonight," he said between gulps.

"It should be. I just took it out of the milk can in the pond about a half-hour ago," she replied.

He finished his milk.

As he grabbed for the cookie jar, she grabbed his hand. "No more, Otto."

Looking at his soiled hand, she said, "You should have washed your hands before you ate."

He examined his hands. "Well, Dad always says, 'you have to eat a bushel of dirt before you die.'"

"If you keep eating with such dirty hands, you'll have a bushel in you before you know it. Now, scoot over there and wash your hands," she said mildly as she motioned to the hand pump on the sink.

As Otto got out of the chair and went to the sink, she grabbed the damp cloth out of the sink and cleaned up the cookie crumbs.

While pumping the water into the sink, Otto asked, "What are the surrey and horse doing in front of the house?"

"I got more potatoes out of my garden than we need or will ever use over the winter months. So, I thought, we'd see if the new neighbors could use them." She began to set the table for supper.

"Are those the new people that we saw in church yesterday?" he asked as he scrubbed his hands in the water.

"Yes, they bought the old McCluthen farm just down the road. While I was talking to Father Kaus after mass, he mentioned they don't have much. So, I thought, we'd see if they could use the extra potatoes."

"How long have they lived there?" asked Otto as he dried his hands on the towel hanging beside the sink.

"Three or four days--I guess?" She left the dirty water out of the sink and swished the sink clean.

"What if they don't like potatoes?" asked Otto as he took his place at the table.

"Well, then we'll sell them to Mr. Erickson. He won't have any trouble getting rid of them," his mother replied.

She took the kettle of potatoes off the stove, drained the water from the potatoes, mashed them, and set them on the table.

The kitchen door opened and in stepped Phillip wearing a soiled bib overall.

"Hi, Dad," Otto greeted.

"Hi, Otto," replied Phillip.

"Hi, honey," Della greeted him with a huge smile as he walked toward her.

"Hi, honey," Phillip kissed her soft cheek. "I loaded the bags of potatoes into the back of the surrey. I think we'll leave right after supper. If we wait until after milking, it'll be dark before we get home. I don't like driving the horses after dark." He washed his hands, dried them, and sat at the table.

"That sounds good to me," Della said as she set the beef roast and gravy on the table.

As the white steam swirled around the center of the table, they folded their hands, bowed their heads, and said a short prayer of thanks before they began eating.

When supper was finished, they headed down the road to the old McCluthen farm. The sun's bright, glaring yellow eye stared into their faces as they traveled.

Soon the surrey stopped in front of a run-down cape cod style house.

They jumped down from the surrey, hopped over the rotten spots in the porch steps, and knocked on the door.

While they waited for the door to open, Della was afraid that any moment they'd fall through the rotten porch boards. This place reminded her of their place eight years ago. How she wished, her neighbors had greeted her in this friendly manner.

The sound of squeaky hinges filled the air as the door slowly opened. In the slightly open doorway stood a frail, barefooted, dark-haired woman dressed in a white blouse and a colorful, full-length skirt.

"What you want?" she asked softly as she examined them with her dark eyes.

"We are your neighbors up the road, the Aslens. We have more potatoes than we can use, and we were wondering if you would like some?" Phillip motioned to the bags in the surrey.

"I ask my husband." She called inside the room, "Pedro."

A few minutes later a tall, brown skinned, handsome man stood beside her. Covering his muscular, masculine body was a pair of dark torn trousers, a soiled white shirt, and worn-out scandals.

"Si, Maria, what you want?" Pedro asked.

"These people--the Aslens--they live down the road away--were wondering if we would like some potatoes." She motioned toward them as she opened the door wider.

Shrugging his shoulders, Pedro replied, "I have no money to pay for them."

"That's all right. If you can use them, I'm glad to give them to you," replied Phillip.

"Si, we can use them," replied Pedro.

"Where do you want them put?" asked Phillip.

"The root cellar. I'll help you carry them." He grabbed a broad-brimmed straw hat, which hung behind the door, and followed Phillip out to the wagon.

"Would you like to come in?" the woman offered graciously to Della and Otto.

"Thank you," said Della as she and Otto walked into the room and closed the door.

The large room was poorly furnished--a table--several chairs--small sink--water barrel--partially empty cupboards--pile of wood--two straw mats lying on the floor beside a large black wood-burning stove.

On one of the straw mats, lay a small boy covered with a colorful Indian blanket. Della remembered seeing them in church with a boy. He must be four or five, she thought, rather early to be sleeping.

Della and Otto each sat on chairs that were near the table.

"Would you like some coffee?" the woman asked as she walked toward the cupboard containing a few metal plates and cups.

"No, thank you," replied Della. As she looked around the room, she thought. If they ate supper, where are the dirty dishes? If they didn't eat yet, why was coffee only on the stove? Oh, my God is that all they were having for supper--coffee? Thank goodness, we brought them those potatoes! Those poor people!

The woman grabbed a cup, filled it with coffee from the coffeepot, and sat by the table.

"Ma, Ma--I'm cold." The feeble voice came from the boy under the Indian blanket.

Della looked at the boy lying on the mat. She thought. How can he be cold? It's nice outside tonight. He's near a hot stove. He's covered with a warm blanket.

Maria got up from her chair and knelt beside the boy. She reached into a bowl of water, which was setting on the floor near the boy, and pulled out a cloth. She wrung the excess water out of the cloth. Lovingly, she wiped the boy's forehead.

"Does the boy have a fever?" Della was deeply concerned.

Maria looked up. "Si, he got it this afternoon."

Della rose from her chair, grabbed a metal cup from the cupboard, dipped it into the water barrel, and handed the filled cup to the woman. "See that he drinks plenty of water to make up for the loss of fluid because of the fever."

Maria took the cup, raised the boy's head, and put the cup by his mouth. "Drink this, my little Pedro." Slowly, the boy sipped a few drops.

The door opened and in stepped Phillip and Pedro.

"I think we better go now, Della. I've got milking to do yet," Phillip said. He looked at the boy and Maria on the floor. "Is something the matter?"

"The boy has a fever," said Della.

"Do you want to stay here and help? I can come back and pick you up later," Phillip said.

"No, that's all right. We can take care of the boy," replied Maria as she rose from the floor.

"Are you sure?" asked Della.

"Si, but thank you anyway." Maria smiled.

Della returned the smile. "Well, okay, we'll be going then. When the boy is better, come and visit us. We have a big sign at the end of our driveway. So you shouldn't have any trouble finding us."

"We'll do that," said Maria.

"Si, we will. Thank you for the potatoes," said Pedro.

Phillip put his hand on Pedro's shoulder. "Glad you can use them." Then he shook Pedro's hand as he said, "Nice meeting you and your wife."

Pedro and Maria smiled. "It was nice meeting you, too," they replied.

The Aslens went out the door and into the surrey. Otto sat on the back seat while his parents sat on the front seat.

As the surrey traveled down the graveled road, Della reached over, touched Phillip's hand, and leaned her head toward him. "I'm glad we brought them the potatoes. I don't think they ate supper tonight, and I wonder how many other times they went without supper," she spoke softly so Otto could not overhear them. She didn't want him repeating things at school, as children often do.

"How do you know they didn't eat supper?" asked Phillip.

"There weren't any dirty dishes from a meal and nothing was set up for them to eat, except coffee," said Della.

"Well, if that's the case, I'm glad we brought them the potatoes. In a couple of weeks why don't you take them some of your canned tomatoes. You've got more canned than we'll ever eat," said Phillip.

"Ya, it was a good year for tomatoes, too. Wasn't it?" said Della.

"Ya, and I don't intend to eat all of them and get a sore asshole," replied Phillip.

Della sighed, gave him a disapproving look, and whispered, "The boy's in the back. Watch your words. Little pitchers have big ears, you know."

Phillip turned his head and looked back at Otto.

Otto was kneeling on the seat. He had his arms folded and resting on the top of the back seat. He was watching the dust fly up behind the surrey.

"He didn't hear me," replied Phillip.

"It doesn't take an intelligent person to use such words. Anyone can say them. But it takes an intelligent person to think of other words to use in a conversation besides such foul ones," Della said.

"Ya, my dear Della," he calmly agreed.

"Do you think that's why the boy is sick because they don't eat all the time?" asked Phillip.

"Could be?" Della shrugged her shoulders. "Who's to say? Kids are always getting sick with something."

Soon they were in their driveway. As they rode toward the house, Phillip looked at the cornfield, which crowded to one side of the driveway.

"If the weather is nice, we're going to start harvesting corn for fodder by the end of this week," said Phillip.

"We've got a very big cornfield this year. It'll take us awhile," said Della as she eyed the passing tall stalks of yellow.

"That's why we should start this week if the weather is nice," replied Phillip.

"I like the sight of those tepee-shaped shocks standing in the fields," said Della.

"Ya, they do look nice. But when you see them, you know winter is not far away," replied Phillip.

"Burr!" Della shivered. "Don't mention that."

"Don't worry. I'll keep you warm. Just like I did all the other years." He reached over, touched her leg, raised his eyebrows, and grinned.

"Ya, I suppose, you will." She chuckled.

"Woo!" He signaled the horses to stop. "I'll see you after milking." He turned around and looked at Otto. "You want to help me milk?"

"Sure do, Dad!" he replied enthusiastically.

"No, you don't young man." Della turned and looked at him. "You have homework to do. I saw those books on the stairs. You're coming in the house with me."

"Ah, Della, why don't you let him help me milk one or two of the cows. He can come in and do his homework then. It'll only take ten or fifteen minutes," said Phillip.

"Well, okay," she replied hesitatingly as she got out of the surrey. "But you better be in the house in about fifteen to twenty minutes, I don't want you rushing with your homework," she ordered.

"Thanks, Ma!" Otto replied ecstatically as he jumped in the front of the surrey and sat next to his father.

Della stood on the porch steps and watched the surrey head toward the barn. She smiled to herself as she thought about Otto. He was a really good little boy and so good-looking. He was going to be just as handsome as his father. She wondered how long he'd keep the blonde curly hair. Maybe they'd never change. Phillip's brother had blonde curly hair. Her smile faded as her mind filled with other thoughts. With all her heart, she had wanted to have had another child, for herself and so Otto wouldn't be so alone. Why did she have to miscarry and lose those four babies? Her heart had ached with the desire to have just a chance to hold and cuddled their soft, warm bodies next to hers. She would have cherished being allowed to kiss their tiny, pink cheeks. She would have enjoyed watching them kick their little pudgy legs, swing their little arms about, and hear their sweet cooing.

Tears filled her eyes as she questioned why she couldn't have had just one of the four, just for a little while? But would she have preferred to lose them later on instead of right away? No! It would have been harder maybe to lose the child after knowing it? It hurts either way. Why did she have to lose any at all? Would it have been so much for God to give her at least one? Oh, her dearest Otto! If something would ever happen to him, she'd just die! Nothing could happen to him! He's all she had--ever could have!

She wiped the tears from her eyes. "Enough of this feeling sorry for myself," she talked under her breath. "It was God's will, and he has a reason for everything," she told herself convincingly. "I should just be thankful that I have my little Otto. I better get those supper dishes done and the table cleaned off so Otto can do his homework." She turned and went into the house.

****

The morning rays burst into the bedroom as Della pulled the white shade all the way up on the window.

Otto turned away from the blinding light and covered his head with the patchwork quilt.

"Time to get up for church, Otto," said Della as she pulled up the other shade and walked to the back of Otto's bed.

He took the blanket off his head. "Do I have to go today, Ma?" he asked wearily.

With hands on her slender hips, she calmly replied, "Ya, you do. I let you stay home last Sunday so you could help your dad harvest the corn for fodder. You're going this Sunday. I'll not let you miss two Sundays. God gives you the whole week. You could at least give him an hour of your time, one day a week."

"My whole body aches. My head is throbbing so badly, and my eyes burn from the pain. My back hurts. I don't feel good at all," complained Otto.

A deeply concerned look crossed Della's face. It wasn't like Otto to make up things to get out of doing something that he didn't want to do. He was always very truthful.

She headed toward the front of the bed to see what she could do to make him more comfortable.

Suddenly, Otto sprang out of bed. The contents of his stomach came out through his nose, his mouth, and covered the braided rug that flanked his bed. His eyes were all watery as he held his hands tightly over his mouth.

"Stay there, Otto," Della said as she raced out of the room. "I'll get you a pail. If you have to vomit again, do it on the rug."

Della flew down the stairs into the kitchen. She grabbed her empty scrubbing bucket and flew back up the stairs.

Otto was hunched over. With one hand he clutched his stomach, while he clamped the other over his mouth.

Just as she set down the pail, he let go again. He felt another one coming. He felt as if his insides were coming out, but nothing came out except slime. His stomach hurt, ached, and was screaming with pain. He could feel it contracting, being squeezed inside, but nothing came out again, except slime. He couldn't straighten up. It felt like a rope around his waist getting tighter and tighter. He was kneeling, hunched over a full, stinky pail. Oh, God, when is it going to end, he thought, as he had another "dry heave."

Finally, it did end. Della helped him back into bed and covered his chilly body with a blanket. He lay in the bed, exhausted. Tears of pain were still running down his pale cheeks. His stomach felt raw, sore.

Della took the soiled rug and stinky pail out of the room. A few minutes later, she came back into the room with a bowl of water in one hand and two pieces of cloth draped over her arm. She dipped the smaller of the two clothes into the water and wrung it out. Soothingly, she washed and dried his face and hands. His forehead was on fire!

She went into their bedroom and took the thermometer out of the top drawer of her dresser. She came back into Otto's room and put the thermometer under his tongue. She left the room again to get a fresh bowl of water.

Upon returning, she read his temperature--103 degrees. She put the thermometer on his night stand next to the bowl of water. While sitting at the edge of the bed next to him, she sponged his face. Slowly, she pulled up the sleeves on his pajamas and sponged his arms. After a while, his exhausted body fell asleep.

Sitting on the edge of his bed, in the silence of the room, she watched him sleep. Occasionally, his eyes rolled under his closed lids or one of his fingers would twitch. Her heart ached for him.

He was getting restless. The sound of heavy, rapid breathing filled the room. She felt his skin. It felt dry. She touched his flushed face. It felt hotter. Oh, my God! He's getting worst. I've got to do something! She was fearful for his life.

She thought of her washtub. Softly, she placed the folded damp cloth on his forehead. Tiptoeing, she went out of the door and down the stairs.

As she opened the kitchen door, she saw Phillip leaning over the sink washing his hands.

When he heard her, he turned his head around. "I've got the surrey and horses ready so we can go to church."

"I'm not going to church today. Otto is sick. He has a terrible fever," she said as she walked across the room toward him. She stopped beside him. "Would you please carry the washtub upstairs in his room when you go up to dress for church?"

"Sure," he said as he dried his hands.

"I want to bathe his body in the water and try to lower his temperature when he wakes." She grabbed for some kettles. "I better make some hot water to mix with the cold water, so the water in the tub isn't too cold for him."

After setting the kettles full of water on the hot wood stove, she grabbed her water bucket and started filling it with water from the kitchen pump.

Phillip put the washtub upstairs in Otto's room and then dressed for church.

Della carried several pails of water up into the tub and then sat next to Otto. She started sponging his body again.

Phillip, dressed in a fine, dark suit and top hat, entered the room. "Are you sure you'll be all right while I'm gone?"

"Ya, I'll keep sponging him until he wakes up. Then I'll give him a bath," she replied.

Phillip walked over to the bed and felt Otto's forehead. "My, God! He is awful hot. I'll stop in by the doctor after church and see if he can come here. Maybe he can give Otto something to reduce the fever."

"That sounds like a good idea." She continued sponging him.

Phillip kissed Otto's forehead, kissed Della, and then went downstairs.

"Ma, Ma--I'm thirsty," said a feeble voice. His blue eyes looked so dull, his eyelids so heavy, his lips thick and dry.

Della looked at the night stand. No glass of water. She had forgotten it.

Putting the cloth into the water bowl, she hurried down the stairs. With lightening speed, she grabbed a glass, pumped it full of water, and ran up the stairs.

As she approached the bed, terror crossed her face. The glass slipped from her hand. Broken pieces of glass and splashes of water scattered the floor.

"Oh, my God, not that again!" Della screamed. She ran to the bed and pulled the covers off.

Otto's body was stiffened and pale. It jerked! He was having a hard time breathing. His eyes were rolled back. His hands were fisted. His teeth were clinched!

"Oh, my God, his teeth!" Della was panic stricken. Horrified! She looked about the room! A piece of wood--I need a piece of wood! His pencil! She eyed his school pencil on his writing desk. She ran over to the desk! Grabbed the pencil! Hurried back to Otto! She squeezed the sides of his jaw together with great force.

"Oh, God, help me get his teeth apart! Please, please help me, God!" she pleaded, fearing he'd die if she couldn't do it.

Finally, his teeth came apart, and she stuck the pencil between. He was biting so hard. She thought he'd bite through the pencil. His body jerked again--and again! His fists were turning blue! She had to get his fist apart! When he does that, Phillip's mother always said it meant he was near death.

"Oh, please, don't let him die! Dear, God! Not my little Otto!" Tears were running down her cheeks. Her vision was blurred. Her heart was pounding. She was sobbing and pleading, over and over again, "God, please help me!" She was trying desperately to push her fingers between his tightly clenched fists. She couldn't do it! The water! Last time Phillip's mother put him into a tub of water. She lifted him and carried him to the tub. Oh, how she wished Phillip wouldn't have left! She lowered him into the tub. His stiffened body wouldn't sit. His body jerked. He was uncontrollable. She loosened his pajamas around his neck and across his chest. His chin rested on his chest. She lifted it up, tried to unclench his fist, and lifted his fallen head again. The water splashed about the room. His body jerked and jerked! He wouldn't sit. His body was stiff!

"God--Phillip--someone--help me! Please, don't let him die!"

Finally, she got her fingers in his blue fists. She pulled his fist apart as his fingernails dug into her fingers. Relief! They're apart! His body jerked--again--again--again--then it was stiff! His body was limp! His eyes closed! His arms relaxed!

"No, no, he's not dead! Oh, no, please God let him be alive." Her heart was pounding faster and faster! Stop pounding! So she could hear! Was he breathing? Yes! Yes! She could hear him! He was breathing! He was alive!

"Oh, thank you, God! Thank you!" She kissed and embraced Otto. "Thank you, God! Thank you!" The tears in her eyes were tears of joy. She picked his limp, wet body up and held it on her lap. She rocked him in her arms. "Thank God. You're alive!" She kissed him again and again and again, clutching his body to hers.

After the passing of a few minutes, she took off his wet pajamas, put on dry ones, and put him into the bed. His exhausted body slept.

His forehead felt cooler. His breathing was slow and easy. His body became moist and he was starting to sweat.

Della wiped the hair on her forehead back. She was tired, physically and mentally drained. She sat beside the bed in her wet clothes and held his hand.

"How is he, Della?" A whispered voice startled her.

She looked up with her weary face, it was Phillip home from church.

"I think the fever has broken. Did you see the doctor?" she asked desperately.

"No, he was out of town. His wife said he went to Belmont to get some medicine. He won't be back for three or four days," replied Phillip.

"Well, I don't think we'll need him then anymore. I think he'll be all right now." She patted Otto's little hand. "I better clean up this floor."

Phillip looked about the floor. "What on earth happened here?"

"He had an attack like he used to get when he was teething," explained Della.

"Oh, no! I should have been here to help you." He held her close and stroked her hair.

"Well, I tell you I was really afraid. Thank goodness I remembered what your ma said and did," said Della.

"I'll help you clean up in here," said Phillip.

Together they cleaned up the room and then pulled down the shades so Otto could rest.

Just as they were quietly going out the door and closing it, Otto's feeble voice was heard. "Ma, Ma, I have to vomit again."

"Oh, the pail! I left it downstairs. I didn't think he would need it anymore," said Della.

Phillip touched her hand. "You go by Otto. I'll get the pail."

Della went over to Otto who was now sitting at the edge of the bed. As she pushed his curls off his forehead, she rested her hand on his forehead. No, it can't be hot again! It was! Oh, no! He had a fever again! He began shivering uncontrollably.

As soon as Phillip entered the room with the pail, it had started all over again. The vomiting--the fever--the chills--the thirst--the rapid breathing continued--hour--after hour--after hour.

Della sat by his bed day and night, sponging his body, giving him water, trying to make him eat. She prayed and prayed. She was exhausted but she had to be by him, taking care of him. She had the idea that if she was by him, he couldn't die. So she never left his side. She'd watch for his body to jerk under the covers. When it did, she'd call Phillip. They'd put him into the tub and stick something between his teeth so he couldn't bite off his tongue. They would hold his head up so he wouldn't gag or swallow his tongue.

As Della sat in the chair, her head began to nod and her eyes close. She'd catch herself and force herself to stay awake. Finally, her head went slowly around and rested on top of the chair. She couldn't fight it. Her eyelids were heavy with sleep and soon closed tightly.

In her mind, she heard the hollow echo of voices.

"How is the boy?"

"The fever was quite bad for three days. Then yesterday he got a rash on his face, neck, and then all over his body. After a few hours the rash turned to pimples, and the fever went down. He stopped vomiting and hasn't gotten any more convulsions. So, I guess, he's getting better."

"Well, I better check him. It sounds like what the Thursmen twins have. I hope it isn't."

"Why? What do they have?"

"I'll check him out before I say any more. No need to get you upset needlessly."

"Della, Della!"

Someone was shaking her shoulder. Her eyes wouldn't open. In her subconscious she was trying to open them, but they wouldn't open.

"Della, Della, the doctor is here."

Someone was shaking her again. Her eyes just would not open. She had to get them open, but she couldn't. It must be a dream. That's it! Someone was calling her in her dream.

"Della, Della."

It wasn't a dream. Someone was calling her. She had to wake up. I hope Otto hasn't got worst, she thought in a partially conscious state of mind.

"What's the matter?" she asked in a dazed matter as she yawned.

"The doctor is here," replied Phillip.

She looked around. Leaning over the bed, opening the top of Otto's pajamas was a short man with wisps of gray hair covering his shiny pink head. Della quickly got control of her senses and sat straight up in the chair. "Oh, Dr. Whitmore, how is he?"

"I'll let you know in a minute as soon as I finish examining him," he replied, without looking up as he examined Otto's neck and chest.

Otto lay quietly in the bed.

The doctor took a slender wooden tube about a foot long with a bell-shaped opening at one end out of his black bag, which stood on the floor beside the bed. He put the bell-shaped object on Otto's chest and the other end of the wooden tube into his ear. He was quiet for a few moments. He took the object and put it back into his bag. Then he rolled up the sleeves on Otto's pajamas and examined Otto's arms. He rolled Otto onto his stomach and examined his back. Then rolled him onto his back again, pushed up the legs on Otto's pajamas, and examined Otto's legs and feet.

He sighed, covered Otto up and smiled at him. "You get some rest now," he said.

Otto returned a weary smile.

Picking up his bag, he turned to Della and Phillip. "Let's go out and let the boy rest," he said.

"How is he, Dr. Whitmore?" Della asked anxiously. She wrung her hands nervously.

The doctor repeated, "Let's go out and let the boy rest." He put his arm on Della's back and helped her toward the door.

Quietly, he closed the door, turned, and looked at Phillip and Della. He shook his head. "I'm afraid the boy is not really any better."

"How can you say that, Dr. Whitmore? His fever has gone down. He doesn't vomit anymore. He seems to be getting better except for the appearance of the pimples." Della was upset. She didn't want to hear that. It wasn't what she expected or wanted to hear. The doctor must be making a mistake. That's what it was, a mistake!

"I'm sorry, Della." The doctor touched her hand consolingly. "The fever and other symptoms are going to occur again when the pimples fill with pus, which will be in about four or five days. The boy has a severe case of smallpox." A sad, helpless feeling surged his soul.

"Smallpox! Oh, my God! He's going to die, isn't he?" Della, already under stress, could take no more and began to sob. Phillip held her close to comfort her.

"To be truthful, it is a very high possibility," the doctor replied.

Thoughts of terror filled their hearts, their mind, their very soul. How could this be happening to them, to their child? It was some kind of a terrible, living nightmare. How they wished they could wake up and find out it was a mere dream. However, they were awake, and it was no dream.

"Have you two had a smallpox vaccination within the last five to seven years?" asked the doctor.

"No," they both replied.

"Well, I think you better get one now. Let's go downstairs," suggested the doctor.

"Can't you give Otto anything?" sobbed Della as she started down the stairs.

"No, I'm afraid not. The disease has to run its course. All we can do is pray now," replied the doctor.

Phillip helped Della downstairs through the foyer and into the living room. There they sat on the sofa while the doctor prepared their vaccinations.

"Where could he have gotten the disease? I thought it was almost completely wiped out by vaccination," said Phillip as he rolled his sleeve up for the vaccination.

"It has been almost entirely wiped out in most parts of Europe and in the United States. However, it's still quite prevalent in places like Asia, Africa, and Latin America. I can't figure out where Otto and the Thursmen twins could have come in contact with the disease. It completely baffles me," said the doctor.

He gave Phillip and Della their shots. "I had to go to Belmont to get vaccine. That's why I wasn't home when you came after church."

"After I leave here, I'll have to go to every house and vaccinate everyone before an epidemic breaks out. Boy, that'll be a job to get everyone vaccinated! I've never seen a smallpox epidemic, but I heard they are terrible," said the doctor.

"Ya, I remember my grandmother talking about the epidemic that swept Europe in the 1700's," said Phillip shaking his head. "Terrible! Terrible!"

"If only I knew the source, I could isolate the person before they infected others," said the doctor.

A serious look crossed Phillip's face as he wrinkled his brow. "Latin America," he thought aloud.

"What did you say?" asked the doctor as he closed his black case.

"You said the disease is quite common in Latin America, didn't you?" asked Phillip.

"Ya, that's right," replied the doctor nodding his head.

"Well, about two weeks ago, we went to visit the new family that moved into the old McCluthen farm and their little boy had a fever. Maybe it is nothing, but they are brown skinned like the people from Latin America and they did speak a little Spanish," Phillip said.

"I had heard that an immigrant family had moved in, but I didn't know that they were from Latin America. Maybe I should investigate and go there first before I go anyplace else," said the doctor as he headed toward the living room door and into the foyer.

"Wait a minute," said Phillip following the doctor into the foyer. "I think it would be a good idea if I came with you. They know me. If you, a stranger, come knocking at their door and investigating them, they might not be too helpful."

The doctor stopped, looked at Phillip. "Ya, maybe you're right. It probably would be a good idea if you did come along," replied the doctor.

Phillip turned to Della who had followed them into the foyer. "Will you be all right?" he asked.

She nodded her head. "Yes, Phillip. You go along. I hope you can stop this before it goes too far."

"I hope so, too," said the doctor as Phillip and he went out the door.

After they left the house, Della stood at the bottom of the stairs. She sighed and then slowly went up the stairs to their bedroom. She reached under her pillow and pulled out a chain of black beads, her rosary. As she held it in her hand and walked toward Otto's room, she moved her thumb from one bead to another. When she reached Otto's room, she sat in her usual chair. While watching him sleep, she silently prayed her rosary--over and over--for Otto's recovery.

Hastily, the doctor and Phillip rode in the doctor's buggy to the old McCluthen farm.

Everything was silent--the bare trees that dotted the yard--the empty corral--the sleeping chimney--the empty child's swing--the brown, dried leaves that dressed the unswept porch.

Carefully, they walked up the rotten steps and knocked at the door.

There was no answer. They knocked again.

Phillip looked toward the barn, with its door slightly open. "I'll look in the barn. Maybe they're in there," he said.

"Good idea. I'll wait here," said the doctor as he watched Phillip jump off the porch and run toward the barn.

As Phillip opened the barn door, a sharp stench blasted him in the face. The strong offensive smell made him sick to his stomach. He gagged. "My, God, what is that terrible smell?" He walked farther into the barn. The stench became worst. He unbuttoned the top two buttons of his shirt and held the shirt on his nose and mouth with his hand.

Suddenly, he stopped. There in the stall was the source of the smell--a dead horse. Its eyes wide open--tongue hanging out of its mouth--every bone in its body showing. It was tied in a stall that had no feed or water. Phillip shook his head. "What kind of person would let a helpless animal starve," he thought aloud. He was furious now! He stormed out of the barn and up to the house.

"Did you find anybody?" asked the doctor.

"Ya, I found a starved horse," he replied angrily. "Come on, let's go in."

They opened the door. Lying on one of the mats near the cold, wood-burning stove was a body. It was covered with an Indian blanket. The doctor turned the body over.

"Oh, my God! His face! It's ugly!" cried Phillip.

"Smallpox," said the doctor as he covered the face up.

"Is that what Otto is going to look like?" asked Phillip.

"If he lives, he'll carry the pockmarks the rest of his life." Nodded the doctor. "We better bury him and the horse."

"I wonder where his wife and boy are?" asked Phillip as he looked around the room. "I'll check the rest of the house."

"Ya, that's a good idea. They're probably lying dead somewhere too," said the doctor.

Phillip checked the two rooms upstairs while the doctor checked the other two rooms downstairs and the basement.

"There's no one else here," said the doctor.

Phillip shrugged his shoulders. "They couldn't have gone too far because the horse is in the barn dead."

"Maybe they had two horses. We're going to have to find them. They're carriers. They could spread the disease all over the country," said the doctor.

"Let's bury him. Shovels are in the barn," said Phillip.

They went out the door and into the barn. In one corner of the barn were two long-handled shovels. They both grabbed one and quickly ran out the back door of the barn.

They stopped and looked at the crest of a small hill, which stood behind the barn. They looked at each other. Their eyes asked, could that be what we think it is? They walked closer and closer. Soon they were staring down at the two parallel mounds of small fieldstone.

"Well, I guess we know what happened to the wife and boy," Phillip said sadly as he looked at the two small wooden markers that stood at the front edge of each pile of stones--MARIA--was carved on one marker--PEDRO--carved on the other.

"We might as well bury him here with his family," said the doctor.

"I've been thinking," said Phillip. "That maybe you should ride on and vaccinate as many people as you can today. You could send a man from one of the houses that you stop by out here to help me bury Pedro and the horse."

"Ya, that sounds like a good idea. We have to get this stopped right here and now," the doctor said as he put his shovel down.

Several hours later, Della heard wagon wheels rumble over the brick driveway outside. She rose from her chair and peeked out between the side of the pulled shade and the window.

She saw Phillip get off the farm wagon seat and come into the house.

"Where was he so long and what happened to the doctor?"she thought aloud as she walked away from the window and out the bedroom door. Quietly, she closed the door and went down the steps.

When she saw Phillip, she asked, "Where were you so long?"

"I had to bury Pedro and his horse," replied Phillip in a tired tone. He walked into his den and collapsed into a cozy, brown upholstered chair.

Della followed him. "What do you mean you had to bury Pedro and his horse?" she asked.

"We found Pedro in the house dead and his horse starved to death in the barn," explained Phillip in an exhausted manner. "How is Otto?" he asked.

"He rested most of the day. What about the boy and Maria?" she asked, afraid of the answer.

"They were both buried behind the barn. Ah!" He shivered. "A mass of death around that place."

Della became nervous. She swallowed the lump in her throat. They had died of smallpox. She wrung her hands as she looked out the doorway at the stairs. Her eyes filled with tears. She had heard smallpox was dangerous, sometimes even deadly. But she tried to convince herself that the disease wasn't really that bad. Nothing is ever really that bad until it hits "home" and "our lives." Well, the impossible had "hit her home." There was a real possibility her Otto could die. Oh, it was so hard to admit it. Things like that happen only to "other people," but sometimes we are the "other people." Just because one doesn't want to admit something doesn't mean it won't happen. Reality can be so hard to accept. She had tried to be a good Christian, a good neighbor and what was her reward? Her boy might die. Somehow it wasn't fair. Surely God would not take her Otto away--would he?

The touch of a hand on her shoulder startled her. It was Phillip.

"I think you should get some sleep, Della," he said.

She wiped the tears off her face and turned around. She bit her bottom lip, her voice cracked. "Oh, Phillip, why us? Why our little boy? Our only little boy!"

She put her arms around Phillip. He held her close and stroked her hair comfortingly. "It'll be all right. Everything will turn out fine." In his heart, he had doubts. He didn't believe his own words. A picture of Otto's funeral passed in his mind. It was hard but he held back his tears and his anguish, for Della's sake.

"I'm going back up to his room," said Della as she pulled away from Phillip. "I want to spend every minute with him that I can. I want to hold his warm hands while they're still warm with life." Her chin began to quiver. She ran out of the room as her eyes burst with tears.

Phillip watched her and then turned toward his bookcase. There on one of the shelves sat Otto's little miniature fire engine. With his eyes glued on the object, he walked toward it and picked it up. He fingered it as he stared out the window at the pond where Otto and he would go swimming. On the pond, sat the white ducks with their spoon-shaped bills. They would always follow Otto to the barn each day for the few handfuls of grain that he would sprinkle about the ground for them. His eyes roamed over to the cornfield filled with corn shocks that Otto's little hands had helped to make.

Phillip's teary eyes looked toward heaven. "Oh, God, he's such a good little boy. Don't take him away. If something would happen to him, it would hurt Della terribly. She's a good woman. Don't hurt her that way."

Upstairs, sitting beside the bed, Della held Otto's hand and prayed with her eyes heaven bound. "God, if you give him his life, I promise you I'll see that he spends the rest of his life serving you. I promise that I'll see he spends his life down here for you. I promise! Just, please, please don't take him from us!" She laid her tear-covered face on his hand and then kissed it.

Chapter 4
****
Seduction

BRRR--ING!

Kate turned over in bed and looked at the deadened alarm clock that sat on her night stand. It was six o'clock.

Usually, she shut it off before it rang itself out, but she was really tired and didn't hear it right away this morning. They had spent all day yesterday painting the outside of the inn, and she was exhausted when they had finally gone to bed. She sniffed the air. Even the inside of the inn was filled with the strong odors of the paint solvent.

She turned over and looked at Hans, still sleeping like a baby and "dead to the world." She pushed her body close to his, slid her arm around his hairy chest, and gently caressed him.

"Wake up, Hans," she whispered in his ear as she kissed him.

Slowly, his eyes opened.

She was now leaning over him, smiling, and looking into his eyes.

He raised his head slightly, gave her a quick kiss, and then dropped his head back into the pillow. As she lay on her side next to him slowly stroking the hairs on his chest, he put his one arm around her shoulder.

"Do you know what today is?" she asked.

"No. What is today?" he replied.

"Today is our second wedding anniversary, and I have a present for you," stated Kate.

"You do." A sparkling glint filled his eyes.

She smiled, rolled out of the side of the bed, and walked over to the dresser. Opening the drawer, she pulled out a cylindrical object that was tied in the middle with a red ribbon.

"What's that?" he asked as he sat up in bed.

"It's your present," she replied as she walked toward the bed. She handed him the object and sat at the edge of the bed beside him.

As he untied the ribbon, he saw that it fastened a roll of papers, which he then unrolled. He laid them on the bed and tried to straightened them with his hands as he examined them.

"Why, they're the deed and abstract for the inn and woods around it," he said, as he looked up at her with a big smile. "That's my present?"

She nodded her smiling face. "I hope you like your present."

"I sure do," he replied.

His face burst with ecstacy as he read the names on the papers, Hans and Kate Duren. He had wanted the inn and the rest of the land for a long time. Now it was his, well half his--for the time being, anyway. Before long he'd have everything that he had wanted from the day he came here. It was just a matter of time now and he had plenty of that--time.

"You are now the equal owner of the inn, my dear husband. I figured since you put the money you have in the bank in both of our names. I could put my property and money in both our names also. Like you said, it's foolish to have everything in only one person's name. We're married. What's mine is yours and what's yours is mine."

Hans put the curled papers on the night stand, pulled her back into bed, and held her against him with a gentle embrace.

"I love you," he whispered.

"I love you too," she whispered back as she returned his embrace.

Her body suddenly jerked slightly away from him.

"Sh," she said as she held herself very still, perked her ears, and slowly moved her wide eyes back and forth.

"What's the matter?" asked Hans.

"I thought I heard someone knocking," she replied.

"I don't hear anything." He pulled her close again and kissed her.

A loud tapping on the bedroom window interrupted their kiss.

"Hey! Hans, we got a lot of work to do this morning," shouted a voice from outside.

"Oh, it's Pete. I better get up." Hans sprang out of bed.

Kate lay in bed watching him hurriedly put clothes on his virile body. "Do you have to go right now?" she asked disappointingly.

"Ya, I forgot that we have to load that furniture I made. I have to have it at Erickson's before nine o'clock," he said as he stuffed his plaid shirt into his trousers.

"Hey, Hans! Are you awake?" A tapping at the window followed the question.

While closing his zipper and buckling his belt, he stumbled over to the window. He pulled back the closed curtain and looked outside.

"Ya, I'm coming," he replied as he looked at the alarm clock. The hands still stood at six o'clock. "What time is it?" he asked.

"Six-thirty," Pete shouted back.

"I'm coming. Meet me at the shop." Hans motioned with his hands. He then grabbed the pocket watch off the dresser, set it to the correct time, and fastened it to his trousers.

"Are you going to be gone all day?" asked Kate as she got out of the bed and began to get dressed.

"I'm not going with Pete over to Beechwood. I got work to do in the shop today. Why?" Hans looked in the mirror and combed his wavy salt and pepper hair and flowing sideburns.

"Well, I thought maybe we could go on a picnic and reminisce about our wedding day," replied Kate.

She walked over to Hans, put her arms around his waist, and pressed her partially clothe body against his back.

He put the comb down, fingered his full mustache, turned around, and put his hands on her shoulders. Looking down and examining her sexually attractive body, he replied, "That sounds good to me."

Giving her a "peck" of a kiss, he headed for the door. He stopped as she grabbed his hand.

"It only takes a minute to do the job right." A pleasing grin crossed her face with that statement.

Putting her arms around his neck, she gave him a long passionate kiss. She clung to him tightly as her breathing started to get heavy.

He gently pushed her away. "I've got to go now. There'll be plenty of time for that later." He gave her a warm hug and went out the bedroom door. His body had started to fill with sexual desires. He knew, if he didn't leave then, he wouldn't be able to leave.

"Do you want breakfast?" she called after him.

"No, I don't have time now. I can wait for the picnic," he called back as he walked through the sitting room. As he went through the dining area, he grabbed one of the red apples that rested in the large bowl on the dining table. After shining it on his sleeve, he took a big bite out of it and went out the door.

Once outside, he stopped at the edge of the porch and looked across the railroad track at the big sign that hung over the depot. The words, SHANDY LANE, covered the sign. Hans nodded his head as he looked at the growing town that was flanked with the stream and woods on one side of it and the railroad track and woods on the other side. "Yup! That's a really nice name for the town," he thought aloud as he took another bite of his apple.

Staring at the woods across the track, he thought about how he was going to own that too, someday. Right in the middle of the cleared woods, he was going to build himself the best house around. He'd be the richest man in these parts. There wouldn't be anything that he couldn't have. But he'd have to be careful, one wrong move and he could lose everything.

"Hey, Hans! Stop daydreaming," shouted a voice.

Hans looked up. It was Pete standing at the edge of the woods with his arms folded and an angry scowl on his face.

"We've got work to do. You know Beechwood is a two-hour drive by wagon," said Pete.

"Ya, ya, I'm coming," replied Hans. He took another bite of his apple as he headed toward Pete.

"You know Erickson wanted the furniture by nine o'clock today. I'll never make it now," grumbled Pete.

"So you'll be a little late. It's not the end of the world. You don't have anything else to do all day--or do you have something planned with Betsy?" said Hans. He threw the apple core into the woods amongst the fallen brown cones and dry maple leaves.

"No, I don't have anything planned with Betsy today. Today is a weekday, and there is work to be done. Betsy has to help her dad in the store; we have to build those new stalls in the barn. Remember Kate asked us to do that a few weeks ago," replied Pete.

"Oh, ya, I forgot about them," said Hans. "I'll start on them as soon as we've got the furniture loaded up for Erickson. I was going to work on Mrs. Carter's chairs, but they can wait. She doesn't need them for several months."

Hans started to head toward the barn.

"Where are you going?" asked Pete.

"To the barn. We've got to hitch up the horses and wagon," replied Hans.

"I did that already. The horses and wagon are at the shop. All we have to do is load the furniture," stated Pete.

They walked toward Hans's carpenter shop. Once at the shop, they loaded the carved curio cabinets onto the back of the wagon. Along with the cabinets, they loaded boards for the stalls in the barn, a hammer, and saw.

Hopping onto the wagon seat, they drove toward the barn where they unloaded the material for the stalls.

Hans carried the boards, the hammer, and saw into the barn while Pete drove carefully down the road toward Beechwood.

The sound of a pounding hammer and the grinding teeth of a saw circled the barn in the still of the morning.

After tidying up the bedroom and sitting room, Kate went out the sitting room door. As she shut the door, a soft voice greeted her.

"Good morning, Kate."

Kate looked up the stairs at the woman shrouded in a black floor-length dress and a large scarf, which covered everything except her lifeless, pale blue eyes.

"Good morning, Molly, how are you feeling today?" asked Kate.

"Fine," Molly replied as she started to walk down the stairs.

"Since we don't have roomers today and Hans and I are going on a picnic, there is no need for you to work. So, why don't you take a day's vacation," suggested Kate.

"Today is washday, isn't it?" Molly stopped at the bottom of the stairs.

"Yes, it is." Kate headed through the dining area toward the kitchen door.

Molly followed her and volunteered, "Well, I can help you."

Kate stopped at the door. "No, that's all right. I'll do it just as I always do. Your job is just cooking and keeping the rooms upstairs clean. Besides rubbing the clothes against that washboard would be quite hard for you with your hand being the way it is. Why don't you spend the day just enjoying it with a walk in the woods, or whatever? It is such a lovely day. There won't be to many days like today anymore. Winter is just around the corner, and then the weather will keep us locked inside the inn most of the time."

"I don't feel right seeing you work while I'm doing nothing," replied Molly.

Lightly, Kate put her arm on Molly's shoulder. "Molly, you don't have to feel that way. I owe you and will never be able to repay you for those extra five years you gave me with my dad."

"Oh, Kate, don't say that. You don't owe me a thing. Your dad treated me well those five years, and you've treated me just as good all these years. What your dad gave me was just unbelievable. I never expected that," replied Molly.

"You deserved more." Kate hugged her. "Now go out and enjoy today before I get mad at you," Kate ordered in a kind manner.

"Okay." Molly headed toward the door but then turned and went up the stairs.

Kate put her hands on her hips. "Say, aren't you going outside?"

Molly stopped on the stairs and looked over at Kate. "You said I should go and enjoy myself, right?"

"Yes, I did," replied Kate.

"Well, I enjoy crocheting. So that's what I'm going to do," replied Molly.

Kate shook her head and smiled. "My dear Molly, you are always crocheting."

"It makes me feel good to know a person like me can create something beautiful to the eye. Please understand, Kate, I will never have the chance to give another person the love that is in my heart. No one would ever want me. I know that. So I crochet the afghans and give some of the love and warmth I have in my heart that way."

Kate's eyes filled with water. The vision of Molly became a blur. "Oh, Molly, I wish it wouldn't be that way. You deserve so much more."

"There is no sense dwelling on what should be. What is--is. There is no way we can change it. So we might as well accept things the way they are and try to be happy with what we do have. I'm happy,

Kate. Really, I am," replied Molly as she smiled reassuringly at Kate.

"I wish you would at least let me tell the women at church that you are the one who makes and donates those beautiful afghans for their ice cream socials. They think I make them, and it's not right. You should get the praise and credit," said Kate.

"No!" Molly snapped. "There is no need for them to know. All those 'good Christian people' do is make fun of me and the way I dress. I hear the whispers when they come here to visit you."

"That's just because you dress differently than they do, and you don't like to socialize with them. They think you're different--odd. If they would know that you make the afghans that they delight in seeing and having, I know they would feel differently. They'd know there was nothing odd about you," said Kate.

"Oh, but they're right, Kate. I am an oddity," said Molly.

"Don't say that, Molly, please," Kate pleaded.

"I know it's important to you what other people think and say about you. So let them think you are the one who graciously donates them. I don't really care what they think of me. In fifty years we'll all be dead, and no one will ever know what we did. They won't even know we existed, and they will care even less. Have a nice day, Kate." Molly turned, went up the rest of the stairs, and disappeared around the corner into her room.

Sadly, Kate went into the kitchen. Her heart was heavy the rest of the morning as she washed and hung the clothes on the clothesline outside.

Her mood changed to carefree and light as she started to pack the picnic basket with last night's leftover cold chicken. She was singing a song as she sliced the leftover potatoes for potato salad.

Visions of the wonderful time that she and Hans were going to have on the picnic traveled through her mind. If Hans felt the same way she did, it was going to be quite a romantic picnic. They'd make love. Maybe this time she'd be lucky, and in nine months she'd have a baby. For two years she had been trying. Surely, she would get lucky soon. How she prayed to have Hans's baby. She loved him so much. She'd be willing to go through all that pain just to have his baby. She was thirty-one already. Her heart and body ached to have the child of the only man that she had ever loved and allowed to make love to her. It would be so wonderful to give life to another human being, a child of hers and Hans's. Hans had never mentioned children to her. Nevertheless, she was sure if he knew she was going to have his baby, he'd be just as happy as she. After all, he was forty-five. Surely, he would like to have a child. A boy, she thought.

****

"Hans! Hans!" Pete came bursting into the barn. He looked this way and that way for Hans.

Hans looked up from behind the stall that he was about to pound a nail into. "What's the matter?"

"I think you're in big trouble." Pete threw his arms up in the air. "I knew this was going to happen! I just knew it!"

Hans put the hammer down and came out from behind the stall. "What on earth is the matter with you?" he asked.

"Erickson said a German woman came to town yesterday on the train, and she was asking about you," replied Pete.

"What did she look like?" asked Hans.

"I don't know. I was so stunned when I heard that, I forgot to ask," shouted Pete. "Who else could it be but Lena?"

"Don't shout. The whole town will hear you." Hans walked past Pete over to the barn door and closed it.

"What did Erickson tell her?" Hans walked back over by Pete.

"Erickson told her that you'd be in town today. He thought you'd be coming along to deliver the furniture. She told Erickson that she was staying at the hotel and that you should contact her there."

Hans slowly slid his hand over his mouth and held his chin as he stood in silent thought. The truth couldn't come out now. He hadn't gotten everything he had wanted yet. If he got caught with two wives now, they might take everything he had, not to mention he could go to jail. He had to have time to figure out a way to get everything and prevent the one who divorced him from getting anything. He had to figure out which one it would benefit him to stay with. If it was Lena, would she divorce him? No, not Lena, she needed the security that he could give her. She would not want to be alone in this strange land. What about Kate? She was so in love with him. Even if she found out about Lena, she'd stay. So the decision would really be his. Which one to keep? First, he had to keep them from finding out about each other. Those little wheels were really turning in his head now. He no longer had plenty of time.

"I better get to Beechwood and in a hurry," Hans said.

"I told you that if I thought Kate was going to get hurt, I was going to tell her and I'm going to." Pete headed toward the door.

Hans grabbed his hand. "If you don't want Kate to get hurt, the best thing you can do is to say nothing."

He pulled away from Hans's grip. "The best thing for you--you mean," Pete snapped the comment back at Hans.

"No, the best thing for Kate. If you tell her now, how do you think she's going to feel about the fact that you didn't tell her right away? I'll tell you how she'll feel. She'll feel betrayed. Betrayed by you. How do you think she'll feel about you after she thinks you betrayed her?" responded Hans.

As Pete thought about that, his eagerness to run out the door and tell Kate slowly disappeared. Hans was right. Kate would probably feel betrayed, but he could explain to her why he didn't say anything. What good would that do? She'd still probably think he betrayed her. It would be hard enough on her when she did find out. Especially if Hans went back to Lena. If that did happen, Kate would need someone, more than any time in her life. Perhaps he should just be quiet. If it did happen that Hans went back to Lena, at least, he'd be around to help Kate through the terrible time--and it would be a terrible time. Kate trusted and loved Hans so much. Her whole world would fall apart.

"I won't say anything, not to protect you, but for Kate's sake. If the person in Beechwood is Lena, what do you intend to do?" asked Pete.

"I don't know yet," Hans replied.

"You could stay with Kate. If you divorced Lena, maybe Kate would never find out," suggested Pete.

"We'll see once," replied Hans.

"You said you loved Kate. If you do, there's nothing really complicated about this. You simply divorce Lena if you love Kate. You obviously don't love Lena anymore. You better divorce one of them before they find out about each other," Pete said.

"I don't know what I'm going to do. So leave me alone," Hans snapped.

"Well, you better do something quick because it is against the law to have two wives," remarked Pete.

"Ya, ya, I know. Tell Kate I had to go and see Erickson. He wanted to talk to me." Hans walked toward the barn door.

"What if she asks why?" inquired Pete.

"Tell her you don't know." He mounted the empty wagon and headed down the road to Beechwood.

Pete sighed and shook his head with disapproval as he watched Hans leave. As Hans and the wagon disappeared in clouds of dust, Pete picked up the tools and started to finish the job Hans had started.

As Hans rode the wagon on the road, which passed the country farms and led into Beechwood, a thousand thoughts filled his mind. It was a complicated situation for Hans because love didn't enter the picture anymore, not for Hans anyway. The feelings he used to have for Lena just didn't seem to be anymore. They got lost somewhere in the ten years. Perhaps the desire for money had taken its place. Kate loved him, and he needed that. She fulfilled his sexual desires, but the feeling of love he once felt was gone. He had become cold. Sure he could be kind, thoughtful, and make love, but he couldn't love anymore. Love never entered into his sexual acts with Kate. She was a companion, someone to fill his lonely nights. There was no concern for Lena's or Kate's feelings. He couldn't bring himself to care about anyone, anymore. The importance of money and property kept creeping in until there was no room for anything else. He had to make a big decision and do it quickly. He had to weigh all the odds. The decision he made would have to be most profitable for him. Any one of them could provide him with love and sex.

Money had become a disease. The more he had. The more he wanted. It didn't matter to him who got hurt as long as it wasn't him. He wanted more money because of the prominence it brought.

The town was growing and soon it would need important people to run it. Since he built the town, he figured it was only right that he'd run it. If he had money, he could pull the "strings" to set himself up in such a position, a position of prestige. But what if the people found out about his marriages, and they would. Well, if he had enough money it probably wouldn't matter. He had enough knowledge of people to know that they were "funny" about certain things. If a person was poor and did a wrong deed, it was not tolerated. But if a person had money, the same wrong deed was considered acceptable. Could that be because people were so naive that they thought people with money might give them something if they were nice to them? Hans laughed to himself. Ya, people were that naive. He wouldn't have any problems getting what he wanted as long as he had the power of money on his side.

And so as the wheels of the wagon turned and headed him toward the town of Beechwood, so the wheels of his mind turned and started to lead him down the path toward a scheme that would give him everything he wanted.

He stopped the wagon in front of Erickson's and went inside.

Erickson, a short man with an oversized head, was setting a bushel full of red apples in front of his counter. When he heard the bell on the door, he looked up.

"Hi, Hans, I'm surprised to see you here. Pete just left awhile ago," Erickson said.

"Pete said a woman was looking for me." Hans walked up toward the counter and stood beside Erickson.

"Ya, yesterday she came in and asked if I knew you. I told her that I did. I also told her that you'd probably be here today. She said if you came in I should tell you that she wanted to talk to you. She's in room five at the hotel," replied Erickson.

"Thanks, Erickson." Hans went out the door and over to the hotel.

He stood in front of the door, marked with a big white five, for several minutes. "Well, here it goes," he thought aloud as he knocked at the door.

****

The front door of the barn opened and in stepped Kate with the picnic basket. She walked toward the rhythmical sound of a pounding hammer, which came from inside a newly built stall. The fresh pine smell of the recently cut wood became more prevalent as she neared the stall.

She stopped in surprise at the end of the stall. Why that was Pete! She had expected to see Hans.

"Where is Hans?" Kate looked about the barn.

Pete turned around and wiped the drops of sweat off his brow. "He had to go to Beechwood." He set the hammer on top of the stall.

Kate was puzzled. "I thought you took the wagon into Beechwood this morning?"

"I did but Erickson wanted to talk to Hans about something." Pete didn't like deceiving Kate. It wasn't a good feeling. He didn't like the fact that he couldn't look her straight in the face when he talked to her. If he had, she would have seen the lie on his face.

"Boy, it surely is a hot autumn day. I don't ever remember it getting this hot this late in autumn," Pete commented as he took the soggy shirt that clung to his sweating body off and slung it over the top of the stall.

"I don't remember it being so hot either especially this time of the year. The heat is just drying everything up more. We could use a good rain," replied Kate.

Pete glanced at the basket. "You and Hans planned on going on a picnic?"

"Yes, we did." Kate sighed. "But, I guess, we won't be going now. You want to join me for dinner?"

"No, thanks, Kate, I really am not very hungry. Why don't you save it for supper? Hans will be back by then," said Pete.

"Ya, I'm not very hungry either. I guess I could save it for supper. It'll be nice out then yet. Would you like some of the cold lemonade that I've got in the basket?" asked Kate.

"Ya, that sounds good," replied Pete.

Kate pulled out a quart canning jar filled to the rim with cold lemonade and thin slices of oranges. She unscrewed the lid and handed the jar to Pete.

While he drank thirstily, Kate pulled an object wrapped in red and white gingham out of the basket. When he handed the jar back to her, she handed him the object. "Here you eat this, and don't tell me you're not hungry. Anyone who works as hard as you obviously did to get this all done has to be hungry." She set the half empty jar on the sawdust-laden floor. "You keep this out here. I can make more for supper."

The unwrapped piece of gingham revealed two large drumsticks. "Thanks, Kate!"

"Would you like more?" Kate reached into the basket.

"No, thanks." Pete shook his head as his teeth tore into one of the drumsticks.

"Well, I guess I'll be going then. I've got clothes to take off the line, fold, and iron before supper. That's one thing nice about this weather, I don't have to worry about my clothes getting dry." Kate chuckled.

"Ya," Pete replied between voracious bites.

"See you later, Pete." Kate walked toward the barn door and disappeared from sight between the small opening in the door.

In a little while he had finished eating. He wiped his mouth and hands with the cloth. Then he washed the leftover food particles in his mouth down his throat with the rest of the lemonade.

Soon the barn filled with sounds of Pete's ambitious hammer and saw.

"My, my, you sure do make a lot of noise when you work." A soft voice fell upon his ears.

He stopped pounding and turned around. It was Betsy.

"Hi, Betsy." He smiled. "Well, I won't get this finished if I don't make a little noise. You can't work and not make some noise."

"Well, I know something you could do that would hardly make any noise at all and you wouldn't get calluses on your hands." Betsy grinned and flipped the bottom of her hair on one side with her hand.

"And just what do you have in mind, Betsy?" he asked.

She walked over to him, took the hammer out of his hand, and threw it onto the floor. Then she put his arms around her waist, put her arms around his neck, and pulled him close to her lips. She held him close and pressed her lips against his.

"Now isn't that much better than what you were doing?" Betsy rubbed her fingertip slowly over his closed lip.

"If you think so, Betsy," Pete replied.

She pulled slightly away from him. "Well, don't you care for me at all?"

"You know I do, Betsy."

"No, I don't know that you do. You always say 'someday we'll get married.' Well, I can't wait for 'someday' anymore. If you really want to marry me, it's going to have to be soon," Betsy stated.

"There's no rush. We have plenty of time," replied Pete.

"No, Pete, we don't have plenty of time anymore." She pulled completely away from him. Angrily, she turned and walked to the end of the stall.

Pete walked over to her, put his arms around her waist, and rested his head against her soft, sweet-smelling hair. "Oh, Betsy, you don't have to get upset. We do have plenty of time."

She turned around with tears in her eyes. "No, Pete, we don't." She held out her left hand. There on the second to last finger was a gold ring, set with a diamond and several smaller gems on each side of it.

"Is that an engagement ring?" Pete almost choked on the words.

"Yes, Todd asked my dad if he could marry me last night, and of course you know what my dad said. Then Todd put the ring on my finger as a sign of his 'intentions toward me.' I thought when a girl becomes engaged she feels some kind of excitement, a thrill, some sought of happiness. All I feel is emptiness, a feeling of loss--a loss of you, Pete." She threw her arms around him and clung desperately to him.

Pete comfortingly stroked her hair. "Did you tell your dad that you don't love Todd?"

"It doesn't matter to him." Betsy sobbed. "Todd's a 'fine catch, I'll grow to love him in time,' he says. It makes me sick to think of Todd pawing at my body and slobbering all over it. I love you, Pete. I want to marry you."

"Your dad is not about to let that happen," replied Pete.

She wiped the tears from her eyes. "Well, maybe we could do something so he doesn't have a choice. Something that would make Todd Bester not want to marry me."

He held Betsy out in front of him. "What are you talking about, Betsy?"

"Well, if you'd get me pregnant, Todd Bester surely wouldn't want to marry me. Especially, if he knew it was you who got me pregnant. My dad wouldn't have a choice but to let me marry you. He wouldn't want a daughter of his giving birth to a bastard."

Pete stared at her. He couldn't believe what he was hearing. He never figured Betsy to say or even think of such things.

"Well, what would be so bad about it. I love you and you say you love me. If that's the only way we can have each another, why not?

It surely won't be the toughest thing you ever did in your life." She put her arms around his neck. "Why you might even enjoy it."

She pulled her body tight to his and pressed her lips hard against his. She pushed her tongue through his teeth until it touched his tongue. Her breathing became heavy as she rubbed her hand through his hair wildly. Pete soon found himself holding her closer and harder to his body as his tongue mingled with hers. They laid their bodies side by side on the pile of dry straw that strewed the barn floor. She held his head tight against her lips with one hand while she unbuttoned her blouse and unhooked her bra with the other. She raised the loosened bra above her breasts, broke their kisses, and pushed his head to her breasts.

"Oh, Pete--oh, Pete, love me--love me!" Her body began to move to and fro with excitement as he kissed and fondled her breasts.

Soon he felt Betsy's hand fidget with his belt then fumble with his zipper. He felt her hand groping inside his trousers between his legs. A uniform ticklish sensation and intense excitement filled his body. He felt a hardness and then her hand left the inside of his trousers. Wildly, she took off her skirt and panty and helped him take off his trousers. As he lay on top of her, their nude bodies touched; she wrapped her legs around him tightly. He felt his hardness within her warm, moist body. It felt tight, and he could feel the friction of his hardness against the inside of her body. His heart pounded against his ribs and felt as though it would explode. It made him breathe rapidly--heavily. He desired to exhale to release himself of the excitement that had accumulated within him. Accelerated, his heart beat seemed to move side by side with the rhythmical movements of his body. His whole body, every inch of his flesh, jerked with numerous violent, involuntary contractions. He felt his chest relax and his breasts merged closer to hers. The uniform ticklish sensation became more and more intense with sudden passion. Suddenly, he felt an irregular twisting movement in his hardness--and then another. Just then a bolt of light sprang on them as the barn door opened. Their nude bodies sprang apart.

In the doorway stood Mr. Cork.

Pete felt his face flush with warmth, and he tried to swallow the lump in his throat.

Mr. Cork eyed the horsewhip which hung from the rafter. He grabbed it and came at Pete.

Pete stared at approaching Mr. Cork as he grabbed at the straw pile for his trousers.

"You dirty raping son of a bitch!" Mr. Cork screamed at him as he raised the whip to lash out at Pete.

Pete quickly pulled his trousers up and put his hands up to protect his face as the whip lashed at him.

Betsy jumped up and violently pulled at her father's arm. "Dad, leave him alone," she screamed.

He threw her off his arm and onto the floor. "Put some clothes on your dam ugly body and get the hell out of here," he bellowed back at her.

Pete clutched his chest where the whip had sliced his skin like a razor. The blood-covered cut burnt and had a sudden pricking pain.

Pete tried to siege the whip. But before he could, Mr. Cork lashed at him again and again and again. The pain tore throughout Pete's body and erupted from every nerve.

Betsy hurried to put on her clothes and then ran up to her father and grabbed the whip.

"Leave him alone, Dad, please," Betsy pleaded with eyes full of tears.

Mr. Cork took the back of his hand and with all the force in his body he hit her across the face.

She fell to the floor. Her nose tingled--stung--ached with pain. It felt ten times its size. It was dripping. She sniffled and when she swallowed, a terrible salty taste filled her mouth. When she touched her nose, her hand felt sticky. She looked at her hand. It was covered with a bright, red liquid--blood!

The blood was dripping all over the front of her blouse, her skirt, and onto the barn floor.

"Oh, Dad, stop! Look what you did!" Betsy cried as she looked at herself covered with blood.

"Shut up and get out of here before I hit you again," he violently yelled at her.

As Mr. Cork turned toward Betsy and ordered her out of the barn, Pete moved toward Mr. Cork. Pete thought now there would be a chance to pull the whip away from Mr. Cork, but his beaten body wasn't quick enough. Mr. Cork had turned away from Betsy and had seen Pete approach.

Mr. Cork clenched the fingers of his hand into its palm and gave Pete a mighty blow between his legs.

Pete let out a shrill, high-pitched cry of pain that pierced the ears as he gripped his hands between his legs. His body hunched with paralyzing pain.

Mr. Cork lashed out violently again with the whip at Pete's back. Again and again, he lashed the whip against his body now raw with long, deep bleeding cuts.

Betsy couldn't bear to hear the lashing sounds of the whip or see Pete's bloody body any longer. She was helpless. There was nothing she could do to save him from her father's violence. A violence he seemed to enjoy inflicting on Pete. Sobbingly, she dashed out of the barn toward her parents' house.

Pete's body ached and burned with intense, agonizing pain. Every nerve pulsated with rage. Oh, how he wished he could die and end the pain. He felt a whirling, dazed sensation. Weakness filled every bone and muscle in his body. His body quivered. Blurred objects filled his eyes. His heart seemed to beat less and then it seemed to stop. His body fell slowly--wilted to the barn floor, and he no longer could feel the razor sharp edge of the cutting whip on his raw flesh. Everything went dark, sound disappeared. It was still and dark in the chambers of his mind. His body no longer felt the pain. He no longer felt anything.

Mr. Cork stopped lashing at him when he saw his body sprawled on the floor. Slowly, he walked toward the body, now a mass of blood. He stared at the body. It didn't move. He kicked its side--still no movement.

"Oh, well, he was no good anyway. He didn't have any right raping my daughter," Mr. Cork said justifiably as he threw the whip down onto Pete's body. He left the barn and headed toward his house.

When Mr. Cork opened the kitchen door to his house, he found Mrs. Cork hovering over Betsy, who was sitting near the table with her head held upright.

Mrs. Cork was applying a wet, ice-cold, folded cloth to Betsy's swollen lip and nose. When she saw her husband, she gave him a piercing look. If looks could kill--he would have been dead.

"Lucinda, make another cloth wet and put it in the icebox," Mrs. Cork said to one of the wide-eyed girls standing near the table. Mrs. Cork put a piece of cotton into one of Betsy's nostril's and then gently squeezed the outside of the nostril against the cotton.

A horrid, scorched smell filled the small kitchen.

Mrs. Cork looked up at the stove. "Oh, the potatoes are burning! Kathleen, take them off the stove," Mrs. Cork said to the other girl standing near the table.

Mr. Cork walked over to Betsy. "Are you all right, Betsy?" he asked softly.

Betsy didn't answer. She gave him a look filled with hate and spite. She wished that fat, ugly man was dead!

Mrs. Cork sighed and whispered to Mr. Cork, "There was no reason for this. I don't say anything when you hit me--but the girls. I'll not stand for that!"

"I told her to stay away from that son of a bitch. Do you know what he did?" Mr. Cork's voice started to raise.

Betsy started to sob.

"Not so loud," Mrs. Cork whispered as she motioned to the two girls standing across the room beside the icebox. "They are too small to hear such things." Mrs. Cork had an idea what this was all about.

"They're old enough to hear such things. Maybe then they'll be smarter than their sister," he said loud enough so the girls could hear.

Betsy jumped out of the chair, threw the cloth onto the floor, and raced upstairs.

Mrs. Cork picked up the cloth, put it on the table, and then started to follow Betsy.

"Just leave her be. Next time she'll learn to listen to me, or I'll give her some of what I gave her friend," he shouted.

Mrs. Cork turned around in the doorway. "I'll be right back."

"You better be. I'm hungry!" he yelled after her.

He turned to the two girls. "You see what happens when you don't listen to your dad?"

Terrified, the two girls nodded their heads. "Yes, Dad."

He pulled out a chair and sat at the table. "Well, sit down and wait for your mama to come." He motioned them over to the table.

The girls scampered to their places at the table. They sat quietly waiting for their mother to come downstairs.

When Mrs. Cork entered Betsy's tidy room, she found her sprawled on her stomach on top of her bed. She was crying loudly and sniffling.

Mrs. Cork sat on the edge of the bed, and comfortingly stroked Betsy's hair now entangled with bits of straw.

"Your dad is really a good man. He just has a violent temper, and he gets very angry when people don't listen to him," Mrs. Cork said softly.

Betsy turned around. "Why doesn't he like Pete? Pete never did anything to him."

"I know that Pete has never done anything to deserve such resentment from your dad. I guess there are some people a person just can't like. No matter how nice they may be, there is just something about them a person can't stand. I don't know what causes it, but it's just something that exists. Your dad isn't like me. I like everyone. There isn't anyone I don't like. I like Pete, but it doesn't matter. Your dad doesn't like him. So I don't say anything. If I did, we'd just argue. Your dad can get quite angry with a person if they don't agree with him."

Betsy sat up and wiped the tears out of her red eyes. "Well, I don't agree with him, and I'm not marrying Todd."

"Betsy dear, Todd is a fine boy. He's well educated and quite financially well-off. He can take you away from this 'humdrum' existence. You could have an exciting life with him. You could have a life of 'peaches and cream.' Servants to clean your house--wash your clothes--do your gardening. You'd never have to wear patched clothes. Your children would never have to wear 'hand-me-down' clothes. Oh, Betsy, you have such a wonderful opportunity for so much. Don't throw it away."

"But I don't love Todd, Mama."

Mrs. Cork touched her hand. "Love will come. When you have money and a good life, love will come. If it doesn't you always have the money to make life good. When you don't have those things and only love, sometimes love leaves and then you have nothing. Then you have to stay with someone you don't love just to survive because that person provides the food on the table and the clothes you wear. So you figure you owe him at least his husbandly right. You let him touch you and make love to you; because, after all, it's part of your duty, as his wife. Oh, my Betsy, it is much better to be rich and not have love than to be poor and not have it."

"Well, Pete has money," replied Betsy.

"Yes, Pete has money, but he's not refined--"

"Oh, I hate that word," Betsy snapped as she put her hands over her ears.

Mrs. Cork gently took her hands away from her ears. "Pete will never become someone important. If you marry him, you'll always be a carpenter's wife. You'll live in his crummy little house, wash his dirty clothes, mend them until you're putting a patch on top of a patch, and scrubbing his dirty floors on your hands and knees." Mrs. Cork rubbed the hair out of Betsy's face. "You're such a beautiful girl, Betsy. You've been offered a chance at the best, take it. Don't end up like me. I got old and ugly from all that work. Don't let that happen to you. You're infatuated with Pete now. That's all. It'll pass. And when it does, Todd may not be around." Mrs. Cork rose from the bed. "Well, if what went on in the barn is what I think went on, I think, you'd better consider getting married as soon as possible. Just in case you got pregnant with that little incident."

"I hope I am, then I have to marry Pete!"

"Don't say such things, Betsy. Your dad won't go for that. When he gets angry, he doesn't always think before he lashes out. If you are pregnant and he does hit you, you could lose the baby. And if you're pregnant that may be the closest you'll ever come to Pete--is having his baby. So don't be foolish and don't provoke him. At least give it a try and marry Todd. If it doesn't work, you can always divorce him. You owe it to yourself to at least try."

"I'm not going to give it a try because I'm not marrying him!"

Her mother walked toward the window and looked out. "I think you should get married within the next two weeks. Then if you are pregnant there will be no way anyone can guess that it isn't Todd's baby. I'll get my wedding dress out of the attic and fix it up. We'll have a small house wedding. Just--"

"Mama, didn't you hear anything I said. I said that I don't love Todd, and I'm not marrying him," Betsy interrupted.

Mrs. Cork turned around and said calmly, "We're not going to argue about this. You're marrying Todd." She started to head for the doorway.

"I'm not marrying Todd Bester," Betsy shouted. Her voice choked with sobs.

Mrs. Cork slowly turned around and looked at Betsy crying on the bed. "Supper will be ready in five minutes--if you're hungry." She disappeared from the doorway, and Betsy heard her shoes clap down the wooden stairs.

Betsy lay in her bed. Her face smothered in the pillow. "I'm not marrying him. I'm not." She pounded her fist on the bed. "I'm not!"

****

A few minutes after Hans knocked on the door, the door opened. A woman stood in the threshold.

A surprised look crossed Hans's face. It wasn't Lena! In front of him stood a young little thing with a small pug nose and cheeks that bloomed.

Who was she? What did she want with him?

"I heard that you've been looking for me. I'm Hans Duren."

"You don't look like him. At least you don't look like I remembered he looked," she replied.

"Remembered me! Remembered me from where?" Hans was puzzled--perturbed--and didn't have time to play games! "Who are you?"

"Anna."

He put his hand on his chest. "Anna! Not my, Anna!" He shook his head. That fully developed young woman couldn't be his Anna. His Anna was a little girl with braids and white ribbons who played with dolls.

"Yes, Daddy, it's me. You don't look the same either." Tears of joy filled her eyes. "I'm so glad to see you." She reached up and hugged his neck.

Hans slowly reached up and put his arms around her. "My little Anna, my little Anna." He stroked the soft waves of her shoulder length hair.

As they stood in the threshold, Hans caught sight of a tall, young man with a heavy boned frame standing in the room watching them. His head was topped with cotton fine hair that had been bleached by the summer sun.

Hans released his embrace from Anna. "Is this my Ludwig?" He walked into the room toward the young man whose skin had been darkened by its exposure to the sun.

"That isn't Ludwig, Daddy." Anna closed the door, walked up to the man, and put her arms around him. "This is Alex Leer, my husband. I'm Anna Leer now, not Anna Duren anymore."

She put her left hand out and showed him the gold band on her finger. Her face was covered with a brilliant, happy smile.

"Glad to meet you, Mr. Duren." Alex smiled and extended his hand.

Hans couldn't believe it as he shook Alex's hand. "But Anna, you aren't old enough to be married yet."

"Daddy, I'm eighteen already and old enough to get married."

"Eighteen." He shook his head. "It's so hard to belief that my little Anna is eighteen already and married. It seems like I missed out on a whole lifetime."

Hans looked about the small one-bedded room. "Where are your ma and Ludwig?"

"Ludwig is in Germany. He's twenty-two now and married. That's why Ma didn't come with us. Ludwig's wife is expecting a baby in about seven months. Ma stayed to help. The poor girl is so sick. She has to stay in bed most of the time. As soon as she does something, she starts to spot bleed. They're afraid she might lose the baby. So Ma thought it would be best if she stayed. The girl's family is dead. We're all she has. Ludwig is so excited about becoming a father, and Ma is just as excited about being a grandma."

"That means, I'll be a grandpa. Is your ma coming after the baby?"

"She's planning to. Ludwig and his wife are going to come when the baby is older. Ma will be coming before them. She'll be coming alone."

Well, that gave him at least seven months time, Hans thought. But what about Anna and Alex, they were bound to find out about Kate. Maybe Anna already knew. No, she couldn't know. Otherwise, she wouldn't be so happy and pleased to see him. She had been closer to her mother than to him. He was really a stranger to her. If a stranger would hurt her mother, she'd be furious. Wouldn't she, if she knew?

"The man in the store said you are a carpenter in a town called, Shady Lane," Anna said as she sat on the edge of the bed.

"Ya, I am. What else did he tell you?" Hans tensely held his breath and hoped. Erickson was one of the few people in Beechwood who knew he was married.

"Just that you do beautiful carpenter work," replied Anna.

The tenseness left his body. He felt relieved. Erickson hadn't told her.

"We had planned to take the train, when it stopped again tomorrow, to Shady Lane. But now that you're here, maybe we can ride back with you to your place," Anna suggested.

That didn't sound like a good idea at all to Hans. For the moment, he was trapped. How on earth was he going to handle this? If they came back to Shady Lane with him, they'd surely find out. He was a stranger to her and her reaction would not be good. It would be best if she got to know him a little better, maybe she would not be so hostile. Hostile! She didn't really have any right to feel that way. They were the ones who stopped writing. What was he to think when he didn't hear from them anymore? Well, that didn't really matter at the moment. The important thing for him to do right now was to do something to protect his interest before anyone found out.

"Do you have any money left after the trip?" Hans asked Alex.

"No, I'm afraid not," replied Alex.

"Well, then it isn't a very good idea to come back to Shady Lane. There aren't that many jobs available there. You'll have more of an opportunity to get work here because Beechwood is ten times as big as Shady Lane," Hans said.

"Well, couldn't Alex help you in your shop? I was looking forward to being with you to make up a little for all the years we were apart," said Anna.

"I've got Pete helping me, and we really don't have that much work for three people. It wouldn't be fair to turn Pete out and let Alex work. Especially since Pete has been good enough to help me from the start."

"You're right, Daddy. It wouldn't be fair to do that to Pete," Anna agreed.

Hans put his arm around Anna's shoulders. "I tell you what I'll do. I'll come into town as often as I can to see you and help find Alex a job here. Why I could even move here. There's really nothing holding me in Shady Lane except my carpenter shop, and I could move that here." That should keep them from venturing into Shady Lane, Hans thought. He grabbed into his pocket and pulled out some crumbled money. He straightened it out and handed it to Alex. "This should help you for a while."

"No, Mr. Duren, we couldn't take money from you." Alex shook his head.

"Why not? Anna is my daughter and her welfare is important to me." He reached over, grabbed Alex's hand, and placed the money inside of it. "No arguments, you keep it," Hans insisted.

"Thank you, Mr. Duren."

"Thank you, Daddy." She touched his hand and gently kissed his cheek.

Hans smiled at her. "Well, I should be going."

"Oh, so soon, Daddy." Anna was disappointed about his early departure.

"Yes, it'll be dark soon, and I'd like to be back in Shady Lane before then."

"Why don't you wait until tomorrow? You could take a room in the hotel here, and we could talk longer. It's been such a long time since we've been together," said Anna.

"I know. But I'm afraid I can't stay any longer. I borrowed the horses on the wagon from a farmer, and he needs them back. I'm sorry, Anna." He gave her a long hug, and then they walked to the door.

"Bye, Daddy," said Anna as she closed the door behind him.

As Hans walked down the hall and the stairs, he wore a pleasing smile on his face and a "tickled feeling" passed through him. His Anna had grown up to be a real beauty. It was just unbelievable how beautiful she was. Even more unbelievable was the fact that she was his daughter.

So Lena was coming in about seven months. How would he feel

when he saw her? Could he keep all his lies straight for that long? He had to move fast now.

As he climbed onto the wagon and headed toward Shady Lane, he looked at the sky. The sun wouldn't set for some time on this warm autumn day. He should make it home just in time for supper. With all the things he had to think about, time went fast and soon he was in Shady Lane.

"Whoa!" Hans said as he stopped the wagon in front of the barn. He dismounted the wagon and unhitched the horses from the wagon. Pete must be done with his work, he thought, as he led the horses toward the quiet barn. As he approached the door, he thought it was strange that Pete hadn't put the bolt in the hasp to keep the door shut. Hans opened the door and led the horses inside. The reins abruptly dropped from his hands, and his eyes became glued to the horrifying sight.

"Oh, my God! What has happened here? Who is that?"

He ran toward the body that lay amid the pile of straw, which was drenched in blood.

As he turned the body over, his face became pale with shock. "It's Pete! What mad man could have done this. My God! Is he dead?" Quickly, he bent down and rested his ear on Pete's raw, inflamed chest. He could feel the sticky blood touch his ear and side of his face. Was there a heartbeat? No, he couldn't hear one. Oh, wait! Yes, there was a heartbeat--a very slight one. Hans's eyes quickly searched about the barn for something to wrap Pete's body in. His eyes stood still. Draped over one of the old horse stalls was a drab, mouse-eaten horse blanket. Hans snatched it off the stall and carefully wrapped Pete's body in it. Pete's blood covered Hans's hands, his clothes, every visible part of his body. He lifted Pete's limp, inert body into his arms. With great effort he started to carry Pete's dead weight up to the kitchen door. Hans was breathing rapidly, heavily; his heart was throbbing and his arms were beginning to tingle, feel numb. He couldn't carry Pete any farther. Thank goodness he was at the door. He peered into the window located at the top of the door. Kate was alone in the kitchen neatly folding towels on her ironing board. Forcefully, he kicked his foot against the bottom of the door.

Kate was startled by the sound. Turning in the direction of the sound, she saw it was Hans. Quickly, she opened the door.

"My, God! What has happened," said Kate as she closed the door behind Hans.

"I don't know. I've been gone all day. I just found him."

"Take him up to his room." Kate filled a basin with water and took some cloths along with her. Hurriedly, she walked in front of Hans opening doors. When they reached Pete's room, she pulled back the blankets on his bed so Hans could lay him in it. She placed the basin and cloths on the night stand and watched Hans unwrap the horse blanket. Kate became queasy at such a gruesome sight. She clamped her hands over her mouth to stop the ejection of her stomach contents. She felt her face turn white and cold.

Hans touched her. "Are you all right, Kate?"

She nodded her head and took her hand from her mouth. Kate looked at Pete. "Who would do something like that?" She shook her head. It was hard for her to believe one "civilized" human being could do something so animalistic to another human.

"I don't know? Some kind of a mad man!"

Kate wet one of the cloths, wrung it out in the bowl, started to sponge Pete's body clean, and wash out the cuts. Taking the other cloth, she gently dried his body. She rinsed the blood-covered cloth in the basin. The water turned red.

"Why would someone treat Pete so brutally?" Kate walked to the other side of the bed to wash the other side of his body.

"I guess we'll have to wait for Pete to tell us," replied Hans.

"Do you think he'll be able to?" Kate was afraid. Was he going to die?

"I hope he can tell us who did this. That person should be hung or at least given the same treatment. I'd like to see how that person would like it." Hans helped Kate gently roll Pete on his chest so she could clean his back. Hans looked at the basin and picked it up.

"I'll get you some fresh water," he said.

"I'll get the salve we have in our top dresser drawer. Dr. Gibbs says that it's really good for wounds and cuts," Kate said.

They both left the room and went downstairs.

Hans went into the kitchen, opened the back door, and threw the bloodstained water out onto the ground. Walking over to the sink, he filled the basin with fresh water and grabbed another cloth for Kate.

Kate tossed about the clothes in the dresser drawer looking for the salve. It was in there! She had seen it so many times before, but where was it now? Oh! There it was. She reached far into the back of the drawer and pulled out a small jar.

She met Hans going up the stairs just as she shut the sitting room door. "I hope this salve helps?"

"It will, don't worry," Hans said reassuringly.

They climbed the stairs and soon were in Pete's room.

"If there is a mad person running about the countryside doing such a thing, I think, we better warn others," Kate said. She set the salve down, reached into the clean water, wrung out the clean cloth, and continued cleaning Pete's body.

"We better wait and see what Pete says, if he says anything!" remarked Hans.

Appallingly, Kate looked at Hans. "Don't say such things. He'll be fine. Don't you think so?" Kate needed reassuring.

"I didn't mean it that way, Kate. Of course, he'll be fine. I just meant that sometimes Pete keeps things inside of himself. If he doesn't want to talk about things, he won't."

After she finished cleaning his body, she opened the jar and soothingly applied the yellow, greasy, jellylike substance to the cuts on his back. When she had finished with his back, they rolled him over, and she finished the front of his body.

Hans darkened the room by pulling down the shades. He then picked up the basin and soiled cloths while Kate covered Pete's unconscious body with the blankets. They left the room and stood outside the closed door for a moment.

Kate sighed. "I do hope he will be all right."

Hans put his arm around her shoulder. "He'll be all right. He will."

"Thank goodness his face didn't get cut. He's got such a good-looking face. I'd hate to see it scarred all up," Kate said as she slowly walked down the stairs.

As they entered the kitchen, Kate took the soiled cloths. "I think I'll throw these away. I'll never probably get the stains out, and I don't want to be reminded each time I see them."

"Ya, I don't blame you." Hans threw the water out the door.

Seeing the picnic basket in the middle of the table, he hit his forehead with the palm of his hand and rolled the hand over his hair. "I'm sorry, Kate. I forgot about the picnic."

She grabbed the basin out of his hand and rinsed it out. "Well, it's to late now to go on one. I'm not even hungry."

"Well, I'm starved. I didn't eat all day." He sat at the table and took some of the food out of the basket.

"What did Erickson want to see you about?" Kate dried her hands on a towel, which hung beside the sink, and then sat at the table.

"Oh, a leg broke off one of the curio cabinets I made him last week, and I had to fix it." He dug into a drumstick with his pearly white teeth.

"Tsh." Kate sighed and shook her head. "Well, I should think Pete could have fixed that."

"Well, you know Erickson." He poured himself a glass of lemonade and gulped it down. "You make the best lemonade."

"Thank you. I'm glad you like it."

"Say you know what I've been thinking, Kate."

"No, I don't. Why don't you tell me?" She smiled at him and then grabbed the other glass out of the basket and filled it full of lemonade.

"Why don't we sell the inn?"

"Sell the inn!" A shocked look crossed her face then a perplexed look. What on earth was he talking about? Selling the inn! "Just where would we live if we sold the inn?"

"We could build a new house. I know how. I am a carpenter. We could use the money from selling the inn to buy material and the land."

"We own land. Why buy more?"

"Because I know a perfect setting for a new house, and it isn't on our land."

"Just where is this perfect setting?" Kate took a sip of her lemonade.

"Across the railroad track in the woods."

"It always comes back to that woods. You are bound and determined to have it, aren't you?"

"Well, it's just standing there. No one is getting any use or enjoyment out of it. I think a nice big white house setting in the middle of the woods would be a beautiful sight. Especially, if it's our big white house."

"I told you the owner doesn't want to sell." Kate fingered her glass.

"Maybe the owner has changed her mind. It's been two years."

Kate was surprised. "How do you know it's a woman?"

"Kate, I'm not stupid. You told me that you know the owner and the only person I've ever known you to be so secretive or protective of is the cook, Molly. Right?"

"Yes, she owns the land." Kate finished her glass of lemonade, rose from the chair, and placed the empty glass into the sink.

"I don't understand. Why all the secrecy about the land?" Hans asked.

Kate sat back in her chair. "Molly doesn't want to be bothered by people who might be interested in buying the land. So she asked me not to tell anyone."

"How on earth does she figure that she's ever gonna get bothered? She's never around. She's always lurking in the shadows and disappears completely as soon as someone comes around," Hans replied.

"She likes to be by herself."

"A bit odd, if you ask me." Hans licked the last bit of chicken off his fingertips.

"That's not very kind, Hans. Everyone has their reasons for doing what they do," replied Kate.

"Are you going to ask her if she'd sell us the land?"

"Yes, I'll ask her." Kate rose from the chair. "Are you finished eating?"

"Ya, it was very good. You make the best fried chicken."

Kate chuckled. "I bet you say that to all the girls."

Hans pulled her onto his lap. "Nope, just to my favorite ones." He chuckled and kissed her cheek.

"I better clean off the table." She got off his lap, threw the chicken bones into the rubbish dish under the sink, and put the basket and gingham cloths on the shelf.

She dampened a cloth and started to wipe the table clean.

"That's three hundred acres of land, Hans. We'll never get that much money from selling the inn. We'll have to take some out of the bank," Kate said.

"So, that's not such a big deal. We've got my savings in Beechwood and yours in Bester's bank. We'll just take the money out of one of our joint accounts," suggested Hans.

"Yes, we could, but what are we going to do for income after we sell the inn?" Kate was concerned.

"I make enough money in my carpenter shop for us to live nicely. I don't like you working so hard in this inn. Especially now that the train stops almost every day, it's too much for you. We aren't that poor that you have to work so hard. If I have a bad year in the shop, we have enough in the bank to help us out." He touched her hand. "I love you, Kate. I just want you to take care of me and our house. Wouldn't you like that?"

Kate thought about what he said as she cleaned the table. He was right. They had enough money to live good. They didn't need the inn for income. His carpenter shop was really doing good. If she became pregnant, she would like to spend all her time taking care of the house and later the baby. The two rooms they lived in now would be too small if they started a family. Also, the inn was too enormous to convert into a house.

"Maybe you are right, Hans. I would like to stop this 'rat race' and just take care of our home and you." She put the cloth into the sink and sat back in her chair.

"Should we sell the twenty acres, too?" she asked.

"We might as well. Otherwise, we'd have to have a new deed and abstract made out and that'll take awhile," Hans replied.

"Well, we have lots of time. If you'd like the twenty acres of woods, we could keep them," suggested Kate.

"No, we'll have enough woods after we buy the land from Molly."

"Well, she might not sell," cautioned Kate.

"I really don't know what she could possibly want with it. If she sells the land, she never has to worry about anyone bothering her about it. She could use the money to build a house somewhere far away from people. She could live quite comfortably off the money that she'd have left after building a house. She wouldn't have to work the rest of her life. She'd have a very nice life," Hans rationalized, hoping that Kate would use the same words in convincing Molly.

"It would be a nice life for her. Wouldn't it? I know it's hard for her working the way she does, especially with her arm being the way it is. However, I'd like her to live nearby. If she needs anything, I'd be right there to help her," Kate said.

"She's a grown woman. Isn't she?" Hans responded.

"Well, yes."

"Well, then why can't Molly take care of herself? Why do you always have to watch out and be so protective toward her," Hans asked?

"I owe her a lot. I owe her for my dad's life," replied Kate.

"You owe her for your dad's life?" Hans was puzzled.

"Yes, she saved my dad's life a long time ago. That's how she got the land."

"What do you mean, 'that's how she got the land'?"

"When my dad died, he gave me the inn and two hundred acres of woods. He gave Molly the three hundred acres across the track," Kate explained.

"Boy, your dad was a right generous man."

"That he was." Kate nodded her head. "But what is the price of life? It's worth a lot more than three hundred acres. Molly lost a lot when she saved my dad."

"What--"

A knock at the kitchen door, interrupted his question.

"Who could be knocking at this hour?" Kate eyed the clock. It was nine-thirty. She rose from the chair.

"You stay there, Kate. I'll get it." Hans motioned Kate back to her chair as he got up. "After what happened to Pete, you can't be too careful. Who knows who's at the door."

Kate was a bit terrified. What if it was the man who beat up Pete! A mad man!

As Hans neared the door, he could see through the window. "It looks like Betsy!" He opened the door and let her in.

"My God, Betsy, what has happened to your face?" Kate was shocked and deeply concerned about Betsy's swollen, black and blue nose and lips.

Betsy clung to Kate and started crying uncontrollably.

Kate embraced her and comfortingly stroked her hair.

"Tell me what's the matter, Betsy." Kate offered her a chair.

Hans pulled the chair out from under the table for her to sit on. "You almost look as bad as Pete." Hans sat in his chair.

"Oh Pete!" Betsy sobbed. "How is Pete?"

Kate and Hans looked at each other in surprise. How did she know about Pete? How?

"You know about Pete?" asked Kate.

"Yes." She continued to sob. "I was there when--when--when my dad beat him."

"Your dad did that!" Kate pointed upstairs.

"That man is crazy!" Hans jumped out of his chair and headed toward the door. "I'll give him some of his own medicine! See how he likes it!" Hans and Pete may have had their disagreements. However, when something like this happened, he was on Pete's side.

Betsy sprang from her chair and grabbed Hans's arm. "No, please, don't go to my dad. If he finds out that I came here--oh, please, don't go! I'm afraid of what he'll do!"

"Good, God! Is he the one who did that to your face?" Kate held Betsy's hand gently in hers.

Betsy lowered her head and nodded.

"Hans, I don't think you should go over to Mr. Cork's house. You'll just make matters worst. Perhaps it would be better for everyone if we just forgot this incident," Kate suggested.

"Ya, maybe you're right, Kate." Hans looked at Betsy. "If your dad feels so hostile toward Pete, why did he let you come here? You obviously came over to see Pete, not us."

"My dad doesn't know that I'm here. I waited until he and my ma went to bed. Then I crawled out my window and down the oak tree that touches the house near my window. I just have to see Pete," Betsy said.

Kate sighed. "It won't really do any good for you to see him. He's still unconscious."

"Oh, please, can't I just sit awhile beside his bed, please," Betsy pleaded between her sniffles.

"Come along." Kate took her hand and led Betsy up to Pete's room.

Hans locked the door, turned out the gas lamp, and followed them up the stairs to Pete's room.

When they opened the door and went in, they found Pete awake.

Betsy ran over to the bed and touched his one hand. "Oh, Pete, I'm so sorry. It's all my fault." She sobbed.

"How are you feeling, Pete?" asked Kate as she and Hans approached the back of his bed.

"I'll be all right. I just hurt a lot. Can I be alone with Betsy?" Pete's weak voice asked.

"Sure, if you need anything you just call," Kate replied.

"You let us know when you're leaving, Betsy. Kate and I will walk you home. You shouldn't be out in the dark alone at this hour."

"Thank you, but that's not necessary. I came by myself, and I can go back by myself."

"Kate and I like to take a walk on beautiful nights like these. There aren't to many of them left. We're lucky it's this nice out yet. A September night that's like a July night is a rarity," Hans commented.

"We'll be sitting on the porch steps," said Kate as they went out and closed the door.

"Oh, Pete, I love you," said Betsy as she gently squeezed his hand.

"Ya, we both look like lovers, don't we? You snuck out of the house, didn't you?"

"That's the only way I could get out to see you. You know my dad wouldn't let me out of the house tonight for sure. Oh, I love you so much, Pete. Let's run away and get married then no one can ever keep us apart."

"I'm hardly in shape for running right now." Pete started to chuckle, but it hurt too much.

"Well, as soon as you're better, let's go--okay," Betsy said eagerly.

"I wasn't the first. Was I?" he asked.

Betsy smiled. "Huh--what do you mean? You weren't the first?"

"You know what I mean, Betsy."

Betsy rose from the bed and pulled up the shade.

"It's really lovely out tonight," she said as she looked out at the starry sky. "Hans and Kate are going for a walk later. Too bad we can't go."

"Betsy, I'm right. Aren't I?"

She turned around, rubbed her hands together, and asked nervously with a smile, "Right--right about what?"

"It wasn't the first time for you, was it?"

"Pete, you are talking in riddles. I should go home so you can get some rest. I think you need it." She headed for the door.

"You let someone else touch you. Didn't you? Maybe more than just once because you aren't the innocent little virgin I thought you were. You're a little bit too experienced. What are you some kind of a whore?"

She turned around abruptly. "Pete, don't say such things about me! You don't know what you're saying."

"I'm saying that a girl who never had an experience with a man would hardly know or have any idea of what probably would excite him, and what would make her body fill with excitement."

Tears filled Betsy's eyes. "It was only once before, and it wasn't my idea. I hated it! Please, believe me, Pete," she pleaded. "It was all my dad's fault!"

"Your dad! You mean your dad?" Pete was shocked. Her own father! It was unbelievable! Repulsive!

"No, it didn't happen with my dad, but it was his fault. He arranged for Todd to take me home. Remember the ice cream social? The night Todd took me home."

"I thought you couldn't stand him! Then you let him touch you that way!" A disgusting look crossed Pete's face.

"It wasn't like that," Betsy replied trying desperately to convince Pete.

"Well, then why don't you tell me the way it was!"

"He made me have sex with him." Betsy sobbed.

"Oh, come on Betsy! No one can make someone have sex if they don't want to," Pete replied in a judgmental tone.

"Well, I didn't want to, but Todd made me." She wept aloud with a break in her voice and short, gasping breaths.

"If you didn't want him touching you, you could have done something to stop him. You could have kicked him or pulled his hair. You could have run off while he was pulling down his pants. A man can't run very good with his pants halfway down."

"I didn't think of that at the time. I was shocked, stunned. He caught me off guard. I just couldn't think. My mind was a blank. Before I knew it, he was all over me."

"Ya, sure! There's no way you're going to convince me that a guy can have sex with a girl against her will. No way!"

"Well, does it really matter? It only happened once. I love you, Pete."

Pete lay still. He didn't answer. He didn't even want to look at her.

"It doesn't really matter that you weren't the first--does it?" Betsy was frightened by what she anticipated his answer might be.

Pete was silent. He didn't know how he felt. His illusion of her was shattered. It was important to him that she'd be a virgin. That he'd be the first and only one to have ever touched her. But why was it so important, he wasn't a virgin. She probably knew that, but it didn't make any difference to her. Why did it make a difference to him? His ego. He wanted to have something no one else had ever touched. If everyone sees it, who wants it. Girls like that are a "dime a dozen." Cheap! If he'd wanted a girl like that he could have had his choice of any of the girls that worked at the Beechwood tavern, but he had wanted a special girl. A girl no one had ever touched. A girl he knew was his very own and one that would make others wish they had. If he wasn't the first and only guy, he felt cheated. He didn't want secondhand things anymore. All his life he had them--secondhand clothes--secondhand shoes. He wasn't going to have a secondhand girl. All of a sudden he didn't know Betsy. She wasn't at all like he had thought. The sweet innocent girl no longer existed--if she ever did.

"Well, it doesn't really matter--does it? All that is important is that I love you, and I do. Oh, so much." She hugged him in bed and kissed his lips. He pushed her away and just looked at her. His eyes spoke "you cheap little whore." He didn't have to say anything. She knew by looking at him. She burst out the door and down the stairs. To have Pete think so badly of her was something she just couldn't bear. She felt about herself the same way he did. Dirty! Cheap! Ugly! God she was so cheap--so dirty--so ugly!

As she stood at the bottom of the stairs, unforgettable scenes from that night with Todd blasted through her mind. She had been sitting under a shade tree with her mother. They were watching Pete, Hans, some of the other men, and older boys playing baseball. Then her father and Todd came over. Before she knew it, she was walking toward the stream with Todd. It was a beautiful evening, and she enjoyed walking through the serene woods. She had wished it was Pete walking beside her. When Todd touched her hand and held it in his moist, cold, sticky hand, shivers went up her spine. Ugh! His hand had felt terrible. Soon they were at the edge of the stream where they stopped and sat down. Then Todd suggested taking off their shoes and splashing their feet in the water. How stupid she had been! How naive of her not to think he didn't have something else on his mind! She still could remember how quiet the air was. Only their splashes of water echoed the stillness. Then suddenly, she felt his arm creep about her and soon he had his thick, moist tongue in her mouth. It felt terrible. His saliva had run down her chin. It was disgusting. She had tried to pull away, to push him away. His strong arms held her tight. She had felt his hands pull her blouse out of her skirt, climb her back, and loosen her bra. After he had laid her down, he put his body on top of hers. Soon he had her blouse unbuttoned and was slobbering on her breasts. A strange feeling shot through her body. She couldn't tolerate Todd, but her body seemed to desire what he was doing. She had said to herself that it wasn't right what he was doing. He was seeing her naked body. They weren't married. He shouldn't be doing that to her. He shouldn't be seeing her naked. She had tried again to push him away, but he would lay harder on her chest. She could feel him struggle with his belt and then his zipper. He took her hand and put it between his legs. She quickly pulled her hand out. She didn't want to touch that thing, but he put her hand back and held it there. Her hand down there seemed to excite him. The more he kissed her breasts; the more excited she became. She didn't want to, but she couldn't control the excitement that filled her body. Suddenly, she felt the thing between his legs get big and hard. She felt him lift her skirt and soon that thing was in her. It hurt. She tried to squirm away from under him, but she couldn't. She didn't want that thing in her body. She couldn't stand him holding her hand much less doing what he was doing to her. But after a while, the more he moved, the more she began to like the feeling. When he had finished, her body seemed relaxed. She had thought how wonderful it would feel to do that with

Pete. Was that sex? The only thing her mother had told her about sex was that it hurts, and a girl shouldn't have sex until she is married. She had told her it hurts more if a girl wasn't married. The hurting was God's punishment for being a bad girl. It did hurt at first, but then it didn't hurt after a while. Pregnant! Her mother also said when a girl has sex she becomes pregnant. Oh, no! She couldn't get pregnant, not with Todd's baby. Then she'd have to marry him. She remembered how frantically she had prayed and prayed that she'd get her period. When she finally did, she felt like having a celebration. Ever since then she was afraid to be alone with Todd. She had thought if he'd do it again she might not be so lucky. The next time she might get pregnant. Then she thought, why couldn't it work the opposite way, with Pete and her. If she seduced Pete and he made love to her, maybe she'd become pregnant. Then she could have Pete. She felt her lower abdomen now and hoped for Pete's baby, but would it turn out that way now? Now, that he felt differently about her. Sure it would, if she was carrying his child, he'd marry her. He wouldn't want a child of his to grow up deprived like he did. The chiming of the dining room clock startled her.

"I better be going home before they find out I'm gone," she thought aloud to herself.

As she reached for the doorknob, she remembered Hans and Kate. She wiped the tears off her face and out of her eyes. Kate and Hans didn't have to know that she and Pete had a disagreement. She stopped her sniffing, opened the door, and went out onto the porch.

Hans and Kate, sitting on the top porch step, turned around and looked at her.

Betsy forced a smile. "Well, I'm all ready for my escort."

As they rose from the steps, they could see her eyes were red. Kate put her arm around Betsy comfortingly. "Are you all right, Betsy?"

"Yes, I just couldn't stand to see Pete that way. I better not see him for a while."

"Under the circumstances, I think that's a smart thing to do," Hans said as they walked toward Betsy's home.

They stopped in front of the white picket fence.

"Thank you," Betsy said as she opened the gate and entered the small lawn area.

Kate and Hans just shook their heads and smiled to each other as they saw her scramble up the tree and into her unlit window.

Hand in hand they strolled through the darkness of the night toward the lighted inn.

"I don't think those two were just talking when Mr. Cork found them in the barn," said Hans as they walked along, "if you know what I mean."

"Oh, I don't think Betsy's that kind of girl," Kate replied.

"No, I don't think she's the kind of girl who would let just anyone touch her. However, I know she cares for Pete, and I wouldn't doubt that she went 'all the way' with Pete. I think that's when Mr. Cork came in," Hans said.

"Well, I really don't think he deserved such a beating for something like that," remarked Kate.

Hans opened the door for Kate. "No, I don't think so either."

"Do you think I should check on Pete?" Kate asked.

"No, there's nothing you can do." Hans opened the sitting room door, and they went in.

They turned out the gas lamps, got undressed, and went into bed.

As Hans lay in the bed with the back of his head resting on his hands, he stared at the ceiling in thought. His scheme could only work if Molly sold her land. He ran his scheme through his mind. He knew every move that he had to make, but he couldn't make a move until he had Molly's land.

"What do you think about children, Hans?" Kate's question broke the silence of the dark room.

"I never thought much about them. Why? You aren't pregnant, are you?" His heart suddenly seemed to stop waiting for the answer. Kate being pregnant would ruin his whole scheme. He hadn't figured on that happening. Well, now that was stupid! They were always making love. It was bound to happen. Especially since he hadn't taken any precautions to prevent it so far.

"No, I'm not, but I would like to have a baby, our baby." She put her arm around him and rested her head on his chest.

His body felt relieved. That was a close scare. "Not right now, it's not the right time."

"Why not?"

"First of all, there is no room here for a baby. I want to build you a house first. Secondly, I don't want you doing anything except taking care of our house when you become pregnant. I don't want you getting run-down because you have so much work to do around here. I think it would be best if we waited until we have the woods bought and our house built."

"I suppose you're right." Her arms slid off his body as she laid her head back on her pillow in disappointment. She'd have to wait.

"It'll be early enough to start our family then. A few months longer won't make that much difference. As soon as we buy the woods, we can start our family. Until we do buy the woods, I think I better use something to prevent you from becoming pregnant." Hans planned his words well. He knew from the little things that Kate had said since they'd been married that she longed to have a child. He figured she'd now convince Molly to sell the woods. She knew the sooner Molly sold the woods, the sooner she could have a baby.

"What do you mean, you'd do something to prevent me from becoming pregnant?" Kate asked.

Hans got out of bed and walked over to where his clothing was lying on a heap on the floor. He reached into the front pocket of his trousers and pulled out a small red box.

"This is what I mean." He tossed the box over to her onto the bed.

She picked it up and looked puzzlingly at the box. "What is this?"

"Safeties--rubber's. I wear them so you don't get pregnant," he replied.

"Oh, you aren't really going to use them, are you?"

"Well, what do you think I bought them for?" he replied.

"Where did you get them?" She handed them back to Hans.

"I bought them from Erickson today."

"I don't know why you wasted your money on them. It's not the most serious thing in the world if I did become pregnant."

"I told you I don't want you becoming pregnant until you don't have to work in this inn, and until I've got a house built so we have room for the baby." He put the box under the mattress.

"A baby doesn't take up that much room," Kate replied.

"Well, I'm using them until things are the way I want them to be." He crawled back into bed, gave her a kiss, and then turned away from her. The plans for his future didn't include having a child with Kate.

Kate just lay there in silence. Quiet tears filled her eyes and ran down her cheeks. It pained her to have to wait longer for a baby, but Hans was only thinking of her. He didn't want her working so hard, and he wanted to provide her with a nice home. It was so sweet of Hans to think of her that way. Well, the sooner they bought the woods, the sooner she could have their baby. She rolled her hand over her cheeks to dry her face of the tears. She'd ask Molly tomorrow--the first thing tomorrow.

****

Hans rolled over and found Kate's side of the bed empty. He threw the blankets off and sprang out of bed. Did he oversleep? Why didn't she wake him? His eyes shot over to the clock. It was only five-thirty. It wasn't time to get up. He looked at the empty hook where Kate had hung her clothes the night before. What was she doing up so early?

He put on his clothes and went into the sitting room. I bet she's with Molly, he thought. Quietly, he crept up the stairs. He tiptoed over to Molly's door. He could hear soft voices coming from behind the closed door.

"I don't know, Kate."

"Well, you won't ever use the land, but you could use the money. You wouldn't have to work so hard then. You could build your own house far away from people, and you wouldn't have to live in fear that someone might see you."

"I don't want to move away from here. You're all I have, Kate. I'd like to stay near you."

"You can, Molly. Why don't you keep a section of the land you want and build a place for yourself on it? Hans could build a house for you."

"I don't need a house just for myself. Could I live in your house with you?"

"I don't see why not. I don't think Hans would object. I would like that very much."

"Well, like you said, I don't really have any use for the land. So, I might just as well sell it."

Hans's face lit up when he heard that his scheme was going to work. He tiptoed back downstairs. Into the bedroom he went and sat at the edge of the bed. When he heard Kate in the sitting room, he started to put on his shoes to give her the appearance that he had just gotten up and was finishing dressing.

"Well, good morning, Hans!" Kate said a bit surprised that he had gotten up by himself. She usually had to shake him after the alarm went off to wake him. He never seemed to hear that alarm.

"You look happy today, Kate." He put on his last shoe and stood up.

"I am." She kissed him. "Molly will sell us her land. She said that you should take care of the legal side of things. She doesn't know anything about such things. She'd like seventy dollars an acre."

"Okay, I'll go to Beechwood today and find a lawyer to handle this. Now, all we have to do is fine a buyer for the inn," Hans replied.

"I really don't like selling the inn." Kate looked around the room. "Dad built every inch of this place by himself. Somehow I'd feel as if I'd be leaving him permanently if I sold it."

"Your dad is dead. We're alive. You can't live your life for people that are dead," Hans remarked.

"I know, but somehow it wouldn't seem right to sell it. We have enough money to buy Molly's land. We don't need the money from the sale of the inn."

Hans thought for a while. His scheme would work whether they sold the inn or not. In fact, maybe it would work better if they didn't sell it.

"I suppose we could keep the inn and hire someone to run it for us," he suggested.

"Oh, Hans, that is a marvelous idea. Thank you so much for not making me sell it." She embraced and kissed him.

They left the bedroom and went into the kitchen where Molly had a hot breakfast waiting for them.

After breakfast, while Kate tidied up the kitchen, Hans stole away quietly into the bedroom. He opened the drawer on the night stand, pulled out the rolled up papers that he had put in there yesterday morning, and put them inside his jacket. He went into the kitchen, sat at the table, and drank coffee as he watched the clock until it was time to leave.

"Well, I'll be leaving now." He kissed Kate "good-bye," went out the door and walked toward the bank, located at the edge of town.

A tall, handsome curly haired man had just pulled up the dark shades on the bank windows and was now unlocking the front door as Hans reached the bank.

As Hans entered the bank, the handsome man went behind the teller window and greeted him, "Good morning, Hans, what can I do for you today?"

"Quite a lot, Todd. First of all, I want a cashier's check for twenty-one thousand dollars," Hans said.

Todd's eyes almost "popped out." That was a lot of money to be withdrawing. "Do you want both your names on the remitter?" he asked.

"No, just mine," replied Hans.

"Okay, I'll be right back." Todd went into the back room where Hans could see him talking to his father. They both looked up at Hans. Mr. Bester nodded his head and Todd disappeared from view. A few minutes later Todd was back in sight. He handed his father a small piece of paper, which Mr. Bester signed. Todd came out and gave Hans the piece of paper. "Here you go. Have a nice day."

"Not so quick, I'm not finished yet," Hans said as he took the check.

"You aren't?" remarked Todd.

"No, I want another cashier's check made out to me," Hans stated.

"Okay, for how much?" Todd asked.

"Everything I have left in the account," replied Hans.

"Everything!" Todd replied shockingly. "I don't know about that. Does Kate know you're drawing everything out?"

"She sure does. You want to run up to the inn and ask her?" Hans replied.

"It's an awful lot of money. Are you sure you want to draw it all out?" Todd asked.

"Ya, stop beating around the bush and give me my money," Hans said.

Todd went into the back room again and had another discussion with his father.

Mr. Bester rose from the chair and came out to the teller window. "Hi, Hans," Mr. Bester greeted him with a big smile on his double-chinned face. "That's an awful lot of money you're withdrawing today. Are you sure you want to draw it all out right now?"

"Ya, I'm sure. What's the matter, don't you have my money?" Hans asked.

"Sure we do." He turned to Todd. "Make out a cashier's check for the rest of his money."

"Okay, Dad," replied Todd. He departed to the back room again.

A few minutes later Todd came back and handed his father the check. Mr. Bester signed it and gave it to Hans.

"Twenty thousand, six hundred dollars," Hans said as he examined the check. "It was nice doing business with you." Hans folded the checks and put them into his pocket.

Hans was in a happy mood. So far, so good, he thought as he whistled a happy tune on his walk back to the inn.

"I'm back, Kate," he shouted as he entered the door.

"So soon?" She propped up the open window with a stick and walked toward him.

"I've got a lot of money here on these two pieces of paper." He pulled them out and showed them to Kate.

"What did Mr. Bester say when you took everything out?" Kate asked as she examined the two checks.

"I don't think that he liked it very well," replied Hans.

"I suppose he wasn't as happy as he was when I put all that money in his bank five years ago," Kate commented.

"No, not quite that happy." Hans chuckled a bit.

"Well, Mr. Blake should be happy when you deposit this in his bank again." Kate gave him the check for twenty thousand six hundred dollars. "I wish I had never changed banks. Mr. Blake was always nice to me and my dad."

"Well, Bester's bank was right here. It was more convenient for you than traveling back and forth to Beechwood. With me it didn't matter, I had to go to Beechwood all the time to take Erickson the furniture his customers always ordered. So, it was never inconvenient for me at all," said Hans.

"Maybe I should go to Beechwood today with you. It's going to be another scorching day. It will be too hot to work, and I haven't been to Beechwood for such a long time," Kate said.

No, that was not a good idea. Anna was there, and he had things to do. Things Kate shouldn't know about.

"Why don't you wait until I go next time? Pete might need you today," Hans said.

Kate looked up the stairs. "Yes, there should be someone around to see how he does today."

"You can come along with Molly when she has to go to sign the papers for the land," Hans suggested.

"Yes, that's a good idea. Molly won't like going into Beechwood at all, but if I'm with her maybe she won't mind it too much. I'll give her this." Kate motioned to the other check in her hand. She ripped off the carbon copy, handed it to Hans, and took the top copy of the check upstairs.

A few minutes later Kate came down and handed Hans some papers. "Here are the abstract and deed. Molly said you should tell the lawyer to start processing them. When her signature is needed to make things legal, she'll go to Beechwood but only at night. She doesn't want people staring at her."

Hans grabbed the papers, examined them, folded them, and put them into his pocket. "If she wouldn't wear that scarf on her face, no one would stare," Hans commented.

Kate shrugged her shoulders. "Well, she has her reasons. Just like we all do." She gave him a good-bye kiss and he went out the door.

****

The two-hour drive over the dry, dusty road had made Hans's throat dry and hot. When he reached Beechwood, the first thing he did was to stop his horse in front of the tavern. It was before dinner so the tavern was not very full. He walked up to the bar and ordered himself a tall, cold glass of beer. The white foam tickled his nose as he gulped down the yellow brew.

"Fill it again, Bart." He pushed the glass toward the edge of the bar.

As he looked in the mirror, he saw his mustache was covered with foam. As he wiped it off, a small woman approached him.

"That looks a lot better, honey. My, aren't you the handsome one." She eyed him up and down.

"I never saw you before." Hans eyed her sexy body. His eyes

rested on her large breasts, which seemed to crowd out of the low-cut dress. The rest of her body features were small. She looked extremely top heavy. Hans liked the look.

"I just came in on the train today," she replied.

"Has the train left already?" Hans grabbed his refilled glass and took a drink out of it.

Shrugging her shoulders, she replied, "Ya, honey, I don't know." She looked about the room. "No, it couldn't have. The conductor is here yet." She motioned to a uniformed man sitting at a table drinking a glass of beer.

"How long have you been here?" Hans questioned.

"I just came downstairs, when I saw you, honey. You're a big man." She rubbed her hand on his shoulder. "I really would like to find out if it's true what they say about a man with big feet." She looked at Hans's feet then smiled up at him.

"How much do you earn in a week in a place like this?" Hans took another drink of his beer.

"I earn a lot more than I would if I worked in a factory, and I have a lot more fun." A big grin covered her face.

"So, no one in town has seen you yet?" Hans asked.

"No, honey, you'd be the first," she replied.

"I have a little proposition for you," Hans said.

"That sounds really good, honey." She put her arm around his waist.

"How would you like to earn fifteen dollars a week and hardly do anything to earn it?" Hans asked.

"It sounds good. But what do you mean, 'hardly do anything'?" She pulled him closer to her.

"I'll pay you fifteen dollars a week for staying out of sight until after you do something for me," Hans said.

She frowned her brow. "I don't quite understand."

"I want you to do something for me in about four weeks or so. Until I want you to do this thing for me, it's important that you stay out of sight and no one around here knows who you are."

"What do you want me to do for you?" she asked.

"There is no need for you to know now. I'll only take five minutes of your time but it's important that you stay out of sight until I need you. Very important! Are you interested?" Hans asked.

"Fifteen dollars a week just to stay out of sight." She raised her eyebrows. "That's a lot of money."

"Believe me, it'll be the easiest money you'll ever make." Hans took another drink of his beer.

"After I do this little thing for you, then what?" she asked.

"Then we go our separate ways," Hans stated.

"And just how am I going to stay out of sight until you need me? I don't think that I like the idea of staying in my room all the time, like a prisoner," she replied.

"You won't be staying here. If you agree to our deal, you'll be staying at an inn in Shady Lane," Hans explained.

"Shady Lane! Where on earth is Shady Lane?" she asked.

"It's about a two-hour drive from here. It's a small town--no tavern but nice scenery," Hans said.

"You part of the scenery?" She took a sip of his beer.

"Ya, but we've got to act as if we've never met. If someone asks why you're staying so long, just tell them you like the scenery in Shady Lane," Hans suggested.

"What if they ask what I do for a living?" she questioned.

Hans looked out the tavern's large window. Across the street was a baker shop. "Tell them you helped your dad in his baker shop. He closed the shop to go on a vacation. So you thought you'd take vacation also."

She put her hands on her hips. "That's all fine and dandy to say but what if they ask me something about baking?"

"Just tell them you're on vacation, and you don't want to talk about work," Hans replied.

"Ya, that's a good line." She took another sip of his beer.

"Well, are you going to go along with what I ask?" Hans asked.

She shrugged her shoulders. "Sure! Why not? Like you said, 'it'll be the easiest money I'll ever make.' "

"I'll give you seven dollars for every week you stay out of sight. The day that you do what I want, I'll give you the rest of your money, eight times the number of weeks you stayed out of sight in Beechwood." He grabbed into his pocket. "Take this and buy some different clothes, clothes a baker's daughter would wear."

She grabbed the money and stuck it down the front of her dress. "Thank you."

"You'll have to take the train to Shady Lane. So I suggest you get your ticket and find out when the train leaves," Hans said.

"I'm on my way." She went out the door and headed toward the train depot.

Hans finished his beer and then went out the door. He stood on the boarded sidewalk as he surveyed the town. He couldn't find the place he was looking for. Maybe Bart knew. He turned and went back into the tavern. Bart was busy washing the bar glasses.

"Where is Fremont's office?" Hans asked.

"Fremont? I heard the name before, but I can't place it right now," replied Bart.

"I saw his name on a 'for sale' sign just before I came into town today," stated Hans.

"Oh, ya, I know now. He's that new lawyer in town. Just keep walking down the street until you come to where the street starts to go off in an angle. His office is right on the corner. Upstairs." He motioned with his wet hand as the water slid down to his elbow and then onto the floor.

"Thanks, Bart," Hans replied.

Hans followed Bart's direction and headed down the street. As he turned the corner, he saw the stairs that led up to a porch. Hans climbed the stairs and knocked on the door marked with FREMONT.

"Come in," a voice called from behind the door.

As Hans opened the door, he was greeted by a sparsely-furnished room. The tidy room appeared empty until a head popped up from behind an immense dark desk.

"Hi," the smiling face behind the desk greeted him. The tall, slender figure of a man then extended his bony hand for a handshake. "My name is Samuel Fremont."

"I'm Hans Duren." He returned the man's gesture and shook his hand.

"Please sit down, Mr. Duren. What can I do for you today?"

"I have some deeds and abstracts to be transferred." Hans reached into his pocket and pulled out the pieces of paper, which he set on Mr. Fremont's desk.

Mr. Fremont reached for the papers and examined them. "This is deeded to Kate and Hans Duren--just recently." He looked up a bit puzzled.

"Ya, I know. My wife would like the whole deed in my name now. She wants to give it to me as a present," Hans replied.

"Why didn't your wife come with you?" asked Mr. Fremont.

"She's not feeling well today. The fact is, she doesn't have too long to live. That's why she wants my name only on the deed. I don't have to pay inheritance tax that way, she said," Hans replied.

"Well, she's right about that. Nevertheless, she'll have to come in and sign the legal papers at a later time in front of witnesses," explained Mr. Fremont.

"Ya, she knows. She'll come in," replied Hans.

Mr. Fremont examined the other papers. "This deed is Molly O'Leary's." He looked up.

"Ya, I'm buying that land from her. Here's a copy of my cashier's check and a binder she signed." Hans handed him the copy of the check and binder.

"This Molly O'Leary will also have to come in and sign some legal papers," Mr. Fremont informed Hans.

"Ya, she knows that too. They figured you could get everything set up and ready for them. Then when it's time for their signature, they figured they'd come in," Hans explained.

"Well, things usually aren't done that way, but I suppose it won't do any harm to do things that way. After all if they don't sign the legal papers, nothing is legally transferred and this deed and abstract are useless to you." He reached into his drawer and pulled out a fountain pen, which he dipped into the inkwell.

"Are the ladies also aware that since they are the grantors in this situation that they are required to pay for my services, registration fee, transfer fee, and for changing the abstract?" Mr. Fremont asked.

"Ya, they know that. However, I told them I'd take care of that for them. So just make all the expense out to me," Hans replied.

"Okay." Mr. Fremont scribbled something on a piece of paper and then looked up. "I'll send you a letter in the mail when everything is ready to be signed. You can notify the ladies, and we'll set up a date for signing the papers. What is your address?"

"Shady Lane," Hans answered.

"I'll have to know the purchase price for each piece of property," Mr. Fremont stated.

"This is for Molly O'Leary's property." Hans showed him the copy of the cashier's check again.

"Twenty-one thousand dollars," Mr. Fremont said as scribbled it down. "And your wife's deed is a gift. Right."

"Right," Hans replied as he put the copy into his pocket.

"Well, I guess that's all Mr. Duren. Everything should be ready in about six weeks. Maybe a little sooner, it's hard to say for sure. However, I'll try to get it ready by then for you and the ladies," Mr. Fremont informed Hans.

"I saw your name on the farm outside of town," Hans commented.

"Yes, my aunt just died and left the farm to me. I don't have any use for the farm so I'm selling it," Mr. Fremont answered.

"How big a farm is it?" Hans inquired.

"One hundred twenty acres," Mr. Fremont replied.

"How much you want an acre?" Hans asked.

"About one hundred ten dollars," replied Mr. Fremont.

Land is a good investment, Hans thought. He could always rent the land out. His money would make more for him on the farm than just setting in the bank. Besides he didn't trust those banks. If there was a fire or robbery, he'd lose that money.

"I'd like to buy the land," Hans stated.

"Okay. You give me a deposit, and I'll start on the legal part of the deed," Mr. Fremont replied.

Now Hans wasn't stupid. He knew it probably would be better to have a different lawyer handle this deal. A different lawyer would oversee the negotiations and execution of a sales contract to Hans's benefit. Another lawyer would also search the records in the county and examine them thoroughly to see if Mr. Fremont really had a right to sell that land. He knew Molly owned the land that he was buying from her. He also knew that she wouldn't cheat Kate. Molly was under the impression Kate was purchasing the land also.

"I think it would be best if I got a different lawyer to handle the transaction with you," Hans suggested.

"That's fine with me," Mr. Fremont replied.

"Okay, I'll find a different lawyer, and he can negotiate with you then." Hans rose from the chair.

"Fine." Mr. Fremont extended his hand to Hans, who shook it.

After leaving the office, Hans walked up and down the streets until he found a different lawyer's office. Beechwood was a large town, so there was more than one lawyer available.

Hans employed a lawyer, gave him a small money deposit, and soon the sales contract was signed. Hans was now committed to purchasing the land. He felt secure that his lawyer would investigate thoroughly if there were mortgages, liens, other people's rights to the property, and if Fremont indeed had a right to sell.

After settling the sales contract, Hans decided it was about time to deposit that other cashier's check in the Beechwood bank.

"Good morning, Mr. Duren," a bright smile from behind the teller's window greeted him as he approached.

"Good morning, Mrs. Benson, how are you today?" Hans asked.

"Fine, thank you." Her eyes had the sparkle of a young girl, but her crow's-feet gave her true age away.

"I'd like to make a deposit in my account." Hans pushed the cashier's check and his bankbook toward her.

When she finished making the proper notations in his book, she handed it back to him. She sighed and shook her head with a grin.

"What's the matter, Mrs. Benson?" He put the bankbook into his pocket.

"The single woman around here must be a little crazy," she said.

"Why?" Hans asked.

"Well, I tell you. If I wasn't married and I saw a handsome, eligible bachelor like you walking around, I surely wouldn't let you get away." She shook her head with disbelief.

"Ha." Hans laughed. "You think so."

"I know so, Mr. Duren," she replied with a definite conviction.

He chuckled. "Good day, Mrs. Benson."

"Good day to you too, Mr. Duren."

After concluding his business at the bank, he decided to visit Anna. As he walked into the hotel door, the train whistle blew. He paused in the doorway for a few seconds. Well, his lady was on her way to Shady Lane. Without her he couldn't pull this scheme of his off. If he wouldn't have needed her so desperately, he would have never offered her so much money. Ah, what he was paying her was nothing compared to what he was going to get with her help. A grin crossed his face. He was pleased with his cleverness.

The clever grin disappeared from his face as he stood outside Anna's hotel room door. Tenseness filled his body again. If only Kate doesn't find out about Anna, and Anna doesn't find out about Kate, for at least two months. After that, he didn't really care. No, he couldn't figure that way. It would be best if Anna never knew of Kate. He didn't want Lena to know that he was ever married to anyone else while he was married to her. He couldn't take the chance, regardless of how minute it would be, of Lena divorcing him. She could legally take a lot of what he had financially. He didn't have to worry about Kate. She didn't have any legal property rights. In fact, legally there wasn't even a Kate Duren. However, she could send him to jail for bigamy.

"Hi, Daddy." A voice came from behind. Hans swung around. It was Anna.

"Hi, Mr. Duren," Alex said with a big smile.

"Well, hi, you two. I was just about to knock," Hans responded.

"Alex found a job." Anna's face was aglow.

"A job! Where?" Hans asked.

"At the blacksmith shop," Alex replied as he opened the door and they all went inside.

"Well, that's good." Hans patted Alex on the back. "Is that what you did in Germany?"

"No, I was a farmer."

"We're going to buy a farm here. But until we do, we need money to live. So, Alex is going to work at the blacksmith shop for a while," Anna explained.

"That sounds like a good idea." Hans didn't mention the farm that he was about to buy. He didn't want anyone to know. If Lena did divorce him, it would be best if she didn't know or find out about the farm. If she didn't know about it, she wouldn't ask or expect half of the farm as a divorce settlement. Maybe he should do that with all his money--buy farms and keep his ownership of such things a secret. If no one knew he had it, no one could put a claim on it.

"Are you going to stay at the hotel until you buy a farm?" Hans inquired.

"Yes, we think so," Alex replied.

"That'll be quite expensive, won't it?" Hans asked.

"No, I got a job as a cleaning lady in the hotel. As long as I work here, we can have our rooms and meals free," Anna said.

"Well, that sounds like a good deal," Hans replied. Indeed it was, especially for Hans. With both of them busy working here in town, it was very unlikely that they'd come to Shady Lane. Nevertheless, he planned to keep himself informed as to what they were doing.

"I'll come to visit you whenever you don't have to work. When would that be?" Hans asked.

"Sunday is the only day we aren't expected to work. So, I suppose, Sunday will be the only day we'll be able to visit," Anna said.

"Well, that's too bad I can't visit you more, but it's better than not being able to see you at all," Hans replied.

"It sure is," Anna said.

"When do you start these new jobs?" Hans asked.

"Right away. I'm afraid you made your trip for nothing. We don't have time to visit," Anna said disappointingly.

"Ah, that's okay. I got to see you for a little while, so my trip wasn't all in vain." Hans gave Anna a kiss, said a good-bye to Alex, and left the room. He had all his business settled in town so there was no need for him to stay around. So he didn't. He mounted his horse and started toward home.

****

Pete, slowly and painfully, sat up in his bed. He glanced at the clock. It was twelve-thirty. That's the latest he had ever stayed in bed. He could barely move his body. Every muscle twinged. Every bone ached. Every nerve stung of pain. Finally, he stood up and reached for the top drawer of his dresser. He slowly pulled the drawer open and took out a clean pair of underwear, some socks, and a shirt.

An agonizing expression crossed his face as he put the clean shirt on his back. He looked in the mirror. His chest was marred with long scab-covered cuts. His body made an involuntary quiver as he thought of the whip stinging his body. That Mr. Cork was "nuts." Huh! He raping Betsy was funny. She had shown him a few things and so had

Mr. Cork. She wasn't even worth the beating he had gotten. He wondered who was better--Todd or him? Todd made her have sex. Huh! That was funny! No way, could a guy make a girl have sex, if she didn't want to. Did she think he was stupid? Well, no way! She wasn't going to get another chance with him and neither was her father. She wasn't the only girl in the world. They all deserved each other, the Bester's and Cork's. He could get sex anyplace. He didn't need that kind of hassle. What difference did it make who gave him his thrills, as long as he got them? It was a lot better that way. No commitments. No responsibilities. Just a good time! He leaned over and looked at himself in the mirror. I'm good-looking. I can get anyone, he thought to himself as he finished buttoning up his shirt.

As he reached for the drawer and started to pull a pair of work trousers out of the drawer, he heard a soft tapping at the door.

"Can I come in, Pete?"

"Just a minute, Kate, I'm getting dressed." He put on his trousers. It was hard. His sore back felt tight and hurt each time he moved.

"Okay, Kate." He sat at the edge of the bed.

Kate entered the room wearing a delightful smile. "I'm glad to see you're up. That means you must be feeling better. Right?"

"No, not really, Kate, I just don't like lying in bed in the middle of the day. It doesn't seem right." Pete slowly rose from the bed. "I better go and finish those new stalls in the barn."

"Don't you worry about them. Hans can take care of them when he gets back." Kate walked over to the window and pulled up the shade.

"Gets back? Where did he go?" Pete asked.

"He went to Beechwood." She walked over to the other window.

Pete remembered the woman. Was it Lena? It must be. Why else would he go back to Beechwood today? "Did Hans mention what he had to do in Beechwood today?"

"We're buying the woods across the track from Molly. So he went into town to see a lawyer." The shade slipped out of her hand as she pulled it. It made a snapping sound as it rolled all the way up tightly on the rod.

"Oh, that scared me!" Kate exclaimed.

Pete was suspicious of Hans. "Whose money are you going to use to purchase the woods?"

"Ours, of course," Kate replied.

Pete squinted his brow. "Ours? You and Hans have separate accounts. Don't you?"

"No, I put everything that I had in both our names several months ago, but I didn't tell Hans until yesterday. I thought that it'd make a nice anniversary present for Hans." She pulled the shade down a bit.

"I bet Hans really liked that present. Didn't he?" asked Pete.

"He was surprised, but it was a nice surprise." Kate smiled. She was so pleased with herself because she had made Hans happy.

"Why didn't you leave things the way they were?" Pete asked.

"Well, I thought about what Hans had said, and I decided that he was right," Kate replied.

"Right about what?" Pete questioned.

"Well, we are married so why have two separate accounts. What's mine is his, and what's his is mine," Kate said.

"So Hans put his money in both your names also?" asked Pete.

"Yes," replied Kate.

"Where? Here in town?" questioned Pete.

"No, in Beechwood," Kate replied.

"How do you know he did?"

"Because he told me that he did. Why all the questions?" She walked over to the bed.

Pete shrugged his shoulders. "Just curious." He had a feeling and not a very good one either. Did Hans really put his account in both their names? How could he find out? If he found out that Hans didn't do as he had told Kate, what could he do about it? Tell Kate?

"Should I make you something to eat?" Kate asked.

"Ya, please, I'm quite hungry." Pete got off the bed so she could make it for him.

"I'll make you some potato soup." She patted the pillow until it was loose and fluffy, then placed it on the made bed.

"That sounds good to me," Pete replied.

They headed out the door and down the stairs.

When they reached the bottom of the stairs, the door of the inn opened and in stepped the woman that Hans had met in Beechwood.

"Hi! I was told on the train that I could get a room here," the woman said.

"The train is here already?" Kate was surprised. "I didn't hear the whistle."

"The new engineer doesn't always blow the whistle," Pete said as he grabbed for the woman's suitcase. "Can I take that for you?"

"Why, yes. Thank you." She smiled graciously at Pete.

Pete smiled back. She was pretty and smelled so good, he thought.

"Pete, could you show her to a room, please," Kate said as she turned toward the woman and asked. "Would you like something to eat?"

"Yes, I would," the woman replied.

"I was just going to make some potato soup for Pete, would that be okay with you?" Kate asked.

"That would be just fine." She followed Pete up to a room while Kate went into the kitchen.

After the woman was settled in her room, she and Pete sat outside on the porch steps. They talked until Kate had their soup ready.

After they had eaten, the woman helped Kate do dishes. When the dishes were done, they sat at the kitchen table and talked over cups of steaming coffee. The woman questioned Kate about all kinds of things. The woman thought perhaps Kate would say something that would give her a clue as to what Hans wanted her to do for him.

Pete strolled out to the barn where he waited for Hans. While he waited, he took a fork and threw some of the bloodstained straw into the stall to be used as bedding for the horses.

While he waited, his mind flashed full of questions and suspicions. He wondered if it really paid to even ask Hans anything. He'd probably just lie to him if he didn't like the question or figured Pete wouldn't like the truthful answer to the questions. Sometimes Pete thought that maybe he should just leave and let things take their own course. Maybe he should take the job Mr. Ewerdt had offered him at his sawmill in Beechwood. There was nothing and no one holding him here. But what about Kate? He couldn't leave her here alone. Especially if Hans was going to hurt her. She'd need someone. Well, she did have Molly. Huh, Molly, she couldn't even handle her own "hang-ups." She merely runs away and hides instead of facing people. He wondered why she was that way. She would hardly be a "tower of strength" for Kate. Poor Kate! It would destroy her when she found out that her marriage to Hans would be regarded by the law as if the marriage had never taken place because Hans was already married. Their marriage was null.

The barn door swung open and in walked Hans leading his exhausted horse to the stall. "Waiting for me?" Hans tied the horse in the stall.

"Ya, who was the lady in Beechwood?" asked Pete.

Hans's face lit up. "My little Anna." Hans took the saddle off the horse and hung it over the stall.

"Anna! I thought Erickson said a woman was asking for you?" questioned Pete.

"Anna is the woman. She's eighteen already."

"You're kidding me now," Pete said.

"No, I'm not. Don't forget we've been here ten years. Anna was only eight when I left. Time went too quick." Hans shook his head.

"Did she come with Lena?" Pete asked.

"No. She came with her husband, Alex Leer. Lena's still in Germany." Hans gave the horse a forkful of hay.

"Is she coming also?" Pete asked.

"In time, I guess," replied Hans.

"What are you going to do about Kate?" Pete asked.

"That isn't really any of your concern. Is it?" Hans walked out of the barn and toward the inn.

Pete stood in the barn doorway and watched Hans. As Hans approached the kitchen door, it opened. Kate, with a gleaming smile, came out and gave him a warm hug and long kiss. They talked for a few minutes and then strolled hand in hand toward the path that led into the woods and down to the stream. Hans was a lucky man to have a good woman like Kate to love him so much, Pete thought, as he watched them disappear.

Chapter 5
****
Scheme and Betrayal

The harmonizing chiming of church bells spread across the countryside. It was a still, warm, hazy day of Indian summer, a beautiful day for a wedding. The church door opened and out stepped a bride in a white dress and a handsome groom in an elegant black suit.

The couple stood beside each other outside the church, shaking hands with each person that came through the church doorway and accepting everyone's wedding congratulations.

At the end of the line was Pastor Clark. He paused and talked to the bride and groom for quite awhile. "Do you think you'll still be around here at Christmas time?" he asked.

"No, we'll be leaving in a few weeks for Boston," replied the bride.

"Why so soon?" Pastor Clark inquired.

"Todd has to start his new job on January first. We'd like to get a place and get settled a little before he starts. After he's busy working, we won't have time to go house hunting," Betsy replied.

"Yes, that's understandable." The pastor eyed Betsy from head to toe. "You look so pretty in your mother's dress."

Betsy smiled. "Thank you. You're so kind."

"No, I just tell the truth." He held her hand softly. "May God bless you with a very happy marriage, my dear Betsy."

Betsy smiled at him.

"And Todd--I guess congratulations for you twice would be in order." The pastor extended his hand.

"Well, thank you, Pastor Clark." Todd shook the pastor's hand.

"I was really surprised when I heard you had accepted the offer at the Boston bank. I surely thought that you'd take over your dad's job at the bank," the pastor commented.

Todd chuckled. "My dad is not about to retire for a very long time. He likes his work too much. Besides, the Boston bank is bigger. There's more of a chance for advancement, and the pay is really good. I'll be earning twice as much as my dad. In addition, life is more elegant. I don't care for the crudeness of these small country towns. I've missed the Boston life. After five years out in this wilderness, Boston is a very welcome change."

"Life maybe is crude. However, I find it less complicated," the pastor replied.

"Well, this kind of life is not for me. I'd like a nice house in a Boston suburb. I'd like to live near Brookline. They've got a golf course there. I like playing golf. You ever play it?" Todd asked.

"No, and I don't think I'd find it exciting to chase around a ball, but to each his own. I wish you much happiness," replied the pastor.

"Oh, we'll be happy, right, Betsy." He put his arm around her waist and pulled her closer to him.

Betsy forced a brilliant smile as her eyes slowly roamed toward the inn. Her heart cried, but she couldn't let her eyes. It was her wedding day. It should be a happy day. Tonight would be her wedding night. Todd would expect his husbandly rights. Could she tolerate letting him touch her again? Sure, if she pretended he was Pete. In the dark and with her eyes closed, she wouldn't see his face. She could pretend the body holding her and wanting her was Pete's. But could she really pretend? Really fool herself? Maybe if she got drunk enough on her wedding, she could fool herself. But what about the next time? Maybe Pete would come, take her in his arms, and say he loved her as much as she loved him. Yes, he would. She was sure. Until then, she could pretend.

"You and Mrs. Clark are coming to the Cork's for the reception and dinner, aren't you?" asked Todd.

"Yes, we are. We'll be along shortly. Mrs. Clark has to frost the cake she made for the dinner," the pastor replied.

"Oh, she didn't have to do that. My mother has been busy baking and cooking all week. She's got enough food to feed all of Shady Lane for a week," Betsy commented.

"Well, I'm glad to hear that. I'm starved." Todd helped Betsy into the back of the surrey.

Seating in the front seat of the surrey was Todd's father. He drove them to the front of the Cork's house. A place was reserved for their surrey right in front of the picket fence gate. There were twelve other surreys and buckboards lined up and down the small street. Mrs. Cork's large, globe-shaped chrysanthemums of white and purple arrayed the newly painted white porch. The strong scent of the chrysanthemums perfumed the air around the house and the yard.

Just as they entered the house, a few more wedding guests arrived in their surreys and buckboards. The house was full of busy chitchat. It was crowded with some people sitting and others standing about.

"Excuse me, Todd. I'll be right back," Betsy said as she went up the stairs.

Once in her room, she looked out her bedroom window toward the inn. Oh, is he going to come? Her heart ached to see him. Her mother had said that she had invited them all personally. Oh, why doesn't the door open? If he's going to come for dinner, he has to come soon. She looked down into the yard. They were setting up the tables for the people to eat outside. As she looked back at the inn door, she saw it open. Oh, he's coming. No. It wasn't Pete. It was Hans and Kate. Oh, he isn't coming. She wouldn't get to see him. As she held her hand over her mouth, her eyes burst with tears. She turned away from the window. She mustn't cry. Her eyes would get red. A bride mustn't have red, swollen eyes. Pulling her tears back, she forced a smile.

"Betsy," her mother called from outside in the hall.

"I'm in here, Mama," Betsy answered her call.

Her mother came into the bedroom doorway. "Betsy, they've got a table set for you and Todd. Come on."

"Yes, Mama, I'm coming." She walked toward her mother.

Her mother touched her hand. "Oh, you look so beautiful. I could just cry. You'll be so happy. You'll see. Your dad and I are right."

"Yes, I'm sure you and Dad are right. Are all the guests here?" Betsy asked.

"Yes, except for Hans, Kate, and Pete," her mother replied.

"Hans and Kate are coming. I just saw them come out of the inn."

"Well, I didn't really expect Pete to come. He knows how your dad feels about him. Considering that, it's better this way."

Betsy smiled. "Ya, I guess you're right. I wouldn't come if I was Pete either."

They went downstairs and squeezed through the crowd until they were outside. Todd was waiting on the porch. He took Betsy's hand and led her over to the table.

The table was decked in a beautiful white crocheted cloth and crystal vases filled with a few of Mrs. Cork's smaller chrysanthemums. Sitting at the table, next to where Betsy was to sit, was her sister, Kathleen. She was Betsy's bridesmaid. Beside Kathleen sat Mr. and Mrs. Cork. Todd pulled out the chair and Betsy sat on it. Todd sat next to her. Sitting beside Todd was the best man at the wedding, Todd's friend. Todd was the only child in his family. Next to Todd's best man sat Mr. Bester and Pastor Clark. Todd's mother was dead.

After Pastor Clark finished grace, everyone sat down to eat. As Mrs. Clark and a few neighbor ladies served the food, Todd's best man stood up and made a toast to them. A few minutes later a loud, sharp ringing sound could be heard. The wedding guests were tapping their spoons against the side of their coffee cups.

"Well, you know what that means," Todd whispered to Betsy. His face was covered with a radiant smile.

"I'm not doing that in public," Betsy whispered back and drank some of her wine. She felt her body become warm and her face flush.

"They expect us to. It's done at every wedding. They'll keep making the noise until we do."

Kathleen gently pushed her elbow into Betsy's arm. "Come on. Everyone will think it's strange if you don't."

Betsy and Todd stood up. As they kissed the clanging noise stopped and everyone laughed and shouted, "Come on, let's see more!"

Ugh, he's a sloppy kisser, Betsy thought disgustingly.

"That's the way, Todd!"

"Hey, do it again!"

Just as they sat down, Kate and Hans approached the table with a big box.

"Congratulations, Betsy." Kate smiled at Betsy while she shook her hand. Turning to Todd, she said coldly, "Congratulations, Todd."

As Todd stood up and extended his hand toward Kate, Hans shook it. Hans knew Kate wouldn't shake it. She would have preferred it to be Pete who was sitting beside Betsy. Kate couldn't tolerate Todd even looking at her much less shaking her hand--heaven forbid!

Kate and Hans took the gift inside the house, came out, and sat at the table with the other guests.

After the meal, the men drank, socialized, and played cards while the woman cleaned up the meal's mess.

While some of the other women washed and dried the dishes, Kate carried the leftover food out of the warm sun into the root cellar, where it would keep from spoiling until it was needed for another meal.

Each time she went down into the dark, cool cellar, she'd leave the door open so she could see her way. Suddenly, darkness burst into the cellar. The door had closed on her.

"Oh, how did that close?" Kate mumbled as she stumbled blindly toward where she thought the stairs where.

From out of nowhere, a hand grabbed about her waist and started feeling up her body to her breasts.

She threw the hand off her body and turned around. She was furious. "For heaven sakes! Who are you?"

"Oh, Kate, don't be that way." A hand rubbed between her legs and started stroking her. "You'll like it. I know you want it. It'll feel good."

She grabbed his hand away. "Keep your filthy hands off me!"

As she felt his body push against hers, she felt the bulge in his trousers as he rubbed back and forth over her groin. She backed away until she could back no more. She was up against the wall. She could feel him breathing on her. Now he had his hands on each side of her shoulders. He had her pinned against the stone wall. She could feel his moist kiss on her forehead, her face, and her lips. Then she could feel him lean over her and kiss her neck and then her tailored blouse where her breasts were. Oh! The filthy pig was slobbering all over her. This had gone far enough! The smutty pig wasn't going to touch her. She remembered what her father had told her to do in a situation like this. She raised her knee and struck a mighty blow between his legs. She heard a yell and then felt his hands leave her shoulders. She had to get out of there quick. He was mad! Who knows what he'd do now! With her trembling hands, she frantically explored the side of the wall until she felt the stairs. She groped up them and opened the door into the welcomed sunlight. She gave a sigh of relief and then closed the door.

"Is something the matter, Kate?" asked Hans who had been looking for her.

"No, let's go home." She forced a convincing smile and grabbed his hand.

As they went around the corner of the house, Kate turned and looked toward the root cellar door. It slowly opened and Todd came out. Kate had figured that it was him. She'd recognize that foul mouth anywhere. Poor Betsy! Mr. Cork should have left things alone. He'll live to regret the day that he first seen Todd Bester. Betsy Bester didn't even sound right. Betsy Hof--now that would have sounded a lot better. She couldn't understand why he even married Betsy. He couldn't love her. A man doesn't try to do what he just tried on his wedding day, not if he loves the girl he married. He couldn't have married her just for sex. The way he operates, he could get that from anyone. Betsy was attractive. Was that why he married her? That must be it. There was nothing else. The Cork's weren't on the "social ladder" like the Bester's, so it wasn't for money.

Betsy was refilling her wine glass again as Hans and Kate passed her. That's not going to help you, my dear Betsy, Kate thought, as she and Hans walked arm in arm past the other guests, through the gate, and toward the inn.

Sitting on the porch steps waiting for them were Pete and Eva. Pete handed Hans the envelope that he had in his hand. "I picked this up at the post office today."

Hans examined it and then stuck it inside his suit jacket.

"Something important, Hans?" asked Kate.

"No."

"How was the big wedding?" asked Pete.

Hans shrugged his shoulders. "A wedding's--a wedding."

"You should have never let her go, Pete." Kate looked down at the Cork's house. "Todd Bester isn't right for her."

"They're perfect for each other, believe me!" replied Pete.

"Well, it's none of my business, is it?" Kate put her arm around Hans's waist. "Let's go for a walk."

"Sure, why not," replied Hans.

"Let's walk up the railroad track for a change. We've never done that," Kate suggested.

"Oh, Kate, only kids do that," replied Hans.

"Well, I'm a kid, and I want to do it." Kate chuckled and pulled him toward the track.

"How long have they been married?" Eva asked when they were out of hearing distance.

"Two years last month," replied Pete.

"Hans is quite a bit older than Kate, isn't he?" asked Eva.

"Ya, I guess so. Kate is thirty-one and Hans is forty-five, I guess. I really don't keep track of their ages. I got more important things on my mind than age."

"You mean, like the girl that just got married today?"

"No, not her either." Pete got up, put his hands into his pocket, and walked toward the barn.

Eva followed him with her hands behind her back.

"Are you mad at me?" she asked.

"No, I just don't like all your questions. Ever since you came here, all you've been doing is asking about Hans and Kate. After listening to that for a month a person just gets sick of it."

"I'm sorry. I won't ask any more questions, except for one."

Pete sighed and gave her an annoying look. "What's that?"

"Do you think I'm pretty?"

"Ya, you're okay."

"Just okay, huh!"

"Ya."

As Pete opened the barn door, Eva turned and looked toward the inn.

"There she goes again."

"Who?"

"The woman you call the cook. She was spying on us again. Why does she dress and act so odd?"

Pete shrugged his shoulders. "Ya, I don't know."

"You mean, as long as you've lived here you never wanted to find out what's under the scarf that hides everything except her eyes?" Eva followed him into the barn.

"Ya, at first I did. But after a while, I figured, it's her business. I don't like people prying into my business either. You and Hans are a perfect pair."

"Why do you say that?"

"Because he's always wondering about her also." Pete put the bridle and saddle on his horse.

"Well, why doesn't he find out?"

"He never had the opportunity before, and now he won't do anything that might ruin his chances of buying her land." Pete tightened the two girths that fastened the saddle on the horse. "Should I saddle a horse for you?"

"No, I don't feel like riding today." She looked out the open barn door toward the window that the cook had peered out. "I think I'll rest for a while."

Pete led the horse outside, mounted it, and rode down the path toward the stream. He enjoyed riding his horse as it traveled in an ambling gait. He felt free as if he had left the world and all its problems behind him. As he looked through the bare branches of the maple and oak, he could see part of the blue sky through the thin patches of the white, semi-transparent clouds.

He stopped his horse in the clearing near the stream. The once enormous stream had shrunk to a mere trickle and was now surrounded by a bed of dry parched mud. It was ugly! Why did things have to change? Couldn't things that were beautiful stay beautiful? No, nothing ever stayed the same, he thought.

Pete dismounted and sat on the stream's bank amidst the tall, dry, brown grass. The breeze seemed to pick up now and by the time darkness came it would probably whistle around the inn again. But now it was soft and felt refreshing on his face. It stroked his hair so gently. Occasionally, he'd pick up a dry fallen leaf and toss it carefully into the trickle of water. It'd bounce and whirl on the small current and then float out of sight. He thought how people in his life were like the leaf. They'd start out so beautiful and green. Even when they were yellow and red they were beautiful, but then they'd fall and become an ugly dead brown. They didn't stay beautiful. He thought of his mother. Life was beautiful when she was alive, but then she died and left him in an ugly world. He thought of Hans. He was a beautiful person, so kind, so good, but had changed into someone ugly who didn't care about anyone. Then there was Betsy who he had thought was so beautiful and innocent but had turned out to be a cheap, ugly whore. Every time he had someone beautiful, they turned out ugly. He hated that! The uncertainty that life always seemed to hold.

The harmonious musical tones of an accordion penetrated his ears. Betsy's wedding dance must have begun. He looked up at the sky. The stars were slowly appearing in the now cloudless sky. He was upset with himself. He hardly got to ride at all. He had wasted his time throwing leaves into the trickle of a stream and thinking, or rather feeling sorry for himself. As he rose to his feet, he felt a hand on his shoulder. He turned around. It was Betsy. His eyes examined her. Was she crazy coming out here with that white dress on? She should be at her wedding with Todd, not here with him. He was annoyed. "What the heck are you doing here?" He saw that her eyes were glassy. "Are you drunk?"

"No, my dear Pete, you know I don't drink." Her speech was slurred. She clumsily embraced him. "Hold me, Pete. Please, say you love me."

Her breath emitted a strong, unpleasant smell--alcohol.

Pete took her arms from around his body and threw then free from his hands. "Get out of here! I don't want anything to do with you!"

He mounted the horse and grabbed the reins.

She grabbed his leg. "Oh, Pete, please don't leave me! I love you!" Copious tears ran down her cheeks.

Pete squeezed the horse with his legs, shifted his weight forward, loosened the reins, and rode off toward the inn.

"Pete--Pete--please, don't leave!" Betsy shouted as she tried tipsily to follow him up the path. It was useless. The horse and Pete soon disappeared. She stopped. He didn't want her anymore than she wanted Todd. She had made a complete fool of herself. Well, at least she had seen him--touched him. Soon she wouldn't be able to see him or touch him. That thought pained her! It was as if he was dead and she could never be near him again. He was so far out of reach and sight. She felt so hopeless, so empty, and so all alone. He was lost to her forever! Forever! There was no way she could ever have him now. He hated her! Oh, that thought wrung her heart with pain and filled her eyes with endless tears. She felt her lower abdomen. In a few days she would know. Maybe all she could have of Pete was his baby. She was late, but that was nothing unusual for her. She was always so irregular. Her period hardly ever came on time. Sometimes she'd even miss a whole month. Oh, if only she was pregnant with Pete's baby. She'd adorn that child with all the love she had for Pete. If she couldn't have him, his baby was just as good. The child would have a life just like Pete would want for his child, a life of never wanting or going without. If she was pregnant, should she tell Pete? No. He probably wouldn't believe her just like he didn't believe her about Todd. She couldn't stand to be rejected again. Besides, he didn't love her. He despised her. Living like that would be worse than living with Todd. At least Todd wanted her, even if it was probably only for one thing--sex. It was better than not being wanted at all. She heard the music and knew that she had to hold back her tears. She had to put on her gracious smile again. Her cheeks hurt from wearing that pretentious smile all day. Well, in a few days they'd be gone from here, and she would not have to pretend anymore. She could be herself. With her body shrouded in a false fulgent manner, she went back to her wedding dance and "her husband."

****

Slowly and cautiously, a pair of feet crept up the wooden stairs lit by beams of moonlight. They went down the hallway and suddenly stopped at a door.

KNOCK! KNOCK!

"Eva, it's me. Open up."

A light shined from under the dark door and then it opened.

As Eva stood in the doorway in her shining satin lingerie, a complacent smile crossed her face. "Well, well, I see you finally gave into temptation."

"Be quiet," he said as he surveyed the hallway and went into her room.

"Not so loud," he whispered as she slammed the door shut.

"My, my, are you afraid the wife might wake up." She began to roll her hands on his shoulders.

He threw her hands off his shoulders. "I came because of our business arrangement, nothing else."

"Oh, Hans, don't be so prudish. There's no harm mixing a little pleasure with business. In my job, I do it all the time." She put her hands around the back of his neck so he couldn't miss her large breasts as they pressed against his nude chest.

He untangled her hands from behind his neck and reached into the front pocket of his trousers. "First business and then fun. After we've got our business arrangement completed, then maybe we'll engage in a little fun and games." He pulled out a piece of folded paper and handed it to her.

"I want you to practice what's written on that paper tonight. Tomorrow morning you're going to ask me to take you into Beechwood. Take everything along you want because you won't be coming back here. Our business deal ends tomorrow."

"So soon! I was just starting to like it here. I thought maybe I could work something up with Pete before I left."

"You stay away from Pete," Hans snapped. He was mad. If she'd mention anything to Pete, he'd ruin everything. There was no doubt about that.

"Well, you don't have to worry about Pete. He's as prudish as you. Maybe it's a good thing I'm getting out of here. Guys like you and Pete are enough to dampen a girl's ego. You make me think I'm out of practice."

Hans's eyes rolled over her sexually arousing body. If he could have, he would have jumped into bed with her right then and there. But he had to be sensible, now was not a good time.

"You're not out of practice, Eva. Believe me, just bad timing. That's all." He headed for the door and then turned as he touched the doorknob. "You make sure you practice that tonight."

"You don't give a girl very much time."

Hans smiled. He had planned it that way. She couldn't tell anyone tonight. The longer she'd have known, the more of a possibility of her accidentally mentioning it to someone. The possibility of her mentioning it now was quite slim. It was Hans' opinion that the least other people know of a scheme, the more likely it was to succeed.

He gave a breath of relief as he stood outside her door. She was a very desirable woman. Pete must have been crazy to turn down something like that.

He heard a key turn in a door. His head automatically turned in the direction of the sound, Molly's door. Well, it wouldn't be long now and he'd find out exactly what she was all about--one way or another. That he promised himself. He'd been waiting long enough. He would wait no longer. Her day had just about come.

Hans tiptoed back downstairs and into the bedroom. Quietly, he slithered back into bed next to Kate who was sleeping soundly. Thank goodness she didn't wake up and find him in Eva's room. It would have been hard to explain. Good thing Pete hadn't seen him. That would really have been the end. The end of everything! He was so close. Oh, so close to having everything! He was afraid to even breathe for fear everything might explode in his face, and he'd end up with nothing. He couldn't wait until tomorrow was over.

He couldn't sleep. He rolled his plan for tomorrow over and over in his mind. He planned every step, over and over and over. His body was tense with anxiety. Soon the beams of the early morning sunlight slid into the room across his face. The day that he had waited for was now starting. Would he feel excitement or remorse after today's deed was done? He could still back out. Ah, why should he? Everyone is used by someone. If he didn't use other people, they'd use him. It's "either use or be used." He had things exactly where he wanted them now. If he didn't move now, the chance might never come again. If people were that gullible, it was better that he'd be the one to reap the rewards than someone else.

As the alarm went off, Kate's arm reached out of bed to shut it off. She rolled over on her back and looked at Hans who was lying on his side with his back facing her.

"Time to get up, Hans." She yawned as she shook his body.

To make it appear as if he had been sleeping, he stretched and yawned as he turned over on his back.

"Oh--good morning, Kate."

"Good morning. Today's Monday, washday again."

They dressed and then went into the dining area where Molly had the table set for breakfast. Pete was standing in front of the window and staring out it when they entered.

"Good morning, Pete," Kate greeted him with a warm smile.

"Good morning, Kate, it's another beautiful day." Pete turned from the window and sat at the table.

"Well, I'm glad to hear that. I've got a lot of wash today." She glanced out the window and then went into the kitchen. The aroma of fried bacon escaped into the dining area, and the cracking sound of eggs frying could be heard through the open door. A few minutes later Kate came out with a plate of toast and bacon strips. After setting them on the table, she went back into the kitchen and returned with two plates filled with crisp hash brown potatoes and fried eggs. She set one plate in front of Hans and the other in front of Pete.

"Pete, would you please knock on Eva's door and tell her breakfast is served." Kate went back into the kitchen.

Just as Pete rose from the chair, Eva came down the stairs with her suitcase. Soon the room was filled with the scent of her lavender perfume. She set the suitcase down and approached the table. "Hans, could you please take me into Beechwood today?"

"Sure." Hans rose from his chair, then pulled out a chair for Eva to sit on.

"Why didn't you take the train last night when it stopped here?" asked Pete.

Eva shrugged her shoulders. "I didn't feel like leaving then."

"Good morning, Eva, you look pretty today," Kate said as she entered the room and placed a full plate of food in front of Eva and another plate in front of herself as she sat down at the table.

"Why, thank you, Kate, I'm going to miss your charming compliments."

"Oh, you aren't leaving us already, are you?" Kate was disappointed. She enjoyed Eva's company.

"Yes, it's about time to go back to work. I'm going to miss the wide-open space when I get back to the city."

Kate reached over and touched Eva's hand. "I hope that you'll come back and visit us again."

"Oh, I will." She looked over at Hans as she put a forkful of food into her mouth.

Hans continued to eat. He pretended that he didn't hear what they were talking about, but he heard and thought to himself, you aren't ever coming back here after today. In fact, you're going to disappear completely after today.

After he had finished breakfast, Hans went into the bedroom. He looked toward the door. No one was coming. He went over to his chair valet where he had hung his suit when they came back from church yesterday morning. He reached into the inside pocket of his jacket and pulled out the letter Pete had given him on Saturday. He folded it and stuck it into the back pocket of his trousers. It would be best if he disposed of that letter as soon as possible.

When he entered the dining room area, the room was empty except for Eva, who was dipping a donut into her cup of coffee.

"Where is everyone?" Hans asked.

"Kate's outside washing clothes and I guess Pete went to hitch the horses and wagon up for us." She dipped the rest of her donut.

Hans pulled the sheer curtain on the window aside. He could see Kate scrubbing clothes on the washboard. Kate wouldn't come in, so he only had to worry about Pete. He eyed the door and then walked over to the potbellied stove. He opened the front door of the stove, pulled the letter from his pocket, stuck it inside the stove, and lit the letter with a match. When he was satisfied it was completely burnt, he shut the door.

"What are you doing? It's beautiful outside. You don't need the stove burning today."

Hans turned around. "Don't worry about the stove. Did you practice writing what I told you to?"

"Yes, I did but I don't understand why I had to practice that." Eva finished drinking her coffee.

"The only thing you have to understand is that I'm paying you a lot of money to do something for me. If you don't do it, you're not getting the rest of the money. In addition, you're paying me back what I've already paid you."

"What if I've already spent it?"

"Well, then I feel sorry for you."

"Why? What are you going to do if I did?"

"You don't really want to know, believe me."

"Oh, Hans, come on now. You don't seem like the kind of man who beats women. I know you a little better than that."

"You don't know me at all, Eva. Nobody really knows anyone, not really. So don't press your luck. I can be a bully bastard when someone rubs me the wrong way. I usually don't get angry but when I do. I really let go."

"Well, don't you worry. I want the money. I'll do what you want." She walked toward him and wrapped her hands around the back of his neck. "Maybe we could even celebrate the end of our business arrangement with a little party, just me and you."

He pulled away. "We'll, see, Eva. We'll see how things go."

"Things will go just fine, just really fine."

"I hope so." He picked up her suitcase and opened the door.

"I'll bring the wagon up here. When you see me in front of the inn, come out, okay."

She nodded her head. "Okay. Why don't you go out the kitchen? It's closer."

"Molly's in there working. The door is locked." He went out the door.

Eva went up to the kitchen door. She heard the clatter of dishes. She turned the doorknob. It was locked.

Eva went up to her room, looked in her dresser mirror, and examined her face closely. She looked drab without her tavern make-up. Grabbing the small sailor hat setting on the dresser, she fixed it on her head. She fussed with her bustle, straightened her skirt-waist, put on her gloves, and grabbed her drawstring purse. She watched out the window for Hans. Soon she saw the horses come around the corner of the inn. As she went to the door, she turned around. Her eyes surveyed the room. She had everything. She went out of the room, shut the door, went down the stairs, and out the front door of the inn. Hans helped her onto the wagon and down through town toward Beechwood they went.

After they had been traveling for about a half-hour, Eva broke the silence. "Well, when are you going to tell me why we're going to Beechwood and what I have to do?"

We are going to Beechwood to sign some papers."

"Well, I kinda figured that after you made me practice writing all night. You know, I even dreamed about that writing when I slept."

"It's very important that you sign the name you practiced instead of your own. It has to appear as if you've been writing that name a long time. It has to be natural."

"Oh, I'll be natural all right. I've got a callus on my finger from all that writing. I don't even know how to write my own name anymore. Why did I have to write her name? Are you pulling a 'fast one' on her?"

"You had to practice her name because for fifteen minutes today you will be her. You will have to sign her name on some papers. That's what you're getting paid for, and that's all you have to know."

"So that's why it was important for no one in Beechwood to know who I was. I couldn't imposture someone else if people knew who I really was."

"Ya, it was really lucky for me that I came into Bart's when I did and that you came into town when you did. That was the only snag in my plan. I needed an impostor to be her. You were a 'god sent.'"

"Well, that's the first time I ever was called that. I have been called a lot of things, but never that." She chuckled.

"I suppose not."

"Just what are these papers I'm supposed to sign?"

"The lawyer will tell you. You just don't say any more than you have to. I told him you were sick awhile back and that you don't have long to live. If he mentions something to that effect, you go along with that."

"Anything you say. You're the boss. A lawyer, it must be something legal, huh! I don't particularly care to get mixed up with lawyers, legally that is. Otherwise, they're really good customers."

"Well, it's part of the business arrangement. Just think of all the money you'll get for just fifteen minutes of your time."

"Ya, I'm thinking and the more I think, the more I like it. But what if she finds out? Could I get in trouble?"

"If she does find out, so what? No one really knows who you are. Who would they look for?"

"Ya, you're right." She paused. "Bart knows me."

"He's probably forgotten you already."

"Oh, I don't know. He's quite smart."

"Oh, you don't have to worry about Bart. Well, there it is, Beechwood."

"It's a welcome sight after all the 'excitement' I had in Shady Lane. A place like that is bad for a working girl like me."

Hans chuckled.

"Well, it is! I'm used to having guys flock around me and pay a lot of attention to me. To all of a sudden have that all taken away and go to a place where no one looks at me is very depressing."

Beechwood was crowded. Today was Monday, the day when the train shipped animals to the stockyards. The streets were cluttered with farmers' herding prime steers, fat hogs, old cows, unproductive dairy cows, and breeding stock with tough hides. Farmers' empty wagons stood in front of every building. Hans couldn't find a place for his wagon anywhere close to Fremont's office. He continued to travel down the street. Finally, he found a place. They'd have to walk quite far. He tied the horses to the hitching post, and then he helped Eva off the wagon. He grabbed her suitcase, and they started down the street to Fremont's office.

Abruptly, Eva stopped and quickly pulled Hans into a narrow dark alley.

"What's the matter with you?" Hans snapped at her.

"Quiet! There's a person coming down the boarded walk who knows me." She pushed Hans back against the side of the building and held him there with her hand. She stood beside him very still, scarcely breathing.

"I thought you said no one in town knew you," Hans angrily whispered. He was so close to having what he wanted and now, all of a sudden, everything could be ruined. He was furious!

"The person is not from here. He's from Shady Lane, and he knows you too."

Hans's anger toward her diminished. If the person knew him also, it wasn't her fault. He never thought that he'd see a person from Shady Lane here, not today. The odds of seeing someone a person knew in this big town were a million in one. How could he get so lucky? Was fate turning on him? Was that a sign that he should give up the scheme before it went any further? His body grew tense. He began to sweat. He could feel the beads of sweat on his forehead. His underarms were wet. What if the person saw him like this with Eva, hiding in the alley? Who was the person? Was it someone who would tell Kate what they had seen?

The footsteps on the wooden boards became louder--closer. Then they stopped. The person was on the edge of the walk. Soon the person would step down onto the ground and walk over to the other boarded walk. The person stepped down. Hans saw him. He didn't know him. Eva was wrong. He pulled away from the side of the building and started to walk out into the street again.

She pulled him back. "What are you doing? He didn't come yet!" she whispered.

Oh, no! Could he get back against the building in time? He must be coming soon. The footsteps on the boarded walk stopped. The person stepped onto the ground in full view of the alley. Hans knew him, and he knew Hans. The man stopped and reached into his jacket. He pulled out a watch and examined it. Would the man look into the alley and see them? The man put the watch back inside his jacket. Hans held his breath. His heart seemed to pound frantically--louder and louder! It felt as if it would pop out any minute. Could the man hear it? It was so loud. He waited and waited. It seemed like it was forever. What would the man do? Finally, the man walked over to the other boarded walk and stepped onto it. Hans felt a heavy weight leave his body as the man's footsteps faded into the rest of the noise of the street.

Hans rubbed his hand up over his forehead. Boy! That was a close call. Hans was surprised the man knew Eva. "How does he know you? I never saw you with him. You never mentioned you knew him?"

"Oh, come on, Hans. You didn't really think I'd spend all my time looking at those four walls in my room, did you? I'm used to some action. When I didn't get any from you and Pete, I looked somewhere else for it. I've got to keep in practice." She chuckled. "That's my living."

"Well, I never had the faintest idea."

"Well, we couldn't exactly advertise it. I mean the guy was engaged and about to be married in a few weeks. We had to be discreet." Eva sighed. "I felt sorry for the guy. His girl wouldn't give him anything before they were married." Eva laughed. "He said that she would not even kiss him. Can you imagine that?" She shrugged her shoulders. "Well, he doesn't really care. He just married her for the money."

"What on earth are you talking about? Betsy's dad doesn't have any money. At least not compared to what Todd and his dad have."

"Betsy's dad doesn't have to have money. Her uncle has enough."

"Her uncle?"

"Ya, according to Todd, she has a rich uncle who is the president of a bank in East Boston. He is a bachelor who doesn't have any relatives except Betsy's dad. He never got along with Betsy's dad so in his will he leaves everything to Betsy and her two sisters."

"Well, how does Todd know all this?"

"Todd's dad is a very close friend of Betsy's uncle. He witnessed the will. Betsy's uncle is the one who helped Todd get the job in Boston."

"Why would Todd tell you that?"

"He probably doesn't even remember that he told me. His tongue really gets loose when he has a couple drinks under the belt." She shrugged her shoulders. "Besides, he probably figured I could care less."

Slowly, they peeked around the corner of the alley. Todd was gone.

They walked a little farther and then went up the stairs to Fremont's office. Hans laid her suitcase against the side of the building. It'd be safe there until they were finished in Fremont's office.

KNOCK! KNOCK!

"Ya, ya, come in!" a voice yelled from inside the door.

As they entered, Fremont was hunched over his desk busily writing. He never looked up, just motioned with his one hand. "Sit down."

After a few seconds he looked up, put the pen down, took off his wire rim glasses, and rubbed his tired eyes.

"Ah, Mr. Duren." Fremont extended his hand. "Good to see ya, really good. I see you got my letter telling you everything was ready for the signatures."

"Ya, I got it Saturday," replied Hans.

"And who is the lovely little lady?" Mr. Fremont smiled at Eva.

"This is Mrs. Duren. Kate, this is Mr. Fremont."

Mr. Fremont rose out of his chair and extended his hand. "Glad to meet you, I'm sure." He smiled again and sat back in his chair. "Where is the other lady--ah--Molly?" He couldn't remember her name and began to search his desk. "Molly--Molly--ah, here we have it." He pulled out a piece of paper. "Molly O'Leary."

"She couldn't come today. She can't make it until quite late tomorrow night. It may be dark when we come," explained Hans.

"Well, that's all right with me. It's just a lot of driving back and forth for you." He looked at Eva. "We don't need your signature on the other papers. That's just between Molly and your husband. So if you don't want to, you don't have to come along."

He put on his glasses, pulled open the top drawer on his desk, and rustled through some papers. Sorting out a few papers, he examined them. "Ya, this is the warranty deed and here's the transfer return." Putting the papers down at the edge of the desk near Hans and Eva, he rose from his chair. "We'll need another witness." He opened the door that was located behind his desk. "Maggie, will you come here, please."

"Okay," a soft voice replied. A few minutes later a woman came through the doorway drying her hands on her apron. Her dress hung loosely over her tall, thin body. If it wouldn't have been for her long hair and beautiful feminine face, she could have been mistaken for a man. She did not have a noticeable waist and her undersized breasts were barely visible. When she saw Hans and Eva, she smiled.

"We need another witness for these papers. Would you mind?" Fremont asked kindly.

"Of course not," she replied with a sweet smile.

"Okay." He examined the papers. "Since you are the grantor, Kate, you must sign here on this warranty deed." He dipped his pen into the inkwell and handed it to Eva.

Eva signed Kate Duren where Fremont pointed.

"Okay, my dear." He took the pen from Eva and handed it to Maggie. "You are a witness so you must sign here."

Maggie signed on one of the lines reserved for witness and Fremont signed on the other line. Fremont stamped the paper with his notary seal, then signed it again, and put it into a folder on his desk.

"Well, that's it for you, Kate. Your arm can rest now." Fremont smiled up at her and then turned to his wife. "Your job is done also. Thank you, dear."

Maggie smiled and then left the room.

"You have to sign the transfer return right here, Hans." He handed Hans the pen, and he signed the papers.

Fremont took them and examined them. "I'll take care of the recording and the federal revenue stamps. I'm to bill you for everything, Hans?"

"Ya."

"Well, I'll see you and Molly tomorrow night then?" Fremont inquired.

"Ya," Hans responded.

Hans and Eva rose from the chairs and departed from the office.

The hardest part, which was getting Kate's signature on the deed for the inn and the woods, was over. It was his now. He could breathe easier. The tense tightness left his body, and he could feel every muscle become loose.

"Well, where's my money?" asked Eva when they reached the bottom of the stairs.

"Don't worry about it. You'll get it."

They proceeded down the street.

"I don't know exactly what I signed. However, I do know that what I did is against the law. I signed someone else's name to a legal piece of paper. That's forgery!"

"Don't worry about it. No one will ever know you did it." Hans stopped. "You wait here." He went into the bank and a few minutes later came out. "Here, you better count it." He handed her the money.

"Don't worry I intend to." She counted the money once and then again. "Ya, it's all here." She folded it and stuck it into her purse. "Nice doing business with you. Feel like celebrating?"

"Why not!" He grabbed her hand as they started to walk across the street to the hotel. In the middle of the street, he turned around and started walking back toward the bank.

"What's the matter? You forget something?" Eva asked.

"No." He couldn't go into the hotel. Anna worked there. She might

Scheme and Betrayal

see him. Besides, there were too many farmers in town. What if some of them were from around Shady Lane and they saw him come out of a room with Eva? He still had to be careful. He didn't have Molly's land yet.

"Where are we going?"

"I think it would be best if you got out of town as soon as possible." He hurried down the street, with her hand in his, toward the train depot.

As he neared the depot, the crowd became more populated, and he had to slow his pace. When he heard the whistle, he knew the train had enough steam to travel. He didn't have much time. Oh, why didn't the people move. If they had their business finished, why did they have to stand around and talk? They were getting in his way and slowing him down. Would he make it in time? If he didn't, Eva couldn't leave town until Wednesday. Leaving her roam the streets for a whole day was dangerous! What if Fremont saw her and found out who she really was? He couldn't stay in town with her to see that she stayed in her room all the time. He wouldn't really mind that but how could he explain that to Kate or to Anna if she found out. Besides, he had to take Molly to the lawyer tomorrow night. Not being able to monitor her, made him feel uneasy. His body felt tightly stretched--taut. As he raced through the tight crowd, he could taste the salty beads of moisture as they ran down from his forehead onto his lips. Ah, there was the depot. People were still lined up waiting to board. Could he get a ticket yet? So many people! Maybe there weren't any more tickets available. Oh, now he had to worry about that. His worries were short. Soon he was at the ticket window.

Hans gave the ticket clerk behind the window a taut smile. "Can I purchase a ticket for Sacramento?"

"Sacramento! I'm not going to Sacramento." Eva pulled her hand out of his.

"Well, can I?" Hans snapped at the clerk.

"Yes."

"Give me one for the lady!" Hans took his wallet from his pocket.

Hans saw the people boarding the train. The line was getting short. The platform was getting empty. "Well, can't you hurry up!" Hans reached into his wallet, pulled out some money, and pushed the appropriate amount toward the clerk as he handed Hans the ticket.

Hans grabbed Eva's arm. She pulled away violently.

"I'm not going to Sacramento."

"Listen!" he whispered. "It's for your own good as well as mine. No one can ever get you for forgery there."

"I'll have to use almost all the money you gave me for travel expenses. I won't have anything left when I get there."

"You'll have enough left."

"Not as much as if I didn't have to travel so far. I'm not going unless--"

"Unless what?" Hans was angry. He grabbed her arm, squeezed it tightly, and gave her a piercing long look.

"You're hurting me. I'll scream if you don't get your hand off me." Her face was full of pain.

As he released her from his grip, she rubbed her sore arm.

"What do you want? More money!"

The line of people waiting to board had disappeared, and the platform was deserted. The conductor shouted, "All aboard." The whistle blew. The bell clanked.

Nervously, Hans reached into his pocket and pulled out his wallet again.

Eva grabbed the wallet and counted the money inside. Fifty dollars. She took it all and grabbed her suitcase out of his hand.

"That's fine, Hans." She ran toward the passengers' car waving her ticket. "Wait! Wait!" she shouted.

The conductor grabbed her arm and pulled her up onto the passengers' car step. After she had caught her balance, she gave Hans a smile and threw him a kiss with her hand. She was pleased with her cleverness. She had gotten more money out of him than they had agreed on. Perhaps she should take on a new occupation!

Hans was angry, but his anger was soon replaced by a feeling of relief. The tension had escaped from his body. An overpowering feeling of joy took its place. Everything was going so well! Then suddenly, his spirits became dampened with some alarming thoughts. What if Eva came back here? What if she didn't go to Sacramento? The train disappeared from view. No, she wouldn't come back! She'd be in just as much trouble as him if anyone ever found out. She had to stay away from Fremont. How could she explain to him that she signed Kate's name but wasn't Kate?

As he headed back to his wagon, he tried to convince himself that he wouldn't have to worry about her. Would he? He figured if she was a logical person she could figure her odds weren't very good around here. But was she logical? Did she figure her odds? Would she come back for more money? If she did, would he give it to her or would he find a different way to end their business arrangement? Well, he wasn't going to worry about that now. After tomorrow night, he'd be pretty well set. He wasn't going to spoil his grand feeling of accomplishment by worrying about something that might never happen. He'd take care of that problem when and if it ever came up. His line of thought was broken.

"Hans, Hans!"

He looked around to see who was calling his name. In the doorway of the tavern stood Todd holding a glass of pale, foamy beer.

"Come on in and have a beer, Hans."

"No, I better be getting home."

"Surprised to see you here," Todd remarked as he approached Hans.

"I had to bring Eva into town. She wanted to leave on the train today."

"You should have told me. I could have brought her in and saved you the extra trip." He stopped in front of Hans and took a drink of his beer.

Hans thought to himself. Yes, I bet Todd would have liked that. Then Hans wondered, could she have told Todd why she came to Shady Lane? No, she couldn't have. Hans was careful not to tell her too much. The only thing she could have told him was that he was paying her to stay out of sight. That was no crime. But what if he told Kate? No sweat! He'd deny it. Kate would believe him. She'd never believe Todd. She despised him.

"What's a newly married man like you doing in town without your bride?"

"I'm making arrangements for our trip to Boston on Friday."

"You could have done that at the depot in Shady Lane. You would not have had to come all the way to Beechwood for that."

"I wanted to get myself a couple of new suits for Boston. I'm sick of the ones that I've been wearing to my dad's bank. A new job--new clothes!"

"Why didn't Betsy come along?"

Todd let out a contemptuous chuckle. "She doesn't know anything about men's clothes."

"Well, I thought maybe she'd be buying some new things also."

"She's got enough clothes. Why does she need anything new? She'll be at home all the time anyway," he replied scornfully.

Boy, he's really a generous fellow and really full of love for his wife, thought Hans. Sounds like Eva was right. He doesn't love Betsy.

"Well, I better be going. See you later, Todd."

"Ya, sure, Hans." Todd motioned with his glass of beer. Then he emptied it hastily and went inside to get a refill.

Hans glanced into the tavern window before he continued down the street. He saw Todd walk back to the bar and to a tavern girl. From the familiarity of their greeting, she had obviously been waiting for him.

Being curious, Hans observed them for a while. He didn't have anything else to do. It was after dinner and by the time he'd get back to the inn, it would be too late in the day to start any work in his shop.

Todd did whatever he pleased. It didn't matter that he was in a public place, what was proper, or who was watching him. He touched her body wherever he pleased and did exactly what he wanted with his hands. Now Hans was perhaps not the most moral person either, but he felt there were things a person just had the moral decency not to do in public. Seeing how his sexual excitement was carrying him a little too far in public, the girl managed to convince him to go upstairs with her. So up the stairs and into a room they both disappeared.

****

After leaving Beechwood, Hans's pace toward Shady Lane was slowed considerably. The buildings in the city had made him unaware of the weather conditions on the open country roads.

His horses were now traveling directly into a mighty and steady Southeast wind. The rainless autumn had caused the topsoil to form into a dry crumbling powder and now the wind was blowing this powdery earth into the air. The clouds of dust blew from the plowed fields across the rest of the rain thirsty land. It blew into Hans's face and made it hard for him to breathe. As the dust particles beat against his face, it felt rough, red, and chapped. The dust blinded his vision and the particles inflamed his eyes and made them itch. It collected on his clothes and soiled them. His whole dust-covered body felt grimy.

After three hours of struggling, he finally stopped in front of the barn. The pine trees in the woods now stopped the dust and protected him from some of the brutal attacking wind. The trees were starting to show their tow of the wind and the hot sun that had beat down on them during the summer months and now during the two weeks of Indian summer. Their green needles had disappeared and been replaced by brown ones that were as dry as paper. After bedding down the horses, Hans went into the house where a warm supper was waiting for him. He washed his face and hands to make himself feel refreshed, and then sat with Kate and Pete to enjoy the delicious meal that Molly had made for them.

After supper Pete went upstairs to read, while Hans and Kate went outside and sat on the porch. The house and woods protected them from the blowing wind. Except for the wind, it was a beautiful evening, and they weren't about to let the wind ruin their enjoyment of it.

"I was surprised it took you so long in Beechwood today. I thought you'd be back by dinnertime," Kate said.

"I thought, as long as I was in town, I'd stop by the lawyer and see how things were coming with our purchase of Molly's land."

"That was a really good idea. How are things coming?"

"As it turns out, it was a good thing that I stopped by him. The papers are all ready to be signed. I told the lawyer that Molly and I would be in tomorrow night."

"Don't I have to go along?" Kate inquired.

"No, he told me that only Molly and I have to sign the papers."

"Well, I'll come along anyway. Molly probably would like me to be along with her."

Hans wasn't worried about what she had said. He had figured on her wanting to come along, and he had planned accordingly.

"How are you going to manage that? You can't be at two places at once, can you?" he asked.

"What do you--oh, I forgot. Tomorrow night is the 'going away party' for Pastor Clark and Martha."

"Since you planned it and are having it here, don't you think you probably should be here and not in Beechwood?" Hans commented.

"Besides that, I'll be terribly busy cleaning and helping Molly with the food. Oh! Molly won't be here to help me."

"She'll be here most of the day. I knew you'd probably need her so I told the lawyer we'd be at his office quite late. He lives behind his office, so it isn't really inconvenient for him."

"Oh, that was really thoughtful of you, Hans." She held his hand and kissed his cheek.

"I figured we don't have to leave until about three o'clock. By that time all the work should be pretty well done."

"Yes, it should be pretty well done by then. However, that means you probably won't be able to come home at night because it'll be too dark to travel with the horses," Kate said.

"Not really, it won't take long at the lawyer. We should start for home right after sunset. That'll give us one and a half to two and a half hours of twilight to travel home in. If it gets too dark, we can always spend the night in some farmer's field until dawn."

"Yes, that would be much better. Molly wouldn't like staying in town all night."

"Maybe, I'll get back in time to visit with some of your guests."

Kate was pleased with that thought. "Oh, that would be marvelous. I only have one problem with the party," Kate commented.

"What's that?"

"After today I don't know what to serve guests to drink with the lunch," said Kate.

Hans was puzzled. "I thought you were going to serve coffee with your lunch."

"I was, but I don't know if I should after today. Couldn't you taste it in your coffee at supper?" Kate asked.

"Taste what? The coffee seemed fine to me," Hans replied.

"Well, I think our well water is becoming distasteful. After drinking a glassful, I felt sick to my stomach. It seemed to me that it tasted and smelled salty." Kate made a disgusting facial expression.

"I haven't really noticed anything, but I suppose it could start to become brackish. It is a dug well and the water level has probably dropped because of the lack of rain."

"Do you think we should dig another well?"

"No, I don't think so. It'll start to snow soon and that'll add moisture to the ground and probably raise the water level again. All the water that has evaporated over the hot summer has to come down in precipitation pretty soon."

"Well, I hope you're right," Kate commented.

The wind was still whistling about the inn when they went inside. It was like a lullaby that lulled them to sleep that night.

****

The next day was another beautiful Indian summer day. The temperature was hot and the trees again bowed their trunks and branches in respect to the wind as it steadily blew about them out of the Southwest.

The day went fast and soon it was time for Molly to leave with Hans for Beechwood. Molly was reluctant to go without Kate. It took a tremendous amount of convincing on Kate's part for her to go with him. Molly was like a little child. She had put off going out into the world for such a long time that now the mere thought of it scared her. She had a strange feeling about Hans. She didn't feel as if he'd protect her like Kate. When Hans offered to help her onto the wagon, she turned from him and mounted herself. She sat so far at the end of the seat that Kate was afraid she'd fall off while they drove to Beechwood.

As they drove on, Hans was constantly wondering what was under the scarf that hid all of her face? Why she wore long-sleeved dresses all the time, especially on days when the weather was so hot and humid? He couldn't find out now but on the way back he had different plans. Before he got her home tonight, he'd have his questions answered.

Molly had always sensed this inquisitiveness in other people about her. That's where her fear came from, the fear that someone would want to see what the scarf and long sleeves hid. Kate and her father knew. It was because of Kate's father that she had to dress that way.

It wasn't Kate's father's fault, but he had always felt responsible. That was the reason for his generosity toward her, guilt. Kate's reasons were different. She felt gratitude at first for what Molly had done for her father. After a while, Molly sensed different feelings. She began to feel the same way about Kate, as Kate felt about her, sisterly love. Kate had never had a sister--and Molly--well she didn't know. She could have had one, but she couldn't remember. Her only memory of family was Kate and her father. Molly trembled at the edge of the seat as she constantly kept an eye on Hans's hand. She'd jump with fright if there was any moment toward her. "Oh, God, please don't let him reveal my shame," she silently prayed.

Her mind was so haunted and troubled with this fear that when the buckboard stopped at Fremont's office, she had no idea how it had gotten there. She looked about the town. She hadn't been in a town this big ever since Kate's father took her to the inn. That was a long time ago, maybe fifteen or sixteen years ago. A lifetime seemed to have passed since then. Except for Kate, her life was really an empty one, a mere shell of an existence.

She looked around. She wanted to absorb everything. The sight of the blazing sun slowly setting over the continuous, endless rows of houses and shops was something she probably would never see again. It was so different from Shady Lane where there were only a few shops and houses clustered in a small area. A person could see the farms and woods beyond the town but not here. There was nothing beyond the town except more shops and more houses. There were no woods only a few huge trees that stood here and there. A person could count the number of trees on one hand. She could never live here. In fact, she wanted to leave as soon as possible. The town seemed to turn loose an unexplainable fear in her heart. Soon her body began to tremble! But why? She had never been in this town. Why did her body fill with this unexplainable fear?

Someone tapped her leg. It was Hans. He wanted to help her down. She shook her head with great protest. He backed away from the wagon, and she got off by herself. She followed him up the stairs to the office.

Fremont thought at first her appearance was quite odd and wondered if Hans and that woman were doing something felonious.

Scheme and Betrayal 183

What else is a person to think about a person who hides their appearance? But then he thought, it's not his job to discover or prosecute fraudulent acts. He was hired to take care of a legal matter for his clients, and these two people were his clients, at least Hans was. The woman was also if she indeed was Molly.

After Molly signed the warranty deed, just for curiosity sake, he looked at the old deed. The two signatures were the same. She was indeed Molly O'Leary. Fremont felt a little bit easier. At least he hadn't been a party to a criminal act.

It did not take long in Fremont's office. When they left, Hans had completed his schemes. He now had Kate's inn and woods, and Molly's three hundred acre woods. He no longer needed Kate. It would be to his advantage to see that Lena didn't seek a divorce when she came. In a divorce, she would be entitled to a part of whatever he had. He had what he wanted, and he wasn't about to lose it all over a divorce. He didn't have to worry about Kate. A court would invalidate that marriage because he had been already married when he married Kate, but he could go to jail for bigamy. How could he get out of that? He'd find a way. It would just take awhile and a lot of thinking.

Well, the worst was over for Molly. She had made it into town and signed the papers. It wasn't as bad as she had thought it would be. The fears that had cluttered her mind, slowly were forgotten and soon she started to enjoy the open countryside as they left Beechwood behind. She relaxed and started to trust Hans. She began to think that maybe she was a little paranoid in her thinking that everyone wanted to see what was behind her scarf. She surely had misjudged Hans. He didn't even make a move toward her.

Out of the corner of his eye, Hans watched Molly. This may be the only chance he'd ever get. He had to see what was under that scarf.

As she looked at him, she could sense what was on his mind. He wasn't different after all. He was just like everyone else! What a fool to let her guard down! Fear overwhelmed her! Oh, Kate! She wished Kate could help her!

Molly jumped off the buckboard just as Hans reached for her. He caught the hem of her skirt and clenched it tightly in his hand. WHAM! She fell face first onto the small, jagged stones of the gravel road. Everything went black for a second. A severe, sharp pain throbbed back and forth through her head. Her vision was blurred-- then doubled. She shook her head, again and again. She still couldn't see properly. He would be coming for her. She had to get out of there but where could she go? She crawled off the road and then stopped. Looking up, she grasped her hands over her scarf. Hans was standing over her. He ignored the pathetic look in her eyes, the look which begged him to leave her alone. He took his strong, broad hand and tore her small hands off her scarf. He then tore off the scarf that had hid her face and hair for all those years.

The scarf fell from his hand. He stumbled backwards with fright. He put his hand over his face, closed his eyes, and turned away from the hideous sight. He felt sick to his stomach.

"What's the matter with you big, strong man? Can't you take what you see? I can. I see that every day of my life. You want to see more? I'll show you more." Angrily she ripped the long sleeve off her dress revealing her left arm.

Hans looked with disgust at the horrid sight. The arm was deformed with irregular streaks and bumps of purplish skin.

"You want to see more--big man!" Her voice cracked as her water-filled eyes released their salty tears. She pulled her skirt up showing her left leg. It was as bad as the arm.

Hans wished he had never been so curious. He knew now why she had wanted her privacy. He looked down at her sitting, sobbing, and holding her face in her hands. He felt a compassion for her as he viewed the ugly purple scars that had replaced the left side of her head where no hair would grow. What could have caused this? What on earth had happened to her to cause such disfiguration?

As he stood over her, she stretched her arm to reach her scarf. She couldn't quite reach it. As she started to crawl toward it, Hans reached for it and handed it to her.

She looked up at him. Hate filled her eyes. "Don't expect me to thank you."

While she spoke, Hans noticed something on her face that he hadn't seen before. It wasn't as noticeable as the purplish scars, but it was there. I was another scar. He could see it quite clearly. It was on the other side of her face, one straight scar from her cheekbone to her jaw. He remembered seeing that hideous scar many years ago.

"Theresa," he mumbled. Could it be her? It has to be! No one else could have a scar like that. He could have never forgotten the sight of that thing.

"Theresa," he said louder as he touched her shoulders.

She pulled away. What was he talking about? Was he going mad? Boy! That would just be her luck. She became frightful and backed away.

"Why did you change your name? In all the years I've lived at the inn, why didn't you ever tell me who you were?" Hans asked.

She shook her head. "I don't know what you're talking about. You've gone mad!" She backed up farther away from him. Frantically, she looked about. Where could she run to? Who could help her? Why didn't someone come down the road?

Hans was puzzled. Why was she pretending not to know him?

"Come on, Theresa. You must remember me. I'm Hans, your brother." He extended his hands for her to come so he could embrace her, but she only backed away farther.

"What on earth is the matter with you? Why did you change your name? What happened to Hugo?"

"Hugo?"

"Yes, your husband, Hugo?"

"Either you have me confused with someone else or you're going crazy. I'm not Theresa."

Hans stepped toward her. "Come on, Theresa. You don't have to pretend with me. Whatever your reasons are for keeping your real name a secret, I don't care. We all have our secrets. If you don't want anyone to know your Theresa Merts, that's fine. I'll keep your secret."

"I am not keeping anything a secret. I'm not the Theresa person you are talking about." She reached toward the scarf in his hand. "Give me my scarf so we can get going. It's going to be dark soon."

He grabbed her hand; she pulled back.

"Don't be afraid, Theresa. I won't hurt you." He tried to reassure her, but he could see the fear in her eyes. She really did not know him. She did not know her own name. Why? What had happened to her? To Hugo? Why had she come here? Why did Kate's father give her the land? He had to know the answers. Who could tell him? Kate! She must have some answers. She had to. He had to find out--tonight!

He handed Molly her scarf. She put it on. They mounted the buckboard and drove toward Shady Lane.

Molly was still trembling from the experience. She was baffled. Why had he called her Theresa?

Every now and then Hans would glance at her. The scarf could no longer hide what he knew was under it. He could see the hideous scars; the head only half covered with hair. That repulsive, unforgettable sight would always haunt his mind. He wished that he had been a little less curious. Now he would have to live with his knowledge and pay for his curiosity.

The dark part of twilight was soon upon them. The crescent, slender of the moon and the numerous twinkling stars in the cloudless sky gave them very little guidance as they traveled in the dusk. Unlike the previous night, the wind was still and silent. Every squeak of the buckboard's turning wheels could be heard as well as the rhythmic clapping hoofs of the horse's easy, ambling gait.

While traveling down the road, a few farmers passed them going home. Hans recognized them and bid them a friendly "hello" as they passed. They were members of Pastor Clark's congregation and probably had been at Kate's party. They obviously felt the same way about traveling in the dark as Hans did and had left Kate's party early. However, they were luckier than he was. In five minutes they'd be home, he had about another half-hour of crawling along the road before he'd reach Shady Lane.

When he stopped the buckboard in front of the barn, Molly jumped off, ran hastily toward the inn, opened the kitchen door, and closed it behind her.

The dining area was still quite full of party guests when Hans entered the inn.

"Oh, Hans, I'm so glad you got here before everyone left." Kate was so happy to see him. She went up to him, gently grabbed his hand, and kissed him on the cheek. She eyed the dining table. "I'll be right back."

"Where are you going?" Hans clung to her hand.

"The cheese is gone. I've got to get more."

Scheme and Betrayal 187

Hans smiled and let her go. She was really a beautiful, desirable woman. How was he going to get rid of her before Lena came? Lena would find out about Kate that was for sure. But if she didn't have to see Kate, it would be easier for her to accept what he had done. There was no doubt in his mind that Lena would probably stay with him once Kate was out of the picture. Staying with Kate would cost him too much. Besides what he had here, there was also the money Lena would have from their property in Germany. Lena was a good woman. She was not as young as Kate, but she was an attractive woman in her own way. At least she had been, he wondered how she looked now. Had she gotten gray like him? Had wrinkles set upon her smooth skin? How old was she? She was three years his junior. He was forty-five. So she would have to be forty-two by now. They were so young when they left each other. Now when they would meet again they'd be older, wrinkled, and gray. In a way he was longing to see her again, to see how she looked, to talk about the children and the lost ten years, to talk about things they had done together as a family before he left. They were both going to be grandparents. He could see himself playing with his grandchild. It would be fun being a grandfather.

"You must be thinking of something nice with such a happy expression on your face. I hope it's me," said Kate.

Hans just smiled and took the glass of sherry Kate had offered him.

"How was the trip into Beechwood with Molly?" Kate asked.

"I have to talk to you afterwards about Molly," Hans replied.

"Oh, it didn't go good, did it?"

"I'll tell you when we're alone," Hans replied.

"I thought so. Molly is so shaken up that she almost cut her finger off when she helped me slice the cheese."

"She's in the kitchen?" Hans was surprised.

"Well, of course. Do you think she was going to come through the dining area in order to go to her room? The way she feels about people, you should know she'd never do that."

"Kate," Martha called and motioned Kate to come over by her and her husband.

"Excuse me, Hans. We'll talk later."

"We sure will." Hans took a sip of his drink and sat in a chair. He watched the people that were standing and sitting in the room.

Dr. Gibbs was sitting next to the potbellied stove leaning toward Pete, who was sitting on the other side of the stove. Dr. Gibbs's mouth was going a hundred miles an hour. He loved telling stories of his early years as a doctor in Chicago. He must be telling a really good tale tonight because Pete seemed to absorb every word Dr. Gibbs was saying.

On the opposite side of the room were Mr. and Mrs. Cork. Standing beside them was Todd, who was making conversation with Mr. and Mrs. Cork. Todd was playing his husbandly role really good tonight. He was standing next to Betsy holding her hand. Well, maybe he was holding her hand for another reason. She didn't seem to stand too steady as she emptied her glass of sherry. She didn't seem too interested in their conversation. Her glassy eyes often roamed about the room and seemed to rest on Pete, who was quite unaware of her. When her eyes left Pete, they settled on the full sherry bottle setting on one end of the table. As she made a move toward it, Todd held her hand tightly in his. Hans couldn't hear, but he knew the word Todd had told her when she looked at him, "No!" An angry look filled her eyes as she pinched her lips tightly together and tried to pull away. Her mother told her something and then took the glass from her hand. Betsy acted like a little spoiled child and thrust out her lips in a pouting manner. Todd said something and then he dragged her past Hans and out the door.

Hans stared at Pete. Perhaps he could get Pete to help him get rid of Kate. But how? He'd have to think of something. Whatever he thought of, he would have to be careful that Pete didn't find out he was behind it.

When Mr. and Mrs. Cork strutted past Pete, they made sure that they said good night to Dr. Gibbs and deliberately ignored Pete. They then bid Hans good night and left the inn.

"Ya, I guess, I'll be going too." Dr. Gibbs's voice rose as he got up from his chair. He walked over to Kate, Martha, and Pastor Clark. "We're going to miss you two." He extended his hand. "You take care, both of you."

"Oh, we will, thank you," replied Pastor Clark.

As Dr. Gibbs left the inn, he said good night to Pete and Hans.

Pete walked over to where Hans was sitting. "Well, how did it go with Molly today?"

"Okay."

"I was surprised Kate didn't have to come along. I thought you both were buying Molly's land."

"We both are."

"Why didn't Kate have to come along then?" Pete didn't believe Hans.

"I don't know why, ask my lawyer." Hans got up and started to walk toward Kate, Martha, and Pastor Clark.

Pete grabbed Hans's arm. "Who is your lawyer?"

Hans pulled away. "That isn't any of your business."

"I'd like to check your story out. You got something to hide that you won't tell me his name."

"I don't have anything to hide. Why don't you mind your own business?" Quickly, he walked over to Kate so Pete couldn't ask him any more questions.

Pete stared at Hans for a few minutes, then went upstairs. He was furious. He wanted to know what Hans was up to in the worst way. It made him more furious that he didn't know.

As Hans watched Pete go upstairs, it suddenly came to him how Pete, without his knowledge, could help him get rid of Kate. He would use Pete's curiosity and his protective feeling toward Kate to achieve his purpose.

Then he looked at Kate who was busy talking to Martha and the pastor. That sweet creature wouldn't want him to go to jail for bigamy. He didn't have to worry about her filing a bigamy charge against him. She'd probably get a quick and quiet annulment. She would not like the idea of too many people finding out that she was living with a man who was married to someone else. Her reputability was important to her.

After the Clark's left, Kate tidied up the room. She carried the leftover food and dirty dishes into the kitchen.

As Hans sat drinking his sherry, he watched Kate walk back and forth into the kitchen. He could hear the clanging of her fine china and silverware as Molly washed them. How ironical life was. For years he had been asking about his sister and a place called Dry

Springs and here she was under the same roof as him. Why didn't she tell him? Why didn't Kate? Why did she have a different name? It was his sister, Theresa, he was sure. He could never forget that scar. His mother had always made a fuss about it. The hair that she did have was blonde, just like Theresa's. Something like that couldn't be a coincidence.

"Well, that's all for tonight." Kate looked about the room. She held out her hand to Hans. "Let's go to bed."

He got up and put his empty glass on the table. With their arms about each other, they walked into their living quarters.

"I think Pastor Clark and Martha enjoyed the 'going away party.' Don't you think so?" Kate began to undress.

"They told you it was a fantastic party about fifty times before they left. So, I guess, a person could figure that they did enjoy it quite a lot." He hung his suit neatly on the chair and then crawled into bed next to her.

Kate moved close to him and began stroking his chest.

"I'm not in the mood tonight, Kate. I'm preoccupied with Molly."

"You said earlier you wanted to talk to me about her. You know I don't like discussing her. She doesn't like me talking about her to others."

"Well, I think that I've got a right to know a few things about her. I think that she's my sister, Theresa."

"Your sister, Theresa! How could you possibly think she's your sister?"

"I saw the scar on the right side of her face. It's just like the one my sister had. I could never forget that hideous thing."

Kate's eyes widened with shock and surprise. She sat up in bed. "You've seen her whole face then, haven't you?"

"Ya, my God, what happened to her? How did she come here and why does she call herself Molly O'Leary?"

"Oh, Hans." Kate sighed. "Do you really think she's your sister, Theresa?"

"Ya, I really think so, but I don't understand why she pretends not to know me."

"I'm afraid she isn't pretending. She probably doesn't know you. Or to be more accurate, she doesn't remember you. She doesn't remember anything except the last fifteen years of her life."

Hans was puzzled. "What do you mean? What are you talking about?"

"Perhaps it would be best if I started from what I know to be the beginning," suggested Kate.

"Ya, perhaps that would be best, maybe I could understand a few things. Right now a thousand questions are running through my mind."

"About fifteen years ago, my dad went along with Judge Emery up North. Judge Emery had told my dad about all the good times that he had with some of the girls who lived in the lumberjack towns up there. My mother had been dead for several years at that time and my dad was a handsome, virile man with sexual needs. He hadn't been with a woman ever since she died and his needs and desires were strong. Especially after the judge told him about all the good times that he had. You probably wouldn't have guessed it of the judge, but when he'd start drinking some of that Irish whiskey with my dad, his tongue would really roll. Ugh! I never could understand how they could drink that terrible tasting stuff straight out of the bottle like that. Well, anyway he'd become so loud and boisterous that a person couldn't help but overhear him. The way he'd describe and talk about some of those women, a healthy man's juices surely would get worked up. Well, they were on their way back home when the train stopped, and they had to stay in this one town overnight. My dad spent the night in the hotel. The judge had a 'lady friend' in the town, and he spent the night at her house. In the middle of the night my dad was awakened by loud piercing screams and frightful cries. As he opened his door to see what was the matter, a blazing flame struck out at him. The hotel was on fire. The hotel was full of flames and smoke. He closed his door and leaned against it while he planned how to get out of there. There was no window in his room. The only way he could get out was through the door. He opened the door and stood there for a few moments. He didn't know which way to go. Then he heard a voice yell. 'This way! Take my hand!' He looked in the direction of the voice. There was a man holding a woman's hand. The man was holding out his other hand to my dad. My dad lunged through the flame and took hold of the man's hand. Together they groped, hand in hand, down the smoke-filled hall. Suddenly, a burning beam came loose and fell amongst them. My dad was knocked into a semiconscious state. He couldn't see anything. There was smoke and fire everywhere. He felt a hand feel about his body and then grab his hand. The person started to drag his body. My dad tried to get up and move on his own accord but he couldn't. His mind didn't seem to obey his commands, and so he had to leave the person drag him. The smoke started to disappear, and he could see the building across the street. He heard a panting voice say, 'We're almost there, Hugo. We will be out of here soon, my dear husband.' When he was in the doorway of the hotel, he heard a scream and the person let go of my dad's hand. Then he saw the person, ablaze with fire, run into the street. People came running. They threw a blanket on the person, and then they rolled the person about on the ground until the fire was out. He heard the person screaming, 'My husband! He's in the doorway--get him out! Hurry up! Get him out! My husband! Get Hugo out--he's in the doorway!' Then everything went silent. When my dad regained consciousness, he found himself in a bed with a big lump on his head. He also found out that the woman who had saved him became frantic when she learnt that she had pulled a complete stranger out of the fire instead of her husband. She could no longer remember anything from before the fire. Her mind seemed to block it all out. She couldn't remember her name, and no one in town knew it. She and her husband had come into town very late that night. The only one who had seen them was the hotel owner, and he had died in the fire. She didn't have anyone anymore. Being so badly burnt and scarred, my dad figured that she'd have a hard time finding a job to make a living. He felt so guilty, as if it was his fault because she had saved him. If she wouldn't have, maybe she wouldn't have gotten burnt so badly. So he brought her back here and arranged with Judge Emery to have a legal name given to her. He called her Molly O'Leary. Since it was because of Molly that he was still alive, my dad left her the three hundred acres of land as an expression of his gratitude. That's the whole story. That's all I know."

"Did I hear you correctly? Your dad mentioned her husband's name was Hugo?" Hans inquired.

"That's the name that my dad heard her call for. Since she had a wedding ring, my dad and I assumed that was her husband's name."

"Well, there's no doubt in my mind at all now. She's my sister, Theresa. Her husband was Hugo."

Kate touched Hans's hand. "Oh, Hans, I'm so glad you finally found your sister. I'm so happy for you."

"Huh, I haven't really found her. She doesn't know me. I have merely found out what happened to her. I haven't found a lost sister. My sister, in the sense of the word, no longer exists."

"I am sorry about that. At least you know what has happened to her, and that she has been well taken care of."

"Ya, you're right about that. It does ease my mind to know she's not dead or living a terrible existence. Perhaps her memory will come back, and she'll remember me."

"Anything is possible. If that's what you would like, I hope that it happens."

As she lay beside him in the stillness of the room, she could hear the ticking of the clock. She wanted him to make love to her, but he just lay there quietly. They had the woods now, soon he could start building their house, she thought. He could have no objections to having a baby now. She felt in the mood, and she wanted to make love. She moved closer to him, leaned over him, and kissed him.

He returned her kiss and put his arms around her. He loved stroking her silky hair and smelling her fragrant lilac scent. Gently and slowly, he rubbed his hands up and down her smooth back and over her fleshy, rounded buttocks. As he caressed her, his body filled with excitement. He remembered that he had used the last of his condoms. He couldn't get her pregnant now. If he did, Lena would divorce him for the sake of the child. Lena had always felt a child needed both a mother and father. Also, he couldn't leave Kate with nothing if she was going to have his child. He couldn't be careless now. He couldn't let one night of pleasure ruin everything. He'd have to stop in time. He lay on top of her and between her legs. His hard male member slipped into her. He could feel the muscles of his male member contract and relax repeatedly. It was time! He jerked it out. He lay on his back. His heart was still pounding, and he was still panting. Had he pulled it out in time? He sat up. His body filled with relief. He must have pulled it out in time. His thick, whitish fluid was spread across her dark pubic hairs and the upper part of her thigh.

"Why did you do that?" Kate asked with frustration.

He grabbed the handkerchief from under his pillow and handed it to her. "I told you. I don't want a child until I've started a house for you."

She sat up and wiped the sticky warm substance onto the handkerchief. "You always have an excuse. First, it was getting the woods. Now it's waiting for the house. Don't you love me? Don't you want us to have children?" She put the soiled handkerchief on the night stand.

He put his arms around her. "Don't get all upset. Everything will turn out fine." He gave her a hug and kissed her cheek. As he laid his nude body down, he covered it with a blanket and went to sleep.

Kate pulled the blankets over her body also. She lay still as the tears moistened the top of her pillow. How long would she have to wait? Would Hans ever let her have a baby? If he wouldn't, what then? She could never have one. What if that was the way it was going to be? What if she never had a child? Never have a child! Oh, she couldn't stand that! She didn't sleep well that night. Her body was to tense, to full of worry, full of fear that she might never have a child. If she couldn't convince Hans to have a child, there was no way that she could ever have one. She loved Hans, and she was not the type of woman who could or would make love with any other man except her husband.

Before Hans fell asleep, he had a few thoughts of his sister. How things had changed. He and his sister had grown so far apart. He felt no love, no fondness, no dislike nor hate toward her. The only thing he felt was pity. A pity that he'd feel for anyone who had experienced such a tragic life. He'd feel as much for a stranger. What if she did remember him and also remembered that he was married and had two children? It didn't matter. It was about time Kate found out. He had to get her out of the way before Lena came. If Theresa did tell her, he wouldn't have to think of a way to use Pete to tell her. He couldn't tell her. It'll be too obvious that he wanted to get rid of her. It had to appear as if it was by "accident" that she found out.

****

With the passing of the next two weeks also went the warm days of Indian summer. The potbellied stove "blushed red" and absorbed the dampness of the air as its warmth replaced the chillness which lingered in the autumn air. Sometimes a sheer white blanket would cover the fields and tips of the trees at night. But as the early morning rays peered down on the blanket, the millions of snowflakes of the blanket would dissolve into the earth and once again the brown parched grasses and powdery earth were revealed.

Hans, who was dressed for the cold weather in a large heavy coat, hat, and gloves, had just mounted the wagon that was loaded with furniture when Kate came out the kitchen door. She had a shawl draped over her shoulders as she walked toward Hans who was sitting on the wagon.

"Couldn't you come to church with me first before you go to Beechwood?" she asked.

"No, I'll get too late of a start and get home too late this afternoon."

Kate sighed with disappointment. "I don't know why Erickson had to change your delivery day to Sunday. For the last two months we haven't been able to spend any Sundays together. Doesn't Erickson know it's a sin to work on Sundays?"

"I don't think he really cares, Kate. I don't like to offend him. I could never sell my furniture here in town like I do in Beechwood at his store."

"I know that, but I don't see why you have to deliver it on Sundays?"

"I'll talk to him, Kate, okay." He gave her a big smile.

"Okay." She smiled back. "I'll see you sometime after dinner?"

"Ya, probably."

Just then Pete came out of the barn and fastened the barn door.

"Are you going along with Hans?" Kate asked as he walked toward her.

"No, I'm going to church with you." Pete paused beside her and waited for her to finish talking with Hans.

"Bye," she said.

"Bye, Kate--Pete." Hans gave the horse a slap with the reins and started moving away from them.

Kate watched Hans travel down the road for a few minutes and then looked at Pete. "Why didn't you say goodbye to Hans?"

Pete shrugged his shoulders. "Let's go inside. It's cold out here." He took Kate's hand and walked her into the inn.

"What's the matter between you and Hans?" Kate took off her shawl and hung it on a hook near the door.

"What makes you think something is the matter?" Pete hung his coat on the other hook and walked over to the hot stove.

"You hardly ever work in the shop anymore when Hans is in there. You usually wait until he's out of the shop before you go into work. Sometimes I can see the light in the shop when Hans and I go to bed at night. If you are in the same room, you don't say anything to each other. Did you two have a fight about something?" Kate rubbed her cold hands together over the hot stove.

"It's nothing for you to be concerned about," Pete responded.

"Well, I can't understand it. You used to idolize Hans and now it seems as if you despise him terribly."

"Don't be concerned about it." Pete walked over to the icebox and pulled out a white pitcher full of milk. "You want some hot chocolate, too?"

"Yes, that'll be nice. It'll take the chill out of the bones." Kate went to the cupboard, took out two tall glasses, and set them on the table. As she sat at the table, she watched Pete mix the cocoa and sugar with the milk, and set the kettle on one of the cast-iron plates of the wood-burning stove. Soon a chocolate smell filled the kitchen.

The steam from the hot chocolate twisted and curled into the air as Pete filled their glasses then sat at the table by Kate.

"I wonder what our new pastor is like?" Kate said.

"Well, we'll find out in about another hour," said Pete as he looked at his pocket watch. "We'll also get a look at the new people that moved into town."

"Oh, yes, I had forgotten about them. He's the new teller at the bank, isn't he?"

"Ya, I guess he is." Pete finished his milk and rose from the table.

"If I had known that Todd was going to leave, I would have never bothered taking my money out of his dad's bank." Kate took the two empty glasses and put them into the sink.

"Ya, you should have kept your money in his bank where you

could keep your eyes on it. You don't go to Beechwood very much."

"Well, it should be just as safe in the Beechwood bank. Hans always had his there."

"Ya, that's just what I'm concerned about."

Kate frowned. She was puzzled by that remark. "What do you mean?"

"Oh, nothing. Just remember, you have only known Hans for ten years. You don't know everything there is to know about him."

"Yes, that's true, but I don't really need to know any more than the fact that he loves me."

"I've learnt from experience that there is nothing a person can ever be sure of, except dying. Trusting too much in one thing or person only leads to hurt when you find out your trust was misplaced."

"Oh, Pete, you still feel bad about Betsy. Don't you?"

"No, not anymore."

****

After unloading his furniture, Hans had dinner and an afternoon visit with Anna and Alex. It was on his way back to the inn that Hans thought of the idea that would make up the last step in his scheme. He would just have to wait for the right situation to come along. With the weather getting cold and everyone staying inside more, the right situation would arise soon, maybe even tonight. Then what? Had he figured Kate's reaction right, or would he end up in jail?

He was so deep in thought that before he knew it, he was in front of the barn.

When he entered the inn, Pete was sitting in one of the "captain's chairs" reading a book. Hans examined the book very closely. Pete appeared to be almost finished with it. That's how he'd get him into Kate's sitting room! He'd have to watch Pete very carefully so he'd know about when he'd be putting the book back into Kate's bookcase.

"Where's Kate?" Hans asked.

Pete looked up from his book. "You really care?" he replied scornfully.

"Well, I'm asking aren't I?"

"She's in the kitchen helping Molly make supper," Pete snapped and then continued reading his book.

"You almost done with the book?" asked Hans.

"Ya." Pete examined the unread pages. "I should get done tonight. Why?"

Hans shrugged his shoulders. "Just curious." He walked toward the kitchen door. "I suppose the door is locked," Hans grumbled.

"No, she hasn't locked it for the last two weeks. Guess she must feel secure no one is going to bother her."

Hans went into the kitchen. He found it empty. The "spatting" sound of potatoes frying in the pan and the open kitchen door told Hans that they must have just stepped outside. He went up to the door and stood in the threshold. Molly and Kate were standing near the corner of the house. Molly had her arm around Kate consoling her.

"Are you okay?" He heard Molly ask.

Kate just shook her head.

"What's the matter?" Hans asked.

He startled them and they turned around.

Kate looked pale and her eyes were watery. "Nothing's the matter. I just didn't feel good. Now that I got whatever was bothering me out of my stomach, maybe I'll start feeling better."

Molly helped Kate back into the kitchen.

"I think it's that greasy smell from the pig lard that the potatoes are frying in. It's a disgusting smell and makes me sick. If you don't mind, Hans, I'm going to skip supper. I feel awfully tired," Kate said.

"Sure, should I help you into the bedroom?" Hans asked.

"No, I'll be okay. I'll feel better after I rest awhile," Kate replied.

Kate left the kitchen and went into their bedroom. She laid her body on the bed and rested.

The situation was getting better, thought Hans. She'll be in the house all night. Now if only he could be sure that Pete would go into the sitting room later on in the evening. Hans went into the dining area.

"Is that a good book you're reading?" Hans sat in the other "captain's chair."

"Ya, it's okay. What's the matter with Kate?" Pete was concerned.

"Oh, nothing serious. So you think you'll get done with the book tonight, huh."

"Ya. Why all the questions about the book?"

"Well, winter is coming and there isn't going to be too much to do. I thought maybe I'd spend some of my time reading a good book now and then," Hans explained.

"Well, I find this book quite interesting so I don't think you will," Pete said caustically.

"You're probably right." Hans rose from his chair and went into the sitting room. He closed the door behind him and looked into the bedroom. Kate was asleep. He slowly and quietly closed the bedroom door. He went over to the writing desk, opened the last drawer, and pulled out a metal box. Grabbing into his pocket, he pulled out his pocket watch chain. Attached to the end of the chain, along with his watch, was a small key. He put the key into the metal box's keyhole, turned it, and then opened the unlocked lid.

The metal box contained the deed and abstract for the inn and Molly's land. Kate had told Hans to put them in there for safekeeping when he received them. Kate had never examined them. She trusted Hans and believed him when he told her the property was "theirs." Hans placed the deeds on the desk, put the abstracts back into the box, put the box back into the drawer, and then closed the drawer.

Hans turned around and looked at the bookcase. Some of the books needed to be arranged differently. There was enough room left on some of the shelves where one or two books could be placed. Pete could squeeze the book into those spaces. For Hans's plan to work, Pete had to put his book in one certain place. So Hans started to place books on each shelf until they fit so tightly that a sheet of paper couldn't fit between any of them. He did this with all the shelves. When he was finished there was only one shelf left where a book could be put. The shelf had only five books on it with room for about ten more. It was behind these five books that Hans placed the deeds. He laid one book flat on the shelf so as to appear that the book had fallen over by itself. As the book lay flat, parts of the deeds were visible. That was exactly what Hans wanted. He was now counting on Pete's curiosity to do the rest. The success of his plan depended on him being right about Pete's reaction. If he had figured Pete wrong, his plan wouldn't work.

Hans walked to the door and then turned around. He was pleased with the bookcase. Pete couldn't miss the deeds. However, he had forgotten one thing, the bedroom door. After walking over to the bedroom door, he quietly opened it a little. Just enough for Kate to hear what was being said in the dining room, but not enough for Pete to notice it was open. With the stage being set, he left the sitting room and went into the dining area. He took a deck of cards from the shelf and sat at the table. He pretended to play solitaire, but his eyes were on Pete all the time. Pete had two or three pages left to read. Hans waited and waited. Finally, he was on the last page. Then he closed the book and rose from the chair. Just then Molly called for supper. Pete put the book on the dining room table and went into the kitchen. Hans would have to wait until after supper.

Molly went up to her room while they ate supper.

"How is Anna?" asked Pete.

"Fine," Hans replied.

"Just how long do you think, you can keep Anna from finding out about Kate and Kate from finding out about Anna?" Pete asked.

"Long enough, I hope," Hans answered.

"Long enough for what?" Pete inquired.

"Just don't worry about my business," Hans stated.

"I'm not worried about you. It's Kate that I'm concerned about."

"There's no need to be."

"There better not be."

After supper they both went back into the dining area. Hans pretended to finish his game of solitaire but all the time his eyes were on that book. He was hoping Pete would pick it up and put it back in the bookcase. He couldn't tell him to put it back. Pete might figure out his plan. If he did, it would be hard to provoke the reaction he wanted. Come on Pete, pick up the book, Hans thought to himself.

Pete just sat in the "captain's chair" with his feet crossed enjoying leisurely puffs on his corncob pipe. He sat so tranquil as he gazed out the window and the wreaths of smoke swirled about his head.

"When did you start smoking?" asked Hans who had never seen Pete smoke before.

Pete took a few puffs and then took the pipe out of his mouth. "Just this afternoon."

"What started you on that?"

"Kate gave it to me."

"Kate!"

"Ya, Kate didn't have anything to do today again so she went into the attic. She looked through her ma and dad's scrapbooks. She asked Molly and me if we'd like to reminisce with her. Molly didn't want to. I didn't have anything to do, so I went up with her. She found the pipe among her dad's things and she asked if I'd like it. She said that she missed the aroma of her dad's cherry tobacco. She always felt so at home when she could smell that in a room. I thought I'd try it, and so far I like it."

"Well, personally, I think you look wacky with a pipe and the tobacco stinks."

"To each his own." Pete put the pipe back into his mouth and began puffing again.

The room was quiet for a while again. That book bothered Hans. Wasn't he going to put it away? It was important that he'd do it tonight. Kate was in the house. No, he wasn't putting it away just smoking that dumb pipe. Hans was getting impatient and a bit angry.

"That damn smoke is enough to give a person a headache. Get out of here with that dumb pipe," Hans shouted.

"Well, if you don't like it, why don't you get out of the room."

"This is my place, not yours. If anyone is going to leave the room, it's going to be you. Not me!" Hans angrily turned a card faceup on one of the seven rows of cards lying on the table.

Pete rose from his chair. "Anything you say, Hans."

"Don't forget your dumb book. Finish reading it somewhere else."

Pete grabbed the book as he walked toward the stairs.

Hans waited and listened to see where he would go, the few seconds that passed seemed like hours. Was he going to put the book away? He was at the bottom of the stairs. He would go either up the stairs or into the sitting room. Which one? His heart was pounding. He listened. He couldn't hear Pete on the stairs. Then he heard the door open. He was going into the sitting room. Hans waited again. Any minute he figured Pete would come bursting out of the sitting room.

While in the sitting room, Pete put the book on the desk and then headed for the door. As he touched the doorknob, he turned and thought. He had read the book; therefore, he should really put it away.

Why should Kate have to put it away for him? She was kind enough to let him use her book, so the least he could do was to put it away for her. He looked about the bookcase. He couldn't remember which shelf he had gotten it from. Oh well, it probably didn't matter just as long as he put it back. There was only one shelf where it would fit and that's the one he walked toward. When he got to the shelf, he placed the fallen book right side up. Then he noticed the ends of some papers sticking out from behind the end of the other books. It looked as if someone had hid something behind them. Oh well, it wasn't any of his business. He placed the book, which was in his hand, next to the fallen book that he had just set upright. On the partially hidden papers, he could now see big, black block letters--DEED. He thought, if that was a deed, what a strange place to put it. He became curious. What were those papers? He pulled them out and examined them. As he read them, he became furious! Everything was in Hans's name! Kate wasn't mentioned on the deed for the inn or Molly's land. Kate didn't own anything!

Pete stormed up to the door and swung it violently open. He rushed violently over to Hans, gave his shoulders a powerful push, and threw the papers down on top of his cards.

Hans looked up. "What the heck you think you're doing?"

"Explain those papers!" Pete demanded.

Hans looked up at Pete with an annoying self-satisfying look on his face. "I don't have to explain anything to you." Hans turned away from Pete, pushed the papers out of his way, and continued with his game.

Pete felt his face turn red, his blood began to boil! He pinched his lips and clenched his teeth. With vehemence he grabbed the cards out of Hans's hand and threw them across the room.

"You're explaining those papers to me. Now!"

"I don't have to do anything if I don't want to."

In a wild rage, Pete took his hand and pulled Hans out of the chair by the scuff of his collar. "You took everything on her didn't you?"

"I don't know what you're talking about?" Hans acted so innocent. Pete was playing right into his hands.

Pete didn't like it when someone acted as if he was so stupid. He clenched his fingers into his palm and struck out violently--again and again--at the annoying, self-satisfying look that covered Hans's face.

The numerous blows knocked Hans onto the floor. His jaw and teeth hurt. He felt his mouth. It felt sticky. He looked at his hand. It was soaked with blood.

Pete's voice rose. "Get up! You dirty son of a bitch!"

Hans just sat there holding his mouth.

Pete stomped over to Hans. "Get up--I said!" He pulled Hans up and struck a forceful blow into his stomach.

Hans's body formed into a hump as he grasped his stomach. He moved jerkily toward a chair.

"You're not sitting down." Pete pushed the chair over so Hans couldn't sit on it. "A son of a bitch like you deserves everything you get."

Hans rammed his head into Pete's stomach.

Pete hunched his body. He grabbed Hans's head. They both went landing on the floor with a loud, thundering noise. Pete quickly threw Hans off his body and onto the floor. Pete leaped on him and hurled his fist into Hans's stomach. Hans plunged his fist into the side of Pete's head and pushed him off his body.

The furniture was toppling about the room as they exchanged violent blows against each other's body.

Above the rumbling and tumbling sounds a voice suddenly shouted, "My God! Will you two stop--right now!"

They looked up. Kate was crying. Her hands were shaking. She was extremely upset to see Hans and Pete fighting. Her voice cracked. "What on earth is going on?" She ran over to Hans. "Look what you've done, Pete. How could you?" She held Hans close to her as she comforted him. "What on earth is the matter with you, Pete?"

Pete was breathing rapidly--heavily--with great effort. "Are you going to tell her, Hans?"

"Well, someone better tell me what this is all about." She looked at Pete blamefully.

Hans was quiet.

"Well, Hans--who is going to tell her--me or you?"

Hans still remained silent. His lip was bleeding. It felt oversized and prickly.

Pete grabbed the papers off the table and gave them to Kate.

"What are these?" She grabbed them and started to examine them. She shook her head. "I don't understand what these papers have to do with the fight?"

"Look at them really close, Kate, and you'll find out," Pete suggested.

She handed them back to Pete. "I really don't know anything about what they say except that they are deeds." She turned to Hans. "What are they doing out here in the first place?"

"Don't ask me? Pete brought them out here."

Kate helped Hans to his feet.

"This is your last chance, Hans. If you don't tell her the whole story, I'm going to."

Hans was quiet. Pete was doing exactly what Hans had planned on. "Tell me what?"

"I'm sorry, Kate. This is going to hurt you, but it's gone far enough. It's all my fault that things have turned out the way they have. I should have said something right away," Pete said.

Kate was puzzled! She didn't understand what Pete was talking about. She grabbed a handkerchief from the pocket in her dress and wiped the blood off Hans's lip. She felt a rage toward Pete for having hurt Hans.

"For God's sake! What has come over you?" Kate asked Pete.

"He doesn't deserve your sympathy or your love."

"Oh, be quiet!" Kate snapped.

Pete sighed. "It's beyond belief that you could let Kate care for you now, after what you had the guts to do!"

"I think you've done enough harm here, Pete. I think you better leave," Kate remarked.

"I'm not leaving until you know what's going on," Pete stated.

"I know what's going on, and I don't like the way you are treating Hans. After all he did for you."

"Ya, good old Hans! He can't do anything wrong! Can he?" Pete's voice was full of scorn. He threw the papers into Hans's face. They fell to the floor. "Tell her now!" Pete ordered sternly.

Hans's silence made Pete furious. With his one hand, Pete grabbed Hans's shirt violently! With his other hand, he made a fist ready to hit Hans in the face.

Kate grabbed for Pete's hair and began to pull. She was desperate! She didn't want Pete to hit Hans again. She started to cry. Her body trembled. "Leave him alone! Leave him alone!" Kate screamed.

"That dirty son of a bitch isn't even your husband." Pete took his hand off Hans's shirt and lowered his fist.

Kate slapped Pete's face. "I'll not have you talking that way about Hans. Get out of here! Now!" She embraced Hans. "Make him get out of here!"

"He won't make me go, Kate, because he knows what I'm saying is the truth. He already has a wife. He just used you to get your money and property. If you don't believe me, just take a look at those papers." Pete pointed to the papers lying at Hans's feet. "You don't own anything. Kate Duren doesn't even exist legally. You were never his wife. You aren't married to him."

Kate clung to Hans more tightly. "Oh, please, make him and his ugly lies go away." She sobbed.

Hans stood silently with his arms at his sides.

Kate loosened her grip on Hans and looked up at his calm, expressionless face. She didn't sense any outrage from Hans toward Pete.

Hans looked down at her with his cold, uncaring eyes.

Kate wrinkled her brow. She was so confused! Why wasn't Hans denying what Pete was saying? Why wasn't he holding her and telling Pete to get out of here? A terrifying feeling suddenly shot through her body. Her body felt a cold chill. As she backed away, the papers crumbled beneath her feet. She took her arms off Hans's body and shook her head.

"Tell me it isn't true, Hans. Please, tell me!" Her voice cracked, her chin quivered, as her tears blurred her vision. She picked up the papers and flung them across the room angrily. "I don't care about them. I don't care if I don't own anything as long as I have you. Tell me I do--please!" Her cracked voice pleaded between her sobs.

Hans's silence gave her the answer.

"Oh, my God! It's true!"

Pete put his hand on her shoulder comfortingly.

She threw his hand off. "Get your hand off me!" She glared at Pete. "How could you go along with his lies--his scheme? What do you get out of this? Some of my money or some of my property? Do you get the inn or the woods?" She slapped Pete. "I hate you. I hate you all!" She swung at Pete again.

Pete grabbed her hand. "You hate him." He motioned to Hans. "Then send him to jail! It's against the law to marry another person when you're still married. Send him to jail!"

Kate was quiet for a few minutes. "No, why should I give him up? Why can't his first wife?" She pulled away from Pete and walked over to Hans. "You could divorce your first wife. Then we could be married again legally."

Hans shook his head. "No, I don't think so, Kate."

"Why not?"

"Because if I divorce Lena, she could take what I have. I have no intentions of giving up anything!"

"I thought you loved me!"

"I love you as much as I could love any other woman."

"Don't you feel anything special for me at all?"

"No, not really," Hans replied coldly. "Now, why don't you two get out of my room."

"Why you dirty--" Pete leaped toward Hans.

"Leave him be." Kate pulled Pete's arm back as he was about to hit Hans.

"No, come on, Pete! I'd like to knock you on your ass. Come on big man!"

"You disgust me, Hans," said Kate.

"Send him to jail, Kate!"

"Oh, I don't think Kate will send me to jail. Will you, Kate?" Han's face was covered with a sickening grin.

"Oh, you know me so well, Hans, don't you? I wish I had known you so well."

"You don't mean you're going to let him get away with this!"

"The fewer people that know about this, the better. It's bad enough the people in this town will know. How can I ever show my face again?"

"The people can't blame you, Kate. You didn't know."

"It doesn't matter. I lived in sin with a man. They'll call me a slut. No, I can't file charges. Something like this doesn't happen every day. If we went to court, everyone would know. I couldn't stand that. It'll be hard enough living here now. I don't know how I'll survive this." She burst into tears and ran from the room. She ran up the stairs and knocked on Molly's door until she let her in.

Pete watched Kate. He wished he could help her. Do something to ease her pain and humiliation. But he was helpless, it made him angry.

As he turned to Hans, the daggers of hatred in his eyes shot out at him. Pete pounded his fist on the dining table. "Damn you! Damn you! I hope you dirty son of a bitch burn in hell!" He stormed out the door and up the stairs.

Hans's eyes shot to the papers lying on the floor. "I've got to put them in a safe place," he said to himself. He walked over to the corner where they had landed and picked up the crumbled papers. With the papers in his hand, he went into the sitting room. Closing the door, he gave a sigh as he leaned against the closed door. "Oh, Pete, you were perfect," he whispered to himself. He walked over to the writing desk, laid the papers down, and spread his hand along each page to straightened out the wrinkles. Then he folded the papers, grabbed the thickest book from the bookcase, and set it on the folded papers to get rid of their wrinkled bulkiness.

He went through the open bedroom door and sat at the edge of the bed. It'd be lonely and cold in the bed tonight. It was too late and dark to go to Beechwood again. Maybe he'd spend tomorrow night at the Beechwood tavern. He undressed and went to bed.

Meanwhile, upstairs, Pete took the pillowcase off the pillow and started to pack his belongings into the pillowcase. He reached into his pocket and pulled out some money. He put it on the dresser next to the bed. That should pay for the pillowcase, he thought to himself. As he went out into the hall and headed for the stairs, he stopped and looked at Molly's door. He turned, walked toward the door, and knocked.

The door slowly opened. "What do you want?" Molly asked.

"Can I see Kate, please?"

"No, she's sleeping."

"It's all right, Molly. Let him in."

Kate was resting on the bed. As Pete entered the doorway, she sat up. She wiped her red eyes. Her face was covered with red blotches from crying.

"Kate, I'm so sorry. Please, believe me. I wish you had never had to find out, but you had to. I'm so sorry I didn't tell you sooner."

"Sure you are! You're a lot richer for it though, aren't you?"

"Kate, don't think that way of me, please. There is no excuse for me not telling you. I'm sorry about that. Is there anything I can do?" Tears of sincerity filled Pete's eyes.

"No, you've done enough, thank you," Kate replied in a sarcastic quiet tone.

"Are you going to stay here?"

"I don't have any place else to go, but I can't stay here. Now can I? It's not my place anymore. Is it?" Kate burst into tears.

Molly, who was standing near the open door, rushed over to the side of the bed to comfort her.

"I think you better leave," suggested Molly.

"Ya, I suppose, I better." He turned and headed for the door in a gloomy manner. He went down the stairs. At the bottom of the stairs, he paused and looked at the sitting room door. He felt like going in and hitting Hans one more time, but that wouldn't change anything. He went out the door and down to the barn. After saddling his horse, he started to head down the moonlit road toward Beechwood. He was going to take the job Mr. Ewerdt had offered him.

As the door closed behind Pete, Kate's eyes flooded with uncontrollable tears. In a matter of minutes her whole life had changed. She was so happy just awhile ago. She had everything; now she had nothing. How foolish of her to be satisfied with what she had. Whenever she had been satisfied with what she had and didn't care for anything else, what she had was taken away from her. It wasn't fair. Why had God done this to her? What had she done wrong to deserve such punishment? Hans was gone from her. He was so close--just downstairs--but so far out of reach. There would be no one to hold her close, to kiss her, or to love her. No one to love her! She was alone! How stupid! She always had been alone. Hans had never loved her. He had made a fool out of her. He had used her. How could she face the people of the town when they found out? She couldn't show her face! Where could she go? How could she live? She had been betrayed by two people that she cared so much about. There was no one she could turn to for help. She was all alone--only Molly was there--but she could only comfort her. She couldn't make the scheme go away, lessen the pain of betrayal, or go with her when she went among people. She would have to find a place to live and also a job. Oh, she could hear the people gossip and see their smug little smirks. She would feel their repulsive, disgusting eyes look upon her in a vile manner. She wouldn't be able to stand it! She couldn't live that way!

Her body was exhausted. Her red, tired eyes grew heavy and heavier. Soon all thoughts of shame and betrayal vanished. Her mind became full of beautiful visions. She could see her parents walking through a green pasture dotted with hundreds of wild yellow and white flowers that danced so softly in the gentle breeze. They were holding out their hands to her--calling her to them. But she couldn't see herself, just the smiling faces of her parents calling her. She wanted to run to them but she couldn't. Where was she? Then suddenly out of nowhere, she came and was walking beside her parents. She felt so loved, so protected, so secure. She didn't need anyone. She had her parents. They were a family again. They laughed and held each other's hands as they walked through the pasture of dancing flowers. Suddenly, Kate's body felt strange. Everything in her stomach seemed to be in her throat. She felt clogged up. She was afraid to swallow, to burp, for fear that everything would come out. She had to get up. Everything in her throat was going to come out! She jumped out of bed and clamped her hands over her mouth. She felt better now that she was standing up. After a few seconds, she took her hand away from her mouth. The terrible sensation to rid her stomach of its entire contents had disappeared. What on earth was the matter with her? Whenever she would lay down today, she had felt the entire contents of her stomach in her throat, ready to come out. She looked over at Molly curled up in a chair. At least she hadn't awakened Molly.

Kate sat back on the bed and looked out the window. The sun was starting to peek over Molly's woods. No, they were Hans's woods now. He had everything. She had nothing. Life was unfair. How she wished that things could be the way they used to be before Hans and Pete came. She thought of her dream. Could there have been a reason for that dream? Maybe that was the answer, the only way to get away from the shame. No one would really care. Her parents were waiting for her. She wouldn't have to worry about anything if she was with them. They loved her. No one else did. No one else cared.

Slowly, she walked toward the door. She didn't know exactly how she would do it, but she would. Her mind seemed clouded. Dazed! Quietly, she turned the doorknob. She heard the door click as it opened and then squeak on its hinges. She glanced over at Molly who was still sound asleep. Good, she hadn't woken up. She slid her slender body through the opening and then carefully closed the door. Stealthily, she moved down the stairs.

The cool October air chilled her body as she opened the door. Her bare feet and the bottom of her flannel nightgown became wet from the early morning dew as she walked to the barn.

She paused at the barn door before opening it. She turned and looked about. Puffs of gray clouds had now covered the sun. The oak and maple trees stood bare among the thirsty brown needled pine. Everything was ugly! Everything had changed. Nothing seemed to stay the same. Life was not worth all this grief. It was ugly! Ugly! Ugly! Everything was ugly! No one ever really cares! A person is always alone! She didn't want to be alone anymore! She didn't want any more pain! No more grief! She couldn't live with the shame the rest of her life. If she wasn't around, who would remember what she had done? No one would care. She'd be forgotten and so would be what she had done. Oh, God! She had slept with a man she wasn't married to. She was so ugly! She was a whore! A slut! No one loved her! No one ever did--except her parents--only her parents. They were waiting for her. She had to go.

She opened the door and went inside the barn. She looked around. There it was what she wanted. It would do the job. Going over to the corner of the barn, she took part of the rope that was sticking out from under a loose pile of straw. Shaking the straw particles off, she walked over to the center of the barn near a tie stall. She fastened the end of the rope tightly around the top board of the stall. With the rest of the rope in her hand, she climbed up onto the tie stall and slid the rope over the long, thick wooden beam that provided horizontal support for the barn. As the rope swung loosely over the beam, she stood motionless and gazed intently with her eyes wide open at it.

With her hands vibrating uncontrollably, she reached for the part of the rope that now hung loosely over the side of the beam. Her hands quivered about the rope as she formed the loop in the rope by making a slipknot. The finished loop fell below her feet. It was too long. She took the loop and wrapped the rope over the beam again and again until the loop hung only a few feet below the beam. She watched the loop swing in the air. She bit her lower lip and held her breath for a second. Her trembling hands seized the loop and put it around her neck. All she had to do was jump and it would all be over. Could she? Would she? She had to!

CLUK!

The rope stung her neck. It squeezed the cords in her neck. It was so painful! Her vision became blurred--dim. Her head felt oversized--numb--it was throbbing loudly. It hurt. She felt dizzy. There was no sound anymore. She couldn't breathe. She kicked her feet about as her hands grasped the rope around her neck. She couldn't get any air! It hurt! Then her body felt so weak--so limp! As the last breathe of oxygen stole out of her body, faintness embraced her. Darkness touched her. Her arms dropped limply beside her body. Her body jerked as her nerves revolted against the ultimate order from her brain. Her body jerked again but now there was no order from the brain to defy and then a mere--just a mere twitch as the last of her body's energy faded into oblivion.

Chapter 6
****
Fiery Death

Anna came bouncing down the stairs whistling as her brown locks of hair danced about the white collar on her brilliant pink dress. She was exuberantly happy today. The day was exactly the way it should be. The sun was shining through a cloudless sky and had made everything bright and warm. Easter Sundays were supposed to be that way, at least Anna thought so.

As she neared the bottom of the stairs, the inn's door opened and startled her. A quick look at the familiar face that stood in the doorway soon brought a glowing smile to her face.

"Good morning, Daddy." She hugged his neck and gave him a big smile.

"Good morning, Anna." He returned her embrace and kissed her forehead like he had done so many times before when she was a little girl.

"Oh, it is a happy Easter." She pulled out of his embrace, took his hand, and walked out the open doorway onto the porch.

The Southwest wind greeted her and tossed her hair about her face. In a quick and sweeping motion, she pushed the hair out of her face behind her ears.

"It's so beautiful here, Daddy. Oh, aren't they gorgeous!" Her eyes had caught sight of rows of flowers growing along the edge of the porch. Each tall stem had a colorful, bell-shaped blossom on its end.

"Who planted the tulips?" she asked.

Hans shrugged his shoulders.

"Was it the woman who lived here with you?"

Hans looked at her in amazement. Who had told her? He really shouldn't have been surprised. She had lived in Shady Lane for six months. It was really a surprise that she hadn't found out sooner.

"What do you know about her?" he asked.

She took her hand out of his and backed away. "So there really was another woman?"

"Just what did you hear?"

"Just that you were living with a woman who called herself your wife," Anna replied.

"It's true. I was living with a woman for the last two years, but she wasn't my wife."

"How could you do that to Ma?"

"There isn't any real excuse, I guess, but I didn't hear from her anymore. She never answered any of my letters. I got lonely. I figured no one cared. I hadn't heard from Ma for the last two years."

"Daddy, please don't lie to me. It makes it worst."

"Lie--about what?"

"Ma wrote you all the time. It was you who stopped writing. It was mean of you to stop writing when you did. Ma needed you then. She was going through a very hard time and your letters would have given her support."

"Wait a minute. Something isn't right here. I wrote your ma every month. It was she who never wrote."

"Daddy, I know she wrote you because Ludwig and I always mailed the letters for her."

"Well, I never got them."

"Well, she never got your letters either."

Puzzled expressions crossed their faces as they looked at each other.

"Well, that is really strange. All those letters couldn't have gotten lost," replied Hans.

"The Count," Anna muttered as she stood staring at the porch floor.

"The Count? What are you talking about?" Hans was puzzled and intensely curious.

"Oh, you remember." She paused. "Oh, that's right he bought Herr von Buren's castle after you left."

"Herr von Buren sold his castle!" Hans raised his eyebrows in astonishment. He couldn't believe Herr von Buren would do that.

"Yes, he married Fraulein Weimar. She sold her castle, he sold his, and then they bought a larger castle that overlooks the Rhine. They own a really large estate just outside of Cologne," she explained.

"Huh, I never thought he'd ever get married, especially to her. They're both older than I am." He paused in thought for a second. "Well, what about this Count? What does he have to do with my letters?"

"You know that about a year after you left Ma sold the house."

"Ya, she wrote me that."

"Well, then you also know that we needed a place to stay. We moved into your carpenter shop, and Ma proceeded to try and sell the forty acres of woods and the shop. It was about this time that Herr von Buren sold his castle that overlooked our woods. The Count von Himmler," she emphasized his name as she raised her eyebrows and opened her eyes wider, "bought the castle. I know Ma wrote you that she was having trouble selling the woods and shop because Ludwig and I always read the letters."

"Ya, I know. I received those letters."

Anna sat on the porch steps. "A lot of people came to look at the shop and the woods. They'd say that they wanted to buy it and that they'd come back in a day or two to make the proper arrangements necessary to purchase the shop and the woods. Ma would wait and wait, but the people would never come back. Finally, three years had passed and nothing was sold. We had to have money to live. The money from the sale of the house was gone. Ma went to look for a job. She'd have the job for a day or two. Then suddenly, the people she was working for decided that they didn't need her anymore, but that wasn't the worst. When they hired someone else the next day for the same job, Ma was really hurt. She wanted to leave town so bad. She began to think for some unknown reason people hated her and she didn't have any friends. People were so unkind. One night when Ma came home tired from walking all over to find a job, there came a knock on the door. It was the Count. With his head held high with pride, he stood in the doorway for a few seconds, then walked into the shop conceitedly."

"Looking at him, I couldn't understand why he had such a high regard for himself. He was nothing to look at. He was a small, skinny unimpressive figure physically. He looked about the room haughtily and then at me and Ludwig. I'll always remember his eyes as he looked at me. They were so wild--piercing--hypnotic. He scared me. When he looked at Ma, I was afraid that he was going to hurt her. I remember standing still and barely breathing. His presence gave me a strange feeling, a perception of something evil. Silently, I prayed with all my heart that he'd leave. I didn't know why he had come, but I sensed no good would come of meeting such a man. He took papers out of his jacket and placed them on the table. Then he took Ma's metal pen nib and dipped it into her inkwell. Holding out the pen to her, he ordered her to sign the papers. Ma was perplexed. What was on the papers? She picked them up and read them. The bewildered look on her face was soon replaced by an angry look, which became angrier as she read on down the page. When she had finished reading, she ripped the papers up into a thousand pieces and threw them into the Count's face. His piercing eyes dilated as he pressed his lips together in anger. In a piercing and high-pitched voice, he yelled at Ma, 'You'll be sorry you did that, you peasant!' With that remark, he stomped toward the door and swung it open wildly. He then turned and just looked at Ma for a few seconds, then he left."

"What did he want Ma to sign?" asked Hans.

"He wanted Ma to sign the woods over to him for nothing. Since our woods bordered his castle, he wanted it," explained Anna.

"Why didn't he just offer to buy the woods?"

"The Count is a member of nobility, one of the upper classes in Germany. Do you actually think that he'd pay us 'peasants' for anything? Ma was really shaking after he left. She felt things couldn't get any worst. No one wanted us there. She wished that she could leave, but we didn't have any money. That night about two o'clock, Ma heard a noise at the back door. Cautiously, she got up to investigate. She was so afraid. Was it the Count? Before opening the door, she waited. When everything was quiet, she opened the door. There was no one there. As she turned to shut the door, her eyes caught a glance of something setting on the top doorstep. It was a cloth with something wrapped in it. Ma picked it up and unwrapped the cloth. It was a jar of pickled pork hocks, a jar of sauerkraut, and a half a loaf of course, dark rye bread. There was also a note, which explained a lot of things to Ma. It appeared that the Count had his eye on the woods ever since he bought the castle. The people, who had looked at the woods and shop and had shown some interest in it, were warned by the Count not to buy the woods or the shop. The people in town were also warned against giving Ma a job. The Count wanted her to feel so unwanted and desperate that he figured she'd sign the papers just to get away from the unkindness of the townspeople. The people in town couldn't show their support for Ma openly. They were afraid of the Count. The Count stopped in at the shop about five times that year with the papers. Each time Ma tore the papers up, and he went away extremely angry."

"Why didn't Ma ever write me about her troubles?"

"She didn't think the Count could really do any harm, and she didn't want to worry you. What could you do? She figured if he wanted the woods and shop badly enough, he'd pay a price for it. Ma at least wanted enough money so we could all come to America by you. Knowing that Ma didn't have a job, some of the townspeople would leave staples on the back steps for us to eat once and awhile. Ludwig and Ma would hunt in the woods and cut wood. Then the Count stopped coming and we figured that he had given up, but we were all wrong. One afternoon we had just come back from mailing you a letter when suddenly the door burst open and several police stood in the doorway blocking the sun. They flung the cupboard door wildly open and took out a very long, dark loaf of bread. We were surprised! We had not put the loaf there. How did it get there and how did they know what to look for and where to look? Another man soon came and stood quietly in the doorway, it was Oslo. The police gave him the loaf of bread and asked Oslo if it was his. When Oslo stated it was the one that was stolen, the police then asked him which one of us had stolen it from his bakery. I still can see Oslo swallowing the lump in his throat. His mousy little face getting red as he pointed his skinny finger at Ma. I clung to Ma with tears in my eyes. I knew what they were going to do. How could Oslo lie? As I looked up at him, he turned and ran down the street. Every day that Ma was in jail, the Count came with the papers for Ma to sign. She wouldn't sign them. It was then she decided to write you about what was going on. The

Count had the police cut off her hair and then lock her in the stocks that stood in front of the town hall. At night the townspeople, who knew Oslo had lied, let her out and burnt the stocks. The Count was furious! He ordered the police to put her in jail again. As the days and months passed without a word from you, Ma became more and more depressed. She wrote you so many letters. Ludwig and I would always mail them to you. The Count probably got a hold of the letters. Your letters as they arrived and Ma's as we delivered them to the post office. That's why you didn't hear from us, and we didn't hear from you."

"I bet that's what happened. How long did Ma stay in jail?"

"Until she signed the papers," replied Anna.

"So she finally signed them and gave him everything he wanted?"

"Ya."

"Did he leave her out then?"

"Ya, he did."

Tears began to fill Anna's eyes. She slowly got up and started to walk away. Her legs were trembling, her hands shaking. She couldn't let him see her tears. He might wonder why and that's one thing she couldn't tell him.

"I don't want to talk about it anymore. Today is Easter." She picked a purple tulip and held it up to her nose to smell. "They are so pretty. I love tulips."

Her father came up and gently touched her shoulders. "I'm glad you all are okay and that you're here."

She reached up and touched his hand on her shoulder. "I'm glad too, Daddy." She was glad--more glad than anyone could ever know. It was her secret and her mother's secret as to what really had happened to make her mother sign those papers. She would never tell and neither would her mother. With Germany left far behind her, so was the secret. No one would ever know.

"I would like to know one more thing then I won't bother you with the past anymore."

Anna held her breath. What did he want to know? He couldn't ask her about it, could he? No, he doesn't know. No one does, not even Ludwig. She forced a smile and turned around. "Sure, Daddy, what do you want to know?"

"Why didn't I receive any letters after the Count left your ma alone?"

"Ma hadn't heard from you for so long that she didn't know what to think. So she decided to save every bit of money that she made to go to America. She was determined to leave a country where such injustice could occur. Ma just didn't have time anymore. She worked all day and most of the night in the hotel as a cook and cleaning lady. We could stay at the hotel as long as Ma worked there. Ludwig worked for a farmer. That's how he met his wife. She was the farmer's daughter. I was the hotel dishwasher. Ma saved everything that we earned. When Ludwig got married, Ma gave him all the money that we had saved so he and his wife could come to America. After that, Alex and I got married. Since Ludwig and his wife weren't going to leave until after their baby was born, they gave Alex and me the money to come here. Ma had enough money for herself when we left, but she decided to wait for the birth of the baby. It's strange that I haven't heard from Ma. The baby should have been born sometime now. Just think as we are talking I could be an aunt and you a grandfather."

"Ya, that's something--isn't it--me a grandfather."

"Do you like the idea of being a grandfather, Daddy?"

"Sure, why not? The only thing I wish is that someday I will be able to see and hold my grandchild."

"You'll get your wish, Daddy, don't worry."

"You really think they'll come after the baby is born?"

Anna was deep in thought and a faint sound seemed to drift into her ears incoherently. "What--did you say something?"

"I said--"

"There you are." A voice broke into Hans's reply. It was Alex.

"Well, I'm ready for church." He made a gesture of his hands as he glanced at his clean dark suit. It made him look so dashing, so handsome. He was a good-looking, virile man. Anna loved him and her eyes gleamed when she saw him.

"Happy Easter." Alex put his arms around her waist.

Anna loved that when he touched and held her. It made her feel so warm and secure in his love. Just holding his hand made her feel wonderful. She loved to have him near her.

The three of them walked to church. There were a few whispers and unkind remarks about Hans and Kate from people who had lived in the community for a while. But the community was changing, a lot of people who had known Kate had moved or died. New people were constantly moving into the community. The one's that made the remarks couldn't prove anything. The pastor was new. After Pastor Clark left, the church was vacant for a while. Hans took that opportunity to dispose of the church's copy of the wedding. The judge had moved to Boston. The conductor had died, and the train's engineer had retired to "who knows where." Pete had left, and he'd never talk about it. Betsy and Todd were gone. Mr. Cork's excessive drinking deterred his credibility, and Mrs. Cork was a quiet person who chose not to gossip about her customers. Mr. Bester wouldn't say anything. Hans had too much money. His tracks were pretty well covered. His story would be believed. Everyone who had been at the wedding was gone. He had Anna and Alex convinced that the remarks were "idle gossip," spoken by people who were jealous of him.

"It was a beautiful church service, wasn't it?" Anna said as they walked up the steps into the inn after the church service.

"Ya, it was. Just think a year ago we walked up steps into a Gothic church. Now, we're walking up wooden steps into a small clapboard church. Things surely do change," remarked Alex.

"They sure do. We'll be married a year next month." Anna paused at the bottom of the stairs as she waited for Alex to close the door behind her.

Hans started to walk into the sitting room.

Anna touched Alex's hand as she called. "Daddy, can Alex and I talk to you for a few minutes before you take off your church clothes?"

"Sure, Anna." He turned around. "What do you want to talk about?"

Anna and Alex walked hand in hand into the sitting room. They sat on the sofa as Hans sat across from them on a chair.

Anna rubbed her hands together nervously. "Please, don't get the wrong idea and please don't feel hurt about what we are going to tell you." A very concerned look crossed her face. She was concerned about her father's feelings. She didn't want to hurt him.

"Alex and I are very grateful to you for inviting us to live here at the inn and for hiring Alex to work in your carpenter shop. I enjoyed these months together and getting to know you again. It was almost like when I was your little girl at home in Germany. I needed to be with you after all those years of separation. However, I'm not your little girl anymore. We aren't at home in Germany. No amount of time can ever bring back those days. They are lost in time. Nothing can ever stay the same, and nothing can be brought back. I'm married now. Alex and I have our own dreams. We want a farm. Alex has always wanted a farm. We've saved as much as we could, and we think we have enough saved for a nice down payment on a farm. Alex doesn't object to doing carpenter work, but he couldn't do it all his life. He wouldn't be happy. Also, I don't like the idea of people always stopping here at the inn. I'm a private person. I like my privacy."

"But the train only stops every other day and only for an hour or so, then the people are gone again. If you buy a farm, you and Alex will be working all the time, every day. You'll never have a day off. You'd have to help him out in the fields and in the barn. That's no life for a woman. A woman should just take care of the house, cook, and do things that aren't so strenuous. Women are fragile and should be treated that way," Hans said.

"Oh, Daddy, women aren't fragile little china dolls. It would be fun working beside Alex. We'd always be together."

"Well, you're together now."

"It's not the same. Alex helps you in the shop, but all I do is watch. I'm not a part of things. On a farm I'd be beside Alex when we milked the cows, made crops, and harvested them. I'd be there because he needed me, and I'd be helping him," explained Anna.

"But Anna you don't know anything about farming, you were raised in town. You've never had to work on a farm."

"I know what it's like, Daddy. I always went out to Alex's parents' farm before we were married. I helped milk the cows, make hay, shock oats, and I liked it. A person is free. You're your own boss and I liked it."

Hans got up and walked over to the bookcase. What about the farm he had? It was just setting idle. He hadn't found anyone to rent it. Of course, who would rent a farm in the fall of a year or winter especially when there was no feed. Should he rent it to Alex and Anna, or should he just give the farm to them? No, he wanted the farm and the land. It meant power. The more he had, the more power he could get, and the more important of a person he could be. But what was he working for really? Wasn't it so his children would have something someday? He couldn't take it with him when he died. Could he? -- No, he had worked and schemed too hard to get what he wanted and now had. Anna and Alex should work hard also for what they wanted. They'd appreciate things more. Giving the farm to her would mean changing all kinds of legal papers, and he had enough of that. He'd rent the farm to them, he thought.

"Daddy, please, don't be hurt."

Hans turned around. "Instead of buying a farm now and borrowing the money you don't have saved, why don't you rent a farm," suggested Hans.

"We had thought of that, but then we figured that the money we'd pay for rent was really lost to us. If we paid the same amount in interest toward a mortgage, then the money would be doing some good for us. Eventually, we'd own the farm," commented Alex.

"What would you say about going into a partnership with me," asked Hans?

"I don't care for carpenter work." Alex shook his head. Couldn't Hans understand that, he thought.

"I'm not talking about carpenter work," replied Hans.

"I don't quite understand." Alex was perplexed.

"I own a farm, but I don't have anyone to work it for me."

Alex and Anna were surprised.

"You own a farm, Daddy?"

"Ya, just outside of Beechwood, I bought it last fall. I'll supply the farm. You supply the work, and we'll split everything in half, the bills, the checks, and whatever else is involved. Someday when I die, the farm will be yours."

Alex pressed his lips together and frowned his brow. He was thinking. Was it a good deal, or not?

"Well, what do you think?" asked Hans.

"Anna and I will have to think about that," replied Alex.

Hans drew up his shoulders. "Okay."

Anna glanced at the clock. It was eleven-thirty.

"Oh, the train stops today. I better get the coffee set up and some sandwiches made. The passengers are always so hungry when the train stops around dinnertime."

Anna hurried into the kitchen. The sound of cupboards and drawers opening, then closing, and the sharp metallic sound of the silverware that she used to make the sandwiches filled the kitchen for a while. Then, the sounds ended. The sandwiches were all made and set neatly on a pewter serving tray. Anna put a clean cloth over the sandwiches so they wouldn't dry out. She carried the tray into the dining area and placed it in the middle of the table. The inn was quiet. The pleasing and refreshing aroma of the coffee filled the room. Anna sat in the "captain's chair" near the potbellied stove. She took a deep breath of the coffee smell and then let the breath out of her mouth. It was a really good smell. She relaxed and waited.

Meanwhile, Hans had gone into the bedroom to change out of his church clothes. Alex had gone upstairs to do the same.

Soon she heard the train whistle. She got up from the chair and went into the kitchen. She took several cups out of the kitchen cupboard and carried them into the dining area, putting them on the table. She did this a couple of times. She paused for a moment and looked at the table. Maybe she had better get out a few more cups and saucers just in case the train was full, she thought.

As she heard the train's brakes screech on the metal rails, she went into the kitchen, took the coffeepot off the stove, grabbed three more cups, and went into the dining area. As she set the coffeepot down on a cloth, the inn door opened.

"Good morning, Mrs. Leer," said the conductor.

"Happy Easter," the engineer greeted her as he followed the conductor up to the table.

"Good morning, guys, a lot of people on the train today?" Anna asked.

"Ya, it's full but I don't think too many are getting off. We aren't staying that long," replied the conductor.

"Don't you have to fill up with water?" Anna asked.

"No, we're carrying our extra water in the tender. The last couple of times we stopped to fill up here and the other places farther up the track, we hardly got any water. All the streams are like yours, mere trickles. The railroad thought the water supply around here would get better after winter, but you hardly got any snow this winter. No spring rains yet, bad news," stated the engineer.

"Ah, we make better time if we don't have to stop and fill up with water all the time. Also, the passengers are happier if they get where they are going sooner," said the conductor as he blew into his hot cup of coffee.

"You mean they usually get more snow around here in winter than what we had this year?" asked Anna.

"They sure do. There have been winters when the train couldn't travel past Beechwood for weeks at a time because the track was so full. This winter was unbelievable." He turned to the conductor. "How many inches of snow did they say we got this winter?"

"Two--three--it wasn't much."

"Heck, no! Hey, really good sandwiches, Anna." The engineer gulped the sandwich down.

The conductor rested his elbows on the table as he held the cup of coffee in his hands. The white steam swirled up and disappeared as he stared out the window. "Some of the trees aren't even pretty this year. Just look at the needles on some of the pine. They're as dry as paper."

The engineer looked toward the window. "Yup, you're right." He sipped his coffee loudly. "It doesn't look as if anyone else is getting off the train. We better be going."

"Holy cow! I forgot a woman wanted to get off here." The conductor set down his empty cup of coffee. Eating the rest of his half-eaten sandwich, he rushed out the door.

"Ha--ha--see what you do, Anna. You're such a good-looking, young thing that you make us old guys forget about our work."

"Where is he speeding off to like lightning," asked Alex as he came down the stairs?

"Hi, Alex. Oh, he forgot about one of his passengers." The engineer set the empty cup down, grabbed another sandwich, and headed toward the door.

Hans was walking through the sitting room and had overheard the conversation through the open door. "Forgot about one of his passengers?"

"I guess he was supposed to let one of the passengers know when we reached Shady Lane," replied the engineer.

"Well, can't the person read? There's a big sign right on top of the depot," Hans commented.

"I guess not. Well, I better be going. See ya." He waved a good-bye as he departed outside.

They all followed the engineer out the door. On the porch they stood, waiting to see who was going to get off. Through the windows of the train, they could see the conductor and someone walking through the aisle beside him.

Soon the door opened, the conductor stepped out with a small bag. He set the bag down on the depot platform. A few minutes later, a gray-haired woman came out the door. They couldn't see her face. She was getting off on the other side of the train, near the depot. The conductor helped her off the train steps onto the depot platform. The woman picked up her bag and examined the small red depot building.

"Okay, let's go!" the conductor shouted to the engineer as he boarded the train. The woman turned around as the train traveled down the track. The passing train cars prevented them from seeing her face.

"Why don't you and Daddy help her with her bag and into the inn?" Anna suggested to Alex. "I think I'll start our Easter dinner now. We won't do anything all day so one good meal should be enough. We'll eat around two o'clock. Is that okay?"

"Sure."

With their reply, Anna turned and went inside the inn.

As the caboose passed, the woman stood alone on the platform.

Alex and Hans started to walk toward her. Suddenly, Alex took Hans's arm and held him back.

Hans looked at him perplexed. "What's the matter?" Hans pulled away.

"Don't you know her?" asked Alex.

Hans looked at the woman slowly walking down the wooden steps. He wrinkled his forehead. He was bewildered. He looked at Alex. He didn't know what Alex meant. Why should he know that woman?

"It's Fraulein Duren, your wife!"

Hans shook his head. "No--not my Lena!" He stood for a moment and watched her coming closer. Tears began to fill his eyes. It was Lena!

She had changed. Her plump figure had disappeared. She had curves in just the right places. Her hair was short and gray, but her face showed no sign of age. It was glowing and free of wrinkles. As she approached, butterflies fluttered in Hans's stomach. He began to feel the way he felt the first time that he had seen his Lena, so many years ago. She was so beautiful--sexy--and she was his. Oh, what was he doing just standing there! He should rush up and hold her soft, warm body in his arms--kiss her moist pink lips--and he did. He held her so tight. He would never let her go again. He pressed his lips hard against hers.

She dropped the bag and held him close. Her eyes exploded with tears. All the loneliness of those ten years was worth it to her for this moment. Oh, could such happiness be a dream? No, it wasn't a dream! Hans was holding her tightly. She was holding him. His arms wrapped around her made her forget the past for the moment and made her feel safe and secure in this new place.

"Anna, Anna, come quickly!" Alex shouted.

Anna flung open the door. "What's the--"

Her ma's eyes met hers.

"Ma, Ma!" She ran down the stairs with tear-blurred eyes.

Hans released his embrace.

Lena ran toward her Anna. They embraced.

"Oh, my Anna! I've missed you so." She held Anna's face in her hand. "My Anna! My beautiful, Anna!" She embraced her again and then looked at Alex. "You are a good man, Alex. You took good care of my Anna."

Alex went over and hugged Lena. "I'm glad you're here."

Lena felt a strong hand touch hers. She turned. It was really Hans!

"Let me take you into your new home."

She squeezed his hand. "Yes, and never let go of me again."

Alex went over and picked up Lena's bag. He took Anna's hand and they followed Hans and Lena into the inn.

Lena stopped in the doorway. After living in the shop and then a hotel room all those years, seeing more than one room to live in, shocked her. The rooms were beautiful. The furniture was exquisite. Hans had done well. For a moment, she felt like a failure. All that Hans had acquired in Germany, she had lost for him. She brought nothing for him. Then she thought, why let it matter? They were together. No more wasted time. Life was too short to waste any minute of it. She loved him and wanted to be with him, and that's what she was going to do--every minute. Nothing else mattered but to love him and be loved by him.

She squeezed his hand and smiled up at him as they walked into the sitting room.

"Sit here, Lena." Hans motioned to the sofa and Lena sat down.

"I'm going to get us all a drink." He headed for the table where the sherry and several glasses were placed.

"This calls for a celebration!" He grabbed the decanter and started to fill the glasses.

"I don't want any, Daddy," said Anna as she sat on the chair.

"Oh, Anna, just a little. It's a celebration! It's not everyday something like this happens." Hans started to fill a glass.

"Are you ill, Anna? You do look kind of pale all of a sudden." Lena rose from her chair and went over to Anna. She touched Anna's hand and caressed it in hers. "What's the matter?"

"Oh!" Anna put her hand on her abdomen.

"Do you have pain?" asked Lena.

"Tell them, Anna," said Alex as he reached for the glass Hans handed him.

"Thank you," said Lena as she took the glass Hans offered her. "Tell us what?"

Anna's face lit up as she touched her abdomen. "I just felt our baby move again." She touched Alex's hand.

"Anna, oh my Anna!" Lena hugged her. "This is the best present anyone could ever ask for. When?"

"About five months from now."

"Two grandchildren in one year, we're getting old, Hans." Lena touched his hand.

"What did Ludwig have?" asked Anna excitedly.

"A little girl. They called her, Heidi."

"Oh, I bet Ludwig would have liked a little boy. He likes fishing and things like that," Anna commented.

"Ludwig was just glad the baby survived. His wife had to be so careful. As soon as she was on her feet, she'd start to pass blood. You are lucky, Anna. You don't have such problems."

"Yes, you're right." Anna got up. "Excuse me, I should really check on our Easter dinner." Anna started toward the door.

"I'll help you, Anna." Lena rose from the sofa.

"No, Ma, you rest. You had a long trip."

"You don't know how nice it is going to be for me to go into a small kitchen and cook a small meal. Now don't deprive me of that." Lena put her arm around Anna as they walked through the dining area.

Anna stopped at the table and grabbed the serving tray still full of sandwiches. "We'll be eating sandwiches for breakfast, dinner, and supper tomorrow."

"Oh, who cares, Anna. There are worst things than that."

"You're right, Ma. We should know."

Lena closed the dining area door behind them as they entered the kitchen.

Anna basted the chicken and turned the dressing in the bowl so it wouldn't burn.

"Well, I see you haven't changed when it comes to making your dressing. You never did like making it in the chicken. Instead you make an extra dish to wash by making it in a bowl," Lena said teasingly.

"One extra dish isn't that much, Ma."

"How have you been feeling?"

"Fine, Ma." She opened a jar of canned beets, took them out piece by piece, and placed them into a bowl.

"Beets, they used to be your daddy's favorite vegetable."

"They still are. Why do you think we're having them? I don't like them."

"Anna, they are good for you, especially now. I'm glad to hear that you are having a baby. I was afraid that maybe what happened would affect your marriage."

"Sometimes it does, Ma." Her eyes became watery. "I don't want it to, but it does. Alex is so wonderful. He never forces or badgers me. Sometimes, I think, I should tell him."

"No, Anna, you must never tell him," Lena snapped at her. "It's our secret. No one else must know. Once you tell someone else it's no longer a secret and before long everyone knows. A husband must never know something like that. It could make things go bad between you, and then he'd always have that to throw back at you."

"Not Alex, Ma, he'd understand."

"No one ever really knows anyone else. We maybe think we do, but not really. I wish Ludwig would come over here, soon." Lena began to pace the floor as she wrung her hands. "I don't like him being over there so long. The longer he stays, the more of a possibility that he will find out our secret."

"Ludwig wouldn't tell anyone if he found out."

"Ya, that's what everyone always says, 'that person wouldn't tell anyone.' Isn't it odd how everyone soon knows about a person's secrets of the past, the skeletons in the closet."

"Ma, you worry too much." Anna touched her shoulder and caressed it gently.

Lena touched her hand. "I worry about you, Anna." She started to cry. "It was my fault."

Anna embraced her. "No, Ma, it wasn't your fault. Things are just in our 'cards of life.' It's the way things just are."

"Oh, why must the ugly past haunt us in the chambers of our mind. The best time of our lives, when we are babies and experience all the love and only the good things of life, are all forgotten. Why can't the ugliness of other things be just as easily forgotten?"

"Ma, don't think of those ugly things. They deprive you of enjoying the good things of life. There are good things too, Ma. Spend your time thinking of them. I do. That's the only way I can go on. If I didn't, there wouldn't be this baby inside of me. It's a good thing, Ma."

Lena wiped the tears from her eyes. "You're right. It is a good thing, this baby. Maybe by experiencing what we did we can protect the baby and see nothing like that ever happens to it."

"Sure, Ma, maybe that's why things happen."

Fiery Death

Anna opened the cupboard door and took out several plates, cups, and saucers. "Would you help me set the table?"

Her mother smiled and reached for the dishes. "My dear Anna, you still don't like to set the table, do you?"

They both laughed.

It was an enjoyable meal. No one really ate too much though. They were all too full of joy and happiness.

Alex and Anna did dishes while Hans and Lena walked outside. Hans took her into his shop. They walked into the woods. Hans felt proud as he showed Lena all that he had acquired. "We will never want again, Lena."

"You have done well, my husband. I am only sorry that I managed your affairs so badly in Germany. You could have much more."

"I also own a farm. Alex and Anna might live there."

"Oh, I bet Alex would like that. He wants to be a farmer, you know."

"Ya, that's why I offered him the farm."

They walked hand in hand back toward the inn.

"It looks like everything is going to turn out fine for us. We will never have to worry about money. We have our lovely daughter with us. In a few months we'll have a little grandchild. America is truly a place where if one makes use of opportunities, you can do anything you really want to."

"You certainly have, my dear Hans."

"For you, Lena, all for you."

"The air is so still now. The wind was blowing during dinner, wasn't it?"

"Ya, a nice warm southwest breeze."

As he walked hand in hand with Lena, he thought of Kate. How often they had walked the very same path. Kate liked to walk and so did Lena. He remembered their walks down the streets in Bremen every night, except when it rained or snowed. As they walked, he looked down at Lena. She really had a shape on her. She had lost some weight. Her face still looked soft and smooth, her lips so moist. He stopped, took her in his arms, kissed her hard, and held her tight. He could feel the excitement in his body. He rubbed the lower part of his body against hers.

"Hans, please, not here! Be civilized! We do have a bedroom, don't we?" She tried to push him away, but he held her too tight. He pressed his mouth on hers. She turned to the side.

"Hans, please, let me go. We have a bedroom. This is not the place." She tried to pull away again as she looked about hoping no one was watching them.

He held her tight and hovered over her. "I love you, Lena. I've waited so long for you." He turned her face toward his and pressed his lips against hers.

The rigidness of her body disappeared. She relaxed in his arms. He backed her up against a tree and rubbed the lower part of his body faster and harder against hers. He kissed her intensely.

She wanted him to make love to her but this just didn't seem right, not here--not like this. What if someone came into the woods? Things like that were done in private. If he couldn't control himself, she'd have to.

"Hans, I don't want our first time together to be like this. Now, please, stop." She tried to push him away again. "Hans, please, please don't ruin our first time after all these years. Animals do it like that. People do it in their bedrooms, in privacy."

"There's no one here," he panted. He kissed her hair, her forehead, her cheeks, her lips, her neck.

Slowly, she felt the pressure of his muscular body on her decrease.

"Okay, Lena," he said softly. "We'll, do it your way."

****

Anna's eyelids were getting heavy. She held the half-crocheted yellow baby blanket up and examined it. She had done enough for today. She rested it on her lap as she watched Alex who was paging through the Sears mail order catalog again. Anna smiled to herself. Her dear Alex was daydreaming about the things that he'd like to have on his farm. That catalog was his "wish book." Oh, her dear Alex! She loved him so much. She'd work day and night so she could help him get all those things and make his dreams come true. He was such a good, kind man. He deserved to have everything that he wanted. She rose from her rocker and stretched her back a bit. It hurt from sitting so long. She walked over to the window and looked out. It was a beautiful clear night. Every star was out. It was so still. There in the northwest sky she could see the kite-like shape of Bootes rising. Bootes, the herdsman, driving his plow around the North Star. She thought of Alex and how fitting that constellation was to him. Somewhere up there was the Big Dipper, but where? Come on now! She should be able to find that. That was the only one that she could ever find when she was small. That was always fun! At night after supper was finished and dishes done, they'd all sit outside and find a constellation. Everyone would always leave the Big Dipper for her to find. They all knew that was the only one she could find. Ah, there it was. She looked at it for a few seconds. Then suddenly her eyes caught glimpse of a light in the distance. Huh, she never noticed that before. Was there a town over there? She had always thought the woods stretched as far as a person could see. It did--then what was that light?

"Alex, will you come here for a moment, please."

She waited a few minutes. It was silent--no squeak of a bed--no footsteps coming toward her.

"Alex." She turned around. She smiled to herself and slowly shook her head. Her dear Alex had fallen asleep. There was a tranquil smile on his face. He must be dreaming of his farm, she thought. Ah, she was tired, too. She pulled down the shade, turned the wick out of the gas lantern, took the book out of his hand, and crawled into bed beside him.

Soon after her head touched the soft feather pillow, she also was fast asleep. Toward morning, beneath her closed eyelids, her eyes began to move rapidly back and forth. She had begun to dream:

She was dressed in a black dress and walking up four steps onto a porch. Holding on to her one hand was a child, but she couldn't see the child's face. It was blank. When she reached the top step, she paused. There were two doors, one to her left and one in front of her. She reached toward the door in front of her and opened it. The room was full of people. As she opened it wider and started to walk in, everyone looked at her. They looked so hatefully at her. Their eyes seem to pierce her soul, and their hatred pierced her heart. Then they all quickly turned away. No one wanted to see her, to talk to her. She could feel how unwanted she was and felt their contempt for her in every bone of her body. As she walked into the room farther, someone grabbed the child out of her hand. They put the child outside and closed the door. She tried to open the door but she couldn't. "Let me have the child," she cried. Everyone turned around and stared at her. They started to walk toward her with their faces full of hate. They pushed her aside and stood in front of the door. They wouldn't let the child in, and she couldn't get out. She looked around desperately. There was another door. Maybe that would lead her to the child. She opened it. A chilling breeze blew at her. She shivered and clutched her arms and hands close to her body. She stepped into the room. There was a big black coffin. She walked closer to the coffin. Who was in the coffin? The coffin was open, but she couldn't see who was lying in the coffin. The body didn't have a face. It was blank. Suddenly, she found herself in the middle of a field. She didn't know where she was. For as far as she could see, the field went on endlessly until it met the blue sky. Then out of the horizon came a herd of horses. They were coming at her. Where could she go? She ran faster and faster! They came faster and faster after her! Clouds of dust from their stamping hoofs flew all about. They were coming faster and faster! Then she saw the faceless child, it was in the path of the horses. She ran toward the child and picked it up but running with the child slowed her. Every time she turned around, the horses were coming closer and closer. They were so close that she could feel their painful nips on her back. Her legs were limp. She could hardly breathe anymore. The child in her arms was so heavy! She tripped and she could see the hoofs coming on top of her and the child.

"Ah! Ah!" She sat up. She was in her bed. Her body was sweating, trembling!

"Anna, are you all right." Alex sat up beside her and put his arm around her. Her scream had awakened and scared him.

"Oh, Alex! I had that terrible dream again, the one with the coffin and the horses."

"It's just a dream, Anna." He said comfortingly.

"Oh, Alex! I'm afraid the dream may mean something. I've had the same dream twice." She began to cry.

"Anna, Anna don't cry. A dream is merely a dream, nothing to take seriously."

"You don't think they can come true, do you?"

"No, Anna." He held her close. "You better get to sleep now. You're sleeping for two now, you know." He kissed her gently on the forehead.

"Oh, Alex, I love you." She hugged him and then laid her body back down.

"What is that roaring noise?" asked Anna.

"Ya, I was just wondering the same thing. The moon is really bright tonight. It seems to shine right through the shade."

"Ya, it sure does." Anna looked at the shade-covered window.

Alex glanced at the clock. Its hands were at three o'clock.

"There isn't too much of the night left. In about three hours we'll have to get up, so we better get back to sleep." Alex turned over and pulled the covers up over his body.

Anna lay there for a while. She couldn't fall back to sleep. That continuous, steady roaring sound kept her awake. What on earth was it? She glanced at the clock. It has to be later than three o'clock. It's so light outside! If she remembered correctly, the full moon was several nights ago. The moon should be going in its last quarter now. It shouldn't be that bright. Oh, who really cares! She was tired! She had the alarm set for six o'clock. If the clock was wrong, it just meant she'd maybe get a few more hours of sleep. Her father wouldn't say anything if Alex came to the shop a little late. Besides, her father might not get up so early either. He might want to spend all day with her mother. It was so nice having her mother near. Her mother would be here when she had her baby. That was so important. She didn't know anything about having a baby. Sometimes the thought had scared her. But her mother was here now to help her and explain things to her. She wasn't alone. Sure she had Alex, but he probably didn't know any more than her about babies. She slid her hand over her abdomen. Their little sweetheart was in there. It made her feel so good when she felt it move today. It was a real baby and it had moved twice today. With sweet thoughts of their baby, she fell asleep.

She hadn't slept very long when she was awaken by loud, thunderous roars and continuous cracking sounds. She sniffed and then sniffed again. Was that the smell of wood burning? She threw off her blankets and swung her legs out of bed. Something was burning!

CRASH!--Broken pieces of glass flew about the room.

The sound woke Alex. He jumped out of bed.

The top of a burning tree had plunged through the window. Red, hot flames leaped into the room. The torn shade and curtains disappeared into streaks of fire. The walls covered with dry wallpaper soon burst into flames.

"My, God! The place is burning!" Alex jumped into his trousers, grabbed Anna's hand, and ran toward the door. As he touched the doorknob, he quickly pulled away. The knob was extremely hot. He touched it again and quickly hurled it open. Monstrous flames, enveloped by smoke, struck out at them with unbearable, intense heat. Alex slammed the door shut. Gray smoke began to creep under the door and steal their oxygen. They began to cough and choke. Their eyes grew red and burned. How could they get out? They had to get out! The flames were devouring the door.

Alex ripped the blankets off the bed. "We have to get out this room. We're going out into the hall and try to make it down the stairs and then out of inn."

Anna was crying hysterically. Her hands were trembling with great fear. "We can't go out there! Everything is on fire!"

Alex threw some of the blankets over her. The rest he wrapped around himself. "If we stay here, we are going to suffocate for sure. Maybe we'll die out there too. I don't know. Our chances maybe are better out there. We'll never know if we don't go out there. We know we don't have a chance in here. If we don't have a chance out there, the end result is the same. At least let's try."

"Our baby! Our baby! Is this the way it ends?" She coughed and choked. "It isn't fair!"

Alex pulled the blankets farther over her hair. "Take my hand! Here we go!"

He opened the door. The flames savagely lashed out at his uncovered face. "It looks like the stairway is all on fire."

"Oh, we're going to die, Alex! I can't breathe!"

Alex pulled her through the glaring, infernos of flames that whirled down from everywhere. The fierce, hungry flames attacked the blankets, and they could feel the burning heat on their backs as they ran through one towering pillar of flames after another. They held the wrapped blankets over their nose and mouth. They held their breath as much as they could to avoid breathing in too much smoke.

Soon they could go no farther. They were at the end of the hall, up against a wall. They might just as well have stayed in their room. The result was going to be the same. Alex threw the burning blankets off their bodies into the flames. He eyed the burning hall. The flames leaped out through all the doors, except one. What was behind that door? Maybe that room wasn't on fire yet.

"Come on, Anna. Let's go back and open that door."

"I'm not going back into those flames! It's useless!" She sat on the floor with her back against the wall and watched the flames come closer.

"It's not that far, Anna. Come on!" He pulled her up and dashed through the biting flames. Alex quickly turned the doorknob and flung open the door. The room was untouched by flames. He pulled Anna inside, ran to the window, and looked out. They could get out here.

"Alex! Alex! I'm on fire! Help me! Help me!" Anna screamed.

Alex spun around. Anna was frantically hitting the flames on the sleeves of her nightgown. Alex grabbed the sleeves and tore them off.

"Come on! Help me! We can get out here!" He threw the blankets off the bed. "Tie them together!"

Quickly, with her hands nervously shaking, she tied the blankets together as the balls of fire jumped farther into the room.

Alex tied one blanket to the leg of the headboard, opened the window, and threw the other blankets, which Anna had tied together, out the window. They weren't quite long enough. Anna would have to jump. Alex didn't think that would be good for her.

"I'll go out first and grab you when you come down," he said.

Anna watched him hustle down the blankets.

"Okay, Anna, come down."

Cautiously, she climbed down. Soon she could go no farther. She dangled from the end of the blanket. She couldn't feel Alex's hands. Wasn't he going to help her down?

"Alex, where are you?" she called frantically.

There was no reply.

"Alex, please! I can't hold on much longer! Where are you?"

"Alex! Alex!" Anna screamed. She became overcome with an anxious anticipation of death as she looked up and seen the flames snap through the window. "Alex! Alex!"

"Hang on, Anna. I'm coming. I went to get a ladder. I couldn't quite reach you from the ground, and I didn't want you to jump and fall."

He set the ladder up against the house. Anna could feel her dangling feet touch a step.

"It's all right, Anna." Alex's hands guided her feet to the step. He hung on to her until she caught her balance on the ladder. He backed down, and she did the same.

Panting and crying, she fell into his arms for comfort and security. Then, quickly, she turned from him and looked at the inn.

"We've got to get Ma and Daddy out!"

They ran to the side of the inn where her parents' bedroom was.

The defiant flames spit out harshly at them through the window.

"Oh, my God! Are they in there?" Anna cried.

"I don't know." Alex stood on his tiptoes and stretched his neck. He tried to see between the jumping streaks of flames and clouds of smoke. He held his arm up to protect his face from the flames, but the intensity of the heat kept him from getting to close.

"Ma, Ma, are you in there?" called Anna.

There was no reply--just the sound of the burning inn cracking and the violent, rotating flames.

"Ma! Daddy! Are you in there?" she cried again.

"Sh! I think I hear something!"

They were very still. They ceased to breathe for a second--then they heard it--coughing and choking from inside the bedroom.

"They're in there. I'll see if I can get inside and get them out." Alex ran to the front of the inn, pulling Anna along with him.

The fire had so weakened that part of the inn that it collapsed into a mass of flames before their eyes. They moved back away from the scorching heat. Her parents were dead! What a terrible way to die! There was no time to cry. The woods around them were ablaze. They had to wake the people in town. Quickly, they turned toward the town. What town? It was incinerated! Only parts of some of the buildings' framework could be seen standing amongst the flames.

Soon these parts surrendered and fell like the other parts of the buildings into the wild craving flames.

"The horses!" Alex shouted. He took her hand and pulled her behind as he ran around the inn toward the barn. He stopped quickly in his tracks. The barn was a burst of flames.

Their only way out now was a narrow path down to the stream. They ran down the path flanked with burning, falling trees. The wind began to blow violently and blew the hot, glowing pieces of wood about. Some of the pieces would touch their unprotected skin and burn it black. Their throats were sore from coughing and inhaling the continuous, charred smell of smoke. The ground was hot and burnt their feet. The gases made them feel faint--tired--like lying down and sleeping.

Would they ever escape the pursuing flames or would the flames' pursuit end when they were wrapped in its arms of death? What was at the end of the path? The muddy stream? A wall of greeting flames?

At the stream's edge, they found that the woods across the stream were also on fire. They looked about. What could they do now? Just wait to be consumed? No! They'd follow the stream. It looked free of falling trees. Of course, they didn't know if the whole stream was passable, but they wouldn't find out by staying there. At this point, their chances were just as good going down the stream as standing there.

Soon they were walking in the muddy remains of the stream. Moving through the mud was slow and oh, so tiring. It was such an effort to pull their legs, knee-high in mud, out to take the next step. Burning trees would topple and fall near the stream's bank.

"Oh, Alex." Anna stopped. "I can't go any farther--. I'm just too tired."

"Anna, don't quit now! The worst is behind us."

She turned her head and looked behind her and then in front of her. It looked the same. Everything was burning! Slowly, she pushed her hair out of her soot-covered face and looked up through the burning trees at the sky. It was covered with heavy masses of dark clouds. They looked like big, black mountains. It looked so gloomy--like a day bringing "death." She felt a drop of moisture on her face--then another. Was it finally rain? It was! Suddenly, the clouds were bursting loose! She soon was drenched and so was Alex. It was a cold rain, but it felt so good.

They looked at each other with a smile that extended from one side of their face to another. They stood embracing each other as the deluge of rain poured down on them.

The thunder cracked and blinding flashes of lightning streaked the sky. The muddy stream was soon filled with water up to their knees. The water began to flow fast and with much force. They clung to each other now so neither one would lose their balance and be washed away with the wild water.

A short distance from them a large rock, worn and rounded by weather and water, stuck out amidst the stream. They splashed through the water toward it. Alex helped Anna up onto the rock and then climbed up beside her.

Cuddled together and cold, they watched the rising water surge by.

The day long downpour slowly diminished the flames. Things were now burning and smoking without the giant flames. Here and there large trees stood--scorched--black--barren of branches and leaves--lonely, amid a gray ash-covered floor now cluttered with half burnt, fallen trees. Whirling clouds of smoke spotted the wretched scenery. In some places, the fertile humus of the woods' floor had been burnt down to bare rock.

As the sun began to set, it began to drizzle. Alex and Anna were extremely hungry. Alex helped Anna off the rock, and they waded their way to the banks of the stream. Where should they go? Where could they go? Everything was gone. Where were they? The railroad track! They should be able to find it. It was parallel to the stream. So they started to walk in the direction of where they thought the track was. They walked and walked. Their feet became burnt and bleed as they walked over the smoldering remains of the woods. It started to get dark and they still hadn't found the track. Where was it? They walked on in the drizzle. Finally, Anna let go of Alex's hand and sat on a drenched pile of ashes.

"I have to rest, Alex. My legs are so tired. My feet hurt." She rubbed the bottom of her feet with her hands. "It's getting so cold." Her lacerated, burnt nightgown offered very little warmth to her shivering body.

"If we keep moving we'll stay a lot warmer than if we sit still."

"I know, Alex, but I just can't move anymore."

He sat beside her. "Maybe it would be best if we rested for a while." He wrapped his body around hers and rocked her in his arms.

Her head fell against his shoulder, and her body became limp. Her eyes tightly closed in sleep.

Her tired body slept for hours in the drizzle. As the sun was rising on a new day, she awoke. Alex was still holding her tightly.

"Do you feel better now?" Alex's loving voice asked.

"Yes, a little better."

"Well, let's go then." He got up and gently helped her up. They could see a lot better now that the clouds of smoke had completely disappeared. Everything hadn't burnt. The burnt area was surrounded by green woods and there was the railroad track. They walked toward it and then started to walk on its crossties.

The sun was high when the track finally led them into a town, Beechwood. They were weary and famished. Beechwood was silent--no horses--no buggies--no wagons--no people! Slowly, they dragged their bodies down the street until they reached the hotel where they had stayed and Anna had worked. Feebly, Alex opened the door and helped Anna inside.

The woman behind the hotel desk recognized them and quickly walked up to them. She helped them both to a small sofa.

"Are you all right, Anna--Alex?" She was so concerned.

"We will be as soon as we get some sleep and food, Sophia," replied Alex.

"Of course, you need rest. Come with me." She helped them into her living quarters. "Margaret, come here, please."

A few minutes later a dark-haired, young woman came into the room. "Were they in the fire?"

"Yes, dear, heat up some water for a bath, please."

"Yes, Mother." She left the room.

"Anna--Alex come into the kitchen. I've got a kettle of chicken soup on the stove, just waiting to be eaten."

"Oh, thank you, that sounds so good," said Anna.

"Well, it's nothing fancy, but it fills the stomach. I find that it's a lot easier to make soup than meat and potatoes on days when I have to run the hotel by myself." She pulled out a kitchen chair for each of them.

"Felix and the other men left yesterday morning to fight the fire." She filled their bowls to the brim and set the piping hot soup before them. "We all woke up coughing and choking Monday morning." She handed them each a spoon. "The wind just blew the smoke right into town. Gray ashes fell like snow. The sky had an orange-purple glow."

The door flew open. "They're back! They're back!" Margaret shouted as she stood in the threshold. She set the kettle of water down and pointed down the street at the large group of men, buggies, and horses marching into town.

"Well, I kinda figured they'd be back pretty soon. The thunderstorm helped them a lot. Thank God, it rained. Otherwise, I think, this town would be gone. They say the town of Shady Lane is completely gone," said Sophia.

"Ya, we know. We were there," said Alex.

"Oh, that's right you moved there with your dad," said Sophia.

Anna broke down in tears.

"Anna's parents died in the fire," responded Alex.

Sophia went over to comfort Anna. "I'm so sorry, Anna."

"How on earth did you get out of that burning hell?" Margaret asked Alex.

"I really don't know. I guess God figured our baby should have a chance to live," replied Alex as he reached for and held Anna's hand.

"Oh, my goodness! What an ordeal for a pregnant woman to go through," Sophia commented.

Sophia turned to Margaret who was putting the kettles of bath water on the stove. "Get the doctor, Margaret, will you, please."

"Sure."

"No, there is no need. I'll be fine once I take a bath and get some rest," said Anna.

Margaret paused in the doorway.

"It won't do any harm for the doctor to examine you. Go ahead, Margaret."

Margaret closed the door as she went outside and into the street to find the doctor.

"Thank you so much for the soup. It was very good," said Alex.

"Would you like more?" asked Sophia.

"Oh, no, thank you. I'm full," Alex responded.

"Would you like more, Anna?" Sophia asked.

"No, I really don't feel like eating."

"I know, but you have to. You've got a baby inside of you who needs nourishment." Sophia went to her icebox, opened it, and poured Anna a glass of milk.

"You drink this." She handed the glass of milk to Anna. "Now don't upset yourself by thinking of your parents. You have to relax and get some rest. You must be happy for your parents. They don't have any cares or worries where they are. They are happy and always will be. As long as you are here and you have that baby, and that baby grows and has a baby, your parents are never dead. Part of them keeps on living from generation to generation. In a sense having that baby would give your parents immortality. So you better take good care of yourself and that baby."

Anna smiled a little and drank the milk.

The steam was starting to rise from the kettle. Sophia took a big copper tub from behind the stove and carried it into the bedroom, which was next to the kitchen.

The kitchen door opened.

"The doctor will be here in an hour or so. He has to treat some of the men for burns," said Margaret. She grabbed a soup bowl out of the cupboard, filled it, and sat at the table.

"Fill one for me, please," said Sophia as she took one kettle off the stove and poured its boiling hot contents into the copper tub.

While her soup cooled, Margaret filled a soup bowl for Sophia. Then she took the empty kettle from Sophia, went outside, refilled the kettle with water, brought it back inside, and gave it to Sophia.

"Your bath is ready, Anna," Sophia said after she dumped the kettle of cold water into the tub. "Should I help you into the tub, Anna?"

"No, that's okay." Anna slowly walked toward the bedroom.

"There are some dresses in the closet. Take any one you would like to have," offered Margaret.

"That's very kind of you, Margaret. Thank you." Anna closed the door and undressed.

Oh! The bath felt so relaxing on her legs and on her back, but the bottom of her feet and arms hurt. Stung! She couldn't tolerate having them in the water. She looked at them. Her arms and the soles of her feet were covered with spots of charred skin. Some of the charred skin had peeled away leaving red open sores that hurt when the water touched them. There were bulges filled with fluid in some places. They hurt also, but not as much as the raw open sores. She just let the dirt soak off her feet while she gently patted her arms to get off the soot and the mud. With each pat of the wet cloth, she clenched her teeth with pain. The pain seemed to cut through her whole body. The repeated surges of pain began to make her sick to her stomach. Nevertheless, she had to clean her arms. Some of the open sores had dirt ground deeply into them. If she didn't get the dirt out, she knew that she'd probably get some kind of infection. Finally, she just rested back in the tub, her arms submerged in the water. She shut her eyes and let the stinging pain take its course. The worst was over, getting out of the fire alive. The sores would heal. The pain would go.

When she felt clean and refreshed, she got out of the tub. After dressing in one of Margaret's dresses, she even felt a little pretty as she looked in the mirror. Well, here she was wasting time looking at herself in the mirror while her dear Alex was patiently waiting to clean himself. How inconsiderate of her, she thought. She opened the door and went out.

Alex was talking to an old man who held a dark bag in his hand.

"Oh, you must be Anna." The old man rose to shake her hand.

"Yes, I am." She extended her arm toward him.

The old man caught sight of her arm. "We must do something about these burns." He offered her a chair and began to apply a soothing ointment to each of her burns.

Meanwhile, Alex helped Margaret and Sophia empty the tub of dirty bath water outside. After Margaret and Sophia had filled the tub with fresh warm water, Alex took his bath. Somehow, his arms and feet didn't get as badly burnt as Anna's. When he had finished his bath, the doctor treated the few minor burns that he had acquired.

As the old man shut his black bag and was ready to leave, the door swung open. A large man covered from head to toe with soot stood in the doorway. He was unrecognizable at first.

"Are you all right, Daddy?" asked Margaret.

"Yes, I'm fine. Thank God for the rain. We would have never been able to stop that fire." He dropped his tired body into a chair then looked at Alex and Anna. "I was sorry to hear about your dad, Anna."

Anna stood still. Her eyes began to water.

"How do you know about her dad?" Sophia asked as she set a hot bowl of soup in front of him to eat.

"The first thing we heard when we came into town was that Anna and Alex had survived the fire."

"Were you that far fighting the fire?" asked Sophia.

"No, we went through where the town of Shady Lane used to be after the rain had stopped the fire. Everything in the town is burnt down to bare rock. That land won't be any good for anything for a long, long time." He rose from the table and washed his sooty hands in the sink.

He turned to Alex and Anna while drying his hands. "You are really lucky. Everyone else in the town must have died in their sleep from the gases and smoke."

"Does anyone know what started the fire?" asked Margaret as she cleaned up the dirty sink after her father finished washing.

"Well, a couple of the men that were farther up than us said that it started in the middle of nowhere. There were no farms, houses, and no towns around. The only thing we all could figure is that a spark from the train yesterday must have fallen on some of the dry trees or grasses and started the fire." He began to eat his soup.

Sophia shook her head. "If only the rain would have come a day earlier."

"Ya, that little word 'if' can make a lot of big changes in people's lives," he added.

"Come along, Anna--Alex, you can rest in Margaret's room." Sophia went into the room and threw the blankets back on the bed.

Alex helped Anna into the room, and there they both finally found a well-deserved rest.

The next day Alex went to the blacksmith shop and asked for his job back. They had to have money to live. Sure they had money saved and in the bank, but they were not going to use that--not if they didn't have to. That was for their farm.

So early every day Alex went to the blacksmith shop where he worked until late. Beechwood was a bustling town and there was a desperate need for the blacksmith. As he hammered the hot pieces of metal into shape on the anvil day after day, his thoughts were a million miles away, thinking of his farm. The days seemed to pass quicker for him that way.

Anna helped Sophia at the hotel again. She was weepy the whole first week. It just wasn't fair! The events of life had kept them apart. Now death had parted them forever. So much time together was lost and now they were dead! How could God be so cruel? What if this was all there was? She'd never be with her parents again! Then she felt her baby move inside of her again. Her grief slowly faded. What a miracle that little life was! For a baby to form out of two minute substances was just a miracle. There had to be a God! There had to be a divine creature to make a baby. Her mother and father were happy, and now they'd be together forever in heaven. A smile replaced her tears. When the day came that she could no longer fit into her clothes because of her swollen abdomen, her joy grew more.

It was about this time that a tall, slender figure of a man, Mr. Fremont came to visit Anna and Alex. He informed them of Hans's will and his wealth. Fremont needed Ludwig's address to inform him of his inheritance. Hans' assets were to be divided equally. Ludwig and Anna didn't want the inn or any of the land around it, so they asked Fremont to sell it for them. With some of her proceeds, Anna paid Ludwig for his share of the farm. Although Hans had said the farm would be hers, he had died before he could change the will.

After everything was settled, Alex and Anna moved out to the farm. There they worked and waited enthusiastically for the arrival of their baby. They used the money that they had saved to originally buy a farm to purchase animals, farm equipment, and to fix up the barn and house. Their dream had come true. However, the happiness of the dream fulfilled was decreased by the realism that someone had to die for it to be that way.

****

Sitting on a chair in his pajamas watching the early sun peek over the hill was thirteen-year-old Otto. His elbows were resting on the windowsill as he held his head in his hands. He hadn't slept all night.

What was going to happen today had upset him extremely. He had hoped that his father could change his mother's mind. But as of last night, her mind had remained unchanged.

The roaster crowed and a few minutes later he saw his parents walk toward the barn for milking. A feeling of resentment rushed through his body. He suddenly felt a surge of hatred for his mother. Why was she really going to do that to him? Did she really want to get rid of him that badly? Did she hate him that much? Well, if she did, he could hate also! She talks so lovingly in front of other people, about how much she loves children. She cuddles and kisses everyone else's children and then she can't wait to get rid of the only child she has. What a great mother! So there he sat all drenched in self-pity as the lonely clock ticked away the minutes of his last morning at home.

Inside the barn, Della sat on one stool milking her cow while Phillip sat on another stool milking his cow.

"Are you sure you won't change your mind, Della? You know the boy doesn't want to go."

"He maybe doesn't like the idea now. But in years to come, he'll thank me."

"I don't think so, Della. He wants to be a farmer. He loves the land too much."

"That's just because it's the only kind of life he knows. Once he experiences this new kind of life, he'll like it."

"Couldn't we wait to take him until after his birthday next month?"

"No, he'll fall too far behind. He should start school just like the rest. It's always much harder to make up what you miss."

"But, Della, he's so small to be that far away from home. Couldn't he go to the one in our diocese?"

"Well, I was told that the preparatory in Worcester is the best. Our Otto is only going to the best. I want him to have the best and to be the best."

"You can't make him be something that he doesn't want to be."

Della was finished and rose from her stool. "When he was almost dying from smallpox, I promised God that if he let our Otto live, I would see to it that he'd spend his whole life serving God. If I break my promise, God will take our Otto."

"Oh, Della, you are too superstitious." Phillip poured his pail of milk into a milk can. He took Della's milk pail from her and did the same.

"I can't take the chance." Her eyes became glassy as they filled with approaching tears. "I'd rather have Otto alive, than near me and dead."

Phillip could see the conversation was upsetting her, so he discontinued it.

They continued milking the remainder of the cows in silence. Phillip didn't like sending Otto to that place. It was so far away. He really wanted Otto to stay here and help him. In a few years, when Otto would be older and could help him more, he had planned to buy more land. Now it didn't look like that was going to happen. Well, maybe in a few years Della would change her mind. Especially, if she saw how unhappy Otto was, and he would be unhappy. Otto didn't care for studying all the time, and he definitely wouldn't like being confined within the limits of a city.

Phillip sighed to himself as he finished his last cow. It was useless trying to explain that to Della. He had tried for the longest time. Finally, he decided to let things take their own course. Maybe, after she missed the boy for a while, she'd become more mellow to his idea.

Della finished milking her cow and left the barn. She stopped to gather some eggs and then took a slab of cured bacon out of the smokehouse. As she neared the house, she looked up at Otto's window. She saw him staring down at her. She smiled a big smile and waved happily to him. He did not return her gesture. Instead, he stared coldly at her.

Her smile faded. She felt hurt. She didn't want to hurt him. She loved him. Why couldn't he understand? If she broke her promise to God, he'd punish her and take him away.

Once in the kitchen, she began making breakfast. The pleasing, distinctive smell of the bacon filled the whole house. The eggs crackled in one pan as the potatoes fried crispy brown in the other.

Della walked through the foyer and stood at the bottom of the stairs. "Otto, your breakfast is done."

Otto just sat by the window. Who cares, he thought? You old bag! Eat it yourself!

She waited for an answer. After a few minutes, she called again. "Otto, I know you are awake. Please, come down for breakfast."

There still was no answer. So she went up the stairs to his room. Standing in the threshold, she said, "Otto, please, come down for breakfast."

Otto didn't move. She walked over and touched his shoulder.

With great physical force, he threw her hand off. "Leave me alone!" he shouted.

"Otto, please you must eat," she softly pleaded.

He got up from his chair and looked at her. The pupils of his eyes were in the corners of his eye sockets. The whites of his eyes showed so distinctly. His eyes burnt with hate! His look pierced her heart.

"Oh, Otto, please don't look at me that way."

He snapped at her, "I'll look at you anyway that I want to." He turned from her and looked out the window again.

"You'll like it, Otto."

"You mean you'll like it. You're such a fake. I can't understand why people don't see you for what you really are. I'm not going any place, especially there!"

"Otto, you have to, I promised God. If you don't, something terrible might happen to you. I love you, Otto."

"Huh! There is no one to impress now, so save your lies."

She held her hand over her mouth as the tears poured forth. She couldn't bear the pain of her own son looking so hatefully at her. Quietly, she carried her saddened heart down the stairs and into the kitchen.

She sat at the kitchen table and stared into the foyer at the stairs. Being in deep thought, she didn't see Phillip come into the house.

"Della, Della, are you okay?" His hand on her shoulder startled her out of her thoughts.

She jumped out of the chair. "Oh, your breakfast." She looked at the pans on the stove. "I hope I didn't burn anything."

"It doesn't smell like anything is burnt." He looked about the room. "Where's Otto?"

"He's in his room. He doesn't want any breakfast."

"Well, he's got to eat something. I'll go get him."

Phillip left the kitchen. By taking two steps at a time as he went up the stairs, it wasn't long before he was standing inside Otto's room.

"Your mother has prepared a nice breakfast. You come down now."

"I'm not going to sit at the same table with someone who wants to get rid of me."

"Your mother doesn't want to get rid of you. She just wants the best for you."

"Just what makes her an authority on what is best for me?"

"She's your mother, Otto."

"Big deal!"

"Otto, you show some respect for your mother."

"Respect! Well, I surely can't respect you, now can I? You don't have a backbone. I thought the men were supposed to run the family. You do everything she wants. You never do anything I want."

"Otto, give it a try."

"Sure, it's easy for you to talk. You're not the one who's going."

"I know your mother. If you oppose her, she'll become very defensive and determined to carry her ideas through. That's why I'm not pressuring her right now. After you are gone, I know she'll miss you terribly. Then I'll convince her to get you back home here, where you belong."

Otto saw a ray of hope. "Do you really think she'll change her mind?"

"When the reality hits her that you are gone, she'll want you back here."

"Oh, I hope you're right, Daddy. I want to help you on the farm."

"I know you do and you will. I promise you. Now come on, let's go down and eat breakfast."

"Okay."

Phillip put his arm around Otto's shoulder as they walked down the stairs into the kitchen.

After breakfast, Della tidied up the house. Phillip helped Otto pack his suitcase. In a short while, they were all dressed in their Sunday clothes and heading down the road toward Beechwood.

Beechwood was crowded today again. It was "stockyard day." Farmers from all around had brought animals that they wanted shipped to the stockyards. Since the train was the only practical way to get them there, everyone used it. No one wanted to drive fifty miles to take their few animals to the stockyard. Since the train only took the animals once a month, it was a crowded occasion.

As Otto waited in line to board the train, his mind went back to the many times that he and his father had brought animals here. He remembered how his father hated to take off work on a beautiful day and bring the animals down here. Taking off on a beautiful day, meant he'd fall a day behind on outside work. Of course, his father hated coming here on rainy days also. All the animals on the dirt street always made it so muddy. Otto didn't mind it. Because after the animals were on the train, he and his father would stop at the store and buy a few sticks of light brown licorice. He really liked chewing that stuff. He was going to miss that. Oh, well, maybe he wouldn't be gone that long. He hoped not.

Suddenly, he was boarding the train and then looking out the window at his parents standing on the depot platform. They were waving a good-bye to him. He raised his hand and waved to them.

It was scary being on the train by himself. What if he got lost? What could he do? Where could he go? Who could help him? He was all alone! He began to shake with fear as he stared down at his ticket--Massachusetts. What was that?

His hands began to perspire. He shot up from the seat and stumbled over the other passengers' feet as he scrambled out into the aisle. He flung the train door open. He wasn't going!

Abruptly, he stopped. The train had started to move. He couldn't get off. He saw his parents walk back to the wagon. He lowered his head in disappointment. They didn't even turn around to take a last look at him. He clutched his small suitcase to his chest. Somehow holding that made him seem less alone.

"Hey, boy! Get in here!" A rough hand pulled at his arm and dragged him back into the car. "Are you crazy standing out there when the train is moving?" The man was shaking him as he held his shoulders tightly in his strong hands. "Sit down and stay sitting." He pushed Otto down into a seat.

Otto began to cry silently. He didn't like this at all. If they had looked harder, they could have found someone to do the farm chores for them so they could have come along with him. He began to fear that he'd never get out of that place. They were going to leave him there forever.

"Ticket," shouted a voice.

Otto deep in thought never heard the voice. Something pushed at his shoulder. Otto looked up. It was the man who had pushed him into the seat.

"Ticket."

Otto didn't know where it was. He pulled the inside of his pockets out, looked on the seat, the floor, opened his small suitcase, and looked among his clothes. He had it a little while ago. What happened to it? He rose from the seat and started to walk in front of the man.

The man's muscular hand on his shoulder quickly stopped him. "Where do you think you're going?" he snapped harshly at Otto.

Otto became nervous. His face flushed red as he swallowed the lump in his throat. "I was sitting up there before. Maybe I dropped my ticket there." Otto pointed to three seats ahead of him. Two men sat there now.

"Stay here. I'll look for it." The man walked up to the seat and said something to the two men. They examined the seat, the floor, the aisle.

Otto sat breathlessly. His heart pounded, faster and faster! It felt like it would pop out! What if they didn't find it?

The man came back to Otto. "There was no ticket."

"Well, I had one."

"Sure you did, kid." The man grabbed Otto's ear and pulled him out of the seat.

Otto felt something crack inside his ear. It hurt!

"Think just because you're a kid, you're going to get a free ride. No way!" As he continued to pull Otto down the aisle, Otto tried to hide his tears. Through the blurriness of his eyes, he saw something on the floor. It was his ticket!

"There's my ticket." His trembling finger pointed.

The man let go of his ear, picked up the paper, and examined it.

"You're going to Massachusetts?"

Otto nodded.

"Well, I don't want any more trouble out of you until we get there. Get to your seat."

As Otto turned to walk back to his seat, the man raised his foot and kicked Otto hard in his one buttock. Otto fell forward and onto the floor.

One of the passengers, sitting at the end of a seat, got up and helped Otto to his feet. "Are you all right?"

"Yes, I am."

"Well, that's good." He brushed the dirt off Otto's pants' knees and helped him back to his seat.

"Thank you," said Otto.

"You don't have to thank me. It was the Christian thing to do."

Otto watched as the man walked back to his seat. At least there was one kind person, he thought.

Every time the train stopped, Otto closed his eyes and prayed earnestly that the kind man wouldn't leave the train. He was so afraid that if the man left the train, there would be no one to help him if that "ticket man" picked on him again. Otto huddled his body together timidly every time he saw that "ticket man" re-enter the passengers' car. He was so big--so ugly!

As the "ticket man" picked up his eyeglasses and put them on his face, Otto noticed that he had only two fingers on his hand. Otto wondered what had happened. As he saw the man's eyes meet his, Otto quickly turned and looked out the window.

They were entering a valley now. The train seemed to slow as they traveled along a river bank. Factory after factory began to pass in view as the train slowed more and more. Finally, it stopped. The "ticket man" went to hold the door open as the people left their seats, aisle by aisle.

"Come on, boy--let's go," ordered the man who was sitting in the seat next to Otto.

Otto got up and waited for the aisle to clear. When the majority of the people had departed from the train, Otto made his way down the aisle toward the door. As he walked through the door, he felt his foot hit something. Before he knew it, his head and all parts of his body were hitting the wooden steps, as he fell down them, one by one, onto the hard compact ground.

He heard a laugh and looked upward. It was the "ticket man." He had tripped him. There he stood, his hands on his hips, cracking out his incisive laughter. "Ha! Ha! Ha! You forget how to walk, boy?"

Otto stood up and wiped the dust off his clothes as he straightened his jacket. The "ticket man" took a step as if he was about to come after Otto. As Otto ran away, he heard the laughter again. The "ticket man" had teased him. He was not about to chase after Otto.

Otto stopped and waited until the "ticket man" disappeared. When there was no sign of him, Otto went back to the depot platform. He sat on a bench and waited. His parents had told him that a man was going to meet him.

Then, suddenly, in this strange place, familiar words fell pleasingly on Otto's ears.

"Otto. Otto Aslen."

Otto turned around in the direction of the voice. There behind him stood a tall man, whose short dark hair was frosted with bits of gray. He greeted Otto with a much needed friendly smile. The man had a stiff, white collar around his neck and wore a black, long close-fitting vestment.

"I'm Father Brown." He extended his hand.

Otto shook it and the grin on his face became wider and wider. He didn't feel so all alone anymore.

"Your parents wrote me that I should meet you here," said Father Brown.

"Yes, I know. They told me. It's scary in a strange place. I'm glad you're here."

"Oh, come now. I find it hard to believe that a big boy like you would be afraid." He put his arm around Otto's shoulder as they walked toward a surrey, which waited for them.

Soon Otto was traveling down street after street lined with houses and shops. Otto could hardly believe that people lived so close together. They didn't have any lawns or trees around their houses, just someone else's house right next to theirs. There weren't even alleys between the houses. They didn't have any backyards either like the people in Beechwood did. Children were fighting in the streets. Babies could be heard crying through broken windows. Was this where he was going to live? It was ugly! People lived like animals, one on top of the other. No privacy!

Besides being crowded with houses, the streets soon became

crowded with horses and surreys. Everyone was getting in each other's way. Everyone was cluttered into one spot. No one could move this way or that. So everyone just stood still.

A shrill whistle could be heard over the profanity being shouted amongst the people caught up in the congestion. Otto had never heard such words nor ever seen a man dressed like the one who was forcing his way through the crowd and blowing the whistle clenched between his teeth.

"Good, a policeman, we'll be out of here shortly now," Father Brown told Otto.

Otto watched as the policeman, by motioning this way and that with his hands, diligently moved the surreys one by one until they were all moving about smoothly.

Finally, he motioned to Father Brown and Otto. Slowly, they moved their way down the street. Approaching in the distance, Otto eyed a vast green acreage. It was lined with tall, green trees of all sizes and decorated with multicolored masses of flowers. Otto was glad to see a bit of farm scenery amongst the gray cages of the city. Otto felt a bit of a chill as the warm rays of the sun were blocked out by the umbrella of trees that lined both sides of the street they now traveled.

The surrey turned off the street and headed down a long driveway flanked with "well-groomed" scrubs of greenery. At the end of the driveway were two large red brick buildings. The fourth-story floor on each had dormer windows. One building had a tall tower with a large cross adorning the top of it. The other had a large clock perched between two of the fourth-story windows. Otto had never seen so many chimneys on a building. One building had ten chimneys. The other had eight. There were so many doors. Which one did a person go into? It was big. He'd surely get lost and who could help him? How would he ever know where to go?

Father Brown stopped the surrey and told Otto to follow him. Otto followed him up the steps and through the biggest door he had ever seen. Once inside there were stairs and doors all over the place. Their footsteps echoed down the long empty halls as they walked along. Just when Otto thought he could rest after one flight of stairs, there was another flight that he'd have to climb. He was totally exhausted as they finally finished climbing the last flight of stairs.

"Here's your room." Father Brown opened a door.

Otto looked in. It wasn't as big as his bedroom at home. There was only space for a small bed and desk. Otto walked in, he didn't like the room. It smelled stale, moldy.

Otto looked out the window. "Is that a barn out back?"

"Yes, it is. We supply all our own food here."

"Can I get to work out there?"

"No, that's just for boys who can't pay for their tuition. You can, so all your time can be devoted to studies."

"I always enjoyed helping my dad on the farm. Can't I help here also?"

"I don't think you really understand how lucky you are that you don't have to work out there."

"Well, couldn't I help just a little bit?"

"The boys that work out there have to get up at four o'clock every day, milk the cows assigned to them, and clean out their assigned stalls. They have to be done with all their work by six o'clock Mass. If they miss the Mass, it means two hours of extra prayers. They spend all day in classes unless there's farm work to do like baling hay or filling silo. Then they have to go to classes at night. It's not an easy task. If you're smart, you'll be satisfied with what you have and keep your mouth shut. Now come along, we'll get you a schedule, show you your classrooms, and whatever else you want to know about."

Otto felt strange, lonely, and scared in this new place. But most of all he felt homesick and being able to look out at the barn always made his homesickness worst.

****

"Mail! Mail!" The voice echoed through the hallways and into the keyholes of the rooms. The incoming letters of the week were kept until Sunday after Mass. That way, the letters couldn't interrupt the studies of the students during the week.

Otto rushed out into the hall. There was a crowd of boys all trying to look at the letters all at once to see if they got a letter. Otto stood back and watched. Letters were tossed about the table and onto the floor. The letters on the floor were stepped on and soiled. How foolish, thought Otto. No one would take anyone else's letter. So why didn't they let everyone take their turn looking through the pile?

As the crowd subsided and the others walked away reading their letters, Otto moved closer. There were only a few letters left on the table. Otto glanced at them. Ah! There was one for him! As he opened the letter, he hoped that his father had convinced his mother to bring him home. But as he read the letter his "ray of hope" became dimmer and dimmer. There was no mention of him coming home. In fact, his parents wrote of how they were going to miss him at Thanksgiving. He wiped the tears from his eyes, angrily crushed the letter together, and tossed it into his wastebasket. He should have known better than to expect his father to talk her out of keeping him here. He did whatever she wanted. That mousy little creature!

Otto slammed the door of his room and sat on his bed. He couldn't cry about his loneliness because his heart was bursting too much with hatred--hatred toward his mother for getting rid of him and keeping him here--hatred also for his father because he wasn't a man and didn't stand up to her. He'd get even with her! She'd regret the day that she put him here!

As the day for the arrival of letters drew near again, Otto let some of the hate disappear so a "ray of hope" could enter his heart again. But his "ray of hope" was again smothered out. In class and at night when he should have been studying, his mind would be filled of thoughts of the farm, and the day when he could leave this place.

His grades began to fail, but he didn't care. Perhaps the school would terminate his stay. Then his parents would have to take him out of this place and back to the farm.

One day the inevitable happened. Otto was summoned to the principal's office. He was a little bit afraid. He didn't like the idea of being scolded. Nevertheless, there was an inner emotion of joy and hope as he thought that perhaps this might be his last day at this place. Maybe his parents were in the office waiting to take him home?

He opened the door into a vast room. It had a coldness about it. Behind a large desk sat a stern-faced elderly man.

"Close the door and sit down, Mr. Aslen." The sternness of the words echoed off the high ceiling and traveled through every bone of Otto's body making him feel weak. His voice intimidated Otto. He felt as a child who had done something wrong and finally got caught.

As the man's eyes surveyed Otto, he felt that the man could read his mind and knew exactly what he had done and why.

"If you would be anyone else, we wouldn't hesitate to throw you out of here on your ears. However, since you can afford to pay the tuition here, we will keep you. Not because we like you, but because we like your parents' money. You can get a good education here if you let yourself. So if you were smart, you'd take advantage of this opportunity and learn as much as you can. You will be staying here, so make your stay here easy for yourself. As long as your tuition is paid, I have no intention of informing your parents of your poor grades."

"I don't want to become a priest," Otto protested.

"Well, then don't," he snapped. "Just studying here won't make you a priest. You have to be ordained to become a priest. Now, let's face the facts. For some reason your parents think that you should become a priest, so they sent you here. It takes money to run this place. Most of you, tuition paying students, don't make good priests anyhow. However, we like to keep you as long as possible so the money keeps coming in. Like I said, we offer a good high school education here. So why not take advantage of it and learn something."

Otto just sat there staring. His plan hadn't worked. He was surprised. They just cared about the money at this place. God didn't even enter this man's thoughts.

"If you have nothing to say, I suggest you go back into your room and study, Mr. Aslen," he ordered with cold unconcern.

Otto, in a trance, rose from his chair and went back into his room. He was just a dollar bill walking around to the people here. They didn't care about him either. Those God-fearing--religious--good people--didn't care about God or people--just money. If those kinds of people were going to go to heaven, he didn't want to go there. Well, his only hope to get out of here now was to try his father again. He'd write him a separate letter and plead with him.

When he had finished the letter, he took it and put it into the box marked--LETTERS TO BE MAILED--which set on the table in the hall.

Otto waited anxiously until Sunday after Mass. Then finally the familiar voice echoed through the halls. "Mail! Mail!"

However, there was no mail for Otto that day. Of course! He should have figured that out! He just mailed it on Monday. His father probably hadn't even received his letter yet.

He waited the following week also. He spent all his time hoping that his father would get up enough courage to tell his mother that they were getting him out of this place.

Sunday didn't come fast enough. It seemed like years had passed. Then there it was, Sunday, and there was his letter. He rushed to his room and quickly tore it open. "Oh, please! Let it say that they are coming to take me out of here."

He read on. "No, No! It can't be!" He sat on the edge of the bed. The letter fell from his hands as he held his head. The reservoirs of his eyes let go and his tears flowed. Oh, so freely! He wasn't even with him when he died. She had buried him already. He couldn't even look at him one last time. He was gone forever! It was her fault! If she wouldn't have sent him here, he could have been helping him. He had always gone up into the silo with his father. His job was always to wipe the silage off the steps so it wouldn't freeze on the steps. His father must not have cleaned them off. He slipped on one of the steps and fell down the silo. It was her fault! If he had been there, the steps would have been clean. She knew his father never took the time to clean them as he came down. He never had time for little things like that. Those little things were Otto's jobs--little but important. He lay on the bed and cried and cried.

The next time he opened his eyes, it was morning. Otto saw the letter on the floor. He hadn't finished reading it. Maybe she would take him home now to help her work on the farm. Quickly, he picked the letter up and read on. No, she wasn't going to get him. She was going to rent part of the farm out to other people, and some of it she was going to sell so she would have tuition money.

He crushed the letter tightly in the palm of his hand and angrily tossed it against the wall. There was nothing left for him now. This place was his home. He only had his books. Maybe he should lose himself in them. Then he remembered what his mother had told him a long time ago, "what you have in your head, no one can ever take away." Well, it looked like maybe she was right. Everything that he had ever cared about had been taken away--his father--the farm--his home. It was all her fault and his hate for her increased day by day.

It was about time for morning mass. He had better hurry! If he was late, it meant two hours of prayer. As he watched the priest do Mass, he thought. It was really an easy job. The pay wasn't bad especially when you figured the only expense a priest had in life was his food. The parish took care of the wood for the stove and fireplace. Some people even brought the priest food. Sure, he'd have to work hard for about twelve years studying. After that, he'd have it easy. When he was twenty-four, he'd be a priest. He'd say Mass for a half-hour out of a day and then be free to do whatever he wanted. It would be almost like being retired except he'd be getting paid. Maybe the "old bag" didn't have such a bad idea, about him being a priest. He might just as well accept things the way they were. There wouldn't be anything left for him to come home to. She was going to sell the farm, piece by piece, as she needed tuition. He really didn't have anything else to look forward to or do anymore. It looked like she had won.

Chapter 7
****
Dreaded Secret From the Past

Anna shot up in bed! Her heart was pounding. She was terrified, confused! For a minute, she didn't know where she was. Then her senses came back to her. She had that dream again. Who was in the coffin? Why were the horses running over her and the child? The child had a face now. It was Amanda! A cold chill went up her spine and shook her whole body. She had that dream over and over. Could it be a warning? Yes, it must be. Amanda was going to be killed by a horse. She started to cry. She had to protect Amanda. She had to make sure that Amanda was never around a horse alone. That had to be the reason why she had that dream over and over again. It was a warning!

She laid her head on the pillow and tried to sleep, but all she did was toss and turn. Throwing the blanket off her body, she sat at the edge of the bed. The clock said five-thirty. I was time to get up. Oh, what was today? Monday? She'd have to wash then. No, she washed yesterday. So today was Tuesday. Amanda's birthday! My how time "flies." Next year she'd be old enough to go to school already. Anna didn't like the idea of sending her to school. She was her baby, and she'd try to keep her at home as long as she could.

Anna pulled her feet back into bed and moved closer to Alex. He was sound asleep. His body was exhausted. God had been good to them this year. The crops were quite plentiful. They had gotten three crops of hay this year. The oat's crop was so good that they didn't have enough room to store half of it, so they had to sell it. For the first time in the five years that they had been farming, the silo was completely full, and they still had corn standing in the fields. The crops were plentiful and so was Alex's work.

Anna had helped him as much as she could, but she had a garden that had been just as plentiful. All through the summer, she had been putting pickles in crocks, canning beans and beets, digging and storing the potatoes and carrots. Most of the garden work was done now, she only had to make sauerkraut. In a few days she would have plenty of time to help Alex but by then his crop work would be done also. Everything always seemed to come at the same time.

She rubbed his back. "Time to get up and milk the cows."

"Ah, that feels good."

Anna kept rubbing his back and then stopped. "That's enough for now. We better get chores done. Today is an important day." She sprang out of bed.

Alex turned over on his back. "An important day?"

"Yes, today is Amanda's birthday."

"Oh, that's right. I think I'll take her along into town with me today and buy her a birthday present." He got out of bed and dressed in his brilliant flannel shirt and gray bib overalls.

"That sounds like a good idea. While you're gone, I'll make her a birthday cake." She stuck her plaid shirt into her farm trousers and zipped them up. "I don't care what you buy her, but please, no more dolls." Anna bent down and put the doll that she had just picked off the floor on the dresser.

"Okay." Alex laughed. He put his arm around her as they walked out of the bedroom.

Anna tiptoed over to Amanda's room. Very quietly she opened the door and peeked in. The little brunet head was lying fast asleep on the pillow. Anna always checked her before they went out to milk the cows. During milking she'd come in several times to check Amanda. There really was no need to always come in and check because Amanda always slept until they had the milking done and the barn cleaned out. Nevertheless, Anna was a very concerned, caring mother.

Outside the air was brisk, sharp, and so invigorating! A few more trees stood black, nipped by the frost last night. In a few days their leaves would turn yellow and brown and then whirl one by one to the ground. In the garden, the great yellow pumpkins stood in their solitude with their green leaves fringed and spotted an ugly, dead brown. A pale yellow was slowly creeping up the green stalks of the corn plants. The yellows and crimsons of fall were slowly opening the door to the bare, ugly death look of winter.

Anna liked the stillness of the early morning hours. Only the soft rubbery noise of the fallen leaves could be heard as they walked over them in the wet grass toward the barn.

"That's going to be our dinner today." Alex stated as he heard a pheasant cackling in the cornfield.

Anna laughed. "You've been saying that for the last week but so far that pheasant has out smarted you."

"His luck has to run out soon and today's the day."

"It's a nice day for Amanda's birthday, isn't it?"

"Yes, a nice day for work also."

"Oh, Alex, let's take off today. Next year she'll be in school, and we won't be able to spend as much time with her as we would like. Let's take advantage of our time together. After you return from the creamery, why don't we eat and then ride about the countryside. We could go to the park. Amanda likes the teeter-totter. It tickles her tummy, she says."

"We'll see once. Let me think about it during chores." He opened the barn door for her, and they went inside. Their milking cows greeted them with hungry bellows. The horses rose in their stalls.

When they had finished milking, they pitched the manure into an old wagon. While Alex drove the wagon out into the field and pitched the manure off the wagon onto the field, Anna gathered eggs and went into the house.

It was seven o'clock. Amanda was still sleeping so peacefully. Anna decided to start making Amanda's birthday cake. She mixed the ingredients for the cake and put the cake into her oven. As the cake baked, she tidied up the house. When Alex came in, she started breakfast.

"Amanda still asleep?" Alex washed up and changed his manure-covered overalls.

"Yes, if she isn't awake by the time I have breakfast done, I'll have to wake her." She placed the fried eggs and bacon in front of Alex.

They heard a little cough and turned toward Amanda's room. There in the doorway stood little Amanda. Her small hand was rubbing her still sleepy eyes. Her hair was all tangled about her head.

"Good morning, Amanda. Happy birthday!" they both greeted her.

A big grin came across her small round face and her big brown eyes lit up with excitement. "Today's my birthday! Oh, boy! Does that mean you don't have to work today? We can have fun today, Daddy." She climbed up onto his lap and cuddled herself close to him.

"Would you like that?" he asked.

"Yes, I sure would!"

"Okay, I'll tell you what we'll do. First of all, you eat breakfast. After breakfast you get dressed and come along to town with me. After we're done at the creamery, I'm going to buy you a birthday present."

"Can I have a doll?"

Alex smiled and looked at Anna. Anna had a big grin on her face as she shook her head--no way Alex!

"We'll see, sweetie. You go eat now, okay." He helped her off his lap.

"When you come back with Daddy, I'll have a surprise for you."

"Oh, boy! Another surprise! Gee, birthdays are sure fun, Daddy! Aren't they?"

Alex chuckled. "Ya, I guess so."

When he had finished breakfast, he went outside and loaded the milk cans onto the back of the wagon. Then he brought the wagon, which was hitched to the horses, up to the house and went inside to wait until Amanda was ready to go with him.

Anna brushed a shine into Amanda's hair, then neatly braided it, and tied the ends with a white ribbon. She dressed Amanda in her prettiest blue dress, which was trimmed with a white collar and cuffs.

"Wow, don't you look pretty," Alex said.

Amanda turned to Alex. "Do you like it, Daddy?"

"I sure do. You'll be the prettiest girl in town." He picked her up and carried her out to the wagon.

With her little hands, she waved a good-bye to her mother. She was so full of happiness. She was going into town with her father! That was a big thing for a little person--to go along into town with their father.

The ride into town was not a quiet, solitude one. Amanda was always talking. There wasn't anything that she didn't see.

"Oh, Daddy, look at that rabbit. Where do you think she lives? Do you think she has babies? Do you think rabbits have birthdays? Oh, Daddy, there's a deer! Aren't they beautiful? They surely do run fast. Are you going to shoot one this year again? Why doesn't Mama like it when you shoot them?"

Alex couldn't get a word in. She just kept talking and talking. He marveled at how her little mind could think.

"What are you going to buy me for my birthday? I'd like a doll, Daddy. Can I have one? Oh, look at the 'honkers,' Daddy. They are flying so low that you could almost grab them out of the sky."

Alex looked up. The sky was black with geese. If only he would have had his gun. Those "damn geese" would probably devour the rest of the standing corn. It didn't bother him too much because he had all the feed he needed, but some of his neighbors didn't. He hated to see the geese land in their fields and consume the corn.

At the edge of Beechwood, Alex stopped the wagon in front of an immense fieldstone building. He helped Amanda out of the wagon onto a large wooden platform, which was attached to the front of the building.

Beside the two huge double doors, which served as the entrance to the building, was a string. Alex pulled it, and a bell could be heard ringing inside the building.

Alex then started to unload his milk cans that were full of milk from last night's and this morning's milkings.

"Good morning, Alex," a husky man coming through the doorway greeted him.

"Good morning," Alex replied as he lifted the last can off the wagon.

"And who do we have here?" the man asked Amanda.

Amanda smiled and lowered her head. Suddenly, she couldn't say anything.

"She surely is a quiet, sweet little thing," said the man.

Alex chuckled. "Ya, until she's around you for a while, then she'll talk your ears off," Alex replied. His heart was so full of love for his precious Amanda.

"Oh, ya." The man laughed. He started to carry the cans inside.

Alex took Amanda's hand and followed the man inside. He emptied all of Alex's milk into a large container. Meanwhile, another man rinsed the cans clean and carried them back out onto the wagon. Alex and Amanda followed him. When all the cans were back on the wagon, they proceeded into Beechwood.

"I want to go in there to get my present." Amanda pointed at the general store.

"Okay, then that's where we will go."

Alex stopped the wagon and helped her down. Amanda ran quickly toward the store.

"Hey, wait for me." Alex chuckled. Her excitement elated his soul. She was such a sweet little person.

She waited by the door until he opened it. With her little hand in his big hand, they went into the store. Her eyes only seen one thing. The big china doll setting on the shelf behind the counter. It's dark hair was arranged with fancy curls and ribbons.

"Can I have that doll, Daddy?"

"Wouldn't you like something else besides another doll? You have so many at home."

"But not any like that. Please, Daddy, please!"

Alex looked at the doll. It was different. It was quite elaborate. Its embroidered, full skirt must have had at least six or seven ruffled petticoats under it. It was a beauty--but another doll! Anna would think he was crazy.

"We have a cheaper doll if you feel that one is too expensive." The clerk pointed to another doll.

Alex glanced over at it. The price was no problem because of Hans's will. They had the farm free of debts and plenty of money in the bank. Half of the money Hans had in the bank was given to Anna. In addition, they had the remainder of her proceeds from the sale of the land burnt in the fire. They would be financially set for the rest of their lives. It would all be Amanda's someday anyway. So, he thought, why not let her have the doll that she wanted.

"I'll tell you what. The doll will be your present from me, okay."

"Oh, thank you, Daddy." She bounced up and down as she clapped her hands with excitement.

"But you have to pick something else out also because your mother wants you to have something else besides a doll. Okay, sweetie."

Amanda nodded her smiling face. "Okay, Daddy! I love you!" She hugged him tightly.

"I love you too, sweetie." He kissed her cheek.

She walked around the store looking at things. Nothing else really interested her.

"What about this Amanda?" Alex pointed to a black slate surrounded by a wooden frame.

Amanda looked at it, made a distasteful face, and shrugged her shoulders. "What is it, Daddy?"

Alex picked up a slender white stick and made a circle on the piece of slate. In the circle he drew a funny face.

Amanda laughed. "Can I do that, Daddy?"

He handed her the chalk. A pleasing and proud smile covered her entire face as she saw her marks on the slate. She had never seen anything like that. It amazed her to see that she could make something.

"Would you like that, Amanda?"

"Yes, I would, Daddy. But I don't have any more room on here to make some more marks."

Alex chuckled. "We'll solve that problem." He reached for a cloth and wiped the slate clean.

"There now you can make some more marks." He turned to the clerk. "We'll take the doll, the slate, and several sticks of chalk."

"Can I carry the doll, Daddy?"

"You surely can, sweetie." He handed the doll to her.

She carried it so attentively outside.

"Well, I guess we can head for home now. I wonder what your mother's surprise is?"

Amanda's face gleamed with the biggest smile.

He took her hand as they walked toward the wagon. A loud BANG and then another BANG made Alex stop. Out of curiosity, he looked up the street in the direction of the sound.

BANG! BANG!

What on earth was that? A buggy without any horses was swerving left and right down the street. People were running out of its way as the man sitting inside the "horseless buggy" was frantically turning a handle, trying to get some control over the moving thing he was in.

BANG! BANG! Puffs of light blue and white smoke flew out from behind it.

Alex's horses were becoming nervous--skittish.

BANG! BANG! The noise grew closer and louder. The horses became more active.

Alex handed Amanda the slate and chalk. "Stay here, sweetie. I've got to calm the horses."

Alex went to the front of the horses and tried to hold the reins.

BANG! BANG!

The frightened horses jumped up at Alex causing him to lose his balance. He fell backwards, helplessly on his back. He could see the horses come over him.

He felt the great force of the horses' hoofs press on his legs and crush them. The metal plates on the hoofs dug into his stomach. He heard a crack and then a continuous sharp pain shot through his chest. Every breath became painful and harder to gasp. The hoofs gashed his face.

As the wagon wheel ran over him, he felt an unbearable surge of pain in his head. He saw yellow spots--red spots--then nothing. Everything was dark.

Amanda screamed wildly as she looked at her father's bloody, motionless body stamped into the dirt. "Daddy! Daddy! Daddy!"

The clerk in the store came out and took the hysterical Amanda into the store away from the gruesome and unforgettable sight.

"Daddy! Daddy! Daddy!" Amanda would not stop crying and screaming wildly. She clung to the doll tightly as if it was the only thing that she had left which had something to do with her father. She wasn't going to let go of the doll that he had just given to her. It gave her a sense of security and closeness to him.

Amanda looked out the window. Through her blurred vision, she could see a crowd around where her father had fallen. The crowd started to move apart as several men carried her father down the street into the doctor's office.

A gentle hand touched her shoulder. "Come away from the window, dear. Everything will be fine," the clerk said reassuringly.

Amanda looked at the wooden sidewalk where she had stood

outside. There were several large, black pieces lying disorderly on the walk.

"Oh, my slate. It's broken, too." She sobbed.

"That's all right. I've got plenty of them," replied the clerk.

"My daddy! Will my daddy be okay?" The words broke through her sobs.

"I'm sure he will be, dear. Now come on, let's sit down."

Amanda pulled away from her and ran outside. Her legs flew down to the doctor's office. She peered into the window. The doctor was in the back room with her father. With her little hands, she opened the door and went inside.

The room had a strange smell, a disinfectant smell. Quietly, she sat on a chair. She felt a little better. Through the partially open door, she could see her father lying in the other room. She cuddled the doll close to her as the silent tears washed down her cheeks.

****

Anna was looking out the window, waiting patiently for them to come home. It was taking Alex a lot longer than she had anticipated. Then she grinned. Her little Amanda was probably having a difficult time deciding what present she wanted.

Then she caught glimpse of dust flying about the road in the distance. That must be Alex and Amanda. The way the dust was flying, they were going extremely fast. Why would Alex go so fast? Amanda could fall off. Oh, she didn't have to worry. Alex wouldn't do anything to endanger Amanda.

Carefully, she surveyed the room. Everything looked so clean and neat. Amanda's cake had really turned out beautiful. It was so large. They'd be eating cake all week. Oh, well, Amanda's birthday only came once a year, and she always got such joy out of having a big cake. Anna had really splurged. She had decorated the white cake with slivers of chocolate. It was expensive, but it looked so nice.

Turning toward the window, she was surprised to see the wagon turn into the driveway already. It wasn't Alex! A strange sensation vibrated through every nerve of her body. For a second she was chilled. Something was not right. Suddenly, the dream flashed through her mind. Why did she think of the dream now? Had something happened to Amanda? No! Not her Amanda! Terror overcame her body! She didn't wait for the man to come up to the house. Wildly, she flung the door open and ran to him.

"What's the matter?" She was terrified of his reply.

"I'm afraid your husband has been badly hurt."

"Oh, no! Alex! What happened?"

"The horses and wagon ran over him."

Anna couldn't believe it! It was unreal! How could something that she had dreamed come true?

"Oh, my God! How bad is he hurt?" Her lips began to quiver. Her body began to shake uncontrollably.

"I don't know. I'll take you into town if you want me to."

She grabbed at him. "Amanda! How is Amanda?"

"She's fine. She was on the sidewalk." He helped Anna onto the wagon, and they rode off to town as quickly as they could.

Anna burst into the doctor's office door.

Amanda ran up to her. "Daddy is hurt." She sobbed.

"Yes, I know, but he'll be okay. You sit out here while I go in by the doctor." Gently, she sat Amanda in a chair. With her hands shaking, she knocked on the partially open door. She could see the doctor but not Alex.

When he heard the knock, the doctor turned around. "Oh, it's you, Anna, come in."

Slowly, she entered the room. Where was Alex? He hadn't died, had he? As she entered the room more, she saw Alex.

Her hand covered her mouth. Her tears flowed. He looked terrible! There was a big white strip of cloth wrapped around his head. A large ugly cut covered one side of his face. His chest was wrapped around with cloth, and he had splints on his one leg.

She ran to him and gently caressed him. "Oh, Alex, I'm so glad you're alive."

She looked at him. His eyes were so strange. He was staring-- looking past her--through her. It seemed as if he didn't even see her--know her.

"Alex, what's the matter?"

Sitting like a statue, he stared coldly ahead, not moving.

"Doctor, what's the matter with him?" Anna asked frantically.

The doctor sighed and shook his head. "I think, when the wagon wheel went over his head, it may have damaged his brain."

"Oh, no! My dear, Alex!" She lowered her head and cried in his lap. "My dear, Alex. What has life done to you?"

The doctor went over to Anna, gently pulled her up, and consoled her by holding her in his arms and patting her back.

"What do I do now? My beloved, Alex. Why?"

"I think it would be best if I kept him here a few days and watched him to see if there is any change."

"Well, couldn't I take him home and watch him?"

"Anna, be realistic. Look at yourself. You're a small, fragile woman. Now look at Alex. He's a tall man with a lot of muscle on that heavy boned body of his. You could never handle him. The way he is now, he'll have to be put into and taken out of bed, carried to the outhouse. There's a million other thing you'd have to help him do. You could never handle that big body."

"Do you think he'll get better in a couple of days?"

"All we can do is hope and pray. I really don't know. I hope so for everyone's sake."

Her voice cracked. "What if he doesn't get any better?"

"Well, if that turns out to be the case, I would recommend that you put him in Jennings."

"Jennings! That's a place for crazy people!"

"It's a place where they take care of people who can't take care of themselves." He looked at Alex. "At this stage, I'm afraid that's what Alex is, a person who can't take care of himself."

"Oh!" She sobbed. "He'd be so far away. I love him. I want him close to me. No, I won't put him there."

He held her shoulders tight and shook her a bit as to shake some sense into her. "Anna, be realistic, please." He turned her toward Alex. "Like this, only his body would be close to you. He's like a piece of furniture. He feels nothing. He knows nothing. You have to understand the care that he's going to need. You can't give it to him. Think of Amanda. How do you want her to remember her father? As a man, or as a thing that just sat in a chair--staring?"

"Oh, God! No!" She sobbed uncontrollably.

"We'll wait a couple of days, like I said. But, please, I beg you, don't fool yourself into thinking that he'll get better. Personally, I've seen things like this before and a couple days don't really change anything, but I'll wait to be sure. When you come back here, if he's the same, I would suggest you sign the necessary papers and have him committed."

"Oh, how things change. One minute I was so happy because I thought I had everything that I ever wanted. Then suddenly, it's all gone and I don't have anything. Was it such a sin for me to think that I had everything and to be satisfied with what I had, that God punishes me by taking it away? Did I think that I was so 'smug' in my world that God decided to punish me?"

The doctor held her close and gently stroked her hair. "No, Anna, I'm sure that God isn't punishing you. Things just happen. You can't see why now. As years go on, you'll see the reason. Then you'll realize why things do happen. You haven't lost everything. You have a beautiful little girl. She's part of Alex and that part of Alex will live on in Amanda. You are luckier than most. I have no living reminders of my wife. There is nothing of hers that will be carried on from generation to generation. As each day passes, we all learn some kind of lesson. Some lessons are harder to handle at first, but we learn and as we get older we become wiser. The only thing is the young people don't want to learn from our lessons. So they learn in their own way. Sometimes the lessons of life are painful, but we all survive. That's what everything is really all about--surviving. Sometimes it's not the way we want to survive, but survival is survival." Lovingly, he kissed her on the forehead. "Now, you go out there and take care of that little princess of yours. She's going to need you so much now."

Anna wiped the tears from her eyes and held her head proud and in control. "It seems as if history repeats itself generation after generation. I spent most of my life growing up without a father too. So I know the feelings Amanda will be experiencing. I guess, I've got a better start than my mother did."

"There you see, something you learnt and experienced years ago will help you and Amanda survive better."

She forced a smile. "I hope so."

"You'll do fine."

As she walked out and into the other room, Amanda ran up to her and clung tightly to her. "Is Daddy all right?"

"He'll be fine. The doctor will take care of him."

"Isn't Daddy coming home?"

"No." She tried to keep her voice from cracking. She had to hold her tears back. Crying now would just upset Amanda. She stooped low with her feet drawn in close to her body. "Daddy will stay here for a while. The doctor is going to take really good care of him."

"After the doctor is done with him then he'll come home?"

"Yes." She held Amanda close. It was so hard to say that. The thought that it might not be true, choked her up inside. It was so hard to keep the tears back, but she had to. "Well, let's go home now." She stood up. "What do we have here?" She stroked the doll's fancy curls.

"Isn't she beautiful, Mama? Daddy got me that as a present."

"Oh, he did." She smiled and then stroked the doll's hair again. "Yes, she is very pretty."

"Daddy bought me a slate too, but it got broke. The lady said I could have another one, but I left before she could give it to me."

"That's all right. We'll get another one." She held Amanda's hand as they went out the door.

"I'll see you in three days, Anna?" asked the doctor.

"Yes, I'll be here."

"Are we going to pick up Daddy then?"

"We'll see."

"Mrs. Leer, over here," a voice shouted as she walked out the door. It was the neighbor who had brought her into town. "The horses are quiet now. I don't think you'll have any more trouble with them. If you are afraid to drive home with them, I'll gladly take you." He pulled the wagon with horses toward her.

"No, that's all right. I think we can manage." She lifted Amanda up onto the wagon.

"The horses usually are so gentle. What caused them to become so wild and run over Alex?"

"Ah, Mr. Stoner, the banker, bought one of those Duryea brothers' automobiles. He doesn't know how to use the dumb thing, but you know how those rich people are. They've always got to have something that no one else has got. The dumb machine stinks up the air and scares people and animals half to death with its loud noise." He shook his head as he helped Anna onto the wagon. "The dumb piece of metal doesn't have a brain. You can't control it like an animal. It controls you. I tell ya, if they make any more of them we'll all be in trouble."

"Thank you for coming out to the farm and taking me into town."

"No problem. I'm glad that I could help. Do you need any help with the chores?"

"No, that's all right. Thank you. You've got your own farm to take care of. Alex has the field work pretty much completed. There are just the daily chores to do. It'll take me awhile to do them, but I'll get them done."

"Well, if you need any help, you just let me know."

"Thanks." She paused. "Oh, there is one thing. Since you drive past our farm every day to the creamery, would you mind terribly taking our milk along? I can't lift those milk cans when they're full."

"Sure. No problem."

"Well, you let me know how much I owe you for that."

"I drive past your place anyway. You don't have to pay me."

"I want to. So, please, let me know what I'd owe you for that."

"I couldn't take your money, Mrs. Leer. It's not right to take money from a woman or anyone when they've got a bit of bad luck."

"Alex was going to sell you that field of corn that he didn't need, wasn't he?"

"Ya, we talked about it."

"Well, if you take our milk into town, the field is yours. I'll not expect a penny for it," she said sternly.

"That's not necessary."

"It is for me. It's settled. That's the way I want it."

"Okay, I'll see you tomorrow morning."

"Fine. Good-bye."

It was a strange ride home. Anna had never driven the wagon. Alex always had. She felt awkward sitting in his place, holding the reins, and driving home. There was no one to help her down from the wagon. She had to get down herself. It was the first thing, among a long line of things, she'd have to do herself from now on. However, what upset her the most was the empty feeling of loneliness all these things would bring if Alex would never be near her again.

Amanda's eyes grew big with excitement when she opened the

house door and seen the cake on the table. "Oh, light the candles, Mama, please," she shouted.

Anna lit the candles. They watched them burn smaller and smaller. With a deep breath, Amanda blew out each of the five candles. Anna cut her a piece of cake.

"Aren't you going to eat some, Mama? It's really good."

"No, I'm not hungry." She rose from the chair and walked over to the window.

With her arms folded, she stared out the window. In her mind of memories, she could see Alex with the horses turning over the soil with his new disk plow and planting the fields with oats and corn. He was a good farmer. He loved farming. A quick smile rushed across her face. Except for threshing, he didn't care for that dusty job. His body would itch constantly, but he never had time to itch it. He always had to be there in the dustiest place right beside the thresher, holding the bags that caught the oats. He'd make restless movements all during supper and milking. When the last cow was finally milked, he'd run down to the stream. He'd soak and soak in there. He had found relief, at last, until the next day, when they'd be threshing again.

Her vision blurred as her eyes filled with tears. He was such a good father and a good husband. Their time together had been so short and now was it over? It wasn't right. They had a lifetime of living left. Why couldn't they spend it together? Would she never feel his arms holding her, feel his love, feel his warmth, and the security of his hand in hers? Would there be no long nightly summer strolls up the road or Sunday picnics under the shade trees anymore? No more "good-bye" kisses before he went to town or out to work? No more "horsie back rides" for Amanda or funny stories? Wouldn't there be the three of them anymore sitting before the fire making and eating popcorn? Would Amanda never be able to pull off his shoes when he told her that he couldn't because he needed her help? Amanda wearing his hat and coat about the house wouldn't be the same if he wasn't there to laugh at her "cute" sight. Wouldn't his laughter ring through the house anymore, his footsteps no longer be heard? Oh, God, don't take him away. He deserves the best. He deserves to know and see his sweet Amanda grow day by day. God, he's earned the right to reap the rewards of his life. He's such a good, loving man. Please make him okay, she prayed within her heart.

Because of her anxiousness about Alex, the next three days seemed to go so slow. Even with all the work that occupied her days, she just couldn't keep her mind off Alex.

Finally, the three weepy and depressing days of waiting had come to an end. Anna hoped and prayed all the way to town. She never heard Amanda and all her millions of questions.

When her eyes met the doctor's, no words had to be said. She knew. Her hand shook as she signed her name on the papers. As she signed Alex away forever, she doomed herself to life without him. She wanted to hold him, to love him, but there was no sense to even see him. He didn't know her. She turned to leave but then stopped and paused.

"Can I go back there?" She motioned toward the door. Her heart wouldn't let her leave. She had to see him--to hold him--to kiss him one more time.

"Yes, you can but why do that to yourself?"

"Thank you. Amanda, you stay here with the doctor." She opened the door and slowly went in.

Alex was sitting so still and lifeless staring at the door. He never even blinked when she walked through the doorway and stood in front of him. She knelt down on the floor in front of his legs and held his hands which rested on his lap. As she kissed them, her tears moistened his hands. Even though he couldn't comprehend, she had to be there and touch him. It was better than not having him at all. At least he was alive. As long as he was, there was always that little glimmer of hope in her heart. Maybe he would come home to her again someday. Their time had been so precious. She never really knew how precious until this very moment when the harsh reality of them never having anytime together again seemed inevitable. She gently squeezed his hand and kissed his forehead. "My dear Alex, I'll always love you," she whispered. She felt a slight movement of his hand as she held it. She looked at him, but he remained still. He had that dead stare in his eyes. She had wanted him to be all right so badly that she must have imagined it, she thought. She turned and went out the door.

The stiff body of her husband did not move. He couldn't move, but he knew how she felt. He could hear her. He could see her and he could cry and that's what his eyes did as he sat helplessly in that chair. His eyes cried for that beautiful woman that he could never hold again. He cried for her tears that he could never kiss away, and for his dear sweet Amanda who he would never see grow into a lovely young woman and who would forget him as time went by. He tried to move his legs, his arms, to call after her, but he couldn't. Oh, how helpless he was. How utterly helpless! He wished he was dead! Then he would never have to suffer the pain of seeing her and not being able to touch her--to love her.

After Anna and Amanda left for home, the doctor drove Alex to Jennings and had him committed into the institution. They gave him a comfortable room and put him into a chair, which was positioned in front of a window. There he sat day after day. He watched the leaves fall one by one. He watched the people travel to and from town. He watched them dig graves and wished the graves were his. He watched the trees stand naked on the winter white blanket. He watched Anna come and then watched her leave. She was a good wife. She came every Sunday and brought him a fresh baked pie. He watched the buds appear on the trees. Then the leafless trees and brown grass turn green. He watched Anna come with beautiful spring bouquets. His room smelled so fresh after she left.

The winter had passed and Anna had survived. Milking and cleaning out the barn was not such a big chore. She could do it and she did. A person can do anything if they really want to, she had always thought. But now spring was coming and planting the crops was more than she could handle. In addition, that place where Alex was, cost money. She had been using the money her father had left her in his will to pay the bills. However, that wouldn't last forever. Eventually, she'd have to sell the farm. Why not sell it now when she didn't need the money so desperately? If she waited until she needed the money, she couldn't hold out for the best price. But before she sold the farm, she had better find a job and another place to live. She'd ask the doctor when she saw him again. He knew everything that occurred in town. If someone needed a helper, he'd know.

Every Sunday after church, ever since Alex's commitment, Anna and Amanda would stop in by the doctor. After Anna made the three of them dinner, she'd leave to visit Alex. Amanda always stayed by the doctor. She never knew where her mother went. Anna wanted it that way because if Amanda knew where she was going, she'd surely want to come along and see her father. Anna didn't want her to see her father in his present condition. She wanted her daughter to have wonderful memories of her father--memories of him laughing, telling funny stories, and singing funny songs.

One Sunday after church, during their usual visit with the doctor, there was a knock at the door. Amanda rushed to open the door. In the threshold stood a petite, white-haired lady.

"Well, hello, my dear. What's your name?" the woman asked in the most charming voice.

"Amanda."

"Well, now that name is just as pretty as the little girl who has it."

Amanda giggled.

"Come in! Come in!" The doctor motioned with his hands.

The room was soon filled with a most pleasing fragrance.

The woman smiled. "Good day, Marcus."

"Yes, that it is." He helped her take off her shawl and hung it over a chair for her. "I want you to meet someone." He took her hand and pulled her over to where Anna was sitting. "This beautiful woman is Anna Leer. Anna, this charming lady is Mrs. Amelia Oker."

"Oh." The woman chuckled. "He has a way with words." She extended her small, wrinkled hand. "I'm glad to meet you. I'm sure."

The doctor took a sniff of the air. "Ah, doesn't that smell good, Amelia?"

She sniffed. "Yes, it does. From the good smell I can guess you didn't make it."

"Ha, ha, you guessed right, Amelia." The doctor offered her a chair. "Would you like something to drink while we wait for dinner to get done?"

"No, thank you, Marcus."

"Anna would you like something?"

"No, thank you. I don't care for that stuff."

"Marcus told me that your husband met with quite a terrible accident awhile back?"

"Yes, it was a most unfortunate accident. He was such a good man. It just doesn't seem right that his life should be wasted like that."

"Yes, life plays mean tricks on us all. Very few things ever turn out the way we want them to."

Anna rose from her chair. "Well, I better check dinner, excuse me." Once in the kitchen, she leaned her back against the closed door. Oh, she didn't mean to be rude, but she didn't want to carry that conversation any farther. She was on the verge of breaking down into tears. She didn't want a scene like that, especially in front of a stranger.

After dinner, Anna left for Jennings. When she came back, she was surprised to see Mrs. Oker was still there. Amanda was sitting on her lap and thoroughly enjoying the story that Mrs. Oker was reading her.

"Hello, my dear. You have such a lovely child," Mrs. Oker greeted Anna as she walked into the room.

"Thank you."

"And you have a lovely child too, Amanda," Mrs. Oker told Amanda as she touched the doll that Amanda held tightly in her arms.

"My Daddy gave me that before he got hurt."

"Well, that was very nice of your daddy."

She nodded her head. "My daddy is nice."

Mrs. Oker helped Amanda off her lap and then stood up to stretch. "I think my legs fell asleep. We were sitting there quite a long time."

Amanda looked down at Mrs. Oker's legs. "How can you be standing and be asleep?"

Anna chuckled. "That's not what she means, sweetie."

As Mrs. Oker headed toward the door, she reached for the shawl that was draped over the chair.

The doctor rose from the chair. "Are you going already?" He didn't want her to leave yet. There was something that he had wanted her to ask Anna. That's why he had arranged for them to meet today. Didn't she think Anna was right?

"Yes, it's about time. I have a busy day tomorrow." She turned toward Anna. "What time could you be at work tomorrow?" She wrapped the shawl snugly around her body.

Anna wrinkled her brow. She didn't understand. "I beg your pardon?"

"Marcus told me you were looking for a job. Well, I'm alone in my bakery. I'm getting too old and the town is getting too big. I can't do it alone anymore. I like you, and I'd like you to work for me."

Anna's face lit up. "Oh, thank you. I'll be there tomorrow at seven, if that's all right? Oh!" She paused and a troubled look crossed her face.

"What's the matter?" asked Mrs. Oker.

"I'll have to find someone to take care of Amanda."

"Ugh, that's nonsense. Bring her along. She won't get in the way. We might even put those two to work." She chuckled, motioning to Amanda and her doll. She leaned toward Amanda and touched her hand. "You never did tell me. What is your doll's name?"

"Sweetie."

Mrs. Oker smiled. "That's a very nice name. Well, I'll be looking forward to seeing all of you tomorrow." She stood up straight and touched Anna's hand. "You do know where the bakery is, don't you?"

"Yes, I do. We'll be there tomorrow."

"Thank you for inviting me to dinner, Marcus, and thank you, my dear. It was delicious. You're a good cook."

Mrs. Oker turned and went out the door.

Anna hugged the doctor. She was so full of excitement. Her heart was beating so fast.

"Thank you so much for mentioning me to her. Now all I have to do, is find a place to live. Then, I can sell the farm. First, I'll have to ship the cows to the stockyard. It's going to be hard to milk and also work in the bakery. Before I go home, I'll stop by our neighbor and ask him if he could take our cows to the train for me."

"If you need any help with shipping the cows, I'll be glad to help. I know Mrs. Oker will understand if you have to take a day off work to do that. She's a very nice person."

"Thank you. If the neighbor can't help me, I will need your help. The cows should bring a good price."

"Anyway that I can help you, I will. I know what's ahead for you. I've had other patients like Alex, who have to live in a place like Jennings. You have to pay for everything as long as you have something. When you don't have anything, then the State will take the responsibility for paying the bills resulting from the care of Alex."

"Yes, that worries me. I'm so afraid that once the money is gone, Alex won't get such good care. I've heard stories of how they make them live in filthy rooms in the cellar, and they don't feed them properly."

"Those stories aren't true, at least not at Jennings. I know that place. They will always take good care of Alex."

"I hope so."

"Don't worry. Why don't you stay for supper?"

"No, thank you. Dinner was quite enough. I should be going. I've got to milk cows yet and talk to my neighbor." She took Amanda's hand and walked toward the door. She stopped and turned. "Thank you again for helping me get the job. See you next Sunday."

"See you tomorrow," he replied.

"Tomorrow?" She was puzzled.

"I've got a sweet tooth you know. So every morning I stop at the bakery and buy some of Mrs. Oker's freshly baked goods. Of course after tomorrow, they'll probably be your fresh baked goods."

She smiled, turned, and went out the door.

She was so anxious about her job that the night hours didn't go fast enough for her. Working at a bakery would be fantastic! She liked to bake and now to get paid for it that was unbelievable! She could get a good price for the farm now. She wouldn't have to almost give the farm away because she was in desperate need for money. There was enough money in the bank to take care of Alex for a couple of years. The money from the cows and the farm would take care of him for several years after her inheritance money was gone. Then what? The doctor told her not to worry, but she couldn't help the concern. The question--how would they treat and care for Alex after the money was gone--constantly entered her thoughts. She wanted the best for him. She didn't want him to be treated like an animal because he didn't have any money.

Well, maybe the doctor was wrong about Alex. Maybe he would get better. Maybe some day he could come home to her and Amanda again. Oh, how she hoped and prayed. Deep inside her soul, she couldn't really admit to herself that Alex was going to stay like that forever. So she prayed and hoped and then concluded that someday everything would be the way it used to be. Until then, she'd pray and give Alex the best care.

A prayer is a powerful tool, but sometimes it gives false hope and keeps a person from realizing the truth--the reality and finality of things. So it was with Anna, she had accepted the change in her life but not the fact that the change was permanent. The change would make her life completely different. Things would happen that she had never thought would ever happen in her family or in her life. She didn't really know what life was all about yet, but she would slowly get to taste it to the fullest extent--and the taste wouldn't be a pleasant one.

****

Early the next morning, out into the crisp spring air they went. Anna had gotten up early to do the farm chores before she left for the bakery. The neighbor and his son were coming over later to take the cows to the train depot for their transit to the stockyard. As payment for his time, Anna and the neighbor had agreed that the neighbor could retain her two best milking cows for himself. All Anna would have to do tonight, when she came home from the bakery, was to clean the manure out of the barn.

The ride into town was as usual, Amanda was busy talking again but this morning it was to her doll. Anna would look over at her and smile. She was so kind to her doll. She would make a fine mother someday, Anna thought.

The town was so quiet and still as they drove down the street. Some of the store owners were just pulling up their shades. They'd wave and have a friendly smile for Anna as she drove past their shops. Then with the reins in her hands, she turned the horses down a narrow alley and brought them to a halt behind the bakery.

As she opened the door, the aroma of fresh baked bread pleased her senses.

Mrs. Oker was busy kneading bread. When she saw Anna and Amanda, she gave them a big smile.

Anna was surprised to see all the freshly baked loaves on the shelf and a counter full of donuts and sweet rolls left to rise.

"Am I late?" Anna asked.

"No, my dear, I'm just early. I thought I'd get most of the baking out of the way so I could spend time showing you where things are and how I like things done." She motioned with her hand. "There's an apron for you and a net for your hair. People want to buy our baked goods not our hair." She chuckled.

Anna put on the large white bib apron and tucked her hair under the net.

"How are you today, Amanda?" Mrs. Oker asked.

Amanda smiled. "Good."

Mrs. Oker reached into a big bowl. When her hand came out of the bowl, it had a smooth white clump in it.

"Here is something for you." She handed the clump to Amanda. "You flatten that out with your hand. Then when I bake the rest of the sweet rolls, we'll put a little sugar and cinnamon on it and bake it. Then you'll have made something too."

Amanda ambitiously started flattening the piece of dough out with the palm of her hand. Sounds of her little hand pounding filled the room.

Anna and Mrs. Oker hustled and bustled about the hot bakery with their white hands and flour-covered aprons. Anna had made a lot of those things at home--sweet rolls, coffeecakes, cream puffs, donuts, and kuchen. So she was no stranger to the task. Mrs. Oker only had to tell her where things were located.

Mrs. Oker eyed the clock. "Time to open the bakery." She untied her apron, washed the dough and flour off her hands. After removing the hair net, she fussed with her hair.

Anna started to untie her apron.

"No, no, my dear, you'll be working back here baking. I'll be in the other room behind the counter taking care of the customers."

Anna retied her apron. "Oh, I'm sorry. I didn't know."

"I know. That's all right."

A bell rang. "Our first customer." Mrs. Oker pulled the curtain aside that covered the doorway and disappeared out of sight.

"Anna, you can wait on this customer," she called from the other room.

Anna quickly took off her apron, washed her hands, and rushed out into the shop. When she was out there, she realized that she still had the funny net on her hair. But, when she saw the customer, it didn't matter. He had seen her at her worst already. It was the doctor.

"Come to satisfy your sweet tooth?" Anna said with a warm smile.

He nodded his head. "And to see my two favorite ladies."

Mrs. Oker gently pushed her elbow into Anna's arm. "He thinks if he flatters us that we'll give him one more eclair than what's in a baker's dozen and he's right. Flattery gets him everywhere." She chuckled and put the fourteenth eclair into the bag and handed him the bag.

"What is Amanda doing?" He put the money for the eclairs on the counter as he tried to peek through the crack between the curtain and door frame.

"She's busy making herself something good to eat," replied Anna.

"Say, do you use that upstairs for anything?" the doctor asked Mrs. Oker.

"Just for gathering dust," she replied.

"Why don't you rent it out?" he asked.

"I used to, but no one likes living up there especially in summer. The heat from the bakery makes living up there unbearable. Why all the interest? You want to live up there so you have easy access to my eclairs?"

"No. I was just wondering and thinking that it would be nice for Anna if she could live up there."

Mrs. Oker looked at Anna a bit surprised. "I didn't know you were looking for a place to live. I thought you lived out on the farm."

"Yes, I do, but I want a place in town to live. I want to sell the farm."

"Oh, my dear, I think you are making a mistake by selling the farm. Once you have land, keep it, don't sell it."

"I can't work the farm myself."

"Well, rent it out then," Mrs. Oker suggested.

"I thought about that. However, renting would not bring in enough money to pay for Alex's bills. Eventually, I'd have to sell the farm anyway to pay for the bills."

Mrs. Oker didn't understand. "I thought the State takes care of a person when they're in a place like Jennings."

"The State only takes care of a person if they don't have anything. If a person has something of value, money or a person owns property, all those assets have to be used first. Then when everything is gone, the State will take care of a person," explained the doctor.

She touched Anna's hand sympathetically. "Oh, I'm sorry. I had no right to tell you what to do, especially since I didn't know anything about your situation. If you want to live upstairs, you can. I won't charge you anything. The rooms are just standing empty anyway."

"Well, that would be nice. I'd be close to work, and Amanda would be right upstairs. I could sell the horses. That would also save on the livery expenses."

"Of course, it would be perfect. It's settled. You'll live upstairs. Every night after work I'll help you get the place cleaned up. Then on Saturday, Marcus will get a couple of men to help him move your things into town." She turned toward Marcus. "Please, watch the bakery for a minute."

Grabbing Anna's hand, she pulled her outside. They climbed at least a dozen steep steps. Then Mrs. Oker opened the door into a large room. A stale, moldy smell hit their faces. The room was draped from wall to wall with cobwebs. Some were unshapely jumbles of threads and some resembled wheels with spokes. The cobwebs clung to their hands as they whisked them out of their way. The floor was carpeted with layers of dust.

Their footsteps echoed through the empty room as they walked over to another door and opened it. This room was much smaller but was brightly lit by a southern window. Another room they looked at was even smaller. The only light in that room came when the door was open.

It was a small but a cozy place. Anna liked it. She could visualize her furniture decorating the rooms. She walked over to the black, wood-burning cook stove and rubbed her hands over its round, rusty plate. She smiled at Mrs. Oker. "I think this will be fine."

The next several nights before they went home, she and Mrs. Oker scrubbed every inch of the rooms. When Anna was at the farm, she worked late into the night packing their belongings and cleaning up the barn and house. Sometimes it seemed that she would never get all the cleaning done, but she managed by sacrificing her hours of sleep.

On Saturday, the doctor and two other men helped her move. As the last wagon load of their belongings left the farm, Anna took a last look at it. The stone farmhouse stood so quiet in its emptiness as the surrounding green-dressed trees waved "good-bye" in the gentle breeze.

Her sentimental heart was heavy with sadness. The sense of lost became deeper as the farm faded more and more from sight. There were so many memories. Amanda was born there. Oh, was she doing the right thing? Once it was sold, she could never get it back. It would be gone forever. Yes, she was doing the right thing. She had to get rid of it. She would need the money for Alex. They couldn't live on sentiment--nostalgia--things that had been--things that might have been. She had to turn away from the farm and leave the past there, along with the dreams that Alex and she once had.

She looked toward Beechwood, her future. She had no dreams for that place, just thoughts of survival. Dreams were foolish. They never did come true.

It was a difficult task carrying the furniture up the narrow steps. Nevertheless, they managed and before long the rooms were furnished with her furniture.

Anna hadn't seen Mrs. Oker and Amanda since the first wagon with their belongings came into town early in the morning. When Mrs. Oker asked to take care of Amanda while she moved, Anna assumed that they'd be in the apartment watching the men move in the belongings.

Then as the men and the doctor were coming down the stairs, they met Mrs. Oker and Amanda.

"All done?" Mrs. Oker asked.

"Yes," they replied.

"I suppose all that hard work has worked up an appetite."

"Carrying everything up those stairs would work up anyone's appetite," replied the doctor.

"Well, I'm glad to hear that because Amanda and I have made a feast for you all. Now come to my house." She looked up the stairs at Anna who had just come through the threshold. "You come too, Anna. We'll finish the rest afterwards."

So off to Mrs. Oker's house they all went for supper. She had a quaint little house at the edge of town. Inside the white picket fence, which surrounded her house, she had two sheep that kept her lawn nicely trimmed. The inside of the house was modestly furnished and immaculately clean. Everything, which was supposed to sparkle, sparkled. Everything, which was supposed to shine, shined. It was so orderly. Everything had its place and that's where things were put-- in their place.

****

Anna and Mrs. Oker got along just fine. Mrs. Oker had such a kind, loving heart. Working for her was a joy. One happy day of work followed another. The only day Anna didn't look forward to was Sunday, the day she visited Alex. She would sit in the room and tell him what she and Amanda did during the week. It was so upsetting. He'd just stare. She felt as if she was talking to a wall. She was so frustrated that she couldn't help him and that in all this time there wasn't any improvement. Her heart ached for him.

Amanda now stayed with Mrs. Oker when she visited Alex. Mrs. Oker has insisted that they spend Sundays with her at her house. Anna didn't think it was right to leave the doctor alone. He had been so good to them when they didn't have anyone. To solve that problem, Mrs. Oker invited the doctor every Sunday also.

Anna had only one problem. She didn't like the idea of Mrs. Oker constantly giving Amanda gifts. When she found out that Amanda was going to school, Mrs. Oker took her shopping. Amanda came home with a different dress for every day of the week. Anna never had that many dresses in her whole life. Mrs. Oker also bought her a pair of shoes for school, a pair for at home, and a Sunday pair. Anna really thought it was quite ridiculous. Amanda would outgrow the shoes before she'd outwear them.

Anna didn't say anything, she just sat back and shook her head.

It made Mrs. Oker happy and who was she to deny an old woman her happiness. She had earned it with years of hard work and probably didn't have too much left in life.

Finally, the day Anna and Amanda had anticipated came, Amanda's first day of school.

Amanda didn't eat too much for breakfast. Her stomach was full of butterflies. Anna didn't have an appetite either. She felt sad. Her little girl was going to school. Amanda wouldn't be all hers anymore. Anna knew it was the first step, in a series of many steps away from her. It was also sad that Alex wasn't there to see that his "little sweetie" was big enough to go to school already. Her eyes became a bit watery. She was going to miss her. Her small hands helping roll out the dough, frosting the sweet rolls, and licking out the frosting dish. The years went too fast. Where did time go? It wasn't right that during the best time of a child's life a parent had to work all the time to survive. Then, when a person eventually had money and didn't have to work so long and hard, the child was gone. So it was with Anna. That time was gone and now she'd see Amanda for only a little while each day.

Anna lovingly washed Amanda's face and hands. After braiding Amanda's hair, they went into her bedroom. There, draped neatly over a chair, was a crisp, white petticoat and a beautiful blue printed dress. They had picked out the dress the night before and laid everything out for today.

When Amanda was completely dressed, Anna checked her over for last minute approval. Just as Anna opened the door, Mrs. Oker was about to knock. They greeted each other with big smiles.

"Come in," Anna said.

"How do I look?" Amanda asked as she turned herself around.

"I think you look grand," Mrs. Oker said as she came into the room. "There is only one thing wrong."

Amanda's smile faded.

"You should be wearing something else." Mrs. Oker handed her a small box. "Open it, my dear."

Amanda's little fingers hurriedly opened the box.

"Oh, it's beautiful!" Amanda pulled out a dainty chain. Suspending from the chain was a beautiful deep blue stone. It was shaped so artistically and sparkled as fragments of light hit it.

Mrs. Oker took it and fastened it behind Amanda's neck and then centered it in front of her dress.

"It's a sapphire. It's the stone for your birthday." Mrs. Oker turned toward Anna. "I know her birthday isn't until next week, but I just couldn't wait to give it to her."

"It's very kind of you, but you didn't have to get her anything for her birthday."

Mrs. Oker stroked Amanda's neatly braided hair. "I know, but I wanted to. I enjoyed buying the necklace for her birthday."

"You're going to spoil her."

"Well, I might as well spoil her. Once she's out in the world, people can be so unkind."

Mrs. Oker noticed Anna's look of disapproval and touched her hand. "Please, indulge an old woman. I've waited all my life for grandchildren, and I have none. My time is getting short down here. Amanda has no grandma, and I have no grandchild. Let us live in our imaginary world and enjoy it. Maybe our imaginary world is more close to reality than you think. I know some grandparents who despise their grandchildren. Just because the same blood runs through the veins doesn't guarantee love. It does no harm for me to love her and think of her as my grandchild, does it?"

Anna caressed her hand. "No, of course not."

"I better go or else I might be late for my first day." Amanda grabbed a small metal box off the table.

"And what do you have in there?" asked Mrs. Oker.

"My lunch."

"Ugh, a cold lunch!" Mrs. Oker shook her head. "You know the school is right behind my house. If it's all right with your mother, why don't you eat dinner at my house every day?"

"Can I, Mama?"

"Oh, that's too much of a bother."

"No, it isn't. I'd love it." Mrs. Oker touched Anna's hand. "Please."

Anna couldn't refuse Mrs. Oker's begging pale blue eyes, nor Amanda's glistening eyes saying "please."

"Are you sure it won't be too much of a bother?"

"No, no, you come, too. We'll close the bakery during dinnertime. No one has a right to come into the bakery. They should be at home eating a balanced meal, not sweets," she said jokingly.

Just then they heard the big school bell ring through the town.

"It's really time to go now," Anna said as she took Amanda's hand.

With one on each side of Amanda holding her hand, they walked her to school. Once again tears filled Anna's eyes as she watched Amanda walk up the wooden steps of the red schoolhouse and disappear as the immense door closed behind her small body.

"Here." Mrs. Oker handed her a handkerchief. "I know how you feel. I felt the same way when my Regina went the first time. You'll be so proud of her when she comes home and tells you all that she's learnt. She'll learn a lot more than you and I ever dreamed of learning."

"Oh, it's so hard to admit she's growing up and growing away from me." She wiped her eyes with the handkerchief.

"Just because she's growing up doesn't mean she's growing away from you. I know how you feel. You're starting to feel unneeded. It's a terrible feeling to think no one needs you. Amanda will always need you but in different ways. She won't always need you to help her get dressed, to take a bath, or to make meals for her, but she'll need you for other things. She'll need you to talk to, to help her solve her problems, to comfort her when others hurt her, and to understand her feelings and moods. In a sense, her real need for you is just beginning. So, don't feel so gloomy. Smile and enjoy the years ahead that you'll share together."

"Mrs. Leer, Mrs. Leer," a voice shouted from down the street. It was Mr. Fremont. He was motioning her over to his office.

"Go see what he wants. I'll start the work in the bakery."

Anna walked down the street and up the stairs into his office.

"I'm glad I saw you on the street. You saved me a trip over to the bakery. I know it's not that far, but the town is getting so big that I've got more work than I can handle." He pulled out some sheets of paper from a drawer and placed them in front of her. He called out his wife. "Maggie, we'll need a witness." He handed Anna a check. "I've sold your farm. All you have to do is sign these papers." He handed her a quill pen.

Anna examined the check. "Gee, that was quick." She dipped the tip of the pen into the inkwell and signed the papers.

"Well, it wouldn't have gone so quick if the farm had been in your husband's name. Considering his current condition, there would have been a lot more work and time wasted."

"Yes, I'm glad that I listened to Alex and only had the farm in my name. At the time I really thought Alex was a little ridiculous saying, 'it was my inheritance and it should be in my name.' He didn't feel right about taking something that was mine, even if he was my husband."

"Ya, Alex was a proud man. If he didn't work for it, he didn't really feel that he had a right to it."

"How is Alex?" Maggie was concerned.

"The same. No better. No worse."

"Amanda with Mrs. Oker?" Maggie inquired.

"No, she's in school."

"Already! My goodness, time really went fast. The last time you sat in this office you were pregnant with her." Maggie took the pen that Anna handed her and signed on the witness line. Taking the pen, Fremont signed on the other witness line.

"Well, that's all." He extended his hand. "Take care, Anna."

"Thank you. I will." She headed for the door.

Mr. Fremont hurried from behind his desk to open the door.

"Thank you."

"Good-bye, Anna."

"Good-bye."

Outside the office, she paused and looked at the check. How long could it take care of Alex? She worried.

****

Dark-gray clouds began to spread across the sky and snow began to fall. It covered the leafless branches, the roof tops, and made white streaks across the brown plowed fields. The wind whistled through the keyholes in the doors and the cracks in the windows. It roared in the eaves and about the bakery.

Anna didn't mind the winter this year. She was inside working, and it was nice inside the bakery. Sometimes it was a little bit too hot, but she wasn't about to complain. Last year at this time, she was hauling manure out into the fields and sitting in a cold barn between cows. She froze her toes, her hands, and her nose. She wasn't making as much money as she had made on the farm, but she was doing something that she could handle. They were living quite nicely. She was happy. Amanda was happy. What more could a person ask of life but to be happy?

With the weather being so bad lately, she didn't visit Alex so much anymore. However, she had to visit him this week for sure. It was

Christmas. Through talk at school, Amanda had found out where Anna went on Sundays after dinner. Now she wanted to see her father. After giving that request very serious thought, Anna had made her decision. Amanda's memories of her father were to stay the way they were. She would not have Amanda remember her father the way he was now. Amanda disagreed with her mother's answer of "no," but there was nothing she could do about it. So as usual, she stayed by Mrs. Oker.

The snow crystals started to float lightly down as Anna left for Jennings that afternoon. During her visit and on her way home, the snow became heavier. She could barely see the road as she traveled. It was a cold, tedious drive but finally she reached Beechwood.

Most of the people had retired for the night, and the street was quite dark. As she approached Mrs. Oker's house, she could see her standing near the window looking out. Before Anna reached the porch, Mrs. Oker had the door opened for her.

"Are you all right, Anna? I was so worried about you." She shut the door behind Anna and helped her take off her wet coat and scarf.

Anna knelt beside the glowing fireplace and warmed her frozen hands.

"Is Amanda asleep?"

"Yes, she fell asleep on the sofa. So I carried her into the bedroom."

"I'm sorry that I'm so late."

"That's all right. It's not too good out there, is it?"

"No, I had to inch my way home."

"I don't want to interfere or be bossy, but I don't think you should travel all the way to Jennings to see Alex when the weather can change so quickly in winter. From what you told me, Alex probably has no perception of time. He doesn't know if you come every day, every week, or every month. You have to think of Amanda. If something would happen to you on the road in weather like this, what would become of Amanda? I love her and I'd take care of her, but I'm an old woman. Who knows how long I'll be here. I'm eighty-two already. I'm just living on borrowed time."

Anna took her shoes off and rubbed her cold toes. "Yes, I was thinking the same thing. I've decided that I'm not visiting him until spring, probably Easter. Easter is late this year. It's sometime in April. The weather is quite nice then."

"I think that's a good idea."

Just then a woman came walking down the stairs. When she saw Anna, she stopped. "I'm sorry. I heard someone come in. I thought it was Arnold returning from his walk." She turned to go back upstairs.

"You don't have to leave. Come down here and meet my dear friend, Anna."

The woman came down and forced a smile when she greeted Anna. She had a petite frame. Her cheeks had a healthy glow, but her eyes were so dull, sad, and cold. They revealed a soul that was void of love--dead. Her hair was odd. If she would do something with them, she probably would be a very attractive person. Anna had seen men with longer hair. Why on earth would a woman cut her hair that short?

"Oh, you are the little girl's mother, aren't you?"

"Yes, I am."

"Remember when I told you a couple of months ago that my daughter and her husband were coming to live with me sometime in January. Well, this is my Regina."

Anna was happy for Mrs. Oker. "I'm glad you're here. You've made your mother very happy."

"That she did." Mrs. Oker put her arm around her daughter. "Can you imagine how surprised I was when I opened the door this afternoon and there my Regina stood? It's going to be a grand Christmas!"

"Well, when you wrote that you wanted to give us the bakery because it was getting too much for you, we just thought why not leave and come right away. Arnold is quite ambitious. He couldn't wait to start working in the bakery." Her mind was preoccupied. She kept looking toward the door.

Anna observed her curiously. So she was expecting Arnold, who must be her husband, to come through that door any minute. She said that he had gone for a walk, on a night like this! Anna eyed the clock--eleven o'clock--and this late! Something was not right. In addition, Anna could sense that Regina didn't like her here.

"I think I'll wake Amanda now. It's time for us to go home." Anna grabbed her shoes that she had set beside the fireplace to get warm.

"Oh, she's sleeping so nicely. I hate to see you wake her and take her out into the cold. Why don't you spend the night here? You could crawl into the bed with Amanda," suggested Mrs. Oker.

"No, I've bothered you enough today."

"You haven't bothered me. I insist you stay, please." Mrs. Oker touched Anna's hand and stopped her from putting on her shoe. "Please, Anna."

Anna looked at Regina. She didn't want Anna to stay.

"No, really, I couldn't impose."

"Don't talk so foolishly. You are staying." Mrs. Oker was getting upset. Anna didn't want to hurt her feelings. So she agreed to spend the night.

Anna crawled into bed beside Amanda. It was cold in bed. She cuddled close to Amanda. Her warm body heat quickly warmed Anna. Soon she fell fast asleep. She had that dream of the horses and coffin again. She had to get closer to the coffin so she could see who was in there. But the closer she came, the farther away the coffin seemed. She tried walking closer and closer. Just a few more steps, and she could see who was in there.

A loud BANG woke her. Darn it! She only had a few steps yet, and she could have seen inside the coffin. What was that noise? She heard another sound. Someone was stumbling about the stairs. Quietly, so she wouldn't wake Amanda, she got out of bed and tiptoed over the cold wooden floor to the door. She opened it a bit. Through the slightly opened door, she could see the shadow of a man, a huge man. He was stumbling about the hall. His hands groped about Regina's bedroom door for the doorknob. When he found the doorknob, he turned it this way and that. Finally, he opened it and staggered into the room. He tried to support himself by hanging onto the doorknob.

"You fool." A whisper came from inside the room. It was Regina. "You're not sleeping in bed. I'm not smelling that awful alcoholic breath again tonight. It gives me a headache."

"Hiccup! Well--that's--nothing--new," he slurred. "Hiccup! Hiccup! Hiccup!"

"Stop that noise. You'll wake everyone up, you fool!" She got out of bed and walked over to the door.

As she started to shut the door, he grabbed between her legs. She threw his hand away. "Leave me alone, you fool!"

He lost his balance and stumbled backwards into the hall against the wall. "Hiccup! Hiccup! That's--all--you--ever--say."

"You get what you deserve, you fool!" She shut the door and locked it.

Anna closed her door and went back to bed. They both were fools, she thought. They had time to spend together; they didn't make use of it. She wished that Alex and she had time to spend together again. They wouldn't waste it by drinking, calling names, or depriving each other of love. How foolish they were not to spend every minute they had in each other's company. Well, it's their life, to each their own. She put her arm around Amanda's sleeping body and fell into a peaceful sleep.

A gentle tapping on the bedroom door was the next sound she heard. "Anna, it's time for you and Amanda to get up."

"Okay, we'll be right down," replied Anna.

Amanda turned over, sat up, and rubbed her eyes. She was confused. "Where are we?"

"Mrs. Oker's. You fell asleep here last night." Anna started to make her side of the bed.

"What took you so long? We waited and waited for you. Mrs. Oker started to worry. She thought maybe something bad happened to you." Amanda got out of bed and started to make her side of the bed.

"The weather was terrible. I could hardly see anything."

"Mrs. Oker's daughter is here," said Amanda.

"I know. Did you see her daughter's husband?"

"Yes." Amanda lowered her voice to a mere whisper. "He's strange. When we ate supper, he just sat in the living room drinking brown stuff out of a bottle. When the bottle was empty, he just got up and walked out the door. He didn't even put a coat on. Don't you think that was odd? It was cold outside."

Anna raised her eyebrows as she spread her hand across the bedspread to smooth it out. "Well, all done let's go."

As they passed Regina's bedroom door, Anna paused and thought her share. If Regina's husband was what she thought he was, a drunk, she hoped that he would stay away from the bakery. He could ruin

Mrs. Oker's business. Also, it would be difficult working if a drunk was stumbling about.

"Good morning, Amanda, you don't have very far to go to school today, do you?" Mrs. Oker said as she put a bowl of piping hot oatmeal in front of Amanda.

"No, I don't." Amanda sat at the table and then looked out the kitchen window. Everything was covered with a blanket of white. It looked so fresh, so clean.

"Think we can build a snowman, Mama?"

"I don't know. I hope so. We've built one every year. We surely can't have a winter without a snowman. Can we?" She smiled at Amanda as she sat at the table beside her.

Regina, already sitting at the table, didn't say a word. She just looked at Anna with her cold eyes. Anna felt uneasy. Regina's smug "better than you" attitude made Anna feel like "dirt."

"I don't think I'll go into the bakery today. I should go to see Mr. Fremont and get the necessary papers written up. Are you sure that you and Arnold want the bakery?" asked Mrs. Oker.

"Yes." Regina nodded.

"Well, you're going to get it someday when I die anyway. You can use the bakery now. So why not give it to you now. Besides with me not being underfoot, you and Anna can get to know each other better. Since you'll be working together, I think that's a good idea."

"We have plenty of time to get to know each other. Frankly, I think you should come to the bakery all the time until I know how to go about doing things," Regina commented.

"You don't need me for that. Anna knows everything. She'll help you."

Regina didn't like that at all. Especially since she thought herself better than Anna. It would be degrading to have that "trashy little thing" teach her something.

After breakfast, Anna bundled Amanda up snugly and then watched her walk to school. Turning from the window, she looked at the clock. "Time to go."

Anna and Regina grabbed their coats, scarfs, and muffs and went out the door.

It was a quiet walk through the soft, fluffy snow and over the small windblown drifts that covered the streets and wooden sidewalks.

When they arrived at the shop, Anna took her hand out of her muff and started to unlock the front door.

Regina nudged her out of the way. "I'll open it and I'll keep the key from now on," she snapped. "After all, it's going to be my bakery." She unlocked the door and then turned to Anna. "You know, I don't think very much of people who use a child to sponge off other people!"

A bewildered look crossed Anna's face.

"Oh, come on now, you know exactly what I'm talking about. You know my mother loves children, so you've been using that knowledge and your little daughter to get free meals and a convenient babysitter for when you go gallivanting about the countryside till all hours of the night." She stormed into the shop.

Anna followed her in and calmly replied, "Before you accuse me of anything, I think, you should have the facts about the way things are. First of all, your mother invited us to eat at her place. Secondly, your mother asked to take care of Amanda. I didn't ask her. Last of all, I don't gallivant about the countryside. I go to see my husband who is in the Jennings home."

Regina put her hands on her hips. "Do you actually think that I'd believe anything a 'trashy thing' like you told me?" Her words were full of hate. Her eyes like daggers.

"Frankly, I don't care if you believe me or not. I know it's true and so does your mother. All I really care about is what your mother thinks."

"Well, you better start caring about what I think. You're going to be working for me. If you value your job, you better be very careful about what you say and do."

With those words, Regina had taken away Anna's sense of security. Regina was going to be her boss before long. She didn't like Anna. Would Anna be out of a job? Would she make Anna find another place to live? Anna needed the job so she'd have to be careful about what she did and said. She couldn't take the chance of doing something that might jeopardize her job.

The days and weeks passed slowly. It was no longer nice working at the bakery. Anna made a point of not visiting Mrs. Oker too much.

She kept Amanda away from her also. It hurt her to do that because she and Amanda had grown so fond of Mrs. Oker, but Regina didn't like them coming to the house. Anna wasn't about to upset Regina, especially, since all the papers had been signed. The bakery was Regina and Arnold's now. There was one thing Anna was happy about. Arnold had never come into the bakery. In fact, she didn't even know what he looked like.

As usual, every night, Regina left home as soon as the bakery was closed. Anna was always left to clean the bakery by herself. One night, while she was sweeping the floor, the back door of the bakery opened. It was dark outside. She couldn't see the person's face. The silhouette told her it was a man. He walked into the room and closed the door.

"Who are you? What do you want here? We are closed. Come back tomorrow."

The man paid no attention to her words. He made no reply, just moved closer toward her.

Anna became afraid. She held tightly onto the broom and backed up as the man came closer. He was in the lamp's light now. She could see him and his face. She recognized him. Terror encompassed her body! It trembled! Her heart pounded and pounded! She started to breathe frantically! Her legs became so weak. She couldn't move. What was he doing here? How did he find her? Why was he here? She never thought she would ever see him again! He knew her secret! He was her secret! The secret from out of her past! The secret that she and her mother had shared! Oh, God, was he going to do it again! No, not again! She wasn't that stupid sixteen-year-old girl now. She had learnt her lesson. Once was enough! She had to think. What would she do? Suddenly, there was no more time to think. His hands were pinning her shoulders against the wall.

"Well, well, we meet again my pretty little one." His huge body hovered over her.

Not again, she thought. Forcefully, she shoved the broom handle under his chin.

He let out a shrill cry as his hands set her shoulders free. Blood began to streak his arm and cover his clothes as he held his hand over his chin.

There was no time to feel sympathy. Even if there was time, she had none for a man who would do to a sixteen-year-old girl what he had done. She threw the broom down and ran to the door. Wildly, she reached for the doorknob. After flinging the door open, she flew up the stairs two steps at a time. After slamming the door to her apartment shut, she locked it. She leant against the door to catch her breath. She was safe now--but for how long? Would he always be in the shadows just watching and waiting for the right moment to get her?

"What's the matter, Mama?" Amanda looked up from her schoolwork that she was doing at the kitchen table.

"Nothing." She was still trying to get her breath back. "Nothing." She walked over and stroked Amanda's hair. "Nothing is the matter." She looked at the door with fear. Would he come after her and knock down the door? If he did, she would kill him! Not so much for herself, but for Amanda! What had happened to her must never happen to Amanda! Never! No one had protected her. Her mother hadn't because she couldn't. Now, she was going to protect Amanda. She had to! Her sweet, innocent Amanda. She kissed her head and then went to the stove to start their supper.

In addition to worrying about the man coming up to their apartment, she was also concerned that the back door to the bakery wasn't locked. Regina had left her keep the key for the back door making her responsible for locking it. What if Regina found out that she left the door unlocked? Would she fire her? She would have to be in the bakery before Regina tomorrow, then Regina would never know. Right now, under these conditions, there was no way she was about to venture down and lock that door.

After that episode, every night after Regina left, Anna locked the back door while she cleaned up the shop. She checked the alley and the stairs before she went out and up to her apartment. Several weeks had passed, but Anna's precautions had not. One night when she started to unlock the apartment door, she found that it wasn't locked. She was furious at Amanda. Ever since that night, she had made such an issue that she should always keep the door locked. Now, here it was unlocked!

As she came through the door, she scolded, "Amanda, I thought I told you to keep the door--" She saw a man sitting at the table.

Amanda stood up from the table. "I had it locked until Regina's husband came. Then I didn't think that I needed to lock it anymore. This is Arnold, Regina's husband." Amanda motioned to the man sitting in the chair.

So finally she was going to meet the "poor" man that was married to Regina. Her months of curiosity as to what he looked like would soon be satisfied.

Her anger with Amanda diminished. Of course, Amanda had to let Arnold in. After all, it was his apartment.

As she walked to greet him, he stood up and turned around.

Anna stopped. She felt her body become chilled. Her eyes stared in total disbelief. She was startled for a moment. Then she walked over to Amanda and put her arms around her as to protect her. "What are you doing here?"

Amanda was puzzled. She could feel the terror in her mother's body and hear the fear in her cracking voice. Why?

"I come to talk to you," the man replied.

"I have nothing to say to you." She held Amanda tightly in her trembling arms.

"We can talk in here or outside. Wherever you want?"

After all these years, why did the past have to come back to haunt her? There was nothing to talk about. What did he want? Oh, she knew. She had an idea. She didn't want Amanda to find out her secret. The quicker she got him away from Amanda, the better. She was tense, if only he didn't blurt out anything.

"You stay in here and start peeling the potatoes for supper. Arnold and I have to talk about something." She kissed Amanda on the top of her head.

Anna closed the door securely behind her and whispered as they stood on top of the stairs, "What do you want?"

"You know the answer to that." He rubbed his hand under her chin.

She flung his hand away angrily. "Don't you ever touch me!"

"Do you like your job?" He rubbed his hands about her shoulders.

As she reached to throw his hands off her body, he grabbed her arm and squeezed it hard.

"I don't want to hurt you if I don't have to. Now be nice to me."

"You could never hurt me as badly as you once did. Now leave me alone."

His eyes, full of meanness glared at her as he squeezed her arm tight. "You know Regina listens to me. If I'd say the wrong thing about you to her, you'd be out in the cold--you and Amanda. Now why don't you invite me in and be nice to me."

"Drop dead!"

He threw her arm loose. As she lost her balance and started to fall, she grabbed onto the railing.

"I'm not forcing myself on you. I've got better things to do with my energy tonight. You think about what I said. Next time when I want you, you better be more willing." As he walked in front of her, he paused and eyed her body up and down.

She could feel him undressing her with his eyes.

"You're well worth the wait, but not too long of a wait." He puckered his lips and threw a kiss at her.

Her whole body shook uncontrollably. Her arms were covered with goose bumps. What should she do? Well, she knew one thing for sure. She would never let his filthy hands touch her. He was repulsive! The only other thing left to do was to find a different job. But where? She had such a hard time finding one last time. In fact, she hadn't even found the job, the doctor had. She couldn't ask him to help her again. He'd wonder why. She could tell him that she didn't like the job in the bakery. No, that wouldn't work. He would never believe that. He knew how desperate she was for a job and a place to live. She'd have to keep her eyes and ears open. Regina's customers were always informing Regina of the latest happenings in town. Maybe she'd overhear a conversation about a job. If someone needed help, they would usually put a sign in their window. She'd just have to get up early, walk up and down the streets in the morning and check all the merchants' windows.

So that is what she did, but she didn't have any luck. There were no jobs for women. Well, there was one and it paid well, but it made Anna "sick to her stomach" to think of all those men touching her and letting their stuff go into her body. Ugh! The way things were going. This was the only job around and the only place she had to live. What would she do if Arnold came back to the bakery--to her apartment?

She didn't have long to think of an answer. As she was about to unlock the back bakery door and leave for the night, she heard a key turn in the lock from the outside. Was that Arnold?

Quickly, she reached for the kerosene lamp and turned its wick down. The room plunged into darkness. She groped and stumbled about the room until she came to the barrels where the flour and sugar were stored.

The moonlight crept into the room as the door opened slowly. It was Arnold! She scarcely breathe for fear that he would hear her. Her heart sounded like a thousand drums.

BANG! He had shut the door.

CLICK! CLICK! He had locked the door.

CLUMP! CLUMP! His footsteps came closer. They stopped.

Light flashed into the room.

WRP! CLUMP! WRP! CLUMP! He pulled the shades down on the back windows.

CLUMP! CLUMP! CLUMP!

Through a crack between the barrels she could see him now. He was standing in the doorway and surveying the bakery. She figured that he'd probably go into the storefront of the bakery and look behind the counters for her. So she waited and waited. Finally, he disappeared into the storefront. She had her key ready. She jumped up from behind the barrels and ran toward the back door.

Something touched her arm.

RIP!

She turned around. There he stood with her torn dress sleeve in his hand.

"Tsh! Tsh!" He shook his head. "That's not the way to treat the person who holds your job and home in his hands."

Oh, God! What could she do now? She took her key and quickly opened the door. She clung to the doorknob for dear life as he tried to pull her away. He was too strong. She lost her grip, and he flung her across the room. He took her key out of the door and put it into his shirt pocket.

"Let's be reasonable and practical about this. Your husband has been gone a long time. You have certain needs. I have certain needs.

So why not satisfy your needs and mine at the same time. There's no big deal about it. You'll have a little fun in the process."

Anna slowly slid her body along the cupboards toward the back door as he talked. But he was quicker than she, he slammed the door shut and stood in front of it.

"Come on, Anna, grow up! It isn't going to hurt you. Give me what I want and you get to keep your job."

She felt his cold hand touch her sleeveless arm. She jerked away.

"Don't be ridiculous! It'll be fun. What's the matter you forget how good it feels. I'll make you remember." He leaned over and started kissing her. He kissed down her neck as he tried to open her blouse. "Take it off, Anna," he whispered.

She didn't want him to see her body. "Turn off the light first." Also, in the dark maybe she could get away from him.

"The light's just fine. If you don't take it off, I'll rip it off."

She swallowed the lump in her throat. Her body quivered with each sob as she moved her head back and forth pleading, "No, no." She could taste the salt of her tears on her lips. "No, no, no." She closed her eyes. "No, no."

She could feel his hands on her body as he unbuttoned her blouse. Then she felt a violent, painful yank on her body as he tore her bra from her body.

She crossed her arms over her breasts to hide them.

He grabbed her arms away from her breasts and pinned her arms against the wall. His eyes glowed with satisfaction as he looked at her large breasts and pink nipples. "Oh, it's a shame to let such things of beauty go to waste."

"No, please don't touch me." Her trembling words broke through her sobs. She could feel his moist tongue moving about her nipples. He released her arms. As his hands caressed her round hips and squeezed her buttocks, she held her hands tightly between her legs so he couldn't violate her there. Then she couldn't feel his touch nor his breath on her. She heard a clanging and a "zip" sound. She opened her eyes to see a huge, naked hairy man standing in front in her. She could see every muscle in his arms and the depraved look upon his face. Her soul screamed with rage.

His nude body came toward her. When she tried to push him away, he grabbed her two small hands and held them tight in his one hand. He began devouring her one breast and painfully squeezing the other. "Lay down," he whispered.

She shook her head. "No, no."

"Lay down," he ordered. His voice was threatening and his eyes wild.

Sobbing, she laid her body on the cold floor. She felt the floor's roughness on her back. He pulled her skirt up and torn her panty from her body. Before long he was lying on top of her. He was so HEAVY! She could feel his hardness stabbing her. She shut her eyes as her tears flowed down her cheeks.

Her mind blanked out the present and went flying back into the past as she felt the pain of that first time again:

It was the time her mother had been put in jail by the Count. Ludwig and Anna had come to visit her like they had many times before. However, this time was different. They sent Ludwig home and only allowed Anna inside the jail. The Count was there with the papers again. He told the guards to bring Anna along. Roughly, they dragged her down to where her mother was. They had moved her mother from her usual cell. She was no longer in a room alone. There were other cells in the room and they were occupied with jeering men. They were so filthy--their minds--their bodies. Anna had never heard such words. She had never seen men with such disheveled hair, clothes, and beards.

As one of the guards opened the creaking door, "cat sized" rats scurried into their big holes located in the ground floor. Anna tried to move toward the open door, but the guard held her tight in his strong hands. She was confused! Why wouldn't he let her go in by her mother?

At that moment, the Count put the papers before her mother and ordered her to sign. Her mother took the pen, broke it, and threw it at the Count.

He was furious! He motioned the guard to open the other cell. Motioning to Anna he shouted, "Put her in there!"

An evil grin crossed the faces of the two unshaven prisoners as the guard pushed Anna toward their open cell door.

"No," shouted Anna's mother. "I'll sign the papers."

The guard held Anna tightly in his grip as Anna's mother signed the papers.

"Let her go now. The property is yours." Anna's mother put the pen down.

After examining the papers and nodding his head in approval of his achievement, the Count ordered Anna thrown into the cell anyway. The Count and the guards laughed as the depraved men tore off her clothes and ravished her virgin body. Anna could hear her mother crying and begging. They just laughed and made dirty remarks. As Anna lay there, their dirty, evil, unwashed bodies moving on top of hers and pounding her body into the dirt floor, she looked into the faces that she would never forget. Now as she opened her eyes, she once again could see the face of one of those prisoners. She was his prisoner now--caged in a cell of survival.

"Now wasn't that fun, Anna, just like old times--hey." He lifted his body off hers and started to get dressed.

As Anna got up off the hard floor, her back shot full of pain. She hurried to close her blouse. As her shaking hands fumbled with the buttons, a hand touched hers. She looked up. Their eyes met. She backed away.

"Don't worry. I won't do it again, at least not tonight." He rubbed his fingers inside her unbuttoned blouse about the uncovered part of her breasts.

"Too bad I didn't know you were in town sooner. We could have had fun together a long time ago." He laughed.

"I curse the day that I first met you. If I had a choice--"

"Well, it's either you or Amanda."

"You monstrous animal! She's only six years old. If you ever talk to her again, I'll kill you!"

"Tsh! Tsh! Such language from a lady. My, my."

As she raised her hand to hit him, he grabbed it, moved his body closer to hers, and twisted her hand behind her back. "Don't spoil a perfect night, Anna."

He released her and walked to the door. Taking her key out of his pocket, he unlocked the door. Turning around, he tossed the key at her. The smirk of a young boy, who had just gotten away with something, flashed across his face. He puckered his lips and threw her a kiss. As he departed from the room, he let the door open. The outside coldness filled the room as the snowflakes fell inside the doorway onto the wooden floor.

Anna stood there staring out into the darkness for a long time. Is this what her life had finally come down to? She felt like a piece of dirty, cheap trash. What if anyone found out? How could she live here if they did? Everyone would call her a whore. She was an adulteress! What if she became pregnant? My, God! What could she do? What would everyone think? She had tried to lead a good life. She had never done anything wrong, not until now. Why was everything turning out so wrongly? She wished she could die. Her skin crawled as she thought of that animal touching her like that. Oh, why did Alex have to leave her like this? How she wished, he was here beside her now. But he wasn't, she was alone! The happiness that used to fill her body died. She wished all her tomorrows would never come because Arnold would be in them.

The next time with Arnold bothered Anna less. By the third and fourth time, she came to accept it as the way things just were. She would just lay there without emotion, turn her head, and stare endlessly at the wall until he was done. It didn't even bother Arnold. He just wanted a body. It didn't matter to him if it moved or not, just so it was there and he got his "thrills."

The first couple of times that Anna visited Alex she felt guilty. However, the guilt subsided as she reasoned with herself that she had to do it to survive.

****

My Dearest Otto,

I can no longer live with this intense loneliness and keep my promise to God. Having you so far away is like not having you at all. It is worse than if you were dead. Longing for you all the time fills my heart with pain. I want you home with me. I know your resentment for me has been the reason that you have never answered any of my letters since your father died. But please, just this once put your resentment aside and answer this letter. Let me know if you still want to come home. If you do,

I'll inform the head of the seminary and stop your tuition payments and tell him to send you home to me where you belong.

I love you, Otto. Please, answer this letter. Please, come home. Please.

Love Always,
Ma

Neatly, Della folded the letter and sealed it in an envelope. The inkwell was dry so she placed the letter on top of the oak desk. Tomorrow she would address it and mail it to Otto.

Time had not been kind to thirty-eight-year-old Della. Failing eyesight made her eyes tire easily. After a couple minutes of reading or writing, her vision would become blurred. Gathering dust on the desk was a pair of wire rim glasses. They didn't help her sight. So she never wore them.

Flaming surges of pain shot through her hips as she got up from the chair. Barely able to walk because of stiffness and pain, she moved slowly down the basement steps to the root cellar.

Rows of canned vegetables sat on the sagging wooden shelves. Setting on the top shelf was a dusty, black enamel kettle. After examining it, Della decided that she'd need a new kettle for canning this year. Rust had caused small, pin-sized holes to occur where the enamel had been chipped off by previous years of use.

Sentimental thoughts flowed through her mind. Her sweet little Otto and Phillip had given her that kettle for Christmas one year. With a big smile on his face, Otto took the kettle from under the tree and gave it to her. It was wrapped in white paper and covered with strands and strands of red ribbons and bows. Otto showed her the finger that he had used to help Phillip make the bows. Gently, she hugged the kettle close to her heart as if it were a child. Never in all the years that he was growing up did she hug Otto. She was afraid hugging him would make him a "mama baby," a sissy. All those years and never once did she really show the boy how much she really loved him, and she did with all her heart and soul. Now, all she wanted was a chance. One chance to show him how she really felt, but was it too late? He was eighteen now. What did he look like? Did he look like Phillip? What kind of a man had he grown into? Was he kind and loving like Phillip?

Placing the kettle back on the shelf, she decided to keep it. She couldn't use it for anything, but she couldn't throw it away. Throwing it away would be like throwing away a cherished memory. It was a part of Otto and Phillip. They had given it to her. It was like having them close to her. That's all she had now, things and the memories that went along with them.

After pausing for a moment to decide what she wanted to eat with her meatloaf, she grabbed a jar of her green beans. Otto didn't like them. Therefore, it was a good idea for her to eat most of them before he came home--if he wanted to come home--and if he really did.

Going back up the stairs with her bad hip was a painful struggle, but she made up.

Scalding steam rose from the kettle full of potatoes as she poured the hot potato water over the beans, which she had just poured into another kettle. Since she had cooked them when she canned them, she saw no need for boiling them again. Letting them set a couple minutes in the hot potato water would warm them sufficiently for her.

Having to eat alone was the loneliest thing of all. She was glad that she only had to sit at the table once a day. Having to eat that one meal was a chore. It was depressing to always eat alone.

After supper, she sat in her rocker and stared out the window as usual. That was all that she had to do. And so, she rocked the lonely hours away.

Most of the land that had belonged to the farm had been sold. She only had five acres left. On that acreage stood the house, barn, a small shed, and the pond. Never in a million years would she ever sell that pond. Otto and Phillip had so much fun in that pond. That pond was the first place Phillip and she had made love in this new land. It was the first time that she had let herself love Phillip to the fullest.

Sixteen years ago, when they moved here, she would have never guessed that Beechwood would almost be at her doorstep, but it was. Most of the land that she had sold was covered with new houses and shops.

A gentle tap on her windowpane broke her thoughts. As she looked down, a friendly smile greeted her. It was Antonio, the little boy who lived next door. Under all that winter clothing his little, brown face was hardly noticeable.

With a smile, she motioned him inside the house.

"Hi, Mrs. Aslen." He came into the house and walked over to her. "How are you today?"

"Oh, I'm just fine, Antonio." She shivered from the coldness that he had carried into the room.

"Here's your Thursday paper."

"Thank you, Antonio." She took the paper from his hands. "There are some cookies in the jar on the table. Go take a few. Take some home for the rest of your family also."

"Gee, thanks. Your cookies are always so good." He rushed into the kitchen. A few minutes later he came out munching on one and stuffing a few more into his pockets.

"See you next Thursday." Out the door he went, leaving her alone inside the quiet house.

Beside the rocker was a brown wicker basket full of multicolored yarn. Out of the basket she pulled a large crochet hook and a ball of yarn. The large loops of crocheting threads used in making an afghan were much easier for her to see than the small loops used in making dainty dollies. So she crocheted afghans until her vision became blurred. When it did, she would stop, close her eyes and rest her head on the back of her rocker. It would be the same when she tried to read the newspaper. It would take her all week to read the newspaper's four pages. She had thought of discontinuing her subscription, but she liked being informed of the local happenings. More important though, it was a reason for Antonio to come and for her to give him her homemade cookies. She had few things in life to look forward to. Maybe that would change with her letter to Otto.

Several hours after darkness, she went to bed only to be awakened a few hours later with a headache that pounded and pounded inside her head. Her stomach muscles began to twist and turn inside of her. She crunched her body into a ball shape to try and stop the pain, but it became worst and worst. Climbing out of bed, she fell onto the floor with intense stabbing pain. She couldn't walk. On the floor she lay all curled up with her stomach twisting and turning inside of her.

She couldn't tolerate the pain. Her insides were being torn apart. Beads of sweat made her pajamas wet and stick to her body. Weakness overcame her body. Paralysis captured her arms and legs. With great effort, she swallowed the saliva in her mouth. The word "help" stuck in her throat. Her lips were glued together, they refused to part and let the word out. Desperately, she wanted to crawl out the door and get someone to help her, but her thoughts were imprisoned within her mind. They wouldn't come out and tell her body what to do.

Soon it didn't matter. She couldn't see the door. A heavy weight was resting on her chest. Every breath in and out became a struggle.

In the darkness of the room, she lay in pain for hours. Only the ticking of the clock and her last gasping breath filled the silence of that room. In that moment, her struggle for life had ended and Della's pain had ceased. Her body was free from the agony of its loneliness. Peacefully, her body lay on the bedroom floor. She had joined Phillip and left Otto alone.

A week later it was Antonio who found Della's body. Seeing something like that is not the best thing for a child. Della wouldn't have wanted it that way, but she couldn't do too much about that.

When Otto was notified, he felt no emotion, no sense of lose. His hatred for her had penetrated so deeply that it now controlled his very soul. His only regret was that she hadn't died six years ago instead of his father.

Otto never returned home to see her grave or to settle her estate. The property was left abandoned and the usual tenants of an abandoned building moved in--rats--mice--deterioration.

Now without any money for tuition and no place to go, Otto would have to work to stay at the seminary. Instead of him watching the other boys from his window, another boy watched from the same window as he worked.

While on the farm at home, he had never experienced such hard work. His father had always let him do the easy jobs. The jobs he knew that Otto would consider fun. Things were different now. He had to do the dirty, backbreaking work along with the other boys. He had to shovel out the wet, unpleasant smelling manure of more than a hundred cows every morning. When that was done, he had to climb up into the silo and throw enough silage down for the morning and evening feedings. The sweet fermented smell of the silage made him sick. When he saw all those cows every morning in their stalls, he thought he'd never finish milking.

When summer came, the acres and acres of hay, oats, and corn depressed Otto. After seeing the hard side of farming and suffering with calloused hands, Otto was glad that he was studying to be a priest. Hard work just didn't agree with him.

Another winter passed and Della's letter was still on that desk collecting layers and layers of dust.

CRASH! A ball came flying through the window near the desk.

"Go in and get it, Antonio," a voice shouted.

"I'm not getting it. You hit it. You go get it!"

"I'm not going in there. There are rats in there. See there are some running beside the house."

"Rats aren't going to hurt you," said Antonio.

"My ma says they can bite and attack people. She said that house is full of them, and I shouldn't go in there."

"Do they really bite?" asked Antonio.

"Yup, that's what Ma says."

"Do you think your dad will buy us another ball?" asked Antonio.

"If he doesn't, we can buy one together. I'm not taking a chance on getting bit."

"Me either," replied Antonio.

So the ball stayed inside the house. Strong gusts of wind would whirl through the broken window and fly about the room. One such wind lifted Della's letter off the desk and tossed it behind the desk out of view.

Otto would never know how much his mother had really loved him. Instead he grew into a man thinking his mother had despised him and only wanted to get rid of him. Intensely, he hated her for that and for her dominance over his life and his father's. Frustration and anger accompanied his flaming hatred because he never had the chance to punish her for what she had done or the chance to dominant her like she had him. He wanted to hurt her, but he couldn't. The frustration grew inside of him. He was a bomb of anger and hate just waiting to explode.

Chapter 8
****
Illegitimate Child

Gently, Anna rocked in the black rocker as she nursed the sweet little bundle resting in her arms. Deep feelings of love surged in her heart for the child even though she despised the child's father.

Such little hands and feet, he was so adorable.

What kind of life would that sweet little person have? People were so unkind. It depressed her when she thought about the rude remarks that people made to her about her illegitimate child. Even the children in school were mean to Amanda. Much too often Amanda would come home from school with tears in her eyes and torn clothes from the other schoolchildren pushing her around.

Her heart laden with sadness, she began to cry--not for herself but for her children. She couldn't block the hurt of the sarcastic remarks. No matter how depressed she was about other people. She never let that depression interfere with how she treated Henry and Amanda. They could always depend on her for kindness and love. Never once did she raise a hand or her voice to her children.

When Henry's hunger was satisfied, he fell asleep. Carefully, she laid him into the bassinet and pushed it into Amanda's room. In about four hours he would probably wake up for another feeding. By that time Amanda would be off to school. There were only a few days of school remaining and soon Amanda would be around to amuse Henry while she worked.

Ever since Henry was born six months ago, Anna had been getting up extra early. By the time Regina came into the bakery, Anna had almost everything done. The only thing left to do was to bake the raised doughs. Anna did this so Regina wouldn't fire her for taking time off during the day to feed and care for Henry. With two small children to care for, she needed that job more than ever.

Arnold hadn't come around to bother her since the child was born, but that didn't ease her mind. She knew it was just a matter of time before he'd show his disgusting face. Day after day she thought of that and tried to think of something that she could do to make him leave her alone if he came back and wanted to resume his relationship with her. She was desperate. She didn't want to become pregnant again--not with his child. If Arnold had come around while she was constantly nursing Henry, she wouldn't have had to worry about it. However, now that she had started to wean Henry, the danger of pregnancy existed again.

Late one July night, Anna's fears were confirmed. As she was about to leave the bakery, a drunken figure swayed in the doorway. Arnold! As he approached and touched her, she pulled away.

"Oh, come on, Anna, we're old friends. Don't be that way."

She raised her eyebrow. Old friends! Like--heck! She thought. You disgusting pig aren't going to touch me--not anymore."

Reeking of alcohol, he huddled over her.

Pushing him away, she ran toward the open door.

Regaining his balance, he staggered over to her. "Come on, Anna, you know you like it."

"You don't know anything about me. So don't tell me what I like and don't like. You disgust me! I hate you! I hate you!"

Stroking her hair, he slurred out his words, "Whether you like me or not, you have to be nice to me or you and your little 'bastard' will be out in the cold."

"He's my child. He's your 'bastard' and you know it." Her angry eyes shot out at him.

"I don't know anything. Like you said, 'I don't know anything about you.' Oh--now--that's not really true--is it? I know you got a great little body." His hand started to slide down onto her breasts and stroke them.

With all her strength, she slapped his face.

Becoming furious, he grabbed her shoulders and shook her violently. "Don't you ever hit me! Don't you ever hit me again!"

"Let me go or I'll scream my head off."

He laughed. "What are you going to say when half the town comes running in here? They'll laugh in your face when you tell them I tried to force myself on you."

"Well, I bet one face won't be laughing too much when I tell her whose baby that is upstairs."

"You can't prove it's mine."

"And you can't prove he isn't."

"You won't tell her. This job means too much to you. You need it."

"You have just as much to lose as I do if she finds out about the baby."

"I won't lose anything."

"Are you that sure that you'd take that chance?"

"Why would you tell her?"

"If you don't leave me alone, I'm going to tell her."

Realizing she was serious, he released her shoulders. A sober look came across his face.

"You don't want to take the chance of Regina kicking you out, then you'd have to work. You couldn't sit around drinking all day and spending half the night with other women then, could you?"

"She won't kick me out."

"You don't know what she'd do for sure. Just to be safe, you better leave me alone."

Surveying her, he said, "Ya, you aren't anything special. I can get the same thing from others without the risk--no sense 'rocking the boat.' I know when to quit--when I'm ahead." As he walked out the door, he turned to her. "It was sweet why it lasted but all things must end." Puckering his lips, he threw her a kiss. "So long, my sweet."

Anna breathe a sigh of relief. A heavy load had just been lifted from her. Finally, she was free--as free as a butterfly. A feeling of overpowering joy saturated her body. She had won. It felt so good to be the victor.

After locking the door, she paused and looked up at the starlit sky. It felt good to be alive! Gleefully, she twirled her body about. Singing, she walked up the stairs and unlocked the door.

Amanda was sitting on the floor with Henry beside her. "Hi, Ma."

"Hi, sweetie, come here." Anna held her arms out to Amanda. "I love you, sweetie." Gently she hugged her and stroked her hair.

Meanwhile, Henry had crept up to them and was yammering at Anna's feet for her to pick him up and she did. "I think you've spoiled him Amanda."

Amanda laughed and kissed him on his cheek.

Putting Henry down, Anna walked over to the stove. "Well, I guess I'll have to order some more wood from Pete Hof at the sawmill tomorrow," she said as she took a couple pieces of wood off the dwindling pile. "It'll be awhile before supper will be done. Why don't we go for a walk?"

Amanda didn't look too pleased about that idea.

"Oh, don't look so sad. I know why you don't like to leave the apartment, but you can't let other people control and ruin your life. Just ignore their remarks. We don't need them. They've never done anything for us, and they never will. We can live just fine without them. They're only words, and you can't die from words." Anna picked Henry up.

"Come on, sweetie." She held her hand out to Amanda.

Hesitantly, Amanda took her hand and got up from the floor where she had been playing with Henry. "Maybe they are just words, Ma, but they surely do hurt."

"I know, sweetie, but the people who are mean to you are not good people. They aren't worth having as friends. You are lucky that people like that don't like you. Someday they'll get their due. Life doesn't always turn out the right way. No matter how much better than us they think they are, the day will come when they'll find out they aren't any better." She held Amanda's chin in her hand. "Come on and show me a smile. It's beautiful outside. God made the world for everyone, and we have just as much right to enjoy it as anyone else does."

It was a sight most of the "righteous" people of Beechwood didn't care to see, a whore walking down their street with her "bastard." When they saw her coming, some people would turn and walk the other way. Others crossed the street, while others got off the wooden sidewalks and walked in the streets. If she looked in a store window, the green shade would quickly come down in front of her. With their noses turned so high, Anna surely thought that they'd trip over something or walk into something that they hadn't seen. But no such luck, "Christian people" like that were always lucky. Nothing ever happened to them in their smug world of righteousness. Oh, there were a few friendly people, men of course, who thought it would be easy to get into bed with her. Anna ignored them. She didn't listen to them nor look at them. They ruined her walk. It was just supposed to be Amanda, Henry, and her.

****

Before long school had started and Anna had to take Henry into the bakery again while she worked. Anna knew Regina had never liked her. But in spite of her contemptuous feeling, she did treat Anna in a civilized manner. Arnold never came around, and Anna was happy in her work again. She enjoyed working with dough and smelling the pleasing aroma of the finished product.

As she kneaded the dough, she'd watch Henry play. He sat in a cardboard box with a pillow propped in front of him. There he'd be so content playing with his toys. Sometimes his toes would interest him more. Often, he'd sit sucking his big toe. He would have liked to crawl around on the floor, but Anna didn't think that was too safe. She was concerned that he'd touch one of the hot stoves and burn himself.

One September afternoon, as Anna had just finished feeding Henry, she heard a deep, pleasing voice out in storefront of the bakery talking to Regina. "You don't have any more?"

"No, I'm sorry. They just went so fast today. They always do on the days when the farmers bring their cattle into town to be shipped to the stockyard. They're usually the only thing that they have time to eat when they're busy loading their cattle," explained Regina.

"Gee, Eva will be disappointed," the voice responded.

"Well, I'll tell you what I can do, if it's all right with you? I'll have Mrs. Leer bake up a batch just for Eva. She can deliver them to your house when she's finished baking them."

"If it isn't too much of a bother, I'd really appreciate that. Eva likes them and if possible I like her to have what she likes. In her condition, there aren't too many of the things she likes that she can have."

"Yes, I understand. We all are terribly sorry something like that had to happen to her--such a fine person."

"Well, I guess that's the way things go. I'm just glad she didn't die on me," replied the voice.

"Yes, that's the most important thing."

"Well, I can expect Mrs. Leer sometime today?"

"Yes, she'll be there," Regina replied.

Making deliveries was ridiculous! If he wanted the sweet rolls so badly, why couldn't he pick them up himself? Who was he? Why was it so important for Regina to please him, thought Anna?

A few minutes later Regina came into the back room by Anna. "You have got a special order of sweet rolls to make and deliver."

"I'll make the sweet rolls, but I can't deliver them. I'm sorry. I can't leave Henry alone." Anna motioned to Henry lying on his back in the box playing with his feet.

"Well, he won't be alone. I'll be here," she snapped.

"Okay. Who are they for?" Anna didn't want to upset Regina. She could fire her.

"Mr. Stoner, he lives at the edge of town in the red brick Victorian house."

"Mr. Stoner--I heard that name before," said Anna.

"You probably heard it more than once. He's the banker."

"Oh, yes." Anna remembered now. However, it wasn't the fact that he was the banker that she remembered but that it was his automobile that was responsible for Alex's accident.

Hurriedly, Anna worked along. She didn't want that special order of sweet rolls to cause her to fall behind in her other work. She didn't want to get done too late tonight. In fact, she had planned on getting done earlier tonight. Tonight was a special occasion. Now with delivering the sweet rolls, she'd get done later. While the sweet rolls were setting out to rise, she washed the pans, cleaned the shelves, and swept the floor.

As she was about to put the sweet rolls into the oven, the back door opened. In the doorway stood Mrs. Oker with a pleasant smile. Even before she said "hi" to Anna, she bent over, kissed Henry, and started talking to him. Henry became so excited. After putting down the package, which she held in her hand, she lifted Henry up and walked over to Anna. "I see the outfit that I gave him for his Baptism finally fits him."

"Yes, but I'm afraid not for long. He's growing like a weed."

"Like a good weed though." Mrs. Oker kissed his pink cheeks and hugged him close to her. "Oh, he's so soft and sweet." She rubbed her cheek against his fine brown hair and then surveyed him. "I still think he's going to have a pug nose like you and Amanda. With all that curly hair, he should have been a girl."

Anna chuckled. "Yes, he does have fine features, doesn't he?"

Mrs. Oker nodded her head. "Can I come over tonight?"

"Sure, you know you don't have to ask." Anna smiled lovingly at her.

"Well, you hardly ever come around to visit me anymore. The only time I see you and the children is when I come to the bakery. I thought perhaps you were upset with me for something."

Touching her hand, Anna replied, "Oh, no, I could never get upset with you. You're too kind to ever do anything to upset me."

"Well, I'm glad to hear that. You know I love your two children very much. They're the grandchildren that I'll probably never have. Oh, I have something for Amanda." She walked over and picked up the package that she had brought into the shop. She handed it to Anna.

"No, it's your present to Amanda. You should give it to her."

"I thought I heard two voices back here."

"Oh, hi, Regina, dear. I thought I'd stop in and see how things are going."

"Things are going fine, Mother." A sense of jealousy and hate filled Regina's eyes. She didn't like her mother flaunting all over that "bastard." A child like that didn't deserve attention or love from decent people. How could her mother lower herself and associate socially with such a scornful woman and her "bastard"? Revolting! Simple revolting! Her mother paid more attention to Anna than to her. Women like Anna--sluts--should not be allowed to have children. They're like animals, going from one man to another. Well, if she had another "bastard," she wouldn't be working in the bakery. She didn't care what her mother said. Next time Anna was getting thrown out of the apartment and the bakery.

"Do you have Mr. Stoner's sweet rolls done?" Regina asked.

"I just put them into the oven. They'll be ready in about a half-hour. I've decided to take Henry along when I deliver them."

"I don't care. Just know your place and deliver the sweet rolls to the back door, the cook's kitchen."

"Okay."

Mrs. Oker's eyes shot up to the clock. It was two o'clock. "You mean you won't be here when Amanda comes home from school today?"

"No, I'll probably be at Mr. Stoner's at three o'clock."

Turning to Regina, Mrs. Oker asked, "Couldn't you take the sweet rolls? Today is a special day for Amanda. Anna should be here when Amanda comes home."

"I have to stay here to take care of the bakery."

"Well, Anna could do that," Mrs. Oker suggested.

"I told Mr. Stoner that Anna was going to deliver them and that's who is going to deliver them."

"Ugh! Mr. Stoner doesn't care who delivers them. I'll take them. It's more important that Anna be here when Amanda comes home."

Anna thought of Mr. Stoner's house. If it was the one she thought it was, a person had to climb a lot of steps in order to get up to the house. It wasn't a good idea for an elderly woman to climb all those steps. It would be stressful. She could collapse from exhaustion.

"No, I'll take them. I'll leave a note for Amanda on the back door," Anna stated.

"Well, I can tell her," suggested Mrs. Oker.

"No, that's all right. I don't want to bother you."

"Well, frankly I don't care what you do as long as those sweet rolls get delivered," Regina snapped at Anna.

"I'll take care of Henry for you. Can I wait in your apartment for Amanda?" asked Mrs. Oker.

"Sure, if you want to."

"Well, I don't have anything else to do." Resting her forehead against Henry's she said, "We'll have fun Henry, won't we?"

Regina rolled her eyes. Disgusting! She went into bakery's storefront and waited for customers.

As Mrs. Oker went out the door, Anna called after her, "Wait! You forgot the package."

Mrs. Oker reached for the package as Anna handed it to her.

"Thank you. Now don't worry about us. We're going to get along just fine."

After closing the door, Anna went to the window and watched the kind little old woman walk up the stairs with Henry. Mrs. Oker was truly a good woman--a living angel.

"I don't pay you for staring out windows. That old woman is truly a fool--wasting her time on people like you." Abruptly, Regina turned and disappeared into the storefront.

Even though Anna pretended it didn't hurt, remarks like that ate down to her very soul. Well, let Regina make her remarks. As long as she went home with her pay every week that was all that was important.

The aroma that filled the room told Anna that the sweet rolls were done. As she rolled some in sugar and frosted others, her thoughts were of her dear Alex. What was she going to do with Henry and Amanda this Sunday when she went to visit Alex? Dr. Whitmore had left for Chicago to attend his godchild's wedding on Saturday. He wouldn't be back until Monday morning. Ever since Regina and Arnold had come to live with Mrs. Oker, the children had been staying with Dr. Whitmore during her visits with Alex. She couldn't ask Mrs. Oker because of the way she knew that Regina felt about her children. Maybe she should delay her visit until next week. No, she couldn't do that. She felt guilty about not visiting Alex the last two weeks. Henry had been teething, and he had been so crabby that she didn't want the doctor to be bothered with him.

What could she do? Why not take them along? Amanda could wait in the visitor's lounge while she saw Alex. Amanda was too small to take care of Henry. So she decided to take Henry along with her into Alex's room. Alex never noticed her. He surely wouldn't notice the child. Perhaps it was ridiculous of her to visit Alex. He never knew that she was there. But it made her feel good to see him. She loved him and needed to be close to him. If this Sunday's visit turned out all right, then in the future she'd always take Amanda and Henry along. She wouldn't have to bother anyone. It wasn't good to rely on others too much.

As she walked up the wooden sidewalk toward Mr. Stoner's house, her feet suddenly stopped in front of the general store. Now, she could visualize the automobile coming down the street--the frightened horses running over Alex--the wagon marring his head. Only a shadow of a man sat in the automobile. Maybe today she'd catch a glimpse of Mr. Stoner, and the shadow would have a face. It was ironic that she should be going to Mr. Stoner's house today. Especially today--it was three years ago today that Alex had been hurt. She could never forget that day. It was Amanda's fifth birthday.

"Hey, what you got in the bag, good-looking." A man's arm went around her waist.

Engulfed with fright, she ran out of his embrace and down the street. His dreadful laughter followed her, but it began to dwindle as she neared the immense Victorian house that set on the top of the pine-covered hill.

Up the stone steps Anna climbed toward the house. At the top of steps, she paused to rest her tired legs. She must have climbed a hundred steps. It was understandable why Mr. Stoner had an automobile. She would have preferred to ride than walk those steps any day.

Around to the back of the house she walked. Once, twice, three times she knocked and then waited. No one answered the door. Again and again she knocked. She heard the school bell ring. The children were being dismissed. She wanted to get home. So around to the front of the house she ran. After only one knock, the enormous black door opened. In the threshold stood a plump woman wearing a black dress, which was trimmed with a white lace collar and white cuffs.

"Yes," she soberly greeted Anna as her eyes comprehensively studied Anna's common appearance.

"I've brought Mr. Stoner's baked goods." Anna held the box containing the sweet rolls out to the woman.

"Who is it?" a voice called from inside the house.

"It's your baked goods, monsieur," the woman replied.

"Is that Mrs. Leer?" the voice asked.

The woman looked at Anna.

"Yes, I'm Mrs. Leer."

"Yes, it's Mrs. Leer, monsieur."

"Please, ask her to come in. I wish to talk to her."

While raising her eyebrows, because she had to leave such a

common person into the house, the woman opened the door wider to admit Anna. "Wipe your feet first," ordered the woman.

Anna did and then entered the house. The large polished oak staircase gleamed as the light from the two, large stained-glass windows shined down on it. Suspended from the ceiling was a large glass fixture with hundreds of branches full of candles. Anna was overwhelmed at the elegance of the house.

"This way." Motioned the woman.

Slowly, Anna walked toward the room. She was a bit afraid. What would a man like Mr. Stoner want with her? She must look awful. She ran her hand about her hair to make it less messy. Then she tried to wipe the blotches of flour off her dark dress, but it was too late. Soon she was standing in a gigantic room. The walls were covered with one bookcase after another. Anna never knew there were so many books. He must have every book that was ever written. There, behind a large desk, stood a broad figure of a man. His well-groomed hands, never touched by a day of hard physical work, were twirling about an immense wooden globe that sat on a carved, wooden stand.

"Monsieur, Mrs. Leer is here." The woman departed and left them alone.

Anna swallowed the lump in her throat as he turned around. He was a fine-looking man. The gray head of hair didn't seem to match his young physique, and his smooth, well-shaven face hid his age well.

"Please, sit down, Mrs. Leer." He offered her a chair and helped her into it. "You are shaking. There is no need to be afraid. Please, feel comfortable here." Walking over to his desk, he opened the small wooden box that set on it. After opening it, he pulled out a big brown cigar. "Do you mind if I smoke?"

"No." Anna was surprised and flattered that a man of his distinction should care about what she wanted.

After taking a wooden match out of a small box and striking it against the decorative stone paperweight, he lit his cigar and took a few leisurely puffs.

Anna felt uneasy as he stood looking down at her.

"Oh, I am sorry. I'm making you uncomfortable." With that he sat in the chair beside her.

"It took me awhile before I placed your name. You are the Mrs. Leer whose husband was run over by horses, aren't you?"

"Yes, I am."

"How is your husband?" he sincerely inquired.

"He's alive--but not really alive."

He reached over and touched her hand. "I'm so sorry. I didn't hear about your husband until I came back here several months ago. I've been out of the United States for the last two years traveling various places trying to find someone who could help my wife. Oh, I'm sorry. You have enough of your own problems without hearing about mine. Well, anyway, I had no idea that my automobile caused such an accident. My son never told me. When I eventually found out about it, I wanted to get in touch with you. However, things with Eva occupied all my time."

Anna was puzzled! Who was driving the automobile? It must have been someone else; otherwise, he would have known about the accident. But who?

"I feel very bad. If I could help your husband be the way he was, I would, but I can't. All I can do is offer you my help if you ever need it. So, please, any time you need help just call on me. It's the least I can do."

Anna didn't like taking favors. She didn't like to owe anyone. Nevertheless, Mr. Stoner was a "light at the end of a tunnel." A tunnel that seemed to get longer with its light getting dimmer. The place in Jennings had cost Anna more than she had figured on. In a few years all her money would be gone. She had always worried about the kind of care Alex would get when it was gone. She didn't like the idea of taking Mr. Stoner's money, but he had offered. She had to forget about her pride and think of Alex. After all, if it wouldn't have been for his automobile, Alex would be with her and Amanda.

"I'm getting along fine now. However, if I ever need help, I'll remember your offer."

"Yes, please do. I really want to help." He was so sincere. "I was just going to take a walk around the grounds. Would you like to join me? I hate walking alone. Perhaps you could tell me more about yourself."

"Please, don't be offended, but today is my daughter's birthday. I'd like to get home by her as soon as possible. I hope you understand."

"Of course, I understand. How old is your daughter?"

"She's eight today."

"You deserve a lot of credit for raising a child by yourself."

"Well, I really don't have a choice."

"Yes, I know. I'm truly very sorry about that." He helped her from the chair and walked her out into the foyer.

"Hey, Dad!" a voice called. A young man came hopping down the stairs and soon was standing in front of them. "Can I take your car to Beloit?"

"Frederick, please remember your manners?" Mr. Stoner stated, a bit embarrassed by the young man's lack of etiquette.

"Oh, hi," he replied unenthusiastically then turned quickly toward his father. "Well, can I use it?"

Mr. Stoner was getting very perturbed with Frederick's continued lack of courtesy. "Mrs. Leer this is my son, Frederick."

Anna smiled and extended her hand.

Frederick looked arrogantly at her hand. He was "too good" to shake hands with a common person. "Well, can I have the keys?"

Besides making her feel like a fool, he made her feel like dirt-- someone not even good enough to lick the dirt off his boots. She would never come back into this house--not to be made a fool of and mortified again! Mr. Stoner could shove his money "where the moon didn't shine"! She survived before, and she could do it again!

"No, you can't have the keys because I'm going to use the car." Reaching into his pocket, he pulled out a small chain with several keys on it. Gently, he put his arm around Anna's waist. "I'm taking this lady home." Out the door they walked, around the house, and into a small building.

There the thing stood, the automobile. Anna stood still. She was afraid to get too close.

"It won't hurt you. It's a harmless thing. It's the driver that's dangerous. Come on! You'll enjoy the ride." His kind voice reassured her.

She let him help her up onto the seat. Anna had never sat on a seat like that. It was so soft. She rubbed her hands across the black leather. It was so smooth, not coarse like the wooden seats that she was accustomed to. An odor filled her nostrils. Turning around, she saw Mr. Stoner pouring a transparent liquid into something on the car.

"There, now we're ready." After setting the can down, he climbed into the car and sat next to her. He smelled like the liquid that he had put into the car. It was a prominent, nauseated smell. After taking hold of a lever, the car made a noise and started to move.

Anna, filled with fright, clung to Mr. Stoner's arm.

He touched her hand. "Don't be afraid. Just sit back and relax."

Quickly, she took her hand off Mr. Stoner. How dare she touch him? She had better remember her place, she thought. "I'm sorry."

"For what? You didn't do anything to be sorry for. I sense that for some reason you think that I'm different from you. Well, I'm not, Anna. I'm made out of flesh and blood just like you. You're just as good as I am, and I'm just as good as you. No, that's not true. I think you're maybe better than I am. You have to struggle from day to day to survive. You're working hard to get what you want. I've always had an easy life and lived in luxury. When my father retired at the bank, I just stepped in his shoes. I really don't have the faintest idea of what survival means. It'll be the same with Frederick. Frederick and I are different though. If he doesn't change his ways, he'll find out what it means to survive. He just doesn't comprehend that if you continuously spend money, it disappears. I wish he'd fine a nice girl and settle down before it's too late and he's too set in his ways."

The ride was different--noisy but comfortable. Mr. Stoner seemed like a very nice person. As they rode down the street, he didn't seem ashamed to be seen with her. He did have a reputation to protect, but it didn't seem to matter. He waved to the people that he knew on the street. Maybe he hadn't heard the town's aspersion about her.

The automobile stopped in front of the general store.

"I don't live here."

"I know." He got out of the automobile, opened the door next to where she was sitting, and helped her out of the seat. "It's your daughter's birthday isn't it?"

"Yes."

"Well, let's buy her something."

"I've already bought her present."

"Well, I haven't. So come on." Taking her hand, he walked her up the steps, onto the sidewalk, and into the general store.

Gawking eyes watched them as they walked about the store.

"Mr. Stoner, I couldn't let you buy my daughter a present."

"Why not?"

"It doesn't seem right. You don't know my daughter. You don't even know me."

"I've always wanted to buy things for a little girl. So, please, let me indulge my wish! Don't you think this is pretty?" He pointed to a dress hanging on a hook.

Anna had never seen such a dress. It was a beautiful red dress with a lace-covered yoke, neck, and sleeves.

"Don't you think the red would look nice with your daughter's dark hair?"

Astonished by the knowledge that he had of her daughter, Anna stood speechless.

"Well, what do you think?"

"You do know all about me, don't you?"

"No, I don't know you. I just know what people say about you. They're two different things."

"Well, most people don't think so."

"Well, that's their problem, isn't it? It's not ours. When you're a business person, you learn to base your decisions on matters of facts not on idle talk. People like to talk. They always have. They always will. In a hundred years from now no one will even know we existed, so why even be bothered by what people say." Taking the dress off the hook, he walked over to the store's counter. "Wrap this in your prettiest paper and put a lot of ribbons on it. I like ribbons." He turned to Anna. "Don't you?"

"Whatever you say. You're paying for it," Anna replied.

The clerk snickered to herself.

Anna knew exactly what she was thinking--"another gentleman friend."

"How is this?" The clerk directed her question at Mr. Stoner.

"Very good, give me a bottle of that perfume over there, please." He motioned to a fancy bottle setting on the shelf behind the clerk.

"No, Mr. Stoner, the dress is too much already."

As the clerk handed it to him, he gave it to Anna. "It's for you."

Anna blushed. She was flattered. An important man like Mr. Stoner had bought her something! She'd cherish that! It would just be used for very special occasions--church on Sundays.

When he stopped the automobile in front of the bakery, Anna didn't know if she should invite him up to Amanda's little party or not. She'd feel embarrassed. Her apartment was nice for her, but Mr. Stoner would probably consider it shabby. However, since he did buy Amanda a present, it would be the decent and polite thing to do. He'd probably refuse anyway. It wouldn't be a good enough place for him to walk into.

"Would you like to come up for a while and have some of Amanda's cake?" she asked as Mr. Stoner helped her out of the automobile.

Glancing up and down the street, he replied, "If you don't care what people are going to say, I'd love to."

Anna couldn't believe his answer. She was at a loss for words.

"Well, do you care?"

"They can't say anything they haven't said a million times before."

"Well, okay, let's go." Extending his elbow for her arm, they walked down the alley and up the stairs.

A cozy and loving sight greeted them. Mrs. Oker was rocking Henry in the rocker while Amanda sat at her feet reading her schoolbook aloud to Mrs. Oker.

"Happy birthday, sweetie!" Anna stood in the threshold with her arms extended toward Amanda.

"Hi, Mama." Amanda put the book down, went over to her mother, and received the warm hug her mother had been saving for her all day.

"Happy birthday--Amanda?" Mr. Stoner wasn't quite sure of Anna's daughter's name as he handed her the present.

Reluctantly, Amanda looked at the present. She didn't know that man. She didn't know if it was right to take a present from a stranger. A smiling nod from her mother told her that it was okay. So she took it and unwrapped it. Her eyes glowed; her heart jumped. It was beautiful! "Can I try it on now, Mama?"

"Sure." Anna's heart felt her little girl's excitement.

Amanda flew into her bedroom. A few minutes later the prettiest girl in town was standing before them dressed like a princess. "Isn't it pretty, Mama!" She paraded about the room.

"Yes, it is. Thank you so very much, Mr. Stoner."

"It's worth it just to see that glow in Amanda's eyes." He smiled with delight. It made him feel good to make a little girl so happy.

Anna walked over to Mrs. Oker. "How were the children?"

"Good--good--a regular joy." She handed Henry, who was sleeping in her arms, to Anna.

After putting him into his bed, Anna returned to the room, and Amanda opened the remainder of her presents. Mrs. Oker had given her an elegantly crocheted, white shawl. Anna had given her several embroidered handkerchiefs. They weren't much, but Anna had put a lot of love into making them. They were embroidered so beautifully with colorful little flowers that they were almost too nice to use. Taking her presents, Amanda disappeared into her bedroom. A few minutes later she came out of the room with a doll. "My daddy gave this to me for my birthday before he got hurt. Isn't she pretty?"

Mr. Stoner's heart became heavy. A father should be with his daughter. That stupid piece of metal had deprived that little girl of her right to grow up with a father. He should have never bought it; then, Frederick wouldn't have been so fascinated with it.

Squatting down, he stroked Amanda's hair. "Yes, she is very pretty. I've traveled all over the world, and I've never seen such a pretty doll."

"She takes such good care of that doll. Her other dolls lay all over the apartment sometimes, but not that one. It's got a special place on her dresser. She doesn't play with it like she does the rest. Instead she'll sit on a chair and just talk and talk to it. It's almost as if she's talking to Alex."

"Well, maybe in her mind she is," said Mrs. Oker as she lit the eight candles on Amanda's cake.

After putting the doll back on her dresser, Amanda sat anxiously waiting for the candles to burn down far enough so she could blow them out.

"Make a wish. If you blow them all out at once, your wish will come true. You can't tell anyone your wish; otherwise, it won't come true," Anna said.

Finally, the anticipated moment came. Closing her eyes, she made a wish.

Three blows of her breath and the candles were out.

"Oh, my wish won't come true now." Amanda started to cry.

Mrs. Oker and Anna went to comfort her. "That's all right you can make another wish next year."

"But I wanted Daddy to come home now, not next year."

"Oh, my dear, dear Amanda, everything will be all right. Don't cry. It's your birthday. Come on let's eat a piece of cake." Mrs. Oker sliced the cake and gave each one of them a piece.

After he finished his piece, Mr. Stoner got up to leave. "Remember, Anna, if you ever need anything, please, just let me know. Thank you so very much for bringing Eva the sweet rolls and for the delicious birthday cake."

"Thank you, Mr. Stoner, for everything," replied Anna.

"You don't owe me any thanks. I'm the one who owes you and that little girl. It was nice seeing you again, Mrs. Oker. Well, take care now. Good-bye."

"He is a very kind man. I feel sorry for him though with his wife being sick like that. It's just a shame something like that had to happen to such a young pretty woman like his wife. There he sits with all his money, and it can't help his wife." Mrs. Oker shook her head.

Anna was about to ask what was the matter with his wife, when she heard a loud THUMP in the bedroom and Henry began to scream--yell in terrible pain!

They ran into the room. Anna hurried to pick him up off the floor and soothe away his tears.

"Well, good heavens! He pulled himself up over the bassinet and fell off it. I would have never thought he could do that," said Mrs. Oker.

"Oh, I hope he didn't damage his brain when he fell." Anna was in tears.

"Let me check him over a bit, while you're holding him." Mrs.Oker examined his head. "No, he didn't hit the back of his head. See the red mark on his forehead. That's where he fell. I'll chop a little piece of ice off the ice block in the icebox, and then we'll put it on his head. It'll keep the bump small."

Henry just screamed as they applied the cold ice to his head. It took about fifteen minutes before he was quiet. Anna held him close, to comfort him, to ease the pain that she felt for him, and to keep him from crying.

"Well, I'll be going home now. It'll be getting dark soon. I think Henry will be all right now. Just remember, don't let him go to sleep for a while. It's not good to sleep right after a blow to the head."

"Why?" asked Amanda.

"They say a baby might not wake up again if it sleeps right after a head injury," answered Anna.

"That's what they say. I don't know if it's true but why take chances," said Mrs. Oker.

"I'll keep him awake." Anna kissed his little head.

"Good, I'll stop in tomorrow and see how he is. Good night, Amanda." Mrs. Oker gave her a big hug and kiss. "Do you feel any older?"

Amanda laughed. "No."

"Well, when you get to be my age your answer will probably be 'yes.' " Chuckling she went out the door.

Sitting in the rocker, holding Henry, and caressing Amanda, Anna was pleased with the wonderful way Amanda's birthday had turned out. Alex would have liked it because it made Amanda so happy. Getting presents and being the center of things always makes children happy, and Amanda was no exception.

****

Sunday was a splendid day. The warm sun caressed their faces as they rode through the countryside to Jennings. Anna was glad it was nice outside. She had dreaded the idea of taking Amanda and Henry out in nasty weather. As usual, her worries were unfounded.

As they traveled the graveled driveway toward the cold gray building, Amanda asked her mother if she could see her father. Anna's answer was the usual "no." Although Amanda's memories of her father were fading more and more as the years went by, Anna rationalized that no memories would be better than a memory of her father sitting like a "vegetable."

Anna was anxious. She always longed to be close to him. Even though he just sat there, she felt good being close to him. Time and the changes it had swept into her life, had not changed her feelings for Alex. He was still her dear Alex and she loved him deeply.

With a drooping posture and disappointed heart, Amanda sat on the cold leather sofa in the waiting room. Although she wasn't a spoiled child, she acted like one now. She couldn't see any reason why she couldn't see her father. To her, what she wanted wasn't that outrageous. But, there wasn't anything she could do, her mother had said "no" and that was it. Amanda was a good child. She always obeyed her mother's wishes.

Down the silent hall and up a flight of stairs Anna walked carrying Henry. He was too small to be let with Amanda.

After passing several rooms, Anna entered one. There was Alex, sitting in his wheelchair and staring out the window. Anna pulled a chair beside him. She turned his wheelchair around so she could look at him while she visited with him. After giving him a slight kiss on his cheek, she sat in the chair and held his hand in hers as Henry sat on her lap. Even though she thought that he couldn't hear, she told him of Amanda's birthday party, how well Amanda was doing in school, and how much she enjoyed her work in the bakery.

However, unaware to Anna, Alex did hear and he did understand.

After setting Henry on the floor, she rose from her chair. As she leaned over to kiss Alex a good-bye, she noticed him slowly moving his hand. He was pointing at Henry who had crawled up on Alex's legs and was now standing in front of him. Ever so slowly Alex began to move his head back and forth.

A feeble whisper came out of his mouth. "Not mine--not mine." His hand fell flat onto his lap and his head stopped moving. Staring down at the child he repeated his words. "Not mine." A tear fell from his eyes.

Anna's heart ached. He knew, and he was hurt. She would have given anything--anything to keep that hurt from him. Oh, God! He was aware of what was going on. If only she would have known, she would have never--never brought the child.

Kneeling at his feet, she took his hands in hers. She kissed them and held them against her tear-covered face. "Alex, it's not the way you think. I only love you. I always have, and I always will."

"Not mine."

The words came out in a slow whisper, but to Anna it seemed as if they were blasted across the room.

"Oh, Alex, I'm so sorry, so very sorry. I never meant to hurt you. I love you! I love you!" She sobbed. "I had to survive. I could explain it to you but what good would it do. It's done, and I can't change it. Please, please, just believe that I love you. You are the only person I'll ever love. Oh, Alex, please believe that."

A soft rap on the door told Anna visiting hours were over. She rose from the floor and wiped her face free of tears, but nothing could wipe the tears from her heart.

"I love you, Alex." Gently she kissed his forehead. Picking up Henry, she walked toward the door. She felt his pain in her heart.

As he sat in the empty room, a shower of tears cascaded down his face. Thoughts ran back and forth within his mind. He had lost everything. His Anna had found someone else. He was truly alone now. There was no reason to live. His reason for living had found someone else. She had his child. The child was a bound between them. Anna had cast him aside. He wished that he could die and make everyone happy. How foolish he had been to think that she came because she cared about him. Obligation! That was the reason she had come. Oh, let me die God! Let me die and make everyone happy!

No! That wasn't his way. He wouldn't give them the satisfaction of seeing him dead. Anna was his wife for as long as he was alive. He had a hold on her. They were married. He loved Anna, and he wasn't going to give her up that easily. He would get well. He had to. Come on--legs--arms--move--move! Let me walk out of here. Move! Move! Move! The struggle inside of him was strong but his legs and arms didn't move. Time! It would take time. But no matter how long it took, Anna would still be his wife. He'd get out of this place and when he did, he'd win himself back into her heart. No one else would have his Anna.

There was a chance, after all, he could move his hand and head a little. That's more than he could do three years ago. He was motivated now, and nothing was going to stop him. He'd walk out of this place and then Anna would be his.

Maybe next year--on Amanda's birthday--yes, that would be a nice present for his little Amanda. He wondered how she looked. He longed to touch her, hug her, and stroke her fine brown hair. She would be a beauty like his Anna.

In time, he'd be coming home. He'd take his little girl and Anna away from that other man. Those thoughts stuck with him day after day and motivated his need to be a whole man again.

Chapter 9
****
The Rape

Fiercely, the early spring rain beat against the windowpanes of the old, red brick house. The cold rain was slowly dissolving the last white remains of winter. Then an unbelievable sound was heard-- someone was knocking on the front door. A husky man, who had been sitting at a desk, went to open the door.

Standing in the rain and soaked from head to feet was a young woman. Her wet stringy hair covered most of her face and water was dripping from the ends of her dress sleeves. Her clothing was tight against her body revealing her mature, sexy shape.

"Are you Father Aslen?"

"Yes." Otto dreaded letting her into the house. She'd get everything wet and muddied, but it wouldn't look good letting her stand out in the rain. What would his parishioners think if they saw that? So he opened the door wider and invited her in.

"What can I do for you?" He shut the door and turned around to look at her. Water was dripping all over the place. She had gotten his rug all full of mud. Simply disgusting!

She extended her hand. "I'm Pamela Bester."

"I don't think I've ever seen you before. Do you go to my church?" He reluctantly shook her wet hand.

"No, Father."

"Why have you come?"

"My mother died yesterday." Her voice cracked. It was hard for her to say, "my mother died."

"Oh, I'm sorry to hear that." He wasn't really, but it was what a person usually said. It sounded good and that was all that was important to Otto.

"You are the only one I haven't seen yet, and I hope you will help me. If you don't, there is no one left." She began to sob.

"What kind of help do you need?"

"I need a place to bury my mother."

"Are you Catholic?"

"No."

"Well, people usually get buried in the church of their religion. The church your mother attended is where she should get buried."

Pamela lowered her head in shame. "My mother didn't go to church, not for a long time."

"Well, she wasn't Catholic. She didn't belong to my parish." He shrugged his shoulders. "There is really nothing I can do to help you. I suggest you go to the church of her religion. I'm sure the pastor there will be able to help you more than I."

"I went there, and he wouldn't help me. He said my mother was a bad woman and couldn't be buried amongst Christian souls."

"Did you attend the church?"

"Yes, but that still didn't change his mind."

"Well, I can't help you either." He reached for the doorknob.

"I have money. I'll pay whatever is necessary. I want my mother to have a Christian burial. It's important to me, please."

Otto's eyes perked open. Money! Well, now maybe he could help her after all. She'd pay any price? He began to think in terms of monetary reward. "Well, maybe it is possible. How much could you pay?"

"Well, for the last ten years my mother and I have been living on the inheritance my mother received from her uncle. I don't know how much is left, but my mother did say there was enough for me to finish this semester at college. It was my mother's money, and I feel that it should be spend on her."

"Well, why don't you find out how much she has and bring it here. If you have an appropriate amount, your mother will have a very nice Christian burial. If not, I'm afraid that I can't help you."

"What do you consider an appropriate amount?"

"Well, I have to consider the facts that your mother was not Catholic, didn't belong to my parish, didn't attend mass, and since you didn't mention you lived with your father, I assume your mother was probably divorced. These are negative facts to be considered."

"No, my mother wasn't divorced. She and my father just went their separate ways. My father liked it that way. Then he wasn't legally obligated to pay alimony or child support. My father couldn't tolerate looking at me much less paying for my survival."

Otto could have cared less about her problems or the way her father felt about her. The money--now that was of great interest to him. "You better go now. The sooner you leave, the sooner you'll come back, and the sooner we'll know if there is something to consider." He shoved her out the door with her clothes still drenched and dripping of rain.

Her teeth clicked together rapidly as her chilled body walked down the streets and alleys toward her mother's apartment. When she reached the door, she reached into the pocket of her wet dress and pulled out a key. She went into the apartment and closed the door. As she looked about the apartment, she thought how ridiculous it had been for her to lock the door. There was nothing in the apartment that anyone would want. There was nothing to steal.

In one corner was a small, neatly made metal bed. That was where Pamela slept. Across the room in the other corner stood another bed. It was unmade and a dent was in the pillow where her mother's head had lain. On the floor, several empty vodka bottles lay strewed about. Pamela thought of her mother dying in that bed. She didn't want to go near the bed, but she had to. Her mother had kept her bankbook under her mattress. Slowly, in the silence of the room, she walked over to her mother's bed and groped under the mattress. Within a few moments, she pulled out the book from under the mattress.

She rubbed her hand over the dent in the pillow as she recalled the pleasant memories that she had of her mother when she, Pamela, had been a child. The memories were of years before her mother had become obsessed with the need for vodka. They were happy years that were full of childhood games, pushes on swings, walks in the park, and birthday parties. Her mother would join right in the fun and games. She was as young in spirit as Pamela's friends. But then her mother's happiness faded and she no longer joined in the parties. She started to stay in her room more and more.

He had changed her--taken away her youth. He had done the most damaging thing a man could do to a woman. What he had done had taken away her desire of caring about herself or anything. It was his fault--her father's. Well, he could be happy now. His "millstone" was dead.

She wiped the tears from her face as her voice cracked. "Well, she's finally free of you, Daddy! You can't hurt her anymore."

Pamela opened the bankbook and looked at the last entry. There was nothing in the book. That couldn't be! Her mother had said that there was still some money left. There had to be! How could she bury her mother without it? Pamela turned to the first page of the book. There was the large five digit number. Her mother had used all that money in only ten years. Pamela groped under the mattress again. She could feel nothing. She threw the mattress off the bedspring. There was a white envelope taped to the bottom of the mattress. Pamela opened it. It was full of money. Pamela counted it. That's all there was! Would it be enough to bury her mother?

Pamela was confused. What had her mother done with all that money? As she examined her conscience, Pamela knew the answer. Her mother had never worked. She had spent most of the money on her vodka and on Pamela. Pamela had always been dressed nicely and sent to the best schools. Her mother had never cooked a meal. They had always gone to the restaurant to eat. Her mother's hands had never touched a washing machine. Their clothing was always sent to the laundry. The only thing Pamela did in their apartment was her schoolwork and sleep.

While Pamela did her schoolwork, her mother would sit in her bed and drink her vodka. Before Pamela would go to bed, she'd take the empty bottle out of her sleeping mother's hand and cover her mother with a blanket. Solitary, was the best description for her mother. She never went into the taverns or picked up men. She'd drink alone in their apartment and never shared her bed with anyone. Pamela always felt there was someone that her mother would have liked to share her bed with but for some reason, she couldn't and didn't. Often at night Pamela would hear her calling his name. Whenever Pamela would ask who the man was, her mother would open a bottle and start drinking. Pamela never did get an answer and now she never would. The man her mother called in her dreams, Pete, would remain a mystery to

Pamela. It was the secret that her mother had taken to her grave.

Realizing she had reminisced much too long, she ran with the envelope full of money back to Father Aslen. The rectory was dark as she approached. Lacking the virtue of patience, Otto had gone to bed. He was not about to lose a minute of sleep waiting for someone. When she came back, she'd knock, then he'd get up.

Pamela was just about to knock when she suddenly paused. If she woke him up, maybe he'd be angry with her. Maybe he'd charge her more or maybe he wouldn't bury her mother at all. He was the only one who had given her a glimmer of hope that her mother could perhaps have a Christian burial. She couldn't take the chance of upsetting him and making him change his mind. So under the porch and in front of the door, she huddled her shivering body and waited until morning came.

The rest of the night went so slow. Pamela dozed off now and then. The constant shaking of her cold body and the uncomfortable position she was in, made it impossible for her to get a good night sleep. Finally, she heard someone moving about inside the rectory.

The rain had ceased, and the sun was starting to peek between the parting clouds of gray. Pamela got up and peered into one of the double-hung windows. Through the sheer curtain, she could see Otto moving about the room. She knocked on the door.

"Oh, it's you, got the money?"

"Yes."

"Well, come in then." Otto opened the door wide to let her in.

"It's in here." She handed him the envelope with the money.

Looking inside and counting it he responded, "That'll do fine."

"You're taking it all!"

"If you want your mother buried, ya."

"I have to pay the mortician and rent for the apartment out of that money too."

"Well, okay then, find someone else to give your mother a Christian burial." He handed the envelope back to her and opened the door for her to leave. He wanted all the money.

Pamela thought, it was her mother's money. It should be spent on her. "No, wait. You can have it all." With that she handed the money back to him. "When can you bury my mother?"

"When is she going to be 'laid out' in the funeral parlor?"

"She's not going to be 'laid out.' She didn't know anyone and no one cared to know her."

"Doesn't she have any relatives?"

"No, they all died years ago in a fire. She has no one, except me."

"Well, we can bury her today if the mortician is finished."

"I'll go to the funeral parlor right now and find out." Pamela dreaded going there. Seeing her mother's corpse would remind her again of her great loss. What could she tell the mortician when he asked for the money for his services?

"Could I just have half the money to pay the mortician, please? There still would be enough left for you."

"You can pay the mortician out of you weekly wages from where you work," Otto suggested. He wasn't about to take the chance of losing the money that he wanted.

"I don't work anyplace. I've been going to school to become a teacher."

"Well, that's your problem, not mine. You know I'm sticking my neck out burying her. She wasn't Catholic, and she didn't belong to my parish."

Otto's stomach began to growl. He was hungry. His breakfast wasn't setting on the table like it always was. Oh, he had forgotten. His housekeeper had quit yesterday. Well, he didn't know how to cook, and he was hungry. "You want a job?"

Pamela was puzzled, what was he talking about.

"Do you want a job?"

"I need a job, yes."

"Well, you got one. Get in the kitchen and make me breakfast. I want some eggs--any kind. From now on you're my housekeeper. After breakfast, go pay the mortician all that you owe him, then give me the rest. I'll take what you still owe me out of your housekeeper wages until you've got me paid in full. As a housekeeper you get to live here, if you want."

Pamela didn't know the first thing about cooking, but she had better learn quick and good. It was a good job Otto had offered her. A place to stay, her food, and a job had all been taken care of. She scurried into the kitchen. Frantically, she looked from drawer to drawer for a cookbook. Ah, at last she found one. Eggs! He had wanted eggs. How does a person make eggs? Running her fingers down the index, she came across "eggs." After reading the recipe over several times, she made him breakfast. She felt pleased with herself when Otto said that breakfast was good.

After breakfast, Pamela went to the mortician. He had finished her mother, but he hadn't done a very good job. At least, Pamela didn't think so. Her mother was so painted up--her bright rouged cheeks --her scarlet lips. It wasn't her beautiful mother. Pamela was disgusted, but she thought maybe that is the way things were done. Nevertheless, she couldn't do anything about it now. It was done, and she wanted this painful ordeal over. Soon she would get her wish; it would be over with.

Standing alone in the cemetery beside Otto and the mortician, Pamela spoke quietly within her heart to her lonely mother. As Otto said the last words of the funeral ritual, a cloudburst poured from the heavens. The mortician ran in one direction while Otto ran toward the rectory. Pamela finished speaking the words within her heart. Hesitating to say that final good-bye to her mother, she stood out in the rain beside the coffin. She didn't care if she got wet. Her tears mingled with the rain. After touching the coffin gently, Pamela walked slowly toward the rectory, her new home now.

When she reached the steps, the rain stopped. A rainbow appeared across the sky. Pamela remembered her mother reading to her out of the Bible about the rainbow. God had put it in the sky after the great flood. It was God's covenant to man. Pamela remembered that the rainbow was God's promise that he would never destroy the world by water again. Her mother had read stories from the Bible to her every evening when she was a little girl. That was the one thing they did together before he changed her.

However, the last several years, during the summer months when Pamela had no school, her mother had turned to the Bible again. Often she would ask Pamela to read to her out of the Bible at night. Even though she drank and didn't go to church, her mother was a good person, in her own way. She always believed in God and never blamed him for her faults. Pamela knew her mother was truly happy now. She had gotten her Christian burial. Pamela felt a comfort within her soul that she had been able to fulfill her mother's last wish.

****

Several days later, while Otto was in church saying Mass and Pamela was making dinner, there came a knock at the back kitchen door. Through the sheer curtains, which covered the window at the top of the door, Pamela could see her visitor was an elderly woman. As Pamela opened the door, she couldn't help but notice the look of surprise on the woman's face.

"Who are you?" the elderly woman snapped.

"I'm Father Aslen's housekeeper. Who are you?"

"I'm his last housekeeper. He can't seem to keep anyone too long. I forgot a few of my things when I left the other day. I knew he would be in church, so I figured it'd be a good time to come. I didn't expect anyone to answer my knock. I had planned to enter, get my things, and leave without him knowing I was here. I don't ever want to see him again. That's my apron you're wearing."

"Oh, I'm sorry. I didn't know." Pamela began to untie the apron.

"Ah, that's all right, keep it. I got plenty at home."

As the elderly woman walked into the kitchen she went straight to a drawer and opened it. She searched inside for something, but whatever she thought was in there, obviously wasn't. With her eyebrows frowned, she looked about the kitchen in a confused manner.

"Are you looking for something?" Pamela asked.

"Yes, I am. I bet he threw it away just to get even with me. He knew it was a heirloom, my great-grandmother's."

"Maybe I can help you. What are you looking for?"

"Never mind. I see it." She walked over to the shelf and picked up the cookbook that Pamela had been getting her recipes out of. "This is it. I see you've been using it."

"Yes, it's been my life saver. I don't know anything about cooking or baking."

Closing the book, the elderly woman gently rubbed her hand over the decorative cloth cover. "My mother gave me this book and her mother gave it to her. I like things that are passed on. After a person is gone, that's all we have left. I'm sorry but I can't leave you use it. It's more than a cookbook to me. I have a daughter also, and someday

I want to pass it on to her. I have to take it with me. I'm truly sorry."

"I understand. It's just that I don't know what I'm going to do now without the cookbook."

"This isn't the only cookbook in the kitchen."

"It's the only one I found."

"Oh, no, there are half a dozen in here. I never used them so I put them way back on that top shelf out of my way." She pointed to a shelf all cluttered with different size bowls.

Pamela couldn't see any books.

The woman put her cookbook down and grabbed a chair. She climbed onto the chair. While standing on her tiptoes, the woman handed the bowls down to Pamela, one at a time. The shelf was soon cleared of all the bowls. Pamela still couldn't see any books. The elderly woman stretched her body. She could reach them now and hand them, one by one, down to Pamela. Pamela wiped the dust off each of them as she placed them on the table. There were six books. Pamela surely would get some help now.

One by one Pamela handed the bowls back up to the elderly woman. When she had finished, the elderly woman stepped off the chair and put the chair back in its place.

"I'll be going now. I got what I came for." The elderly woman grabbed her cookbook off the shelf.

As the elderly woman was about to leave, she turned and gently caressed Pamela's hand. "You seem like a very nice person. If you were wise, you'd take my advice and leave here as soon as possible. Father Aslen is not like a man in his position should be like."

"What do you mean?" The woman aroused Pamela's curiosity.

"I am not one to malign others. I just give advice. I don't want you to learn a lesson the hard way, like I did."

"I need this job."

"Ya, I thought, I needed it too. Father Aslen thought I did too. He thought that he had me because I needed the job, but no job is worth that. I'm not that kind of person. Well, I've said too much already. I have to go now. Good-bye and please, take my advice."

With that the woman left, leaving Pamela in a confused state. What on earth was the woman talking about? She wasn't going to leave this job. Maybe that's what the woman really wanted. The woman probably thought that she could scare her into quitting so she could have her housekeeping job back. Yes, that must be it, Pamela thought. Well, she wasn't falling for that. Father Aslen was a good religious man. He was kind to her. Priests were good people. Besides even if he wasn't nice to her, she still would have to keep the job. She owed him money for her mother's funeral.

As the days passed, even though she was kept busy with the usual housekeeping chores, Pamela often wondered if the woman was really trying to warn her and what she was warning her about.

****

Valiantly, Alex had struggled over the last eight years, but his struggles were in vain. His heart was now heavy with despair and a sense of failure. In all those years the only thing he had accomplished to do was move his one hand ever so slightly. Years were passing into years. Time was slipping away so fast. Anna was getting older. He was getting older. Time stops for no one, and it waits for no one to catch up. Things would never be the same. He would never get better. It was hopeless. It always was, but he never could admit it. Anna wasn't his. No matter how much he loved her, it didn't matter. She didn't love him. She had someone else. She had his baby. He could never win her back--not like this. He was nothing--not even a whole man anymore. Just a vacuum that absorbed air and swallowed the food that was fed it. No man lived like that. He wasn't a man! Oh, how Anna must hate him. Hate him for making her live with the man she loved out of wedlock--for having his child out of wedlock--for depriving the child of his father's legal name. Obsessed with these thoughts of Anna's hate, he longed to do something to rid himself of her. Maybe her hate wasn't too strong yet. If he set her free, maybe she wouldn't hate him each time she thought of him. He didn't want her to have that feeling when she thought of him. If only, he could do something. It just couldn't be anything. He had to do something so she would know that he did it to set her free. Then maybe she wouldn't hate him. He could never live with her hate.

The thoughts whirled and whirled in his mind as he stared out the window. The trees were starting to bud. It was time for a fresh, new year to start. It was time for Anna to start a new life--one without his yoke around her neck.

"Well, how are you this afternoon, Alex? It is getting nice outside. All the snow is gone now, you know. Did you like your dinner?" asked the nurse. In her one hand she carried a bowl of warm water. In the other hand she had a metal mug with a shaving brush and soap inside. Over her arm she had draped a wide, heavy strip of leather.

She babbled on and on. Alex often thought that she was crazy. She knew that he couldn't talk. She thought he couldn't hear, but still she babbled on. Ridiculous! So Alex thought.

After setting the items, which she had carried into the room, on a small table near Alex, she reached into her shirt pocket and pulled out a white object. From inside the white object came a thin, fine steel blade with concave sides. Taking hold of the white handle, she stroked the blade several times on the strip of leather.

Alex hoped that she'd sharpen it enough before she started to shave him. It hurt when the blade wasn't sharp enough. It pulled his whiskers.

Satisfied with the sharpness of the blade, she set it down. She moved his chair away from the front of the window to beside the small table. Dipping the shaving brush into the warm water and then into the mug, she made a lather and spread it over his cheeks and jaw. It felt warm and refreshing on his untouched face. No one ever touched him anymore except to shave or bathe him. There were no loving warm kisses or comforting gentle hugs left for him in the world anymore. Anna's kisses and hugs, whenever she came to visit, could not soothe away how he thought that she really felt about him.

"Your whiskers really grow. I really should almost shave you every day." Picking up the straight razor, she began to shave him. She had sharpened it enough and Alex was glad.

"Help! Help! Someone, please help me!" The piercing cry came from out in the hall.

Laying the keen-edged razor on the table, the nurse darted out into the hall. "Oh, my God!" Came her cry as she disappeared from the threshold and out of sight.

Alex eyed the razor setting on the table. It was an opportunity. How could he make use of it? He would have to. He might never get such an opportunity. Could he move his arm that high to reach it? Slowly, he moved his arm--one inch off his lap--then two--then three.

His arm wouldn't move any farther. It had to. He could do it. He would just have to try harder--try harder--try harder--four inches. Finally, he could rest it on the arm of the wheelchair. A tight pain filled his arm and the ends of his fingers. Just a little bit farther then he could reach it.

Painfully, he inched his arm up closer and closer to the top of the table. Finally, it reached on the top of the table beside the blade. He was exhausted--moving that arm was the hardest work that he had ever done. His fingers gripped the blade. Securing it firmly in the palm of his hand, he let his hand drop back into his lap.

While letting the razor rest on his lap, he used his movable hand to turn his other hand over. There were the puffed blue veins on his wrist that would help him with his deed. It would be the deed that would free Anna so she could be with the one whom she really loved.

Taking the razor, he dashed out at the veins. For a moment he felt a sharp sting and then the warm, sticky, opaque red liquid inside his veins erupted. The red liquid spurted across the room, the floor, and bathe his body in its warmth.

Suddenly, he could see Amanda and his beautiful Anna running from the house to meet him when he came home from a day of planting in the fields. He could see Anna's love for him in her eyes, feel her love for him in her kiss, and feel her body caressing his. Next he could see himself pushing Amanda on the swing and hearing her laughter as the upward swing motion tickled her stomach.

The days of his life ran before him as he relived each for a brief moment. They flashed before him like a kinescope in a matter of seconds and then they were gone and so was he. This was the last thing that he had done because of his love for his Anna.

The anguish that had darkened his soul fled. Somehow he could feel Anna's warm love in his silent heart and around his cold body. Peace! At last he felt peace. Finally, he was going home to rest. His soul was leaving the earthly shell that had trapped it. Anna would love him now. She'd know why he had done it. He had set her free! With those last thoughts, the final sounds of life around him faded and ended.

****

With her heart beating frantically, Anna jumped up in bed.

Flinging her feet out of bed, she ran to Amanda's room. As she threw open the door and seen Amanda in the bed, a relaxed feeling of relief passed over her body. After closing the door, she leaned against it and tried to regain her senses.

It had been a dream, but it hadn't been an ordinary dream. It was the dream about the coffin with the faceless body again. Only this time the body in the coffin had a face--Amanda's face. Why was she dreaming such terrible dreams about Amanda? First, the horses tramping her and now her face in the coffin. The dream with the horses had come true except it was Alex not Amanda. She had dreamed about something that was going to happen but it had happened to a different person. Was Amanda going to die? Or was someone else that she knew? Ah! That was foolish! No one can dream what is going to happen, but yet she did about the horses. She had that dream so many times before Alex got hurt. After he got hurt that part of the dream ceased and only the coffin kept coming back into her dreams.

Fear overwhelmed her, not only of the dream and the worry if it would come true but thoughts about herself. Was she possessed? Is that why she could dream about things that would happen? Maybe the people in town were right. Maybe she was an evil woman filled with Satan. Or, maybe she was crazy--believing in dreams coming true. No normal person believes in dreams. Perhaps it was in her mind. She couldn't control her dreams. Was she going insane? If she was, somehow she'd have to fight it. She had Amanda and Henry to take care of. Well, Amanda didn't really need her that much anymore. She was sixteen and did have a job at the bakery. On her own she could probably survive, but Henry was only nine. She had to take care of herself for him. That was one thing which she couldn't expect Amanda to do--taking care of Henry if she wasn't around. It's not that Amanda wouldn't because she would. Amanda loved that little boy, but something like that was too much for a young girl to handle. Anna had a hard time raising him herself, and she was twice as old as Amanda. Keeping her wits about herself was important now. If she was going insane, how could she keep others from finding out?

She had to stop such thoughts! If she went on thinking like that, she probably would go crazy. She was just as sane as anyone else. It's just that she had weird dreams. That was all! She had convinced herself and wasn't going to worry about it anymore. It was Saturday. She didn't have to work today. As long as the children were still sleeping, she was going back to bed.

Later, Anna was awakened from her well-deserved sleep by a loud rapping at the door. Who on earth is that? Anna thought as she hurriedly tossed off her nightgown and put on her dress. She didn't like answering the door wearing clothing that she wore to bed.

"Come on! I don't have all day," the impatient voice shouted through the door.

Anna hurried, she didn't like him shouting. He'd wake up the children. With her hair uncombed and bare feet, she ran to open the door.

"Well, it's about time! What kept you so long?" He stretched his neck to see if there was anyone in the room.

Anna knew what he expected to see--a naked man running around. "What do you want?"

"I've got a telegraph message for you." He handed her a yellow piece of paper and stretched his inquisitive neck again.

Anna grabbed the paper and looked up at him. A pleasing smirk covered his face. Anna turned around to see what he found so indulging. There Amanda stood in her bedroom door threshold. Even though she was fully clothed in a dress and shoes, he seemed to undress her with his eyes.

Anna stepped through the doorway and slammed the door shut. "Don't you ever think those things about my girl! She's a good girl. My life is almost over, and I don't care what people say about me. However, I'll not have people thinking and saying untrue things like that about my daughter. She's a good girl. You hear! There's nothing here for boys like you. Tell your friends the same. Now get out of here!" she sternly ordered him.

As he ran down the steps two at a time, Anna opened the door. Standing in the threshold, she started to unfold the telegraph message.

The boy stopped at the bottom of the steps. "Slut!" he shouted back at her and then ran down the alley.

Anna raised her eyebrows. Even though she had heard that so many times before, it still hurt each time it was said. Just like it hurt the first time. However, what even hurt more was the idea that people were starting to think that of her Amanda. It wasn't fair. She hadn't done anything for them to talk about. She hadn't even gone on a date with a boy. Anna wouldn't let her. Amanda was still too young to think about protecting herself. She had no idea what life was all about. So Anna protected her the best she could. The only way that she knew how, was not to let her date boys. Sometimes this caused arguments, but Amanda always eventually listened to her mother. Especially, after Anna explained how things sometimes can happen beyond our control and the result can be a child like Henry.

Constantly, Anna emphasized the fact to Amanda that she didn't want her to go through life living with that mistake. People never let a person forget it nor the child as it gets older. It hurts even more to hear the child that you love being called a "bastard." Consequently, if Amanda couldn't control her desires because of herself, she should at least think of the child that could result from such uncontrollable desires. Of course, sometimes a person doesn't have a choice when someone forces their uncontrollable desires on a person, as they both knew.

From first hand experience, Amanda knew what pain it could cause. At school, she often heard the other children tease Henry unrelentingly. Her memory of the remarks that were made to her and her mother were always quite vivid. After careful thoughts, she'd always listen to her mother because she knew that her mother was right and only thinking of her. Anna was pleased. Amanda was really a good girl.

"What's in the telegraph message, Ma?"

"Oh, I don't know. I was thinking about something else." Quickly, she finished unfolding the message and read the contents.

"Oh, my God! How could he do something like that?" Stunned Anna sat in a chair. It was unbelievable--too hard to comprehend! Alex was dead! He had committed suicide. He was gone forever! She cried.

"What's the matter, Ma?"

"Um--" She shook the cloud of haze out of her mind. She had to think quickly. There was no need for Amanda to know that her father had killed himself. Crumbling up the telegraph message, she replied,

"It's your dad. He's dead." The tears flooded her eyes and face.

"Daddy, dead! How?"

"He just died. That's all."

"You know, Ma, I don't even remember him anymore, and now I'll never get a chance to see what he even looked like." Amanda sobbed. "I wish you had let me visit him. It wasn't right of you to deprive me of seeing him." With her heart laden with loss, she ran into her room and closed the door.

As Anna sat there crying, Henry came over to her. "Daddy's dead?"

"Yes, he's gone to see God. He'll be happy now in heaven." She stroked his shoulder length brown curls and held him close to her. Giving him a kiss on the head, she rose from the chair.

Henry didn't cry. "Daddy" was just a word to him.

Slowly, Anna opened Amanda's bedroom door.

Teary eyed, Amanda sat on the edge of the bed stroking her doll's hair. With a look of anger in her eyes, she looked up at her mother.

"I know why you're angry with me, but you really don't have a reason to be. You're old enough to understand now, and I owe you an explanation." Sitting on the bed next to Amanda, she touched her hand and continued. "Your dad was a handsome, intelligent, active man. He'd play child games right along with you--hide and seek--tag--everything. You were his pride and joy." Softly she stroked Amanda's hair. "You say you don't have any memories of your dad anymore and if I had left you visit him you would. That's probably true, but you wouldn't want those memories of him. After the accident, your dad was not the way he wanted to be. He didn't like himself that way, and I don't think he would have liked you to see him that way either. In fact, I know he would have never liked you to remember him that way. No memories at all are better than bad ones."

Amanda rose from the bed and set the doll back in its place on the dresser. "I feel so deprived. Is that the right word? I mean I would like to have touched him--seen him--kissed him one more time. My hope has been stolen away from me. As long as he was alive there was always the hope that he'd get better. Now--all of a sudden--it's all over. He's gone. What if this is all there is? Then he's gone forever. I'll never see him again."

Anna rose from the bed and held Amanda tight in her arms. "We must believe that this isn't all there is. We'll see him again, and he'll be the way he wants us to see him."

"Oh, Ma, life isn't fair, is it?"

"No, but whoever said it was supposed to be. We just have to live it the way it comes. Nothing can change what happens. What's done is done."

"When did Daddy die?"

"Yesterday afternoon, I think I'll go there now and make all the arrangements or whatever I'm supposed to do. I want him buried here in our parish cemetery close to us--not in their cemetery." As she walked toward the door, she paused, wiped her tear-covered face, and turned around.

"You know we are really crying for ourselves. We're crying because of our loss not because we're sorry for him. We're selfish. We are only thinking about ourselves, and what we wanted. I wanted him to stay alive for me because I loved him, and I wanted to be near him. What did he want? He didn't want that kind of life. He wasn't happy. I think he's happy now, and maybe we should be happy for him. He's better off than we are. We're still stuck in this hell."

"Mom, I'm hungry." Henry stood near the open bedroom door.

Anna looked at the clock--ten o'clock. "Amanda, will you please make Henry his breakfast. I want to leave right away so I can get everything finished before visiting hours begin at the place. I want to be home for supper." Seeing the woodbin was empty beside the stove, she told Henry to run down the steps and bring up a few pieces of wood to burn in the stove, so Amanda could cook breakfast. They kept their wood piled under the outside stairs.

"Amanda after breakfast will you and Henry please fill the woodbin up for me." Anna put on her shoes.

"Sure, we can do that. Right!" Amanda ruffled Henry's hair. "We don't have anything else to do."

"Good." After combing through her hair quickly, she gave Henry and Amanda a kiss, a hug, put on her coat, and flew out the door.

After renting a buggy from the livery, she set off toward Jennings. She had only traveled a short way when she noticed one of the wheels was about to fall off. Seeing it was unsafe to travel farther, she tied the horse and buggy to a tree that was near the edge of the woods.

After looking up and down the road, she started to walk toward the closest farmhouse. When she finally arrived at the farmhouse, she was informed that the person who could help her was out in the field planting oats and couldn't stop his work to help fix the buggy. He had to get his crops in while the weather was nice.

Anna waited and waited until he came home for supper. Dusk was upon them by the time he had the buggy fixed. Being too dark to travel, the couple offered Anna a room for the night. Reluctantly, she accepted. Nothing had gone the way she had planned, but she couldn't travel now. So she had to stay.

Early the next morning, she rose before the couple and left for Jennings. Being extremely grateful for their help and hospitality, she left some money on the table for them. Being independent, she never liked to owe anyone anything.

The Sunday church services were just ending as Anna arrived at the institution. Immediately, she noticed Mr. Thorton, the institute administrator. He was taking a casual walk around the grounds enjoying the briskness of the fresh spring air. The sun peeking through the clouds was a welcomed sight in such a dreary place.

Anna climbed off the wagon and walked over to him. It was then she found out that there were no plans to be made and no coffin with Alex in it to be taken home.

"I really can't understand why you couldn't have waited until I arrived." Anna was upset. She had different plans for Alex's remains. She was his wife. She had loved him and thought that she should have had at least a say in what happened.

"Mrs. Leer, this is an institution and in order for it to run smoothly certain rules must be maintained. If we are lenient with the rules for one person, the next person will expect the same leniency. We sent you a telegraph message the same afternoon your husband passed away. We waited the rest of the afternoon and all day Saturday for some word from you. When we didn't receive a response by Saturday night, we decided to make the necessary arrangements. We didn't know if you were coming or not. It is our policy not to let the dead remain in the institution for more than three days. Monday would have been the fourth day. Surely you can comprehend the condition of the body by then. It is our rule to bury the dead promptly. We didn't know if you were coming or not."

"I didn't receive your message until nine o'clock Saturday morning and then I had trouble on the way with the buggy."

"I am sorry, Mrs. Leer, but we did send you the telegraph message on Friday, and we had no idea of your problem while you were traveling here. We've had plenty of experiences in the past where relatives don't even care to visit people here when they are alive much less take care of the arrangements when they die. They completely forget about them and want nothing to do with them."

"Mr. Thorton, you should have known better when it came to me. You know that I visited my husband almost every Sunday afternoon. You know that I did because I often left you my husband's monthly payments when I came."

"It's done, Mrs. Leer. There is no sense talking about it."

"Can I see his grave?"

"Of course, come on." Putting his arm around her waist, he guided her through the cemetery to where a pile of fresh ground rose above the newly sprouting green grass.

Silently, she stood staring at the pile of ground as she talked in her mind to Alex. Then she looked around the cemetery. It made her feel so cold--so empty. It was a desolate place. The dead weeds of last year's autumn cluttered the small white stones, which marked the graves of people who had died that no one cared enough about to visit and keep the graves free of weeds. She wouldn't let that happen to Alex's gravestone. No weeds would ever clutter it. She'd never desert his place of rest.

"Do you allow flowers?"

"You can plant some if you want to, but you should talk to the caretaker about that. He might not like to cut around them."

"Where can I find him?"

"He's not here now. I saw him go home after church. He's always here during the week and on Saturdays. Why don't you come back then and ask him? Do you want to take Alex's belongings back with you?"

"Oh, I don't know. All he had was his clothing. I really have no use for them. Why don't you give them to some needy person at the institution?" Anna paused. "How did he do it?" Her lips quivered.

"With a straight razor."

Anna's body shook, her stomach turned upside down as she suppressed the sudden surge of nausea inside of her. "Oh--my God!" The words choked in her throat.

"There was very little pain. When you cut your wrist, it's over in a matter of seconds."

"How on earth did he get hold of something like that?"

"The nurse, who was shaving him, ran out into the hall to answer a cry for 'help.' Apparently, one of the patients in a wheelchair had lost control of his chair, and it started to roll down the steps. The patient grabbed onto the railing, and there he hung hollering for someone to help him. While the nurse was helping him, somehow Alex managed to get the razor off the table. The more I think about it, the more I believe that Alex was always aware of what was going on around him. I don't think his brain was damaged, maybe just his nerves. Well, we'll never know now."

In a flashback, Anna could see Alex pointing his hand, slowly shaking his head, and mumbling "not mine--not mine" at Henry. From that moment on, she had known that Alex could comprehend his surroundings. Was the child the reason that he had taken his life? Did he feel that she had betrayed him? That she no longer loved him? She came almost every Sunday, surely he must have known that she cared. She began to sob. Did he die thinking that she didn't care or love him? Did he feel so empty--so alone that no one cared if he lived or died? She had always told him how much she loved him. Didn't he believe her? No, he probably didn't not after seeing Henry. If only she wouldn't have made that mistake of taking Henry, then maybe he wouldn't have been so hurt and felt so dejected--so betrayed. All her words couldn't erase what he must have thought to be the truth.

Mr. Thorton handed her a handkerchief. "Mrs. Leer, please take comfort in knowing that it was what Alex wanted. He wasn't happy and maybe now he is."

Wiping the tears away, she replied, "That's just what I told my daughter. The tears are for ourselves when someone dies. We cry because we aren't going to see them or have them around. We cry because we should have done this or should have done that."

"We shouldn't waste our time thinking about death. It comes when it's ready. There is nothing we can do to prevent it. All we can do is live each day to the fullest and dream of the future. Don't let death come without the taste of living. Don't stay in the darkness before you have to. Alex gave you a chance at what he couldn't give you anymore. Take it and let the warmness of life touch everything you do. Don't lock yourself in the cold darkness of the past. When you're dead, you have no choice. You're alive and there are as many choices as chances out there for you. Let Alex go. He's gone."

Anna knew what he was talking about. She should find another man. No, she couldn't do that. She never would. Alex was her only love. She'd never love anyone else. She didn't want anyone else. No one could ever take his place, and she would never think of having someone take it.

Gently, she rubbed her fingers over the gold ring on her left hand-- "till death do us part." No, not her and Alex, they'd never part. Her heart and soul would always love him. He'd always be a part of her.

"Well, I should be going home. My wife is probably waiting dinner." Mr. Thorton extended his hand. "Take care, Mrs. Leer."

"Thank you, I will." She returned his hand gesture.

For a moment she stood still and watched as he disappeared behind the institution. Turning she looked at the pile of ground and then walked toward the buggy. She had a feeling of leaving something so irreplaceable behind as she left the institution that day. Even though she had seen his grave, it was hard for her to believe that he was really gone.

****

"Henry, don't do that! There is enough wood in there already. Now put that plate back on the top of the stove and leave it there. You aren't supposed to put the piece of wood in there anyhow. You're supposed to open the door in front of the stove and put the wood in there." Amanda grabbed the piece of wood away from Henry and threw it into the woodbin.

"We better fill the woodbin up again before Ma comes home. I wonder what is keeping her so long. I hope she didn't get hurt or anything. She did say she would be home by yesterday afternoon, didn't she?" asked Amanda.

"Ya, she did. I heard her say it a couple of times. Are you worried that something might have happened to her?"

"Yes, I am. It's not like Ma to leave us alone so long."

"What are we going to do if she's not back by tonight?"

"I don't know. Maybe we should go by Dr. Whitmore and ask him what we should do."

"Ya, let's go."

"No, not yet, we'll give her a few more hours. I'll clean the house up, and we'll fill the woodbin up first. If she isn't home by then, we'll go over to Dr. Whitmore," Amanda suggested.

Amanda picked the scattered rag rugs off the floor, took them outside, shook the dirt out of them, and hung them over the stairs' railing until she had finished sweeping the house.

"Here." She handed Henry the feather duster. "Dust the furniture while I carry wood in for the woodbin."

Henry started dusting but stopped as soon as Amanda disappeared outside and down the stairs. A cold damp breeze came through the open door. Henry didn't close the door. He wanted to be sure that he could hear Amanda coming up the stairs. A mischievous idea entered his thoughts. Getting caught for doing what he was thinking about would result in a punishment.

The fire in the stove fascinated him. The dancing flames attracted him. He took the plate off and watched them. They weren't high enough for him. Taking another piece of wood from the woodbin, he stuck it into the round hole where the plate had set.

Hearing Amanda's footsteps on the stairs, he quickly put the plate back on and covered the hole. He ran into the bedroom. His little heart was pounding. He stood behind the door and waited until Amanda went down the stairs again.

Slowly, he moved through the kitchen and looked down the stairs. Seeing Amanda was busy loading pieces of wood into her arm, he went back over to the stove and took the round plate off again.

Wildly, a large fiery flame shot out of the hole and struck out at his face and brown hair. As the room filled with the distinctive smell of burning hair and flesh, the shrill scream of the burning child pierced Amanda's ears.

When Amanda heard the frightful cry of agony, she knew

something terrible must have happened to her brother. Dropping the wood, she ran to the bottom of the stairs.

At the top of the stairs, Henry stood engulfed in flames. Amanda didn't know what to do. Instinctively, she darted up the stairs toward Henry. Before she could reach him, he fell and rolled down the stairs like a ball of fire. Amanda screamed and screamed and screamed as his blazing body rolled past her and lay at the bottom of the stairs.

Upon hearing her frightful screams, a man from the street dashed back into the alley. Seeing the burning child, he took off his jacket and smothered the flames on Henry's body with it.

Useless were his efforts. The charred body lay lifeless at the bottom of the stairs. The man had merely prevented the body from burning completely.

Soon the alley was full of gawking spectators--standing--whispering.

Amanda stood paralyzed in time. Her body felt warm and then cold--then warm and then cold again. She felt sweaty. Her head became numb. It felt like it was going around and around. The voices of people seem to fade into the distance.

"Are you all right, Amanda?" The voice seemed so far away. She couldn't comprehend--then there was nothing to comprehend. It was dark and quiet.

When she opened her eyes, the white ceiling stared down at her. Where was she? In a few seconds she recognized the familiarity of her surroundings. She was in her bedroom in her bed. Seeing Dr. Whitmore beside her bed, she asked, "What happened?"

"You fainted. Fortunately, I was there to catch you; otherwise, you'd have a few bruises and bumps on yourself," replied Dr. Whitmore.

"Henry--how is Henry?" She clutched for the doctor's hand.

Dr. Whitmore shook his head. "There was nothing anyone could do. He was dead by the time I arrived."

Uncontrollably, Amanda sobbed.

Dr. Whitmore held her tight. She saw the affluently dressed man, who had smothered the flames, standing briefly in the doorway.

"Who is that man?" she asked.

By the time Dr. Whitmore turned to see who she was referring to, there was no man in the doorway--no man anywhere in sight.

"I was surprised to find out that you and Henry were here alone. Where is your ma?"

"Daddy died. Ma went to pick up--" She swallowed the lump in her throat. She could barely say the words, "His--his--body." She broke down into an explosion of tears.

"Oh, my God, and now this on top of that! How is your ma going to handle this?" He rose from the edge of the bed and walked about wringing his hands. "I'm worried about how your ma is going to take this news. It's an awful lot for one person to accept--the loss of two loved ones."

A loud voice from the other room interrupted his thoughts of concern.

"Well, what can you expect when a mother goes off with her 'men friends' and leaves her children home alone."

Filled with rage, Dr. Whitmore stormed into the other room. "How dare you malign her in her own house and after something so tragic has happened to her!"

"My! My! What does she do to promote such loyalty in you? I never thought you would--"

"Get out of here before I forget I'm a gentleman and kick you out of here!"

Amanda heard footsteps and then the door slam. She heard Dr. Whitmore talk to himself as he walked back into the bedroom. "Fools, darn stupid fools think they know everything but don't know a thing about anything! The only commandment they keep is the third. They don't even know the other nine exist, then they have the gall to judge others!--Oh, I'm sorry. They just 'ruffle my feathers.' I usually don't get mad but when I do, I make up for the times when I don't." He tucked her under the covers. "When will your ma be back?"

"I don't know. She was to be back yesterday afternoon sometime."

"Well, that's not like your ma at all. She's always reliable. When she says that she'll be back at such a time, she usually is. I think I'm going to notify the constable. Something must have happened; otherwise, she'd be here."

Looking at Amanda, he could see talking like that had upset her. "Oh, I'm sorry Amanda. I should have kept those thoughts to myself.

I'm sure your ma is fine." Lovingly, he patted her hand that was lying on top of the blanket.

"You get some rest now. Everything will be fine." With that he left the room and closed the door.

Alone--she was alone in the darkness of the room. Her brother was gone--gone forever. She'd never see that smiling face again. Oh, what a terrible way to die! He was such a good little boy. He didn't deserve to die and then such a painful death! Oh, why did that sweet little boy have to die? He never hurt anyone. Rolling over on her side, she grabbed her pillow and held it tight to her. The pillow muffled the sounds of her distressful cries. Anguish was tearing her afflicted heart apart. With the pillow wet with tears, she drifted into a land of slumber. The pain of reality was freed from her mind.

A loud scream awoke her. Springing up in bed, she was in a daze. It took a few minutes before she could comprehend where she was. She recognized the voice that belonged to the screams and cries that were coming from the other room. It was her mother. Hearing her mother's cries stirred up Amanda's emotions again. Freely, the tears flowed forth. She needed her mother and her mother needed her. She got out of bed and opened the door.

Comfortingly, Dr. Whitmore was embracing her mother. When she saw Amanda standing in the threshold, she ran toward her and embraced her tightly. Their tears mingled.

Dr. Whitmore's eyes filled with tears as he watched them soothe each other's pain.

"Why is this happening to us? Why?" asked Anna. She sat in a chair near the table. Pulling out a handkerchief, she wiped her dripping nose. "Wasn't it enough of a punishment to lose my husband? Did I have to lose my child as well?"

"Death is not a punishment, Anna." Dr. Whitmore tried to console her.

"Well, what the heck is it then? I have so very little--sob--and the little I do have--sob--is taken away from me. Oh, God! Why? Why didn't you take me instead of my boy? He had his whole life ahead of him. My life is almost gone, and it's worth nothing!"

"Oh, Ma, I'm sorry. It's my fault. I should have watched him better. I'm sorry. I'm so sorry, Ma." Amanda knelt at her mother's feet and cried in her lap. Her anguishing sobs filled the room.

Anna stroked Amanda's hair. "At least I still have you. God hasn't taken you away from me. He's taken everyone else. I think I really would die if he took you away too. I feel so dead already. My heart is bursting with pain. I couldn't take losing you!" As she sat in the chair, her stomach began to turn this way and that. Her hands began to tremble uncontrollably. Her body started to feel warm.

Dr. Whitmore saw the "white sheet" cover her face. "Are you all right, Anna?"

"Oh, I'm just so tired--so tired of living. Alex had the right idea."

"What are you talking about?" the concerned Dr. Whitmore asked.

"Oh, nothing." She had almost let it slip. No one must ever find out how Alex died. That would be another thing people would throw in Amanda's face if they knew about it.

Helping Anna out of the chair, he walked her toward her bedroom. "Come along, Amanda, help your ma get ready for bed. I'm going to make some warm milk for her. It'll help settle those nerves and help her sleep."

Anna was drained--empty. There were no more tears left. The will had left her soul.

Monday morning had come quickly. She said her last good-bye to her little boy as they lowered him into the deep, dark hole in the ground. Her bulging red eyes could cry no more. The tears and her wishes couldn't bring him back. It was hard to accept. The empty places that used to be filled by Henry pushed the cold truth of reality down her throat.

It was a small service--Dr. Whitmore--Mrs. Oker--herself and Amanda. Reluctantly, she left the hole in the ground, which was now Henry's place of rest, and proceeded to walk out of the cemetery. As she walked past the last row of graves, a hand touched her and stopped her. She was startled at first, but as she turned around to see who had touched her--surprise gripped a hold of her.

"I'm truly sorry, Mrs. Leer."

"Thank you."

"I know that I hardly know you, and I didn't know your boy at all. But like I said, I do feel that I owe you something because of what happened to your husband. Therefore, if it would be all right, I'd like to get a nice gravestone for your boy. Will you let me do that?"

"No, thank you, Mr. Stoner. He was my child. I took care of him the nine years that I had him all by myself, and I can take care of him now too. When I needed help, there was never anyone around. I don't need anyone now either."

"Please, Mrs. Leer, it's for me that I want to do this."

Anna thought. It would be for Henry. She hadn't given him much when he was alive, and she really couldn't give him much now either. She couldn't afford a gravestone. At least if Mr. Stoner got one, he'd have one. Why should she let her pride and bitterness at life deprive Henry of a gravestone? When a person is dead, that's all that is left.

"Please, Mrs. Leer, you can help me pick it out if you wish?"

"Okay. Please, let me know when you want to pick one out."

"If you feel up to it, we could pick one out now."

"No, I'm sorry, but I don't feel like it today. I really have to get more used to the idea that he's really gone. My mind is cloudy. I don't feel like making a decision like that now."

"I can understand that. Would you like a ride back to your place?" He motioned to his automobile.

"No, thank you. I want to stay here awhile."

"Sure, would it be all right if I came by your place in a week to pick you up so we could look at some gravestones?"

"That would be fine. I'd prefer a Saturday because I have to work during the week."

"Oh, I'm sure Regina wouldn't mind if you took a day off for that."

"I don't want to press my luck with her. Besides, I really can't afford to take a day off work."

"Of course, how foolish of me to even suggest such a thing. Would you mind if I gave Amanda a ride home?"

"No, not if she wants one."

"Good-bye for now." Putting his black hat back on his head, he climbed into his automobile and started traveling slowly down the road. As he approached Amanda, he stopped and talked to her. A few seconds later, they were both in the automobile riding into town.

Anna went inside the church and sat in the back pew for a long time. She felt at peace there. A great pillar of anguish seemed to be lifted off her body. Her emotions had calmed a bit. It was done, and there was nothing anyone could do about it. There was a good reason God made things happen. Perhaps she couldn't contemplate the reason now, but she'd eventually know the reason--why? She'd see Alex and little Henry again. It was just a matter of time, and when she did see them, they'd never part again. They'd have eternity together. Their days together would be like the stars in the universe--too numerous to count and always there. Tranquil thoughts such as those helped her to live from day to day.

The day Mr. Stoner came to pick her up to look at gravestones came quick and went just as quickly. Little Henry had the biggest and most elaborate gravestone in the cemetery. Mr. Stoner had insisted on it. It was rather ironic! In the years and generations to come no one would remember that Henry Leer was referred to as the "little bastard son" of the town whore. No, in a matter of years everyone is soon forgotten. The only thing that remains is a person's gravestone. In Henry's situation, most generations will assume that Henry must have been quite an important person to have such a gravestone. Well, he was important! Maybe only to two people--but sometimes that's more than some people have.

Ever since Amanda had graduated from eighth grade, she had worked in the bakery. She considered it drudgery. However, it was a job, and she had the satisfaction of looking forward to Friday, the last day of work and payday.

Anna had always figured that she had supported the family before Amanda got a job, and she could do so afterwards as well. Worrying that she might not always be around to support Amanda and Henry, Anna had always insisted that Amanda put her earnings into the bank. Anna bought all of Amanda's clothes and other necessities with the understanding that Amanda would provide for Henry if something happened to her. Anna knew Amanda loved Henry deeply, but she didn't think it was fair for Amanda to use her money to provide for Henry. So Anna thought, if she didn't ask Amanda to provide for anything that she wanted after she had a job, then things would come out even, if Amanda ever had to provide for Henry until he was old enough to find a job.

Well, that worry of Anna's would never come to pass now. Neither would her other worry--the worry about what kind of care Alex would receive after the money was gone. Which it was, after she finished paying the last monthly bill and burial expenses. Looking over the bills she couldn't believe things had actually cost that much. Well, if a person has the money, they'll take it, she thought. Alex had been in that place eleven years. Almost half of his life and twice as long as they had been together.

After Henry's death, there was a face that haunted all of Amanda's thoughts and a curiosity that longed to be satisfied. Working in the bakery, she had come to associate every face in town with a name, every face except one. She had never seen the man who had smothered the flames on Henry's body until that day. The face was young, well shaved, and pleasing to the eyes. She had never seen a man with such a crop of hair--so thick--so black. Who was that man? Something inside of her would not let the curiosity disappear. She wanted to see him again. She wanted to know who he was.

****

The damp days of spring had quickly drifted into the warm nights of summer. Pamela liked her housekeeping job with Father Aslen. He had been so kind to her. He had made her feel at home at a time when she needed to have such feelings.

From the moment she awoke until she went to sleep at night, she longed to be near him, to see him happy, and to do all that she could to please him. Within a few weeks, he had become her life. She no longer cared to visit her college friends or make new friends. Being near him was all she wanted or cared about. Her heart sang of the joy this man's presence had brought into her life and into her very heart.

It was Sunday and she had made dinner exactly the way he wanted it. When she saw him come out of the sacristy, she placed the piping hot dinner on the dining room table. By the time he'd get into the house and would sit at the table, the meal would be just right to eat. Sunday mornings always seemed to drag on and on for Pamela. It was the two Masses that he had to perform. She didn't get to spend any time with him until dinner. During the week, after early morning Mass, he would be around all morning.

"This looks and smells really good, Pam," Otto said as he sat at the table, still wearing his black vestment and Roman white collar.

Hearing him call her Pam made her heart flutter.

"You'll have a rest for a couple days this week," Otto said.

Pamela was puzzled. "Why?"

"I'll be gone for a few days. My mother is sick, and I feel that I should visit her. She is quite old."

Pamela could understand that, but she didn't like it. The house would be so empty without him. She'd miss seeing him sit by his desk and work over the church papers, miss making him meals, miss seeing him sit across the dining room table from her, and miss waiting for him to come in for breakfast after Mass. It would be so lonely without him. The thought of not being near him was more than she could tolerate at the moment.

"Excuse me." Pamela rose from the chair and left the table.

"Aren't you going to eat anything?" He noticed her empty plate.

"No, I'm not hungry." She forced a smile and went into the kitchen. In a depressed state, she stared out the window. She didn't comprehend anything that was going on outside. Her mind was too full of other thoughts. What were the feelings she had for Otto? Constantly, she desired for him to kiss her, to hold her, and feel his body tight against hers. She wanted them to be as one; she wanted to give herself fully to him and have him completely. Yes, she knew. She was in love with him. She had a burning desire for him to make love to her--oh--so passionately. What was she thinking? He was a priest. It was not right to think that way about a "man of God." What could she do? He must never find out. Being the good man he was, he'd make her leave. Even though it was wrong to think of him and want him as her lover, she couldn't control the desires that filled her daily thoughts. Cautious! She had to be cautious. She couldn't jeopardize her stay with him. If he found out how she felt, he'd surely send her away. But worse than that is what he would think of her. A harlot! Oh, to have him think that of her would be worse than not seeing him.

It was foolish for her to be in the kitchen by herself, she thought. She should be spending as much time with him as she could. Why should she waste time feeling depressed about not being near him, when she could be near him now? With her face all aglow with a radiant smile, she joined Otto at the dining room table.

"I see you feel hungry now," he commented.

"Yes, I just had a bit of an upset stomach. Where does she live?"

"Who?"

"Your mother."

"Oh--in Chicago."

"Oh, I know where that is. That'll be quite a trip."

"Yes, it'll take a few days."

"What about Mass every morning?"

"I've informed the parishioners that if they wish to attend Mass during the week they'd have to attend Saint Martin's. Father James will be available for emergencies if they should occur."

"When do you leave?"

"Right after dinner." He pulled out his pocket watch. "In exactly one hour."

Pamela's heart fell--so soon.

"That was a good meal." Otto pushed himself away from the table. Making the sign of the cross, he whispered a prayer and then excused himself from the table.

Pamela sat there, picking at her food with her fork. She wasn't hungry.

A few minutes later Otto came down the stairs in a dark suit and tie. In his hand he held a small suitcase. He looked more like a businessman than a priest.

"Well, enjoy your vacation. Before you know it, I'll be back and your vacation will be over." He took a dark top hat out of the closet and put it over his blonde hair. Waving a good-bye gesture, he went out the door.

The loneliness of that long week finally came to an end when Otto walked through the door on Saturday afternoon. Pamela's heart leaped, and she felt like she was floating on air. Seeing him again was like seeing him for the first time. He was such a sexy man. Oh! How she wanted to go to him and kiss him--hold him--love him--claim him as her own! Instead, all she could do was smile and say, "How was the trip?"

"Like any other trip."

"How is she?"

"Who?"

The Rape

"Your mother."

"Oh, she's fine." He put his hat into the closet and then went up the stairs with his suitcase.

Shortly thereafter, he came downstairs dressed in his usual priestly attire. Sitting down at his desk, he began opening the mail that had accumulated while he was gone.

Although Pamela considered him a man of good virtue, she knew that he was not the tidiest when it came to hanging up his clothes. Contemplating it was strewed about his bedroom. She proceeded to walk up the stairs.

"Where are you going?"

"Upstairs to hang up your clothes."

"I'll take care of that. I'm quite hungry. Would you please make supper."

Pamela was surprised--not that he was hungry--but that he'd hang his own clothes up. In the three months that she had been his housekeeper, never once had he hung his clothes up. She'd have to see him do that before she'd believe it! Very well, he was hungry, so she'd make supper.

While they were eating supper, a loud knock came on the door. As Pamela opened the door, a frantic man pushed his way past her into the dining room.

"Father, I'm sorry for bothering you but it's my mother! I think the end has finally come! Please, come and give her the last sacraments!"

Otto rose from his chair. Leaving an unfinished plate of food on the table, he sped out the door with the man.

Pamela took his unfinished plate and put it into the oven to keep the food warm for him. After doing dishes and tidying up the room, she decided to go up to her bedroom and crochet until Otto came back. While passing Otto's room, she glanced inside. It was just as she had suspected--a mess.

Smiling to herself and shaking her head, she went about tidying the jumbled room. As she picked up his suit jacket and examined it for a possible cleaning, an object fell out of one of the pockets.

Stooping down, Pamela picked the object up. It was a small brown book. Etched on the front cover were the words, BEECHWOOD BANK. Curiously, she opened the book and started to read the first yellow page in the book. It was a bankbook belonging to OTTO ASLEN. As her eyes surveyed the page, she was astonished at the large amount of each deposit. There was one deposit every three months. She thought, he only made some four hundred dollars a year. How on earth could he deposit three times that in a year and still manage to have money left to live on? It was strange! Where did he get that money?

Her state of confusion was broken when suddenly the book was ripped out of her hand. There stood Otto. His burning, angry eyes glaring at her. She had been too absorbed in thought that she hadn't heard him come back into the house. There she was snooping in his private belongings.

His hand came hard down against her face. The harsh blow made her fall against the bed.

"How dare you look through my private things! How dare you!" he shouted at her.

The slap hurt, but not as much as the fact that it was Otto who had hurt her and that he disapproved of her.

Being in a rage, he hit her again. Now she was becoming afraid. She had never seen Otto like that.

"Didn't I tell you to leave my things alone? Well, didn't I?"

Crying, she nodded her head.

Violently, he began shaking her. "You snoopy little thing! When I say something, I want you to listen! Do you hear me? Do you hear me?"

The words stuck in her throat. She could hardly see him through her teary, blurred eyes. "Yes, yes." She sobbed.

She felt him release her shoulders. Even though he had stopped hurting her, she still hurt deep inside. She had lost him! He'd surely ask her to leave now. She'd never see him again. Despite the fact that he had hurt her, she still cared about him--loved him. After all it was her fault, she had no right snooping in his things. He had every right to get mad at her.

Sobbing, she ran into her room and closed the door. If only she would have gone to her room first, none of this would have happened.

From underneath her bed, she pulled out a small black suitcase. Setting it on the bed, she opened it and started to pack the things from inside her dresser into the suitcase. She'd leave before he told her to. It would be more than she could coop with to hear him tell her to leave.

It didn't take her long to pack. She didn't have too much. As she clutched the suitcase handle in her hand and headed for the door, it opened. There Otto stood in the threshold. His eyes shot down at the suitcase.

"What are you doing?"

"I'm leaving."

"I'm sorry. I didn't mean to hurt you. Please, don't leave."

Not heeding what he had just said, she walked past him into the hallway.

He grabbed her hand. "Please, don't leave. I'm sorry. I promise. I'll never do that again."

"Just leave me alone. It's better this way."

"Better for whom?"

"For everyone, please, let go of my hand."

Reluctantly, he set her hand free and watched her walk down the stairs. The realization of that moment hit him. Emptiness and a sense of loss gripped him. He felt different about Pamela leaving. He never felt this way when the others had left. His emotions began to take control of him.

"Wait!" he shouted as he raced down the stairs toward her.

As she turned to see what he wanted, her eyes met his. She could see a reflection of her own desires in his eyes. Was she right about the feeling that just surged through her body? Did he want her like she wanted him? She felt his hands touch her shoulders again, but this time it was a gentle touch. His lips felt warm and so moist on hers. The warmth of his body embraced her as he held her so gently in the security of his arms. She felt herself become as light as air. There was no concern about what was morally right or wrong. She wanted him, and it was right. She'd give herself completely to him if he wanted her to--and he did.

Flinging her into his arms, he carried her up the stairs into his bedroom. It was the first time that she had made love and given herself completely to a man. The passion of that moment was all that was important. There was no one else in the world--just them.

Something that made a person feel so warm inside--so needed--and loved--couldn't be wrong. She felt no guilt. She could never feel guilty about loving someone. He was the only man who had ever touched her and whoever would. She loved him! Love was good! Love was pure ecstasy!

From that night on, Pamela warmed Otto's bed ever night. However, her love for him didn't halt her curiosity. Where did he get that money? After that night the bankbook was never mentioned again until one Sunday, three months later.

"I'll be leaving this afternoon again to visit my mother," Otto announced while they were eating dinner.

"You say you love me but yet you don't trust me."

"What are you talking about?"

"Are you really going to visit your mother or are you putting another deposit in the bank?"

"That's really none of your concern."

"Love is just a word to you, isn't it?"

"No, it isn't. I do love you but love doesn't last forever. I'll not bare my soul for love's sake. What I do when you're not around has nothing to do with how I feel about you."

Being terribly upset, Pamela rose from the table and stormed upstairs crying. If he didn't trust her, he didn't love her.

Otto was puzzled. There was nothing to get upset or all "teary eyed" about. It was really none of her concern what he did in Beechwood.

Nevertheless, Otto was concerned that she had seen the bankbook and obviously the amount of deposits. Would she tell anyone? Whom could she tell? Who would believe her? People would believe him. Unless, of course, they started investigating, then he'd be in trouble! He'd have to be cautious in his actions toward Pamela. It was important that she didn't fall out of love with him. As long as she loved him, she'd never cause trouble for him.

After he finished his dinner, he cleared the table and did the dishes for Pamela. It was about time for him to get changed for his trip. So up the stairs he went and turned the knob on his bedroom door. Pamela had locked herself inside. Being extremely upset that he didn't trust her enough to confine in her, she had locked him out of his own room. Everything he needed for his trip was in that room.

Having a quick temper, Otto began pounding on the door with his fists.

"Let me in, Pam," he yelled.

"Go away."

"Pam, let me in. I have to change my clothes for the trip."

"What's the matter with the clothes you have on? Don't you want anyone in Beechwood to know that you're a priest?"

She was absolutely right about that. Being dressed as a priest was conspicuous. Everyone always likes to talk to a priest. Another factor was that if he deposited that money as a priest, people could get suspicious. They'd question where a priest would get such money. However, as a businessman, they were just glad a person chose their bank to deposit the money in.

Pounding on the door was getting him nowhere. He had to control his burning anger. If he let it get out of control, he could hurt her. If he did that, she might turn against him and tell everyone.

"Come on, Pam, honey, open the door, please."

"Are you going to tell me what you're going to do in Beechwood?"

"Yes, I'll tell you."

"Well, I'm waiting."

"I'm not going to talk to you through a door. Please, unlock it."

"You promise you'll tell me."

"Yes, I do."

The key turned in the door and then it opened.

Otto grabbed her and laid her on the bed.

"Well, tell me."

"I love you, Pam." He laid his broad body beside hers and started to kiss her.

She pushed him aside. "No, first you tell me what you're going to do in Beechwood."

"Beechwood isn't important. All that's important is that I love you."

Every time she tried to talk, he'd smother her with his kisses. His body next to hers stirred up her emotions and desires. He had won that "round" and gotten his "going away present."

Although he had avoided her questions, he hadn't dulled her

curiosity. If anything, he had made her more ardent to find the answer out herself. While he was gone, she searched every dresser, desk, and book in the house. There was no clue to be found. He was clever all right. The money just seemed to come from nowhere.

****

The heat in the bakery that July day was just unbearable. Anna and Amanda couldn't wait until it was time for them to leave. They had plans for after work that day. They weren't going to spend all evening in that stuffy apartment. No, they were going to pack a lunch, go to the park, and stay there until dusk. But first, they had to finish at the bakery.

Because of the humid heat of the day, Regina left for home earlier than usual. Anna didn't care for the extra work, but she was glad Regina had left. The heat had made Regina very irritable.

As Regina neared the porch of her mother's house, she heard loud voices from inside. It was her mother and Arnold. They were quarreling--but about what?

Regina walked up the stairs to the door, stood outside, and listened.

"Why don't you damn fool drop dead!" Arnold shouted.

"Oh, I'm sure you would like that. Then there would be no one around to keep you in line."

"I don't need to be kept in line. I'm doing just fine."

"Sure, you are with my money and my daughter's."

"Well, what else is your daughter good for?"

Mrs. Oker slapped his face.

Arnold punched her shoulder and knocked her onto the floor.

"That's your style isn't it? Manhandling women!"

"Ah, drop dead." He started to leave the room.

Mrs. Oker scrambled to her feet and violently grabbed onto one of his arms. "You're not going anyplace until I'm done with you!"

"I don't have to listen to you. I can go anyplace I want and do whatever I want." He pushed her away and started to walk out the room.

"You walk away from me and you'll be walking away from your free meal ticket. You better get back here and listen to what I say now or tonight you'll be out of this house and out of my daughter's life without anything."

"What the heck are you talking about?"

Mrs. Oker walked over to her desk, opened the drawer, pulled out an envelope, a piece of paper, and a quill pen. Out of the envelope she pulled a stack of five hundred dollar bills. She flashed the stack in front of his face.

"This can be yours if you get out of my daughter's life right now and stay out of it forever."

"Ha, Ha! Do you think I'll settle for 'chicken feed' when I can have it all someday?"

"You take this because it's all you'll ever get. I swear. I'll see you never get any more!"

Arnold continued to chuckle. "Just how do you plan to do that?"

"I want you out of my daughter's life! For the last nine years I've seen the way you've treated her. You come home to her bed after leaving someone else's. You're asleep when she leaves in the morning and if you're here yet when she comes home you're always drunk. She has no companionship from you. You give her nothing! You just take! You're a parasite! Without you she could find a better life and I intend to help matters along." She reached for the paper and pencil. "Here's a piece of paper. I want you to write her a letter telling her that you've decided to leave and you want a divorce. You send me your address and I'll notify you when you're to come back and sign the legal papers. The day my daughter is legally free of you, I'll give you the same amount of money that I'm giving you now."

Arnold chuckled again. "Just what makes you think that I'll do such a stupid thing and give this all up?"

"Because if you don't write that letter tonight, tomorrow I'm going to my lawyer. I'll make a codicil in which I state that my daughter, Regina, cannot inherit any of my belongings until she meets the condition of the codicil. The condition being that on the day she is legally divorced from you she'll inherit what is mine."

Arnold laughed hideously at her. "You, damn old fool, actually think she'll give me up!"

"I know my Regina. She was born with a 'silver spoon' in her mouth. She's accustomed to a fine life without the toils that make it possible. If she has to choose between a life of luxury without you and a life of scrimping and working just to have your name, she will choose the life without you. She doesn't have you anyway. Besides, you wouldn't stay around too long if you'd have to work."

"You old bitch!" He slapped her face.

She dropped the money and fell against the desk. Suddenly, she felt so nauseated--a whirling sensation filled her head. She felt herself vacillate! Sensing she had no control over what was happening, she groped for a chair and sat on it. A surge of pain stabbed the center of her chest. She grasped her chest. She felt a squeezing sensation--tightness--a heavy pressure on her chest. The pain shot up to her neck and down her left arm. She could hardly breathe. "Help me--help me." The words struggled out of her throat.

Arnold picked up the money. "Die you old bitch!" he shouted at her as he left the room.

Being outside, Regina didn't hear her mother's faint cries of help. However, she sensed from the conversation that something was suddenly wrong. Quietly, she walked over to the window and peered inside. There in the chair her mother's body lay still. Swiftly, she ran into the house.

"Mother! Mother!" she shouted as she ran to the chair and threw herself at her mother's knees. Clutching her mother's hand, she begged, "Please, be all right! I love you! I don't want you to leave me! I do love you!"

Regina's tears felt warm as they fell on her mother's hands. They were warm tears of love. At that moment near her death, Mrs. Oker heard the words that she desired to hear from her daughter all her life but never did.

"I--love--you--too." Her mother's feeble hand touched hers.

"Arnold! Arnold!" Regina screamed. "I know you're here. Arnold! Come in here--now! Arnold!" Hysterically and with tear-filled eyes she watched the doorway for Arnold to appear.

A few minutes later he appeared in the doorway, but not alone. His usual companion was in his hand--a bottle of booze.

"Get the doctor!" she shouted.

Arnold merely stood in the doorway and took another drink from the bottle.

"Damn you! Get the doctor now!" Regina had never talked to him like that. Never once in all the years that they were married did she ever swear or raise her voice like that. She meant what she said. He had better leave and avoid getting her more upset. Putting the bottle down, he raced out the door to get Dr. Whitmore.

"Regina--I want you--to get rid of him. He's--no good--for you." The words slowly tumbled out.

"He's my husband, Mother. I care for him."

"How much humiliation--are you going to take--because of him?"

"I've never seen him with my own eyes with other women and until I do, I'll not believe what others say."

"My dear Regina--please--take off the blinders. Life is too short to never experience happiness. Everyone has a right to be happy at least once in this hell of an existence. Arnold will never give you that happiness. Please--get rid of him before it is too late--please."

"In all the years we've lived here you never once ever said anything bad about Arnold. You've never interfered at all with our life or made comments about it. Why all of a sudden now?"

"Because I won't be around to watch out for your interest too much longer."

"Oh, Mother, don't say such things. Why you'll probably live longer than all of us."

"Regina--please--take your blinders off. Stop looking at life through rose-colored glasses."

Regina kissed her mother's hand. "You'll be all right. I know it."

"Anna--would you please get Anna. I want to see her."

"Why do you want to see her?" Regina asked in an adverse manner.

"Please, just go get her for me. For me, please."

"I don't think I should leave you alone and I won't."

Just then Dr. Whitmore came into the room. Regina rose as the doctor walked over and examined her mother.

"Help me lay her on the sofa." He motioned to Arnold to help him carry her over to the sofa.

"We must lay her on her back."

"What's the matter with mother?"

"I think she's experienced a slight heart attack."

"Will she be all right?"

"Anna--please, I want to see Anna."

"Go get Anna before she gets too upset again," Dr. Whitmore ordered Regina. "You have to relax, Amelia. Take things easy. It'll be all right."

After tidying up the bakery, Anna and Amanda climbed the stairs to their apartment and packed their picnic lunch for the park. As Anna grabbed the brown wicker basket filled with cold chicken and buns, a knock was heard at the door.

Amanda opened it. She was surprised, in the doorway stood red-eyed Regina. Her face was covered with red blotches from her intense crying.

"What's the matter, Regina?" Amanda asked as she opened the door wider and let Regina in.

Concerned, Anna helped Regina into the room and offered her a chair.

"No, I can't stay. Mother wants to see you." Regina sobbed.

"Regina, what's the matter?" Anna sensed something had to be very seriously wrong for Regina to be in such a state and then to come and see her.

"It's Mother--sob--sob--she's dying!"

"Oh, no, not your mother! What happened?"

"Dr. Whitmore thinks she had a heart attack. She wants to see you, Anna."

"Come on!" Anna said as she grabbed Amanda's arm.

The three of them sped out of the apartment, down the stairs, and down the sidewalk to the edge of town where Mrs. Oker's house stood. As they burst into the house, they were greeted by the sight of Arnold sitting on the bottom step of the stairs.

"How is she?" asked Regina.

"Dr. Whitmore hasn't come out of there yet." Arnold motioned with his hand toward the two closed sliding doors.

Regina and Amanda stood quietly in front of the doors waiting anxiously for the doctor to come out.

Anna wrung her hands in worry and walked about nervously. Her worries and concerns were for Mrs. Oker. Her nervousness was because of Arnold. She didn't like being in the same room with him. His glassy eyes watched her every move. Every time she turned around his eyes were surveying her. She felt as if she was under a microscope--naked. She couldn't leave, so she wished he would.

Finally, the door opened and Dr. Whitmore came out.

"How is she?" asked Regina as she looked at her mother lying quietly on the sofa.

"Well, I think she'll be all right now. She needs rest."

Regina walked into the room and sat in the chair next to the sofa. "There, didn't I tell you that you'd be all right." She patted her mother's small, wrinkled hand.

"Yes, you did." Mrs. Oker smiled slightly.

Seeing Anna, Mrs. Oker asked her to come into the room.

"I'm so sorry, Mrs. Oker," Anna said as she approached the sofa.

"It wasn't your fault. There is nothing for you to be sorry about." Turning to Regina, she said, "I want to talk to Anna alone, please."

Regina didn't like that. A lot of emotions surfaced--hate--spite--jealousy--but she forced a smile and pretended to be understanding.

"Regina, please close the doors," Mrs. Oker requested as Regina crossed the threshold.

Regina forced another pleasing smile and shut the doors behind her.

"Come sit here in the chair beside me." Mrs. Oker smiled. "I want to talk to you."

"I don't think you should exhaust yourself by talking too much. You have to rest and get better."

"I won't get better. This is it. I've had more than ninety years. I'm not greedy. That's enough."

Sentimental Anna couldn't keep her eyes dry.

"I must admit this came sooner than I wanted it to. There is one thing I didn't accomplish--one very important thing. It's not for me but for Regina. I've waited too long to try and get that parasite out of her life."

Anna was surprised to hear Mrs. Oker talk like that. Never once did Mrs. Oker ever say anything bad about anyone.

"You're my last hope. Will you help me, please?"

"I would if I could but there's nothing I can do."

"Yes, there is. You hold the 'ace,' and I would never ask you to use it if there was any other way. You've used it before now, please, use it for me to help Regina."

Anna was bewildered. Ace! What was she talking about?

"Mrs. Oker, I'll not interfere in Regina's life. She's old enough to make her own decisions. She's put up with everything that he's ever done--his drinking--his women. She doesn't want to leave him."

"Regina will only take so much, and I'm hoping your 'ace' will be her limit."

"I'm sorry, but I don't know what you are talking about. What 'ace'?"

"The one you used to keep Arnold away from you."

Anna pretended that she didn't know what Mrs. Oker was talking about. Anna felt her face flush. She began to feel uneasy--like a child caught in a lie.

"Anna, Anna, I'm old but not blind. Henry, he was your 'ace.' I know whose boy he was--Arnold's."

"Well, according to the town, he could have been anyone's," Anna spoke softly.

"Anna, my dear Anna, I know you so well. I pride myself on being a good judge of character. That's why I know my daughter has to rid herself of that man. He'll take everything from Regina and when it's all gone--he'll be gone also. He isn't anything but a 'drinking stud.' That's all he knows how to do."

"What do you think I can do?"

"I want you to promise me something."

"Before I make a promise, I want to know what I'd be promising. I won't make a promise unless I know that I can keep it."

"I know you wouldn't. I know your heart. It's good but no one ever gives you a chance to show that. It's their loss not getting to know someone like you. If I die this night, I want you to promise me that you'll tell Regina that Henry was Arnold's boy."

Anna was shocked at such a request. "Regina won't believe me. She thinks the same way the whole town thinks about me. According to this town, I have a constant flow of men coming in and out of my apartment. Telling her something like that won't accomplish anything. She'd fire Amanda and me and kick us out into the cold."

"If you tell her that, there will be just as much doubt as there will be a ray of belief. That little bit of probability could be enough to make her find disgust in him to get rid of him. There is nothing more scornful than a man who deprives his wife of a child but gives a child to another woman."

"I'm sorry, but I can't do that. Amanda and I have to survive. I can't lose my job and our place to live."

"I'm afraid you may lose that anyhow."

"What do you mean?"

"Regina has always felt an antagonism toward you. I don't know if it is because she is jealous of you because you had children or if she despises the way you 'stand on your own two feet' and survive. Maybe it is none of those reasons. Sometimes there are people others dislike for no apparent reason. Anyway, if it wouldn't have been for me, Regina would have never let you keep your job or the apartment. She wouldn't have hired Amanda. She let you stay because I asked her to. After I'm gone, I don't think she'll let you stay at the bakery or the apartment. I'm sorry, Anna."

"I've always felt that Regina didn't like me, but I thought as long as I didn't provoke her or upset her, she'd never fire me."

"Maybe she won't, but I think you should be prepared. Will you tell her about Henry if she does?"

"It's useless to tell her. She'll never get rid of him."

"It's the only thing that I have left. I have to believe that it'll upset her enough to bring her to her senses and get rid of him."

"Don't you understand, Mrs. Oker? Regina doesn't want to get rid of Arnold. I'm not going to tell her about Henry. I'm sorry but it won't accomplish anything."

"Oh, Anna, please. I'm sure it will. I know when she finds out it'll be the end of him. It's worth the try. Please, tell her."

"I can't."

"What if she fires you and you no longer have anything to lose? Will you tell her then?"

"Oh, I don't know. I really don't think that it'll do any good."

"Oh, please, Anna. Please, you're my last 'ace'--my last hope!"

Anna sighed, rose from the chair, and walked over to the window. As she stared out the window, she contemplated about what she should do. What would be the right thing to do? "Okay, if she fires me, I'll tell her about Henry. I don't think that it'll do any good, but I'll tell her--just for you, okay." Anna waited for a reply. When none came, she turned around away from the window. "I said I'd--"

Mrs. Oker's eyes were staring wide open at her. The look of death sent a chill up Anna's spine and enveloped her body in a paralysis. Seeing someone so close die, had frozen her mind for a second. When reality reached out and revived her senses, an emotional--intense--uncontrollable suffering ripped her apart. "Dr. Whitmore! Come quickly!" she screamed.

The doors flew open and soon everyone was crowded about the sofa.

Placing his fingers gently over Mrs. Oker's eyes, Dr. Whitmore closed them.

No one had to say anything--everyone knew.

Regina bellowed out a loud cry, then she lashed out at Anna. "She was getting better until you came into this house. You made her die! Death follows you around like a shadow! You're evil! Get out of my sight! I don't ever want to see you little whore again! Get out! Get out and don't you dare show up at my mother's funeral! I'll not have anything more to do with you whore. Get out! Get out! Get out of my house--my life--get out!" Regina screamed as Dr. Whitmore refrained her from physically striking out at Anna.

"She's upset. She doesn't mean it. Maybe you should go now. She'll feel better in a little while," said Dr. Whitmore.

"I meant every word I said. I don't ever want to see you whores again! Now get out! You're evil! You bring death to everyone! Get out! Get out! Get out!"

Being made aware so bluntly of her defects, Anna, with Amanda at her side, lowly departed from the unexpected scene of such hatred. The vile words echoed in Anna's thoughts. Was she really evil? Is that why death seemed to plague her?

No! She wasn't evil! Things were meant to happen the way they happened. Anna would refuse to start believing what people thought and said about her. She knew that she wasn't a whore. She was a good person! She had only done one thing wrong--submitting herself to Arnold so she could keep her job. How foolish! Arnold never had a thing to say about her job. Regina didn't even have any control over her job. Mrs. Oker, that kindly, elderly lady, was truly an angel. She owed her a lot, but she couldn't do what she had asked. She wouldn't tell Regina. Henry was dead--let him rest. Things were bad enough without opening old wounds.

When they were inside their apartment, Anna looked about the barely furnished room. "I suppose tomorrow we'll have to start looking for a new job and a different place to live."

"I don't think she really meant that, do you?" asked Amanda.

"Yes, Regina meant ever word. She's been waiting nine years to let me know how much I disgust her--how I'm not worthy to even kiss the ground she walks on."

"She needs us in the bakery. She can't do all that work herself."

"Amanda, don't ever make the mistake of thinking you're absolutely necessary for anything or anyone. There's always someone around who can take your place and who maybe can do the job better than you. Nothing is for sure except death. No one ever absolutely needs you. You're only important to one person and that's you."

"You're important to me, Ma. I love you." Amanda gave her mother a long hug.

"I know, Amanda. I'll always love you. It's just us against the world."

"Yup--and tomorrow we'll look for jobs--just you and me." Amanda saw the basket on the table. "Do you still want to go to the park and eat our supper?"

"No, I'm too tired to go to the park, but I am hungry. Please, hand me a couple pieces of chicken out of the basket." Anna sat in a chair at the table. As she reached for the chicken, her hands trembled uncontrollably.

"Are you okay, Ma?" Amanda was deeply concerned.

"Yes, I'm just a little shook up. I guess."

"Well, you don't look good at all, Ma. Your eyes are so bulgy."

"I'm tired. That's all."

"Yes, besides the work, the heat is really tiring."

"Maybe it's a good thing that we move out of here. The heat is unbearable during the summer," Anna commented.

"It probably wouldn't be so hot if the heat from the bakery wouldn't rise up here."

"She'll have a hard time renting this apartment. Mrs. Oker commented once that no one stayed too long because of the terrible heat from the bakery. Regina will find that out soon enough."

"Well, in winter it's nice. You don't have to carry so much wood up here to feed the stove and keep the place warm." When Amanda looked at the stove, the burning sight of Henry flashed instantly in her mind. "I think it's good that we're leaving." Amanda got up from the table. She wasn't hungry anymore. "I'm going to start packing a few things. There is no sense waiting for the last minute. I suppose Mrs. Oker will be 'laid out' tomorrow and then buried the next day. Regina will probably be harping at us to leave after the burial. I hope we're gone by then."

"I hope so too." Anna grabbed into the basket and took out several pieces of chicken. "Gush! I'm so hungry lately."

Amanda smiled. "You might as well eat it all. Otherwise, it'll go to waste because I'm not hungry."

"Are you sure?"

"Yes, Ma." Amanda grabbed one of the empty boxes, which was set beside the stove to be used as burning material, and departed into her room. She didn't have too much to pack and before long she was finished.

Taking her doll off the dresser, she stroked its hair. The memories of her father were dim. His face had vanished, she no longer knew what he looked like. All she remembered was that he had given her the doll on her fifth birthday. The doll was all she had of him now, and she cherished that doll for that reason alone. Carefully, she placed the doll on top of the box filled with her belongings. She undressed and went to bed.

The hot, humid night passed slowly as Amanda tossed and turned trying to capture a few minutes of sleep. But sleep wouldn't come and soon the early dawn gave way to another hot day. The whistle of the arriving train revealed to her that it was foolish to try and sleep now. She got up and started breakfast. The early morning noises didn't wake Anna, so Amanda had to wake her again for breakfast.

Dragging her feet and yawning, Anna came to the table.

"Didn't you get much sleep either?" asked Amanda.

"I slept well all night. In fact, I think maybe I got too much sleep. I still feel tired. I went to bed right after you left the room."

After breakfast, they started walking down the street. Amanda went one way and Anna the other, both seeking a job. They decided that after they found a job, they'd look for a place to live. It was not practical to get a place to live until they were sure that they had a job to pay for the rent.

Across the street in Mrs. Morris's restaurant window, Anna seen a sign, DISHWASHER WANTED. Gee, could she be that lucky to find a job already? She hoped so as she ran across the street toward the restaurant. Looking into the window, she could see Mrs. Morris draping a fresh tablecloth over one of the tables.

With high hopes, Anna went into the restaurant and walked up to Mrs. Morris. "Excuse me. I'd like that job as a dishwasher."

Mrs. Morris turned around all smiles until she saw it was Anna. Suddenly, her smile disappeared. She cleared her throat. "Oh, I'm sorry, you're too late. I just hired someone. I must have forgotten to remove the sign from the window."

"Are you sure you don't need any other help?"

"No, I'm quite sure," Mrs. Morris replied sternly.

"Well, thank you anyway." Disappointed, Anna went outside and sat on the bench that stood in front of the restaurant window. The smell of the food made her hungry again but eating at home was cheaper.

As she sat there, she heard an argument commence. Mrs. Morris's voice rose above the clattering of the dishes and clanging of the silverware. "You get in there right now and wash those dishes. You don't have anything else to do."

"I told Greg that I'd come over and we'd go fishing today," a voice replied.

"You'll have plenty of time to go fishing after I hire someone to wash dishes around here. Now get in that kitchen!" Mrs. Morris ordered.

"No, I don't want to."

"Don't you sass me! As long as you live under my roof and eat at my table, you'll do what I say!"

"Ah, dishwashing ain't for boys," he grumbled.

"I don't care. You get in there right now!" Mrs. Morris had the final word, and the boy went into the kitchen. As she turned around, Mrs. Morris's face looked right into the face of Anna, who had come into the restaurant while Mrs. Morris and the boy were arguing.

"I thought you found a dishwasher, and that's why I couldn't have the job."

"I don't have time to talk to you." Mrs. Morris turned from Anna. Anna grabbed her arm. "Why did you lie?"

"I don't want a person like you working in my establishment. That's why!" She pulled loose of Anna's grip.

"A person like me--you don't know me then you dare to judge me!"

"I don't have any intentions of getting to know a person like you any better. Now, please, leave. I have descent people to talk to and wait on."

"Well, excuse me! Far be it from me to deprive a descent person like you from making a good living!"

Anna held her head high and proud as she walked out the door. She heard the snickering laughter and the slanderous tongues flapping. She wasn't the way they talked; therefore, she wouldn't act ashamed. She was just as good as all of them, and she wouldn't let them make her think otherwise.

There was only one thing left to do and that was to continue down the street in hopes of finding a job. The answer was the same at each place--"no." Weary and exhausted, Anna started back to the apartment in the midafternoon, parching sun. Her stomach rumbled with hunger and her feet burnt with a pinching pain. Hopefully, Amanda had been more lucky with finding a job.

Finding the apartment empty, Anna took off her shoes and soaked her feet in cold water. As she waited for Amanda, her eyelids became increasingly heavy. With her feet still in the water, she folded her arms on the table and rested her head on them. Within a few minutes she was asleep. The squeaking of the door woke her. Turning around, Amanda's sad face met hers. She didn't have to ask. She knew. Amanda hadn't had any luck either.

"Hand me the towel, please." Anna pointed to the towel hanging near the sink.

"What are we going to do, Ma?" Amanda handed her the towel and flopped herself down into a chair.

"Something will come along. Don't worry." Anna dried her feet and then went over to the icebox. She pulled out a carton of eggs and then proceeded to make them something to eat.

"Don't make me too much. I don't really feel like eating. Make me only one egg, please." Amanda went to the counter and cut herself a slice of bread. "You want a piece too, Ma?"

"Yes, please, cut me two."

After setting the table, Amanda sat in a kitchen chair, buttered her bread, and then watched her mother.

Into a bowl Anna broke one egg, then two, then three, then four.

"Ma, I only want one egg."

"I know. I only made you one. It's in the frying pan. I'm making myself scrambled eggs."

"You're going to eat all of them?"

"Well, I didn't eat anything since breakfast, and I've been walking all day in that hot sun. Maybe you're not hungry, but I am."

The meal passed in silence and so did the washing and drying of the dishes. Instead of packing the dishes back into the cupboard, they packed them into boxes. Their usual talks didn't prevail tonight. They both were too occupied with the thoughts of where their next meal would be coming from and where they would lay their heads after tomorrow night.

"Do you have everything of yours packed?" asked Anna.

"Yes, I've got everything that was in the dresser, on the wall, and on the floor packed. I just have to pack the blankets that are on my bed. I'll pack them tomorrow morning," replied Amanda.

"While I'm packing up things in my room, would you pack up the things in the kitchen here?" asked Anna.

"Sure, it'll only take a couple of minutes then I'll help you. Do you think we should wash the walls off before we leave?"

"I suppose. We don't want to leave the place dirty."

"Well, then I'll start that when I'm finished packing in here."

The rest of the afternoon and early evening hours were spent scrubbing the walls and floors. As twilight approached, they were finished. All ready to move--but where?

"My clothes are just sticking to me. I'm going to take a bath," Amanda said as she sat on the chair to rest for a few minutes.

"I'll be back in a little while." Anna headed toward the door.

"Where are you going?"

"I just thought of where I might get a job."

"Well, surely you're not going like that, are you?"

"Why do I look that bad?"

"After sweating from scrubbing and washing walls in this hot apartment--how do you think you look? How do you think you smell? No one will hire you looking like that."

Anna looked in the mirror on the hall tree. Her sweaty, stringy hair and perspiration spots under her arm pits were something to be desired.

"I'll get a bucket of water in so you can wash yourself and put on a clean dress. Why don't you wear a short-sleeved dress when it's so hot outside? Your arms aren't that bad," Amanda commented.

After Amanda left with the bucket to get some water, Anna took off the sweaty dress that clung to her. She examined her arms that were covered with ugly purple scars. The forest fire hadn't spared one part of either arm. Rubbing her hand over her face as she looked in the mirror, she thought how fortunate she had been that her face had been unscathed.

"So where are you going, Ma?" Amanda asked as she set the bucket of water into the sink.

"Well, there's a person who offered to help me if I ever needed it. I need it now, and I'm going to find out if his words were real or just whiffs of hot air that he just felt like blowing out." Anna began to wash herself. The cold water felt good--so refreshing--so soothing.

"Aren't you going to tell me who he is?"

"Mr. Stoner. I'm going to see, Mr. Stoner." She brushed the snarls from her hair and tied her hair neatly in back with a white ribbon.

"Mr. Stoner offered to help you?" Amanda's voice was full of bewilderment and surprise.

"Yes, a long time ago, he felt some responsibility for what happened to your dad."

"Well, he should. He caused the horses to go crazy. Is that why he bought Henry the gravestone--to ease his conscious?"

"I suppose, but it wasn't Mr. Stoner who was driving the automobile. It was his son. Mr. Stoner wasn't even in town when the accident occurred." Anna put on a clean dress, buttoned the bodice, and pulled her hair out from inside the back of her dress.

"Mr. Stoner has a son!"

"Yes, an ill-mannered, spoiled brat! He's the reason I never really thought of taking Mr. Stoner up on his offer. His son made me feel like dirt when I met him. I thought, that will be the day I'd lower myself, swallow my pride, and ask them for help. Well, I really don't have a choice now. It's getting dark already. I better hurry."

The long walk through town and up the stairs to Mr. Stoner's house was exhausting. Before knocking, Anna rested a few minutes "to catch her breath."

Nervously, she banged the decorative clapper against the large door. He was her last hope. If he said "no," what would she do?

The door opened. A uniformed maid greeted her, "Yes, how can I help you?"

"Could I please see Mr. Stoner?"

"Whom shall I say is calling?" the maid asked.

"Mrs. Leer."

"Wait here for a moment." She closed the door in front of Anna.

Anna turned away from the door and gazed at the stars while she waited. However, she was unable to enjoy their beauty. There were more important things on her mind.

The door opened, but it wasn't the maid. "Oh, Mrs. Leer. How good to see you, come in, please, come in." His greeting was ecstatic. He was genuinely glad to see her. "Eleanor, please bring us some coffee. You do like coffee?"

"Yes, but not tonight, thank you," Anna replied.

"Yes, you're quite right. It's hot enough without drinking coffee. Would you care for anything else?" asked Mr. Stoner.

"No, thank you."

"That'll be all, Eleanor, thank you."

"Wee." Eleanor bent her knees, dipped her body slightly, and departed down the long hallway.

"Please, sit." Mr. Stoner offered Anna a chair in his study.

The red leather felt cool as Anna leaned back into the chair.

"I am sorry to hear about your friend, Mrs. Oker. She was a fine lady--a very fine lady."

"Well, in a way, she's the reason that I'm here."

"She is?"

"Yes. Now that Mrs. Oker is dead I no longer have a job or a place to live."

"Oh, I suppose her daughter is going to sell everything and that leaves you in a bad situation."

"As far as I know, her daughter isn't going to sell anything. The reason I don't have a job is because she doesn't want me working in her bakery."

"Oh." The puffs of cigar smoke whirled about his head.

"You once mentioned to me that if I ever needed any help, I should just come and ask you for it. Is your offer still good?"

"Yes, if you need help, I'll gladly help."

"Well." She paused. "I was wondering if you needed any extra help around here?"

"Well, to tell you the truth everything runs pretty smoothly around here."

"I understand. I'm sorry I bothered you." Anna rose from the chair and started to leave. Words--empty words were all he had offered her --how foolish of her to think otherwise.

"Where are you going?" he called after her.

"I've bothered you enough. It's time to leave."

"You haven't bothered me. Please, come back here. I like talking to you."

"It's very kind of you to say that, but sitting here doesn't really help my problem."

"I didn't say that I wouldn't help you. I just said things run pretty smoothly around here. I don't need any more house help. However, I could use your services for something else."

"For what?"

"A companion."

"If you're offering me a job as your mistress or live in whore-- forget it!"

"No, no, Mrs. Leer, the thought never even entered my mind. I would never dishonor a lady like you by even suggesting such a thing."

"Well, what else am I to presume when you offer me a job as a companion?"

"I'm sorry. I should have made myself more clear. I meant a companion for my wife."

"Your wife?"

"Yes, it's terrible for a woman like my wife to be confined the way she is. The servants are quite busy operating the household, and they don't have the time to talk with her or be with her. She's stuck inside this house all day by herself until I come home from work. She never complains, but I know that it's not easy for her."

"Just what would I do?"

"Be with her. If she wants to go out into the gardens or into town or just wants someone to talk to. You'd just have to be around for her. You could live right here if you wished."

"Me--live here? I really don't think that I'd fit in. It's much too elegant for me."

"Nonsense! You're no different from me or anyone else here. We're all people. We all need to live somewhere. Quite a few of the other servants live here--those without a family. They all have their own private room upstairs."

"I'm not like them. I do have a family, Amanda. Remember?"

"She can stay here too. There's plenty of room. Does she have her job in the bakery yet?"

"No."

"Well, I need another teller at the bank. If she would like the job, please ask her to come to the bank at nine o'clock tomorrow morning. Otherwise, I'll get someone else."

"Mr. Stoner, I appreciate your job offers but they are really charity offers--aren't they? I mean you made the jobs for us."

"No. I didn't get to where I am by giving jobs to people that I didn't really need. Even if I did, they wouldn't be charity jobs. If it wouldn't have been for my automobile, you wouldn't be worrying about a job. Your husband would be. I owe you and I always pay my debts. Would you like to meet my wife, Eva?"

"If I'm going to be her companion, I guess it would be a good idea."

"Come along then."

Up the oak staircase they climbed. They stopped in front of one of the doors that flanked the enormous hallway.

Mr. Stoner knocked. "Can I come in, Eva?"

"Yes, I've been waiting for you." Came a reply from within.

He opened the door. Combing her copper hair was a woman about Anna's age sitting in a wheelchair.

"This is Anna Leer, Eva." He kissed Eva's lips and took hold of her hand.

"Hi." Eva smiled graciously.

"Remember, Eva, once you told me how lonely it was for you during the day when the servants were all so busy."

She chuckled. "It must have been quite awhile ago because I don't remember saying that."

"It was awhile ago--too long ago, in fact. I should have thought of your needs a long time ago. I'm eleven years too late. I'm sorry."

"Oh, Charles, you've been a good husband. You took me all over Europe trying to find someone to help me. What more could you do?"

"What I should have done then, I hope you'll let me do now."

"You know I always let you do anything you want to. What is it?"

"I'd like to hire Anna as your companion to help fill your lonely days."

"Oh, my dear Charles, what a splendid idea! It would mean so much to have someone around to talk to. Would you really want to be my companion? Oh, please, say 'yes.' "

"If you really want me to, I don't see why I couldn't be your companion."

"Oh, that's just splendid! Thank you, Charles! Thank you so much! You are indeed a good husband." She held his hand to her face and kissed it. "When can you start?" Eva was so excited.

"Tomorrow, if that would be all right?"

"Oh, yes! Tomorrow would be great!" replied Eva.

"Would you like to show Anna the house?" Charles asked.

"Oh, tomorrow is early enough. It'll give us something to do. Don't you think so, Anna?"

"Yes, tomorrow would be fine. It is getting late, and I should really be getting home."

"Yes, I can imagine it's quite hard for horses to find their way in the dark," replied Eva.

"Oh, I didn't come with a horse and buggy. I walked."

"Where do you live?"

"In town above the bakery."

"That's quite a distance to walk." She looked to Charles. "Why don't you take her home in the automobile?"

"No, thank you. It's very kind of you to offer, but it's such a beautiful night. I'd prefer to walk."

"I wish I could." Eva smiled.

"Oh, I'm sorry. It was thoughtless of me to say that."

"You don't have to be sorry. It's not your fault that I can't walk. You have the right to say whatever you think. That is the most important thing in a relationship--being honest--saying what you think and feel."

"It was nice meeting you, Mrs. Stoner. I'll see you tomorrow."

Eva extended her hand. "Yes, I'm looking forward to tomorrow. It was very nice meeting you. I'm sure we'll get along really well. Good night."

"Good night." Anna smiled, returned Eva's friendly hand gesture, and left the room.

Eva grabbed Charles's hand. "Why don't you walk her home? It's a long way back to the bakery."

"Are you sure that it's all right that I leave you for a while?"

"Yes." Eva paused. "So that's Anna Leer."

"I suppose you've heard what they say about her?"

"People like to talk. I really don't care what she does or doesn't do as long as she treats me okay. That's all that I care about."

"Well, if you know about her reputation, aren't you afraid that with her being in the same house that it'll be a lot easier for her to jump into bed with me?"

Eva chuckled. "My dear Charles, if you want to be unfaithful there is nothing I could really do about it. If it wouldn't be here, it'd be somewhere else."

"I love you, Eva. I'd never hurt you that way."

"I know you wouldn't. I don't have to worry about Anna. After seeing her I don't believe those things they say about her. I've known whores and she doesn't seem like one to me. For that reason, I really think you should walk her home."

"You're sure it's all right?"

"Yes, I think it's proper for a gentleman to walk a lady home."

As Charles departed a "well pleased" smile came across Eva's face. Yes, Anna would be perfect. She would fit into her plans perfectly! Turning her wheelchair around, she pushed herself over to the window. Through the window, with the help of the outside lamp, she could see Charles running after Anna.

From first hand experience, Eva knew how the townspeople treated women like Anna. The only difference between her and Anna was that Eva had been what they called her, whereas, Anna wasn't. The Beechwood people had not scorned Eva. They never had a chance to know what she was like before Charles met her. However, she had experience with other townspeople's treatment of whores. There were always the same bunch of "holier than thou" people living in every town. If Eva's plan succeeded, it would be funny to see those same people "eat" Anna's dirt, like Anna had "eaten" theirs.

Eva felt a strangeness about Anna. It seemed as if she had met Anna somewhere before, but she hadn't. The feeling was confusing. Why should she have that kind of feeling about someone she never met? A feeling as if she should know Anna.

When Anna and Charles had faded out of view from the light of the outside lamp, Eva called Eleanor and asked her to help her into bed. While she lay in bed in the darkness and silence of the room, she contemplated the various steps in her scheme.

****

After washing herself, Amanda went into her bedroom and closed the door behind her. To escape the heat of the night, she lay nude in her bed. Being exhausted from lack of one night's sleep and from walking all day, it didn't take long for her to fall asleep. She was unaware of the amount of time that had elapsed from the time she went to sleep until a knock on the apartment door woke her.

Who is that? She wondered as she crawled out of bed. Putting on her bathrobe, she walked toward the apartment door as she tied the bathrobe's belt snugly around her waist.

Yawning, she opened the door.

"Who are you?" she asked the husky man who stood outside the door.

"Are you Anna?" he asked.

"No, she's not here now. Who are you and what do you want?" As she became more awake, she noticed the man's glassy eyes. He was drunk! Not wanting anything to do with a man in his condition, Amanda slowly started to close the door.

"Hey! There's no need to do that!" He stuck his foot into the doorway and grabbed his hand onto the door. "I'm not going to hurt anyone. Some guys told me Anna was good for some fun. All I want is a little fun."

"Well, you won't find it here. So leave!" She held the door tight against his foot but a frail young thing like Amanda stood no chance against a big man like that. With one mighty shove, the door flung open and Amanda fell against the wall.

"Get out of here! Those men were lying! You won't find anything here!" Amanda shouted.

"Oh, no, you're the one who's lying. You see I've found something already!" With a smirk on his face he eyed Amanda's body up and down. Taking hold of the doorknob, he slammed the door shut.

"Get out of here or else I'll scream!"

"Go ahead. I don't think anyone will really care."

Filled with intense fear, she walked backwards away from the approaching man. Terror! This couldn't be happening to her! Terror! How could she get out of there? Terror! She had to think of a way! She scrambled about the table to keep him at a distance. When she had managed to have him follow her around the table away from the door, she made a sudden dash toward the door. A huge hand suddenly grabbed onto her bathrobe, ripped off her sleeve, and then swung her across the room with a tremendous force.

As her body hit the edge of the cast-iron stove, her body fell onto the floor. Her back stung for a moment. She couldn't move! As she saw him come closer and closer, she crawled up the front of the stove. Her trembling feet moved along the stove away from him.

Grabbing hold of the belt on her bathrobe, he pulled her closer to him. He slopped kisses on her face as she struggled to get away.

"Let me go, please!" The belt dug into her waist as he pulled it tighter about her. His mouth slopped down her neck to her breasts. Violently, she began to kick and kick. She now knew what he was going to do. She couldn't believe this was happening to her! A dirty pig like that looking at and kissing the private parts of her body!

When she pulled his hair, he became furious. Releasing the belt, he took her hands and held them in back of her. "It's more fun this way. I like it when you fight." His raucous voice instilled a motionless terror within her. With his enormous hand clamped around her two petite hands like a vise, he dragged her into the bedroom. Throwing her against the metal tubular footboard, he tore the bathrobe viciously from her body.

Sobbing and trembling she pleaded, "Oh, please, please, leave me alone!" She held one arm over her bare breasts and the other between her legs. As he started to take off his clothes, she slowly edged away from the bed toward the dresser. Beside the dresser, she slouched down and cuddled her body. Resting her head on the top of her knees, she sobbed uncontrollably. "Oh, Mama--help me--please--help me --please come home and help me! Mama--help me! Sob--sob--sob--sob--sob!"

"Come on, honey," called the raucous voice.

Through the teary haze, she looked up. There he stood in his hairy, naked ugliness! A big red thing protruded below his stomach. He grabbed her hand and started to pull her up to her feet. Desperately, she tried to pry her hand loose from his.

"No, please, no! Leave me alone! Please--no--no--no--"

Pulling her up, with a violent rage he threw her onto the bed. Before she could scramble out of the bed, his huge body was hovering over hers. With no avail, she tried to push him away. He pinned her arms against the bed as he beastly bit at her breasts--first one--then the other. He'd viciously suck on one, violently pull it up into his mouth and let it go. Then he'd do the same to the other. Sucking--pulling--biting--her tender, virgin breasts were tortured with repeated pain.

Using his knees, he forced her legs apart. Then he placed his legs between hers and pounced down on her inflicting bruising pain on her inner thighs. Painfully, she felt him thrust something hard between her legs. It was that ugly--red--thing! He was trying to put it into her! No! She didn't want that inside of her! She tried to twist and turn her body away from him.

The Rape

Angrily, he brutally lashed at her face with his fist. "Stop it! You old bag!" he shouted. "Hold still! You're doing what I want!"

She saw yellow spots in a black foreground. Her jaw stung. Again and again and again--he thrust that hard thing between her legs--harder and harder and harder. Suddenly, she felt it tear through her dryness. Her body screamed--screamed--screamed of the pain--pain--pain--as he ripped into her body. He laid the heaviness of his body completely on top of her. He was crushing her chest. She could hardly breathe! Vigorously, he pounded and pounded and pounded his body up and down--up and down--up and down on hers. The stabbing pelvic pain--the abdominal pain--the constant pain was unbearable. Pain! Pain! Unbearable pain! Harder and harder he pounded and pounded against her. The piercing pain--pain--pain brought more tears to her eyes. He was tearing her insides apart--pain--pain--pain! When would he stop? He was hurting her so badly. She could barely breathe! That horrid feeling of him pounding and pounding against her bones--of him tearing inside of her. When would the pain stop? The pain--pain! She couldn't tolerate it any longer! His sweaty chest clung to her. The salty drops of sweat fell off his face onto hers. His breath of stale beer made her want to regurgitate! Then she felt a "gush" inside of her as he held his body still for a second. He was putting something from his ugly body inside of hers. How revolting! To have something of his inside of her made her want to die and end this terrible thing that was happening to her! It wasn't right that he did that to her body! It was her body--her private possession! He had spoiled it! Made it dirty! It was ugly! No one was to see it much less do that to it. He had no right! He had no right! The pain--the pain--oh, the pain--when would it end?

Then she felt relief come to her chest. Slowly, he started to lift himself off her. Then he stopped and chewed at her breasts for a few seconds. She could feel the thing pull out of her. His hideous face all covered with small pits stared down at her. The ugly, distended thing had disappeared, only a little shriveled thing hung between his legs now. Anna lay there for a minute, then not wanting him to see her naked body anymore, she threw the blanket over her abused body. Clenching the top of the blanket in her fists, she held the blanket over her body and prayed that he'd leave--soon.

Her pain filled body sobbed and sniffed. It seemed like "hours" before he left the room, and she finally heard the apartment door slam shut. She listened for a few minutes. Everything was still. He had gone. She was safe now.

Slowly, she climbed out of bed. Everything ached. She couldn't stand upright. It felt like her whole insides were going to fall out. She held her hands between her legs. As she took a step, a piercing pain stabbed in her groin on each side of her abdomen. Her abdomen ached like a muscle aches the first time it is used. Crouched over with pain and with her hands still between her legs, she inched over to the chair where she had laid her clothes earlier in the evening before she went to bed. Each step stabbed her sides with pain. Suddenly, she felt something seep out of her, and she felt a moistness in her hands. Taking her hands out from between her legs, she could see they were covered with blood. She began to cry again. That animal had hurt her. She was bleeding now! Oh, God why did he have to do that to her? She felt a strange sensation run down her leg. More blood! Was she going to bleed to death? What had he hurt inside of her? What was she going to do?

Grabbing her panty, she held it between her legs to absorb the blood. Pulling the blanket off her bed, she wrapped it around herself. Sobbing--crying--she inched her way into the kitchen. Her only hope now was that her mother didn't come home. She didn't want anyone to ever know about what had happened. Shame filled her soul. She didn't want anyone to know someone had seen her naked body--touched her breasts--stuck part of them inside of her. It was so degrading not to have a say over one's own body--to be held down while someone did that to one's body.

When she reached the sink, she grabbed the wet cloth that was lying in the sink. Seeing the unlocked door, frantically, she locked it so he couldn't come back. She also didn't want to be disturbed until she had washed her body and had disposed of her torn bathrobe.

Using the cloth and a bar of homemade lye soap, she began to scrub her body. She'd scrub his smell off her--his sweat--his salvia-- his touch. Scrub--scrub--scrub--scrub! Her body would never be clean of him. Sob--sob--scrub--scrub--sob--sob--scrub--scrub! Her body was scrubbed red but still she could smell him--feel him. Scrub--sob

--scrub! She couldn't wash away what he did. She couldn't get back what he had stolen--her innocence--her virginity. It was hers to give, but she could never give it to the one she would someday love. It was stolen--ripped from her! She wasn't pure anymore. She had been violently thrown into the adult world of cruel reality. Innocence could no longer be her virtue.

While holding the wet cloth between her legs, she threw the bloody panty into the wood-burning part of the stove. She went into her bedroom where she picked up the torn bathrobe. She cringed at touching something that he had touched. After putting the bathrobe into the stove also, she set the clothing on fire. She watched until everything was burned and the flame disappeared.

Wrapping the blanket around her body, she unlocked the door so her mother could get into the apartment. Going into her bedroom, she closed the door and secured it by placing a chair's backrest under the doorknob. As she sat on her bed, she could see her reflection in the dresser mirror. She looked so ugly. She was so dirty. Sex was so degrading. No one would ever humiliate her like that again--hurt her like that again!

With the cloth still between her legs, she lay in her bed in an embryo position. Lying like that seemed to ease the pain that burned inside of her. The constant surges of pain on each side of her lower abdomen felt like the stabs of a knife.

When sleep came, she could finally escape from the horror of that hideous face and repulsive body that had smothered her.

Chapter 10
****
Deception

Standing in the center of the gothic style altar, he looked so demure as he turned around and faced his congregation. The alb appeared so crisp and fresh under the green chasuble. Green represented hope. Hope was for what? That he would be successful in his scheme and never get caught? Hope that his congregation would be very generous today again--or hope that he would soon have enough money to call an end to this farcical existence? These were the thoughts that flashed through his mind as he stood before his parish representing God.

Slightly extending his right hand, he moved it in the form of a cross as he said, "*Benedicat vos omnipotens, Deus, Pater, et Filius, et Spiritus Sanctus.*"

"Amen," was the loud uniform reply from his parishioners as they stood in their church pews.

With the words, "*Deo Gratius,*" one of the two altar boys handed Otto his black biretta, which Otto placed on top of his blonde hair. Carrying the cibrorium with the burse resting on top of it, the altar boys and Otto departed from the sanctuary into the sacristy.

The bellowing tones of the pipe organ penetrated the entire church from its hardwood floors, to its fine vaulted ceiling with molded ribs and arches, and its windows made of ornamental lead glass. The sound drowned out the clatter of the people leaving the church.

When the altar boys had their surplices and black cassocks hung in the oak wardrobe, Otto asked them to bring the two wicker collection baskets into the sacristy.

In the sacristy, they placed the baskets on top of a husky pedestal desk. "Is that all right there, Father?" asked one of the boys.

"Yes, that's fine," replied Otto as he folded his stole and green maniple into one of the bottom drawers of the oak highboy.

"Would you like us to do anything else for you, Father?" asked the other boy.

"No, that's all. You can go now," replied Otto as he removed the cincture from around his waist.

"Good-bye, Father." The boys hustled out the door and ran across the lawn to where their parents had been waiting for them.

From the sacristy window, Otto watched them leave as he took off his alb and amice. After putting the remainder of his vestments away, he pulled the shade down on the window and locked the outside door. He then walked over to the other door and surveyed the church pews and vestibule. The church was empty and so quiet. For a few moments, he stood there motionless as he drank up the serenity of the church. With the serenity came emptiness--loneliness. It was good for a man to be alone and have his privacy--sometimes but not always. Right now Otto needed privacy, and he was glad that he could have it. However, he couldn't cope with the loneliness if he knew it was going to be forever. That's why he was so glad that he had Pamela now. She filled the empty void of loneliness for him. He could choose now. When he wanted to be alone, he could be. If he didn't want to be, Pamela was there. He liked having control over things and people. There was only one person he couldn't control--his mother. Still now yet, he hated her for dominating his life and making him leave his father. Thinking of her made him frustrated. He never got a chance to get even with her. Oh, how he hated her for dying before he had his revenge. Violently, he struck out at the wall with his fist. For a few seconds the anger that surged inside of him hid the pain of his fist hitting the wall. When his hand finally stung of the pain, he shook it about as to shake away the pain. Then he caressed it in his other hand and rubbed it for a few seconds. After the pain had ceased, he closed the door and locked himself inside the sacristy.

Grabbing beneath his black cassock and into his suit pants pocket, he pulled out a small key. With the key he unlocked the tambour roll top of the desk. After rolling up the desk top, he sat on the sturdy ladder-back chair.

He grabbed one basket off the top of the desk and began to count the money. There were several white envelopes with names written across the front. These were envelopes with money inside for church dues. Otto put them on a separate pile.

After counting out the money, he jotted the amount onto a piece of paper. Then one by one he tore open the envelopes and counted the money inside. On a piece of paper, listing the parishioners, he wrote down the amount of money that was in the envelope next to the name that had been written on the envelope. Everyone was given credit for the amount that they had paid toward their assigned church dues. That amount had to be accurate for the church bulletin that was issued at the end of the fiscal year. After placing that money on a separate pile, he jotted the amount onto a piece of paper and placed the paper near the pile.

Since the parish paid him seven hundred dollars annually, the nuns five hundred, the organist five dollars, and the janitor eighty, he had to be sure there was at least that amount in the bankbook to pay those expenses. That meant he'd have to deposit at least so much to cover those expenses and that is exactly what he had been doing for the last four years.

He counted out twenty-five dollars in change and put it into a brown cloth bag. Before zipping the bag shut, he reached under his cassock again and into the pocket of his suit pants. Out of the pocket he pulled two small brown books. He opened one and examined it, then he tossed that one onto the desk. After examining the contents of the other brown book, he put it into the cloth bag with the twenty-five dollars. Zipping the bag shut, he put it into one of the pigeon holes located in the roll-top desk. The remainder of the money he put into the other brown cloth bag, which by now was bulging from three months of Sunday collections. It was about time to go to Beechwood again. He'd talk to Father James tomorrow.

He added up the totals--ninety dollars and fifty cents minus the twenty-five. He stuck this piece of paper into the bag, zipped the bag shut, and put it back into its pigeon hole.

The outside doorknob began to turn. Someone was trying to get into the sacristy. His eyes shot to the clock. It must be an early mass server for the ten o'clock Mass, he thought.

Hurriedly, he pulled down the desk's roll-top cover and locked it securely. After unlocking the inside sacristy door, he took the two empty baskets and set them outside the sanctuary against the wall where the communion railing ended.

The church was still empty.

He then proceeded to unlock the outside door. As he opened it, he saw a little boy patiently sitting on the steps. "Good morning," Otto greeted him.

The startled boy sprang to his feet. "Good morning, Father."

"A little bit early, aren't you?"

"Yes, I'm sorry."

"That's all right. The important thing is that you are here." Otto motioned him into the sacristy.

After the High Mass, when the church and sacristy were once again empty, Otto locked everything again and proceeded as before. The only exception was that this money went into the bulging brown bag. He took the brown little book that he had tossed onto the desk earlier and opened it. Taking a date stamp, he adjusted it to Monday's date, pressed it onto the ink pad, and stamped the date into the bankbook. Next, using an eye dropper, he filled his fountain pen with ink. After examining the piece of paper, where he had figured out this Sunday's totals on, he jotted down the total into the bankbook and then added that sum to the amount he already had in the book.

That little book was the book he showed to the trustees at the monthly church meetings. For as long as he had been a priest in the parish, which was five years now, he had managed to talk the trustees out of expensive repairs. How long he could do that, often troubled him. If they ever decided to do expensive repairs, they would find out the total in the book was not accurate. In fact, they'd find out that he hadn't submitted that book to the bank for more than four years.

Smugly, he smiled to himself as he thought how clever he had been to get the other bankbook. All he had to do was to tell the clerk that he had lost the old bankbook and she issued him a new one. The new one was the one in the cloth brown bag filled with the twenty-five dollars. The one he always took to the bank. The one the trustees never saw. The one he used to fulfill the duty the lazy trustees had given him. The duty to withdraw the money and pay the salaries of the parish's employees.

Vanity filled his soul. There was no remorse. Even if there had been room in his soul for remorse, he wouldn't have felt any. His parishioners were the elite of Boston's society. Most of them had more money than they knew what to do with. Why shouldn't he have some of that money? He knew what to do with it.

Out of the bottom drawer he took a large black book, an old Bible. Lifting the cover revealed the hollowed out inside of the book. Only the borders of the pages remained. Into the hollowed out pages, he placed the bulging brown bag and bankbook. Once he closed the cover, it appeared as a Bible again. Reaching into the desk, he grabbed the other brown bag and rested it on top of the Bible. After checking to see everything was in order, he went out the door.

When she saw Otto come out of the sacristy, Pamela knew that the Masses for the day were completed. It was a beautiful day in April. It was not at all like the day a year ago when she first met Otto. That day turned out to be the most important day of her life.

Quickly, she set the table. She had it decorated with a vase full of tulips and had baked his favorite desert--apple pie. Everything had to be special today. Today was the day she had decided to tell him and everything had to be just right. It had to be today. She couldn't put it off any longer. He had to help her decide what to do. She couldn't make that decision alone.

Constantly, she had worried about how he would react and what he would do. That was why she hadn't told him before--why she had delayed telling him--but she could no longer do that. Something had to be said and it had to be today!

Pamela greeted him with a warm smile as he entered the house. After placing the Bible and the brown bag on his desk, he sat at the table.

All during the meal, Pamela waited for the right moment to tell him but it never seemed to come. After dishes she joined him in the living room where he was sitting on the sofa reading the Sunday paper.

Pamela sat beside him. "I have to talk to you."

"Well talk. I'm listening." He continued to read the paper.

"Please, I have to have your full attention."

"Okay." He folded the paper and set it on the arm of the sofa.

"Do you really love me, Otto?"

"Yes, I do. I love you deeply." He put his arm around her.

"I don't know how to tell you." She paused. "I guess I might just as well blurt it out. I'm pregnant."

"Oh, boy! I didn't count on that happening." He was surprised. "How many months are you?"

"Five."

"What are you going to do?"

"Me? It's our baby so it's our decision."

"Well, you can't stay around here and have it. Now can you?"

"You want me to go away? I thought you loved me."

"I do."

"Then why do you want to get rid of me?" Her eyes became watery.

"Be realistic! You cannot have that baby in this house. People never see you out. They'll put 'two and two' together. They'll run us both out of town."

"Well, where should I go? What should I do?"

Otto sighed. "I have to think about this." He rose from the sofa and walked about in deep thought for a few seconds. Suddenly, he grabbed the Bible and the cloth bag.

As he headed up the stairs, Pamela called after him, "Where are you going?"

"Upstairs."

"But we haven't decided what we're going to do."

"I've got to have some time alone to think about it."

"Then you will help me decide what to do?"

"Yes--after while--not now!"

Pamela sat on the sofa. Had she waited this long for nothing? Was he going to let her make the decision by herself or was he really going to help her? What if he didn't help her? What could she do? She couldn't stay here, but she had no place to go--no money! She'd have to have money! She'd have to live! Worry--worry--worry!

She felt her lower abdomen, in another month she'd start to show. No one would hire a pregnant woman. It was hard enough for a woman to get a job if she wasn't pregnant. Oh, God, what would she do? He was a priest. He couldn't come with her. She'd be alone and after the baby came--then what? She could never come back here--not with a child! Maybe she should give the baby away? She had heard of women doing that. If she did that, she could come back and no one would ever know. Maybe that would be the best thing. She would have no resources for supporting a baby. If she gave the baby away, someone with money would probably adopt it. It would be better for the baby. As she looked up the stairs, she wondered if Otto was really thinking of her.

Upstairs Otto sat at his desk. A thousand thoughts bombarded his mind. What was he doing here--what was he really doing? He was no real priest! Sure he had been ordained a priest but he wasn't one--not really--not in his heart. Being a priest was his mother's idea--not his. He only continued because it seemed like an easy life. It was an easy life until Pamela came along. Oh, there had been women before but there was something about Pamela. She seemed to wrap him in a "spell." He felt different about her--that was the difference. He had feelings for her. He longed to be with her--not just for sex but because he wanted her close. Was that love? Was that the different feeling he had for her? It was that feeling that couldn't let her be alone now. It was his child she was carrying. If he didn't help her, what would become of them both. He didn't want to spend a day without her. He always wanted her close to him.

"Damn it! I love her!" He rose from the chair and walked over to the window. He gazed at the church. He knew how he felt about Pamela but his feelings for the church were mixed--confusing. Somehow he couldn't make himself feel about the church the way a priest was supposed to feel. His feelings for Pamela and the child were greater.

Maybe her pregnancy was a sign. A sign that maybe he should leave before he got caught at what he was doing. If he stayed here now, he'd lose Pamela and the child. But in time, he'd eventually lose his church also.

Biting his lip and deep in thought, he walked back to the desk. Taking the brown cloth bag, he opened it and pulled out the bankbook. After setting the bag down, he opened the hollowed out Bible and pulled out that bankbook. With the two books in his hand, he walked over to the cold potbellied stove, which centered one wall.

After placing the bankbooks inside the stove, he reached for a match and ignited them. He watched the flames consume the books and turn them into mere dark-gray ashes.

He opened his closet and pulled a suitcase off the top shelf. After placing the suitcase on his bed, he opened it and put both of the brown cloth bags inside. He concealed the bags by covering them with various pieces of clothing from his dresser drawers. When the suitcase was full, he closed it.

Throwing his cassock and white Roman collar onto the bed, he put on a suit jacket and matching tie.

Pulling one of the drawers completely out of the dresser, he turned it upside down and removed the tape, which fastened the Beechwood bankbook to the underside of the drawer. Putting the bankbook into his pocket and grabbing the suitcase, he opened his bedroom door. He paused in the threshold for a second as his eyes surveyed the room. Had he taken and disposed of everything that could incriminate him or help others to find him? Yes--he had! With that reassuring thought, he closed the door.

When Pamela seen him coming down the stairs, she rose from the sofa. Butterflies fluttered inside of her stomach. Her legs trembled as she eyed the suitcase. He had decided the inevitable! Uncontrollably, her lips trembled--her chin quivered--her eyes filled with tears. He wanted her to go so badly that he had packed her things for her?

Otto, being extremely concerned about her trembling and misty blue eyes, ran down the remaining steps. Throwing the suitcase down, he embraced her.

"What's the matter?"

Pamela pushed him away. "What do you care? You couldn't wait to get rid of me! Could you?"

"What are you talking about?" Gently he put his hands on her shoulders to try and calm her and stop her from crying.

"You were in such a hurry to get rid of me that you couldn't even wait for me to pack my own suitcase! You had to do it for me!"

"That's my suitcase."

"Oh, so you were the one who was going to leave. It doesn't really matter who leaves. The end result is the same. I'm left alone."

Gently he put his hands on her face and wiped it free of the tears. "Pam, I'm not going to leave you. I love you." He held her body close to his and lovingly rubbed his hands over her shoulders and back.

It felt so good to feel him hold her again and to say those words, but what good were words--empty words! No matter how they made her feel, they couldn't change the situation she was in.

"Words are cheap, Otto!" She pulled out of his embrace.

"Not when I say them they aren't."

"Boy! When I do something stupid, I really do it well. I should have known our relationship couldn't go anyplace. Now I'm pregnant and the father can't marry me! Oh, that's funny--isn't it--Father. Oh, God--now that's even funnier--call on God to help me after what I did--went to bed with one of his priests!"

"Pam, please, don't get so excited. Let me explain my decision."

"I shouldn't get excited!" She snapped. "Well, damn it all! I surely do have something to get excited about!"

"No, you don't. Now sit down, please." Lovingly, he helped her over to the sofa. "I want you to calm yourself, then go upstairs, and pack what you want to take along. We're leaving tonight."

Pamela was puzzled. Was he leaving his parish--the priesthood? Or was he just taking her somewhere? "Where are you taking me?"

"I'm taking you along with me."

"Just what are you saying? Are you going to stay with me or are you just dumping me off somewhere?"

"I'm saying. Let's leave Brookline. Let's leave Massachusetts. Let's leave everything behind and start a new life together as husband and wife."

"You can't marry me. You're a priest."

"I'm a priest here but not anyplace else. There's a big world out there and plenty of space for us to get lost in. No one need ever know about what I was."

"Where could we go?"

"Beechwood."

"Where and what is that?"

"That's a town in Wisconsin."

"Wisconsin! That's so far away!"

"The farther, the better. We could have a whole new, fresh start--the three of us."

Pamela felt a warm flicker inside of her when he said "the three of us." He really did love them and he did want them in his life.

"We can get married when the train stops in Chicago, then we'll be Mr. and Mrs. Aslen when we start our new life in Beechwood."

"Are you sure that's what you really want to do?"

"If it wouldn't be, I wouldn't have suggested it."

Overcome with ecstasy, Pamela clasped him in her arms.

He held her close for a minute. "We shouldn't be doing this when the curtains are open."

She pushed away and examined each window. No one had seen them.

"Maybe you should go up and pack now," Otto suggested.

"Yes, the sooner I get packed, the sooner we can leave."

"No, I don't think we should leave until it's dark. However, I do think I should go and purchase our tickets now so we will be able to leave tonight for sure."

"What if someone sees you?"

"I'll be careful. If someone does ask, I'll just tell them I'm visiting my mother in Chicago. See you later." He went out the door.

After she had her suitcase packed, Pamela set about tidying up the house. For some reason she didn't want anyone to think that she was a sloppy housekeeper.

It was getting to be suppertime and Otto was still not back. Pamela was getting hungry. Browsing in the icebox, she decided to eat the remaining eggs and made herself some scrambled eggs.

After she had her meal and everything cleaned, thoughts of worry began to possess her. Why wasn't Otto back yet? Was he even coming back? Maybe he had planned all along to leave and never come back? No, he was coming back. His suitcase was still here. Well, he didn't really need that, did he? He could always buy new things. Had he really left her? Had he never cared for her--just made a dumb fool of her?

With her coat on, she sat in the darkness and the damp chill of the evening air--alone in her thoughts of despair.

Soon a flash of light came through the open door and a shadow of a man appeared and then disappeared as the door shut.

"Pam, Pam," called a voice. It was Otto. He had come back.

"I'm in here." She sprang from the sofa and went to meet him.

"Are you ready?" He walked over to the bottom of the stairs and picked up his suitcase.

"Yes." She stood anxiously holding her suitcase.

"Well, let's go then." He opened the door.

With their suitcases in their hands, they stole out into the black darkness of the night.

"Where were you all the time?" asked Pamela as she trotted down the street.

"Hold up! You don't have to go so fast. We've got plenty of time."

Pamela stopped for a second to wait for Otto to catch up. He didn't seem too sure of his steps. As he neared, Pamela could smell his inebriated breath.

"My goodness, were you in a tavern drinking?"

"Nope."

"Come on, Otto, I'm not stupid. I can smell the alcohol on your breath."

"I didn't say I wasn't drinking. I just said I wasn't in a tavern."

"Well, where else does one drink!"

"I was in the sacristy. I finished the last couple bottles of wine." Otto began to chuckle.

"What's so funny?"

"You know they never even noticed it when I'd drink a bottle or two in the afternoon."

"Well, I never noticed either."

"Of course not, I was too smart for all of you. I knew just how much I could drink without showing."

"Well this afternoon you didn't know."

"It doesn't matter now. I don't have a reputation or priesthood to protect. I might as well take all I can from them."

"Well, you surely picked a fine time to drink. A time when you're supposed to have your head together and you're drunk!"

Otto grabbed her arm and held it tight. "Don't ever tell me what I can do or can't do!"

"You're hurting my arm. Let me go!"

"Did you hear me?"

"Yes, I did. You're hurting me!"

Flinging her arm loose, he repeated, "Don't ever tell me what to do or what I can't do! I'll do what I want--when I want!"

By the time anyone would find out they were gone, they would be far away. The parishioners would never see their money, Father Aslen, or Pamela Bester again. They would be as the darkness of the night is--you know the darkness was there but there is no trace of it after dawn comes. So it would be with Otto and Pamela, at least that's what they had hoped and planned on. However, time has a way of making us all pay our "just dues," if not now, then later--if not in this life, then in the next. No one ever gets away "scot free." It's just a matter of time. It's only the fool who thinks he can fool others.

The long swaying train ride made Pamela's stomach turn. The black smoke from the stack blew into the passengers' car and made her nauseated. She spent the majority of the train ride in the small room at the back of the car. Puking through the open hole onto the track made her stomach feel raw and her sides ache.

Relief finally came when the train stopped in Chicago. They were going to spend a few days there before going to Beechwood. Pamela needed the rest and welcomed it.

After a few days of rest and being able to keep food in her stomach, Pamela felt and looked much better. The whitish complexion that had characterized her face the last several days, since they had departed from Brookline, had disappeared.

"How do you feel today," asked Otto?

"Much better," Pamela replied as she lay in the bed.

"Think you feel good enough to get married."

"Yes, I do."

"Good, because that's what we're going to do today."

"Really!" Pamela sat up in the bed. Her face was aglow. They were really going to get married--no more waiting--no more wondering if and when they really would. She and the baby weren't going to be alone.

From out of the dresser drawer, Otto pulled a box. It was wrapped in white paper and decorated with brilliant red ribbons. "A little present for you, Pam."

"Oh, thank you, Otto. You didn't have to do that."

"I know I didn't, but I wanted to."

"It's wrapped so beautifully! I hate to rip it apart."

"What's inside is even prettier."

Slowly, she took off the ribbons and wrappings. "I didn't see you bring this in. When did you get it?" She smiled at him.

"Yesterday when you were sleeping."

"Guess I did a lot of that the last couple of days, didn't I?"

Out of the box she pulled a beautiful white satin dress. It was so smooth to the touch and its lustrous surface was decorated with delicate white chantilly lace.

"Otto, it's beautiful--almost too beautiful to wear!"

"Well, you're going to wear it this afternoon."

"This afternoon? It's too pretty to wear just anyplace."

"You're not wearing it to just anyplace. You're wearing it to the justice of the peace."

With Pamela glowing in her dress of white and Otto truly dignified in his elaborate suit, they were married that afternoon in a justice's chamber. To keep the way they looked that wedding day always vivid in their memories, they went to a studio and had a black and white photo taken.

They stayed in Chicago a few more days waiting for the photo.

On the day the photo was to be finished and available to be picked up, Otto went to get it while Pamela packed their things. Otto had only been gone for a few minutes when suddenly Pamela hunched over from terrible pain in her lower abdomen. After a few seconds the pain ceased and Pamela continued to pack their suitcases. Suddenly, another pain stabbed her in the lower abdomen and soon spread to the groin on both sides. This pain lasted several minutes. When it finally subsided, she slowly walked over to the bed. She sat for a few minutes at the edge of the bed and then she lay down. Another pain shot through her abdomen. She pulled her knees up, but that didn't alleviate the pain. Another pain stabbed her--then another--then another. She felt a strange sensation flow. Her body seemed to have expelled something. She felt a wetness between her legs. Reaching her hand between her legs, she felt something oozy on her hand and found that she had passed a very large clot of blood. What was happening? Was her baby coming? No! It wasn't time! It couldn't come now! Maybe if she lay still, the pain would go away. The clot of blood didn't seem natural? What was happening? Something was wrong! The pain ceased and she tried to remain still--so quiet--quiet--quiet--but the pain came again and again. The pain and the fear of not knowing what was happening made her call out--

"Help me! Somebody, please, help me! Help me!"

A few minutes later there was a knock on the door. "Is something the matter in there?"

"Yes, please come in and help me! Something is the matter with my baby!" Pamela was becoming overwhelmed with fear.

The man rushed into the room. Seeing Pamela huddled in pain, he called loudly, "Elsie! Elsie! Come quickly!"

Soon a middle-aged woman was standing over Pamela. "My God! I think she's going into labor! Get Dr. Raleigh! Hurry!"

It seemed like hours before Dr. Raleigh came.

"Oh--doctor, please tell me it's not the baby--please!"

With gentle hands he examined her. "I can't. It's coming. There's nothing I can do now but watch and hope everything goes okay."

"Otto--where's Otto?"

"Who's Otto?" asked the doctor.

"Must be her husband." The woman shrugged her shoulders as she stroked Pamela's forehead.

Pamela gasped her hands onto the side of the bed with all the force that she had as more tight--stabbing pain pulled through her abdomen and now her back. Then with another sharp pain came a sudden gush of warmness. She felt the contents of her womb leave her body and her body felt relief. The room was filled with silence--silence. There was no cry of a baby. She sensed there was no baby anymore. The doctor turned his hand into the lower part of her abdomen. It hurt! She felt some more of what was inside of her flow out. It was over and her eyes filled with tears--tears of pain--pain--pain! Never would she have another child. The pain wasn't worth it.

They stayed another week in Chicago and then departed to Beechwood. Pamela enjoyed the trip now. Never again would she let herself get tied down with a pregnancy that prevented her from doing what she wanted and enjoying things like other people did. But worst than that was how sick she had been and that terrible pain--never again.

"Are you upset about the baby?" Pamela asked Otto as the swaying passengers' car traveled on the railroad track toward their distination.

"No, it was meant to be. Maybe it was for the best. Now we can really start a new life. We don't have to worry about anyone finding out that you were pregnant before we married. We can start our new life as the perfect couple. I'm going to start my own business in Beechwood. It's important that we appear as honest, God-loving people."

"What kind of business?" asked Pamela.

"Cattle trucking and milk hauling business."

"Cattle trucking and milk hauling business? What on earth is that?"

"You've seen those horseless carriages?"

"Yes, they were starting to be used all over Brookline."

"They are the coming thing. It's just a matter of time before horse drawn buggies will disappear completely."

"Oh, I don't know about that. I wouldn't care to ride in them. They scare me."

"Well, you better get used to them because they are a big part of my idea. I plan to buy two of those horseless trucks and haul the farmers' milk and livestock for them."

"I don't know anything about farmers and I don't really know what you are talking about."

"Every day the farmer has to haul his milk into town to the creamery. That daily chore wastes a lot of his work time especially during the planting and harvesting season. My idea is to buy a truck, pick the milk up from the farmers and haul it into town for them."

"I don't understand how that can make you any money?"

"Let's say. I can haul milk for ten farmers to the creamy in my truck. I only have to make one trip into town. So if I pick up milk from ten farmers and charge them a fee for the service, and I only make one trip into town then the fee from the other nine would be profit. My other idea is to haul livestock. If a farmer wants to ship any livestock now in Beechwood, he has to take the livestock through town to the train and from there the train hauls the livestock to the stockyards. My idea is to pick up all livestock on a certain day with my truck, charge a fee, and haul the livestock to the stockyards in my truck."

"They sound like good ideas, but there is one thing wrong with them that you really should consider," Pamela commented.

"What's that?"

"The success of your ideas doesn't depend on how hard you work but on what the farmers do. What if they don't care for the service you offer? Maybe they have more time to bring the milk into town than they have money to pay you for such services."

"That's why now is a good time to start my business. The farmers like to spend every hour of daylight getting their crops in now. Going into town ruins the whole morning for them especially if they live quite a distance from Beechwood. I'm hoping that by the time they have their crops planted, they'll be spoiled and will want me to continue providing my services."

"Your idea sounds pretty 'iffy.' "

"Well, if that one doesn't work, I know the livestock hauling will work."

"How can you be so sure of that?"

"Because I'm going to charge them the same fee the railroad charges them. The only difference is that I'll pick the livestock up at their farms. Letting me haul the livestock would be to their benefit."

"That idea sounds like it could work a lot better than the other one."

"The other one will work too--just wait and see."

"Why don't you just buy one truck now and see how things go before you buy another?"

"I've got the money to buy two of them. That's what I want to do and that's what I'm going to do. I'm going to get my business going before anyone else gets the same idea as me. The first one in makes the most money, and that's what life is all about. I'm also going to build a new house."

"Where did you get all that money? I know you couldn't have saved it all out of your yearly salary as a priest."

"There is no need for you to know that--to ever know that. As of this minute, I don't ever want the past to be brought up again. We're going to have a new life and a new start. Bringing up what happened before now would only cause trouble in our new life. For our new life to success the way we want it to, the old must be buried and never dug up. You forget about my past, and I'll forget about yours."

"You make it sound like blackmail."

"In a way it is. If you ever think you can or want to ruin me by bringing up my past--just remember--I know about yours and I can talk too. No one ever crosses me and gets away with it."

Pamela sat completely motionless and speechless for a second. She was amazed--astonished! She thought that she knew Otto, but now he had just revealed a side of himself that she had never known--a side of revenge toward anyone who went against him. Seeing that side of him frightened her, especially when he reached over, grabbed her hand, and squeezed it tightly.

"Do you understand?"

"Yes, I do. Please, let go of my hand. You're hurting it."

With a flaming look in his eyes, he let her hand go.

The rest of the trip was spent in silence.

Pamela sat thinking, what else didn't she know about this man?

Otto thought of his ideas and the dreams that he would make come true.

Soon the train stopped and they both stepped off the train into what was to be their new life. A new life with the shadow of the old always present--the shadow that bonded their future together.

After renting a buggy and a horse from the livery stable, they rode down the street toward the edge of town. The buggy stopped and they both looked at the weather-beaten sign that arched the entrance to a driveway. The letters were half rotted away but a person could still distinguish what it had said, ASLEN.

Pamela looked at the house that stood at the end of the driveway. The gray repulsive house, which sagged on its foundation, had not been Pamela's vision of the place that she was going to live in.

The house didn't fit into the tranquil scene of the sparkling pond and tall green trees that shaded it and dotted what once must have been a trimmed, well-groomed lawn.

A short distance from the house stood a gray barn. If Pamela had a choice, she'd have preferred to live in the barn. It looked more inviting.

"Boy, this place really has changed." Otto motioned to the horse to proceed down the driveway. "Of all the times I've come to Beechwood, I never once could bring myself to come out here."

"Why?" asked Pamela.

"I don't know. No, that's not true. I guess I thought coming out here would bring me closer to her and I didn't want anything to do with her."

"Who? Your mother?"

"I was just 'cutting off my nose to spite my face.' I was only hurting myself. This place is mine and I'm going to use it to suit my wants and needs."

"It isn't very much if you ask me."

"There's five acres here and land is always worth something, especially here at the edge of town. You see those last houses we passed?"

Pamela nodded.

"That land used to belong to this farm. The 'old bag' sold almost everything to pay for my education as a priest."

"Who? Your mother?" Pamela asked again.

Otto stopped the buggy and stepped down off it. He looked around for a moment and then walked up the decaying porch steps.

The double-hung front doors creaked as he opened them. Standing in the threshold, he turned and motioned Pamela to come up by him.

Soon they were both standing in the foyer looking at the cobwebbed and dust-covered interior of the house. As Pamela touched the handrail on the stairs, it fell off its rotten foundation and crashed to the floor.

Rats scrambled from all directions into the holes that they had gnawed into the wooden baseboards.

Pamela screamed!

"They're just rats. Don't be ridiculous! They're more afraid of you than you are of them."

"Let's get out of here! I'm not living here! No way!" She headed toward the door.

Otto's hand grabbed tightly onto her arm. "You'll live where I tell you to live."

As he released her arm, she could see the red imprint of his hand where he had grabbed her. With her hand, she held the spot that now stung of pain. He had hurt her again. What kind of a man had she married? Either she did things his way or he hurt her.

Her eyes roamed about the foyer as Otto walked into another room. Her spine shivered. She didn't want to live in such a place. Surely Otto wouldn't either, not after the nice place that he had in Brookline. Was she wrong about that also? Had she misjudged him again?

"God, damn it!" A yell came from the other room.

Pamela rushed through the threshold. There was Otto hanging onto the windowsill for dear life. One of his feet had fallen through the floor. The floor had rotted from years and years of exposure to elements of the weather that had come through the broken window.

Pamela approached him very cautiously. With every step she took toward him, she was afraid the same thing would happen to her.

"Stay away from here. I can get up myself," he yelled.

Pamela stood still in her tracks.

With a good grip on the windowsill and with the help of his other leg, he pulled himself out of the hole away from the weak part of the floor. After examining his leg, he found that it hadn't been hurt seriously. He had only a few scratches on it. He'd survive. Pamela was glad that he hadn't been hurt, but in a way she was glad that it had happened. Maybe he'd change his mind about living here, she hoped.

"Let's look at the rest of the house," he said.

He must be crazy, Pamela thought. "No, I'll wait outside in the buggy for you. We are going to town to eat and sleep, aren't we?"

"We'll see." He turned and went up the stairs.

Pamela held her breath as he took each step. What if he fell through the stairs? She decided to wait inside just in case he had another accident. Outside she wouldn't hear him if he yelled for help.

Being there in the silence of the old house made her nervous--gave her the "jitters." Sometimes the silence was broken by the sound of rats moving between the walls--gnawing on wood. Sometimes she'd hear the boards moan beneath Otto's feet. It seemed like she had waited ages for Otto to finally say, "Let's go."

****

"Good morning, Mr. Hof." The friendly greeting along with the warm smile came from the girl behind the teller window. "How are you today?"

"Fine. How are you today, Miss Leer?"

"I feel just like the May weather. Wonderful!"

"I missed your pleasant smile the last couple of weeks that you weren't here."

"Thank you. How very kind of you to say that." Amanda smiled.

"It's the truth. Otherwise, I wouldn't say it. How is your baby? Oh, I'm sorry. I didn't mean to offend you."

"You didn't. I'm not ashamed of him, he's a find little boy and I wouldn't have missed having him for the world."

"It must be hard working all day and then taking care of a baby at night."

"I think for most women it would be, but it isn't for me. My mother and Eva fuss over him constantly. I don't know who the real grandmother is once and awhile. This morning they told Eleanor to make a birthday cake for supper to celebrate his month old birthday. Can you imagine that? We're all going to get fat if they make birthday cakes every month."

Pete chuckled as he opened his wallet and pushed several dollar bills through the teller window. "Put it all in my savings account, please."

"Excuse me, please." A woman's voice interrupted Amanda as she was entering the proper deposit amount in Pete's bankbook.

"Yes," Amanda greeted the woman with a smile.

"I'm sorry to intrude on you, Pete, but all I want is one little thumbtack. I want to tack this piece of paper on the bulletin board by the door," said the woman.

Pete smiled. "That's okay, Mrs. Westlar. I have more time than money."

Mrs. Westlar looked at Amanda. "Could I have one, please?"

"Sure." Amanda opened a small drawer and with a pleasant smile handed Mrs. Westlar two thumbtacks.

"Oh, I only need one," Mrs. Westlar commented.

"Take two, then you'll be sure it won't fall off each time the door is opened and closed," Amanda suggested.

"Oh, that's a good idea. Thank you." Mrs. Westlar smiled. She took the thumbtacks and walked over to the bulletin board.

Amanda smiled and then continued with her work. "There you go,

Mr. Hof." She pushed the bankbook toward him. "Have a nice day."

"Thanks, the same to you, Amanda," Pete replied with a smile.

After putting the bankbook into his pocket, Pete proceeded toward the door and then stopped. Curiously he examined what Mrs. Westlar was tacking onto the bulletin board with her plump little hands.

A friendly smile crossed her smooth face as she looked over at Pete.

"That's a lot of money to be paying a month for a farmhand," Pete remarked.

"I need the help. I figured if I pay a good wage, I'll get someone real soon."

"Ya, the work on the farm is just starting now--all the planting and later on the harvesting."

"I know and I can't do it alone. I won't sell the farm. Mr. Westlar worked so hard for it and that's all I have left of him now."

"Ya, it's too bad about Mr. Westlar. He was a good man."

"That he was." It was hard to hold back the tears but she did. She was not going to make a scene by breaking down in tears.

Pete read over the piece of paper again. Gee, that was good money! It was more than he was making at Mr. Ewerdt's sawmill but it would be every day. So what, he didn't do anything on Sundays anyway. He didn't even go to church anymore.

"You know, Mrs. Westlar, I think I just might like that job. The only thing is that I really should wait until Mr. Ewerdt finds a replacement for me. I don't like to leave him just like that without someone to help him. Could you wait until then?"

Mrs. Westlar sighed. "Not really, Pete, I need the help right now. I'm sorry but those crops have to get in, especially the oats. The corn could wait until the end of May or beginning of June but not the oats. The lowland is dry now. If I wait too long, I'm afraid the rains will come and then I'll never get in there to plant."

"Gee, I really would like that job."

"I'd like you to work for me, but I really can't wait."

"What if I came over to your place right after work at Mr. Ewerdt's and did the plowing until it got too dark?"

"You'd never get done."

"Sure, I could. The moon is going full. There'll be a lot of light."

Reluctantly she replied, "Well, okay, I'll give you a try. However, if you can't do it, I'm getting someone else."

"Oh, I'll do it. Maybe Mr. Ewerdt will find a replacement for me in a couple of days."

As Mrs. Westlar reached for the doorknob to leave, Pete asked, "What about the piece of paper, aren't you going to take it down?"

"No, not until I'm sure that you can come and get the work done."

"In other words, if someone else applied, you'd hire them without giving me a chance?"

"I'm sorry, Pete, but I'm all alone now. I have to think of myself. Please, understand."

"I can and I will do the job. There's no need for you to keep the piece of paper on the board."

"I want to keep the piece of paper on the board. I really don't have time to argue with you. We'll see how things go. Are you going to start tonight?"

"Yup, I'll be there after work."

"Okay, I'll see you then. Good-bye."

After she was out of the door, Pete looked about the bank. It was empty except for Amanda who was busy writing behind her teller's window. The other teller had disappeared into the bank vault. No one was watching him. Quickly, he tore the piece of paper off the bulletin board and shoved it into his pocket. He wanted that job! No one else would get a chance at it. It was a lot of money and no one else was going to get it.

After leaving the bank, he went over to the sawmill. It buzzed with the sound of the biting teeth of a disc-shaped headsaw. He waited until Mr. Ewerdt had finished and the saw had been silenced.

He approached Mr. Ewerdt. "Karl."

"Yes, Pete." Mr. Ewerdt took the cut piece of wood and put it on the timber dock.

"I want to quit, but I won't leave until you've found someone to take my place."

"You want to quit!" Mr. Ewerdt was surprised.

"Yes, it has nothing to do with you. I've suddenly got an opportunity at a better paying job and I'd like to take it."

"I'm really surprised. You've been here longer than anyone that ever worked for me. I just thought you'd be here forever."

"I hope you aren't mad at me. We can still be friends."

"No, I'm not mad. It's your life. You have to live it the way you want. After eighteen years here, you're really a good experienced sawmill operator. Which town are you moving to?"

"I'm not moving out of town."

Baffled, Mr. Ewerdt replied, "I've got the only sawmill in town, who else would hire an experienced sawmill operator like you?"

"I'm not going to work in a mill. I'm going to work for Mrs. Westlar on her farm."

"Mrs. Westlar? I thought she was going to sell the farm after George died?"

"No, she has no intentions of selling it. She wants to hire someone to help her run it like George did."

"Ya, George was a hell of a good worker. You'll have some big shoes to fill."

"I can do it. I'm not afraid of work especially for that kind of pay."

"I know that you're not afraid of work. You're a good man too." Mr. Ewerdt patted Pete on the back. "I'm going to miss you. After eighteen years I've grown accustom to having you around. It's like losing a right arm."

"You'll find somebody else just as good."

"I hope so, but I doubt it. Besides being a hell of a good worker, you're a good person and wonderful friend. I'm going to miss that most of all."

"Oh, I'll still see you around."

"When does she want you to start working for her?"

"She'd like me to start today. I told her that I owed it to you to wait until you found a replacement for me."

"I do appreciate that. I couldn't handle this mill alone. I'll post a sign out front and put an ad in the paper today. Maybe we'll find someone soon."

To the left of Pete, tacked on a crude wooden wall, were several pieces of yellow paper. Pete tore one off and examined it. "Holy cow! When does this guy want this order filled?"

"Let me see. Who is it for?" Mr. Ewerdt bent forward and examined the piece of paper. "Oh, that's for Mr. Aslen. He's building a new house. From the size of the order, it's going to be big."

"Mr. Aslen? I never heard of him."

"He's new in town. He arrived with his wife sometime last week. You remember last Thursday when the fire department had a fire drill at that house. The house they set on fire to test their new gasoline-powered pump." Mr. Ewerdt pointed toward the edge of town.

"Ya, the house just outside of town near that small pond."

"That was his parents' house," Mr. Ewerdt replied.

"Oh, ya, I remember them. I thought they only had one boy and he was a priest."

"That's the boy. He did go away to a seminary in the East somewhere, but he must have never seen it through. He's married and, I guess, was some kind of a wealth business man back East. At least, that's what Mrs. Benson told me. He's been making rather large bank deposits on a regular basis for the last four or five years."

"Does Mrs. Benson miss her job at the bank?" Pete asked.

"No, she was glad when Mr. Stoner hired Amanda last summer. In fact, after Amanda learnt the job, Mrs. Benson wanted to quit but then Amanda was so sick during her pregnancy that she couldn't work all the time, so Mrs. Benson had to stay on. She just couldn't quit on Mr. Stoner. But after Amanda had her baby and could be at the bank regularly, Mrs. Benson decided to quit permanently."

"Well, I better get at this order. I'll drop the order off tonight and then take the wagon out to Mrs. Westlar. Is that all right with you?"

"Ya, that's okay." Mr. Ewerdt started the headsaw as the carriage moved the log toward its gashing teeth.

Pete went out into the massive lumberyard and started loading the dried lumber onto the back of a large wagon. When he had the wagon loaded with Otto's order, he hitched the horses to the wagon and left for Otto's.

It was late when Pete arrived. The men who were working on the foundation had already left. There was no one around to help him unload. It was twilight when he arrived at Mrs. Westlar's farm.

She was still milking the cows and wasn't too pleased with the fact that Pete arrived so late. However, she was glad that he had come. He was better than no one.

Mrs. Westlar looked different than when Pete had usually seen her in town. Her frilly dresses had been replaced by an old worn out flannel shirt, and manure covered her bib overalls. Her auburn locks were stuffed under a red bandanna and her blue eyes were hardly visible under her drooping tired eyelids.

Besides showing Pete where the equipment for plowing was, Mrs. Westlar had to show him how to use the equipment. Pete never thought plowing could be so complicated. The plow wasn't the problem. The tractor was. Whatever happened to the days of horses when things were simpler? First, step on the gas peddle--shift this--step on another pedal--shift again--jerk here--jerk there. Then the thing would choke off and he'd have to step on the pedal--shift--step on the pedal again--shift--jerk--choke off. He was beginning to have second thoughts--maybe all the money wasn't worth all this hassle. He wouldn't get anything done tonight. He couldn't keep the "dumb" tractor moving!

When she finished milking and came out of the barn, Pete--the plow--the tractor were still setting in the yard.

"Well, you didn't get too much done, did you?" Her voice showed an air of disgust and sarcasm.

"No, I'm sorry. I guess I didn't, but I know how the thing works now. If it's all right, I'd like to start plowing as soon as the sun comes up tomorrow. I don't have to be at the mill until seven o'clock."

"That sounds good! I hope you get more done tomorrow than you did tonight."

"I will, don't worry."

Wearing her manure-covered barn boots, she slowly dragged herself up to the house. As Pete mounted the wagon, she turned around and called to him, "Did you eat yet?"

"No."

"Well, come on in then." She motioned him into the house with her hand.

As he opened the door to the house, a distinctive odor filled his nostrils. The house was filled with a barn smell. It was a different smell and to his astonishment, he didn't mind it. In fact, he liked it.

"Just sit down. I'll be right out," Mrs. Westlar called from another room.

Pete pulled a cane chair out from under the claw-foot table and sat on it. The warmth from the stove made the small, simply furnished and extremely neat room, feel cozy. On one wall was a crucifix, on another was the Last Supper, and on the other wall were several hooks. Mrs. Westlar had hung her bib overalls and flannel shirt on two of the hooks. Directly below her clothes, lying on the floor was an old newspaper where she had set her barn boots. His eyes roamed back up to the two empty hooks. That must have been where Mr. Westlar used to hang his clothes. He thought how lonely it must be for her to be out here by herself.

A perfumed scent filled the air and Pete turned in the direction of the scent.

"I hope I don't give you a headache." Mrs. Westlar smiled as she walked over to the stove where a cast-iron kettle set on one of the stove lids. As she took off the kettle's lid, white steam spiraled up and disappeared into the ceiling.

"Give me a headache?" Pete questioned her statement.

"Yes, I accidentally tipped over a bottle of perfume on my vanity and the cap wasn't on tight. So half of the perfume spilled all over my skirt." She pointed to the wet spot in the lower part of her skirt.

"I think it smells nice." Pete smiled at her.

"I hardly ever wear perfume. That bottle was a present from George on our first wedding anniversary some fifteen years ago. I thought it smelled nice too. That's why I only wore it on special occasions, mostly every year on our wedding anniversary. I figured that way it would last me until out fiftieth wedding anniversary. Guess I saved it for nothing. George is gone and half the bottle spilled out. It really gets me quite angry. I wanted to keep it forever as a keepsake and now it's half gone because of my carelessness."

She placed a soup bowl and spoon in front of Pete, poured the hot soup out of the kettle into a tureen, and placed it on the table. "I hope you don't mind soup?"

"No, it smells good." Pete filled his bowl.

"It's a simple meal to make when there is a lot of farm work. I don't mind eating soup alone. A heavy meal of beef roast, potatoes, and another vegetable like George and I used to eat is no fun to eat by oneself. So, I make myself soup. I like soup, and it always taste better each time a person reheats it. The flavor pulls through more."

"It's very good." Pete slowly sipped the hot soup.

"I'm glad you like it." After placing biscuits and butter on the table, she sat and ate supper with him.

When they had finished eating, Pete helped her with the few dishes they had. Then over a piping hot cup of coffee and a sweet tasting pecan twist roll, they talked.

"So, you want to start early tomorrow morning," said Mrs. Westlar.

"Ya, I think I could get something done. The sun rises around four-thirty. I could work until six-thirty. It only takes a half-hour to get back to Beechwood."

"It sounds like a good idea. If I get up early, then I'd be done with all the chores in the barn and I could plow all day until you come at night. When you arrive, I could do chores and you could plow again."

"I think I know how the tractor works now."

"It took me a while to learn too. George thought I'd never learn how to drive it. Did you see it in the July fourth parade last year? We were the only ones who had one then. So, to promote the tractor and his business, Mr. Jacob gave us a discount if we'd drive it in the parade with a big sign on it saying, COMPLIMENTS OF JACOB'S IMPLEMENTS."

"Ya, I remember it. I never thought then that I'd be learning how to drive it."

Mrs. Westlar sighed. "Isn't it funny how things you never really give a second thought to suddenly become a big part of your reality. When we drove in that tractor together, I never thought there would ever be a day when George and I wouldn't be together. Fate seems to pounce down and leave its unexpected mark that changes everything. George always would say, 'do anything you want as long as you don't ever hurt anyone--do it--because you're the one who has to live with the regrets of not doing what you wanted to.' There is only one thing I know George regretted and that was that he couldn't give me a child."

Pete looked puzzled. "I thought Abe was your son?"

"Abe was George's son from a first marriage. His first wife died. When I met George and later married him, Abe was seven already. Shortly after we were married, Abe became sick with the mumps.

Several weeks later George became terribly sick with them. The doctor mentioned the fact that George could be sterile because of them. I guess the doctor was right. At least I did have Abe. It was better than not having a child at all."

"What does Abe do now?"

"Well, you know he's been married for two years now."

"Ya, I saw him and his wife at George's funeral in November."

"About a year ago her father died and they bought his farm. George wanted them to move in with us and help us work the farm, but she didn't want to leave Illinois. They also wanted to own their own place. So, he's out there and I'm here looking for help to keep my farm. I don't have any hard feelings. A young couple has a right to run their own lives and have their own place."

"Well, I better get back to town. It's getting later and darker outside." Pete finished drinking his coffee, rose from the chair, and started walking toward the door.

"Wake me when you come tomorrow morning," said Mrs. Westlar.

"Okay, I'll do that. See you then."

"Bye."

At first it started out to be a drab old "rat race" for Pete. Getting up at the break of dawn--plowing--planting--rushing back to town--rushing back to the farm--back to town--but then his feelings started to change. In time it was all that motivated him. He couldn't wait to get out to the farm--couldn't seem to spend enough time out there. Why? It was more than the work or the money. For the first time money was second place to Pete. In fact, the money didn't seem to play a role this time in his life at all. He longed to be near Mrs. Westlar, to have her companionship at meals. He longed to talk with her and have her listen to what he said. He enjoyed listening to what she had to say. He wanted to know her desires--her wants--her dreams--what she had done--things about her family.

She listened and understood how he felt--what he wanted and why. She made him feel important. She needed him not only for work but as a companion, someone to share her time with. He found himself spending all his time away from her wanting to be near her. The only thing that made him endure the long hours of work was the fact that at the end of workday he would be with her.

Finally, after two months he couldn't take it anymore. He gave his regrets to Karl and left the sawmill permanently. He moved out to Mrs. Westlar's farm. Now every moment would be spent with her.

In the house he occupied Abe's room. Lying in his bed each night, knowing she was in the next room--so close--yet so far from his arms--was beginning to be unbearable. If he let her know how he felt, what would she do? Would she send him away? She was a moral woman. George wasn't even dead a year. Would she consider it disgusting for him to let her know how she felt? How did she feel about him? He hadn't seen any sign of her having the same feelings about him. He sensed that she liked him but probably only as a friend. He felt more than friendship toward her. As he contemplated what he should do and how he could endure hiding his strong emotions, he heard her bedroom door open, heard her go down the stairs, and then heard the outside door slam.

Enticed by curiosity, he put on his trousers and went downstairs. Through the window he could see her strolling about peacefully in the soft breeze of the July evening. Her auburn locks, freed from the usual bun, flowed softly over her shoulders and glistened as the moon's rays caressed each strand.

Emotions overpowered his thoughts of reason as he stepped out into the July evening. With bare feet, he walked over the dew-covered grass to where she was standing. "Beautiful--isn't it?"

"Oh!" She jumped from fright.

"I'm sorry. I didn't intend to scare you."

"Oh, it's not your fault. I was just very deep in thought." She smiled at him.

"Want to share your thoughts with me?"

"Oh, just memories of the past." She touched his hand for a second. "I'm glad you're out here. It's not good to dwell on the past. One has to deal with the future and find the things that make new memories. Memories of the past can sometimes only bring sorrow if a person dwells too long and makes them your life. New memories enhance the old." She began to walk slowly toward her flower garden. "Those flowers are so beautiful during the day, aren't they?"

"Ya, they are." Pete followed her.

"Nature holds a lesson for us all. It takes a long time for an acorn to grow into a mighty oak. I guess that's nature's way of telling us to be patience and let things go the way they will and they'll turn out fine--just like those flowers. They bring beauty and joy in summer but when winter comes they die. It doesn't mean we should die also. We should wait and more will come in spring and bring us beauty and joy again. I think nature does this to show us a lesson in death. Just because one thing may die, it doesn't mean everything has to die. When one thing of beauty dies, there is always another thing of beauty to come and take its place. Not all life stops at the same time. There is a time for death and sorrow and there's a time for new life and joy. Oh, I bet you think I'm crazy." She stopped walking and stood at the edge of the flower garden.

"No." He touched her shoulders with his hands. As their eyes met, he gently pressed his lips against her moist mouth.

For a second she stood spellbound. Could someone care for her again? As he held her in his arms, she wanted to return his embrace but couldn't. Was she betraying George? No, he had died and left her. She didn't want him to die. If he would be alive, she wouldn't be in this situation. She'd never do anything like this if she was married, but she wasn't married. George had left her. She hadn't left him. For a moment she returned his kiss and embrace. Then, not wanting to get him too passionately involved because she knew that she couldn't let him complete his passion, she pulled away from him.

"Do you love me?" she softly whispered.

"Yes, I do." He tried to kiss her again.

"Love isn't cheap and I'll not do anything to make it cheap and vulgar." She turned away from his kiss.

"I've never felt about anyone like I feel about you. I think of you every minute of the day. I can't stand to be away from you. I want to share my whole self with you. I love you. I love you." Pete was overflowing with passion.

"I won't do something only married people have a right to do."

"If marrying you is the only way I can love you completely, then I want to marry you."

"But I don't know if I love you."

"I love you enough for the two of us. Oh, please, marry me. I can't live much longer without being able to hold you and kiss you."

"Marriage isn't all sex you know."

"I know that. If it was just sex that I was interested in, I wouldn't have to get married. There are plenty of women around who give it out without the string of marriage being attached, and I've known most of them. That's why I love you. You're special to me. Sex is only a small part of the way I feel about you. I need to be near you and to know you are mine. I love you." He embraced her and kissed her again.

"Let's get married--now!" Pete exclaimed.

"Now!"

"Why not?" Pete responded.

"I'm not sure how I feel about you. I don't know if I love you."

"Well, do you hate me?"

"No."

"Well, then you must love me."

She pulled away. "I have to have time to think. Things are moving too fast." She walked toward the house.

Pete followed her into the house and sat at the table across from her. Reaching over, he touched her hand. "I love you, Amy, and I'm going to marry you."

"It's not right yet. George hasn't been dead that long. What will people say?"

"Waiting won't bring George back and what does it matter what people say. You have to do what you want to, because you are the one who is going to live with the regret of not doing what you wanted to do. Remember, that was George's advice about life."

"I have to live here. It matters what people say."

"People are going to talk no matter what you do. You can never please everyone and why try. What you do with your life is your business."

"Oh, life is so complicated." She rose from the chair and walked over to the window where she gazed out at the moonlit night.

Soon she felt Pete's arms around her waist and the warmth of his body so close to hers.

"You make it complicated. It's simple from my viewpoint, either you want to marry me or you don't want to marry me. Nothing else is really important."

She did like to be near him and deep inside her heart she did like it when he had held her and kissed her. Even now as he held her, butterflies fluttered in her stomach and her heart leaped with excitement. She wanted him to kiss her again. She did want him to love her. Turning around she hugged him. "Yes, I'll marry you. I do love you, Pete."

Pete's body throbbed with excitement--ecstasy endowed his soul. He squeezed her tightly and held her as if he'd never let her go.

****

"Well, hello, honey. We meet again."

Amanda looked up from her teller's counter. Her pleasant smile disappeared. Fear gripped her and held her steadfast to the floor. Her trembling legs were unable to move. Faster and faster her heart began to throb. A scream stuck in her throat. Except for the memories of that night, her mind was blank. She couldn't think of what to do. Surveying the bank lobby, she could see there was no one to help her. Mr. Stoner was in his office if she screamed he'd surely come out--but she couldn't scream.

"I want to withdraw this much." He pushed a little brown book and small piece of paper toward her.

Amanda's fixed eyes couldn't move from his face of pitted scars. After that night, she never--ever thought that she'd see that face again except in the nightmares, which she often had of that night, but there he was--staring at her again.

"Don't worry, honey. I won't try anything in here. I just want to withdraw some money." He snickered at her. He was pleased with the fear that she had of him.

Amanda swallowed the lump in her throat and with trembling hands, grabbed for the book.

Suddenly, his hand grabbed hers. "It was nice that night, wasn't it?"

As Amanda pulled her hand away, his hideous laugh sent chills up her spine. Onto the counter her nervous hands counted his money as each dollar bill repeated the movement of her hand--ten--twenty--thirty--forty.

After he had put the money into his wallet, he looked up and with a smirk said, "See ya, honey--real soon." He laughed under his breath.

Amanda watched him closely as he went out the door. Her eyes filled with tears as she thought about how he had hurt her and decided her future for her. She loved her baby but that wasn't how she had wanted things to be. She had always dreamed of saving herself for the man she would marry. How she would go down the aisle a virgin and have a baby in wedlock who would have a father. He had taken that all away from her. Including the respect she had always wanted from other people.

"It's time to close," stated Mr. Stoner as he came out of his office. His voice startled Amanda.

"Oh, I'm sorry Amanda. I didn't mean to frighten you." Seeing her tears he asked, "Is something wrong?"

"No, nothing."

"Are you sure?"

"Yes." She forced a gracious smile.

"Are you looking forward to having tomorrow off?" He walked over to the door, locked it, and then pulled the shades down over the windows.

"Yes, it'll be nice to be around little Alex all day."

"He sure is a cute little guy. You can be proud of him."

"I am and I love him so much."

Mr. Stoner chuckled. "I think everyone at the house does. I have to finish a few things up in my office before we can leave."

"I want to buy a few things at the store for tomorrow so I'll walk home."

"That's all right. I can wait for you."

"No, that's okay. It's such a nice day. I think I'd enjoy a walk home. Thanks anyway."

"Okay, see you at the house."

After locking the money from her teller's box into the vault, she left for Erickson's grocery store.

"Hi, Mr. Erickson." Gleamed Amanda as she entered the store.

"Hi, Amanda." Mr. Erickson smiled at her.

"Do you still have some watermelons left?" Amanda asked.

"Sure do." He walked over to his enormous icebox and opened one of the doors.

A whisk of cold air gave Amanda a sudden chill. "Can I have the one that's cut in half?" Amanda pointed to the one she wanted.

"Sure can." He took it out and wrapped it as Amanda laid the money on the counter.

"Thank you, have a nice day," said Erickson.

"Thanks, you to, Mr. Erickson."

As Amanda headed toward the door, she came to a sudden stop. It was that man again. She didn't want to meet him. She didn't want him to see her. She was afraid of what he might do. Rapidly, she glanced about the store. Where could she hide? There were several barrels full of things and several tables full of merchandise but nothing she could hide behind. Then--there in the corner she saw her answer! Quickly, she scooted away from the door and hide behind a rack of dresses. She scarcely breathe for fear that he'd hear her. As she heard his footsteps, she peeked between two dresses. He was in the store!

"Good day, Mr. Erickson," said the man.

"Oh--hi, Otto. How are you today?" replied Mr. Erickson.

"Fine." Otto walked up to the meat counter where Mr. Erickson was placing several sticks of summer sausage into the meat compartment of the counter.

"What can I do for you today?" Mr. Erickson asked.

"I'd like a dozen of eggs," Otto replied.

"Sure thing. I'll get them for you." With that Mr. Erickson disappeared down the stairs into the cellar.

Otto looked around. Seeing no one in sight, he walked behind the meat counter and pulled out a stick of summer sausage. He pulled the bottom part of his trousers up to his knee revealing the top of his unbuckled boot. Into the boot he slipped the stick of summer sausage, then pulled the trouser leg back down over the boot, concealing the sausage. He did the same with another stick of sausage, putting it into the other boot.

As he heard Mr. Erickson coming up the stairs, he went back to the other side of the counter. He greeted Mr. Erickson with such a pleasant smile as he laid the money for the eggs on the counter. Taking the eggs, Otto left the store.

When she was sure he was far enough away, Amanda slowly came out from behind the dresses. Her eyes were still fixed on Otto walking down the street--farther and farther and farther away from her.

"Amanda! I thought you left?"

Mr. Erickson startled her. "I--I was just looking at the pretty dresses."

Mr. Erickson smiled at her. "They are pretty, aren't they?"

"Yes, they are."

Mr. Erickson went about his work of stocking the shelves with canned goods.

As Amanda watched him work, she wondered if she should tell him about Otto. No--he wouldn't believe her anyway. Mr. Erickson didn't really like her. He was just nice because she was a customer and knew Mr. Stoner.

With the watermelon under her arm, she headed toward the door. Before she ventured out, she paused and examined the street. Otto was nowhere to be seen. Now she wished that she had gone home with Mr. Stoner. Every time that she approached an alley or a merchant's store she was deadly afraid that Otto would come out in front of her, and she'd be face to face with him.

Anxiety, which had filled every nerve in her body, disappeared as she stood safely on the Stoner's front porch. Relief overwhelmed her as she entered the house. For a moment, she leaned against the closed door. With a few deep breaths, she could feel her body relax and the feelings of fear disappear in the security of the house.

If she could have, Amanda would have left Beechwood that day. Knowing she'd probably see Otto again and again terrified her. However, she couldn't leave. She had little Alex to think of now, and she couldn't leave this place of security. She could never raise Alex and keep a job also. Therefore, she couldn't give thinking about leaving another thought, and she had to live with the fear of meeting Otto again.

****

The heavy dew glistened as Anna and Eva sat on the white wrought-iron patio furniture enjoying the stillness of the early morning hours.

"I really envy you, Anna," Eva said as she put her empty coffee cup on the wrought-iron table.

"Me--why?" Anna was puzzled by the remark.

"You can eat anything you want and you don't gain a pound. Me--I can't even enjoy my favorite sweet rolls anymore. I'm getting fat. Especially since I've been confined to this hideous wheelchair."

"You look fine, Eva." Anna finished her piece of jam toast and reached for her cup of steaming coffee.

"What's the matter, Anna?" Eva asked as she saw Anna's hand tremble.

"Oh, nothing. My hands always do that."

"Are you cold? I can tell Eleanor to bring you a sweater."

"No. Really I'm fine. In fact, I feel quite warm."

"Are you sure?" Eva was deeply concerned.

"Yes. Would you like us to stroll through the flower garden to pass the time until Mr. Stoner comes back?"

"Yes, I'd like that. I'm glad Frederick decided to come home over the July fourth weekend. It means so much to Charles when Frederick comes to visit. Charles hasn't seen him for over a year now."

"That's a long time. I don't know what I'd do if I didn't have my Amanda with me, much less not seeing her for over a year."

"Charles would like him to live here but Frederick has different ideas. I don't think he likes me. I suppose it is hard to see someone else in the place of one's mother. He was ten when I married Charles. Just old enough to remember his natural mother and old enough to despise anyone he thought was taking her place."

Anna got up and took a hold of the handle bars on the wheelchair and began pushing Eva through the garden filled with masses of brilliant flowers and well-trimmed hedges.

"Don't they smell fragrant, Anna?"

"Yes, they do. I think July has to be the prettiest month. The flowers come into bloom, the lawn, and trees are their greenest. Everything is so full of life--so radiant."

"So full of life--radiant--like I used to be."

"You're still radiant and full of life, Eva."

"Oh, your words are very kind. I know you mean well but I'm not like I used to be."

"None of us ever stay the way we are. I'm different from what I used to be. Time and fate change all of us. We have to accept it and live the best we can. You are alive and you are still very beautiful."

"Eighteen years ago when I met Charles, I never thought I'd be like this. Of course, I never thought I'd ever come back here after I left either."

"You mean you are from here originally?"

"Well, my first stay in Beechwood wasn't very long. It was profitable--but not very long. My first day in town, I met this man who talked me into doing something that would be quite profitable for me. It was profitable and after I had done what he paid me for, he put me on the train with a one-way ticket to Sacramento. I often wondered what he'd say if he ever saw me back here. But in all the years I've been here, I've never seen him."

"Who was he?"

"I forgot his last name. His first name was Hans. He was a good-looking man. It's probably good that I didn't stay around him too long. I don't think he was the most honest person. He probably ended up in jail."

"Weren't you afraid to go to Sacramento by yourself? Didn't you worry about how you would live in a strange city like that?"

"No, not me. There was always a demand for the kind of job that I was most experienced in."

"Yes, Sacramento is a big city. I suppose there are plenty of jobs for women. A lot more than are around here. They've got more hotels and bakeries." Anna was a bit naive. She never thought the worst of anyone. That's why it had always hurt her when others had always thought and said the worst of her. People who don't think badly of others don't expect others to talk or think badly about them. It's hard to accept a fault in others when a person doesn't possess that fault. People who don't gossip can't accept gossip. People who don't lie can't accept that others do lie.

Eva looked up at Anna in disbelief. Anna didn't really know what she had been. But then she shouldn't have really been surprised because it was that perception of Anna's quality that had attracted her to Anna--along with another feeling that she couldn't explain. A feeling of some kind of bond but there wasn't any, was there? Even though Eva couldn't think of any bond they may have had, that still didn't erase the feeling that always seemed to be there--at least where Eva was concerned.

"Yes, they sure do have a lot of hotels there. That's where I met Charles, in the hotel restaurant. They had a banker's convention in the hotel, and the hotel was full. When he came into the hotel to eat, all the tables had been occupied. Seeing I was sitting alone and knowing how I made my living, the waiter asked Charles if he'd mind sharing a table with me. Charles naturally being a perfect gentleman said, 'if the lady didn't mind, he'd be honored to share the table with her.' So that's how we met." With that Eva rested back in her wheelchair as a pleasant smile swept across her face. "That night was like no other. I'll always remember it. The charming way he talked and treated me. I couldn't believe a man was treating me with such respect. He made me feel important and proud. Made me feel as if I was someone to be respected. I remember how I truly enjoyed listening to him talk. He had a way with words--so educated--distinguished. How long we sat and talked I don't know, but I do remember we went dancing that night. How he loved to dance and dance. Charles is a good dancer. We used to go to every dance there was until this happened to me. I feel so sad about him being deprived of dancing. He is a good man. He doesn't indulge in a lot of other things other men do. He doesn't gamble or indulge in the liqueurs. He's not a carouser and doesn't sleep with other women. Oh, he's a 'fine catch,' Anna, almost too good for me."

"Don't talk that way! You're a good person and Charles loves you deeply. You can see that by the way he looks at you. His eyes sparkle with love for you. You being in the wheelchair doesn't change how he feels about you. When you love someone you don't stop loving them because things have changed them physically. I never stopped loving my Alex, and we were even separated.

"But I'm not a good wife to him."

"Why--because you can't give him sex? I think you put to much emphasize on something that I don't think bothers him. Just being close and having the one you love to hold and embrace is worth so much. It's so much better than not having that person at all. Life on earth is too short. We waste our few precious moments together worrying about senseless things instead of holding and loving someone we care about. To find someone who really loves you is the most important thing in the world--forget the rest of the world--it's not important--not really. Love while you have the chance. Don't waste a second; because, before you know it, the person is gone and you may never know love again."

"Don't you think you'll ever find love again?"

Anna shrugged her shoulders. "I don't know. To tell you the truth, I guess I've been too busy trying to survive."

Just then a loud--HONK--HONK--interrupted their talk. They turned their heads in the direction of the noise. There coming up the driveway, echoing their arrival with a horn, were Charles and Frederick in a black model T.

Taking his one hand off the steering wheel, Charles waved wildly to them. A grin spread from one side of his face to the other.

As Anna and Eva returned Charles's smile and wave, Frederick forced his arm up into a half-hearted wave. If he was glad to be home, he surely didn't show it. If his face had been any longer with gloom, he would have surely stepped on it as he got out of the Model T.

Charles walked down to meet Eva and Anna as they made their way out of the garden toward the house.

"Eleanor! Eleanor! Get my bath ready!" Frederick shouted as he stormed into the house and up the stairs.

He mumbled under his breath as he wiped the dust off his suit jacket, "Damn trains are the filthiest things around!"

Being so preoccupied with wiping the dust off his suit, he wasn't watching where he was walking.

After slowly closing her bedroom door, so she wouldn't wake Alex, Amanda turned around and bumped into Frederick.

"Oh, I'm sorry." Amanda said apologetically. "Please, forgive me." Amanda recognized a familiarity in his face. But at that moment, she couldn't place the face with the place where she had seen it.

Frederick quickly checked her over--her breasts--how her dress hung at certain body curves. When he saw an attractive woman, there was only one thing that filled his head--prurient ideas. Putting his arm around her, he said, "If you're the new maid, you can come in my room and turn my blankets down for bed anytime."

Amanda pulled away. "I'm not the maid. I live here. Who are you?"

"I live here. This is my house."

"Your house? I've never seen you before."

"Well, I've never seen you either. Who are you? My dad's concubine?"

"How utterly disgusting." Amanda turned abruptly and started to walk away.

He grabbed her arm. "Hey, I'm sorry." He wasn't really. "My name is Frederick. I'm Mr. Stoner's son--prodical son--I guess you could say." With that he extended his hand in a gesture of friendship.

Amanda paused for a second and then broke the icy look on her face with a warm smile. "I'm Amanda Leer. Your father and mother were kind enough to ask me to come and live here after they hired my mother."

"She's not my mother. No, not that harlot!" Frederick snapped and took back the hand that he had offered in friendship.

"My--don't we have a descriptive vocabulary for women."

"I just speak the truth. The way things really are."

"If you say so--excuse me. My stomach tells me it's time for breakfast." She wasn't really hungry. She just didn't care for his comments.

With lustful ideas he watched her walk down the hallway and disappear down the back stairs into the kitchen.

Eleanor was busy filling the tub in the other room with water. When she saw Amanda, she nodded a welcoming smile. "I'm sorry. I can't make breakfast for you right now. I have to get this bath ready for Monsieur Frederick."

"That's all right, Eleanor. I do hope he washes where the dirt really is."

Eleanor gave a puzzled look.

"His mouth--he has a very foul mouth." Amanda poured herself a cup of coffee. Seeing the tasty watermelon as she reached inside the icebox for the milk, she asked, "Eleanor, you will join us for the melon this afternoon?"

"Sure."

"Good. The melon will make the fourth a little more special."

"I'm glad that's done. I better call him right now; otherwise, he'll complain that it's too cold." Putting the pail down, she went up the stairs and softly rapped on Frederick's door. "Your bath is ready,

Monsieur Frederick," Eleanor spoke very softly.

"Okay, I'll be right down."

His loud reply woke up little Alex. Soon the hallway and all the upstairs were filled with Alex's high-pitched cry.

Eleanor went into Amanda's room and picked Alex up. "Shhh, that's all right my little sweet one." She gently kissed him and began to slowly rock him in her arms.

"My little sweet one." Came a voice with a sarcastic note. It was Frederick standing in the hallway--snickering. "Really, Eleanor, I didn't think you knew what the word sex meant much less to even know how to go about doing it."

"Your bath is ready, monsieur. I suggest you take it before it gets cold."

"Huh! You're too old to have a kid. Whose is it? My old man's?"

"No, it's not your father's."

"I'm glad to hear that. I wouldn't like to divide anything with someone else someday when the old man kicks the bucket."

Eleanor raised her eyebrows in disapproval.

"Well, whose is it?" Frederick was extremely curious.

"It's Amanda's."

"Oh yeah." Well, at least he wouldn't have to break her in, he thought.

"Her husband lives here too?"

"She doesn't have a husband."

"She doesn't? What happen? He leave her?"

"No, she's never been married."

"Oh, yeah." He looked toward the stairs that led down to the kitchen. So she's that kind. She'll be easier than he had thought. A pleasing smirk crossed his face. "Ya, I better take my bath."

At the bottom of the stairs, Frederick paused and watched Amanda at the sink washing the dishes. She was going to make his July fourth holiday well worthwhile--how convenient to have her in the same house and in the room next to his. It was a "playboy's" dream. The best part was that his dream was going to come true--today--tonight--soon!

"You want to help me with my bath?"

Frederick startled Amanda. She jumped involuntarily. Her heart seemed to stop for a second. She turned around and looked at him.

"No, you're old enough to wash yourself." Amanda despised his lewd remark.

"Oh, I don't know about that." He put his arm around her.

"I have work to do. Leave me alone." She threw his hands off her. Taking a wet cloth, she walked over to the table and proceeded to wash it off.

"Come on." His hand touched hers. His eyes motioned toward the room where his tub of water waited.

"Leave me alone." She pulled her hand away and continued cleaning the table.

"Is everything okay, Amanda?" Eleanor walked down the last few steps. She had figured Frederick was there, and she knew how he talked and thought.

"Yes, just fine," replied Amanda.

"Good, you can help me with the coffee out on the terrace."

"Sure."

With her fingertips, Eleanor felt the coffeepot. It was still hot.

"Don't you think you should take your bath before it gets cold?" Eleanor told Frederick who was still staring at Amanda and indulging in his usual illusions that he had about every girl he met.

"Oh--ya, I guess I better."

Taking the coffeepot, Amanda and Eleanor went out to the terrace to join the others.

"Is the coffee all right?" Eleanor asked as she filled their empty cups with the steaming black brew.

"It's just fine," Mr. Stoner replied as he took a few leisure sips.

"Come, sit by us." Eva motioned Amanda and Eleanor to sit down and join them.

"What are you going to do today, Eleanor?" asked Eva.

"I suppose what I do every day."

"No, you're not. You take today off, go to the parade and picnic," Eva ordered in a most caring way.

"Oh, I couldn't. What about little Alex?"

"What about him?" asked Eva.

"I have to stay and take care of him."

"No, you don't have to. I'm home today, and I don't plan on going anyplace. I'll take care of him. He is my son, and I don't get to spend as much time as I want with him." It was true Amanda did feel that way about Alex, but she would have liked to go for just an hour. They had a ride at the picnic this year. A big wheel that turned around as people sat in it. She had heard it was fun. She would have liked to seen it. However, she didn't want to go alone, and she didn't feel right pushing Alex on others. Depriving them of their fun just so she could do what she wanted. It would be fun being with Alex all day. She had looked forward to that also.

"Ugh, what does an old woman like me want at a picnic," said Eleanor. "I'm staying right here. You go and have some fun, Amanda."

"Eva and I are going." Charles reached over and touched Eva's hand affectionately. His face was aglow with love for her.

"Oh, Charles, I'm sorry to disappoint you, but I really don't feel that good. I don't want to go to the picnic. I am sorry."

"What's the matter, Eva?" Charles asked compassionately. "We haven't missed a picnic since we moved here."

"I have this splitting headache." Eva rubbed her hand on her forehead.

"Oh, I'm sorry, Eva. Then I don't want to go either."

"Sure you do--you should. All of you should go."

"Yes, I agree with Eva. You should go too, Amanda. You should go out and have some fun. I know you'd like to try that ride. Eleanor can go with you. There won't be a celebration like this for another year. You both go. I'll stay here with Eva and Alex," said Anna.

"No, you won't. You go to the parade and picnic with Charles," Eva said.

"No, I don't want to go if you aren't with me," Charles protested.

"Don't talk so foolishly. I know you enjoy watching the parade and socializing at the picnic. I'd feel terrible if you didn't go because of me."

"It won't be any fun without you, Eva," replied Charles.

"Sure, it will. You make your own fun."

"Madame Eva is right. You all go and have a good time. We can take care of things here," Eleanor said.

"You go to, Eleanor. You go with Amanda," Eva suggested.

"Nonsense, Amanda can go with Monsieur Stoner and Anna. I'll stay here with you."

Eva didn't like that idea of Amanda going with Charles and Anna. "Eleanor, you go with Amanda."

"No, I'm staying here. You can't take care of Alex alone, not with him upstairs and you down here," Eleanor stated.

"Bring his bassinet down here, then I could take care of him. I can handle him."

"No, I won't leave you alone. I'm staying and that is final," Eleanor insisted.

"The parade isn't for an hour yet. Maybe you'll feel better by then," Charles commented.

"While we're waiting, how about some of that watermelon I bought yesterday?" Amanda suggested.

"That sounds like a good idea," Charles said. "Would you like some, Eva?"

"Yes, please."

"Maybe you'll feel better after you eat something." Charles was hopeful.

"Maybe I will." Eva smiled as Charles caressed her hand.

As Amanda rose to get the watermelon, Eleanor blurted out, "I'll get it."

In the split second Eleanor remembered that Frederick was still taking a bath. Knowing how vulgar he usually was and probably had already been to Amanda, Eleanor didn't think it was the best thing for Amanda to be alone with him. Handling Frederick was easy for Eleanor. He didn't really bother her. She didn't have what he wanted--a young sexy body.

Everyone found the sweet, juicy watermelon refreshing.

"It was good Amanda. But as I told you once before, I don't like you buying food for the family," said Mr. Stoner.

"I didn't mean to offend you. I just wanted to do something to make today a little different. Besides, I was hungry for watermelon."

"Well, I think it was a very nice idea." Eva smiled.

"How do you feel now, my sweet Eva?" asked Charles.

"I still have a terrible headache. I'm going to rest. Maybe then it'll go away."

"I'll come home right after the parade and spend the rest of the day with you," said Charles.

"Oh, that's so very kind of you, but I really would like to rest for a while. You go to the parade and the picnic. I want to get rid of this headache. You can tell me all about the parade and picnic."

"Are you sure?"

"Yes, I am."

"It's going to feel so strange going without you."

"Well, there are some things that we all have to get used to. You go now and have a good time." Eva looked at Amanda. "Amanda, will you take me up to my room, please?"

"Sure."

"We'll wait for you," said Anna.

"No, that's all right. I don't think I'll go," Amanda replied.

Eva was glad to hear that. She didn't want Amanda going along with Anna and Charles. It wouldn't help her plan one bit to have a third party hanging around.

"I'll take Madame Eva up," Eleanor offered. "You go along. Alex will be fine."

A disapproving look crossed Eva's face. She could see her plan crumble like the ancient walls of Jericho. Good-hearted Eleanor! Well, she would just have to try again. It was for Charles's own good.

Down the stone stairs, which lined the hill, the three strolled toward the park where the parade and picnic would be held. From the terrace Eva could see the double-rimmed framework of the large, steel wheel that towered high above everything else. She took a bit of consolation thinking that maybe Amanda would ride that thing all day and leave Anna and Charles to fend for themselves. Well, there was no sense worrying or contemplating things now. What would happen couldn't be changed or altered.

"Did the old man leave already?" Came a voice--it was Frederick.

"Yes, there they go," replied Eva.

Frederick looked in the direction Eva had motioned. "Good, she's going too," he mumbled under his breath.

"Pardon me. I didn't hear what you said," Eva responded.

"You didn't have to. It didn't concern you," Frederick snapped. With that he ran down the hill toward them.

Eleanor shook her head. "Don't mind him, Madame Eva. If he had manners, he'd actually be dangerous."

"Eleanor!" Eva chuckled.

"It's true, Madame Eva. He has no respect for anything or anyone --except, of course, himself. I feel sorry for the woman that he marries--if he ever marries.

Frederick was almost out of breath when he joined them at the bottom of the hill. "Hi!" came his unexpected and seemingly pleasant greeting. He was panting hard and trying to catch his breath.

Amanda just looked. She didn't like him. Where had she seen him before?

"Hi." Anna extended her hand. "I'm Anna Leer, Eva's companion."

"And my dad's?"

"No." Anna stopped. "I'm going back to the house. I don't want to go to the parade or the picnic."

"Oh, come on, Ma. We'll have fun." Amanda gave Frederick a piercing glare.

"If that's just the beginning of the remarks, it won't be any fun."

"Come on, Ma. Don't let others ruin your fun."

Charles shook his head and gave Frederick a disapproving look.

"Hey, I'm sorry. I didn't mean it." Frederick extended his hand.

Anna paused and then with a reluctant smile shook his hand.

Large crowds had filled the sidewalks and lined the edge of streets. Everyone was waiting anxiously for the parade to begin. However, the only view they had were the backs of everyone else's head. None of them particularly liked that, but that's usually the result of getting to a place late. The best seats are always taken.

"Come on." Charles seen the stairs going up to Mr. Fremont's law office were uncluttered.

As they squeezed through the tight crowd, scowling faces and caustic remarks greeted them. People, who had come early to get their good seat, didn't welcome the idea of some "late comers" trying to budge their way into their seat and knocking them out of it. Moving through the crowd was like swimming upstream.

When they finally reached the stairs, each one took their own step from where they watched the parade. The bands and floats pranced in front of them in perfect view. The parade was enjoyed by everyone.

After the parade, Frederick pulled Amanda so quickly through the crowd on his way down to the park that she soon lost sight of her mother and Charles.

Finally, pulling loose from Frederick's hand, she stood still as her eyes searched the crowd for her mother and Charles. She didn't like being alone with Frederick. He made her feel uneasy.

"What's the matter--you a 'mama baby'?" asked Frederick.

"No," Amanda snapped.

"Well, come on then, let's have some fun. Let's try that ride over there."

Amanda looked in the direction Frederick pointed. There it was the large wheel that she had wanted to ride, but suddenly, it seemed so large. All those people on the ride were screaming. The ride didn't look so inviting anymore. She stood steadfast as Frederick tried to pull her toward it.

"Come on, Amanda. It's fun on there!"

Amanda looked amazed. "You've been on it?'

"Sure, a lot of times! They're called Ferris wheels. Come on, it's fun!"

Hesitatingly, she moved closer to the ride. Before she knew it, she was sitting in a seat next to Frederick going around and around--up and then down. It was fun! Her hair blew about--her stomach tickled. It was funny to see all those tiny people moving about below. They rode the ride so many times that she lost count.

Then there were the games, Amanda considered spending money on them a waste because no one ever won anything. If a person did win, it was usually an item that a person could have bought several times over with the money that they had spent at the game. However, Frederick enjoyed them, and he insisted that she play. By the time it came to eat supper, the cold feeling between them had vanished. Frederick and Amanda were full of fun and laughter.

The sound of music from a nearby tent soon started Frederick's feet tapping to the beat. Before long they were dancing to the quick two quarter time of the polka's.

Amanda never knew life could be so much fun. She had never experienced such excitement. She felt like Cinderella!

Whisking by them, among the other dancers, were Charles and Anna. From the look on their faces, Amanda could see that they were having a good time. She was glad for her mother. However, she would have preferred her mother having a good time with someone else. It wasn't that Amanda didn't like Charles. She thought very highly of him. If Amanda had a chance at having another father, Charles would be her first choice. However, Amanda really felt her mother's time tonight was wasted. Charles was married and nothing would ever come of tonight but a memory. She would have preferred her mother to be with some eligible man. Nevertheless, Amanda's preference was of no importance. That her mother was with any man was really something in itself. Well, maybe in a way it was good that she was having fun with Charles. Maybe it would wake her up, like it had Amanda, to the fact that life can be fun. Maybe it would encourage her mother to accept the advances of other men.

"Whew! All this dancing made me thirsty. Come on, let's get a beer!" Taking Amanda's hand, Frederick led her out of the tent toward an area that was fenced in with a red snow fence.

The noise from inside the fenced area was boisterous and profane. Most of the people were intoxicated. Their eyes were glassy and they moved about in an unbalanced manner.

Amanda pulled back. "I don't want to go in there." Fear gripped her soul as she saw Otto standing inside the fence drinking with some other men. She began to shake uncontrollably. She thought her legs would collapse beneath her. She had to get out of there! With her heart throbbing, she rushed into the crowd. She had to get away before Otto saw her! Oh, God, she hoped that he hadn't seen her already--get out of my way--I have to get out of here--were the thoughts that fuzzed her brain. There was no room for cool, clear thoughts. Panic encompassed her. Had he seen her? Was he following her? Who could help her? No one! She had to get away. Where was he now? She had to move more rapidly. Her heart was pounding faster--faster--faster.

"Ah!" Amanda screamed as she felt a strong hand grip her arm.

"What's the matter with you?"

"Oh, Frederick, I want to go home, please!" She was trembling.

"Sure, that's okay with me if that's what you want to do. Let's go."

Taking Amanda's trembling hand in his, they started toward home.

****

Eva had spent the early part of the afternoon helping Eleanor take care of little Alex. The rest of the day she spent losing herself in reading, "Sonnets from the Portuguese." No matter how many times before she had read each of the poems, each time they moved her deeply. Elizabeth had a way of expressing in her poems the way that Eva felt in her heart about Charles. As the light through the window dimmed, Eva closed the pages and put the worn book back into her night stand.

"Would you like me to get you ready for bed now?" Eleanor stood in the threshold of Eva's door.

"Yes, Eleanor, please. That sounds like a good idea."

"They all must be having a grand time at the picnic." Eleanor helped Eva take off her dress and then put on her nightgown for bed.

"Yes, they must be. Otherwise, they'd probably be back already. I'm glad." Eva smiled.

"Should I help you into bed?" Eleanor hung Eva's clothes neatly on a hanger and placed them into the closet.

"No, I want to sit here for a while. I like to look at how the town lights up in the dark."

Eleanor leaned over to look out the window. "Yes, it is pretty. The sky is all lit up also, so full of stars."

"Yes, it's so beautiful," Eva replied.

"Well, I'm going to retire for the night. I just fed little Alex. I hope he'll sleep through the night for Amanda."

"If he doesn't, we'll know about it." Eva chuckled.

"Should I close your door?" asked Eleanor.

"Yes, please."

"Good night." Eleanor closed the door.

In the still air of the night, Eva could hear the music from the picnic float up the hill. Its beat made her wish that she could get out of that chair and dance like she used to. Memories flashed of Charles holding her so gently. How smoothly they danced. She felt as light as a feather as he'd whirl her about the dance floor--dance after dance. Then there were the waltzes when he'd hold her so close and whisper so softly into her ear, "I love you, Eva." She would give anything to have those days back. Those days of long ago--oh, so long ago!

Voices in the dark brought her back to reality. Someone was walking up the long flight of stone stairs. Who?

Eva sat very still, almost holding her breath. She perched her ears closer to the window. It didn't take long for her to recognize the voices. They belonged to Anna and Charles. Eva was surprised--actually disappointed--they were back so early. Quietly, she sat and listened. The footsteps stopped on the front porch right below Eva's window. She could hear everything as clearly as if they had been in the room with her.

"I'm sorry for ruining your evening."

"You didn't ruin it. I had a wonderful time," Charles replied.

"I know you would have liked to have stayed longer and danced more. I'm sorry I got so tired. I guess it's a sign of getting old. Everything just seems to tire me out these days."

"I understand. Please, don't think you ruined my evening. I had a wonderful time--all day."

"I did too. Thank you for taking me."

"I should thank you for going with me."

"You don't have to thank me. After all, I do work for you."

Somehow Charles resented that remark coming from Anna. "Is that the only reason you went because you thought it was your duty?"

"No, of course not, I went because I wanted to. I just meant--"

"I don't ever want to hear you talk that way. I consider you a friend. Don't you think of me that way?"

"Yes, but you're still my employer."

"When you're not working and even when you are working, I still would like you to think of Eva and myself as your friends. We consider you one."

Anna was surprised. She had never thought the Stoner's felt that way. She didn't think that they really cared for her personally. She had thought that they just considered her as another person who did work for them.

"Okay, then--friends it is." She extended her hand as for a handshake.

Charles gently caressed it in both his hands. "Friends." He patted her hand and returned her smile. "Well, I suppose, we better go inside. Standing out here isn't going to help you feel less tired."

"No, I guess not." Anna chuckled.

Hearing that, Eva knew that she had better get into bed. She couldn't call for Eleanor. They would hear her. Quickly, she wheeled herself to her side of the bed and pulled back the bed covers. How was she going to get into bed? She had to get into bed! She didn't want to see or talk to Charles, not right now. It had upset her to hear that Charles had a good time with someone else. Even though it was what she had wanted, it still hurt. Thinking and hoping for things is one thing, but when suddenly a person sees what you think and hope for come true--the initial reality of it hurts. She had hoped that the day would bring the results it did, but there was a tinge of jealousy. She could resolve that. She had to--and she would--but not right now. Tomorrow she could cope better.

Taking her hands, she sturdily grabbed hold of the brass spindle that comprised the headboard of the brass canopy bed. With all her strength she began to pull the lifeless bottom part of her body into the bed. Her hands that gripped the spindles turned blue, and her arms began to ache. She couldn't make it--but she had to--she just had to!

With determination she finally dragged her whole body onto the bed. Her arms fell to her sides, tired--aching. As she lay panting trying to catch her breath, she heard footsteps in the hall. Quickly, she groped for the covers and pulled them over herself. The footsteps stopped and she heard the doorknob turn. It was Charles. She had made it in time--thank God! Breathing a sigh of relief, she closed her eyes. Quietly, she lay on her side pretending to be asleep as she heard him move quietly about the room.

As he snuggled himself into the bed and under the covers, she felt his arm slide around her waist and caress her tenderly. She felt his other arm slide beneath her pillow. The closeness of his body warmth her. She was glad that he couldn't see her face and the salty tears that moistened her cheeks.

As he slept, her heart wept and seemed to break in a million, scattered pieces. The yearning to love him completely crept inside of her, but she couldn't do it. He deserved better than her. Now with her plan in motion there could be no turning back. It was the best for Charles. When her plan was completed, he'd find the happiness that he deserved and she could no longer give him. Thoughts like that tore and ripped her heart apart. She dreaded leaving him, but she had to do it. Her plan had to succeed, and Anna was perfect for the plan. She no longer was the woman that he had married, and she hated the woman she had become.

Before retiring to her room, Anna quietly checked Alex in his room. Seeing him sleeping so peacefully put her mind at ease and she soon retired to her room.

Sitting before her mirrored vanity, she combed a luster into her dark hair now streaked with a few strands of gray. Slowly, she put the boar bristle brush down and stared at herself in the mirror. Gently, she rubbed her trembling hand up by her eyes. Her eyes were so ugly--so swollen. She tried to make her hand stop trembling but she couldn't. "Mother time" was not being kind to her. Her youth was slowly slipping away and being replaced with bulging eyes and trembling hands of an old woman. Nothing could be done about it. So why should she waste time pouting about things that couldn't be changed.

Feeling uncomfortably warm, she opened both her bedroom windows before retiring into bed. It felt so good to finally rest her tired body. Within seconds, her mind plunged into a state of rest where all conscious thoughts had vanished. Her tired body had left reality behind and exchanged it for the images and thoughts of her dreams.

****

"Would you like to sit out here for a while before going inside?" Frederick asked as they climbed the steps onto the porch.

"It's a lovely night, isn't it?" Amanda said as she gazed at the star filled sky.

"Well, let's sit down and enjoy it." Frederick sat on the steps and then pulled Amanda down beside him.

As he put his arm around her, Amanda's body became rigid. She didn't want his hand to go any farther than her shoulders. Putting his other hand around her chin, he turned her face toward him and soon his moist lips were on hers and his tongue was trying to squeeze inside her mouth. The pain of a man touching her again filled her with an overwhelming fear--hysteria! With all her strength she pulled away from him and sprang to her feet. Before Frederick knew what was happening, Amanda was in the house and racing up the stairs toward her room. Once inside her room, she leaned against the closed door to catch her breath.

A few minutes later, there came a gentle tapping on her door.

"Amanda, I want to talk to you," a voice whispered.

Knowing it was Frederick and still gripped with fear, her hand searched above the door's frame. After finding the key, she locked her door.

"Oh, come on, Amanda. Don't be childish. You didn't have to do that," Frederick said as he heard the key turn in the door.

Amanda was taking no chances. Once again she could see that hideous, scar-pitted face looking down at her. She could feel the pain of that horrid red thing being thrust inside of her again and again. In desperation she quickly covered her face and eyes with her hands, but that couldn't erase the memories of that night. Tears drowned her eyes as her hands slowly slipped down her face. Was that the way it was always to be? Was the memory of that night going to haunt her forever? Would her fear of men and the memory of the pain of that first encounter with a man make her live her life alone--without a man? So what if it did? She didn't need a man. She had someone--her baby. He'd always love her. She was his mother. Children love their mother's forever! But it wasn't enough--not really. She did need other love--a love of a man--but she couldn't tolerate the physical part of that relationship with a man. It was so painful!

"Come on, Amanda, open the door."

"I have to get up early for work tomorrow. Good night, Frederick."

After hearing his footsteps fade down the hall and into his room, Amanda went to bed. As she lay in bed, it suddenly came to her where she had seen Frederick before. He was the person who had tried to save Henry--the stranger who had run into the alley and smothered the flames that engulfed Henry's body.

Poor little Henry! Why did he have to die? He was so sweet. Thoughts of Henry made her heart weep. Amanda cried herself to sleep that night reminiscing of Henry.

Frederick's ego was deflated. That was the first time he had ever "struck out" with a girl. He had figured Amanda for an easy night of sex--a girl with an illegitimate child. Man! How easy could they come? It really bothered him that she had let others touch her but not him. He wasn't giving up. He'd get her. To make himself feel better, he began to figure that she did want it. It was just the wrong time of the month. He could wait five days. Maybe he wouldn't even have to wait that long. She could be over "the curse" tomorrow. Well, he wasn't going to give up, not until he "made it" with her--and he would! That he promised himself. He always got what he wanted-- one way or the other.

The wailing cry of hunger from little Alex woke everyone up the next morning. Soon the whole house was bustling with activity. The aroma of fresh fried bacon tantalized everyone's palate and made their stomach's growl.

Before long almost everyone was sitting around the patio table enjoying the well-prepared breakfast and the warm rays of the sun that reached down and touched each of them.

"It's going to be a hot one today," Charles commented.

"Yes, it must be seventy degrees already," Eva said.

"Sixty-eight--to be exact." Frederick stood, arrogantly, in the threshold.

"Up already? I thought your train didn't leave until this afternoon?" Charles remarked.

"My train may never leave. I've decided to stay here for a while, maybe a week or two."

Charles was glad to hear that. "Why don't you stay here permanently? I need another experienced person at the bank. With Beechwood growing so fast, I've got more work than I can handle."

Frederick shrugged his shoulders. "No, I don't think so." He squeezed between Anna and Amanda so he could sit next to Amanda.

"What would you like for breakfast?" Eleanor asked Frederick.

"I never eat breakfast--got to watch my weight. Just a cup of coffee," Frederick replied.

"It isn't healthy to skip meals," said Charles.

"There's nothing the matter with me. I'm as healthy as can be."

"Wait until you get older. It'll catch up with you--skipping meals like that." Turning to Amanda, Charles asked, "Think you can handle the bank alone today?"

"I hope so." Amanda was nervous about having charge of the

bank. "I do wish Mrs. Benson was still there, especially today."

"There is nothing to be nervous about. Just do what you always do. If somebody wants more, tell them to come back tomorrow when I'll be there. We'll drop you off before we leave for Milwaukee."

"I don't have anything to do today. Why don't I drive Amanda to the bank and help her out," offered Frederick?

"If it's all right with Amanda, it's all right with me," Charles responded.

Sensing Frederick had ulterior motives, Amanda didn't like that idea. However, she didn't like being at the bank alone either. Well, maybe she could be wrong about him. "It's all right with me." It was better than being alone.

"What are you going to Milwaukee for?" Frederick inquired.

"There's a banker's convention there," Charles answered.

Amanda rose from the table. "Excuse me, I want to check on Alex before we leave."

"I forgot something in my room." Frederick rose and followed Amanda up the stairs.

A loving smile crossed Amanda's face as she saw little Alex sleeping so peacefully.

Turning around she was startled to see Frederick standing in the doorway. She gave him a quick smile. "Well, I'm ready. Let's go," she spoke softly as she walked past him in the doorway.

Down the stairs, out the door, into the car, and off to the bank they went.

Meanwhile, out on the terrace, Charles rose from his chair. "I suppose we better leave so we get there on time." Charles took hold of the handles on Eva's wheelchair to push her into the house.

Eva grabbed back and touched his hand. "I don't really feel good today. I don't think I can travel all that way."

"Oh, Eva, I was looking forward to having you along and to taking you to one of those expensive restaurants we used to go to." Charles was disappointed.

"I'm sorry, Charles, but I really don't feel good."

"Should I call Dr. Whitmore?"

"No, I'm not that sick. I just don't feel like traveling."

"I was also looking forward to going shopping with you. What about the new dress you wanted to buy?" asked Charles.

"Anna can get it for me. She can go along."

Anna looked up from her meal with surprise.

"How can Anna buy a dress for you?" Charles was getting disturbed.

"She's the same size as me. Whatever dress you like. You buy. It's really quite simple."

"It'll be a lot simpler if you'd come along."

"I would--believe me--but I just don't feel good."

"Ah, I don't have to go to that convention. We can go shopping in Milwaukee another day when you feel better."

"But Charles you've paid your registration fee, and they're expecting you. You really have to go. Besides, I want a new dress for the Benson wedding this weekend. Everyone has seen all my other dresses. Please, take Anna along and buy me a dress that the town will talk about for years. Please, Charles, do that for me."

"Okay, if that's what you really want." Charles gave her a kiss and then turned to Anna. "Well, you heard the lady. I guess we better leave. See you tonight, Eva."

"Have a good trip and remember, I want the most elaborate dress there is."

Anna caressed Eva's hand. "I'll get you the best dress anyone has ever seen. I hope you feel better when we come back."

"I will." Eva smiled. "Good-bye."

"Good-bye, Eva." Anna smiled.

As Eva watched them drive away and disappear, she thought about how that was the way she had planned for things to be in the future.

"Maybe if you lay down for a while, you'd feel better," Eleanor suggested as she began to clean the soiled dinnerware from the table.

"No, I know what will make me feel better." Turning the wheels on her chair with her hands, she slowly made it down to the edge of the pond.

Eva sat for hours just staring into the glistening blue pond and contemplating--about her plan--about the future--about Charles.

****

Things had gone slowly at the bank. That was to be expected. If Amanda had been alone, the bank would have been jammed with customers. Things seem to go that way--Murphy's law!

After checking the day's receipts, Frederick and Amanda locked the bank and left for home. But instead of turning up the hill toward the house, Frederick took the other road that led out of town.

"Where are you going?" Amanda surged with panic. She didn't like this and she was afraid.

"I thought a nice drive would be relaxing."

"I don't want to take a drive. I want to go home."

"I'm surprised this car runs. This was the first car my old man bought. He keeps it so I have something to drive when I come home. I know he doesn't take care of this car like he takes care of his new one."

Amanda could really have cared less. She wanted to go home. She was afraid out there alone with him. The terror of that night was with her again. He was going to hurt her just like that other man, Otto!

"Take me home!"

"Oh, come on. Don't hand me that goody-two-shoes routine. You want me just as much as I want you."

Her heart began to throb and pound. Was it going to happen again? No! It wasn't! She wouldn't let it! She'd die first! Following her first impulse of survival, she pulled the latch up, opened the door, and jumped out. Her feet stung as they hit the gravel road. With her balance lost, she stumbled uncontrollably to the edge of the road. Finally, she fell on her hands and knees. Seeing that Frederick had stopped the car, she scrambled to her feet. Pain seized her legs. Fear forced her to try and run down the road away from him. Turning around she saw him coming down the road in the car after her. Her heart pounded and pounded. It felt as if it was going to jump out. Breathing became harder and harder. Her legs were so tired. They felt as if they were going to collapse beneath her. She couldn't go on but she had to--she had to--and so her legs moved--how--she didn't know but they did. Closer and closer he came. Finally, she could no longer go on. She fell on her knees onto the graveled road. Panting--panting--panting! Her chest felt so tight and lightening streaks of pain followed each gasping breath. She was so weak! She could never get away! She couldn't stop him now!

Out of the car he came, closer--closer--closer!

She dreaded the worst! Trying to get up, she fell again. Her body was drained of all energy--limp with fatigue! Closer he came until she felt him touch her.

"Come on, let's go." He helped her stand up.

Being in no position to fight or argue, she let him take control of her. To her surprise, he walked her over to the car and helped her into it. Was he taking her home? She couldn't trust him! She had to be on her guard! He could be tricking her--waiting for her to trust him and let her guard down.

After a few minutes, he asked, "Are you okay now?"

Amanda nodded.

Frederick sighed. "You're something else! You're strange!"

Was she strange? She just didn't want to experience that pain. Frederick was attractive, and she was flattered that he found her pretty--pretty enough to be with, but she couldn't give him more. Was he right? She questioned herself.

Frederick's ego took another blow. He knew that he could have taken her there, but that would have been rape. He was a sex-loving guy--but not that way. He preferred his girls willing. That was his ego trip--knowing girls wanted him and would do anything for him. Nevertheless, he hadn't given up on Amanda. He'd break her down. She'd just take longer than most.

Glancing over at her, he grinned as he meditated on the pleasure that he would have when she finally gave in to him.

"Hey, I'm sorry. I didn't mean it when I said you were strange." Calling her names would get him no place. Maybe she was one of those girls a person had to "butter up" with gifts. Well, that was no problem. What else was money good for if one couldn't buy what one wanted.

Chapter 11
****
The Suicide

The weeks of flowers and candy giving went and still Frederick had no results. Taking her to dances, fairs, buying her clothes, didn't help either. Frederick began to think of Amanda as unreal. One kiss on a date and that was it. She never wanted to be alone with him. Being deprived of something made Frederick want it more. Sometimes it made him furious to think that she had let others--at least one for sure, Alex's father--touch her but she wouldn't let him do anything. That made him more determined to have her. Finally, it came to him that maybe there was one gift that would "win her over." But was he ready for what that gift implied? Why not? He'd eventually end up that way anyhow. Amanda was attractive--her face--her body. She was no "charity case." If it didn't turn out, there was always a way out--one way or another. With those thoughts, he gave her the ultimate gift--a diamond engagement ring.

Amanda was shocked--along with everyone else.

Accepting the ring meant accepting the inevitable responsibility that went along with it--marriage. She could be a wife in every room except one--the bedroom. She knew that she shouldn't really accept the ring for that reason. Was she being a bit childish? Other woman got married. They didn't seem to mind the pain. Why should she pamper herself? Maybe it was about time that she grew up and accepted things the way other women had. Life was full of pain. She knew Frederick was a "good catch." Any girl in town would "jump" at the opportunity to just go on a date with him. Here she had the opportunity to marry him. He was attractive and he had been so kind to her. She enjoyed his company and loved to be near him. She did miss him when she was at work and didn't like the possibility of losing him, which could happen if she didn't accept the ring. She dreaded being alone again and would miss the attention that he had lavished on her. He did make her so happy and she couldn't wait to be with him. Was that love? She had never experienced the kind of love a woman has toward a man, so maybe that was it?

****

"What do you think?" Amanda positioned the white veil on top of her hair.

"It's okay," replied Anna. "What do you think, Eva?"

"I think Amanda is the most beautiful bride that I've ever seen," Eva replied.

Anna's eyes were bursting with tears of joy as she fussed about Amanda's light-blue dress, straightened her collar, and draped her locks of hair over her shoulders.

There was a knock at the door. "It's Eleanor. May I come in? I have Amanda's bouquet."

"Of course, Eleanor, come in," replied Eva.

As Eleanor entered the room, a delicate aroma of a tea like fragrance scented the air. In her hand she held a bouquet of red roses tied together with a large white ribbon.

Amanda's eyes gleamed as she reached for the bouquet. Carefully, she took the bouquet out of Eleanor's hand. "They are lovely." She gave Eleanor a kiss on her cheek. "Thank you."

"I just picked them. Hose deserves the thanks. He's the one who grew them. Pastor Davis and his wife just arrived."

"Well, I guess it's about time then." Anna gave Amanda a kiss. "You're on your own now. Remember when you hear the piano that's your signal to come down the stairs."

Out the door they went and down the hall toward the staircase. Hose, dressed in an elaborate tuxedo, was waiting there. After helping Eva out of her wheelchair, he picked her up in his sturdy arms and followed Anna and Eleanor down the stairs.

Once at the bottom of the stairs, he placed Eva into another wheelchair. Within a few minutes, they were in the parlor joining the rest of the quests who were all anxiously waiting for the beginning of the wedding.

Sitting around the room was Mr. Ewerdt, Mr. and Mrs. Benson,

Dr. Whitmore and his wife, and some of Frederick's friends from town and their girlfriends.

The foyer doors were opened wide so all could see Amanda come down the stairs. At certain intervals, the oak railing was decorated with white bowed ribbons. At the foot of the stairs, where Frederick now stood waiting for Amanda, was a large, ornamental silver floor vase filled with red roses and large white chrysanthemums. Wherever a person looked there were bouquets of massive colors.

Pastor Davis, standing firm and straight with his opened black church book griped in his hands, cleared his throat. This was a signal for his wife to begin the wedding march melody on the piano.

With her hands properly positioned on the ivory keys and her foot on the appropriate pedal, she began releasing the melody and harmony that had been trapped within the piano.

As the music fell on Amanda's ears, her stomach began to twist with nervousness. Her hands and knees began to shake. Suddenly, at that moment, the actual reality of what was happening griped her. There had been so much to do since her engagement two weeks ago that with all the rushing and planning she hadn't really had time to consider the actual reality of this day. In a few minutes she would actually be married--married to Frederick. Was it what she had really wanted? Marriage was forever. She hadn't known Frederick very long--just since July--only two months. Maybe she should have waited longer? What if she couldn't tolerate the pain of having him touch her--to see her--dirty--ugly body. Would she ever want him to touch her? No--not really! But if they were married, she would have to let him. Oh, why did she accept his ring and agree to this? Now, it wasn't what she wanted at all, but it didn't matter what she wanted. She couldn't "back out." Everything was ready. If she "backed out" now, Frederick would surely hate her. He was the only man who had ever paid so much attention to her and had made her feel so wonderful--so happy. She couldn't lose that part of their relationship. She had to go through with the wedding.

When Mrs. Davis began to play the march again, everyone began to look at each other and ask the unspoken question. Where is Amanda?

Anna was just about to leave her chair in the parlor and go up the back stairs when Amanda appeared at the top of the front stairs.

The only thing on Amanda's mind now was the question--could she make it down the stairs without falling? Her legs were shaking and felt so uncontrollable. How she made it down, she'd never remember. Before long she was at the bottom of the stairs, and Frederick and she were walking arm in arm up to Pastor Davis.

The words of the ceremony brought tears to Anna's eyes. Those seventeen years had gone too fast. Yesterday Amanda was her little baby. Today she was a woman--leaving her and starting her own family. Time moves too fast and waits for no one. During most of their life, it had been only the two of them. Sure, they had Alex for a while, but then he was gone--and it was just the two of them again. Then Henry came--but he left too. They had been closer than most mothers and daughters for that reason. But even with their closeness, there were secrets that they each had kept from each other. Anna had never told Amanda who Henry's father was. Likewise, Amanda had never told her mother who little Alex's father was. The need to know had never really seemed very important. They were both together and cared about each other and that's all that really mattered. Now Anna would be alone. For the first time she wouldn't have her Amanda. Amanda had grown and had found another to share her life with. Anna was so very happy for her Amanda. It was what life was really all about. Anna knew Amanda would find someone else to share her life with--the man she chose to be her husband. It is sad and cruel but the truth is that a parent raises children only to have them leave them. Why can't they stay small forever, so we can have them forever. Why does the time when they exchange the innocence of childhood for independence of adulthood have to come so soon? They are the centers of our life for such a short time and then they are gone. The childish laughter silenced and even in memories the sound can't be heard anymore. There is a cradle, a bottle, and perhaps a toy here and there that tells us they were really small and "all ours"--once upon a time--

> Oh, little one so soft and sweet,
> Come and sit here by me for a while.
> Let me touch your tiny hands and feet,
> Let me enjoy your sunshine smile.

For soon you'll be too big to sit on my knee,
And you'll have no time left for me.
No time for me--no time for me--

A soft hand caressed Anna's. It was Eva. Eva's eyes told her that she understood. Her eyes were full of tears also.

After the superb meal, the guests mingled and talked with each other. Charles, Mr. Ewerdt, and Mr. Benson left the table and walked over to a small table filled with various liquor bottles. After pouring themselves a drink, they stood about talking business.

While Eleanor cleared away the dirty china, Amanda and Anna carried on a conversation with Pastor Davis and his wife.

Seeing Mrs. Benson was sitting alone, Amanda went over and talked to her.

Frederick followed Amanda.

"Thank you for taking over at the bank for me," Amanda said to Mrs. Benson.

"That's all right. I'm glad I can do it. In fact, it'll feel good to do something different for a while. Doing the same housework day after day was getting to me. I need a change for a couple days."

"I hope my dad finds a permanent replacement soon so you aren't tied down with two jobs again." Among certain people, Frederick watched his terminology--now it was "dad" not "old man."

"A permanent replacement? You're coming back to work after you come home from your honeymoon, aren't you?" Mrs. Benson asked Amanda. She was quite concerned by Frederick's remark. She had planned on working only a few days. A permanent job wasn't in her plans.

Amanda was also concerned about what Frederick had said. She and Frederick had never really discussed what they'd do after their honeymoon. Amanda assumed things would remain as before except for the fact that she had a husband.

"When we come back from our honeymoon, we're moving to New York," Frederick informed them both.

"New York! Why on earth do you want to move so far away for?" Mrs. Benson's eyes slowly moved toward Amanda's abdomen. Where they moving to New York to conceal the early arrival of a baby? The wedding was quite sudden, so Mrs. Benson thought.

Amanda stood spellbound as she listened to find out what her future held for her.

"I've got a business in New York," Frederick stated.

"A business? Oh, yes, I remember now. Your dad mentioned it to me once," replied Mrs. Benson.

"Well, how does it feel to be a married man?" Frederick's father put his hand on his shoulder.

"I don't know. I'll let you know after I've had my husbandly privileges."

That remark caused a lusty laughter among Frederick's friends, Mr. Ewerdt, and Mr. Benson. Charles simply smiled.

Mrs. Benson felt uneasy about the remark.

Amanda felt terrified. "His privileges"--could she make it through this first night?

"Frederick was just telling me that they'll be living in New York." Mrs. Benson decided to change the subject.

"New York?" Mr. Benson was the amazed one now.

"I wish you would consider my offer." Charles directed his comment to Frederick.

"For the last five years you've been telling me that and my answer has always been the same. I've told you over and over. I like my business in New York. I make a lot of money and I enjoy my job. I'm my own boss."

"You'd be your own boss at the bank too."

"No, I wouldn't. You'd be over me."

"Not really, you'd have your responsibilities and I'd have mine. In fact, if you'd be there, I wouldn't have to come into work as much. I'm getting older and it's getting harder."

"I'm sorry. Besides enjoying my business, I make a lot of money."

"Well, you must make enough money. I don't know of anyone else who could take two months off work," Mr. Ewerdt commented.

"I've got a good manager taking care of things while I'm gone."

"What kind of business do you do?" asked Mr. Benson.

"I'm a distributor. People want certain things and I sell it to them."

"What do you specialize in?"

"Satisfying my customers."

"No, I mean, what do you sell the most of?"

"It varies. Sometimes my customers want one item, and next time they want sometime else. Whatever they want I try to sell it to them. Would you like another drink?" Frederick noticed Mr. Benson's empty glass. In addition, that was all the farther Frederick had wanted the conversation to go. The less they knew about his business--the better.

"I think you've had enough," Mrs. Benson commented to Mr. Benson.

"I've only had one," replied Mr. Benson.

"That's enough."

"We've got a second Carry Nation here." Mr. Benson chuckled.

That remark got a chuckle out of Frederick and Charles also.

"She had the right idea. A person should take a hatchet and wreck every tavern around," replied Mrs. Benson. "They corrupt men and steal food from children's mouths."

"How awful! Who does that?" asked Eva as she and Anna approached.

"Those taverns--they should all be closed!" Mrs. Benson replied ardently.

"If things keep going the way they are, you'll have your wish," replied Eva.

"Well, it couldn't be too soon for me," Mrs. Benson responded.

"It'll never happen." Frederick shook his head.

"I don't know about that. Volstead of Minnesota is pushing for some kind of prohibition," Eva commented.

"They've got prohibition in some places already, don't they?" asked Anna.

"Yes, ten or eleven states are completely dry already," replied Charles.

"Some places in Wisconsin are dry too, aren't they?" asked Anna.

"Yes, there is a lot of local option prohibition around," replied Charles.

"It'll never go any farther than where it is now," Frederick stated with stern confidence.

"I don't see anything wrong with a man having a drink occasionally," Charles commented.

"After I work hard all day, I look forward to having my nice cold glass of beer. What's the matter with that?" asked Mr. Benson.

"It's the work of the devil," replied Mrs. Benson.

"What's the work of the devil?" asked Pastor Davis as he and his wife approached.

"This is." Mr. Benson held up his empty beer glass.

"Today's a wedding and that's a work of God. We should be happy and enjoying ourselves. Tomorrow is another day to talk about such things," Pastor Davis interjected.

As the brilliant, expressive tone of a violin filled the room, Pastor Davis turned to Amanda. "May I have this dance?"

Amanda looked at Frederick.

Frederick smiled and nodded his head in approval.

Gracefully, they danced about the area cleared for dancing.

Mr. and Mrs. Benson soon joined them.

"Well, if he can dance with the bride, I can dance with the groom," Mrs. Davis told Frederick and then dragged him out among the rest of the dancers.

Eva looked at Charles. His face was covered with a pleasing grin.

Gently she touched his hand. "Go ask Anna to dance," she whispered.

"No, I enjoy being by you," Charles replied. Holding her hand, he watched his son dance. He couldn't have asked for his son to marry a better person. "I hope they are as happy as we are," said Charles.

Eva smiled and patted his hand. Wasn't her plan working? Why wouldn't he dance with Anna? The marriage between Frederick and Amanda was perfect for her plan. Charles and Anna had something in common now. She had never expected something like this marriage to happen. Nevertheless, it was a welcomed event for her plan.

As Eva was about to tell Charles to ask Anna again, she saw Anna was dancing with one of Frederick's friends.

When the little old man tapped his foot and drew his bow across the strings, everyone exchanged partners. Soon everyone had danced with everyone else at least a half a dozen times, except for Charles. As he sat by his Eva, he seemed to totally enjoy watching everyone else having so much fun. Sometimes he would move the tip of his one foot up and down to the rhythm of the music.

Time seemed to go so fast and everyone was surprised and deeply disappointed when the old man mentioned the inevitable--the last dance had come.

Frederick danced that one with Amanda, gently holding her body tightly to his.

Mr. and Mrs. Benson were in total agreement when it came to their uniform dance steps.

As close as Pastor Davis and his wife danced, one would have hardly guessed that he was a "man of the cloth."

Frederick's friends had enough dancing for one night and had departed from the dance, leaving Anna without a partner.

"Would it be all right if I danced this last dance with Anna?" Charles asked.

"Sure, go ahead. I know how much you like to dance." Eva smiled.

As she watched them dance, Eva despised herself more. She was depriving Charles of so much by being a paraplegic. He deserved so much more. Charles and Anna looked so good together. The way she and Charles had looked before she became this bothersome burden making him a slave to her incompetence.

After the dance, each guest congratulated Amanda and Frederick once again before they left and told them how nice the wedding had been.

As they bid farewell to the last guest, Frederick closed the door and then turned to Amanda. "I suppose we should get packed if we want to make our train to Niagara Falls."

"Niagara Falls!"

"Yes, that's where we are going for our honeymoon. Are you surprised?"

"The whole day has been full of surprises."

"We did talk about going away for a couple of days--on a honeymoon."

"Yes, I know but we never talked about where."

"I know. I just decided for sure today. I thought we'd spend a couple of days there. Before we come back here, I'd like to check in on my business and see how things are going. I also thought we could look for a place to live. My business isn't far from Niagara Falls."

"What about little Alex? Are we going to come back here and pick him up?" asked Amanda. She was not sure of anything, anymore.

"Yes, when we pick up the rest of your things. Don't worry, he'll be okay while we're gone."

"What time does the train leave?"

Frederick pulled at the gold chain that hung from his vest pocket and pulled out his gold pocket watch. "In about an hour."

"I better get packing then."

Just as she began to step onto the bottom step and ascend the stairs, Frederick touched her hand. "You won't need much."

Amanda smiled as she looked at him. Her smile faded as she turned away and continued up the stairs.

Her hands shook as she packed a few things into her suitcase. She wanted to scream and release the fear of the inevitable pain from her body. The scream stuck in her throat and seemed to choke her. Her mind seemed in a daze. For most brides, their wedding day is filled with overwhelming happiness and magnificent plans of the future--but not Amanda's--her day was sealed in an envelope of fear.

She heard her bedroom door close. Turning around, she saw Frederick had entered.

Setting his suitcase down, he walked over to her.

Before she knew it, he was smothering her with kisses.

Losing her balance, she fell backwards onto the bed with Frederick falling on top of her. Oh, no--not now--she needed more time to prepare herself. Pushing at him, she said, "Not here, Frederick. Someone might hear us."

"So what--we're married." Intensely, he kissed her neck.

"Please, Frederick, not here." She became frantic!

A bit angry at being put off one more time, Frederick got off her. After straightening his tie and suit jacket, he clenched her arm strongly in his hand. "Next time you're not putting me off. We're married now and I have a right to certain things--and I'll have them. If I have to rape you, I will."

With anger gleaming in his eyes, he picked up his suitcase and left her room.

Slowly, Amanda rose from the bed. After tidying up her dress and tucking a few strands of hair back into their proper place, she picked up her closed suitcase and quietly walked into the room where little

Alex was sleeping. Standing beside his bed, she watched him.

A few tears floated in her eyes. This would be the first time that she had ever been away from him. She was going to miss his warm smile, his coo's, and his strong little grips on her finger. Not being around that cuddly, loveable little sweetheart was going to be unbearable. She hoped that they wouldn't stay away too long.

She threw him a kiss, quietly closed the door, and went downstairs. Everyone was sitting in the parlor when she entered.

As she stood in the threshold, Anna got up and hugged her. "Have a good time. I love you, and I want you to be happy." Taking hold of her shoulders, she added, "You hear."

"Yes, ma." Amanda hugged her.

"Don't worry about little Alex. Your ma and I will take care of him," said Eva. "You enjoy yourself. You only go on a honeymoon once, so make good memories."

"We will." Amanda felt her smile quiver.

"Well, we better go. I just seen Hose drive up to the house." Frederick took her bag and out to the model T they went.

The ride to the depot was short and quiet.

Amanda could sense the anger that still radiated from Frederick.

When they were on the train, Frederick quietly looked out one window while Amanda looked out the other.

Guilt filled Amanda. She knew the strangeness and strain between them was her fault. Frederick had been so nice to her. Now that they were married, all he wanted was what any man expected from his wife. She was mean to deny him that. He had given her so much. He deserved to be repaid for his kindness--for his love. So much love he had given her--now it was her turn. How could she not love someone who had been so good to her? Someone who obviously loved her tremendously.

Amanda turned away from the window and looked at Frederick. He was a very handsome man. She was so lucky to have someone as good-looking and kind as him care for her and love her. A slight tear came to her eyes as she thought about how badly she had treated him. Slowly, she reached over and touched his hand.

He turned and looked at her.

She smiled and moved closer to him.

Taking his hand away from her touch, he put his arm around her shoulder and held her closer. So he had been right, all it took was a ring and he'd get her in bed, he thought.

No matter how hard she tried, she couldn't wipe away the fear that still possessed her. She pretended to like being held in his arms because it made him happy. All he wanted to do was love her. The least she could do was please him and let him love her.

As the train rattled on in the darkness of the night, they slowly fell asleep in each other's warm arms.

When they awoke, daylight was upon them and the train was decelerating.

As they stepped outside the train and onto the depot platform, the thundering sound of the Falls consumed all other sounds.

A few steps away from the depot revealed the gigantic Falls.

Amanda stopped. Her eyes were filled with astonishment. She had never seen anything so marvelous! The plunging waters created a fine mist which seemed to reflect rainbows. God had truly shown his magnificence by creating such a masterpiece of imposing beauty and grandeur!

"Shall we go to our hotel?" Frederick put his arm around her to guide her toward their hotel.

"Oh, do we have to go now? I want so much to see more of it. Please, I'm so anxious!"

"Okay, wait here for a minute." Frederick took their suitcases inside the depot. After talking to the clerk, he set down the suitcases, opened his wallet, and passed some money to the clerk.

"Everything is arranged," Frederick said with a pleasant smile as he returned to Amanda. "The clerk will have someone take our suitcases to our room."

They were the typical honeymooners and tourist--full of happiness --enthusiasm--and totally enjoying every minute of such a beautiful, spectacular place.

A tough little ship took them in front of the American Falls and then upriver right into the horseshoe of the main Falls. The noise was deafening and the spray from the Falls hit like a tropical rain. The hooded raincoats they had been given to wear were obviously not for "show." Water dripped from all over. Their faces were totally wet and even though the spray blinded them for a few seconds--it was fun!

For the first time someone besides her mother was sharing part of her life. It made Amanda feel warm. It expelled some of her fear and replaced it with a warm--giving feeling. The fear that remained seemed so unimportant in the midst of how wonderful she began to feel. She felt important and why shouldn't she have that feeling. Suddenly, to be loved seemed to be the only important thing in the world--nothing else mattered. Her feelings for Frederick were becoming stronger. She felt herself surrendering to those feelings for him. There seemed to be no fear left to hinder her emotions.

Hand in hand they walked through the rock-cut tunnels behind the Falls and watched the tremendous waters thunder by.

Time seemed to vanish. Every moment was filled with something new and exciting! One minute they were admiring the splendid Falls; the next minute they were riding down the quiet lanes and slumbering old main streets that echoed to the crash of hammers and laughter of playing children. The model T traveled past nineteenth-century churches, schoolhouses, and old mills.

"Where are we going?" asked Amanda.

"You'll find out in a few minutes." Frederick gently pressed his lips against hers and held her tight.

Amanda started to pull away for a second. What would the driver of the model T think? Oh, who cared! His kiss made her feel like she was drifting on a cloud. Suddenly, she didn't care what anyone thought or what was considered "proper" in public. She loved Frederick and there was nothing wrong with that. She wrapped her arms around him, closed her eyes, and kissed him.

Feeling the model T stop, Amanda opened her eyes and peered out the back-seat window.

Nestled among the tall white pines was a stone bistro with a pleasing antique charm.

Scattered here and there, amongst the brilliant blooming gardens, were small patio tables and chairs.

The driver cleared his throat. "We're here, sir."

Handing the driver his fare, they got out of the model T.

"Pick us up in about three hours." Frederick closed the door.

"Yes, sir." The driver backed the model T up and then disappeared around the bend in the road leaving a lingering cloud of dust.

A few minutes after they had sat down at a table, a young woman appeared and handed them each a decorative card. After lighting the two candles on the table, she departed.

In the stillness of the country evening, while they waited for their prepared dinner, they enjoyed the pleasure of a mellow wine and each other's company.

After the meal and a leisurely walk about the well-groomed flowered yard, the model T driver appeared. They left the bistro and headed toward their hotel.

As the bellboy opened the door to their room, Amanda's eyes fell upon the bed--the place where the final act of the day would be performed. It had been such a marvelous day. Frederick had shown her such a wonderful time. She couldn't hurt him by saying "no"-- and she wouldn't.

As Frederick made love to her, she lay rigidly under him.

"Hold me--hold me tight!" he said full of passion.

She did as he desired. The tears rolled down her cheeks as pain pierced one side of her groin. She prayed it wouldn't be that way--but it was.

"Move--move--I love you!" He caressed her tightly.

She tried to move but when she did the pain tore through her more. It was unbearable! She tried to keep her tears inside. She didn't want Frederick to feel them on her face. Oh, God, let it be over, she screamed inside of herself! She couldn't let Frederick know of her intense pain. He might feel guilty about hurting her. She couldn't let him feel that way. He was such a good man. He shouldn't be made to feel guilty about something that was natural for a man to want. Other woman put up with the pain for their husbands, didn't they? Why shouldn't she, she thought?

It seemed like hours--then it was over.

Frederick now lay beside her quietly.

Turning away from Frederick and onto her side, she brought her knees up to her abdomen to try and stop the pain that she still experienced in her groin. Quietly, she cried until the early morning hours when the pain ceased and she finally fell asleep.

Hours later when she awoke, she found Frederick sitting on the edge of the bed reading a newspaper that he held in his hands.

"Good morning," she said.

Frederick didn't turn around, he was deep in thought as he concentrated on what he was reading.

Amanda got out of bed and got dressed. Sitting on the edge of the bed, she brushed her hair as she waited for Frederick to finish reading. She didn't like it when someone interrupted her when she was reading and for that reason she wouldn't interrupt Frederick either.

Slowly Frederick folded the paper and then stared down at it. "Prohibition?" was the huge headline on the front of the *Times*.

"Is something the matter, Frederick?"

He was silent--then with a slight vagueness of mind, he turned to her. "Did you say something?"

"Is everything okay?"

"Um--" He paused. "It will be." He tossed the newspaper onto the bed and grabbed his suit jacket off the oak valet.

"I'll be back by tonight." Hurriedly he buttoned his jacket and then reached into his pocket.

"Here, take this and have a good time today." Onto the bed he tossed one twenty-dollar bill after another.

"Where--what--" Amanda was in a state of confusion!

"I'll see you tonight." Quickly, he kissed her on the cheek and then ran out the door.

Amanda stood stunned for a second or two. When her mind cleared, she ran to the door to stop Frederick and ask him what was going on. However, when she entered the hallway, he was nowhere in sight. She went back into the room, locked the door behind her, and then looked out the window. From the window, she could see Frederick get into a model T which speeded down the street and out of sight.

Turning around she eyed the folded newspaper on the bed. Picking it up she examined it and wondered what Frederick had been reading. Maybe if she knew, she'd know where he had gone. Now that was stupid! Even if she knew what he had been reading--that's all she would know. All she knew about Frederick was how kind and loving he had been to her. Other than knowing he had a business, she didn't know anything else about him--not really!

Sitting on the bed, she looked at the money that he had tossed on it. Would he even come back?

****

Charles helped Eva get dressed and then helped her into her wheelchair.

As she brushed her hair, Charles dressed to go to the bank.

"How are things going at the bank?" asked Eva.

"Oh, fine. Mrs. Benson is glad that I hired another girl to take Amanda's place, but she wishes the girl was trained already."

Eva chuckled. "She doesn't like to train people, does she?"

"No, she just likes to do her work. She doesn't like to be interrupted and have to stop her work to teach someone else how to do their job. She usually gets so involved in helping them that when she goes back to what she was doing, she's forgotten where she left off adding or subtracting."

"Well, five more days and then they'll be back. I miss Amanda."

"Yes, when a person gets used to having someone around and then suddenly they aren't around a person misses them. I wish Frederick would stay here and come to work at the bank. That's what I sent him to college for. Instead he goes into business with a classmate. A business he never talks about except to say how much money it makes for him."

"It's his life. He does have a right to do what he wants. You can't force him to like what you do."

"He used to like what I did until that Jackie Larson filled his head full of ideas."

"Jackie is his friend. Don't speak badly of his friend. It'll alienate Frederick more."

"Yes, I suppose, you're right." Touching her shoulder, he gave her a kiss on her cheek. "I'll be right back to carry you downstairs."

"Where are you going?"

"Just out into the hall. I'll be back before you're finished brushing your hair."

Curiously, Eva wheeled herself up to the closed bedroom door. Slightly, she opened the door. Through the small crack in the slightly opened door, she could see Charles gently tapping on Anna's door.

The door opened and Charles disappeared inside.

So she had finally gotten what she had planned, thought Eva. Now it was time for the last step of her plan. Anna would be there for Charles, and that was how she had planned things all along. Anna would be good for him. It wasn't for herself that she had wanted Anna hired but for Charles.

Once inside Anna's room Charles asked, "Have you thought about what I asked you last night?"

"Yes, I have."

"Well, will you do it?"

"Yes, as soon as Amanda and Frederick come back. I don't want to miss these last few days with little Alex. I don't know when I may see him again."

"I understand that. Next Monday would be fine," said Charles.

"That's okay with me also," replied Anna.

"Good, I'll make the arrangements for then. You'll stay overnight in Milwaukee."

"It'll take that long?" asked Anna.

"I hope that is all the longer it will take. I'm paying them well. So I hope it will be done that quick. If they want the money, I'm sure they'll figure out some way to do it quickly." Finally, Charles realized Anna was still in her nightgown. "I'm sorry I bothered you this early in the morning but I wanted to stop off and make the arrangements before I went to the bank."

"That's okay. I was going down for breakfast anyway."

"Things wouldn't be such a rush now if I had thought of it sooner."

"How did you even know something like that was possible? I've never heard about anything like that."

"I read about it in one of the newspapers."

"I think Eva will like it. I hope it turns out."

"Oh, it will. I'll make sure of that. I better get back to Eva. If I stay away too long, I'll have to make up some excuse."

Slowly, Charles opened the door and peeked out into the hall. There was no one in sight. He didn't want Eva to see him coming out of Anna's room. That would have called for an explanation--a lie--and he didn't like that.

Eva was sitting in front of the mirrored dresser tucking a few loose strands of hair into place. She had her hair combed up and neatly piled on top of her head. "How do you like it?"

"You always look nice, Eva," replied Charles.

"That doesn't answer my question. Do you like it?"

"Well, to tell you the truth, I liked your hair like that." Charles motioned to their wedding picture which stood at the corner of the dresser.

"You like my locks hanging over my shoulder?"

"You have such beautiful natural curly hair. I hate to see you hide them by putting your hair up like that."

"You like Anna's hair like that." Eva was a bit scornful.

"Anna's not you. I like your hair down. It's prettier that way."

"Help me take it down."

"If you like it that way, leave it, Eva."

"No, I want to wear it the way you like it."

As Charles started to take out the bobby pins that held up her hair, she grabbed a hold of his hand. Putting it up to her lips, she kissed it.

"I love you, Charles. I always will." Gently she caressed his hand to her cheeks. "I love you so."

Charles stooped down and hugged her to him. "I love you too."

"You'll never forget me? No matter whatever happens?"

"Eva, I love you. I always will. Of course, I'll never forget you."

"Even if you ever would love someone else someday, please, don't forget me and how much I love you."

"Why all the silly talk. I love you now and I always will. I could never forget someone I love. My love for you grows each day and it always will."

"Even when I deprive you of so much?"

"You don't deprive me of anything. I have you and that's all I want."

"If I ever did anything that might hurt you, please, don't hate me because I would never hurt you deliberately. I love you so much, and I want you to be happy. I would never hurt you because I wanted to be mean to you."

"Eva, what on earth are you talking about?" Such talk was completely bewildering to Charles.

"I love you." She put her arms around his neck and pulled him closer. She gave him a kiss that would last for all time--an eternity.

Feeling a tear on her cheek while they kissed, Charles pulled away. "Eva, are you all right?"

Quickly, she wiped the tear away. "Yes."

"Eva, what's the matter?" Charles was deeply concerned.

"Nothing, it's one of those days. You know how weepy I get lately. Must be my change coming. I'm forty already--you know."

With that Charles pushed her wheelchair to the end of the stairs. Lifting her into his arms, he carried her down the stairs.

Eva enjoyed every minute of that warm closeness to the man she loved so deeply. After today, he'd be out of arms reach and she'd never feel his arms about her again or feel his moist kiss on her lips.

Not having much of an appetite, Eva didn't eat much. She just moved her fork about on her plate.

"Eva, what is the matter?" asked Charles. "Would you like me to stay home today with you?"

"No, that's all right. I'll be fine." She had to do what she had planned--today. The situation was perfect and waiting to do it just made it harder to do. Today had to be the day--for once and all--it had to be done!

"Are you sure?" Charles questioned again.

"Yes, Charles." She smiled. "Besides, if you stay home today, you'll fall much farther behind in your work."

"That doesn't matter. If you want me here, I'll stay."

"I'll be all right. Everything will be fine. You'll see when you come home."

"Well, if you're sure?"

"I am."

"Good-bye then, see you tonight." Charles's kissed her.

His kiss was too short for Eva. She'd preferred the kiss from the man that she loved to be longer--especially since it would be her last kiss. However, she couldn't very well tell that to Charles. So it would have to do. No, it wouldn't!

"Charles!" she called after him.

"Yes." He turned around to look at her.

"I'd like to go along to the car with you--if it's all right?"

"If it's all right? I'd like that very much." Walking back over to her, he took hold of the two handles on the back of the wheelchair.

"No, I want to move it myself, please." She didn't want his last memory of her to be like that--with him pushing her in the wheelchair--her hideous wheelchair!

"The flowers are so beautiful this time of the year, don't you think so?"

"Yes, they are," replied Charles. "Let's take a stroll through them tonight. I'll have more time then."

"Well, here we are." Eva smiled up at Charles.

Charles stopped at the side of the car. "See you tonight."

As he opened the car door and was about to step inside, Eva grabbed his hand.

"Kiss me again, Charles."

She held him tightly to her--never wanting to let go. But as he pulled away, she gently released him from her grasp.

Puzzled and concerned by her unusually tight hold, he asked, "Are you sure you are okay?"

"Yes, you better get going."

"Right." Climbing into the car, he started it and drove down the driveway. As he turned to look at her, she waved.

Turning her wheelchair around, she watched Anna finishing her breakfast at the table.

"Should I come down and wheel you back up here?" Anna called.

"No, that's all right. I want to be alone for a while. I'll be up in a few minutes."

After wheeling her chair behind a hedge out of everyone's view, she sat for a few seconds and stared at the glistening pond. Water--the gift of life--for Charles, yes--but for her it would be the gift of freedom--freedom from the guilt that haunted her heart--freedom from the lifeless legs that imprisoned her in that repulsive wheelchair. It would also give Charles his freedom--his life once again.

Slowly, she wheeled her chair to the edge of the pond's bank. For a second, the finality of the last act of her plan frightened her--but then she felt her body experience a freedom--a sort of relief! A satisfying smile came across her face--for you my dear, dear Charles--my love. I set you free! The hands that held her chair steadfast released the wheels and set them free. The wheelchair sprung forward--

SPLASH!

A breath brought water into her nostrils--it stung--burnt. The survival instinct told her to try to get out--climb out of the water--swim--do something to save herself. But it was too late. Faces and things of the past flooded the numerous rooms of her mind. Little things she had never given a second thought to--a picture in a wallet--the reason she had sensed the familiarity of Anna--the picture was in Hans's wallet--the picture was of Anna. Hans had explained her as his daughter. The faces of her mother--her father--the room she slept in as a child--her doll--Charles--Charles--

****

Frederick knew that his long drive over the dusty, gravel roads was finally coming to an end when he saw the sign, ROCHESTER--2 MILES.

His buttocks were sore from being bounced around on the seat as the model T hit one bump in the road after another.

As the model T turned the bend around some woods, he found himself entering the city. At last!

Down a couple of streets, around a corner, and into an alley between two buildings the model T went and stopped. As he approached the front door of the three-story building, the door flung open and a middle-aged plump man zigzagged out onto the sidewalk. There the man stood with glassy eyes. He tired unsuccessfully to focus on Frederick as Frederick walked past him and into the building.

Once inside the dimly lit building, he walked up to the dark colored bar. With his hands, Frederick motioned the huge man, who was drying glasses behind the bar, to come over by him.

"Hi, Fred, where have you been for the last two months?" he greeted Frederick with a jovial grin.

Considering the question not of importance, Frederick didn't answer the man. It was none of the man's business, Frederick thought.

"Where's Jackie?" asked Frederick.

"Upstairs in the office."

The Suicide

Next to the bar was a door marked PRIVATE. Frederick opened it and departed from the barroom. To the left was a stairway, lit with little red lights. Up the carpeted stairs he went. As he reached the top of the stairs, he paused. He saw one of the many doors, which lined the hallway, open.

A woman with lips painted fire red and dressed in a mere slip stepped into the threshold.

A man followed her out and then stopped beside her in the hall. While he finished buttoning his jacket, his lustful eyes gazed at her nipples that showed through her thin slip. Once his coat was buttoned, his hands began to caress her breasts.

The woman backed away. "You already got what you paid for. If you want more, you pay more."

"Well, maybe I don't think I got my money's worth yet." He started to press himself closer to her.

"It doesn't matter what you think. It's what I say." She pushed him back. "You want another piece. You pay again."

"Hum--you're good. I'll be back. See you later, honey."

"You bet, big boy." As she watched him walk down the hall, she noticed the man standing at the top of stairs.

"Hi, Freddy, honey!" With her breasts flopping and hips swinging, she walked down to greet him.

"Where you been? We missed you," she talked slow and soft.

"It doesn't matter where I've been. I'm here now."

"Right!--and it's good to see you."

"How has business been?"

"Well, you know how it is. The more 'tricks'--the better the business. You and Jackie are good people to work for. Since I've been here, no 'tricks' have run out without paying and none of them have beaten up on any of us girls."

"I think you can thank, 'Bulldog,' downstairs for that. Everybody knows that they won't get by him if one of you girls ever started yelling."

"Ya, 'Bulldog,' he's all right. Sometimes I think I'd like to get a man with a body like that in bed. But then I think of his face and I don't know if I could stand looking at that while I was getting laid by him."

"He used to have a good-looking face."

"You're kidding!"

"No, he was quite the 'ladies man.'"

"What on earth happened?"

"Got into the boxing ring once too often."

"Really?"

"Yup, I'd like to talk more but I'm really pressed for time. I've got to see Jackie."

"Sure, see ya later." The girl strutted back into her room.

Frederick turned and knocked on the door beside him.

"Come in." A voice came from inside the room.

As he entered the room, the voice attached him verbally.

"It's about time you son of a bitch show up! I thought we were partners! Here I am doing all the damn work and paying all the damn bills for the last two months while you're--who knows where! What you come back now for? Want your pay for the last two months? Well, you're not getting it! You didn't work for it!"

"I came back to sell you the place."

"Sell it! What makes you think I want to buy?"

"If you don't buy it, I'll sell it to someone else."

"Before you left you were talking about buying another bar? What changed your mind?" Jackie was puzzled.

"My old man offered me a job."

"Oh, come on, Freddy, who you trying to fool? Your old man has been offering you that job ever since I've known you and you never were interested before. In fact, you told me a thousand times that he could shove that job up his pompous ass." Jackie was angry! She hated it when someone thought she was stupid enough to be lied to and tried to con her.

"That was before I was married."

"Married! You're kidding! You married!" Jackie chuckled.

"Yup, I'm on my honeymoon."

"Well, that's the funniest thing I've ever heard. I suppose I should be jealous. But knowing you, I know a little band on a finger won't keep you from going to bed with whomever you want. Right?"

"Right." Frederick chuckled.

"It's been two months. Why don't you show me what I've been

missing." Jackie eyed his erotic--masculine--physique up and down.

"First things first. You want to buy the place?"

"I've got to think about that for a while." Slowly she began to rub her hands up and down on his lapel. "Why don't you entertain me while I think about it?"

"I'm not in the mood right now. Why don't you say 'yes,' that will get me in the mood."

"How much you asking?"

"My share of what I paid three years ago."

"That's all! The place is worth more than that now. What are you up to?"

"Nothing. The yearly profits from this place have repaid me six times. I want to get rid of the place before my old man finds out. He wouldn't like it one bit if he ever found out that this was where I invested the money I asked him for. Who knows what he'd do. He's getting older and I can't risk getting him upset. His estate is too valuable to lose."

"Well, he hasn't found out yet and he might never find out."

"I'm not alone now. I've got a wife who might start asking questions and she is close to my old man. If she ever found out, she might let it slip out about this place. No, this place has served me well. I made enough money. I'm quitting while I'm ahead. I'll never make as much on this place as what I stand to inherit. I don't have long to wait. He's old. Why lose it at this late stage of the game?"

"Well, I can understand that, but somehow I can't see you settling down in a town like Beechwood. There's just not enough women there for you."

"Oh, come on, Jackie. I think of other things besides that."

"How often?" Jackie chuckled.

"I'm thinking about something else right now--what you should be thinking about."

"If I don't buy it, then what?"

"I'll just find someone else to buy my share."

"Oh, shit! That doesn't sound so good. Especially if you sell it to some asshole. Ah, I've got the money. I might just as well buy it. Then I don't have to contend with some asshole I might not get along with."

"You'll make all the arrangements then and write me when everything is ready to be signed?"

"Everything can be ready by tomorrow. Why make an extra trip? Stay tonight."

"I was going back tonight."

"Back to where?"

"Niagara Falls."

"Oh, my, how romantic. Is that where the blushing bride is?"

"I told her that I'd be back by tonight."

"Is she better than me?"

"No, no one could be better than you, Jackie."

"Then why not spend the night here with me--for old times sake. Let's call it--my wedding present to you." Embracing him, she rubbed her large breasts against him.

He felt a surge of excitement rush through his every nerve. She had always excited him. But because he was married and wasn't supposed to have or want anyone else, she excited him more. It was more fun doing what one wasn't supposed to do. Passion seized him and the hardness between his groin could no longer hold it's excitability. Jackie knew how to make the blood run hot in his veins--how to erupt the intense--emotional excitement within him. What he had with Amanda could never compare with this. It was more than his bodily appetite for sex. It was the idea that he wasn't supposed to be doing it with Jackie that caused such excitement this time. It was fun to get away with something like that.

****

After feeding little Alex and getting him settled in his bed for his midmorning nap, Anna went to find Eva. As Anna came around the dark-green high hedge, her feet stopped fast in their tracks. Jutting out of the pond were two wheelchair wheels. A sudden, unreasoning fear spread quickly through her.

"Eva--Eva!" Anna screamed as she ran up close to the pond.

Through the clear pond she could see Eva's body lying on the floor of the pond. Without thinking, she screamed and then plunged into the shallow pond. As she bent over into the water to reach Eva's arms, Anna's nostrils filled with water. Feeling herself suffocate, she raised her head out of the water in a desperate attempt to breathe.

She felt Eleanor pull her from the water as she saw Hose retrieve Eva's body from the pond.

As Anna regained some of her strength, she tried to move toward Hose and help him with Eva, but Eleanor held her fast.

"Let me go! I have to help her!" Anna was hysterical.

"There's nothing you can do, my dear Anna."

"Yes, there is." Anna tried to free herself from Eleanor's grip.

"Please, Anna, let's go back into the house. There's nothing we can do out here." Eleanor pulled the reluctant Anna toward the house.

The sight of Eva lying lifeless on the grass became blurred in Anna's eyes that were now heavy with tears.

No matter how many times a person sees death, each time is like the first. Unbelievable is the reality that someone a person loves is gone--gone forever! That sorrow drains one's body--one's very soul of all its strength. The body becomes limp and suddenly nothing in this world matters very much. There suddenly is no sense to strive for things--for all things come to an end--so why bother. Let today come and go as it will. Tomorrow comes when it comes--if it does--if it doesn't--what is lost? Who will remember what we did or didn't do in fifty years--who will even know who we were. Perhaps we are all like little grains of sands on the beach. Each like the other--we are all born--we all die. We all are special to someone--someone loves us--someone's heart will ache with pain when we are gone. The pain is always deep and unbearable because the lose is permanent. The breath of life is gone and nothing--nothing can bring it back. None of us realize how precious a breath is until it's not there. How helpless we suddenly are. We can't help the one we love--we can't put the breath back once it is gone--and so life is gone.

"Will you be all right now?" Eleanor helped Anna into a chair.

"I'll be okay." Anna would be as "okay" as she'd ever be. Eva was a good friend to her--like a sister she never had. How close they had become in only a year.

Eleanor went up the stairs and opened the cedar chest which set in the hallway. Out of it she took a neatly folded white blanket. With the blanket in her hand, she went out the door toward Hose.

"I think you better get Monsieur Stoner." Eleanor began to cover Eva's body with the blanket.

Hose helped her cover the body. "My, God, what do I tell him!"

"The truth--what else! Eva lost control of her wheelchair, fell into the pond, and drown."

"She came out here a million times. I can't understand how that could have happened."

"It only takes one time."

"Si, you're right about that, but you'd think that she could have stopped the wheels."

"Well, obviously she couldn't. Otherwise, this would have never happened."

"I suppose I have to go and tell Senor Stoner--the sooner the better. He has to be told. This is not going to be easy."

"She was a good person." Eleanor began to cry.

Hose comforted her in his arms. "That she was. At least where she has gone to now, she can walk and dance again. She loved to dance. We should be happy for her. Her death has made her whole--no more hassles of this life--just the rewards of a life in heaven."

"Do you really believe in heaven?" Eleanor wiped the tears off her cheeks.

"A person has to. It's the belief in heaven that makes this life bearable. I don't think I could stand this life if I didn't believe there was something better somewhere else."

"But what if there isn't?"

"There is."

"How can you be so sure, Hose?"

"Well, my believing isn't hurting anything or anybody. If I'm wrong in my belief, I really don't lose anything. I mean--my belief doesn't do any harm--but it might do me some good. If a person believes in God, he will reward us someday. If there turns out to be no God, I haven't lost anything. If there is a God and I didn't believe--I've lost all of eternity. That's a long time compared to these few years here on earth."

"I hope you are right about Eva being whole and happy now."

"I am. In fact, I bet she danced all the way through those pearly gates. If you're going to be okay now, I should really get Senor Stoner."

"I'll be okay. You get Monsieur Stoner."

"Just think about how happy Senora Eva is--and you won't be so sad. You know she hated that wheelchair and the life she could never have anymore because of it."

"I know you are right. She was never really happy anymore after she was confined to that chair?"

"Sure, you're sad because you won't see her again, and she won't be here for you. But think about her, she had nothing of what she really wanted anymore. I think God knew that and didn't want her to suffer inside anymore. So he decided it was time for her to come home by him."

For a moment, Eleanor was puzzled. Then she realized, for the first time, the marvelous way Hose had of looking at life--and death. His words of heaven were comforting and reassuring. Anna could use such words of comfort, Eleanor thought.

The chair she had seated Anna in was empty. Up the stairs her eyes shot to Anna's open bedroom door. Although she didn't completely believe everything Hose had said, the words were comforting and Anna needed comfort.

In the threshold of the bedroom door, Eleanor's footsteps ceased. Anna was sitting in a chair reading a tattered, old black book. The words, THE HOLY BIBLE, were etched in gold on the black cover.

Anna had found her comfort. She didn't need Eleanor's words. She had God's.

****

As Hose entered the bank, he saw Mr. Stoner sitting behind his desk busily working. Hose hesitated for a few seconds as he contemplated what he was going to say to Mr. Stoner.

Mr. Stoner looked up. "Hose, what are you doing here?"

Mr. Stoner had seen him before he had completely prepared himself as to what he was going to say. Blankly, he stared at Mr. Stoner.

"Hose, what is the matter?" asked Mr. Stoner.

Nervously, Hose walked over to Mr. Stoner. "It's Senora Stoner."

"Eva?"

"Si, I'm afraid she had an accident."

"An accident!" Mr. Stoner was becoming quite excited.

"Her wheelchair fell into the pond."

"Oh, my God! Is she okay?"

Hose was silent.

"She is okay?" Mr. Stoner asked again.

"I'm afraid she is--dead."

"Dead!"

The heart inside of him began to pound rapidly. Suddenly, just under his breastbone, he became seized with a terrible sharp--pressing--squeezing--pain. Quickly, it shot up to his neck and then down his left arm. His body felt weak--numb. Suddenly, his vision blurred into blindness. The tightness in the center of his chest became worst. The constant squeezing sensation made it hard for him to breathe. Each breath was a painful struggle. Clutching his chest, his body began to collapse over his desk and then tumble to the floor.

****

Sitting in a chair surrounded by solitude, Amanda watched the darkness of the night crawl more and more into the room. Finally, the darkness overwhelmed her.

Where was Frederick?

As the clock ticked--ticked--ticked--one hour after another away, Amanda became concerned. Had he been in an accident? Was he lying hurt somewhere? Oh, God, please let him be all right, she prayed.

Over to the window she walked. For hours she gazed out into the deserted street.

Finally, realizing that staying awake during her usual hours of sleep was not going to bring Frederick back any sooner, she decided to retire to the bed.

Worrying about Frederick halted the arrival of sleep for a while. However, eventually, with a prayer on her lips, she dozed off.

Chapter 12
****
The Abortion

In front of the window sat the paper-cluttered mahogany desk. Resting her elbows on the desk was Pamela. Once again she waited for the mailman to deliver the mail. It was important that she got the mail before Otto did. She didn't want him to see the letter--if it came. It had been two months since she sent her letter away. She was becoming impatient waiting for a reply. Surely, he could help her. He had to! She was not going to see this situation to its final end. The mistake had to be eliminated! She was desperate and had contemplated doing it herself but that very thought made her stomach turn and her body shake with fright. Doing something like that was always dangerous, but to do it yourself more often was fatal. Nevertheless, she'd rather be dead than to have the mistake go on any farther.

Slowly, the clock ticked away the seconds--the minutes.

Today was Tuesday. The day Otto hauled his customers' cows to the stockyards.

In another fifteen minutes he'd be coming home from the creamery with the empty milk truck. Before he came in for dinner, he always checked the mailbox for mail. She had to get to the mailbox first. No one was ever going to know about it. No one--never! If that man answered her letter, she'd do everything on her own. Just she and that man would be the only one's who would know.

Nervously, she tapped her fingers on the desk. Where is that mailman? Come on hurry up! For two months now she had been waiting nervously for the mail. How much longer she could take this anxiousness, she didn't know.

Oh, God, let him bring that letter today and have that part of it all over with. Huh! How ridiculous to ask God's help for something like that, she thought. What would God do to her for doing something like that? Condemn her soul? No one has ever seen God. Maybe he doesn't exist. Maybe he was just something that rich people made up to keep the poor people righteous so they could cheat and steal from them. She had asked God for help before, but he never answered her. She had asked him to make this situation of hers not true--but he hadn't. Maybe this is all there was? If it was, she was going to live it the way she wanted. This mistake didn't fit in HER plan. Two mistakes were enough!

Pamela jumped from her chair. There he was! With anticipation, she peered through the sheer window panels. He was putting something into the mailbox. It looked like a big white letter, but she wasn't sure. She hoped with her heart that it was what she wanted.

As the mailman drove away from the mailbox, she ran out the door toward it. Opening the mailbox door revealed several letters. Quickly, she fingered them through her hand. Her eyes immediately fell upon the letter postmarked Chicago. The address in the upper left-hand corner told her it was from the man she had written.

A honking sound startled her. Turning around, she saw it was Otto entering the driveway. Stopping the truck, he got out.

Folding the letter, she put it into her bib apron pocket.

"Hi, Pam," Otto called with a smile as he approached her. "Anything of interest today?"

She swallowed the lump in her throat. "I don't know. The letters are for you."

Otto reached for the letters and examined them. "Nothing important."

"How was your day so far?" He put his arm around her waist as they walked up the wooden front porch steps and into the house.

"Okay."

Once in the house, Otto's eyes roamed about the kitchen. "Where is Margie?"

"She fell asleep on the sofa in the parlor."

"How is Mikie today?"

"His fever broke after you left. I think he's getting another tooth."

"It's probably a good thing that they are only a year apart. That way, they have someone to play with. They aren't always alone. I hated being alone."

"Huh, you can talk smart! You don't have to chase after them and clean up after them all day long. As for playing together, huh, all they do is fight. They drive me crazy!" Pamela grumbled as she took the hot casserole out of the cast-iron oven and placed it on the crocheted potholder that centered the neatly set table.

Pamela didn't eat much--just picked at her food with a fork as she watched the clock. Time went so slowly. Finally, it was time for Otto to leave and Pamela couldn't wait until she saw Otto and the cattle truck leave the yard.

Apprehensively, she ripped the letter open and read its contents--

Dear Mrs. Aslen:

This letter is in regard to your recent letter to me. Pertaining to the information you are requesting, I am afraid certain situations make it very essential that I be very discreet in my reply.
Perhaps more information could be obtained at the following address:

    1314 North Rush Street
    Chicago, Illinois

I hope this will be of help to you as I am unable to supply you with any more information.

Oh Gods! Just an address! She couldn't afford the time to send another letter and wait two more months. What was she going to do now?

She sat on the cane chair and stared over the desk out the window. Stared and thought--stared and thought--

She'd go to the address and wouldn't leave Chicago until her situation had been put to an end. Chicago was so far, but that was good. Her chance of meeting anyone that she knew was not very great. The majority of the people from around the area often went to

Milwaukee. No one ever went to Chicago. At least, she had never heard anyone talk of going there.

How would she explain her trip to Chicago to Otto? When would she go? It had to be soon. Real soon! Otto would be home from the stockyards late tonight. She'd have until then to think of something.

Grabbing a pencil out of the middle desk drawer, she tore a page out of the address pad on the desk and jotted the address from the letter onto the piece of torn-out page. Rising from the chair, she walked over to her cast-iron stove, lifted one of the lids, threw the letter inside, and lit a flaming match to it.

She watched the flame devour the letter. Within a matter of seconds, only a small black substance remained. No letter--nothing for Otto to find and ask questions about.

"Mama, pottie--pottie." Margie tugged at Pamela's dress.

Pamela quickly took her over to the little trainer pot in the corner.

As Pamela began to pull down Margie's trousers, she became aware of a sharp smell. Pamela guessed what the smell was and within a few minutes, her suspicions were verified. Margie had excrement all over her legs, socks, and the inside of her trousers.

"For Gods sake, when are you going to go on the pot!" Pamela began the distasteful chore of cleaning her.

"Twenty-four months old and still you go all over the place except in the pot. All I do is change shit diapers and wash them." Pamela's harsh grumbling made Margie cry.

"Oh, shut up! You'll wake the other little creep."

Stern words like that only made Margie cry more loudly. Soon another wailing sound filled the house.

"God, damn it! You woke him up now!"

Margie cried and sniffled as Pamela washed her up, put clean trousers and socks on her.

Going over to the icebox, Pamela opened the door and pulled out two bottles.

"Here drink this and shut up!" She gave one bottle to Margie who went into the parlor, rested her body on the sofa, and drank from the bottle.

Meanwhile, in the bedroom, Mikie was bellowing out his lungs.

Pamela took the cold bottle and stuck it into his mouth.

"Hold still!" Pamela yelled as she tried to change his soiled diaper. Amidst the wailing came a sudden--sharp scream.

"I told you to hold still. Now the pin poked you, didn't it? Well, that's your tough luck."

After throwing a few blankets onto his kicking feet and crying body, she went out of the bedroom and closed the door tightly behind her.

The closed door muffled his cry and that was just fine with Pamela. She didn't have time to fuss with him. It was his own fault that the pin had poked him. He should have held still. Now she had to do the dishes and get things ready for tomorrow--washday--again. Every other day she had to wash or else she'd run out of diapers. Let him cry. She had no time!

****

"Pete, wake up it's about time to pick the girls up from school." Amy gently shook Pete as he lay sleeping, so soundly, on the kitchen sofa.

"Ya--okay." He opened his eyes for a second and then closed them again.

"Pete, you have to get the girls from school." Amy shook him again.

"Ya--ya--I'm getting up." He still rested on the sofa with his eyes closed.

"Pete, please, the girls will be waiting."

"Okay." He sat up on the sofa and stretched his arms in the air.

"I love you, Amy Hof." He pulled her near and kissed her gently on her lips.

"This isn't the time. You have to pick up the girls. Come, I've got some coffee on the table."

Pete looked at the table. The steam from the cups towered up to the ceiling. "It's too hot yet." He embraced her and kissed her again.

"Come on now! Those poor girls will get sick waiting outside in this cold weather for you."

"Okay." He sighed and got off the sofa. While his coffee cooled, he put on his hat and coat.

"Whoo--it's hot yet!" His eyes watered as he quickly swallowed the sip and put the cup back on the table. "You want to come along?"

"No, not today, tomorrow I'll go along. I figure we'll leave early--right after dinner. We'll stop at the bank and cash the milk check and then go shopping." Amy handed him an opened envelope.

"It's early. I thought it would first come on Friday." Pete examined the contents of the envelope. "You want to put some of it in the bankbook again?"

"We might as well. We don't need all that to live, and I don't like having money at home."

"You going to buy another farm when we have enough money saved?" asked Pete.

"We might as well. Land is a good investment. I was thinking about the McCullogh farm, down the road."

"Ya, that's all good and fine, Amy, but we aren't getting any younger. These two farms are almost all we can handle."

"We can rent the farm. Young people are always looking to rent. They usually borrow money to buy the cows and machinery and then rent until they have that paid for. When they have that paid, then they usually borrow to buy a farm."

"I don't know if I like renting out our property," Pete commented.

"Other people do."

"Ya, sometimes renters don't take care of things because it's not theirs."

"We can always hire someone to help us if you don't like the renting idea."

"It sounds as if you have been giving this a lot of thought."

"While you were sleeping, I was thinking about it. In fact, yesterday when I was at the feed mill, I talked to McCullogh about it."

"You didn't tell me you saw McCullogh."

"I was going to tell you at milking but then with the excitement of the cows getting out, I completely forgot about it."

"What did McCullogh say?" asked Pete.

"He told me his arthritis is really getting bad and that his son-in-law doesn't want the farm. So he is seriously thinking about selling, retiring on the money, and living in town."

"How much does he want for it?" Pete inquired.

"If everything goes well, within a few months we should be able to meet his price and maybe have enough to do some needed repairs."

"Prices are so high now," Pete commented.

"They might go higher. I'm not going to wait hoping they'll go down. Prices may never go down. These might be the cheapest prices we'll ever see."

"I think you should wait. Prices will come down."

"No, I think we invest that money into something solid. I don't like the bank playing with our money. It's our money and if anyone is going to play with it--it's going to be us."

"We should buy stocks," Pete suggested.

"No, I don't like that. You just got paper in your hand."

"You have to admit. I've done pretty well on my Electric Company stocks. Look at all the new farm machinery I've been able to buy with just the dividends that I receive each year."

"Yes, that was a good idea you had back then, but with the ever growing demand for more electricity, the shares of stocks aren't so cheap anymore. You bought the stock when it was cheap and the success of electricity was a gamble. Now the cost of stock doesn't equal out to the dividends. You have received the cost of your initial investment over and over again. The market is so crazy now. It's too unstable. If it would fall, it wouldn't really matter to you. Your stocks have paid for themselves a hundred times over. You can touch land. You can see it. It doesn't burn away or blew completely away like paper."

"Ya, that's true. Gosh! I better pick up the girls." Gulping down the rest of his coffee, he dashed out the door and into the car.

At school, the girls were sitting outside on the wooden school steps. When the girls saw the nineteen twenty-two Lincoln drive into the yard, they leaped to their feet.

Lucy's auburn locks bounced about her round shoulders as she dashed toward the car and opened the door. "Hi, Dad." Quickly, she scooted beside her father to make room for Lori, a wisp of a girl.

"Hi, honey." Pete gave her a hug and kissed her forehead.

"Hi, Daddy." Lori's smile spread from cheek to cheek.

"Hi, sweetie." Pete reached behind Lucy and lovely stroked Lori's short, mousy brown hair for a second.

"Well, how was school today?" Pete turned the steering wheel and drove the car out of the tree-studded schoolyard onto the main road.

"It was swell! Mrs. Parks let me ring the bell at all three recesses! Boy was that fun!" Lori's eyes gleamed of excitement.

Pete chuckled.

"We had a spelling test today. Guess what I got?" said Lucy.

"From how excited you are, I'd say you got a hundred."

"Nope, guess again."

"Ninety-nine."

"Yes, I only got one wrong. I really studied hard for the test."

"You must have--to get only one wrong."

"Don't you think I should get a reward for that, Daddy?"

"Well, I suppose that would be nice. What would you like? A treat at the drugstore--a root beer float?"

"Just me and you?"

"Lori can come along."

"Why? I'm the one who got only one wrong," Lucy protested.

"Well, she wants something too. Right, Lori?"

Lori smiled timidly and nodded her head.

"Well, should we stop now?"

"No, I changed my mind. I don't really like ice cream that much. Why don't you just give me some money then I can buy what I want?"

"Okay." Pete leaned to one side and reached into his bib overall pocket. "Here you go. Here's a nickel."

"Only a nickel," Lucy grumbled.

"Only a nickel! You can buy a lot with a nickel. If it's not enough, give it back, then you'll have nothing."

"No, that's okay." It wasn't really but why should she make a fuss. She'd get more. Just like she had done a few times before. She got away with it then. She'd get away with doing it again. She always got what she wanted and what she thought was rightfully hers.

"No schoolwork tonight?" Pete glanced down at their laps where their school lunchboxes rested all by their lonesome.

"Nope, guess the teachers were in a really good mood today," replied Lucy. "I hope Ma has supper ready when we get home. We played pom-pom-pole-away at recess and all that running really made me hungry."

"Well, you'll find out in a second." Pete turned the car into the driveway.

As soon as the car stopped, the girls scrambled toward the house where Amy was waiting with a big warm smile.

"Hi, Ma! Is supper ready?" asked Lucy.

"Heaven's no! It's too early! There are some cookies in the jar if you're that hungry--but only take a few. We'll eat supper in about an hour after your dad is finished with first chores."

Lucy threw her lunchbox onto the table and hurried to the cookie jar. With her wide hand she pulled out three cookies. From the icebox she took a pitcher of milk and filled a cup with the white substance. She began dipping the cookies into the milk and stuffing the soft part of the cookie into her mouth.

"Hi, Ma."

"Hi, Lori, you want a cookie too?"

"No thanks, I can wait until supper. I'm tired. Can I lay down for a while?"

"Sure, if you fall asleep, I'll wake you for supper. Put three cookies aside for yourself. I don't want to hear any grumbling after while that one got more cookies than the other one did. Lucy you watch the potatoes. I'm going out to help your dad feed silage."

"Okay, Ma."

Lori piled three cookies beside the jar and then left the room.

With Lori in her bedroom and her parents walking toward the barn, Lucy decided to indulge in a few extra cookies. Who would know? It wasn't her fault that her mother made the best gingersnaps in the world. Besides she was older, and she deserved more than Lori. Also she was watching the potatoes--that merited a payment--what better payment then a few extra cookies.

After supper Lucy washed the supper dishes and Lori dried them while Amy helped Pete milk the cows. When they had the kitchen tidied up, they both got ready for bed. With their flannel nightgowns keeping them warm, they sat at the table, each silently reading a book. They both became lost in the world that came vividly alive on each page of the book.

CLICK!

The noise shattered the silence as a flash of light startled the girls.

"Sorry about that, but you know you shouldn't read in such dim light. We do have electricity now," said a soft voice.

"We aren't used to it yet, Ma. It seems so strange to flick a little switch and have a room light up," said Lucy.

"Yes, it does seem strange but I think we can force ourselves to get used to it," replied Amy.

They all chuckled.

Out in the den, Pete took off his soiled and manure scented overalls. He let them fall beside the floor register so they would be warm and dry for the next day when he would wear them again.

Into the kitchen he came wearing his cream-colored long johns, plaid flannel shirt, and gray woolen socks. The smell of barn was still prevalent but not as sharp. He stuck a few pieces of wood into the stove to fed the dwindling fire.

"Who wants popcorn?" Pete rolled a crude bar of white soap in his hands beneath the running water.

"I do," replied Lucy.

"What about you, Lori?" He dried his hands on an old rag.

"I don't care," replied Lori with a smile.

"Okay, it's popcorn we'll have then." Grabbing a kettle, which hung above the stove, he went out into the entryway. After removing the board from the top of a large stoneware crock, he took his hand and scooped out a soft, greasy white substance--lard. He threw the lard into the kettle and then set the kettle on the hot stove. While the lard melted, he wiped his greasy hands once again on the rag. Reaching into the cupboard, he pulled out a covered metal container. From the container he took rice popcorn and put it into the kettle.

When a few kernels began to explode with a popping sound, he put the cover on the kettle. For a few minutes, the room was flooded with exploding sounds, then silence. It was time to enjoy the fluffy white mass, seasoned with salt and a little bit of fresh churned butter.

With the bowl of popcorn empty, it was time to wash the greasy hands and retire to bed.

The lights went out and stillness filled the house.

Lori fell asleep, but not Lucy. She lay wide awake in her bed watching the minute hand move slowly pass one number and then another. She knew her parents sometimes talked for a while before they went to sleep. So, patiently, she waited until she thought they'd be asleep.

When she thought enough time had elapsed, she crawled out of her bed. From under her mattress she removed an item, which she clutched in her hand as she proceeded out of her room.

With the help of the moonlight, which peered through the hallway window, she quietly stole down the stairs.

Ever so carefully, she turned the doorknob on the door at the bottom of the stairs. Then slowly, she pushed the door open and tiptoed into the den. The moonbeams lit up the room like a lightbulb.

Over to the floor register she crept. With her ears alert and keeping a constant eye on the doorway, slowly she picked up her father's overalls. Then, oh so cautiously, she examined each pocket. Naturally, it was in the last pocket where she found what she had wanted.

One by one, she took each coin out of the pocket and diligently deposited it into her little coin purse. Rationalizing, she told herself that she had done well on her test and had done the dishes; therefore, she deserved that money.

However, realizing others might not think that way, she turned the pocket inside out and tore a little hole in it. Her father was always losing things through holes in his bib overalls' pocket--why not his coins. He hadn't caught on the other times she had done it. He wouldn't catch on now either.

Softly, she laid the overalls back on the floor. To her astonishment, as she turned the corner, she bumped into something. Her mother! Her body was numb with shock. A lump stuck in her throat. How could she explain being out of bed and roaming about the house? Worst yet, what if her mother had seen what she had done! How could she explain that? Her mother despised liars and thieves. It was her mother's opinion that they were the "scum of the earth."

As her mother flicked on the light, Lucy squinted her eyes. The light had hurt them for a second.

"Did you go to the outhouse like that?" her mother asked.

"Ah--ya--I had to go really bad." What a relief--her mother had supplied her with her answer.

"Gosh, girl, you should know better than to go out in this damp weather dressed like that. You'll catch a 'death of a cold' with just your nightgown on."

"I'm sorry, Ma. Did I wake you?"

"No, I was just lying in bed when suddenly I realized that your dad hadn't filled the stoker bin before he went to bed. I held my hand over the floor register and there was no heat coming out. So I figured, I better fill the stoker bin or else the house is going to be awful cold by morning. I thought I'd just slip your dad's bib overalls on so I don't get my nightgown full of coal dirt."

"They're beside the register." Lucy pointed to them.

"Ya, I know. He's been putting them there ever since we put the furnace in last month."

"He likes them warm in the morning." Lucy chuckled.

"Ya, I don't blame him. Well, you better get to bed. You got school tomorrow."

"Good night, Ma."

"Good night, honey." Amy hugged her and then gave her a good night kiss.

****

KNOCK! KNOCK!

Amanda looked over the sink full of dishes and out the window. Through the window she could clearly see the back porch. A boy was standing on the porch. "Steven is here, Alex."

Alex jumped from his chair.

"Not so fast, you finish your glass of milk first."

"Ah, Ma!"

"Ah, Ma--nothing! Twelve-year-old boys need their milk. Steven will wait."

Alex opened his mouth and let the full glass of milk slide down. "All gone--bye, Ma." Hurriedly, he kissed her.

"You'll get a stomachache drinking so fast." Her words fell on deaf ears. He was out the door and down the street before she finished the sentence.

Through the window she could see them scamping down the street, laughing and talking about boyish things. "Hum, those boys." Amanda chuckled, smiled to herself, and then went about tidying up the kitchen.

"You got some more nails?" asked Steven.

"Ya, I found some more." Alex pulled a handful out of the pocket in his trousers.

"Good! Man, that's really fun! Those heads really get flattened out."

"Ya, they do. Boy, if Frederick ever found out what I did with his nails, I think he'd kill me." Alex put them back into his pocket.

"If you don't tell him and I don't tell him, he'll never find out."

"Ya, you're right." They both laughed at that.

DING! DONG! DING!

The big bell on top of the white limestone building tolled the news loud and clear. It was time to get into school and into their desk.

Up the steps they ran. Mrs. Roth, their teacher, closed the big oak doors behind them.

Inside the classroom, Alex sat in one part of the room and Steven in another. It wasn't always that way. Mrs. Roth had started the school year with the taller children sitting in the back of the room and the smaller children sitting in the front of the room, so they could see the blackboard. Being the taller children in the class, Alex and Steven had originally sat in the back of the classroom. However, because they talked to each other instead of listening to her teach, she had separated them and moved them both to the front of the class on opposite sides of the room. Needless to say, that didn't stop those two from communicating. Whenever Mrs. Roth would turn her back to the class to write on the blackboard, Steven and Alex would pass notes to each other--

What about recess? Are we going down to the track?

Alex folded the note. When Mrs. Roth wasn't looking, he passed it to the person sitting in the seat to the left of him. That person also watched and waited until Mrs. Roth wasn't watching and then passed the note on. So it was with each classmate until Steven had the note.

Alex would look over at Steven and watch for the reply--

No, 10:00 recess is to short. We can't do that much in

fifteen minutes. Let's wait until lunch at 11:30 then we'll have an hour.

Steven folded the letter and passed it to the classmate on his right. The classmate followed the same procedure as before and as every day ever since Alex and Steven had been separated. The classmates considered it fun doing something behind Mrs. Roth's back.

Alex looked at the clock--only nine o'clock! Language class was next. He disliked language--nouns, pronouns, verbs, subjects, adverbs--who needed that. Time dragged and dragged and dragged on. Finally, the bell rang! It was ten o'clock. Recess! Hooray!

Out the classroom he ran and down the cement steps he flew. At the bottom of the steps, Alex waited for Steven. Together they walked under a tall oak where they sat and ate part of their lunch.

"Let's eat all of our lunch now, so at eleven-thirty we can run right down to the track," suggested Steven.

"Ya, that's a great idea," replied Alex.

They both gobbled up their lunch. When the bell rang, the two boys put their arms on each other's shoulder and walked back into the classroom. They talked up to the last second until they were told to be quiet by Mrs. Roth.

Reading class was next. They had to keep their eyes on the page. If Mrs. Roth called their name, they had to continue reading from the exact word the previous person had stopped at. Alex would very quickly look at the clock--ten-thirty--ten-forty--ten-fifty--eleven--eleven-ten--eleven-twenty--eleven-thirty. The bell didn't ring! They sat anxiously waiting--waiting. Finally, it rang.

Like lightning they went out the door, down the steps, and down the hill to the railroad track. Once at the track, they stopped and both tried to catch their breath.

"You got them?" asked Steven.

"Sure do." Alex reached into his pocket and pulled out a handful of nails.

"Come on, let's put them on the rails!" Steven held out his opened palm.

Alex gave his handful to Steven then reached into his other pocket and pulled out another handful of nails for himself.

One by one, they laid the nails on the metal rails of the track, so when the train would come, it would flatten the nails. Alex laid some on one rail and Steven laid some on the other rail. Whoever had the most flattened nails would be the winner. The loser would owe the winner twenty-five cents.

"How many do you have, Steven?"

"I have twenty."

"Okay, that's all I'll use too. Otherwise, it wouldn't be fair."

"Ya, that sounds good, Alex."

The nails were laid; they sat and waited. In the distance they could hear the train start at the depot.

CHUG---------CHUG--------CHUG------CHUG-----CHUG------CHUG----CHUG---CHUG---CHUG---CHUG---CHUG--CHUG--

The train was picking up speed. In a few minutes it would be there.

The vibrations of the track had knocked off some of Steven's nails. Steven got up and went over to the track to pick them up and put them back on the rail. If all his nails weren't on the rail to get flattened, he could lose. Twenty-five cents was a lot of money. He'd have to find some extra lawn cutting jobs if he lost again.

"Steven, get off that track! Now!" yelled Mrs. Roth who was standing at the top of the hill with her hands on her hips.

Seeing the stern look on her face, the two boys swallowed the lump in their throat. Boy! Were they in trouble!

Alex waited for Steven to come across the track and then both walked up the hill toward Mrs. Roth as the train behind their back rattled by on the railroad track.

They both turned and looked at where the nails had been. It was always fun having the train flatten the nails, but not today. Mrs. Roth had ruined their fun.

"School will be out soon, then we can come down here whenever we want."

"Ya, she'll be gone all summer."

"Boys! Boys!" Mrs. Roth shook her head in disapproval. "You stay on school property when you're in school. You can't go wherever you want. Soon others will go wherever they want and then no one will know where anyone is."

"Yes, Mrs. Roth," they replied sullenly.

Back to the limestone schoolhouse they all three walked. The playground was empty. Recess was over and the other children were in the school. As they entered the school hall, they saw the time was twelve-fifty. That explained why Mrs. Roth had come to look for them.

Their classmates looked at them as they entered the classroom and sat at their desks. The rest of the day went so slow. They were anxious to go down by the track again, but first Alex had to go home and get more nails.

DING! DONG! DING! It was three o'clock. Alex waited beside his desk for Steven. They walked together to Alex's house. Behind the house was a small wooden garage painted white. They went inside and stopped at a huge, clumsy workbench cluttered with wrenches and oil drenched work rags. Alex pulled a large rusty coffee can off the workbench.

"Grab a handful, Steven."

"Ah, Alex, why don't we take the whole can."

"Ya, Steven, that's a good idea."

"Hi, Alex." A soft voice came from behind them.

Alex and Steven turned around. In the garage door opening was a fragile little girl dressed in frilly lace and bows. Her blonde hair was tied with ribbons. Her smile revealed the lost of two front teeth.

"Oh, hi, Rosalia," Alex responded with a smile.

"Hi," said Steven. "Do you think she'll tell Frederick?"

"No, not if I tell her not to."

"What you doing, Alex?" asked Rosalia.

"Oh, nothing."

"Come on, Alex, let's go," said Steven.

"Can I come too, Alex?" asked Rosalia.

"No, you better stay here. You'll get your dress all dirty."

"Ma said I can take my dress off after the pictures are taken."

"The pictures?" replied Alex.

"Of you and me and my birthday cake."

"Oh, that's right. Today is your birthday. Happy birthday, Rosalia." Alex went up and kissed her on the head.

"Come in so Ma can take some pictures. Then we can have some cake, I can change my dress and we can go," suggested Rosalia.

"Come on, Steven, my ma makes the best birthday cakes." Alex put down the coffee can full of nails and motioned Steven toward him.

"Ya, that sounds good," Steven responded.

"You really look pretty, Rosalia." Alex put his arm on his little sister's small shoulders.

"Thank you, Alex, you're the best brother anyone could have."

Opening the kitchen door flung the sweet hickory-smoked aroma of cooked ham into their nostrils. The aroma teased their hunger.

"Hi, Ma." Alex smiled.

With a smile, she returned his greeting. "Hi, Alex, you're home from school, good. Hi, Steven."

"Hi, Mrs. Stoner."

Seeing his mother was just about finished decorating Rosalia's birthday cake with chopped nuts and maraschino cherries, Alex asked, "Can we have a piece of cake, Ma?"

"Oh, Alex, you know the rules. We wait until Frederick, Grandpa, and Grandma come and we're done with supper. Besides, you know the 'birthday person' always gets the first piece."

"But Ma, Steven won't be here then. He has to go home soon for supper."

"Why doesn't Steven go home and ask his parents if he can have supper here then he can have a piece of cake also," suggested Amanda?

"Ya, that's a great idea! Come on, Steven, let's go and ask your parents."

Alex and Steven went out the door with Rosalia following them. As they passed the garage, they heard the train whistle.

"The train's back," said Steven. "Let's get the nails!"

"Right now? I thought we were going to ask your parents about you coming to my place for supper."

"Ah, there's plenty of time for that. The train will leave before your ma has supper done. Besides, Frederick has to come home from work before you eat. Doesn't he?" Steven ran into the garage.

"Ya, we always eat supper together." Alex followed him into the garage.

"Well, let's go then." Steven took the can of nails off the bench and started to walk down the driveway in the direction of the railroad track.

"Can I go along?" Rosalia had followed the two boys.

"Rosalia, you better stay here. You'll get dirty and ruin your pretty dress. Don't you tell Ma," Alex ordered.

"No, I won't. Please, can I come along."

"Well, I suppose, if you stay up on the grassy hill."

"Oh, I'll stay up there. I promise."

"Okay, then you can come along."

"Thanks, Alex." She grabbed his hand and the three of them walked down to the railroad track.

At the top of the grassy hill overlooking the railroad track, Alex set Rosalia down. "You stay here. Okay?"

"Yes, Alex." Rosalia didn't like the idea. She'd prefer to go walk on the railroad track. She could never come down here by herself and now she was so close to walking on it but she couldn't. With a pouting face, she rested her chin in the palms of her hands as she rested her elbows on her knees and watched Alex and Steven.

Oh, so carefully they laid the nails on the rails of the track. Then the train whistle blow and the sound of the train moving on the track became louder and louder.

Alex looked up. "I got forty. How many do you have?"

"Only thirty."

"Well, we better get off the track. We won't count this one. It'll be just for fun." Alex began to walk off the track. Turning, he saw Steven was counting out ten more nails to put on the rail. Alex went back on the track and grabbed Steven's arm. "Come on, Steven! The train is coming! Let them go! Let's get off the track!"

"Ah, we've got time."

The engineer, seeing the boys on the track, blew the whistle. When he saw they were still on the track, he blew it again and again. "For God's sake they better get off! I can't stop!" he said to himself as he applied the metal brakes of the train to the metal rails of the track.

The metallic scream of the shearing metal filled the air with a continuous deadening sound. With his head still protruding out the window and his eyes glued to the boys still in the path of the train, whose explosive energy couldn't be stopped, he blew the train whistle again and again and again. When he saw the whites of the boys' eyes, he knew there wasn't any time left. He dropped his head. Could he dare to look back?

He looked up at the grassy hill where he saw a little girl moving frightfully--crying--screaming. He saw a crowd approach the hill, then stop, and stare in the direction where the two boys had been. He dared to look back and his stomach began to turn and twist inside of him. The sight nauseated him. He regurgitated. He cried. He had stopped the train but it was too late.

In the silence of the moment, a sound came from the crowd.

"He pushed him!" yelled an old woman at the front of the crowd.

Then came a roar from the crowd that now began to move down the hill past the crying little girl.

****

She sat motionless in the black leather seat and stared out the train window. She watched the farm fields, now green with young oats and neatly planted corn, pass quickly in view. Sometimes it reminded her of her life--how it just kept moving and moving--passing from one day to another--to another. What she was doing now would break fate's roll in her life. She was taking control of her life. Fate took a "back seat" on this matter. It was her life--her body. She'd made this choice.

Was it right what she was doing? Could she live with it? Would she regret the decision?--No!-- It was the right thing to do. She didn't want any more. She had to pay the price for his pleasure. She had the pain. She was the one whose life was inconvenienced. She was the prisoner. He was always free to do and go wherever he pleased, but not her. To continue the same way and let it happen would make her a prisoner so much longer.

The hardest thing was thinking of a believable excuse to be gone. She had told her husband that she wanted to go to Milwaukee to do shopping in some of the big stores. She had told Mrs. Benson, who was taking care of the children, that she was getting something special for her husband. She had already done that in Milwaukee to cover her lie. Now she traveled on to her real destination.

She was a good neighbor and friend to Mrs. Benson. Mrs. Benson always appreciated the extra produce that she'd given her from her garden. Also, she had often taken care of Mrs. Benson's children when Mrs. Benson and her husband had wanted to go places. In addition, their children always played together, so it was no "big deal" if she was gone a couple of days.

In about an hour she'd be there--then what? How would she find the place? Surely, someone at the depot would know. This would be her second time in that place. The first time was God's choice. This time it was hers. She had vowed then--never again--the pain had been too bad. Yet, she had endured it twice after that. She had loved him then. Now--sometimes she hated him so much--for his total dominance of her--the physical pain that he inflicted on her when she'd disagree with him or she didn't do what he wanted. This would be her defiant act against him. A rejection of something that was his--and he couldn't hurt her because he'd never know--at least not right now. Maybe in time, when he couldn't hurt her, she'd tell him--to hurt him. Tell him how she destroyed something that was his because she hated him so much. Of course, that wouldn't be all true. She was also doing it to be free.

As the rural area disappeared and the factories, shops, and houses started to appear one right after the other, she thought of her mother. Her mother had grown up in the city and had often talked about how she had loved it and despised the fact that they had moved from the city to that small town--the place where her mother had met her father. Her father--that son of a bitch! How she hated him for what he had done to her mother. Men just used women. Well, not this woman--not anymore! She vowed.

She rubbed her hand over the diamond ring on her finger. The ring had been her mother's. How often her mother cursed the day that she had accepted it from her father. She remembered the last day that she had seen her father. He was coming down the stairs with luggage under his arms and in his hands.

Running down the stairs after him was her mother with tears in her eyes. "Why are you doing this to me--sob? Why did you marry me--sob? You have never treated me as if you loved me--sob? What have I done that made you hate me so--sob? To treat me like a piece of furniture--sob! Don't you think I have any feelings--sob? I've tried to love you--sob. Why can't your try to love me--sob? Why--sob?"

"The money is why I married you--you little, 'country-hick' girl. I should have known you'd never fit into this type of life. Why should I come home? You're so boring. Besides, you never loved me. It was the other one you wanted. It was just a game to me--to get you away from him." He laughed as he opened the door and proceeded to go out it.

Her mother took the ring off her finger and flung it at him. "I curse the day that you gave me this ring."

The ring hit his back, fell to the shiny hardwood floor, and then rolled under a small Victorian table setting near the edge of the stairs.

Her father closed the door and left for the last time. Her mother dragged herself slowly--dejectedly up the stairs and into the bedroom that had been the source of her loneliness for years.

She had picked the ring up that day. It glistened in the light and she had thought how beautiful it was. When she had tried to give it back to her mother, her mother had thrown it back onto the floor.

"I don't want anything that reminds me of him!" Then she hugged her and held her so tightly. "I love you so much, my little Pammie. You are the best thing that ever happened to me." She kissed her and held her again. "You are the best thing that ever came out of my life." Then she felt her mother's tears moisten her face.

She'd get rid of that ring now, but the memories wouldn't be that easy. The memories of that sad, lonely woman whom she loved so deeply made her cry. She concealed the tears from others by looking out the train window.

The train stopped and she departed from it. Asking the depot clerk where the street was, she walked in its direction. She had never seen streets so full of hurried people for a long time, ever since Brookline. The close shops were clean and their merchandise was arranged so neatly in their display windows. Her small bag of luggage was starting to get heavy. Then she saw a jewelry shop and entered it. Taking her mother's ring off, she asked what cash value it had. The amount was surely enough to pay for what she wanted. So she left the ring, full of tattered memories, at the shop and put the cash into her purse. While at the shop, she asked how far she'd have to go to get to the address that she was seeking. The jewelry clerk informed her that it was only two blocks to the right. Pamela felt the clerk survey her appearance and then she raised her eyebrows as if she knew. Pamela "brushed off" the clerk's prejudgement. It didn't matter. It was her life. The clerk's opinion of her was not important.

Within a few minutes, Pamela stood outside the door marked with the street address that the doctor had given her. Through the huge windows, which flanked each side of the door, she could see tables topped with gingham red and white material and chairs neatly set beside each table. Up the cement stairs she walked and entered the building. Two counters were now visible. One counter to the right had stationary metal stools equidistantly placed and topped with cushioned red leather seats. There was a huge glass icebox with assorted containers of ice cream and glass bottles of soda behind the counter. To the left was another counter. The shelves behind this counter were full of bottles of pills, cough syrups, laxatives--all sorts of medical remedies.

There was no one in the room. It was quiet. She sat on one of the stools. Beside a small, round metal item setting on the counter was a sign, RING FOR SERVICE.

DING! DING! Was the sound made when she tapped the pin that raised above the round metal object.

A door opened and out stepped a large woman. "How can I help you?"

Pamela bit her lower lip and thought. How could--how should she word what she wanted to say? She was silent.

"Is there something I can help you with?" The woman approached.

"A doctor gave me this address. I have a--a menstrual blockage. Can you help me?"

The woman stood silent for a moment. "I'll get the druggist." She departed.

Pamela became nervous and fidgeted with her purse. Was this the right place? What if she came all this way and no one could help her? She had to resolve this situation before she went home. Oh, let this be the right place.

The woman soon returned with a man. He was ugly. His nose was quite predominant on his thin face. He only had a few gray hairs left on his shiny head.

"I'm Dr. Samson." He extended his bony hand to Pamela.

Hesitantly, she returned his gesture. Was this the man who could help her?

"You have a female problem?" he asked.

"Yes, I do," replied Pamela.

"For how long?"

"About four months now."

"That would be sixteen weeks?"

"Yes."

Seeing her luggage, he asked, "You need a room for the night?"

"Yes, but that's not why I'm here."

"I know. We have rooms. Why don't you take one?" He motioned to the woman. "Put her in room three." Turning to Pamela, he said, "It will cost you fifty dollars."

"For the room?"

"For the services you obviously came here for." He paused. "Yes or no?"

At first Pamela was a little confused by the man talking in riddles. Thinking a few seconds, she replied, "Yes."

As he held out his hand, Pamela grabbed into her purse and pulled out the money that she had gotten for the ring. She counted out the amount and gave it to the man.

He grabbed it and shoved it into the pocket located inside his trousers.

"Come along then." The woman returned through the door and led Pamela down a hallway to a door marked with a three. Reaching into her skirt pocket, she pulled out a key and unlocked the door.

The open door revealed a small, dark room with no windows.

CLICK! A little bulb, hanging from the high ceiling, lit the room and revealed--a gray painted metal bed, strewed with a dark pillow and several blankets--a wooden table with leaf ends--two spindle backed wooden chairs--a washstand with a chipped enamel washbowl and a porcelain pitcher with a broken spout.

The woman grabbed behind the door. "Put this on." She handed Pamela a dark-green, ugly gown. "Take off all your clothes. You never know what can happen. No sense getting blood all over your good clothes."

Pamela's eyes grew wide open with astonishment. How messy was this going to be? She was becoming apprehensive. Should she really do it? She could still leave. No! She'd see it through!

The woman left and closed the door leaving her in the small room with its cold, depressing dark-green walls. Slowly, Pamela unbuttoned her dress, took it off, folded it, and then placed it on the back of the bed. She took her slip off and did the same, then her shoes, nylons, and panty. She left her bra on. Somehow she didn't feel comfortable with that off. The gown with its open back made her feel so vulnerable in her nakedness. Sitting on the edge of the bed, she waited and waited and waited. No window to look out or let some light in--just four drab--cold walls. The room engulfed her in its gloominess--its quiet, eerie emptiness. She was alone. Nervous with anticipation of what was going to be done. She wished he'd come and get it over with.

The door opened and the woman entered pushing a table on wheels. The table had a handle on each end of it. On top of the table to one side, sat a large glass jar with tubing connected to the jar and to a machine, which sat on the bottom part of the table. Another long tube projected from the jar. This one had an elongated tip. Inside the jar, hanging from the lid, was a bag made of a white gauze. On the other side of the table, next to the glass jar lay a white cloth with items lying on it. Instruments that would be used on her--bent spoon handles--pen holders with wire attached--hair curling tongs made to look like a pincer--and different sized long metal tubes, which from base to tip gradually narrowed making the diameter tip less than the base.

The woman set the portable table in the middle of the room. She then pushed the small table, which was setting against the wall with its two leaf ends extended, to the middle of the room under the light.

"Lay on here." Her fat hands helped Pamela onto the battered table marred with cigarette burns.

As she lay on the table, the coldness of the table climbed up her back, which was exposed through the opened back of the gown.

The woman put a chair on each side of the table. Taking one of Pamela's legs, she straddled it on top of the back of the chair. Then taking a piece of leather, she tied Pamela's leg to the chair at mid-calf and at mid-thigh. The woman then did the same with the other leg. She then dropped the leaf of the table, which had supported Pamela's legs. Pamela's legs were now strapped into a spread eagle position. The woman lifted Pamela's buttock and placed a small piece of cloth under it. To hide Pamela's now exposed, moist vagina surrounded by dark pubic hair, the woman draped a small blanket over Pamela's straddled legs.

Pamela's body became taut. How long was she to stay in this uncomfortable position? Her back was starting to pain her from lying on the hard table. Oh, get this over with, she thought.

After what seemed to be "forever," the man from the drugstore entered the room. He went straight to Pamela and lifted the blanket.

Pamela's rigid body could feel his hand entering her body and feeling inside--once--twice--three times. She closed her eyes. It was an uncomfortable sensation. It hurt!

"Yup," he said, "sixteen weeks--at least."

His hand left her body. She opened her eyes and then saw him extend his palm in the direction of the woman.

The woman moved to the side of the portable table and placed an instrument into the man's extended palm.

Pamela could feel him place the instrument on the upper part of her vagina forcing it open. He then took another instrument into his hand. She could feel him grasp her cervix and then she felt a pinching sensation. He then removed the instrument that he had just used to force her vagina open.

"Number eight, please." Pamela heard him say.

The woman slapped one of the metal tubes into the man's hand. Pamela felt him push the metal tube inside of her. It hurt and she began to squirm, thinking to get away from the pain.

"Don't move!" the man ordered her. "She's starting to bleed." He pulled out the metal tube. "Number 10, please." He held out his hand and grasped another metal tube.

Pamela could feel him stick that inside of her. The pain was getting worst as she felt him stretch her body open, but she remained still --hoping it would be over soon.

He pulled it out quickly. "Number 11."

"Number 12." He was moving with great speed now.

She felt him stretch her more and more--pain--pain--pain! It was hurting so unbearably! She began to cry tears of pain. Then she could feel the warm, stickiness of her blood creeping up her back as she lay there. She closed her eyes and gripped her hands tightly to the side of the table. The pain--pain--it tore her inside and out.

"Number 13."

She screamed inside--the pain--when would it be over!

"Number 14--I broke her water." He pulled out the metal tube and put it back on the table. "Suction tip, please."

Pamela could feel him enter her again. Then she heard the noise of a machine. She could feel him vacuuming deep inside of her. She opened her eyes. There was blood everywhere--the man was covered with blood--the table dripped of blood--the floor was painted with it--the air smelled of it. Blood was swirling into the glass jar.

"I'm not getting anything. Shut off the machine, please." Pamela heard the man say and then the noise ceased.

"Forceps."

The woman slapped the instrument into his hand. Pamela felt him push it inside of her--then come out again. He slapped something onto the table. Pamela saw it. It was a miniature arm--with a ripped shoulder--five little fingers--an elbow--upper and lower arm.

"I have a leg now." She heard him as he slammed it down onto the table.

Pamela turned away, closed her eyes that were swimming in tears. Her lips quivered. "Get it over with!"

"Okay, I think I've chopped it up enough. Turn the machine on again."

The noise filled the room again and she could feel him suck inside of her, moving the tube back and forth briskly.

"Turn off the machine--sharp curette, please." She heard him say.

She felt him scrap inside of her again.

"Suction."

Pamela heard the machine again and felt him inside of her again. It only took a second and then she felt him leave her body and the machine was silent.

"All done."

Pamela left out a sigh of relief--a relaxed feeling flowed from her body. She opened her eyes and turned toward the portable table. She saw the woman take the fragmented miniature body parts and wrap them into a newspaper which she tossed into a pail. Caught in the gauze of the jar, Pamela seen parts of what was vacuumed from inside of her that were too big to strain through the gauze.

Taking a wet cloth and soap the woman washed Pamela's bloody exposed genitals and surrounding area. Then she sponged the area with a brown substance from a small bottle and then attached a pad between her legs. Taking the bloody cloth from beneath Pamela's buttock, she tossed it into the pail also. After putting the pail on top of the portable table, she opened the door and pushed the table out the door.

The man poured water from the pitcher into the enamel dish and washed himself. Taking off his bloody gown, he tossed it on the floor. Walking over to Pamela, he untied the straps that had secured her legs. He raised the leaf in the table and then put her legs one by one on the leaf. He then covered her with the blanket and left the room.

As Pamela lay quietly on the table staring at the light bulb that dangled above her, she could feel the stickiness of the blood where it had crept up part of her back. She could smell its sweet scent lingering in the air. A sudden, painful contraction of muscles jerked her abdomen, her groin, and flashed to her lower back. She turned on her side, curled her body into a ball, and clutched her knees to her chest. The pain was unbearable! She felt so cold! Her body shivered!

The woman returned with another washbasin. After setting the basin on the seat of one of the chairs, she helped Pamela sit up on the table.

"No--leave me alone--the pain is so bad!"

"It's just cramps. They'll come and go for a while then you'll be okay." Slowly and gently the woman washed Pamela's blood-covered legs--one then the other--then her arms--one then the other--then her back. The woman scrubbed the table. "I'll be right back." She took the washbasin filled with bloody water and the soiled towels out of the room with her.

Another stabbing, abdominal pain ripped at her. She held her abdomen and hunched over.

"They'll go away." The man entered the room. "You'll stay here tonight so we can keep an eye on you. If everything goes well, you can leave tomorrow. If not, you'll have to stay longer. No one leaves here until I think they are okay to leave." He helped Pamela into bed and covered her with a blanket. As he sat on the edge of the bed, he held his hand on her head. "You sleep now." Then he left the room.

Alone she lay in the silence of the room. She could visualize the little arm and cried--for now she felt regret at what she had done. Despair--emptiness in her soul--an eternal loss of part of her--gone forever--forever--it could never be replaced. The pain--the agonizing pain came again and again and again! She cuddled her body together and cried into the pillow. What had she done?

How long she had cried, or when she fell asleep was unaware to her. In fact, when the woman came into her room again, Pamela didn't know what time of day--or night it was.

Carrying a small glass tube, the woman shook it down, and read the markings on it. "Open your mouth, please." She stuck the glass tube into Pamela's mouth under her tongue and then left the room.

Pamela could feel the saliva form in her mouth as she moved the glass tube back and forth under her tongue. Sometimes the glass tube would slip out from beneath her tongue and she'd work it back with her tongue.

The woman returned, took the glass tube out, and read the numbers. "Well, we'll try it again." She shook the glass tube again, checked the readings, and put it back into Pamela's mouth. "Keep it under the tongue, please." The woman stood beside the bed like a stern guard waiting for the time to remove the glass tube. After a few minutes, she pulled the glass tube out and examined the red line. Putting the glass tube back into her blouse pocket, she pulled the blankets off Pamela's body and examined her for profuse bleeding.

"Everything seems okay. You can leave." The woman departed.

Slowly, and with pain Pamela got up from the bed. The abdominal pain was piercing--stabbing--piercing--stabbing! She sat back down on the edge of the bed, crunched her body together, and grasped her arms around her knees. There she rocked her body back and forth--back and forth in pain--pain--pain! When it finally subsided, she rose from the bed and slowly walked to the back of the bed to get her clothes. Suddenly, she felt a gush of blood flow from her body.

Taking off the green ugly gown with hardened blood on it, she dressed in her clothes. Slowly she walked toward the front of the drugstore. As she was about to enter the store, the woman stood blocking the doorway. "Use the back door, please." She motioned with her head.

Pamela turned, seen the door, and with a slow pace walked toward it. The midafternoon sun hit her face as she opened the door and went outside. The brightness of the sun seemed to erase the saddened feeling that she had woke up with. The backyard was full of garbage cans. Some covered tightly with their metal lids--others uncovered with stray cats feeding from them. She wondered what they had done to the little body that they had removed from her? It wasn't a body anymore, just torn parts of flesh. What had she done? She began to cry as she walked along in a dazed trance. How long or far she had walked before she questioned where she was, she didn't know. Was she lost? She didn't recognize anything! Yes, she was going the wrong way! Oh! Which way should she go? Stopping in a shop, a kindly old shopkeeper directed her in the direction that she needed to go to get to the depot.

The train ride back was so desolate--so full of downheartedness as she felt that she had left something irreplaceable back in Chicago. Oh, she'd get over the regret that now filled her with depression. Once she was home with the other two, she'd be so pleased that she had done what she had done. She thought of those two crying--changing their diapers--their night feedings--all the work. Oh, yes! She'd made the right choice. In a couple of years they'd both be in school and she'd have some of her freedom back. As the train traveled farther and farther from Chicago, so faded her feelings of sadness of what she had done. The feelings of disgust, of Otto touching her again, filled the part of her soul that had been consumed with regret. Contempt began to flourish there again.

Getting off the train, with her luggage in her hand, she stood alone in her thoughts on the depot platform. There in front of her stood the town--her life--so full of emptiness--so full of regret. Back she'd go to that house where she'd spend the rest of her days cleaning--taking care of those two kids--being Otto's slave.

With such desolate thoughts, she walked in the direction of the house. It seemed like she had walked for hours. She was exhausted.

Then out of the front door of the Benson's house, Margie came running. She ran to Pamela and hugged her so tightly around her legs. "Mama--love you--love you."

"Let go of my legs. I can't move." Pamela pulled away from her and walked toward the house with Margie following and clinging to the edge of her skirt.

"Let go, Margie!" Pamela had no patience with her hanging on her skirt and slowing her down.

As she walked up the wooden stairs, Mrs. Benson opened the screen door and held it open until Pamela and Margie were inside. "How was your shopping?"

"It was okay--very tiring." She set the luggage on the floor, pulled out a kitchen chair, and sat on it.

Margie came up and hugged Pamela again. "Love you--Mama."

Mrs. Benson left the room and came back in a few minutes carrying Mikie. She hugged him and kissed his cheek. "He was such a good little boy." She hugged and kissed him again. "Weren't you, little Mikie?"

"I was good too, Mama." Margie turned to Mrs. Benson for approval.

Mrs. Benson looked at the kitchen window. It had cardboard taped to it to keep the summer flies from coming through the broken pane.

Margie looked in the direction of the window then at her mother. "Mikie broke--he didn't catch ball."

Mrs. Benson shook her head and kissed Mikie's cheek again. "Poor little Mikie gets blamed for everything." She set him on the floor.

Mikie toddled over to Pamela and rested his pudgy hands on her lap.

Margie pushed him away.

Mikie fell on his buttock. Slowly he got up and toddled over to Mrs. Benson who picked him up again. "Oh, here comes your daddy." She carried Mikie over to the window so he could see Otto drive into the driveway with the big, empty cattle truck.

"Well, he's home early," Pamela remarked with a bit of criticism as she rose from the chair. Grabbing her luggage, she walked toward the door with Margie following. Mrs. Benson, who was still carrying Mikie, followed Pamela over to her house.

"Daddy--Daddy!" Margie yelled as she ran to Otto who was also walking toward the house.

"Hi, sweetie." Otto picked her up in his arms and hugged her. "You a good girl today?"

Margie nodded her head. "Ya, Daddy."

Inside the house they all went. Mrs. Benson set Mikie down. "I'll be going now. My kids should be waking from their nap soon."

"Thanks, Lillian."

"No problem, Pamela. See you later." Mrs. Benson left the house.

Otto went over to kiss Pamela.

She pushed him away. "Leave me alone. I'm tired." She took her luggage into the bedroom and closed the door.

Otto made supper for Margie and Mikie. After supper he did the dishes, gave the children a bath, put them to bed, and then got ready for bed also. Seeing Pamela lying in bed, he couldn't understand why she had covered herself up with so many blankets. It was summer and the gentle night breeze was warm. As he crawled into bed and touched her, he could feel that her body was burning with heat. He could feel her curled up body shiver under the sweat drenched blankets. He felt a stickiness on the sheet as he lay beside her. Getting out of bed and turning on the light revealed a sheet covered with a massive amount of blood.

"Pam, what's the matter?"

"The beans should be picked--"

"Pam, what's the matter." He shook her body to wake her.

"Ya, ya, I'll pick them--"

"Pam, what's the matter?" Realizing she was delirious, he shook her more hoping to make her coherent.

"I'll pick them--leave me alone. Oh--the pain--stop the pain!" She began to cry and curled her body more until she could curl it no more.

Otto dashed out of the bedroom and phoned Dr. Whitmore for help. He stood near the window watching--waiting for the doctor. When he finally arrived, Otto flung open the door and ran out to meet him.

"Doc, the bed is full of blood. I think she's dying!"

Together they ran into the house.

Touching her, Dr. Whitmore immediately ordered Otto to fill an empty water bottle with ice. Pulling off the blankets, he saw the pool of blood. He began to examine her.

As Otto came through the door with the ice-filled water bottle, Dr. Whitmore took it and placed it on Pamela's forehead.

Pamela grabbed his hand. "Can you help me? Am I going to die?"

"Otto, could you please get her some water in a glass and also a washbowl full of cold water and a cloth."

"Sure." Otto hurriedly left the room.

Dr. Whitmore shook his head. "Pamela, what have you done?"

"What do you mean?" The words were heavy on her tongue.

"Pamela, I'm a doctor. It's quite obvious what you've done. Does Otto know?"

"No--no one does." She feebly reached for his hand. "No one must ever know--please!"

"You really should be put in a hospital."

"No--then everyone will know. It has to be our secret--please."

Dr. Whitmore was silent as he thought about the situation. "I'll take care of you here. No one will ever know. You might never be able to have any more children because of this."

"I just don't want to die."

"I'll do all I can to see that doesn't happen." He gently caressed her hand.

She forced a weak smile as his face faded away into darkness.

****

He watched her silently through her partially opened bedroom door. He thought he would never love again, but he found himself loving her. He didn't know how much until he found himself beside her hospital bed several months ago praying that she'd live. She had lived, but she was not his. So he loved her from a distance, never mentioning how he loved her for fear of making her leave. She loved someone else and so his heart ached and his eyes cried. They were the dearest of friends and that closeness he cherished with his whole soul.

Unaware of him watching, she stroked her gray streaked hair with her brush. She was done--a hundred strokes. She put the brush down beside a picture, framed in an old carved wooden frame. Her brother had found the frame amongst his things and had sent it to her. She rubbed her hand around the top edge of the frame. The frame held memories. Her father had made it for her. He was an excellent carpenter. Would her grandson follow in her father's footsteps and be a carpenter? It would be hard with the way he was now. Then she touched the picture inside the frame and smiled to herself. If she could go back in time, it would be when the three of them were together. Sentimental tears filled her eyes. How she loved him and all these years she had never thought of another man until recently. With her hand she stroked the scar that extended from the left front side of her neck to the right front side. This other man was good to her, and she had grown fond of him. Since his wife's death and his heart attack, they had become very close. In addition, they shared the same grandchild, but all that was really irrelevant. How did she feel in her heart about him? Was it time to put her dead husband where he maybe now belonged--still in her heart--in her memories--but not a part of her life? He was gone. She would always love him, but he was only a memory. He was dead and couldn't love her--hold her--be her companion through the good and bad times. Now there was someone else who was always with her. It would be hard to let go. Wanting to be close to someone else would be her final act in admitting "once and for all" that her husband was dead--but would that be betrayal?--to his memory?--to his daughter?

Rising from her vanity chair, she grabbed the long chiffon scarf hanging on the scrolled corner of the vanity. She wrapped it around her neck to conceal the ghastly neck scar. Turning toward the door, she was startled to see him standing there.

He smiled. "You look so beautiful." He held his hand out to her.

With a gracious smile she reached for his hand. "Will you take me to Jennings today?"

"Sure." His smile vanished. He could never compete with a dead man. She was going to his grave again.

Holding his hand, she caressed it with her other hand. "It's all right, Charles. It's my good-bye. It's time for me to move beyond the past."

Letting go of her hand, he held her in his arms. His heart fluttered. Should he ask her? He was frightened. Of all the things he had done in his life--as a banker--a businessman--this moment made him nervous--like a schoolboy on his first date. "Can I kiss you, Anna?"

Softly she replied, "I would like that very much, Charles."

With his heart bursting with joy, he held her face ever so lovingly and kissed her with pure elation. Then gently holding her and never wanting to let her out of his arms, he worried about what he was about to say. He whispered, "I love you. Will you marry me--my dear--sweet Anna?"

****

The door opened and the bell rang. The two children went up to the counter and patiently waited while the two women talked. The woman on the same side of the counter motioned to the woman behind the counter that the children probably wanted to be served.

"What do you want?" The woman behind the counter was annoyed at the children's presence.

"We'd like two of those, please." The boy, the older of the two children, pointed to what they wanted.

"First, let me see your money," the woman behind the counter snapped.

Cumbersomely, the boy reached into the pocket in his trousers, pulled out some coins, and laid them on the counter.

The woman counted out the coins she wanted, put them into her cash register, and then gave the children what they had paid for.

"Thank you," they both said and then left the shop.

"Such trash! Trash breeds trash!" said the woman behind the counter.

"The children can't help who their mother is," commented the other woman.

"The people should have run both of them out of town years ago, then maybe Steven would still be alive."

"Did you really see him push Steven?"

"Do you think I lie?"

"Well, it's just that if he did, why didn't they put him in a reformatory or why didn't he get some kind of punishment?"

"Do you really have to ask? How do you think Anna and Amanda get everything they want? Do you really think he kept Anna at the house after Eva died to help with the housework and gardening?

They're little whores and some men will do anything for them. Old man Charles probably paid someone off to protect his whore's grandson--that little bastard."

"Don't you feel sorry for him having to live with what the train did to him?"

"He's a lot luckier than Steven, now isn't he?" The woman came out from behind the counter and walked over to the window.

"You're right." The woman nodded her head in agreement, picked up her box of sweet rolls, and walked toward the door. "See you tonight at the Christian Mother's meeting."

"Ya, see you then." Through the window she watched the children disappear down the street. Piercing hatred raged in her eyes. The hatred burnt through her heart. Feeling someone was watching her, she turned around. There in the back doorway stood her husband. "You drunken son of a bitch!"

"Ya, you're right and I enjoy every minute of it."

"I could just kill you!"

"Go ahead--Regina, the husband killer." Arnold raised the bottle in the air to mockingly "toast her" and then took a drink from it.

Regina stormed out the front door, slamming it behind her.

He took the bottle and smashed it violently against the wall. Glass scattered the floor, and the remaining liquor in the bottle splashed onto the wall and the floor. "We'll, see who kills who--you bitch! Without you, I'd have a lot more money--all yours." His monstrous laughter filled the room as he tumbled to the floor in a drunken stupor.

Chapter 13
****
Child Abusers and Bootleggers

Quietly, Mikie lay snugly in his bed. Outside he could hear the rhythmical beat of the rain drops against the windowpane and on the tin roof. Mikie liked to lie in bed and listen to the rain. At night it was the gentle sound that would lull him to sleep, and during the day it made him feel calm and at peace.

Downstairs, in the kitchen, he could hear someone moving about, closing cupboard doors and rattling the silverware in the drawer. The sounds were familiar early morning sounds. His mother was getting breakfast ready for him and his older sister, Margie.

The downstairs door opened. "Get up for school," called his mother from the bottom of the stairs.

Then he heard the door slam shut again.

Mikie sprang from the bed, slipped his slippers on, and ran into the hall. As he passed Margie's room, he saw that she was still fast asleep with her head buried under the covers. "Margie, get up. Ma has got breakfast ready."

"Ya, ya."

"You better hurry. You know how mad Ma gets if we come late for breakfast."

"She won't say anything if I'm late."

"Hurry up or else she'll yell at me." Mikie flew down the stairs.

As he opened the door, the familiar smell of burnt toast filled his nostrils. Mikie crumbled up his nose. Just one morning he wished that she wouldn't burn the toast. It tasted so terrible. Even the thick layers of jelly that he always put on it couldn't hide the horrid taste.

Mikie hurried to his place at the table. The steam was rising high from his bowl of oatmeal.

"Well, hurry up and eat. I want to do dishes before I leave for work. I don't want to come home to a sink full of dishes after a hard day at work," his mother barked at him.

Mikie quickly stirred the oatmeal to cool it off.

"Will you start eating! Where is Margie?" She yelled up the stairs again, "Margie!"

Mikie ate the toast first then tried to gobble down the hot oatmeal as quickly as he could. It burnt the tip of his tongue and the inside of his mouth. It was lumpy. As he bit the lumps, he could taste the particles of oatmeal that hadn't cooked. Mikie knew that he shouldn't complain or act like he didn't like it. Such things would make his mother angry, and she wasn't very nice when she was angry --especially to him!

A few minutes later, Margie came down the stairs dragging her feet and still half asleep.

"Margie, honey, will you please hurry up. I have to leave for work in fifteen minutes." Pamela scrambled about the house, tidying up one room after the other.

When Mikie had finished, he put his dirty dish into the sink. After washing his hands and face, he went up to his room to dress for school.

Neatly hung over his chair were the clothes that he had worn to school the day before. Mikie only had one pair of trousers. He treated it with care--not wrinkling it or getting it dirty. He had to wear it all week and his mother wouldn't like it if he got it dirty. Up until two weeks ago, he had only had one shirt also. However, Murray, his godfather, bought him a beautiful plaid flannel shirt for his tenth birthday. Mikie thought the world of that shirt. It was the only present that he had received for his birthday. After he had it completely buttoned, he stood for a while and admired it in the mirror. He looked really nice. He hoped Susie Benson thought so too.

"Hey, Mikie, come in here for a minute." Margie walked past his bedroom door and went into her bedroom.

Mikie knew what she wanted. He wished that he had such problems.

"Well, which one?" she asked as she held one dress in her left hand and another in her right hand.

"That one." Mikie pointed to the dress that she held in her left hand.

"Are you sure you don't like this one?" She motioned her head to the dress that she held in her right hand.

"No, I like the other one. Why do you even ask me? You'll wear what you want anyhow. I like this one better than both of them." He took a dress out of the closet, handed it to her, and then went downstairs.

As he neared the bottom of the stairs, he heard voices. They belonged to his mother and father. They were arguing again. Not wanting to get in the middle of things, he sat on the bottom step and listened. When they'd stop, then it would be safe to venture out into the kitchen.

Their voices pierced the door.

"Where's my breakfast?" shouted his father.

"Fix it yourself. I have to go to work," his mother snapped.

"Your first job is at home taking care of me and the kids."

"Well, if I didn't have this part-time job, we'd all starve over the winter."

"There was always enough food on the table all the other years and there'll be enough this year too."

"Ya, that's all there is money for. Well, I want a few extra things too. My furniture is twenty years old and it looks like trash. The linoleum is worn in spots. The curtains are going to fall apart if I wash them one more time."

"Well, don't wash them."

"You smart son of a bitch. I want nice things just like other women have. I'm not going to get them if I don't have a job. You spend all your money on your prostitutes in Milwaukee. You have a bed at home, but it isn't good enough for you. You have to spend your nights and money on harlots! They can afford to buy things that I want and they buy those things with your money!"

"Maybe they're worth more than you!"

"You're just like my old man."

"Well, here's a couple of bucks I have left. Buy yourself a bottle of booze and drink yourself to death like your old lady did." He flung the money across the table at her.

"Drop dead, Otto." She grabbed her raincoat and ran out the door.

"Bye, Pam," he chuckled as he called after her.

Just then the telephone rang--two long rings--one short ring.

"Hello, Otto Aslen here."

"This is Murray. I got four that I want to ship tomorrow," the voice from the other end said.

"Sure thing, Murray, I'll be there sometime in the afternoon. You'll be my last stop tomorrow."

"Good, see you then. Bye."

"Bye, Murray."

As he hung up the phone, Mikie opened the door and came out into the kitchen. "Hi, Dad."

"Hi, Mikie."

"I have to serve Mass this morning. Do you think you can drop me off at school on the way to your milk route?"

"Well, we better leave now or else you'll be late. Is Margie ready?"

"Margie, are you ready?" Mikie called up the stairs.

"No, not yet," she called back.

"Well, I'm not going to make two trips. You better walk up. I'll drop Margie off whenever she's ready."

"Okay." Mikie was disappointed. The rain was nice when a person was inside but not so nice when a person was outside. After putting on his coat and rubbers, Mikie went out the door and started walking down the muddy street toward school and the church. It wasn't far. They often walked to school and church in the rain and snow. However, because he served Mass today, he wanted to look nice--not like a "drowned rat" with wet hair and trousers.

As Mikie walked up the cement stairs in front of the church, he saw his father's big milk truck pull into the churchyard. Margie was looking out the window--snickering at him.

While Mikie served Mass, his body shook now and then from the damp clothes that chilled his body. The huge church was not very full during the weekday Masses. Only the schoolchildren, three nuns and a few elderly ladies attended these weekday services. After the half-hour service, the children followed the nuns into the schoolhouse where the day's classes were taught.

The red brick schoolhouse was a two-roomed school. Mikie was in the room where grades one to four were taught, the "little room," so it was called. Margie was in the "big room" where grades five to eight were taught.

The rain pounded into the ground all that morning and early afternoon. At recess all the students stayed inside the school. The smaller children amused themselves by playing "Simon says" and "button--button--who's got the button." Those games were too childish for Mikie and his friend, so they went into the "big room" and played a card game, sheepshead, with the three fifth-grade boys.

Margie and her friends played "hang the butcher." After being "hung several times," Margie quit in disgust. When Margie quit, everyone did. Soon all the girls were sitting around talking and giggling among themselves.

Mikie found it difficult to concentrate on his card game with the hideous giggling ringing through his ears. Finally, to his joy, the laughter ceased. Looking up to see what had stopped them from making their girly noises, he saw that Margie was nowhere around. She was the "big mouth." Without her being around, none of the other girls knew what to do. They were a bunch of monkeys-- "monkey sees--monkey does."

"Hey, you two fourth graders get out of here!" shouted two big eighth-grade boys as they approached the desk where Mikie and the other boys were playing cards.

"Why?" asked Mikie's friend.

"Because we want to play," one eighth-grade boy replied.

"I thought you guys had your own games," one of the fifth-grade boys said.

"Ya, we did until Chuck and Jerry left."

"Where did they go?" asked another fifth-grade boy.

"The 'cubby hole.' "

"What do they want down there? Are they helping Sister Francis Mary rearrange her brooms and mops again?" asked Mikie's friend.

"Sister better stand in the doorway and shine the flashlight inside the room. Cause if she goes inside that small room, she'll surely squash them both," an eighth-grade boy commented.

The boys all laughed.

"They aren't helping Sister. They're helping themselves, and it ain't to brooms and mops they're helping themselves to either." The eighth-grade boys laughed obscenely.

"Meow--meow." With his hand one eighth-grade boy nudged the other in his arm.

That brought another loud roar from the eighth-grade boys and also brought Sister into the room.

"Boys! Boys! Must you laugh so loudly?" said Sister Francis Mary, the cook and recess supervisor.

"Sorry, Sister," they all replied.

"You better put the cards away now and settle into your own desk. It is almost time for class to resume." She surveyed the room. "Where are Chuck and Jerry?"

"They went to the bathroom," an eighth-grade boy replied.

"Well, you better go get them. Sister Marie will be out soon to resume class."

"Yes, Sister." The boy opened the classroom door, which led out into the hall. Once out in the hall, he closed the door.

His body filled with anxiety, if only Sister didn't follow him and find out where he was really going. The door to the bathroom was down the hall. The door he had to take to get Chuck and Jerry was opposite the classroom door.

Quickly, he opened that door and closed it behind him. It was dark. His hand grasped the wall until he found the switch. A bright light now lit the narrow basement stairs. At the bottom of the stairs, he stopped. In front of him was a very narrow door. The door to the room referred to as the "cubby hole."

"Guys, you better come out. Class is starting." He tapped on the door.

A few minutes later the door opened and they came out. Margie was still buttoning her blouse.

Quietly, they tiptoed up the stairs. At the top of the stairs, they stopped and held their breaths. Boy! If Sister caught them, they'd really be in trouble.

Blonde haired Chuck turned out the light and very slowly turned the knob on the door. Then he carefully pushed the door open to a mere crack. It seemed like ages had passed. It was so quiet. They could hear each other's heart beat. They were cuddled so closely together that they could feel the sweat of uneasiness on each other's brow.

All was clear!

They quickly dashed out into the hall. If Sister caught them now, it wouldn't matter. They could explain being in the hall.

"I better not go in with you. I'll wait in the bathroom for a few minutes before I go in," Margie suggested.

Leaving Margie with a nod of approval, the boys entered the classroom.

Finally, Sister rang the last bell of the day and the children hurried out the door. Outside they scattered in all directions, everyone traveling a different way home.

The rain had ceased. A large arch of colors--red, orange, yellow, green, blue, indigo, and violet--stretched across the afternoon sky. The sun's warmth had erased the dampness of the air. The ditches were bursting with excess water. Everything smelled fresh and clean.

As Mikie stood outside the school talking to his friend, a voice called to him.

"Mikie! Mikie!"

A quick turn of his head in the direction of the yell revealed the person who belonged to the yell. It was Margie! She had her shoes in one hand and her socks in the other. Her bare feet were wading in the water-filled ditch.

Mikie ran to her. "You better get out of there. If you get wet and muddy, Ma will be mad."

"Ah, I'm not going to get wet or muddy. Come on in! Look! The ditch is full of water all the way to our house."

Mikie looked down the ditch. For as far as he could see, the ditch was bulging with water.

"Come on, Mikie, Ma is at work. She'll never know. It's fun!"

"I don't think so."

"Chicken! Chicken!" Margie teased as she tossed her socks and shoes beside the road.

Biting his lip, he looked down at the water. It would be fun walking in it but what if he got caught? Ma didn't like them to play in the water. While he seriously contemplated what to do, he suddenly felt a tight grasp on his hand.

SPLASH!

There was nothing to think about now. Margie had pulled him into the water. His clothes--shoes--everything was wet!

"My book! It fell in the water."

"Well, go get it out." Margie laughed.

Mikie picked up the book soaking with water and drenched in mud. "What am I going to do now?"

"Let it lay and tell everyone you lost it. Or better yet, tell everyone someone stole it."

"That's lying!"

"So, who would know?"

As Mikie started to climb out of the ditch, Margie reached for him and lost her balance on the slippery mud. On her buttocks she fell. Water splashed all about her.

"Oh, I'm all wet!" She began to sob as the water ran off her wet hair into her face. Her copper curls were now like strings of wet threads. "I'm cold." She shivered.

"Ya, so am I. I'm going home." Mikie started to walk down the gravel road. Their house was only four houses away. His shoes squeaked as more water squeezed out of his soles with each step. His wet trousers clung to his thin legs. As he rubbed his hands over his warped book, he wondered how he was going to explain that.

"Wait for me! Wait for me!" shouted Margie.

Mikie stopped and turned around. Patiently, he waited while Margie sat at the edge of the road putting on her socks and shoes. With her shoes on, she stood up and he could see the wet blouse clinging to her young breasts. As she ran up to him, her breasts flopped about in a repulsive way.

As they neared the house, their mother turned into the driveway.

"Oh, oh! What do we do now?" asked Mikie.

"It's to late to do anything. She's seen us," replied Margie.

After shutting the car door, their mother stood beside the car and looked at them very sternly. With the fire of anger blazing in her eyes, she pointed them to the house door.

Knowing they had done wrong, they walked up to the house with their heads lowered.

Their mother followed them. Once inside the house, she slammed the door behind them. "You God damn stupid kids! Just look at your clothes! Get upstairs, Margie, and change! Then you get down here and help me with supper."

Margie flew up the stairs.

"Just look at those shoes, you little bastard." She took a firm hold of Mikie's head and pushed it down so he could see his shoes. "Do you know how much they cost? A lot more than a damn penny--I can tell you that! You don't care about anyone but yourself, you little bastard! It wasn't enough you got wet, but you had to ruin your sister's clothes too."

"But I--"

Her hand flew forcefully across his face.

"Shut up! I don't want to hear any of your lies! You wrecked those good shoes." With her fist, she pounded him violently on his shoulder blades as she clenched her rolled up tongue between her teeth. Taking a hold of his shirt, she ripped it madly from his body.

Seeing his good shirt torn into shreds, Mikie started crying.

"Stop your crying, you damn bastard!" She hit him across his face again then pulled his hair tightly into the palm of her hand. "Take those damn shoes and wet clothes off. Then get upstairs and don't come down until tomorrow. You aren't getting any supper!" She pushed him away from her and then kicked him hard between the buttocks.

With each cautious step, his hurt tailbone ached of pain. He could barely take off his trousers. His shoulder joints hurt so badly. However, despite the pain of his now bruised body, he hurried to get his clothes off. Fear had gripped him. He didn't want her to get any madder. While she was peeling potatoes, he slowly crept up the stairs. At the top of the stairs, his face met Margie's. He could hardly see her through the flood of tears.

"Cry baby," she snickered and teased at him.

He would have run away into his room, but he could barely walk. His injured tailbone stung him so badly. Pain! Pain! Pain!

As he lay upstairs on his bed, he could smell chicken frying. The smell teased his stomach. It began to rumble and be tormented by sudden sharp, brief pain.

"Daddy's home," Margie said as she saw the big cattle truck turn into the driveway and enter the garage, located behind the house.

"Well, that's a first. He's home on time for supper--for a change!" Pamela remarked.

As Pamela put the steaming bowl of potatoes on the table, Otto walked into the room.

Margie ran up and hugged Otto. "Hi, Daddy!"

"Hi, Margie." Otto kissed her head.

"You're home early today." He looked up at Pamela.

"They sent us home early. The fields were too wet. The trucks kept getting stuck." Pamela took the pan of hot gravy off the stove.

"Where's Mikie?" With his eyes, Otto looked about the house.

"That little bastard is upstairs!" Pamela responded.

"What did he do now?" asked Otto.

"Walked home in a ditch full of water."

"You're kidding!" Otto's voice was full of disgust.

"No, I wish I was!" Pamela angrily replied.

"Doesn't that kid know how much shoes cost?"

"He doesn't care about anyone but himself. He got Margie's clothes all wet and dirty."

Otto shook his head. "That kid doesn't have a brain in his head."

"Just look at those shoes!" Pamela pointed to the mud-covered shoes.

"Tell him to get down here. Right now!" Otto began to remove the belt from his trousers' loops.

"Mikie, get down here!" Pamela yelled up the stairs.

Mikie had heard his father's truck come into the driveway. He had also heard their loud voices in the kitchen through the register in his floor, which was directly above the kitchen.

"Mikie get down here--now!" she yelled again.

Mikie knew what would happen when he came down the stairs. He had to hide! But where? The attic! Frantic and with pain, he sprang from the bed and dashed toward the door.

There at the top of the stairs was his father, the belt in his hand.

Mikie slammed his bedroom door shut and locked it.

"Open this door," his father shouted from the other side of the door as he turned the doorknob, trying to open it.

Mikie's body began to shake and shiver.

"Damn it! Open this door!" His father began to pound violently upon the door. "When I get a hold of you little bastard, you'll wish you were never born!"

Mikie wished that already. If he opened the door, he'd get hit with the belt. If he didn't open it, he'd get hit also.

Otto began to kick at the door.

Knowing in only a few seconds he'd bust down the door, Mikie scrambled under the bed.

CRASH!

Otto had broken the door latch off the door molding. Screws and splinters of wood flew across the floor.

From under the bed, Mikie could see his father standing in the threshold. Mikie lay breathless and motionless. The seconds passed like hours as his father searched his closet. Fear throbbed in Mikie's heart. Then something startled him. His father had his foot grasped in his hand and was yanking him out from under the bed.

Wild with fear, Mikie kicked and kicked. He reached for the bed leg. Desperately, he hung on. His grip on the leg became less as his two-hundred-pound father pulled harder and harder at his foot.

"I'll get you little bastard out!" he shouted.

With one last jerk, he flung Mikie's body out from under the bed.

With tremendous force, Mikie's head hit the back of the bed's leg. For a few split seconds, he was unaware of what was happening. When he felt the razor-sharp edge of the belt strike his buttocks, he knew. As he lay on his stomach, he put his hands over his red-beaten buttocks.

Over and over and over the belt slashed at his hands and wrists.

Mikie lay passively still. He held the pain inside and didn't utter a cry. His face was wet with tears as he tried to bury it in the linoleum floor.

"That should teach you not to get your shoes all wet and muddy. Next time I'll kill you little bastard. You're no good anyway!"

Somehow those words cut deeper than the belt. Kill me, I don't care, Mikie thought.

For a long time, he lay there crying from the pain. It wasn't his fault, but he had been blamed for it. Why did they hate him so? Why did God hate him? How could anyone care for him? God didn't even care about him. He must really be no good! Why else would God let that happen to him? He was the "scum of the earth." He wasn't fit to breathe the same air as other people. He was a "piece of trash"!

He reached over and pulled the remains of his birthday shirt over by him. His nice shirt--all ruined. He didn't deserve nice clothes either. With the shirt he wiped his face dry of its tears. He laid the shirt on the floor and then rested his head on it. With every bit of strength beaten from his body, he fell asleep.

After supper Pamela and Margie tidied up while Otto read the newspaper. The quiet evening went quick and soon it was time to go to bed.

In bed Otto lay facing one way and Pamela faced the other, their backs to each other. Tomorrow was Thursday, cow day. Otto would pick up cows from the farmers after his milk route and then take the cows to the stockyards. After that, he'd make his usual stop at a "speak easy" and spend part of the night with a harlot before coming home.

Pamela's memory was clear and vivid. She was a little luckier than her mother had been. At least Otto eventually came home sometime during the night. Even though he did nothing but help warm the bed. Her father--"the old stud"--was never home. Her mother's bed was always empty, but Pamela wouldn't fill her loneliness with a bottle of booze. No, that she wouldn't do! Her mother had only hurt herself--not her father. He would just laugh at her in her drunken stupor--the few times that he'd come to get his belongings. No, that wouldn't happen to her. She'd find something else to fill her loneliness.

By the time the alarm clock woke Pamela the next morning, Otto was already shaved and dressed.

"Hurry up and make me some breakfast," Otto ordered as he combed his hair.

"What's your hurry?" asked Pamela.

"I want to get an early start today."

"Why? You won't come home any earlier tomorrow morning, will you?" Pamela got out of bed and stretched her nude body.

"Put some clothes on your ugly body!"

"If you don't like the way I look--don't look at me."

"I don't--and I won't."

"I hope the cops raid the 'speak easy,' and I hope they throw you and your harlot in jail for a long time!"

With that remark, Otto stomped over to Pamela.

As he approached and not knowing what he was going to do, Pamela became afraid and reached for her dress to hide part of her body. She held the dress up against herself as she backed away from Otto.

As the cold wall touched her bare back, he put his hand tightly around her neck. "You better hope that never happens. Our reputation is the only thing we got going for us. If my name gets dragged in the mud, so does yours, honey. Right now we are highly regarded in this religious community. They've elected you the president of the Christian Mother's Society and me a church trustee. When the reputation goes, the trucking business goes. We have to live in winter too, and you don't have a job in winter."

With his hand still squeezed tightly around her neck, he pulled her neck away from the wall. Angrily, he pushed her down onto the bed.

"The sight of you makes me sick!" Otto stormed out the door, slamming it as he closed it.

She wished that he had hit her instead of saying those things. The bruises from his punches eventually disappeared, but his cruel words had a way of coming back and tormenting her over and over again.

While she dressed, she heard the telephone ring continuously. Otto had built up a good business. He made good money. If only he wouldn't spend it all on drinking and prostitutes, she wouldn't have to work outside the home. She hated him for making her have to go out and work. She really had enough work at home, with her large garden and taking care of the children properly, but she wanted nice things too. They had been married twenty years. Most married women were getting new and modern things, but not her. Her new things of twenty years ago were nothing but junk now. How could a man be so insensitive and spend everything on his own lustful pleasures?

Was she really that ugly? Is that why he went to the prostitutes because he couldn't stand the sight of her ugly body? She looked in the mirror. The light-blue stretch marks were ugly! They covered most of her abdomen. She had a few run down the top of her thighs.

Her breasts had a few stretch marks also, but she couldn't erase them. They were from having children.

After she had her bra and panty on, she grabbed the yellow tape measure out of her sewing machine. With it she measured herself --hips thirty-five--bust thirty-seven--waist twenty-eight. Gosh! Her waist was big! Before she was married, it had only been twenty-five. She was fat!

Gloomily, she finished dressing and then made breakfast.

"Breakfast is ready. Get down here!" Pamela shouted up the stairs.

Mikie, still lying on the floor, woke up. With his body stiff and aching, he crawled to his feet. While sitting on the edge of the bed, he put a clean pair of socks on and the only shirt he now had. Like an old man, crippled by age, he walked into the hall and down the stairs.

His trousers and shoes were in the same place where he had put them last night, near the floor register. The trousers were dry. The shoes were as hard as wood. They pinched his toes but he was not about to complain. Especially after he saw the scowl look on his mother's face.

He hurried to the table where he swallowed his lumpy oatmeal and burnt toast hastily. As he got up from the table, a knife-stabbing pain attacked the right side of his abdomen. Quickly, Mikie moved forward, jerkily. He arched his back as he held his hands over his abdomen to stop the pain.

"What's the matter, Mikie?" asked Margie.

"He ate to fast! That's what's the matter! Eat like an old pig some more! I don't feel sorry for you." His mother removed the dishes from the table and began washing them in the sink.

"Drop us off at school, Dad?" asked Margie.

"No, got to leave now. Bye." Otto went out the door.

"Bye, Dad." Margie was disappointed.

"When was the last time you took a shit?" his mother asked disgustingly.

"Yesterday." Mikie felt the pain ease and soon it was gone. He could stand straight again.

"Take this castor oil." His mother handed him the bottle.

Mikie turned up his nose. "I feel better now. The pain is gone."

"Well, then off to school." She put the bottle back into the small cupboard. Returning to the sink, she finished washing the dishes.

Mikie grabbed his book. It was all warped and the pages were stuck together.

"You're paying for the book, not me," his mother uttered a deep guttural sound of anger.

"Yes, Ma, bye," he replied.

"Bye." Margie shut the door.

As they walked to school, the sudden pain again plagued Mikie. He hunched his body and then fell to his knees, gripping his abdomen with his hands. He began to vomit and vomit.

"Mikie, you better go back home. You're sick." Margie made a disgusting face and turned away from the regurgitated matter now sprawled all over the side of the road.

"No, I'm okay now." He rose to his feet. The pain had disappeared again. He felt a little warmer than usual. Otherwise, he felt fine. Even if he wouldn't have felt better, he couldn't have gone home. His mother wouldn't like missing work because of him. Besides, it was his last day to serve Mass. Maybe if he prayed harder and served Mass really well, maybe God would love him more and be nicer to him. If God loved him, maybe his parents would also love him.

****

The beads of wet, grimy sweat ran down her face. She raised her forearm and rubbed it across her forehead removing part of the sweat that ran down into her eyes. Her blouse and slacks clung to her. The conveyor line had run continuously today. There were no breakdowns. She worked with the speed of the line, picking out debris from the corn that rushed by her on the conveyor. The noon whistle blew, but she couldn't leave for lunch until the relief lady came and took over her job. So she waited for lunch. She saw the relief lady come down the line, relieving one person then another. She was at the end of the line today, so she wouldn't get her lunch until around one o'clock. So she waited and waited and waited--

Now it was her turn. She grabbed the small brown bag that contained her lunch and went outside through the immense opened doors. Near the parking lot was an enormously old oak tree, under which she sat. Resting her back against its rugged bark, she closed her eyes and totally enjoyed the gentle breeze as it blew across her face--drying the sweat, relaxing her body, and refreshing her soul.

"Hi."

A voice startled her. Opening her eyes, she saw a man standing, looking down at her.

He sat next to her. "It's nice out here, isn't it?"

"Yes, it is." She smiled at him. Grabbing into her brown lunch bag, she pulled out an apple and started eating it.

"On your lunch break?"

"Yes, it's so hot and humid in there today." She began to notice the man's beautiful blue eyes and his gorgeous black wavy hair. His face had such fine features. He was one good-looking man!

"You work on the line, don't you?" he asked.

"Yes. How do you know?"

"I've seen you."

"You have?"

"Ya, I often walk through there on my way to the office. My name is Tony and you're Pamela. Aren't you?"

Pamela was again surprised. "How do you know my name?"

"One of the ladies told me. That's a pretty name--for a pretty lady."

Pamela smiled. Did he like her? He must. He came out by her. A handsome man talking to her made her feel warm inside. Maybe she wasn't as ugly as Otto had made her feel.

"Here, you like something to drink?" He handed her an unopened, glass bottle of coke.

"Yes, that's my favorite drink, thanks."

Grabbing into his pocket, he pulled out a metal opener, pulled off the metal cap, and handed her the bottle.

"Don't you want some?" she asked before she took a drink.

"No, thanks, I drank enough waiting to dump my load before."

"You're a truck driver?"

"Ya, when they're short a driver. Otherwise, I work in the warehouse."

"Which do you like better--driving truck or working in the warehouse?"

"They're both okay. I usually don't have very much work during the winter months, just a few days during the week in the warehouse or working on machinery."

Pamela looked at her watch. "Time for me to go back to work." She started to get up when he touched her hand.

"You have a few minutes yet--stay here."

"Why?"

"Because I want you to."

She smiled. She was flattered that such a handsome man like him would want to hold her hand and want to be close to her. He made her feel good.

"You like working during the corn pack?" he asked.

"It gives me extra money."

He smiled and then got up still holding her hand. "I better let you go inside." He helped her up. "I'll take that back." He grabbed the empty bottle that she held in her hand.

Pamela smiled. "Thanks."

"Anytime, good-looking. See ya." He smiled and winked at her. Turning, he walked toward a row of parked trucks.

She watched his firm, small buttocks move this way and that as his long legs walked toward the truck. His slender waist tapered up to his broad shoulders that moved in rhythmical unison with rest of his masculine body. As he grabbed the truck door and pulled it open his large biceps flexed. After climbing into the truck, he closed the door. Resting his tan arm on the open window, he turned his head in her direction, smiled and waved to her.

She watched as he drove away. Would she ever see him again? Did she want to? Was he just teasing an "old married lady"? Thoughts like that filled her mind the rest of the workday. She couldn't seem to think of anything or anybody else but him. Often she'd look through the open door thinking that she'd see him, but she didn't. She probably would never see him again.

When Pamela saw the second shift employees arrive, she knew that it would only be a short time before she'd be out of that "sweat hole." She was glad that it was only a couple of months that she had to work in the factory. The extra money was nice. She'd start to look at new furniture for the living room after she received her next check.

The factory whistle blew, and into line she went following the other workers up to the time clock to punch out her timecard.

"Hey, Pamela! Wait up!" a masculine voice yelled at her as she walked out of the building into parking lot toward her parked car.

Turning around, she saw that it was Tony. She stopped and waited for him to approach her. Her radiant smile revealed how delighted she was to see him again.

"Going home?" he asked as he approached with a smile that spread across his bronzed face.

"Yes," Pamela replied with another smile.

"Are you working tomorrow?"

"If it doesn't rain, I guess so."

"Good! I'll see you then. Have a good night." He opened the car door for her.

"Thank you, see you tomorrow." She sat in the car.

"Ya." He shut the door and waved to her as she drove out of the parking lot.

****

"Mikie! Mikie! Wait for me!" a voice shouted.

Mikie and Margie stopped their walking pace and turned around.

"What does she want now?" Margie asked, disgusted it was Susie.

"Hi, Susie," Mikie addressed her with a cheery smile.

"Hi, Mikie, how are you feeling now?"

"I feel good right now. Thanks for asking, Susie."

Margie rolled her eyes. In her opinion, Susie should be more of a friend to her because they were in the same grade and both girls. There was intense jealousy in her heart that Susie preferred Mikie instead of her as a friend.

"I'm glad that you're feeling better." She smiled at Mikie. "It's nice we're neighbors so we can walk home from school together."

"Ya, really nice," Margie's reply was one of sarcasm. "Mikie should walk with the boys."

"There is no way that I would walk with Chuck and Jerry." He motioned his head toward the two boys walking in front of them.

"No, silly, I mean the little boys walking in back of us. Susie and I will walk with Chuck and Jerry. Come on, Susie!" She grabbed Susie's hand so she could run up to Chuck and Jerry with her.

"No, I'm not walking with them." Susie pulled her hand loose from Margie's grip.

"Stay with the little runt then." Anger with Susie's decision,

Margie kicked Mikie in the leg and then ran up to Chuck and Jerry.

Chuck and Jerry immediately put their arms around Margie and in no time they were whispering and laughing among themselves.

Mikie bent over and tried to rub away the pain that his leg now ached with.

"I'm sorry, Mikie. Do you want to hang on me?" asked Susie.

"No, that's okay. I'll be fine." Mikie hobbled next to her as they went down the street toward their homes.

"Do you have a lot of homework?" asked Susie.

"No, I just have a little arithmetic to do. That won't take too long."

"Ya, you're really good in arithmetic. I don't have any homework tonight. You want to go fishing in your pond again?"

"Ya, that would be fun, but I don't know if I'll have time to dig the worms," replied Mikie.

"I can do it as soon as I get home. You do your homework so after supper we can go. Okay?"

"Ya, that sounds like a great idea."

As they walked on the driveway, which extended beside Mikie's parents' house into their backyard, they saw Margie go with Chuck and Jerry into the side garage door and close it. The only thing in the garage at this time of day was Otto's milk truck. The cattle truck Otto was using to haul cows to the stockyard and Pamela was still at work with the car.

"Let's follow them into the garage," suggested Susie.

"I don't think Margie would like us following her." Mikie knew better than to do anything that might get Margie mad at him. When she'd get mad at him, she'd tell their parents things about Mikie that weren't true. Then she'd snicker when Mikie got a beating from their father.

"Oh, come on, Mikie." Susie grabbed his hand and pulled him along as she opened the garage door.

The light from the open door revealed Margie and the two boys sitting in the truck on the seat. The boys were opening Margie's blouse and looking under her skirt. When the light entered the garage, their eyes turned away from Margie and in the direction of the light.

"Get the hell out of here!" one of the boys angrily shouted at them.

Susie quickly closed the door.

"I hope she isn't mad at me." Mikie's voice revealed the terrible fear that he had of the consequence of Margie's anger.

"Ah, Mikie, don't worry about things that may not happen. Go do your homework so we can go fishing after supper. See you later." Susie walked across the lawn to her house.

Mikie stood still for a minute staring at the garage, then went up the back porch into the house. The clock showed three-thirty. He set his books on the kitchen table next to the filled cookie jar. Usually, he had a glass of milk with some cookies when he came home from school, but this afternoon he didn't seem to have an appetite. He immediately sat at the table and started his homework. He wanted to get done before his mother came home and Margie had a chance to tell her lies. If he was outside when they called him, he could hide where they couldn't find him. There were many nights that he had hid outside until they had all gone to bed. Then he'd sneak into the house and take things from the refrigerator to eat. Later he'd sneak back out to his hiding place until he saw Susie in the morning. When he saw her, he would come out of hiding and walk with her to school. Well, enough of thinking about that, he had to get his homework done. He was so engrossed in his homework that he never realized anyone was in the house until someone punched him in the arm. "Ouch!"

"You better not tell Ma about the garage."

Mikie rubbed his sore arm. "I won't. Just leave me alone."

Margie walked around him and quickly punched his other arm. "You better not." Her eyes of hatred and jealousy pierced his soul.

"Ouch! I won't say anything. I promise. I'll do the dishes for you. Just leave me alone and don't tell Ma lies about me."

"You'll do dishes?" Margie raised her clenched fist as to hit him again.

Mikie pulled his fear charged body away from her and nodded his head. "Ya, I promise."

"Okay, you do dishes tonight and tomorrow night too."

"Okay." He felt relief.

"What is she doing out there?" Margie was looking out the back porch window."

"Who?" asked Mikie.

"Susie. She's digging with a shovel in her ma's flower bed. What a silly little fool. No, she's more than silly. She's stupid too."

Mikie didn't say anything. He didn't want Margie to know that he and Susie were going fishing. He was afraid that she'd ruin their plans because of her intense jealousy. Mikie didn't know why she should feel that way about him. She was the favorite in the family and got everything she wanted.

Margie turned from the window and disappeared upstairs.

Mikie hurried even more with his homework so he could get outside by Susie. They'd have fun fishing.

As he was finishing his homework, his mother came home. "Get the schoolbooks off the table. We're going to eat," she blurted out in a high-pitched tone.

"Ya, Ma." He quickly gathered his books and papers into his arms and carried them up to his bedroom.

"You hurry up and get down here and help me with supper," she yelled up the stairs after him.

"Ya, Ma, I'll be right down there."

As he set the cluttered mess in his arms down on his bed, he had a sudden, stabbing resurgence of the pain in the right side of his abdomen, below his navel. The unbearable pain hunched his body into a ball as he sank to the floor. His body felt chilled. He tried to pull the blankets from his bed to wrap his cold body in, but the pain was too intense. He lay there waiting for the pain to subside, but it didn't. He began to crawl through his doorway. He needed help. Someone stop the pain--pain--pain! Margie wasn't in her room, so he slowly crawled down the hall to the top of the stairs. Someone help stop the pain--pain--pain! "Ma," he feebly called.

There was no reply. She couldn't hear him over the sound of the sizzling-frying meat.

"Ma, Ma, help me!" he tried to yell louder.

"What's the matter with you?" his mother yelled up the stairs.

"I don't know. I have so much pain."

"Ah, just growing pains. They'll go away," replied his mother.

"He's just pretending so he can get out of doing dishes," remarked Margie.

"Doing dishes?" Her mother didn't understand the comment.

"Ya, Mikie said that he'd do dishes for me tonight and tomorrow night. In fact, he not only said he would, he promised he would."

"Mikie if you promised to do dishes for Margie than you're doing them. This pretending isn't going to get you out of your promise." His mother turned away from the stairs and went back to the stove.

"I'm not pretending, Margie. Help me, help me!" The pain twisted and tightened every muscle in his abdomen.

Margie walked up the stairs to Mikie's body crippled in pain. "You better keep your promise--or else you'll be sorrow."

"I'll keep my promise." He shivered with chills as his body sweat from the burning heat of his body's high temperature. Slowly, he unwrapped his cuddled body and stood in a hunched position. The pain had not subsided, but he decided that he had to move to get help. No one would help him here. He crawled down the stairs backwards, one step at a time. Then he crawled even slower, like a wounded dog, across the kitchen floor toward the back porch door.

"You can pretend all you want, Mikie. You're not getting out of dishes and if you continue this outrageous behavior, you'll do the dishes always. It's simply ridiculous!" said his mother.

"Ma, make him stop pretending!" shouted Margie.

"Ah, the hell with him! I'm not wasting my time on him." His mother continued cooking at the stove.

Mikie's eyes were starting to become blurred. He had to get to the door--get outside--get help. The pain was getting worse.

Outside he found himself alone. Susie was gone. He crawled down the porch steps onto the grass. He grabbed the blades of grass as he pulled his body closer to Susie's house. He only had a few porch steps to climb, than he'd find help--not from his own family--but from neighbors--friends.

Through the screen door, Susie saw him climb the stairs. "Mikie! Mikie! Ma, something is wrong with Mikie!"

Susie and her mother scurried out the door. "Get your dad, Susie, hurry up!"

Susie rushed into the house. Soon the entire family was on the porch--her mother--her father--her brother.

Noticing how he crunched his body in pain, Susie's mother asked, "Where does it hurt the most?"

"Here." Mikie showed her as his body wallowed in pain.

"Susie, go over and get Pamela. Bob, please help me put him in the car. We've got to get him to the hospital right away!"

Susie began to cry. "Ma, what's the matter with him?"

"I think he has a ruptured appendix. We don't have much time."

"Are you sure, Lillian?" asked Bob.

"I'm almost positive. My sister had the same thing. She died. We have no time to waste especially if it's ruptured, which I think it is. Hurry, and get Pamela! She has to come along. He's her child!"

While Susie ran into Mikie's house to get Pamela, Lillian and Bob carried Mikie into the car where Lillian held Mikie on her lap.

Pamela came storming out the door. "What's the matter?"

"Mikie's got to get to the hospital as soon as possible. Hurry up and get in the car! You kids stay here together until we get back." Lillian ordered the children as they came out of the house running toward the car.

Before Pamela had her car door closed, Bob was speeding out the driveway.

Susie and her brother stood there crying while Margie stood in total bewilderment.

The speeding car disappeared down the street out of sight.

****

The clouds of dust flew about the truck as it turned one corner then another traveling down the old country gravel road that was more like a snake's trail. After the next corner, he'd be there. He had taken some clean clothes along this morning when he left the house. After Murray had called, he knew it would be another night of drinking and women. Prohibition was great! It hadn't stopped him and Murray from having fun. In fact, it gave them extra money to spend on drinking and on women--prostitutes--or as Pamela would call them--harlots.

There was Murray's place nestled amongst a great stand of trees that hide the house, barn, and outbuildings from the road. It was ideal for their "other business." Secluded, no one could really see what he was doing unless they'd drive into the yard. However, no one was ever that nosey. Sig'em, seen to that. He'd bark up a storm and frightened people away. However, he didn't have to worry. The dog just wagged his tail when he saw him--Murray's good old friend.

Stopping the truck in front of the house, he opened the truck door, stepped onto the running board, and looked about as the truck swayed from the bellowing cattle moving inside the truck. He couldn't see Murray out in the fields and the closed barn door indicated he wasn't in there. There was no movement in the outbuildings either. Of course not, there was only one place he would be now.

Getting off the truck, he walked toward the outside cellar doors, opened one of them, and walked down the cement steps until he stood on the ground of the cellar floor. A familiar thumping sound was coming from a stone structure where inside the thing stood. The thing was made of copper and was heated inside the stone structure. His concern, as he entered the cellar, was that the wire was strapped across the thing's cap to keep the cap from blowing off during the cooking process. To his relief it was, and there was also rye dough paste on the cap. Next to the stone structure was a fifty-gallon barrel attached to the copper thing with a copper pipe. Attached to the other end of the copper pipe was a "copper worm." At the end of the "copper worm" was a funnel filled with hickory coals which according to Murray removed the "bardy grease." The funnel was set into a jug. There were at least seven wooden barrels scattered about the room and just as many wooden boxes filled with empty bottles. Against one wall of the house's stone foundation, set several sacks of sprouted corn.

At a wooden table, Murray sat grinding some of the sprouted corn in a cast-iron sausage mill. "Ah, hi, Otto, pretty soon now."

The thumping stopped and a gush of steam was heard--then a strong surge of liquid which quickly subsided to a trickle--then a second surge came.

"She's coming for good." Murray walked over to the barrel where the jug was now filling with a pure white liquid.

When the jug was full, Murray removed it and put another empty jug under the funnel.

Otto took the full jug and poured the liquid into one of the wooden barrels that was almost completely full of previously made liquid.

Every now and then Murray would taste the liquid. "We'll keep running her yet. I still can taste the alcohol. Seven runs--seven to ten gallons of pure corn whiskey. I'd say that I got one to one and a half gallons of whiskey from a bushel of corn. Not bad, huh, Otto."

"It's done." Murray tasted the liquid. "High shots--two hundred proof, Otto." Murray went over to a cluttered shelf, grabbed a glass tube, and a pail of water setting near one of the barrels. He added the water to the alcohol until it held a good steady bead in the glass tube, diluting with about one-third water. After diluting all the alcohol, he added drops of rye flavoring to give it a yellow tint and rye flavor.

They took the empty bottles out of the wooden boxes and filled them, corked them, and then put them back into the wooden boxes. When the boxes were full and sealed, they began to carry them out to the truck. After setting the wooden box down, which he had been carrying, Otto removed several boards from the side of his truck. The removed boards revealed a hidden compartment into which they now loaded the wooden boxes full of liquor bottles.

"You want to change your clothes now, Otto?" Murray asked as they walked back into the cellar.

"No, I'll wait until after I've got the cows unloaded at the stockyard." Otto grabbed another filled wooden box that was in the cellar.

Murray grabbed the last filled wooden box and followed Otto out to the truck. With the four wooden boxes in place, they nailed the previously removed boards back onto the side of the truck.

"Otto, you check that everything is okay in the cellar and lock the cellar up tight. Here is the key for the padlock on the cellar doors." Murray handed him a key. "I'm washing up and changing my clothes. We should be able to leave in about fifteen minutes. Grab a bottle for us to drink on the road. It'll make the hour drive seem shorter. Besides, I want to get in the mood for tonight. Booze--women--gonna be a great time, Otto!"

"Just like always," replied Otto.

Sharing the bottle of liquor, they drove to the stockyards, unloaded the cattle, and then went to a "greasy spoon" to eat. It was here that Otto cleaned up and changed into his other clothes--a dark-gray, pin striped, double-breasted suit, a white shirt, and a multicolored tie. A gray felted porkpie topped his attire.

They stayed there drinking coffee until it began to get dark. The business transaction they were about to conduct was best done in the darkness. In fact, they both found their excitement in doing things that they weren't supposed to do, and the darkness added more to the intrigue.

Leaving the "greasy spoon," they traveled down the streets with the cattle truck then turned into an alley. They traveled down the narrow alley very slowly. Sometimes the sides of the truck would scrape the sides of the tall, dark brick buildings. The alley wasn't made for a truck that size, but they knew that they'd make it through just like they had so many times before. Soon they came to a large parking area where they stopped the truck and parked it. Getting out of the truck, they walked up to a back door. They rapped a code on the door and then waited.

Soon the door opened very slowly and only as far as the inside chain on the lock would allow it. They could see one eye through the opening. "Oh, it's you, Otto--Murray." The person opened the door.

Inside they walked. "We won't be seeing Al anymore will we?" Otto remarked.

"No, I don't think he'll be stopping here on his way up North to his place anymore. They got him on income tax evasion. They couldn't get him on killing Bugs Moran's seven men, so they settled for that." The man locked the door behind them. "Got another load?"

"Ya, four boxes full," replied Otto.

"You should get a good price for that." Taking a key out of the pocket in his trousers, the man unlocked the door opposite the outside door that they had just come in through.

The open door revealed a dimly lit hallway which led to another door. "See you two later on." The man closed the door behind them and locked it.

In a few seconds, they opened the other door into a crowded room filled with a mixture of sounds all melted together making one big noise. There was a band playing--women with uncovered breasts and G-strings covering their shaved genitals dancing on the huge mahogany bar--drunken men cluttered at the bar grabbing at the dancers and shouting. Otto and Murray smiled at each other. After their business, they'd be right up there with those other men. With that lascivious attitude, they pushed through the shouting crowds at the blackjack, craps, and poker tables.

"Would you like a drink?" asked one of the barmaids who was carrying a tray of drinks and dressed in nothing more than a glittering black swimsuit.

"Sure, sweetheart." Otto grabbed a drink off the tray, put his arms around her waist, and pulled her close to him. "You miss me?"

"Sure did." She rubbed her hand over the flap that covered his zippered suit trousers. "See you later." She winked and threw him a kiss as she started to move through the crowd with her tray of drinks.

Otto took a drink of liquor from his glass as he watched her provocative, "hour glass" body shape wiggle flirtatiously through the crowd. Her long blonde hair cascaded over her bare back and rounded, smooth shoulders. He'd snicker with lust when he saw some of the men rub their hands over her buttock or deliberately rub up against her large breasts. In a few hours, he'd have that sexy, hot body in his arms and wrapped around his body. Otto finished his drink, walked up to the bar, and motioned the bartender to come over by him.

As the bartender approached, he nodded his head at Otto.

Otto returned the nod. It was their usual signal.

As the bartender walked out from behind the bar, he stopped beside Otto and spoke softly, "I'll meet you outside. You parked near the basement door?"

Otto nodded. "The same as before?"

"Okay, let's go." The bartender left the room.

Otto walked back to the red leather booth where Murray had sat when Otto went up to the bar. Murray was intensely kissing a brunette as his chubby hands moved about her sensual body like an octopus.

"Come on, Murray. They'll be plenty of time for that later on. Business first--then you'll have money to buy any kind of fun you want." Otto pulled him up.

They left the building through a different door than they had come in through. Nevertheless, the exit was guarded with as much security as the entrance was.

Once outside, they waited for the basement door to open. When it did, the bartender and four other big, muscular guys came out. The four other guys went up to the end of the alley with their guns in their suits ready for quick use. They guarded the parking lot with keen ears and alert eyes that watched the street and the tops of buildings.

Otto, Murray, and the bartender quickly removed the boxes from their hidden compartment and carried them into the basement. When the last box was unloaded, the bartender whistled to get the four guys attention, and then motioned them to come back into the basement. In the basement, the bartender took a claw-head hammer and pulled the wooden covers off all four boxes. He examined several bottles to ensure they were all full. Pulling off the cork of one of the bottles, he tasted the liquor. "Good stuff, guys--really good stuff." Putting the bottle down, he reached into the back pocket of his trousers and pulled out a leather wallet. He counted out numerous fifty dollar bills to Otto and Murray.

"See you in a couple of weeks again." Otto put the money inside his wallet.

"At this point, Otto, I don't know what's going to be happening in a couple of weeks. A lot of people want to repeal the eighteenth amendment and enact the twenty-first amendment. They all know they can't enforce prohibition. Young or old, we all like breaking that law. Hoover doesn't like to repeal, and I don't either. My reason is different from his. The money won't be there if prohibition is over."

"Not only that--what we gonna do for excitement?" Murray chuckled.

"Come on, let's get out of here and go where the excitement is now. We'll worry about that tomorrow." As the bartender started to walk up the stairs, they all followed.

Otto's and Murray's bulging wallets bought them lots of companionship. The dancers on the bar would come off the bar and dance in front of them. They would wrap their half nude bodies of soft flesh around their masculine physiques and rub their bodies erotically against their bodies. The barmaids would patronize them and convince them to buy them drinks. They would gamble with Otto's and Murray's money. They'd persuade Otto and Murray to gamble and continue to gamble even though the odds of winning were against them. Booze--women--more booze--more women! Their speech slurred. They stumbled forwards, then backwards. Their bodies swayed. They were like limp puppets on a string. The dancers and barmaids dangled them anyway that they wanted. Judgement was eradicated. More booze--more women--more booze--more woman--

"Otto, you have money for me yet?" the blonde woman he had seen earlier asked.

With his body swaying, he fumbled his hand trying to remove his wallet from his pocket. Rocking back and forth with an unsteady balance, he slowly opened his wallet revealing the money inside. "Yup--I still have some--for you, sweetheart." He put his arm around her shoulder to help him stand without falling. With his glassy eyes viewing her exposed breasts, he rolled his hand over and over their softness.

She grabbed the wallet out of his other hand and thumbed through the green dollar bills inside. "This surely is enough, Otto." She took the money out, removed his hand from her breasts, and stuck the money into her cleavage.

"Do you two want some more drinks?" the blonde asked.

"Ya, get us another one before we leave." Murray handed her their empty glasses.

The blonde put the empty glasses on the tray and went up to the bar where she was joined by the brunette that had been with Murray. "I hope you took enough money to make up for having to look at that pitted face when you're in bed with him later on."

The blonde snickered. "I close my eyes then he's just like any other 'john.' "

"Guess we can't have it all. Otto's got a great body but his face is something to be desired. Whereas, Murray's got a damn good-looking face but that gut on him--oh well, their money's good."

****

He stood still gazing at the cold bronzed-colored coffin. He couldn't seem to rationalize that she was lying in there--so still--so cold--so lifeless--so far out of reach from him--gone forever! How could he live without her? Twenty years they were together. They had worked side by side from sunrise to sunset. They were constant companions--went every Sunday to church together--community gatherings together--went shopping together. They had been inseparable--until now. And so he wept his tears of grief. He didn't care if perhaps it didn't seem "manly." She was gone, and his heart and soul were drowning in an endless despair. He wiped away the tears that flowed down his face. Slowly, he moved closer to the coffin. He reached into the coffin and touched her cold hands--hands that had worked so hard all her life--hands that he had held when they had walked--hands that had held him with love--hands that had nurtured their children--hands that were now cold and lifeless--hands that were forever gone. Oh! How could this be? It was his fault! If only he had listened to her and let her do what she wanted to do that day. No, instead he had to do things his way. Oh, God! Let him go back! Let him go back! Let her be alive, God! This couldn't have happened. He collapsed onto the kneeler that was set in front of the coffin. He rested his arms on the top of the kneeler, lowered his head onto his arms, and cried, "Oh God, take back the days of this unrealness. Let me go back and do things differently so this would never happen. Oh, God! Please!"

In the back of the funeral home the two girls stood and whispered, so he couldn't hear their conversation as he knelt by her coffin. For him to hear such talk would have torn his heart out completely.

"I don't know why he had to buy her a new dress. It's just going to rot in the grave with her."

"How can you say that--sob--sob--? She worked hard all her life and never really ever bought anything for herself and now you would deny her a new dress for her own funeral--sob--sob--sob--sob--. My God! What kind of a person are you?"

"I'm obviously the only person around here with any common sense. I would have gotten more out of new dress than her. Then there is the meal after the funeral! Every freeloader from miles around will come for the free meal. Some more money spent foolishly! I think the old man is going crazy! I seriously think we should have someone assigned to his assets, so he doesn't squander them all away now that she isn't around to watch out for them."

"How can you--sob--sob--sob--be so heartless--sob--sob--? She is our mother--sob--sob--sob--and all you can think of is money--sob--sob--sob." She wiped her eyes now red from crying and blew her nose.

"I'm realistic. Ma worked hard so we could have something--not so he could be so stupid and buy her a new dress that is only going to rot. Ma never seen the dress. Why not bury her in something that was really hers? Then to have a free meal for people who probably never liked her. How stupid! Simply Stupid!"

"How cold you are--sob--sob--sob--. Doesn't it make you sad to know that she's gone--sob--sob--sob?" Her hands shook and she felt her legs tremble with weakness. She loved her mother so much. She couldn't cope at this minute with her sister's uncaring attitude toward their mother. Her sister's words had multiplied her grief, a grief that had drained her body and soul. Her fragile body could barely support itself, but she was determined to join her father at the side of the coffin. When she reached him, she put her hand on his shoulder.

Her father raised his head and touched her hand. She knelt beside him, and they held each other's hand with the little strength that they both had left.

When they had finished their prayers, they both rose from the kneeler. Her father put his arm around her and helped her to the chair where they were to sit to greet the people that would come and offer, in respect, their "deepest sympathy."

It was a long, depressing time, the next four hours as neighbors and friends came one by one to "pay their last respect." It always was the worst when the best friends came. The tears became uncontrollable at that time. Even Lucy cried, but were her tears real? Lori didn't think so, but there were more important things on Lori's mind. She found it very hard to accept what was truly going on. It was like a bad dream where things were floating by in the air. Like things were really happening but not to her--not here. She was in a haze. At this time of day they were milking the cows--her father--her mother--herself--and Lucy--but no more. She'd never be there again--to talk to as she sat between the cows, milking them. Now it would just be her father, Lucy and herself--for a little while.

"How are you doing, Lucy?" A tall, impressively virile man sat next to her and held her hand so gently with the only hand he had.

"I'm okay, thanks," replied Lucy.

He bent over in front of Lucy and Lori to address their father, "The chores are all done."

"Thanks, I do appreciate your help." Pete's voice was laden with sadness.

"No problem. You all were good to me. You're fine people. I'm glad that I could help in this little way," the young man spoke softly.

"She was so looking forward to the wedding." With that Pete broke down in tears. There was no one in the funeral parlor so he went outside to get away from it all.

"I'm going outside by your dad." The virile man left his seat beside Lucy and departed.

Once the man was out of sight, Lori asked, "You and Alex aren't still going to get married next Saturday, are you?"

"Why not?"

"Because it's so soon after Ma's death. Out of respect to Ma I think you should wait."

"Lori, be realistic! Everything is planned for next Saturday."

"Everything is at the Stoner's. I'm sure they wouldn't have a problem postponing things, considering the circumstances."

"I don't care if the Stoner's don't have a problem. I don't want it postponed because the day I'm married I get to choose the farm I want as a wedding present. I want the farm Dad and Ma always referred to as 'the old McCullough farm.' I've wanted that farm every since the day they bought it, and I'm not waiting any longer."

"I just don't believe you." Lori shook her head. She just couldn't tolerate being in the same room much less sitting beside her own sister. She had to leave. Getting up, she joined her father and Alex outside.

There they all stood in silence. Lori had her arm around her father consoling him. Alex was holding a cigarette in his only hand and leisurely puffing on it--slowly drawing on it and then slowly exhaling the smoke out through his mouth.

The silence was broken by an old man's voice. "My deepest sympathy, Pete." The old man extended his crippled, aged hand.

"Thanks, Karl."

"My deepest sympathy to you, Lori."

"Thank you, Mr. Ewerdt."

"I hated to see you leave the mill when you went to work for her, but I'd say that's the best thing that ever happened to both of you." Karl patted Pete on the back. "The sad part is the loss, but the best part is that you loved. I regret never loving. It's a sadness worst than death. It's a lucky man who can love." He touched Pete's hand one more time then turned away. He was old man who grew up with the ideology--men don't cry--and if they do--no one must see. So he left with the deep sadness of his lonely life--known only to him.

He was the last of the parade of people that had come that evening to the funeral home. The sun had set with its yellow and red hues spread across the horizon. The trees stood black against it as did the houses and shops of the town. It was time to leave and go home to rest for tomorrow. Tomorrow would be the verifier--when the coffin would be closed and put into the ground.

Lori went home with her father. Lucy drove with Alex, who would spend the night, so he could help them with the morning chores on the three farms. Church services were at ten o'clock, so every helping hand was needed to feed and milk the animals before the church services began. Alex would be taking Amy's place.

Alex lay on the living room sofa. Before he fell asleep, he couldn't keep from shedding a few tears. He was going to miss her. She had been so kind to him even before he started dating Lucy. Since he had been dating Lucy, she had treated him like a son.

Upstairs Lucy lay in her bed and thought of her wedding day. She thought of the farm that she would be receiving and how rich she would be after the wedding. She had wanted Alex for herself and had pursued him to this end result. It was easy getting Alex for herself. The other girls hadn't wanted anything to do with him because he lacked a right hand and also because of the rumor that went along with how he had lost that hand. However, Lucy had looked beyond that--beyond love. She had looked to the practical side. Since Frederick had adopted Alex, he was a Stoner and as such, Alex was entitled to the Stoner wealth. After the wedding she'd not only be closer to that wealth, she'd also have one of the most prominent names in the county. Alex didn't have very many friends but Frederick and Charles, being bankers, did. She had heard some of the names that were coming to the wedding. Oh, there were going to be many prominent, wealthy people there, and she'd get to know them all. She'd be friends with them all. She'd socialize with the important people and be rich like them. How wonderful to have money! With such thoughts, she fell asleep with a most pleasant smile on her face.

Lori, weakened from days of the grief that had consumed her, fell asleep only to be haunted with dreams filled with the visions of things that had happened that day. She had been hanging some washed clothes on the clothesline, when she looked up into the field and seen the accident happen. Dropping the clothes onto the ground, she sped out into the field. When she neared where her mother lay, her father stopped her in her tracks and pulled her close to him to hide the scene from her. However, she had seen it and would never forget. Her mother's eyes were wide open--motionless--with an intent gaze. Blood was slowly leaking from the side of her open mouth. Blood dripped from her ears. Her smashed body was covered with fragments of mud, corn, and blood. Lori awoke shaking and crying--afraid to sleep anymore. But her body would not stay awake, so she slept again only to have the visions reappear and reappear all through the night.

In the privacy of what was once "their room," he sat on the edge of the bed with his arms resting in his lap. For Pete the worst had come now. In the still of the night--the loneliness--the emptiness-- showed its true meaning. Great mental pain came from knowing her death could have been prevented if only he would have listened to her. If only, she would have been driving and he would have sat where she did then he would be dead. It would have been better that way. Amy was a good person; she deserved to live more than he did.

In his mind he relived that day--their last day together. Dark, ragged clouds had layered the sky that morning as the rain lingered on until midmorning. Figuring the fields were too wet to go into with a tractor and wagon, Amy had wanted to do some work in the house. However, Pete was determined to haul another wagon of green cornstalks into the pasture for the cows to eat. As the clouds began to scatter and the sun revealed itself, he convinced her to go with him. With a hand sickle, they chopped the green cornstalks from their roots and threw them onto the flat, wooden wagon. When the wagon was full, he climbed up onto the tractor seat. "Come on up, Amy," he had said as he held his hand out to her to help her climb up beside him. "No, I think I'll walk until we're at the bottom of the hill," she had replied. "Come on, Amy. I'll go slow." Hesitantly, she grabbed his hand and climbed next to him. She clutched her hands to the back of the metal fender that covered the iron, back wheel of the tractor. Pete started the tractor and proceeded down the hill slowly. About halfway down the hill, one of the tractor's back wheels slid into a gully made by the torrential summer rains that had eroded that part of the cornfield. The tractor's sudden tip into the gully caused Amy to lose her balance and fall forward into the path of the huge back tractor wheel. Instinctively, Pete grabbed for her, but he wasn't fast enough. He felt the tractor wheel roll over her body. Before he could get the tractor stopped, he also felt the front wheel of the wagon roll over her body. When he finally stopped the tractor, he jumped from it. He was praying and hoping for a miracle, but it wasn't a day for miracles. He saw her body, pulled it from under the wagon and held it close. He cried. He knew. She was gone. She hadn't wanted to ride on the tractor--if only he would have listened to her.

Unable to sleep, he went to sit outside on the front porch swing. The September night was full of the sounds of the night--crickets--owls. The full moon shone on the cows lying in the pasture. He and Amy had worked so hard--lived so simply--for what? All the money--all the farms they owned didn't stop death from knocking at their door. He would give it all to God if he'd give her back to him. He'd do things so differently. They'd sit more on this porch swing and enjoy the summer nights. Instead of working till dark to get all the work done--so they could earn more money--save more money--buy another farm--work some more--earn more money--save more money--buy another farm--earn more money--money--money. What a "merry-go-round" they had made of their life all for the sake of the "almighty dollar." She was gone and it all meant nothing!

Sometime during the night he must have fallen asleep outside on the swing because the next thing he knew someone was shaking his shoulder. "Are you okay, Dad?"

With his eyes still full of sleepiness, he grabbed the person's hand never wanting to let go. "Amy, it's you--I knew it couldn't be true--you are alive."

"It's all right, Dad." The person lovingly touched his hand.

"Oh, it's my Lori."

"I'm sorry, Dad."

"No, I'm glad it's you. You look so much like your mother." He rose from the swing and hugged her as she returned his hug.

"I suppose we should get started on chores so we get done on time." Her voice cracked as she felt herself start to cry.

"Oh, my Lori, it isn't worth all this. All my life I let things that I really wanted go for the sake of making money or having enough money before I did anything. Things had to be always right regarding money. I couldn't do this until there was enough money--money excuse for this--money excuse for that. Now I've got the money and she's gone. What good is it without her? I didn't learn from my first mistake and now I've made the mistake again." His eyes became red and watery. "Always the damn money!"

"Dad, maybe you should sell one of the farms and enjoy life," Lori suggested.

"What kinds of foolishness are you telling Dad." A voice came out the door and onto the wooden porch.

"Good morning, Lucy, I'm just thinking maybe Dad shouldn't work so hard anymore."

"If he doesn't mind, why should you? Besides, what is he going to do if he doesn't have the farms?"

"Let's get our chores started." Lori didn't want to argue again with Lucy. Every time she had suggested that their parents retire and sell one of the farms so they could enjoy life and not work so hard, Lucy would respond negatively. Besides, this was hardly the time to be arguing. Lori was drained with grief. The little energy that she had would be needed for more important things.

"I still have my suit on from last night. I better change." As he reached for the door, it opened.

"Good morning," said Alex as he walked past Pete over to Lucy.

"Good morning, Alex." Pete went into the house and closed the door.

Alex grabbed Lucy's hand. "Come let's get going to the other farms so we get done. Once the young stock is taken care of at those farms, then we can come back here and help them finish milking."

Lucy pulled free of his hand. "Why don't you go and start the car? I'll be there in a few minutes." She waited until Alex was out of hearing distance. "You keep your foolish ideas to yourself. Dad's going to need watching and I'm the one who is going to do it. So bud out!" She turned and ran down the wooden porch steps and across the dew-covered lawn to where Alex waited in his car.

Lori cried. Her poor father would never have any time to enjoy his life. He'd die of work just like her mother. Lori had no one to talk things over with now. Her best friend--her mother--was gone. Lucy and her were never close. Lucy never had time for her. Everything was the way Lucy wanted it. Lori learnt not to argue. Lucy always got her way. In a way, Lucy was like their father. Money was important to her. She did work hard, but she'd prefer to manipulate for it--even steal. Lori never told and no one else knew, but that's how Lucy often got things. In that way, Lucy was different from their father. He had worked for every penny that he had. Being honest and for people to consider him an honest person was always very important to their father. He always preached honesty, but some how when it came to Lucy that message fell on deaf ears. If he would know about her, it would break his heart.

As Lucy and Alex drove down the road to the farm that Amy had owned before she married Pete, Lori started to walk toward the barn. The cows were already lined up in front of the barn door waiting to get inside to be milked.

They all scurried to get the farm chores finished before the funeral Mass. With so much work to do, the time went fast and there was very little time to think until the Mass. However, once at the Mass, that's all a person did was--think--remember--regret--cry.

Lucy cried, but Lori knew that those tears only came at convenient times. The tears served a purpose. Alex would cuddle her and people would see what a "loving daughter" she was. When Lucy almost fainted and Alex had to carry her out of church into the fresh air, the people whispered, "Oh, that poor girl." As the words fell upon Lori's ears, she thought, that "poor girl" was a good actress.

After the funeral Mass and meal, Alex drove them home and then left. Lori and her father sat outside on the porch swing that creaked with the rhythmical, slow movement of the swing. There was work to be done but neither thought anything was really worthwhile anymore.

Their sad silence of despair--loneliness--was broken by sounds of someone rambling about inside the house. Since there was no one else around, it had to be Lucy.

Curiosity beckoned Lori to investigate. The sounds were coming from her parents' bedroom. Upon entering the doorway of the bedroom, she saw Lucy taking their mother's clothes out of the closet and dresser and putting them into a cardboard box setting on the bed.

"What are you doing, Lucy?" Lori entered the room and stood beside the bed.

"I talked to Mrs. Erickson about the possibility of selling some of Ma's things. She told me that because some people are having a hard time, they are buying nice used clothes instead of the expensive new clothes. She said she'd be glad to sell the things for us." Lucy continued to fold things into the box.

"Stop it right now!" Lori shouted in a voice that cracked from crying and pulled the dress from Lucy's hand. "You're not selling any of Ma's dresses." She caressed the dress to her body.

"Don't be ridiculous! What use do we have for Ma's clothes? Ma was a big woman. We'll never fit into her clothes." She grabbed the dress from Lori's hand and folded it into the box.

"I want to make a heirloom quilt out of her dresses just like Ma made from the clothes that we grew out of when we were small."

"The more they lay around, the more Dad will see them and be reminded of Ma." Lucy grabbed another dress from the closet.

"No, I won't let you sell her things." Lori grabbed the dress.

"Get out of here." Lucy again pulled the dress from Lori's hand and gave her a shove. She looked up and stood still, staring at the door entrance.

Lori turned to see what she was staring at.

There in the doorway stood their father. His eyes told of the sadness in his heart of hearing such a conversation between his children--Amy's children. He lowered his head, turned, and walked slowly away. His heart bled with agony. Their daughters were fighting over their dead ma's things. She wasn't even in the ground a day. A parent raises children--sacrifices for the children--and all a parent wants in return is love. Is that too much to ask especially when a parent had given them life? No, life is never enough! The children want more! All during a parent's life the children think their parent owes them more. The parent will give them more and all the parent wants is love. Just love! Guess that was too much for Amy and him to ask for. What did they do wrong?

****

The sky-blue chiffon dress flowed along her body curves as she walked into the immense room made of shining hardwood floors and decorative wood walls. She stopped in the middle of the room and marveled at the grandeur of the room. It was furnished with the best carved and upholstered furniture money could buy. Her husband always bought only the best--for the house--for her--for the children. She often wondered if he did things out of love or did a sense of guilt prevail over his kind deeds. Well, today was not the day or time to rehash such thoughts. She walked over to the French doors draped in, of course, the best satin curtains money could buy. She opened the doors and stepped out onto the terrace. She admired the beautiful flowers that adorned the terrace, the sides of the house, and that were scattered about in flower beds on the lawn. Just two days ago she was so concerned about a hard frost killing all the flowers before today. Her fears were unfounded, for now, the blue ageratum, red salvias, yellow marigolds, and bronze and purple mums all accented each other. In addition, the trees were starting to dress in their autumn coat--some yellow--red--orange leaves intruded amongst the green. She took a deep breath in satisfaction of mother nature's exquisite beauty. She enjoyed planting and taking care of the flowers as well as the vegetable garden. It filled her days now that the children were older and didn't demand so much of her time. They still needed her, but not in the way they did when they were smaller and sometimes that part of them growing up was sad. Her oldest was leaving this place today--going on his own with his wife. Her baby had started high school this fall, and in a short time she'd probably be leaving also.

From the terrace she could see her husband talking to her. She remembered the first time that her husband had introduced her as his cousin. She was so impressed with his cousin's charming smile and her elegant clothing. She had worn a navy blue hat with a big rim that she had tilted to one side on her black hair. Her color co-ordinated, navy blue dress was accented with a belt that fit ever so trimly at her waist. The matching gloves extended to her elbows. Resting on her shoulders was a mink stole. She was so exquisite--just like a queen! After that first meeting, the cousin would come to the house to visit her husband several times a year.

At first she was puzzled at her father-in-law's coldness toward the cousin and how quiet her father-in-law was when her husband was in his presence. However, one afternoon she found out the reason for her father-in-law's unexplained reactions. She had gone to visit her mother. However, when she arrived, she found that her mother wasn't at home. Upon returning home, she heard voices upstairs. This was surprising--it wasn't the cleaning lady's day--the children had gone to school--her husband was at work. Perplexed, she curiously moved up the varnished, wooden open staircase toward the voices. As she approached the bedroom, where the voices were coming from, she recognized one voice. It was her husband's. Further movement toward the room revealed that the woman was obviously not a cousin but a very willing bed partner.

She never confronted her husband. He never knew that she was aware of the truth. She was afraid if she mentioned what she had seen that he might make a choice. Her greatest fear was that he wouldn't choose her. She couldn't take the chance of him leaving her. She didn't want to raise the children alone. She had started to raise one child alone. When he married her, she found having a complete family was so wonderful. She didn't want to lose that. So she kept her silence when he ventured off on some weekends by himself to New York. He told her that he needed the excitement of the city occasionally; otherwise, he could never stay in such a quiet place like Beechwood. She couldn't criticize him. He had given that life up when he married her. She also considered that perhaps she had driven him into the arms of someone else. She wasn't a very good wife in the bedroom. She found sex physically uncomfortable; her husband had probably sensed that.

He was a good husband. He treated her with kindness and gentleness. After being married several years, it was his idea to adopt her son. He loved the boy and was a good father and friend to him. At night after work, they'd go to the little league baseball games, or sometimes they'd like the solitude of fishing. In winter they'd play cards, checkers, or go ice fishing together. He had given the boy his first job, which he'd be leaving now to work with his wife. Earlier, during the wedding ceremony she had caught a glimpse of a few tears in her husband's eyes. The boy was growing away and her husband felt sad about that. Maybe it wasn't right, his adultery, but she could and did overlook that. There were more important things--the happiness that as a family they all shared, the children loved him, and she loved him. So she'd smile, be happy, keep her silence, and know that even if he went to bed with that woman, he always came back to her. He was her husband, and he obviously wanted to remain that.

"Your flowers are beautiful, Amanda." A hand gently touched her shoulder.

"Thanks, Ma." She turned and smiled at her. "It simply amazes me how you design that long scarf about your neck to hide that scar and still look so elegant. Actually, I think it's the long flowing scarf that adds the elegance."

"The scar is unattractive, but I'm glad I'm alive. If I wouldn't have had the goiter surgery--who knows--maybe I wouldn't be here."

"We can thank Charles for that." Amanda hugged her mother.

"Ya, he really got upset with me didn't he?" replied Anna.

"Well, your life was threatened. All you were concerned about was the cost of the surgery and how you could never pay for it."

"He's a good man. He paid for it all."

"He loved you, even way back then, but you could never see it. You were too blinded with your loyalty to Dad." Amanda paused and looked in the direction of her husband and the woman. "Does everyone know? Is everyone laughing at me, the stupid wife?"

Anna grabbed her hand. "No one knows--except that she is his cousin. Charles and I know the truth, but no one else does."

"How can you be so sure?"

"Charles gets around and comes in contact with a lot of people, and he's never mentioned that anyone has ever questioned Frederick's story. Frederick is very discreet. All they do in public is talk like they are now and if you ever notice there isn't that 'loving gleam' in his eyes when he talks to her or is with her. His eyes are cold. He's just using her for one thing."

"All these years? Why would a beautiful woman be satisfied with only that?"

Anna shrugged her shoulders. "Maybe that's all she wants. Maybe she thinks something is better than nothing."

"So this is where you two are?" Charles stood in the doorway, dressed in a black pin striped tuxedo, black bow tie, and white shirt. "The guests are all here and the cooks would like to start to serve the meal in the dining area." With his usual mannerly style, he stepped to the side of the doorway and motioned for them to enter the room in front of him.

As they entered the dining area, a voice called, "Ma, Ma, wait for me." A young woman, dressed in a brilliant rose-colored dress, which outlined her svelte, young figure, came moving buoyantly through the crowd of eminent guests.

Amanda stopped and waited for her. "Rosalia, you sit with us."

"Oh, Ma, isn't Lucy just so beautiful!" Rosalia's blue eyes gleamed with a gentle charm when she saw Lucy and Alex sitting together at their wedding table.

"Yes, she is and so are you." Amanda fussed with Rosalia's shoulder length, blonde curls that framed her small, round face.

"Where is Dad?" Rosalia surveyed the room.

"He's out there with his cousin, Jackie." Amanda motioned in the direction where he was still talking to Jackie. "Maybe you should tell them that dinner is served. Do you mind?"

"No, I'll go." With adolescence energy, she bounced outside to where her ma had pointed her dad out to her.

"Hi, Dad, dinner is being served." Her peach complexion face radiated with a brilliant smile as she grabbed her father's hand.

"Thanks, Rosalia, you go join your ma at the table. I'll be there in a minute."

"Okay, Dad." Rosalia let go of his hand and went back into the dining area.

"So you'll be leaving right after dinner?" Frederick questioned her.

"Yes, I'd like to stay longer but that's the latest train back to New York until Monday morning. I can't stay that long. I've got an important business meeting early Monday morning." She watched Rosalia walk into the dining area. "She's thirteen now. When are you leaving?" She turned to look at Frederick.

"I've changed my mind. I'm not leaving until she's married. I'm staying to make sure that if she needs me, I'll be here for her. She's my 'little girl.' I want to walk her down the aisle and make sure that the guy I give her to, will love her and treat her good. After she's married, she won't need me to look after her." A trace of a sentimental tear filled his eyes.

Jackie raised her eyebrows in disapproval. "First you said, 'when she's in grade school'--then you said, 'when she's thirteen'--now you're saying, 'when she's married'! Will you ever really leave?"

"Yes, Jackie, I will, but the time is not right. When it's right, I'll leave," Frederick spoke reassuringly.

Jackie turned from him, took a few steps toward the door, paused, and then turned to look at him again. "I'll see you in two weeks?"

"Yes, that would be best."

He and Jackie separated as they entered the dining area. Frederick sat on the side of the table designated for Alex's family--Charles, Anna, Amanda, Rosalia, and himself. Jackie sat on one of the tables designated for distant family relatives and friends. After dinner Frederick became so involved in socializing with the other guests that he never noticed Jackie had left until he began to look for her.

"What's the matter, Charles?" Anna asked as she joined him on the terrace where he had stood in solitude for the longest time--so quiet--so withdrawn. It was not like him to be that way. He always enjoyed parties. In fact, he had invited many of his old friends just so he could visit with them. Instead, Anna had noticed quite a contrary attitude from him all day. As his eyes looked at hers, she could see the sadness that they projected.

"I'm afraid, Anna. I've never been so afraid in all my life." He grabbed for her hand and held it tightly.

"What has gotten you so upset?" She placed her hand on top of his hand that was now holding hers.

"The 'deposit demands' that are taking place lately. So many banks have failed."

"Is there a chance your bank could fail?"

"I'm afraid, Anna, so afraid. What if we lose everything?"

"Charles, there are worst things that can happen. If it happens then we start over--together."

"Oh, my Anna, I do love you." He pulled her close to him and held her so gently in his arms. "Things aren't that simple. What about Frederick, Amanda, and Rosalia?"

"Problems at the bank could be so serious as to affect them?"

"I've let Frederick do a lot of things at the bank that I would have never done. I didn't say too much because I had been trying to convince him to come back here to live for so long. When he finally agreed to do it, I didn't want to question his actions for fear that he'd leave again. This time I'd also lose Amanda and the children."

"Charles, you are probably worrying about something that will never happen."

He didn't reply, just held her close.

She could feel his body tremble.

Chapter 14
****
Deadly Accident

Through the open window, which let in the crisp air of early morning, the loud noise of a door slamming also flowed through. Half asleep, she slowly raised her head from the soft, white feather pillow and looked at the time on the alarm clock. Ah! It was only eight o'clock. She had just gotten to bed a few hours ago. Tired and not wanting to leave the comfort of the bed, which she had all to herself now, she positioned her head snugly back into the pillow. She pulled the dark-colored blanket over her head to block out the sunlight that filtered itself through the closed curtains. In the quiet of the room, she could now hear the sound of a radio playing outside. She wrapped the pillow around her head to keep the sound from entering her ears so she could fall asleep again. With her eyes closed, she lay there. Her mind filled with a million things to do. Things that she would never get done if she continued lying in bed. Since she found it impossible to get back to sleep, she decided to get up. Walking over to the window, which faced the garage, she peeked through the crack that had formed where the two curtains met.

A cattle truck was parked in front of the garage. The truck's hood was open and a body of a man was bent over the fender as he was examining the truck's engine. She could tell it wasn't her husband, Otto. Therefore, it must be the new driver and mechanic Otto had hired several days ago. Otto had achieved the dreams that he had first talked about so many years ago when they were first married. His trucking business was constantly growing.

Otto and she got along really well now. They hardly saw each other anymore--except on Sundays, and that time together was short. After going to church as a family--for appearance sake--they'd each go their separate way. Otto would socialize with his customers either by drinking in the Beechwood taverns or by going to the local baseball games. If the church required his assistance, he'd help. It was good for his business to help in church activities.

Sundays were different for Pamela. She'd use the time on Sunday to get the work done that she couldn't get done during the week because of her full-time job outside the home. The local shoe factory had started a second shift and she was on it. In addition to this new responsibility, she had kept her old one's as well--mowing the lawn, keeping a garden to supply them with all their food for summer as well as winter, which meant canning, and of course, doing the regular household chores of laundering, cooking, and keeping the house clean. To follow Otto's example, she was also active in the church.

RING! RING! RING!

She went out into the kitchen to answer the phone.

"Hello." While she listened, she looked at a schedule Otto had set on his desk. "Just a minute, please." She grabbed a pencil off the desk and jotted a name in one of the empty spaces on the schedule. "Okay, Alex, I have you written down for two calves on Tuesday. Is there a special time that you would like them picked up?--Thanks, good-bye." She paged through the schedule. "Hum. He's working on Saturday again. He must be going to Jennings. Milwaukee isn't open on Saturday. He'll need another truck and driver by next year."

She looked about the house. A lot of her dreams had come true also, at least the materialistic ones. She had a beautiful home with nice furnishings but there was something missing. She felt an emptiness in her heart. She filled that void by working. The money was nice because it gave her the freedom to buy what she wanted, but her job wasn't for purely a financial purpose anymore. She had it because for her there was nothing else. She and Otto had drifted so far apart. There was no hope for them anymore. Their marriage was like everything else--for appearance sake.

KNOCK! KNOCK! Someone was at the door?

She scurried into the bedroom and tossed on her housecoat.

KNOCK! KNOCK!

"Just a minute, I'm coming." Looking in the mirror of her dressing table, she quickly brushed through her disorderly hair. "Oh, good enough!" She tossed the hairbrush onto the oak dressing table.

KNOCK! KNOCK!

"Some people can't hear! I said I'm coming," she mumbled under her breath. She opened the door. Her eyes widened with disbelief.

"Hi, Pamela, good to see you again."

"What are you doing here?" His presence made her self-conscious of her appearance. She fussed a bit with her hair. He surely wouldn't think that she was beautiful now. Oh, he probably never did. They were "just words" to make an old woman feel good.

"I work for your husband."

"I didn't see you yesterday or the day before."

"When I came in the morning, you were still asleep. I spent yesterday and the day before on the road with Otto. At night, when we came back here, you had already gone to work."

"What can I do for you?"

"Just wanted to see you again."

"Ya, sure! What kind of a game are you playing?"

"I don't play games, Pamela."

"Well, you better get back to work. My husband isn't paying you to talk to me."

"No one would ever have to pay me to do that." He started to walk away and then turned around. "See you later, Pamela."

As she watched him walk away, she felt a strong physical attraction for him. Closing the door, she went into the bedroom. She dressed in one of her prettier dresses, combed her hair, and put make-up on. If he came to the house again, she wanted to look attractive. While doing her household chores, she'd often discreetly stare out the window at him. She started to imagine him coming into the house, lifting her into his strong arms, and carrying her into the bedroom where he'd lay her on the bed. Then he'd lay with her and make love to her. It was so long. She didn't know what it was like anymore to be made love to. Oh, how silly of her! She was married and he was just a young guy teasing an old woman. It was time that she came back to the real world. She had fantasized away most of the day, and now it was time to go to work at the factory.

HONK! HONK!

There was Lillian waiting in the driveway for her. Pamela flew out the front door and scurried into the car. As Lillian backed her car out of the driveway, Pamela looked toward the backyard to see if she could see the young guy. She couldn't. The side of the house blocked her view of the garage and truck.

During their fifteen minute drive to work, Lillian talked about what she had done during the day. Pamela sat still and quiet. Lillian probably thought Pamela was a good listener. But in fact, Pamela was thinking of the young guy, Tony.

They arrived early so they got a parking place close to the factory. As they walked through the factory door, the familiar smell of leather and the rat-tat-tat of the sewing machines welcomed them. Women were sitting at machines with huge spools of thread rising above the machine. The woman hurriedly sewed one piece of leather together with another. The completed piece was put into one bag while they grabbed two new pieces out of two other bags. They worked with mechanical speed. Moving like programmed robots, they did the same thing over and over and faster and faster and faster.

Pamela was glad that she was the "floor lady." She didn't have to sit at a machine hour after hour doing the same thing over and over. Her job was to keep the women at the machines supplied with bags of leather parts that needed to be sewed and remove the bags of sewed leather parts that the women had completed.

While Pamela watched the women work, Lillian walked over to a cork board tacked full of little white pieces of paper. "Pamela, come here and look at this." She examined one piece of paper after another.

"What's the matter?" Pamela walked over to the board.

"Job postings for the day shift. I'm putting in for this one." Lillian grabbed a piece of paper off the board. "Pamela, grab one."

"No, I don't think I want to go on days--not right now."

"Well, I'm not missing out on this chance. Bob, the kids, and I would be together at night like a family again. With the kids in school, I don't get to see them anymore, except on weekends. It's the same with Bob. He's getting up and I'm going to bed."

"If I go on the day shift, there won't be anyone to answer the phone during the day for Otto's business."

"Oh, Pamela, you're always thinking of helping Otto. Think of yourself and how nice it would be to see your family more. I'm going to the office now before there are too many people in there. You better grab a posting quick or else you won't get any." Lillian disappeared into the office.

For Lillian it was the best thing but not for her--no not for Pamela. Seeing Otto more would mean going back to a life filled with threats--fights--and more fights. No, things were best the way they were. Besides, she got more work done during the day when she worked on the second shift, so it would stay that way.

Pamela punched in her timecard and went to sit in the lunchroom until the "buzzer" sounded for the first shift to leave and for the second shift to start work.

"Pamela." A short, plump woman stood beside her table. "When you've got your shift going, please, come up to the office. Harley has a new employee that has to be trained and since your foreman isn't here tonight, you'll have to do the training."

"It does matter if the foreman is here or not, it seems that I'm the one who does all the training of new people. I'll be up about four-thirty. Thanks, Lorraine."

"See you then." Lorraine smiled and walked away.

"Well, I got it, Pamela! Harley said I can start Monday at seven o'clock in the morning." Lillian's smile radiated with excitement. "Oh, Bob will be so happy! Pamela, come on, take one of the day shift postings up to Harley. He'll put you on days--no problem."

"I told you things are better this way. Besides, if I went on days I'd probably lose my 'floor lady' job. I don't want to go back to sitting eight hours at the machine again."

"You always complain about how you hate doing the foreman's work, like training all the new employees. This would be a way out of that situation."

"If I was given a choice between the worst of two evils, I guess being a 'floor lady' outweighs the hassle of training new employees. Of which, I have another tonight."

"With all those first shift postings, you'll be training a lot of new employees on second to take the positions of all of us that are going on the first shift."

Pamela shrugged her shoulders. "It'll only be for a short while."

"Hi." Three other women joined them at the table.

Deadly Accident

"Heard you're going on days Monday," one of the women, Marian, a short fat woman, said as she sat beside Lillian.

"You lucky thing," Sylvia, a tall thin woman, remarked as she also sat at the table.

"Why don't you three try for some of the postings?" Lillian asked.

"They're all gone," stated the third woman, Dorothy.

"See, Pamela, I told you to do it right away!" Lillian was disappointed. "Now who knows how long you'll have to wait."

"Lillian, it doesn't matter."

"I saw a new woman go into the office tonight," said Sylvia.

"Ya, they hired a new one. I have to go get her at four-thirty and start training her."

"You'll never guess who it is?" Sylvia had a smirk on her face.

"Who?" they all asked, eager for the gossip.

"Amanda Stoner."

"You're kidding!" They all looked at each other in total disbelief.

"Huh, that little whore thought she had it made when she married Frederick. Guess things really changed after the bank failure. Frederick is working at Ewerdt's lumberyard now. I suppose he doesn't make enough for them to live the way they did before. So the poor little whore has to work with her hands now. No one would want her body," Sylvia commented.

"I surely thought one of us three would have ended up with Frederick. We all dated him at one time," said Marian.

"You dated him the longest." Sylvia turned to Dorothy.

"But you dated him last, you should have hung on to him better."

Not liking that remark, Sylvia changed the subject. "What is Frederick doing at his house?"

"I think he's putting in a septic tank so they can have a toilet inside the house," commented Pamela.

"Oh, the little whore can't use the outhouse like the rest of us," remarked Sylvia.

"That whole family is full of whores and money grabbers. Look at who Alex married," Pamela noted.

"I still can't believe Lucy married him. Looking at that cut off hand makes my stomach turn." Marian quivered.

"Alex is a very polite person. Personally, I do think that he's very good-looking. I admire those blonde natural curls," remarked Lillian, who didn't care to listen to the gossip.

"I suppose, Lillian, you never say anything bad about anyone," Marian interjected.

"It's just that the Stoners' have been long time acquaintances of our family."

"Oh, that's right your mother-in-law used to work at the bank for Charles. Bet she knows a lot of what really went on with Charles and Anna. How convenient for Eva to die so they could get married. I've often wondered about Eva's drowning accident." Pamela added some extra "spice" to the conversation.

"Ya, well knowing Anna, there isn't too much to wonder," Sylvia commented.

"Don't put Amanda near my machine," Marian said seriously.

"Ya, I don't want to work next to her either," Dorothy said.

"Maybe we can make sure she doesn't stay here long. Who wants a whore working here? It'll give the factory a bad name," said Pamela.

A loud noise filled the lunchroom and factory. It was the buzzer.

"Time to go to work." Lillian was glad because the conversation was beginning to develop into a plan for actions to be taken against Amanda. Lillian had heard such conversations before about other women they disliked and within several weeks the disliked women had quit their jobs. Lillian had seen how Pamela and the other women treated women they didn't care for. Whenever they did that, it upset Lillian and she never was a party to their mean actions. Suddenly, she was doubly glad that she was going on the first shift. She didn't want to see Amanda treated that way.

At four-thirty Pamela pranced into the office. Seeing Amanda sitting there, she gave her a haughty look and examined her from head to toe.

"Pamela, this is Amanda Stoner," the secretary, Lorraine, introduced her.

Amanda rose and extended her hand to Pamela.

"Ya, I know." Pamela just looked at Amanda's extended hand. She didn't acknowledge Amanda's gesture. "I'll be your 'floor lady.' If you need anything pertaining to your work, I'm the one to ask. We work on a rate. If you don't make the rate, you're out the door. Follow me. I'll show you your machine." Arrogantly, Pamela went out the door. Letting the door slam behind her, she continued walking at a fast gait never looking back or waiting for Amanda to follow.

"Good luck, Amanda." Lorraine knew Amanda needed it. It was quite obvious to her that Pamela didn't like Amanda. If Pamela didn't like her, the other women would follow Pamela's lead.

"Thanks." Amanda smiled and hurried out the door after Pamela. Sensing Pamela's hostile attitude toward her, Amanda began to feel an agitation within her stomach. She became nervous. As they walked past the other women at the machines, Amanda would smile at them as they looked up from their work at her. No one smiled back--not one woman. Amanda began to feel like an unwelcomed "piece of dirt."

Walking to a machine in a corner, isolated from the other machines, Pamela sat on a stool. "Watch me. I'm only showing you once how to work this machine. I don't have time to babysit new people so you better learn now! It's pretty much like other machines. Here's your lever for regulating the pressure foot. Here's the pedal for starting and stopping the machine." Pamela put two pieces of leather together, put them on the machine on top of the metal teeth, lowered the pressure foot, and with her one foot she applied pressure to the pedal under the machine. The pieces of leather moved rapidly across the metal teeth as the pressure foot held the leather pieces down. When the pieces were sewed together, she took her foot off the pedal, raised the pressure foot, and cut the threads that still attached the sewed pieces to the machine. She put the finished piece into a bag that was setting beside the machine. "There, your first piece is finished." Pamela got up. "Okay, the machine is yours."

Pamela started to walk away.

"Excuse me, where is the bathroom and the lunchroom?" inquired Amanda.

Pamela stopped and turned around. She reinforced the disgusting look on her face by rolling her eyes. "The bathroom is over there." She pointed to an opening in the wall. "It's the second door on the left. You can only leave the machine at your two ten-minute breaks and half-hour lunch. Otherwise, you stay at the machine and work. As for the lunchroom, follow the other women!" Pamela walked down the aisle of women and machines. At the end of the aisle, she stopped to talk to several of the women.

Amanda sat at the machine. Putting her good memory to work, she repeated everything the way Pamela had instructed her. She was so involved in her work that the first "buzzer" for break came quickly. She followed the other women into the bathroom area where she waited in line for her turn to use the bathroom facilities. Despite her earlier encounters, she continued to give the other women a friendly smile. Their reply to her friendly gesture was to stare her down with their looks of spite. While waiting in line, they'd talk to each other but not to her. They'd talk around her as if she wasn't there. The ten-minute break ended just as Amanda finished using the bathroom.

Lunchtime was no different. They slammed the lunchroom door in her face. When she entered the room, she could see them look at her and then talk among themselves. When she joined some of the women at a table, the women left the table leaving her to sit alone. As she ate, she could feel their eyes stabbing at her. Why should they hate her so? She hadn't done anything to them. She didn't even know some of the women. Her hands began to tremble and her eyes started to cry. No, she wouldn't let them see her upset. If she did, then they would have won. They had wanted to upset her, but she wouldn't let them have the benefit of knowing they had succeeded. She thought of happy things, ate her lunch, and went back to her machine. She was at the factory to make money and not friends. If she made friends--fine--if not, it wasn't because she didn't try. She could handle this. It was just a repeat of the way things were before she married Frederick. Those years had hardened her and she'd be fine. But what about Rosalia? This was her last week at teaching school, and she had been hired to work during her summer vacation from school at this factory. She had been hired for the first shift. Amanda wouldn't be around to help her if the women on the first shift were like these second shift women.

Prior to lunch Amanda had been working slowly. She was getting acquainted with the machine and working on a technique to increase her skill and speed. By the time second break came, she was working quite efficiently. The second break was a repeat of the early break and lunch. There wasn't one friendly face.

At midnight, the "buzzer" blew and instantly the machines were silent. The women pushed past Amanda shoving her out of their way as they rushed to get to the time clock to punch out their timecard.

After punching her timecard, Amanda began to search her purse for the car keys. She knew that she had put them in there. Where were they? She took everything out--piece by piece. She searched through everything again. The keys were nowhere to be found. Putting her things back inside her purse, she retraced her steps of the evening. The office was locked and dark. She couldn't get in to see if she had left them in there. No--she remembered that she had the keys in her purse at lunch. She must have lost them after lunch. She crawled about the floor by her machine--lifted up the bags full of leather pieces--searched through the leather items on the table--retraced and retraced her steps. She went into the bathroom and searched each toilet stall. Where could they be? She started to become frantic! Oh, God, help me find them. She began to cry. What was she going to do? Her purse was always with her. No, it wasn't! During the last break, when she used the bathroom, she had placed her purse on the counter near the sink. Could someone have taken the keys from her purse? No--would they? Yes, that was the only answer. My God! What kind of people were these? Oh, Amanda--you know, she thought. You've lived here all your life. Life with Frederick had shielded you from these people and their hateful deeds, but now your situation has changed. Your status has changed. Frederick was no longer the bank president, so people didn't have to be nice to his wife. That's what it had been all about. People weren't really her friends, just pretending while Frederick held a position of power. Now these same people displayed their true hidden feelings of spite and hate. She couldn't run from their ill deeds because they needed the money. Poor Rosalia! How could she protect her? She didn't know how--but she had to and she would.

She had a lot of time to think during her walk home. What would Frederick say? What would he do? Frederick had changed since the bank failure.

As she approached the house, she saw the kitchen was aglow with lights. From experience, she was completely aware of the familiar sight that would greet her as she entered the house. Disheartened, she climbed the wooden steps onto the porch and opened the door. As usual, there he sat at the kitchen table which was covered with empty brown bottles scattered about. As she entered the room, he looked up at her with his glassy eyes that carried with them a look of incoherence.

"Oh, Frederick, you are drunk again." The disapproving look on her face was reinforced in her voice.

"Leave me alone."

Amanda shook her head and softly commented, "I don't know why you drink like that, Frederick. It doesn't make things better. The problems are still there when you wake up tomorrow."

"Shut up! I don't need your lectures!" He swung his hand about and knocked a few of the empty bottles off the table. As they hit the wooden floor, they cracked and pieces of sharp-edged glass flew about the floor. Getting up from the chair, his body oscillated as he tried to focus on where he thought he wanted to go. Starting to move in the direction of his destination, he stumbled awkwardly into the living room where he flopped onto the sofa. "I know I've got to sleep down here tonight--right?"

"You know I don't like to smell that awful beer breath."

"Ya, that's just one of your excuses--. You got a million of them for not giving me sex--. What am I doing here?" he mumbled to himself. "No money--got to work that lousy job at Ewerdt's lumberyard--people laughing at me. Man! I had it all. I still could--yup! I still could have it all! Maybe I could--. Maybe I couldn't--. Got to dress in these old clothes for work--"

"Oh, Frederick, we can make it. I do love you. I've got the job at the shoe factory and Rosalia starts on Monday." She sat beside him to console him. "I do love you." She kissed his cheek.

"Rosalia--my sweet Rosalia--little Rosalia--what have I done to her life?" He began to cry. "I wanted so much for her--my sweet Rosalia. I'll take Rosalia with me--. Yup, that's what I'll do--. Jackie has money--. She can see Rosalia lives good."

Amanda jumped up from the sofa. "What are you saying? You're not taking my Rosalia!" She was getting distraught.

"Shut up! I'll take her if I want--. She's my daughter too--. I only stayed for her." He got up from the sofa.

Amanda had assumed that for many years, but to hear him verify it pierced her heart. She began to cry. "She won't go with you."

"You watch me take her." He began to topple back into the kitchen.

"Frederick, you're drunk. Where are you going? What are you doing?" She pulled at him.

"Leave me alone!" He pulled away from her and lost his balance. He fell against the table and then onto the floor. As his hands hit the floor, the sharp pieces of glass cut the palms of his hands. "Look what you did." He looked at his blood-covered hands. "Jackie, will take care of me--. I'm going in by Jackie."

"Jackie's not here."

"Yes, she is--. She's upstairs in the bedroom." He grabbed onto the chair and pulled himself up. "I'm going up by Jackie."

"Frederick, you don't know what you're doing." She pulled at him as he wobbled toward the stairway and onto the steps. Unable to stop him, she followed his staggering body up the stairs. Being alert to his condition, she was ready to catch his body if it fell.

"I'm going in by Jackie--. She always gives me what I want." He headed toward a bedroom door.

"Frederick, that's Rosalia's room." She tried to hold him back.

He threw off her hands. "No, it's Jackie's." His body swayed. He widened his eyes, then widened them again to focus on the bedroom that he wanted to enter.

Gripped with an overbearing sense of terror of the consequences of him thinking the person in the bed was Jackie, Amanda ran frantically in front of him to block his path to the bedroom door. As he stepped toward her and the door, she pushed at him and his uncoordinated body stumbled backwards, losing its balance. As his body fell and tumbled down the steps, she heard his head crack as it hit the bottom step. His body lay quiet.

Horrified at the unexpected occurrence, she dashed down the steps to his body. "Frederick, are you okay?"

Her body trembled with panic. She took his hands and tried to pull him up. His pliant head fell back. "Oh my God!" Her tears were of terror. Lifting his head to push his body up, she felt a wetness on the palm of her hand. Removing her hand from his head and examining it, she found her hand covered with blood--Frederick's blood.

"Oh God! What have I done--. Frederick, please don't be dead! Please, God! Don't make him be dead--sob--sob--sob!" She knelt over his body. "Frederick--Frederick--sob--sob--. I'm sorry--. Please, wake up! You can't be dead! Is he breathing? Oh, God! I don't think so." She took his wrist into her hand and held her thumb on the inside of his wrist. "I can't feel a pulse--. Oh--sob--sob--where is it? There has to be one--sob--sob!" She let go of his hand and rose away from his body.

Watching his head become surrounded by a pool of blood, she tried to collect her thoughts. Should she call the doctor? If he was dead, there was nothing a doctor could do. If he was dead, she was a murderer. She'd go to prison. There would be no understanding from anyone in this town. She was and always would be the "town whore" who had married one of their "favorite son's." They would all relish the idea of her "getting her just due." She had to get the body away from the bottom of the stairs--out of view. She did not want Rosalia to awake and see her father like that. She had to hide the body! But where? Their basement still had a ground floor. She could bury him there. But could she live in the house knowing Frederick was buried in the basement? The new septic tank! It was made of cement. They had just put it in. Everything was connected. They were going to cover it with ground early this morning. She could remove the cement cover from the hole, push his body through the hole, and close the hole with the cover. No one would ever see the body because it would fall to the bottom of the cement septic tank. Oh, it was so gruesome! How could she do that to Frederick? Put his body in with the sewage waste of a septic tank! Maybe prison would be better than to do that to Frederick's body? What should she do? Who could help her? No one! Her body vibrated nervously. She wrung her hands over and over. She walked to and fro--to and fro.

"Oh, God!" She didn't want it to be this way. Her vision blurred. Tears covered her face. Her nose dripped. She sniffled and cried and cried. She loved him and never would she have ever wanted him dead. She only wanted to protect Rosalia. In his drunken stupor, he didn't know what he was doing. "Oh, Frederick, I love you. I do love you. Please, forgive me for this."

Grabbing Frederick's feet, she began to pull his body. It was a physically draining chore. He was a heavy man. His injured head left a trail of blood. She pulled him away from the stairs, through the kitchen, and into the entrance. From the entrance she could take the body into the basement or outside. For the time being, however, she'd let the body lay in the entrance. She couldn't look at it anymore.

Going into the kitchen, she grabbed a metal pail and filled it partially with water. Putting a scrubbing brush and rag into the pail, she walked over to the pool of blood. She stopped and gazed steadily at the blood. Could she clean up his blood--touch it--rinse it away in the pail of water? Should she? She held her quivering hand over her mouth to prevent the contents of her stomach from being expelled. Her body felt a limp emptiness. Setting the pail on the floor, she sat on the stair step. Taking her hand, she wiped the tears from her face.

In the disbelief and total confusion of it all, she knew a decision had to be made soon, before daylight. If she cleaned up his blood, the evidence of it being an accident would be gone. She realized that she had already made one mistake by moving the body. Cleaning up the blood would be another--if she intended to report the accident. If she cleaned up the blood, she could never tell anyone. She would have to bury Frederick and live forever with the hideous knowledge of how and where she had disposed of him. Whether she went to jail or not, she would always be a prisoner to this deed.

****

The old model T truck stood idling very loudly on the dew-covered lawn next to the old farmhouse's wooden porch. On the porch lay a black cat nursing her kittens as the other cats stood at the edge of the threshold of the open kitchen door. Inside the smell of bacon and eggs from the early morning breakfast seemed enticing, but the kitchen was too full of people for the cats to safely venture inside.

On the kitchen table a young boy was vigorously sucking his thumb and peering inside a white wicker bassinet. "Ma, Jeffery did it again."

"What did he do again?" His mother handed a small cardboard box to the man who just entered the room. "There are enough bottles and diapers in the box for all day. Tell Anna we'll pick the kids up after milking--around eight o'clock." She walked over to the bassinet. "Oh, he uncovered himself again." She gently laid the blanket on the baby that was smiling, kicking his feet, and moving his arms about with excitement.

The little boy on the table laughed. "Look Daddy, he's smiling at me!"

"Yes, he is." The father looked inside and then took the cardboard box outside and placed it into the back of the truck. Coming back into the house, he grabbed the two handles of the bassinet and took it off the table. "See you later, honey." He kissed his wife and then walked toward the kitchen door. "Come on, Eddy, we're going to Great-grandma's."

The young boy's eyes glistened and he quickly jumped off the table onto the floor.

Inside the truck, the father set the bassinet near the passenger's door while Eddy sat next to him. He waved a good-bye to his wife as she stood in the doorway watching them leave.

As the truck approached the Stoner house, Anna, who had been waiting anxiously, came walking down the sidewalk. Her long neck scarf flowed in the breeze.

Charles stood in the doorway supporting his body on a wooden cane. With his other hand, he waved a welcome to Alex.

Stopping the truck, Alex paused and smiled to himself as he recalled some of the memories that he had of his childhood at this house. Things were pretty much the same, except Grandmother had gotten older along with some of the trees and himself.

As Anna opened the truck door, Eddy squeezed between the bassinet and the truck's dash. He jumped out of the truck. "Hi, Great-grandma!" He hugged her legs.

Anna ruffled his blonde curls. "You are a little sweetheart." She bent over and gave him a big hug and kiss. "I love you."

Seeing Charles standing in the doorway, he broke from Anna's hug. As fast as his little legs could travel, he ran to Charles. "Hi, Great-grandpa."

"Come on, you and I are going fishing. I got everything ready." Charles put one arm around the little boy's shoulder and they disappeared into the house.

"Where's Lucy?" Anna asked as she took Jeffery out of the

bassinet, held him close to herself, and kissed his soft pink cheeks.

"She wanted to get part of her wash hung on the clothesline before we go out into the fields today. Among the three farms, we've got more than two hundred acres to plow yet. If the fall weather wouldn't have been so wet, we could have done some plowing then. It really helps out that you and Charles take care of the kids so Lucy can help out in the fields all day. Pete has been plowing since five o'clock this morning and Lori's been harrowing since she finished milking. When I get back, Lucy and I will start picking stones until the constant sitting bothers Pete. Then Lucy and Pete will exchange jobs."

Anna shook her head. "How many acres do you work?"

"Each of the farms is one hundred acres now and Lucy is trying to convince Pete to buy Murray's eighty acre farm."

"There are only four of you. How 'on earth' are you going to work all that land." Anna rested Jeffery against her shoulder and patted his back gently.

"Cash crop it. The canning factory is always looking for land to plant sweet corn, peas, and sugar beets on."

"There aren't any buildings on the land. They blew up along with Murray," Anna commented.

"It doesn't matter. We don't need more buildings. Land always increases in value. Buildings depreciate unless you stick a lot of money into fixing them all the time."

"I can't understand why Murray continued to use that 'still.' Prohibition has been over for at least eight years," said Anna.

"Not to speak badly of the dead, but I never did see Murray sober. Even with prohibition being eliminated, there were many places he could sell his moonshine to. We were working in our field that bordered his line fence that afternoon. You just wouldn't believe how fast that place went up in flames." Alex grabbed the bassinet and walked to the house with Anna. "We appreciate you and Charles taking care of the kids." Alex set the bassinet on a small table located in the foyer of the house.

"No problem. We enjoy them." Anna hugged Jeffery and kissed him again. "Just look at those two." She motioned for Alex to look out the window.

Walking beside Charles was Eddy with two fishing poles, one in each hand--one fishing pole for Charles and one for Eddy.

Anna laughed to herself. "They'll go to the pond and sit there all day."

"The pond?"

"Yes, the pond," replied Anna.

"But there's no fish in the pond."

"I know that. You know that. Charles knows that but little Eddy doesn't. Charles likes it that way. He says, 'it saves on the worms.' Charles just likes to sit and tell Eddy stories. Eddy likes the stories and the candy that Charles always seems to have enough of in his pocket. When the candy is gone, then they come back to the house. I'm glad they don't catch any fish. I'd end up cleaning them, and we'd have fish for supper every night. I like fish but not every night."

"Well, I better get going. I'd like to visit more. When the crops are planted, we'll come and spend a Sunday with you and Charles." He gave Jeffery a kiss and Anna a hug.

"See you tonight." Anna returned Alex's hug. "Don't work so hard."

"We won't, Grandma." He dashed down the steps and out to the truck.

Anna watched him and the truck disappear down the graveled road. Carrying Jeffery, she went into the living room where she sat in a rocking chair. She placed Jeffery on her lap and let him gently rest in her arms. While rocking in the chair, she watched Charles and Eddy through the window. Within a short time, Jeffery fell asleep. Nevertheless, she continued to rock in the solitude of the empty room as her mind filled with thoughts. Thoughts of the future--no--she had no dreams for herself. She had what she wanted. In fact, more than she had ever thought of having. Not material things, because she never had been that concerned with things of that nature. Living to see two of her great-grandchildren was something very valuable to her. She could enjoy them the way she could never enjoy Amanda. She was too busy surviving and then suddenly Amanda was grown. When she and Alex had come here, so many years ago, she never thought her life would be as it was. So many things had happened that had brought her to this moment--in this house--with the people that now had become such a big part of her life--people that were her life.

Thoughts--thoughts of things so far in the past--forgotten--or at least filed somewhere in her memory--that surfaced and seemed to bring more tears of reminiscence to her eyes. Ludwig--she would have to write him again. He never answered, but the letters never came back. So he must have received them. It was almost a half a century since she had seen him. Then her thoughts came more back to home--of two people that were dearer in her heart. It was time for her Memorial Day ritual. She'd ask Charles to drive her tomorrow. First, she'd stop at Erickson's store and buy some flower seed for marigolds. She smiled to herself as she thought how Alex had always liked the marigolds that she had planted in her vegetable garden at the farm. The flowers didn't have a very pleasing smell, but he liked the sight of the yellow and bronze colors amongst the green foliage. Her smile faded as the thought--of those neatly arranged rows and rows of the same white graves--depressed her. There was nothing that marked his grave differently than anyone else's except for the flowers. They made his grave different and special because he was special and different from the rest. He was her first love and the father of her daughter. Yes, she'd ask Charles and they'd go tomorrow. How fortunate she was. She had been blessed twice with the love of two good men.

Life had also blessed her with the gift of two children. Although Henry's name was never spoken, he always remained in her heart and soul. Often when Charles would take a nap after dinner, she'd walk to the church cemetery and spend those quiet moments with him. The tulips at his grave were beautiful this year and the rose bush had survived the winter. How strange she often thought it was to see so much life in a cemetery--the dead, brown grass of winter turning an emerald green--the barren, gray trees sprouting new green leaves --multicolored flowers pushing themselves through the earth to bloom again. In many ways, a person's life was like the spring of a year. Through the tragedies we survive to also start new and bloom again. Now here she was holding her great-grandson and wondering what life would be like for him. Whatever his life would be, he'd survive also. We all do.

The day had gone fast. She thought how strange it was that her thoughts of the past had monopolized so much of the day. With so many other things to do, she had spent the majority of the day holding Jeffery and rocking from one moment to the next. The rocking seemed to soothe her and fill her with an inner tranquility.

Supper had come and gone. Their time together with the children was coming to an end. Anna gave them a bath and dressed them in their pajamas. So if they fell asleep, Lucy and Alex could just put them into bed when they got home.

Eddy, sucking his thumb, sat on the sofa next to Charles. He watched Charles read in silence from one of the books that he had taken from his library. Before long, Eddy's eyelids became heavy. His body would jerk as he tried to catch himself falling asleep. But he was no match for the sandman and soon his head of blonde curls was resting on Charles's lap.

Charles set aside his book and very gently laid Eddy on the sofa. Grabbing for the colorful quilt, which Anna had draped over the sofa's arm, he covered the little boy's sleeping body.

Once again Anna sat contentedly rocking Jeffery. She enjoyed looking at Charles and realizing how much she loved him. Occasionally, Charles would look up from his book and she'd smile at him.

The room was silent except for the squeak--squeak sound of the rocker.

When Jeffery was asleep, she laid him inside the bassinet. For a few minutes she departed from the living room as she went into her sewing room. She returned to the living room carrying a small brown wicker basket. Sitting in the rocker, she opened the basket, pulled out some yarn, knitting needles, and a mitten which she had started and now proceeded to finish.

Charles raised his eyes from the book. "How much do you have left to do?"

"I've got Eddy's finished. I should complete Jeffery's tomorrow. No, I won't have time tomorrow. Oh, it doesn't matter. I've got a lot of time before their birthdays in September."

"Why won't you have time tomorrow?"

"I thought if the weather is nice, we'd go to Jennings." She started to knit.

"Sure, it'll be a nice drive." He smiled at her. "Memorial Day again. The older a person gets, the faster time goes."

Anna looked up to smile at him. Through the window behind him, she saw two headlights coming toward the house. "I think they're here." She put her knitting back into the basket and got up from the rocker. Opening the house door, she stood in its threshold to greet Lucy and Alex.

Charles followed her and stood beside her with his arm around her waist. "I love you, Anna." He hugged her waist.

"I love you too, Charles." She smiled at him and then watched the truck come up the driveway and stop at the edge of the sidewalk.

Alex got out of the truck and then walked over to the passenger's door and opened it for Lucy. He helped her down the running board.

As they walked to the porch, Lucy asked, "How were the boys?"

"They were fine. They're asleep now."

Quietly, they all went into the house.

Lucy grabbed the bassinet and Alex very carefully picked Eddy up into his arms and carried him outside toward the truck.

Anna and Charles walked with them to the edge of the sidewalk where the truck was parked.

Lucy placed the bassinet in the middle of the truck seat. She sat next to the bassinet, and Alex placed sleeping Eddy on her lap. She secured his body by wrapping her arms around him.

Anna left the edge of the sidewalk and walked with Alex to the driver's side of the truck.

"Thanks, Grandma." He gave her a hug.

"Anytime, Alex, we always enjoy those two little sweethearts." Anna returned his hug.

Alex sat inside the truck and closed the door.

Anna stood beside the truck as Alex started the truck's engine.

As the truck moved forward, Anna felt a tug on her neck. Suddenly, her body was flung to the ground. The long neck scarf that had flowed so freely in the breeze was now caught in the closed truck door. It was pulling her body on the graveled road beside the moving truck.

"Stop, Alex, stop!" Anna could hear Charles yell as he hobbled after the truck with his cane and crippled leg.

In desperation, Anna tried to position her fingers between the scarf and her neck to facilitate breathing, but the scarf torque tighter around her neck. The pain caused by the coarse, irregular gravel stones that ripped at her skin and her nerves--was secondary. She could survive that pain but she couldn't survive if she couldn't breathe. The scarf was like a tourniquet. There was no passage of air. She felt her life slip away as her body was dragged into shredded pieces of flesh and small stones became embedded in her layers of exposed, raw skin. Suddenly, there came a hard blow to her head as it collided with a large stone in the road. Charles's yelling--the sound of the truck--the pain of being dragged--the panic of being choked--ceased--and with the silence of that moment--her body and soul was at peace.

****

With his desiring blue eyes, he watched her through the filmy-covered glass windowpane as she hung the washed clothes on the clothesline. Her hair glistened in the midmorning sun and her moist lips, painted red, made his lips droll for the moment when he could feel those lips on his. As she bent over to retrieve clothes from the wooden wash basket, it pleased him to see her large breasts hanging inside her blouse and confined in her lacy, white bra. As she stood securing the wash to the line with the wooden clothespins, he restrained himself from wanting to go and caress her round, soft buttocks that filled her tight slacks. As she picked the empty wash basket up and walked toward the house, he watched her shoulders and hips sway in a manner that was sexually alluring to him.

He worked for a while until he heard the house door slam, then he'd steal a few seconds from his work to watch her again. He'd watch her--hoeing the weeds and picking vegetables in her garden--hoeing the weeds in her flower beds beside the house--mowing the lawn--taking the dry clothes off the line. Day after day he'd discreetly watch her. The more he saw her, the more his voluptuous appetite for her grew.

He had wanted her from the first day that he had seen her almost eight years ago. He never forgot her. Unable to have her, he satisfied his libido with others' bodies. When he was with others, he closed his eyes and pretended it was she that he was making love to.

Getting a job here was no coincidence. He had seen and talked to her husband many times in the tavern. In fact, he had established an amicable relationship with her husband. To his rationale--first get close to the husband and the friendship with the wife will be easy. However, he wanted more than friendship from her. Time was becoming his adversary. Each day he saw her it became more difficult to contain his lust for her. With the lust raving inside him, sometimes he just wanted to seize her body--consume it--devour it. Nevertheless, he put aside these animalistic desires. He not only wanted her, but he wanted her to want him in the same desirable way. However, he didn't know how much longer he could control those utmost, deep sexual desires or how much longer he would even try.

"Hi." A feminine voice came into the garage.

Startled, he turned away from the window in the direction of the voice. "Oh, hi, Margie."

"What you looking at out the window?" She pranced into the garage and paraded her young, womanly body in front of him. She deliberately rubbed against his body as she stood beside him looking out the same window. "Looking at Susie?"

"Susie?"

"Ya, the neighbor girl, she must have just come home from that teachers' school she's going to in Jennings."

He turned in the direction of the neighbor's house. "She's your age, isn't she?"

"Ya, but I'm better to look at, don't you think?" She flaunted her breasts, which were unusually big compared to most girls her age.

"You look older."

"Well, I'm not. I'm just more experienced. Probably know as much as you." Provocatively, she walked around him as she quite obviously examined every inch of his fine, masculine structure. "Well, I've got to go." She started to walk away then turned and walked back to him. She opened her purse and pulled out a red package about the size of a half dollar. "You know what this is, Tony?"

"Ya. What are you doing with that?"

"I always carry one or two along with me, just in case I want to have some fun. Just because I like having fun doesn't mean I can't also be smart. The dumb ones get caught. I'm never getting caught. No one will ever say, 'I had to get married.' No one. When I go down the aisle, let the people start to count the months. Everyone is going to say, 'I was a virgin.' A person always has to think about one's reputation. The appearance of a good reputation is very important, if you want people to treat you right."

"What about the boys? Don't you think they brag about 'making it' with you?"

"The boys I go out with know me, and they know better than to ever tell. There aren't that many girls who would give them what I do. So if they want what I give them, they keep their mouths shut. Otherwise, they don't see me anymore and the fun is all over with. Well, like I said, I better go." She put the condom back into her purse. "I've got people to see, and things to do." She kissed the tip of her index finger. Touching his cheek, she moved her finger down the side of it. "See you later--maybe?" She spirited out the door.

He followed her and then stopped in the doorway of the garage. He watched her join her mother who was walking from the garden to the house.

"Hi, Ma, got lettuce for supper?" Margie observed the head of fresh lettuce from the garden that her mother held in her hands.

"Do you want a salad or sandwich?"

"Lettuce sandwiches. Don't have time to make a salad." Margie turned around in the direction of the garage. "He's still watching me."

"Who?" Pamela turned in the direction Margie was looking.

"Tony?"

"Ya, I think he likes me."

"He's too old for you," Pamela quickly snapped back.

"Ah, Chuck and Jerry are too young. They're so immature." Margie held the door open for her mother as they entered the house.

"Stay with your own age." Pamela took the head of lettuce over to the kitchen sink.

"Why? You're younger than Dad--a lot younger."

"That's why I'm telling you--stay with your own age." Pamela rinsed the lettuce under the running water.

"If that's what you want, can I use your car for a while?"

Pamela glanced at the clock. "If you're back here by three-thirty. I've got to leave for work by then." She reached into the bottom cupboard, pulled out a metal colander, and placed the lettuce into it.

"Why don't you drive with Lillian?" Margie grabbed her mother's black leather purse, which was setting on the paper-cluttered desk.

"Lillian is on the day shift." Pamela grabbed a bowl and placed the drained lettuce into it. "Where are you going?"

"I'm going by Jerry's place and then we might go over by Chuck." After searching her mother's purse, she pulled out a set of car keys. "Thanks, Ma." The door slammed and Margie was gone.

Pamela was putting the lettuce into the refrigerator when she heard the door open. Turning around and seeing who it was, she was surprised.

"Ma, these keys don't fit in your car." Margie tossed the keys onto the kitchen table and searched through her mother's purse again. "Are these the right keys?" She held up another set of keys.

"Ya, I guess so."

"Whose are those?" Margie pointed to the keys that she had just tossed on the table.

Pamela paused to think. "They're probably for one of your dad's trucks." She couldn't tell the truth and no one needed to know.

"Well, what were they doing in your purse? You don't drive the trucks."

"You better be back here at three-thirty." Pamela grabbed the keys off the table. Later, she would put them into the garbage barrel and burn them. No more keys--no more questions.

"Ya, I'll be here." She let the screen door slam behind her. Walking past the garage, she looked in to see where Tony was. Seeing him she smiled and waved. "See you later, Tony."

"Ya, Margie." He waved then continued working on the truck engine. The rest of the afternoon went slow for him. He knew Pamela very seldom came outside in the afternoon. She usually worked in the house before she went to work. It was about time for her to leave. His heart yearned to see her one more time today. That would have to be enough until tomorrow.

Inside the house Pamela had done some ironing, tidied up the house, and then got dressed for work. Time didn't seem to be too much of a concern until she was dressed and found herself waiting for Margie to come home. Looking at the clock and watching out the window for her to come, didn't make her come any sooner--three-thirty--look out the window--watch and wait--three-forty--. Where was Margie? Five more minutes and Pamela would get to work late! Damn that girl!--three-fifty--watch and wait--watch and wait--

KNOCK! KNOCK!

Through the screen door she could see it was Tony.

"Aren't you going to work, Pamela?"

"Ya, Margie was to be back here at three-thirty." Pamela walked toward the door. "I'll be late now." She threw her hands up in frustration.

"I can take you in my car." He opened the door.

"Oh, would you? Thanks!" She went through the door and followed him into his car. Pamela was anxious about being late. They'd deduct her thirty minutes just for being five maybe ten minutes late. Maybe if he went faster, she would not be that late. However, she didn't think it was appropriate to tell him to go faster. After all, he was nice enough to drive her to work. Nevertheless, as an employee, he was getting paid. "Do you think you can go faster?"

"I'm sorry, Pamela. If I go any faster, I'd be speeding. I don't feel like getting a ticket." He smiled over at her. He wanted to reach over and touch her, hold her in his arms, feel her lips on his, but it wasn't the time. He didn't want to get aroused now. He knew that he would not be able to follow it through.

When they drove up to the factory, there was no one outside. The first shift was gone and the second shift had started working. She was definitely late! The car stopped.

"Thanks, Tony." She opened the car door. "Please, tell Margie to pick me up tonight at twelve o'clock." She got out of the car. "And tell her not to be late. I don't like waiting outside in the dark."

"Okay, bye, Pamela." He watched her run through the open factory door and wondered if he could ever have her. He could not wonder any longer. He'd have to find out soon. He could not live like this too much longer.

At work Pamela was busy with all the new employees and time went fast. When the buzzer rang at twelve o'clock, she felt relief. She could rest on the way home because Margie would be driving. Outside the factory she waited. One by one she watched the cars leave the factory parking lot. When the cars were all gone, she stood alone with only a few pole lights lighting the now deserted area.

There was a bit of a chill in the midnight air. She rubbed her arms to keep herself warm. She thought aloud, "Where is that girl? Did Tony forget to tell her?" She looked at her watch, almost twelve-fifteen. Should she start walking? If she did, then maybe Margie would never find her. She would wait five more minutes. She decided that was the last time Margie would ever use her car. Then she saw a car's headlights coming down the road. Maybe that was Margie? The car turned into the factory parking lot, but it wasn't her car. Who would be coming into the parking lot at this late hour?

The car came closer and then stopped. The driver leaned over and opened the passenger's car door. "Sorry, I'm late, Pamela."

"Where's Margie?" Pamela looked inside the car.

"Last time I saw her. She was at home. Come on, Pamela, get in. I don't bite!"

"Why didn't Margie pick me up?" Pamela got into the car.

"Because I told her, I'd pick you up." He started to drive out of the parking lot and down the road.

"Why would you do that?"

"So I could be alone with you."

"Ya, sure." Pamela chuckled--a big joke! "What time did she finally get home?"

"She was there when I came back from taking you to work."

"What was her excuse for being late?"

"She had a flat tire. I saw it. She had a nail in it." He turned onto a side road.

"Why are you turning here? This isn't the way home."

The car continued down the secluded, narrow country road. After driving a short distance, he slowed the speed of the car and coasted onto the grass that skirted the road. The low branches of the trees that canopied the road could be heard scratching the side of the car. He turned off the car and shut off the headlights. Alone they sat in the darkness of the car--closer than they had ever been to each other --totally alone.

Pamela was silent. She felt fluttering and nervousness in her stomach. Was he stopping for the reason she thought? No, this could not be happening. Would he kiss her? She wanted him to. If he did, would she make a fool of herself? Maybe she did not know how anymore? What if he wanted to make love? She had fantasized him making love to her. If he did, could she? She had not made love for so long. What if she could not respond to him? What if her passion was gone, dead from all those years of never having anyone make love to her? Oh, how foolishly she thought, he would not want her that way. Who would?

He moved beside her and put his arm on top of her shoulder. He snuggled closer to her.

"Tony, I think you should take me home." She was so afraid that she would not know how to perform. Fantasizing was better than making a fool of herself. She turned away from him.

Gently taking her face, he turned it toward him and pressed his moist lips against hers. He closed his eyes and enjoyed the exquisite pleasure of kissing her. Releasing his lips from hers, he pulled her closer to him and held her quietly. Just to have her this close was pure ecstasy! "Pamela, I want to make love to you. Please, let me," he whispered.

Oh! How she wanted to, but if she could not perform? He'd know what a fool she was and if she said "no." Would she lose maybe her only chance left for love?

"Don't be so tense, Pamela. Relax. Let me love you." He kissed her again and again and again. He was getting caught up in the excitement of fulfilling his long hidden desires. Passion was erupting from every cell--corpuscle in his body. He felt he could not stop until his satisfaction was achieved.

Pamela's heart raced a thousand miles a second. Could this be happening to her? Oh! Yes, it was! She could feel the passion in his kiss--in his touch. Should she stop him? Could she stop him? Did she want this erotic situation to continue until they reached a condition where she could no longer ask him to stop or she no longer desired him to? At that "point of no return," what if she found out?--or worse yet, he found out that she was an empty woman who could no longer feel love or give it.

Chapter 15
****
The Explosion

The hot, humid air of the island flowed along the coastal grasslands through the encampment, in one end and out the other end of the tents that had been quickly set up at the edge of the dense, forest-covered jungle and high, jagged mountain ranges that ran the entire length of the island. The sounds of riflemen's bullets--the drone of airplane motors--whistling of falling bombs--and burst of fire from flame throwers had temporarily ceased. Left in the aftermath, between the shore and the edge of the forest, was a brown, scorched earth with its smoldering ruins and a shell-pocked beach sprawled with bodies of the dead enemy. Some bodies were carried and drifted by the tide. Others were half buried in the sand and still others were being devoured by maggots. The silhouette of a sole surviving cylindrical palm, with its fan-shaped leaves spread out from its tip, stood against the sky's orange and red horizon. The peaceful sounds of the ocean's white waves rushing up onto the sandy beach and then receding back was now lost in the sounds that came from the tents.

Inside one of the tents, a wooden supply box served as a table. On several other supply boxes, sat four military men involved in a ritual that helped pass the lonely night hours that they were away from their families. Also for a while, it made them forget the smell of death that lingered in this place--this place so far from their home. This place, where they prayed that they would not die.

"I'll raise you five bucks." One of the men threw the money onto a pile already heaping with green dollar bills--one's and five's.

"Ah, come on, John, you don't have anything. Five in to see ya." One of the other men threw a five-dollar bill onto the pile.

"Ah, Jesus Christ, I'm getting out!" Another player angrily hurled his cards onto the table. "All I ever get are the damn shit cards!"

"Ya, me too!" Another hand of cards was thrown onto the table.

With a foxy snicker on his freckled-covered face, John laid down his cards very slowly, one at a time--a red king--another red king--a black king--a red queen--

"Ah, holy shit, you son of a bitch got a full house again?" replied the only player left in the game with John.

"You bet your sweet ass." John laid down a black queen and grabbed for the pile of money. "Thanks, guys. Want to play another game of poker?"

"You smart son of a bitch! You have all our money," remarked one of the guys that stood up and stretched himself. "I'm going to my tent to get some sleep. See you guys in the morning."

"Ah, come on guys! Your 'IOUs' are good until next payday."

"Go to hell, John!" The other player got up and stormed out of the tent.

"Guess the game is over. What a bunch of sore losers! It's all right when they win and I lose, then it's a big joke." John gathered up the cards and stacked them onto a pile. "Here are your cards." John handed them to the only player left.

"Thanks, John. I'm going outside for a cigarette." Putting the cards into his green military trousers, he then reached into his shirt pocket and pulled out a pack of cigarettes. "Want one, John?" He held the pack out to John.

"Thanks." John grabbed a cigarette as they walked out of the tent.

Outside they stood leisurely puffing on their cigarettes as they surveyed the part of the island that they had secured from the enemy today. Some of the men had tied ropes between the stubs of broken trees and were hanging their wash up to dry. Others were unwinding by playing cards. Some were just lying on the rubble-covered ground, their arm over their eyes resting. Others were sitting and reading their "V" mail.

Amongst their divisions tents were the tents of the mustached Aussie veterans--sprightly--erect and tall in posture. They were sociable people and good companions on the battlefield.

Some of the dark-skinned, kinky haired native tribesmen were carrying stretchers of wounded and sick soldiers into the medical tents. Others were standing in groups with their hands behind their backs, quietly examining the situation. Their presence revealed the distinct stone-age culture that still existed on this island. Although some wore shorts, the majority were naked except for the small piece of cloth which they wore to cover their genitals. They were all barefoot, and their bodies were decorated with tight bands on their biceps and elbows. Some also had tribal jewelry in one of their ears.

"Tomorrow maybe the See bees will come and by tomorrow night we'll have a fairly good camp to come back to--if we come back." John slowly puffed his cigarette wanting to enjoy every moment of it.

"They're out there--hiding--waiting for the right time to attach us --ambush us."

"Looks like a fire up in the hills." John tossed his cigarette and with his foot ground it into the earth.

"The 'Japs' are probably cremating their dead. The Aussies have been coming down hard on them the last three days."

"Maybe the Aussies will finish the 'Japs' off, and we can get out of this disease infested hell." John walked back into the tent and sat on one the supply boxes. "Come on in here, pal." John searched through his belongings and pulled out a small box. He opened it and held it out in front of his pal. "Help me eat these. They're getting stale fast in this climate."

"I suppose. What are pals for? You helped me eat mine. The least I can do is help you out now."

"The next time you write home, ask your ma to write down the recipe for those cookies she sent last time. I'll send it back home to my grandma so she can make them when I get home." John bit into the cookie and savored the taste.

"My ma didn't make the cookies." His pal grabbed a cookie and began to eat it.

"Who did?"

"A girl I know back home."

"Ah, a girlfriend! You shy fox! You never told me you had a girl-friend." John gave him a teasing shove.

"She's not a dating friend. She's just a very special friend. I've known her all my life. We're very close."

"She's like a sister, huh. Wish I had a sister."

"No, not like my sister. There is no one like my sister." The tone of his voice clearly reflected a strong dislike.

"All the times we've fought side by side, been card playing pals, talked about a million things, and this is the first time I find out you have a sister. Do you have parents?" John reached into the box for another cookie.

"Ya, I've got parents."

"You get a lot of things from them--cookies--salami--letters?" John continued to munch on the cookies.

"No." He reached into his pocket, pulled out the pack of cigarettes, pulled out a cigarette, and lit it.

"The neighbor girl writes you and sends you things, but your family doesn't?" John was confused.

"They're probably too busy." He knew that wasn't the reason. His parents and sister were probably glad that he was gone. In fact, after finding that letter on his father's desk from the selective service, he knew they didn't care about him.

"Too busy to write to you?" John shook his head--unbelievable!

"What about your family, do they write you?" He didn't care to discuss his own family. What went on within his family was of no one's concern. It was private--no one else's business. Also, talking about it was like rubbing salt into his wound. A wound caused so long ago when he first realized that his family hated him with a passion. Now that feeling had been reinforced by that letter. Sometimes those feelings of hate were too hard to actually accept and live with. Sometimes he thought that maybe if he died his family would be happy. Such feelings ripped at his soul and filled it with an echoing emptiness.

"My ma is dead. She died two years ago. My dad was never one to write. My grandma writes me a lot and of course bakes a lot." John held up a cookie and passed the box over to his pal.

"No, thanks. You're close to your grandma."

"Ya, she's always lived with my ma and me. My dad's a general in the army. I never saw him too much before the war. So I don't think I'll see him or hear from him until this war is over."

"Your dad's a general in the army?" His pal was impressed.

"Ya, he's forty-five. In a couple years he plans to retire. He figures he'll get a really good pension from the army. Me, I can't wait to get out of the service and go back home. When I was small, we moved with my dad from one place to another until I started school. Then my parents decided that perhaps it would be better if my ma and I stayed in one place. So my dad bought a house in Jennings."

"Of all the places your dad must have traveled, why Jennings?"

"That's where my dad grew up. I'm counting the days till I'm out of here."

"You're that anxious to go home to Jennings? I'm not that anxious to go home." He tossed his cigarette butt and took another cigarette out of his pack. "You want one, John?"

"No, thanks. When we get home, we've got to see each other, go out together, and find us some girls. Hey, we don't live that far from each other."

"Ya, before the war I went to Jennings quite a lot on business for my dad." His face became sullen. He thought of that letter again. How could they do that to him? Choose someone else instead of their own son.

John noticed the changed look. "Hey, what's the matter, Mikie?"

"Let's go help Gibbie." Mikie started to walk toward the tall, thin man struggling to put a tubular metal pole into the ground.

With three pairs of hands helping, it wasn't long before the star-spangled banner of red, white, and blue was waving in the middle of the encampment. A hush fell upon the men as one by one they all stood up and gave a military salute to the flag. The Aussies and tribesmen also stood and followed the example of respect by placing their right hand over their heart. Then out of the silence came a voice. "Oh, say can you see . . . . " The whole division began to sing.

When the singing stopped, one soldier shouted, "Horii, this island is ours! We'll bury you here!"

Early the next morning, the infantrymen began to advance from the encampment into the jungle thickly covered with short trees, tall branchless coconut trees, and trees entangled with great--twisting--savage vines. Trees filled with nesting birds. Birds dressed in brilliantly, colored feathers--long flowing plumage combinations of purple, orange, scarlet, and glossy black. The more they advanced the thicker the jungle became. Above them they could hear the strafing and bombing, but in such a thick jungle little damage was done.

Steadily they continued to move--the alert and cautious infantrymen and the rumbling tanks.

RAT-TAT-TAT--RAT-TAT-TAT--RAT-TAT-TAT--RAT-TAT-TAT--RAT-TAT-TAT--

"Machine guns!" John pulled Mikie down to the ground. Flat on their stomachs they lay--afraid to move--afraid to breathe. Bullets cleared their backs within only inches to spare--again and again. Their heads were buried in the carpet of thick, velvety green moss. The angle of death could be felt blowing cooly on their shirts, drenched with sweat.

RAT-TAT-TAT--RAT-TAT-TAT--RAT-TAT-TAT--RAT-TAT-TAT--RAT-TAT-TAT--

When would it stop, they couldn't move. They were pinned down--helpless. The Japanese could advance and kill them as they lay there. They listened. The rapid rate of fire was not getting louder. Obviously, the Japanese weren't advancing. John and Mikie crawled on their bellies behind a short scrub-like palm. From there they dared to look up and find the source of the machine gun. It was a sniper in a tree.

RAT-TAT-TAT--RAT-TAT-TAT--RAT-TAT-TAT--RAT-TAT-TAT--RAT-TAT-TAT--

John aimed his automatic rifle and shot into the tops of the trees where he thought the sniper was.

RAT-TAT-TAT--RAT-TAT-TAT--RAT-TAT-TAT--RAT-TAT-TAT--RAT-TAT-TAT--

The Japanese machine gun ceased. A body fell from among the trees and thumped to the ground--only one?

The sweat from John's forehead ran down into his eyes. He wiped the sweat away. His vision could not be obstructed. His body trembled with nervous anxiety. He watched--not a leaf moved--not a blade of grass flickered--stillness. He listened--silence. Then he saw the tribesmen and other infantrymen slowly move from behind their shelters and move toward the fallen body.

Cautiously, John and Mikie approached the body which had been camouflaged by a green uniform and green leaves stuck in the net of the helmet.

"John, how the heck did you ever see him up there?" asked Gibbie.

"He's a good 'Jap' now. He's dead!" One of the men kicked the deadman's legs.

John felt a sickness in his stomach. Seeing the dead eyes staring up at him filled John's entire body with a sweeping coldness that made every cell--every atom--in his body quiver. He had to get away from the body with its life blood oozing out of it. He felt his stomach twist. He desperately needed to be alone. With his eyes still glued to the body of the man that he had killed, he slowly moved away. His boot camp training had not prepared him for this gruesome reality of war. He regurgitated--again and again and again--until he could no more. He had killed his first man, and it didn't feel good. It felt empty. A life was gone, and he could never bring it back. This wasn't like the army games that he had played when he was small. Here, no one got up, walked away, and started over. This was death and it was forever.

John felt a hand on his shoulder. "It was either him--you--or maybe one of your army buddies. Get it out now, and let it pass. You did good." The huge man patted him on the shoulder. "The first time is always the worst. Next time it'll be easier. Come on, let's get out of here." The general walked back to the rest of the men.

Mikie waited for John and together they joined the others.

Onward they marched with their automatic rifles and loaded down with machine gun ammunition. Following them were the Aussies with their tommy guns. The jungle became thicker and thicker. Even at midday they still walked in half light of dusk. Between the mountains and deep ravines that roared with swift torrents, they marched. On a very narrow path of jagged stones, they had to tread over Japanese infantrymen's cadavers crawling with the larva of the dead. Dying of starvation or jungle fever, they had been reduced to mere skeletal figures with shaggy and whiskered faces. Some wore uniforms soiled with mud and blood. Others had no uniforms and were clothe in only blankets and straw-rice bags and had no shoes.

It began to rain. They became soaked through their boots, underclothing, and to the skin. On the muddy downward track, they would slip and slide. They were covered with mud. Into the swampland, full of flesh-eating crocodiles, poisonous snakes, and skin-piercing mosquitoes they went. Each man watching out for the safety of the other. Their bodies knotted in fear--when and where would the Japanese attack? They crossed a forbidding stream with small canvas boats. Then they laid pontoons, and the anchored boats became stepping stones on which the tanks rumbled to the other side.

RAT-TAT-TAT--RAT-TAT-TAT--RAT-TAT-TAT--RAT-TAT-TAT--RAT-TAT-TAT--

The machine gun bullets on the water caused John and Mikie to be sprayed with water. They scrambled behind the tanks on the pontoon. Crouching, they followed the tanks up to the shore. The glancing rebounds of bullets from the tank whisked past their heads. White and red machine gun fire was coming from barricades and entrenchments where the machine gun was emplaced. The rain poured down harder, and the Japanese fired more and more. Once the tanks were on shore, John and Mikie quickly rolled to cover, each behind a huge coconut palm. For a second, they caught their breath as they lay with relief against the sheaths that marked the trunk of the tree with rough rings.

From behind the trees, they fired their automatic rifles as they moved alertly from one tree to another, ducking just in time the bullets from the Japanese guns. Through sheets of rain, they kept firing in the foreground. Then a burst of flaming liquid was hurled at the Japanese position, and it exploded into thundering towers of red flames.

They advanced with their tanks through the smoldering jungle, knocking down towering trees in their path, grinding shrub-like palms into the muddy floor of the jungle. To look back was to see a path that resembled God's parting of the Red Sea for the Israelites. Amongst the heavy machine gun fire and mortars, three Japanese bulge calls rang out.

"All right, they're retreating!" Mikie threw his helmet into the air. The rain now began to soak the only part of his body that had been dry--his head.

"Well, Mikie, we made it through another day." John put his hand on Mikie's shoulder. "Do you think you killed any?"

"I don't know. I was just firing where I saw the fire from the guns coming. I think I did, but I'll never really know."

"I see that dead guy's face every time I close my eyes."

"John, don't dwell on it. Just remember we didn't ask to get into

The Explosion

this war. They started it when they bombed Pearl Harbor. Until then, we minded our own business."

"Ya, but he was a guy just like me. Fighting because his country wanted him to. I'm sure he'd rather be home just like the rest of us."

"John, you better stop thinking that way. If you wouldn't have shot him, he would have gotten one of us. Which one of us would you have wanted shot?"

"None of you guys."

"There's your answer. It was him or us."

"I suppose the guys all think I'm a coward because I couldn't look at his dead body without getting sick?"

"The guys haven't given the incident another thought. You're the one who is dwelling on it. All the rest of us really care about is getting home in one piece. Whatever makes that possible is all we're concerned about. After this is over, you will never see any of those guys. The only one you will see is me, and in my books you're a number one guy. Let's get some rest before they attack again." Putting his arm on John's shoulder, they walked over to the others.

The rain had ceased.

Among the fallen trees and muddy ground, littered with coconuts, torn palm leaves, and palm shrubs, they sat with the rest of their division. Their bodies had lost their agility--briskness. Some were so hungry that they actually consumed their "C" rations without the usual complaining. Others gnawed at their "D" bars.

"We were lucky today, guys." The general stood tall and proud in front of them. "We didn't lose one man. To make sure our luck holds, we're going to dig ourselves in. Don't fool yourself. Those 'Japs' aren't done with us. To them it doesn't matter if they die. Either they fight to the death or they kill themselves. You'll never take a 'Jap' as a prisoner."

All through the night they dug themselves in, shovelful after shovelful of heavy, soaked jungle ground. Their bodies were fatigued, but survival meant that they push their bodies to the ultimate. They were in charge of their destiny--their life.

With their machine gun emplaced, they waited inside their newly dug trenches. Awake--gripping their filled rifles in one hand and a grenade in the other. Silent--each wondering if this was the day they would die--each praying it was not and wondering if God even answered a pray in this hell of a place. If they did die, who would miss them? Who would cry for them?

John thought of his grandmother. Yes, she'd miss him. She would probably wish it was she who had died instead of him. How many times he had heard her say when his mother died, "why didn't God take me? She was so young. I'm so old. I've lived my life." His grandmother would cry again. His father would maybe feel a loss, but he probably would not miss him. How could he miss someone he rarely saw? His father maybe would feel regret that they had not spent more time together. When he was growing up and even now as a man, John regretted the time that they both had lost.

Even in the depths of his heart, Mikie tried to convince himself that maybe his family would miss him, and maybe they were praying for him. He could wish and pray for that, couldn't he? Yes, he could pray and wish for that, but he had done that all his life. It had not made them love him. Why? He often thought they must have cursed the day he was born. The neighbors, his old classmates, and even the guys in his division showed more concern for him than he ever experienced from his family. It was the time before an imminent battle when he should be concerned about living, and all he could think about was "why should he fight for his life"? It was of no importance to his own family. He wiped the tears from years of never being loved from his face. The thought of that letter again wrung his heart empty of any caring that he had for himself. He would fight to his death to save the men in his division. Their life's were important. He started to feel unusually cold. Chills encompassed his uncontrollable, shaking body and chattering teeth. He had to take charge of his body. He began to repeat inside his head to himself, "I feel fine, I feel fine." He could not let down the men who had befriended him.

In the sinister darkness, streams of light suddenly flashed upon them, instantly blinding them. The Japanese had lights on their tanks and could see where they were. Within seconds, they saw a string of hand grenades roll in front of their entrenchment. John and Mikie immediately threw the grenades, which they had held so long and tight in their hand, at the tanks and then flung their bodies down onto the ground floor of their entrenchment. Instinctively, they covered

The Explosion 597

their heads with their hands. The Japanese grenades at the edge of their entrenchment exploded, and they could feel the fragments hit their bodies. They scurried to their feet to join in the rifle and machine gun fire. White tracer bullets arched and crisscrossed from all directions--from overhead. A grenade landed in the trench. Wild flying fragments hit Mikie's head. It felt like a brick was slammed beside his head. His balance became uncoordinated, and his vision was doubled. Suddenly, things began to spin. Out of control, he fell to the ground.

"Mikie, Mikie!" John shouted.

"I'll be okay. Just worry about yourself. I'll be okay." He lay still for a second. His vision became normal, and he struggled to his feet. He had to help the other men.

A brief, dazzling orange light shot up from behind the Japanese lines and suddenly a swarm of screaming Japanese bounced into view. Their arms swinging wildly, with a bayonet in one hand and a grenade in the other, they charged toward the trenches. Their faces were covered with mud--their bodies wrapped in gory bandages that were loose and flying about.

One jumped down into the trench and with his knife ripped open the stomach of the machine gun operator, Gibbie.

John, hearing Gibbie's unearthly scream, looked over to see Gibbie's intestines oozing out with blood covering everything. In the split of a second that John stood in shock, the Japanese infantryman pulled the knife out of Gibbie's body and quickly plunged forward at John. John responded with his survival instinct and lunged his bayonet into the man's body. Pulling it out, the man fell at John's feet. Seeing Gibbie lying in his own blood, John rushed over to him. He crouched beside him and held him in his arms. "You'll be okay. Hang in there, pal."

"No, it's over for me, John." His limp body lay in John's arms as his warm blood covered John's hands and clothes.

For a mere second, he felt his tears as he gently laid down Gibbie's body. Then pulling back his tears, he let rage grip every part of his body and soul. He sprang to his feet and with his adrenaline boiling, he took control of the machine gun. "This is for you, pal." As the Japanese approached, he mowed them down with a vengeance as if they were cornstalks in a cornfield--one after another they fell.

As the light of day started to approach, the sounds of battle had ceased. The sight from the trenches revealed the carnage of war. The carpet of human bodies--the wounded grasping for help and relief from the pain of inflicted wounds, dismembered limbs--the dead lying in silence as their blood gurgled from their bodies. Hopefully, now, their souls were out of hell.

Mikie helped John carry Gibbie's body out of the trench.

"Mikie, are you okay?" John noticed how unusually red Mikie's face and ears were.

"Ya, I'm okay." He wasn't. His head throbbed and throbbed. He had vomited several times during the fierce fighting, and now he felt very weak. However, he wasn't one to complain. He'd survive it and tomorrow would feel better. There were a lot of men who needed help and that was his primary concern, helping the wounded get treatment and relief from their pain.

One by one, they found their comrades and helped put them on stretchers to be taken to the medical tent. With their hearts heavy, they wrapped the dead in blankets. Having the unpleasant tasks behind them, they sat resting for a while. Thinking--all the energy man puts into killing one another, energy that could be used for helping others, growing food, building instead of destroying. Would man ever learn to use his intelligence and energy for the betterment of others?

Every inch of Mikie's body ached with constant pain. His head continued to throb intensely. When he rose to salute the passing general, his weak body collapsed.

Seeing Mikie's unusually sweated body and anemic looking face, the general knew. He had seen this many times before on these tropical islands. Malaria!

Grabbing a stretcher, they placed Mikie on it and carried him into the medical tent.

"Sir, with the shortage of medical help, I'd like to stay and help take care of Mikie."

"Sure, John, no problem. There's nothing we can do now except wait for the reinforcements to come. I've got to contact them again and request that they bring more quinine for the Malaria. Mikie is just the first one in a long line of men that will probably get it, including, probably me and you." The general contemplated the worst.

"How long before the reinforcements get here?"

"Well, we cleared the jungle for them. I'm hoping that hastens their arrival. If the 'Japs' decide to attack before they arrive, we'll never survive. We don't have that many 'able bodied' men left to fight. Pray, John, for us all." The general touched his shoulder and then left.

Mikie opened his eyes and smiled at John. His voice was weak. "John, you take care of them for me." He tried to move his hand up from his side, but he was too weak. It fell back down.

"Take care of what?" John leaned closer to understand what he meant.

"My pocket--you take care of them."

John grabbed into Mikie's pocket and pulled out the deck of playing cards which Mikie always carried with him. "Mikie, they'll be fine with you. You keep them until we play again." He returned the playing cards to Mikie's pocket.

"No, you take them and remember me. Please, I need to know someone will remember me."

"Hey, pal, we'll play again as soon as you get better and you will." He took the cards out of Mikie's pocket. "I'm just keeping them so next time we're together, I can look at the cards instead of your face."

Mikie gave a weak smile. "I don't think there will be a next time."

"Sure, pal." He touched his arm. "You're going to be fine."

Mikie's body began to shiver, and his skin became cold and bluish. His eyes were so hollow. His body so tired that it drifted into sleep.

They treated him with quinine and then waited. Waited--for the reinforcements--for more medicine--for more to become sick with the disease.

When the reinforcements came, Mikie and the wounded were moved to a better facility. Some would live. Some would die.

John stood alone holding the deck of cards in his hand. He had never played any card games until he met Mikie, the guy who seemed to live for a good game of cards. He looked down at the cards. "Hang in there, pal." His eyes were glazed with soft tears. "I'll never forget you--cards or no cards. I promise."

****

Hobbling along with his wooden cane, the tall, broad shoulder, gray-haired man moved down the streets, ripped open by bombs and now cluttered with mounds upon mounds of bricks and stones. Subdued, he passed the skeletal remains of buildings that were gutted and roofless. Some of the buildings were still burning and glowing. Red flames still were coming from their hollow windows and doors. Other buildings had been completely smashed, and older couples were standing in the dust of the ruins--dazed from the bombings and loss of their much loved property that they had worked so hard for all their lives. It was all gone. It was unbelievable, especially, when victory had seemed so near for so long and now this defeat. Lying on some of the streets were bodies of human beings who had been killed by a bomb or falling building debris. Mothers were crying over the bodies of their dead children. Children were crying over the dead bodies of their mothers, sisters, and younger brothers. There were no older brothers or young fathers here. They had been sent to war. Only old men like him, no longer good for war, were left here in this desolate place that was made more desolate each day with the continuous bombing.

He paused in front of a rubble of smoldering glass splinters and remnants of tiles that used to be Oslo's bakery. Oh, it hadn't been Oslo's for quite sometime, but somehow he tended to keep the familiarity of the old name with a place even long after it had been owned by other's. Oslo had died several years ago and shortly thereafter, his wife. The bakery had been sold after her death for payment of back taxes. The runaway inflation after the first world war had hurt them financially. Both of them crippled with age and unable to work, they just could not survive. It was too bad that they had not treated their nephew better. Maybe he would have stayed and in their old age helped them. He was only twelve, but he remembered little Pete Hof and how he had to live on the streets. He wondered how Pete was doing? Had he found a better life in America? America had never had a world war on its soil. Therefore, it had to be better.

Onward he went, then stopped. He stood in silence and tears came to his eyes. He looked at the ruins from which clouds of smoke still hovered over the remains of charred pieces of wood that now rested in the building's pulverized stone foundation. Not a wall remained,

The Explosion

only memories. This had been his father's carpenter shop, so many years ago. It had survived the first war but not this one.

Home he now headed, out of the city--the jungle of collapsed concrete debris and lost lives--a city that had died and been buried in its own ruins. Through the railroad yards mangled by bombs and past the ball bearing and aircraft factories that had been leveled into extinction, he walked. Taking a short way home, he crossed the fields that once were hay and pasture. Now only battlefields pockmarked with shell holes and crisscrossed with trenches. Scattered about were rusty parts of army tanks, guns, helmets, and rotted bodies of dead soldiers--German--French--British--American? The war did not discriminate when it came to death. He remembered the ancient, huge, spreading black walnut and oak trees that now were bare stumps. Wherever he looked, the countryside was dotted with roofless, burnt-out, farm buildings. Man was so good at taking something beautiful and turning it into a piece of hell--destroying things of antiquity that could never be brought back--taking away the heritage of a country and leaving only a legacy of death and wanton destruction. Why?

He left the fields and walked down a short, dirt driveway, then up some wooden porch steps. Once on the porch, he sat in his old, hand-carved rocking chair and looked now from a distance at what he had just viewed close-up. As he sat slowly rocking in these early, quiet morning hours, he remembered the war that he had been in some twenty-eight years ago. The "war to end all wars," so they said, but obviously not true. They had been a well-supplied, confident army; they all had been conditioned for years to expect the inevitable--war. He had been in General Kluch's army when he was in Belgium. There he had fought against Belgium's main army which was under the command of King Albert. Although Belgium's attempt to block their advance had failed, they had lost almost a month in time. He remembered them burning numerous Belgian Villages and the famous library at Louvain. He regretted a lot of things that they had done in the war. The burning of the library was one regret, because there was no military reason to do that. In his mind, he could see the trenches--rifles on the parapet--comrades in arms. He remembered sending stockings from Belgium back home to his wife. His wife--she had died here. She never ventured off this farm. This farm was where she was born and had died. So it would probably be for Heidi. Being their only child, the farm would pass to her someday when he died. Someday when Heidi would die, how would that ever work with Bertha and Helmet?

He just shook his head in disapproval. Such deceit could never stay hidden forever. Could it? He prayed that he would never live to see the truth be revealed. So many people would be hurt.

He heard noise inside the house, the opening and closing of cupboard doors, the clanging of kettles. He rose from his rocker, opened the old house door, and walked into the kitchen.

When he opened the door, a plump woman turned and instinctively hid what she had on the counter by standing in front of it. "Oh, Pa, it's you." Relieved, she turned and continued what she was about to start before he entered the room. With her small, fat hands, she opened a brown cloth bag and took out some small brown beans and put them into an old grinder. As she turned the crank, ground brown particles came out one end and fell into a small bowl. When she had finished grinding, she took out a small metal pot, measured four cups of water into the pot. Putting the pot on the hot stove, she waited until the water boiled. With the water boiling she added four heaping teaspoons of the ground brown particles. She then took the pot off the heat and with the ground particles settling to the bottom of the pot, she poured out the black-colored water into two large mugs. She placed the steaming mugs on the table, one in front of where her father was sitting and the other where she was going to sit.

She then covered the unused ground particles and put the small bowl, which they were in, into the cloth bag of unground beans. Tying the bag shut, she put it into the cupboard, hiding it behind some of her dishes and bowls.

With the aroma filling the air, she joined her father at the table.

"Oh, doesn't it taste so good, Pa." She took a small sip so she could truly taste the flavor.

"Ya, what's the special occasion?"

"I guess I just woke up and thought how lucky we were that our buildings are all standing. Besides, here I am guarding this precious commodity, and if we're bombed it will be gone too. So, I thought, maybe we should enjoy a cup. If we're still here tomorrow, we'll enjoy another cup. We'll keep on enjoying another cup until either the coffee is gone or we are." She raised the mug as if to toast to her comment and took another lingering taste of the fresh brew.

"Ya, we are lucky. I took a walk this morning to see what damage was done in the city. It is sad, Heidi, so many of the century old buildings are gone." His eyes were full of sadness. All he could do was shake his head.

"I just pray that my Holde comes home alive. So many of the neighbors have lost a husband or son." Tears filled her eyes at the thought of losing her beloved husband.

"With all of us praying, I know he will come home safe." He took another drink of his coffee. "We better open some windows and doors. We don't want any soldiers coming here and smelling the coffee. Then we will have to tell them where it is hidden, and then it will be their coffee."

"Oh, I don't like them coming here."

"I don't either, but we have to give them shelter and help them anyway we can. They are our soldiers."

"This whole war has turned everything upside down. I worry again, Pa, every time they come." She finished her coffee and took the empty cup to the sink.

"I know you do, but maybe she has learnt from last time." He handed Heidi his empty cup.

"Oh, Pa, I don't know. What a disgrace it would be if anyone found out. That's why I did what I did, to save us all from the shame." She walked over to the old house door and opened it. She put a kitchen chair in front of it to keep it open. For a moment, she stood in the doorway looking out at the green pasture. "I suppose we should put the cows in the barn and start milking."

"Ya, I'll wake up Bertha to help us." He rose from the kitchen chair.

"Na, let her sleep. We can handle the milking ourselves. We'll wake her up after milking. She's younger than both of us. Let her clean the barn out today." She excited the door and went into the pasture to chase the cows into the barn.

Ludwig walked to the end of the kitchen. There at the bottom of the stairs he paused, looked up, thought for a moment, then shook his head. He opened the door next to the stairway. The door opened into the barn which was connected to the house.

After milking and feeding the pigs, Heidi filled a pail with water into which she mixed some ground oats and corn. "You keep watch now, Pa." She took the pail into the house and then into the basement. In one dark corner of the basement was a small pen. Inside the pen was a pig. She poured the contents of the pail into a wooden trough. She heard the pig's snorting as she walked back up the stairs. "Any day now, I think, we can butcher it." She locked the basement door behind her. "I hold my breath until it is done eating. Hoping that no one comes and hears it."

"It was a good idea you had, Heidi, to hide one of the litter." He closed the door to the barn and walked through the kitchen out onto the porch.

Heidi walked with him. "Well, it's ridiculous! First, they come out and keep a record of everything we have. Then we have to get a permit to butcher our own animals, and we can only butcher what they allow us to butcher. My God, we've got to feed ourselves. How foolish to only allow so many to butcher. We all have to eat."

He sat in his rocker again. "That's another reason I don't like those soldiers coming around here. What if one of them would find out what we've been doing?"

"Such things make me feel bad about Bertha. We were pleased when the soldiers were distracted." As Heide sat on the top porch step, her heart became saddened.

"Ya, that's true, but I never thought it would go that far."

"I didn't either. Oh, well, it's done. There is nothing we can do about it now."

A distance down the road, they saw some figures walking on what remained of a gravel road that had been bombed more than once. As the dark figures approached, they could be recognized as a woman with three small children.

"Who is that?" Ludwig stopped rocking trying to distinguish the people.

"I think that it is Frau Schwienhurt. I saw her last week after church. She said that she'd come one day this week to visit and see the baby." Heidi stood on the porch step to get a better view.

"Helmut is a year already, kind of late to be coming to see a baby, isn't it?" He rose from the rocker.

"Well, she's been busy, much more than the rest of us. Her husband has been in the war over a year just like my Holde. The big difference is that she has three small children to take care of. I have you, Bertha, and only one small child." She walked down the porch steps.

"You don't have to convince me it's your child. I know the truth, remember. I'm also the one who thinks it's not right what you did." He followed her down the steps.

She stopped and abruptly turned in front of him. "Hush! Keep your mouth shut. It's better this way. Don't you spoil everything with your big mouth," she whispered and then proceeded toward Frau Schweinhurt. With a gracious smile, Heidi extended her hand. "So good to see you, Hela."

"Hi, Heidi." Hela followed her up the steps carrying her youngest in her arms. The other two children followed, clinging to their mother's dress. "Hi, Ludwig."

"Hi, Hela."

"I see you didn't get hit by the bombing yesterday." She stood surveying their property. "I'm glad for you."

"We were lucky. The people in the city weren't so lucky. I walked there early this morning. The sight is one that brings tears to a person's eyes." Ludwig followed them inside.

Once inside, Hela sat the two small girls on the wooden bench near the door. Heidi offered Hela a chair. She sat on it, placing her youngest girl on her lap.

"I was not so lucky yesterday. Everything was destroyed. The children and I were lucky to get out of our bombed house alive. The chicken coop is the only thing standing. We slept there last night." Her voice revealed her tiredness. The vibrant glow had disappeared from her young face and was replaced with a weary look of total despair.

"Oh, Hela, I'm so sorry." Heidi took her hand and comfortingly held it.

"That's not the worst of it. Yesterday, I got word that William was killed two weeks ago in Russia." Spontaneous tears filled her eyes and poured down her cheeks.

Her two daughters, seeing her cry and sensing her terrible sadness, ran over to her, grabbed onto her, and began crying endlessly.

"Oh, my dear, Hela, you are so alone now. You are welcome to live here. We'll all help you raise the girls," Ludwig offered.

"Oh, yes, do stay here." Heidi comforted Hela with a hug. She thought of how terrible it would be if it had been Holde who had been killed. Her eyes also became watery, but she could not cry. It would make Hela and the girls wept more. In her heart, she wept for Hela and those three fatherless girls.

"It is very kind of you--sob--sob--but I'm going to live with my parents--sob--sob--. There is nothing here for me now. You were good neighbors to William and me. I wanted to bring you a gift for Helmut like you always brought for us when we had our children, but I just didn't have the means or time. Right after my youngest was born, my William was called away." She burst into tears again. "At least he did get to see her. Holde never got to see his child did he?" She tried to compose herself.

"No, my Holde was taken to war about eight months before Helmut was born." Heidi offered her a handkerchief.

"Thanks." She took the handkerchief and wiped her face dry. "Does Holde know he has a son?"

Heidi looked over at her father's face and looked straight into his eyes. "No, he doesn't." She continued to look at him until he lowered his head in silent disapproval.

"If only I could have had a son to carry on my William's name. His name is dead now just like him." Her regret brought tears. Her composer was gone.

"Hela, why don't you and the girls rest here today and tonight. Tomorrow I'll walk you to your parents' home," Ludwig offered.

"Thanks, but I couldn't impose."

"Please, Hela, I don't think it's safe for you and the children to go that far alone."

"Pa, is right." Heidi touched Hela's hand. "You rest here until tomorrow then Pa will accompany you."

"What's the matter?" A petite brunette stood at the bottom of the upstairs steps holding a small, chubby-faced boy in her arms.

"Hela's husband has been killed." Heidi walked over and took the boy from the girl's arms.

"This is Helmut." She kissed him on the cheek and walked toward Hela.

The young girl slowly approached Hela. "I'm sorry, Hela." Her blue eyes showed her sadness.

"Thank you, Bertha. You're such a sweet, young lady." She reached out and touched Bertha's hand.

"How fast they grow." Hela smiled at Helmut. "He's younger but bigger than my little one." She touched his fat little hand.

"He eats like a horse," Bertha commented.

"He has natural curls." Hela stroked his head covered with massive curls.

"Ya, isn't he just such a sweetheart." Heidi kissed his soft pink cheek.

Ludwig's eyes met Heidi's then Bertha's. He shook his head and then went outside. Soon a creaking, rocking sound was heard.

"Would you and the girls like something to eat?" Heidi put the boy down on the floor. She took a black cast-iron frying pan from its hook above the stove, plumped it onto the wood-burning stove, and slapped a tablespoon of lard into the pan.

"No, thank you."

"Oh, please. I've got to make Bertha and Helmut something to eat anyway." Grabbing two eggs out of a chipped enamel bowl, which set on the counter, she cracked the eggshells and dropped the contents into the pan, sizzling with hot melted lard. She spooned the hot lard over the eggs until the whites were solid. Putting each egg on a separate plate along with a slice of dark bread, she placed the food on the table.

Bertha sat down at the table and grabbed one of the plates.

"I'll feed Helmut. You go clean out the barn when you're finished eating." Heidi took the other plate, set Helmut on her lap, and mashed the white with the soft yellow of the egg. With a spoon she started to feed Helmut. "Are you sure the girls don't want something?"

"No, thanks. I think we'll be leaving." She put her arms around the girls who still clung to her.

"Oh, no. Please, stay today," Heidi pleaded.

"It's very kind but no." Hela rose from the chair. The two girls were clinging to her so tightly that she could hardly move, but at least they weren't crying. When Hela ceased crying, they also did.

"It was nice seeing you, Hela." Bertha finished eating and put her empty plate on the sink's counter. As she opened the door that led to the barn, she turned, smiled, and waved to Hela. Then closing the door, she disappeared into the barn.

Hela smiled back. "You can be so proud of her. I hope my girls grow up to be as nice and so beautiful also."

Heidi just smiled. She felt relief that no one knew the truth. "Why don't you wait a few minutes? I'm almost finished feeding Helmut. I'll walk with you then, since you are so determined to leave today."

When she had finished feeding Helmut, she washed his face. "I'll take Helmut in the barn by Bertha so I can walk with you." Within few minutes, she had returned.

Out onto the porch she walked with Hela and her children. "Pa, she wants to leave today."

Ludwig rose from the rocking chair. "I've been thinking about your journey. Sit down here." He motioned Hela over to his rocker.

Hela sat in the rocker with the youngest in her arms while the other two hung onto the rocker's arms.

"Up in the attic we have an old wooden wagon. Remember, Heidi, I made that for you to pull Bertha around in."

"Ya, I remember. Why? You want to get it down for Helmut?" Heidi was confused. Why would he think of that now? It was irrelevant.

"No, for Hela, she can put at least two of the children in it. It will make the trip easier for her."

"That's a good idea, Pa. I'll help you get it down."

"No, I couldn't take something you made for your daughter. You can use it for Helmut."

"Please, you just sit there and wait while we get it. I can make another one if Helmut needs one." Ludwig went into the shed and came out with an old ladder that he had made out of two-by-four's. Into the house he carried it.

"We'll be right back." Heidi went into the house, took a flashlight

The Explosion

out of a drawer, checked it for a beam of light, and followed him.

He carried the ladder upstairs into his bedroom. There in the ceiling was a trapdoor. He pushed the trapdoor open with the ladder and then rested the ladder to one side of the hole. Taking the flashlight from Heidi, he climbed the ladder and disappeared into the dark, stuffy attic.

Heidi followed him up into the attic to help him.

The beam of light from the flashlight searched the attic, one section at a time. In one corner of the attic the red wagon sat, cluttered with boxes full of things--old clothes--papers--letters.

Their hands became dirty from handling the dust-laden objects. With the wagon empty, the boxes were now strewn all about the attic floor. They heard someone climb the ladder. Turning, they saw it was Bertha.

"Boy, I never knew all this stuff was up here." She climbed into the attic onto the floor.

"Where is Helmut?" Heidi asked as she placed the last box on the floor.

"He's by Hela. She told me you were up here. What's in the boxes?" She started to open one of the boxes.

"I don't remember anymore." Ludwig picked up the wagon and carried it to the trapdoor opening. "When I'm halfway down the ladder, please, hand me the wagon, Heidi." Setting the wagon down, he stepped onto the rungs and started to descend the ladder backwards.

"Okay, Pa." She handed the flashlight to Bertha, went over to the opening, and watched her father climb down the ladder.

He stopped. "Hand it to me, please." He reached up to grab it.

Heidi moved the wagon slowly downward through the trapdoor opening. "Do you have it?" She hung securely on to it.

"Ya, I've got it." He secured the wagon in his hands. Then very slowly continued backwards down the ladder--one step at a time.

"Ma, this box is full of old letters." Bertha shined the light into the box. Taking one letter out, she examined it.

"They're probably your grandpa's letters." Heidi took one out of Bertha's hand. Holding the light near it, she examined it. "I think it's from his sister."

"I didn't know Grandpa had a sister." Bertha pulled the letter out of the envelope.

"Grandpa doesn't talk a lot about his life. There's a lot I don't know, but I know he had a sister. When the letters would come, he'd often read them to Ma and me."

"Is this from America--United States?" Bertha held the letter close to make out the stamping on the yellowed envelope.

"Probably, that's where she lives--in a town called Beechwood, I think. I'm going down by Hela. Pa and I are going to walk with her for a while. You better come down and take care of Helmut." Heidi started to back down onto the ladder.

"Wait, Ma, I want to take these down and read them."

"No, leave them alone. They're your grandpa's. Now come along and take care of Helmut."

"Ah, Grandpa won't care. They're setting up here gathering dust. Here take this box." She handed the box down to her mother.

"I suppose." Heidi reluctantly grabbed the box and went slowly down the ladder. At the bottom of the ladder, she set the box on the floor.

Bertha put the trapdoor in place so when the ladder was pulled out, the trapdoor would fall on top of the opening, closing it.

Heidi took the ladder down the stairs and gave it to her father who returned it to the shed.

Bertha followed her mother with the box of letters. She placed the box on the kitchen table and began to take the letters out one by one and read them.

"We are leaving with Hela and the children now." Heidi brought Helmut into the house. She took the chair from in front of the old house door and closed it as she left.

Helmut climbed up onto the chair that stood in front of the window and watched them walk into the distance until they disappeared from view. Climbing off the wooden chair, he went onto the soft sofa where he fell asleep.

Bertha became so entranced as she read one letter after the other. The letters informed her of a great-aunt, Anna, who was married to a banker. Wow! A banker! She must have money. Her first cousin, Amanda, was married to a banker also. Boy! America must be full of rich men. She thought how nice it must be to be married to someone with money. Bet they never had to clean out cow shit or pig shit or worst yet the sickening sweet smell of chicken shit. All they probably have to do is look pretty. Must be nice! At that moment, she decided that she was going to go to America. She'd get herself a rich man also. She wondered how much it would cost to go there. She knew that she'd never make any money on this farm. Huh! She'd never make any money anywhere with this damn war! Determination would get her what she wanted. Grandpa always said, "where there is a will, there is a way." Those were the words that she would live by. Nothing would stand in her way, nothing!

Out of the silence of the afternoon, she heard loud, rumbling noises and boisterous voices outside getting closer and closer. Putting down the letter, which she had been reading before she had reveries about America, she went to the window. Pulling back the sheer curtain, she looked outside. There was a group of Germany soldiers. She was appalled at how differently they looked from the soldiers that she had seen over a year ago. At that time, their uniforms were kept so neat--clean--stylish. The buttons on their double-breasted coats had sparkled and their uniforms had fit so attractively. Now the uniforms were tattered and filthy. They even walked differently. Now they limped along probably because of sore feet from walking in their worn shoes. Some shoes even appeared to be stuffed with newspaper. They were pictures of frustration and wretchedness.

As she saw them come closer, she put back the curtain, moved away from the window, and quietly waited.

KNOCK! KNOCK!

She went to the door and opened it, a mere crack, just enough for her to see the soldier.

"Good afternoon, Fraulein, may I please speak to the owner of this property?"

"He's not here now. How may I help you?" Bertha noticed the tall, lean soldier's beautiful, light-blue eyes.

"I just wanted to inform him that my soldiers and I will be camping in his yard tonight. Is there water in the barn?"

"Yes, there is a hand pump near the cow's drinking trough."

"Good, then we will clean up in the barn and there will be no need to bother you in the house." The soldier turned and walked away.

Bertha closed the door. Walking back over to the window, she watched through the sheer curtain. Some of the soldiers went into the barn while others sat on the porch steps and lawn resting. When the others came out of the barn, the one's that had rested while waiting, went inside. When they were all cleaned, they ate and then leisurely sat around--some in their trousers and white tee-shirts, others were shirtless, revealing their masculine, hairy chest. They sat drinking beer and smoking their precious cigarettes down to the smallest butt. They had fought hard. Now in this short, unexpected period of calmness, they enjoyed what they could--while they could.

Bertha watched them one by one. Some of them were actually attractive now that they had cleaned and shaved themselves. In fact, the one that had come to the door had blonde, gorgeous curls to go with those magnificent blue eyes. Smoking and drinking with his bare chest showing, he began to look quite desirable to Bertha.

With Helmut sleeping, Bertha decided it was time to go out into the pasture and bring the cows into the barn. It was an excellent opportunity for her to promenade in front of the soldiers. She ran upstairs to her bedroom where she sat at her vanity in front of the mirror. There she took the hair out of the roll on her head and let it cascade over her shoulders. After brushing it, she took two barrettes out of her wooden jewelry box. She put one on each side of her head to hold her hair behind her ears that were pierced with small earrings. She took off the trousers and the old shirt that she had worn to clean out the barn earlier. Reaching into the closet, she grabbed out her Sunday dress. This was a special dress that she only wore when she went to town for church, shopping, or visiting. She deliberately left the first two buttons open revealing her cleavage. She was very pleased with her big breasts. Looking in the mirror, she straightened the belt that flattered her small waist. Being satisfied with how beautiful and enticing she looked, she went down the stairs, opened the door, and walked out onto the porch. She knew all the soldiers' eager eyes were watching her as she walked in front of them. She eyed the blonde soldier and smiled at him. He was the "catch" that she was after.

"Where are you going?" One of the soldiers with a beer bottle in his hand got up and walked with her. He couldn't help but notice her partially opened blouse. He stretched his neck and strained his eyes to see more.

"I'm going to get the cows and put them inside the barn for milking. You want to help?" Teasingly, she smiled at him and then quickly glanced at the blonde.

"Sure." He continued to follow her. His thoughts were of getting her alone in the barn.

"Great!" She had hoped that maybe her being with him would get the blonde jealous. After all he was their leader and she was "the only hen with all these roosters," so to speak. Who should really have her but the leader, "the main rooster."

As they spirited down the lane to get the cows, she turned and smiled at the blonde.

The blonde smiled back and watched her as he indulged in his bottle of beer and casually smoked his cigarette.

The young soldier shared his beer with Bertha as they walked and smiled at each other. He'd put his arm around her; she'd put her arm around him. He'd hold her hand; she'd hold his hand. All the time she had her eyes on the tall blonde. She made sure that he saw how wonderfully the soldier and her were getting along. In her thoughts, she was hoping that the blonde would come out into the pasture and send the soldier back to the rest so he could have her. They were nearing the barn. When was the tall blonde going to make his move? Bertha was getting frustrated. The blonde soldier only seemed interested in drinking, smoking, and watching them. Didn't he know that her smile at him was a sign that she wanted him?

Once inside the barn, the cows moved routinely into their wooden stalls. At each stall there was a rope, which Bertha used to tie the cows into the stall.

Darkness filled the barn as the soldier blocked out the sunlight by closing the large barn door. He then locked it with its latch. The soldier leaned against the door and watched her as he drank from the beer bottle until he had emptied it. Setting the bottle down, he began staggering away from the door toward her.

She moved out of his touch. "Let me tie up this last cow." She had to put him off. Surely, any minute now, the one she really wanted would come through the door. Oh, my God, he couldn't. The door was locked. Would she have to follow her teasing through? How could she get out of this situation?

When the last cow was tied in its place, she felt the soldier's hands around her waist. "Are you ready now?" He captivated her in his arms and kissed her. His passionate kiss excited her and suddenly it did not matter who she was with. Her libido had to be satisfied. If not by the blonde, this soldier would have to do. They became caught up in the overmastering desire of the moment. Their bodies vibrated with wild excitement. They had to finish what their passion had started. He unzipped his trousers, and she wildly grabbed inside.

"Bertha, Bertha," a voice called from inside the house.

"Oh, it's my grandpa." She pulled away and with nervous fingers she buttoned the top buttons which she had deliberately left open earlier. Quickly, she straightened her dress and belt.

"So what." He grabbed at her. He could not stop now. He was at the height of his excitement.

"No." She pulled away. "Get out of here--now!"

He zippered his trousers, but the zippered trousers could not hide the protruding hardness inside of them.

The door opened and in the threshold her grandfather stood--silent and observing. He knew Bertha. As such, he knew exactly what would have happened if he would not have come home. He saw the soldier's swelled area inside his trousers. Looking at Bertha, he saw the guilty look on her face. The look that prevailed when she knew, she was doing something that violated certain rules.

"Hi, Grandpa, the soldier was helping me tie the cows in their stalls." Bertha smiled.

"Well, looks like they are all tied up so he can leave, can't he?" Ludwig looked at the soldier and with a hand gesture motioned him toward the door.

"Take your empty beer bottle with you," Ludwig ordered.

"Yes, sir." The soldier smiled at Ludwig. As he walked past Bertha, he gave her a lusty smile. Picking up the bottle, he unlocked the huge barn door and went outside.

"Come in the house, Bertha." He held the door open for her.

"Yes, Grandpa." She smiled at him as she swiftly walked past him through the doorway that connected the barn to the house.

When she entered the house, she saw her mother was in the chair rocking Helmut. Helmut's eyes and nose were cherry red; he was still sniffing.

"What's the matter with him?" Bertha asked.

"Ya, that's what I'd like to know." Her mother was upset. "We come home, and he is crying. You are nowhere in sight. Well, I guess we don't have to ask you where you were, or what you were doing, do we?"

"I was getting the cows in the barn for you and Grandpa so you wouldn't have to," Bertha snapped.

"Don't you talk like that to your mother," Ludwig interrupted.

"I just wanted to be helpful and then right away I get criticized for it. Do I get a 'thank you'? No!"

"You never were so concerned about helping us before. I wonder if your desire to be seen by the soldiers didn't influence your helpfulness?" her mother sternly questioned.

"Don't judge me by yourself," Bertha quickly snapped back.

"You should be half as good as your ma was, and we wouldn't have to live this lie," Ludwig commented.

"Well, I tell you this much, Bertha. If it happens again, I'll not do what I did in the past. My husband isn't here now, and I'll not bear the shame that isn't mine. It'll be all your shame, and it won't be under this roof either."

"You can't throw me out. You wouldn't dare."

"I'll even help her. So you better keep your pants up," Ludwig interjected.

"I didn't do anything."

Helmut began to cry from the loud words.

"No, not yet." Heidi tried to soothe away Helmut's fear in hopes that he would cease the crying.

"Oh! When this war is over, I'm getting out of here. I can't stand this place or you two anymore. I wish you were all dead!" She stormed up the stairs. With a mighty swing, she slammed her bedroom door shut and flopped herself onto the bed. Lying on her stomach, she propped her head in her hands. In this position, she could see quite clearly out her bedroom window. Once again her desiring eyes fell upon the blonde soldier. The more she watched him--the more overwhelming became her desire.

"Bertha, come down here and take care of Helmut. We have to milk the cows," Ludwig called up the stairs.

Bertha rolled her eyes and with a scowling face rose from her bed. Sullenly, she walked down the stairs into the kitchen.

"He's quiet now." Her mother gently handed Helmut to her.

Bertha grabbed him but then placed him down on the floor. "He can walk, why should I carry him." She flopped her body down onto a kitchen chair.

Her mother shook her head. "Come on, Pa, let's go do our milking chores. Some people should never have children."

The two of them departed from the kitchen and entered the barn. While they were milking, Helmut amused himself by playing on the floor's rag rug with a wooden train, which Ludwig had made him. Meanwhile, Bertha resumed reading the old letters in the box on the kitchen table. After milking, Bertha took the box and letters upstairs to her bedroom where she secluded herself, only coming downstairs to eat the supper her mother had made. After supper Bertha returned to her room, Heidi washed the dirty dishes from the meal while Ludwig dried them. Later, Heidi gave Helmut a bath and retired him to his bed in Ludwig's bedroom. It was the end of the day now, and as usual, she retired to her chair to do her mending. Tonight she was darning the holes in her father's socks.

After helping Heidi with the dishes, Ludwig had retired out on the porch sitting in his rocker. He watched the young soldiers--talking --smoking--drinking. He smiled thinking no matter how much things may change--human nature stayed pretty much the same. The young boys do what all young boys do. It is expected of them to "sow their young oats." However, girls were to be the virtuous ones. Ah, yes, he remembered girls that weren't virtuous. But when it came to marriage, the guys wanted the virgins. He was the same, but for his Bertha to be that way, troubled him. He shook his head. Why?

Then one by one, he saw that the soldiers had ceased talking and were staring upward. They would take a swig of their beer, a drag on their cigarette, and then make a remark that caused a dirty chuckle among them.

The Explosion

Ludwig turned to see what they were staring at and making remarks about. His heart fell to see such a sight. He was embarrassed. Shocked! His pride had been stomped into the ground.

With the light on in her bedroom, Bertha had chosen not to close her curtains. Therefore, whatever she did in front of her window was clearly visible to all who looked up into her room.

Ludwig, filled with a fury, rose from his rocker. Grabbing his cane, he stormed into the house.

"Pa, what's the matter?" Heidi looked up from her work.

"She's strutting in front of the window while she undresses." Ludwig shook his head. "That girl is unbelievable!" Ludwig swung his cane wildly in the air. "I'll beat some decency into her!" He dashed toward the stairs.

"Pa, leave her be. She is old enough to know exactly what she is doing. If you confront her, you'll only upset yourself more. Please, sit down, Pa. I meant what I said earlier. Next time she's out of here." Heidi continued with darning the holey socks.

He paused at the bottom of the stairs, thought a moment, walked over to Heidi, and touched her shoulders. "You're right. You're her mother--her parent. I've no right to interfere. I'm sorry."

"You don't have to be sorry, Pa. I know you mean well." She smiled at him and lovingly patted his hand, wrinkled from age.

He smiled back. "I'm tired. I'm going to bed."

"Ya, walking Hela home to her parents was tiring, but I'm glad we did it." She took the thimble off her finger, stuck the darning needle into the sock, and then put the sock into her sewing basket.

"Ya, I'm glad also, good night, Heidi." With his cane he thumped up the steps, one at a time.

Heidi put the sewing basket in its proper place, locked the front door, and the door that led to the barn. Turning out the lights, she also went upstairs and retired into her room.

While she was lying in bed just about to fall asleep, she heard Bertha's door creak open. She heard each stair step creak as Bertha stepped on it. Then there was a time of silence. Heidi was too tired to be bothered by what she knew Bertha wanted to do. She turned on her side and fell asleep.

Bertha, scantily dressed in her nightgown, stepped outside onto the porch and then walked down the steps straight toward the man she was staring at, the tall blonde. Taking the beer bottle from his hand, she held it to her mouth and guzzled down its contents. She handed the empty bottle to one of the soldiers standing beside the blonde.

"Come on, I want to show you something." She took his hand and walked him toward the house.

"All right, Joe." Some soldiers raised their beer bottles in the air encouraging him.

"Ya, warm her up for us." A roar of lusty laughter traveled in the warm night air.

As they walked, suddenly a hand gripped itself around her arm and held it firmly. "Don't you think you should finish with me before you start a new adventure?"

"Let go of my arm. He was the one I wanted all along."

Violently, he swung her arm loose. "You little slut!" He spit a mouthful of beer at her.

Taking her hand, she wiped his sticky saliva from her face and continued walking with the blonde. After walking up a few porch steps, she stopped. "I think maybe you should take your shoes off out here." She sat on a porch step.

He sat beside her and in his drunken stupor took off his shoes.

Quietly, she maneuvered his drunken body up the steps, into the house and upstairs into her bedroom. Lasciviously, she tore the clothes from his body. Admiring his body, she knew that he was worth waiting for--but not too long. After tonight she would probably never see him again, but after tonight it did not matter. She would have made love to him and would always remember the pleasure of it.

The rhythmically creaking of the bed and the panting from inside Bertha's room, woke Heidi. She tossed and turned trying to fall asleep again, but all she could do was cry silent tears. Her daughter was a slut and that broke her heart. Why hadn't Bertha learnt from the last time? The consequences could not be any clearer than "the writing on the wall"--a shameful reputation--pregnancy--disease--illegitimacy. She felt so helpless. Why hadn't she been able to convince her? She had been a failure as a mother. She cried herself to sleep.

A loud, roaring sound sprung Heidi from her bed. She was unable to maintain her balance as the floor shook beneath her feet. Glass from her bedroom window blew out at her, cutting her arms and hands. Ceiling plaster fell on her head as the walls cracked and moaned with the violent oscillation of the house.

"Heidi!" Her bedroom door flung open. "We've got to get into the cellar, hurry!" Ludwig had Helmut in his arms as he raced toward the stairs.

Bertha's door flung open, and the blonde soldier burst out. "Damn, Allies!" Zipping his trousers, he flew past Ludwig on the stairs as he ran outside to join his men.

Heidi grabbed sleepy Bertha, who was standing in the threshold of her bedroom, and glided down the stairs after her father and Helmut.

Above their heads they could hear the high, shrill sound of more falling bombs, their violent bursting upon impact, and then the rushing sound of fire. The stairway shook--cracked--and fell. With nothing to grip on to, they all tumbled head first onto the cellar floor.

Helmut was crying loudly. He had hit his head in the fall and the loud noises made him fearful. He desperately clung to Ludwig.

Bertha was hysterical with fear and bellowing in tears. "Oh, Ma, I don't want to die. I don't want to die! I'm sorry about what I said before. I don't want you or Grandpa to die. I didn't mean it, Ma. I didn't mean it."

"I know, Bertha." Heidi hugged her daughter close to her and gently stroked her hair. She didn't like some of the things Bertha did, but she always loved her. "It'll be all right. It'll be all right." Heidi prayed inside her soul--not for herself--but for Bertha, Helmut, and her father that they would survive and not be harmed.

With death lingering over them, they huddled into a corner, crowding their bodies into the smallest area feasible.

Outside the thunderous pounding of the bombs landing grew louder--closer. Singly at first, then several at once as whole groups of bombs fell together. The cellar resounded with their explosions as the howling of the antiaircraft guns reverberated through every inch of their bodies. Their bodies were tight with fear. Hearing the soldiers' gunshots mingling with the other sounds gave them relief in knowing that they were not alone.

They could see the house shake on its foundation. They heard the plaster fall from the walls and ceilings, the booming sounds of the walls falling to the floor, and now crashing through the cellar's ceiling. The pig left out his final sharp, high-pitched cry as a falling wood beam hit him, killing him instantly. Clouds of blinding and suffocating dust accompanied the partial collapse of the ceiling opposite the corner they were in. They coughed and gasped for each breath.

Ludwig draped his body over Bertha, Heidi, and Helmut to protect them from the ceiling directly above them, which was now starting to collapse from the weight of the falling debris of the upper walls, ceilings, and floors. Particles of dust were now falling on them. How long before the entire house would be in the cellar? Would they be buried alive? Closer and closer they huddled. If they were to die, at least they would not die alone and in a strange place. That gave them comfort. When joy is shared, it is doubled. When fear is shared, it is lessened. What could be more fearful than death? Ludwig and Bertha could accept death for themselves but not the children. The children had so much of their life to live yet. It would be such a waste to have their lives end. Bertha could not accept death. Not hers, because she was so young and beautiful, and there was so much she wanted to do. Not her mother's or grandfather's, because of the shadow of guilt that clung to her soul as a result of the careless words she had thrown at them earlier. Oh, God! She did not want anyone to die!

The large center support beam snapped, and the remainder of the house crashed into the cellar. Boards, plaster, heavy beams beat upon Ludwig's back and head. Blood poured down onto his face from a deep gouge in his head. A splintered two-by-four's sharp edge pierced his back. More warm, sticky blood dripped from his body onto Bertha and Heidi.

"Grandpa--Ma--are you okay?" Silence! She heard no reply--felt no movement. Her mouth filled with dry, gagging, plaster dust.

Amongst the rubble covering her body, she could feel part of someone's body--her mother?--her grandfather?--Helmut? She could not see anything. To open her eyes would to have slivers of wood or pulverized plaster get into her eyes and irritate them. Each breath suffocated her as it filled her nose with dust of the pulverized house. Her body was immobilized by the weight of the debris on it. She could not move an arm--a leg. She was entombed in this grave alive. Was anyone else alive? All were silent around her.

The sounds of the battle above were still raging. As long as the fighting continued, there would be no consideration toward someone digging them out. It was getting more difficult for her to breathe. Would she die?

****

The headlights' beams guided her down the familiar road. The red blinkers flashed, the automobile slowed as it turned off the main road onto a tree-canopied side road. The automobile passed the location where he had first made love to her. That night, some two years ago, had resulted in these nightly rendezvous after her work shift. Following a curve in the road, she went up a small hill. The automobile stopped. Its lights went off. She stepped out onto flat slabs of limestone that made a path to a small house. A small, yellow porch light guided her way up to the porch. Through the wooden screen door and into the unlocked house door she went. Flicking on the lights, she glanced at the sofa. Sometimes he'd be sitting there drinking beer and smoking a cigarette when he'd greet her entrance into the house. Other nights just an empty bottle and an ashtray full of cigarette butts setting on the marred end table greeted her--like tonight. She concluded that he probably had a hard day at work and had gone to bed early.

She looked about the two small rooms as she walked through the house. There were dirty dishes in the kitchen sink, crumbs of food on the kitchen table and floor. Clothes lay on the dark-green upholstered living room chair. His soiled work shoes were scattered about. He wasn't the best housekeeper, but he loved her. She had needed someone like that for a long time. He made her heart happy. Sometimes she'd even find herself smiling and singing songs as she listened to the radio and thought of him. He was the best thing that had ever happened to her.

When she reached the bedroom door, she turned off the inside house light. Entering the bedroom, the moonlight flowing into the curtainless window lit her way. She knew the room by memory. If she had to, she could maneuver in that room blindfold. Stopping at the side of the bed, she loosened her clothes from her body and let them drop onto the linoleum floor. Climbing into bed, she snuggled her nude body next to his.

Her touch and kiss woke him. Gently, he held her in his arms and kissed her.

It felt so heavenly to be in his arms and have him cuddle her. Oh, nothing else existed but this precious moment in time. They tantalized each other's erotic zones until their bodies exploded into these uncontrollable surges--one after another--after another. Their bodies mingled in each other's warm moistness, a moistness that induced her to want more and more. She could never let it stop at once--never. It was as if she was trying to fill the void of all those empty years, or as if she was afraid it would end. She wanted to get all she could while she had a chance at it. With him, she held back no desire. When the desire was satisfied, she would lay quietly in his loving arms. This time with him passed too fast and soon it was time for her to leave. She regretted that, but that was the reality of the situation. So with a good-bye kiss on his lips, she left his arms to leave for the place some might call her home. But it was not, it was only a house. This place, right here was her home, the place where she felt love. All of the elegance of her house, never made her feel as she felt in this place. Here she was loved and desired by the man that called this place his home. She felt no emptiness here.

Within a short while, she was at the place where she lived with her husband and where her children had grown up. Once it had been a new house--so full of dreams and promises--now only regrets and hatred filled the house. As she walked into the bedroom, she knew the smell that she would find. His alcoholic breath made the room smell of a brewery. She hated that smell. She left the door open and made sure that the window near her side of the bed was opened enough to let fresh night air circulate into the room. In winter she often slept in one of the children's beds upstairs if neither of them were home. However, in summer it was too hot upstairs for her to sleep comfortably.

With her nightgown on, she lay next to him in bed making sure her back was to his face so she would not have to breathe those fermented fumes coming from his intoxicated body. Lying as such was the extent of her "wifely duties." He was the one who had wanted it that way--so be it. With the years, he had mellowed. He no longer stayed in Milwaukee until the early morning hours. Of course, with age, it was harder for him to get up for work with only a couple hours of sleep. That "old stud" must have someone, she thought. He could never survive as a monk. He must get a "quickie" in Milwaukee before he comes home. Or could he be having something with Lyra, the middle-aged woman who had bought "old man Stoner's" house. She had heard that Lyra had converted part of the house into a tavern, and the rest of the house she had left as an elaborate wedding reception area. She had seen her husband's truck there on occasion when she had taken vacation days from work at night. Of course, her husband had never known, because she had spent that time with her lover while he thought she was at work--if he thought of her at all. Needless to say, it did not matter to her what he did. She had someone else also. She was glad that she had been stronger than her mother, and that she had not reverted to drinking. She would not give her husband that satisfaction. Thank God for Tony. Huh, God would hardly approve of what she was doing, but what her husband had done to her was not right either. The condemnation of her eternal soul was worth the happiness that she finally found. How she wished her husband would die, so she and Tony could be together always. If her husband was gone, would Tony marry her? Yes, he would. Death was the only way she could ever be free of her husband. Divorce was out of the question--always was--always would be in this totally Catholic community. So things would remain as they were until she would be blessed with her husband's death.

 She awoke in the morning to a quiet house. Her husband had left for the day's truck route and the telephone was unusually silent. For a change, it had not woke her up as it usually did every morning. It felt so refreshing to be able to sleep a little late. The first thing she did, after getting up from the bed and stretching her body, was to look outside her bedroom window into the backyard. All the trucks were gone. Disappointed, Tony was gone. Lately, he had been spending the majority of his time hauling animals instead of doing mechanical work on the trucks. She would have liked to see him more during the day, but maybe it was better this way. If they saw each other during the day and were unable to control themselves, they might get careless and get caught. Oh, if only she would be free. But until then, those few stolen hours would have to be enough. She dreaded Friday nights because it meant two days without him. She agonized until Monday night came.

RING! RING! RING!

Going into the kitchen, she reached for the phone. "Hello, Aslen Trucking. How can I help you?"

"Hi, Ma." A gleeful voice came from the other end.

"Well, hi, Margie, how are you?"

"Oh, Ma, you'll never guess what happened?"

"From the excitement in your voice, it must be something really special."

"Ma, Paul gave me an engagement ring for my birthday! Oh, you should see it! It's so beautiful!"

"Congratulations, Margie, I'm so glad for you. I can't wait to see the ring. Have you set a wedding date?"

"Not yet, it won't be for at least two years. Paul wants to graduate from college first."

"Good, we will have plenty of time to plan the best wedding this town has ever seen. When you know the wedding date, the first thing we must do is rent a hall, the most elegant around. There'll be so many people to invite because of your dad's business. Oh, I'm so excited and happy for you! My little girl is engaged. Will you be coming home this weekend?"

"No, I don't think so."

"Are you working this weekend again?" She was disappointed. Weekends were lonely without Margie. There was no one to talk to or do things with.

"That's when I make the most money on tips. I'm so glad Dad talked to his friend at the club about giving me this hostess job. The customer's are so affluent. The other night one customer gave me a ten-dollar tip because he liked my smile. Can you imagine that, Ma?"

"Yes, I can. You are very pretty, Margie. How does Paul feel about the male customers liking you?"

"He doesn't say anything. You know Paul is a man of few words."

"Yes, he's very quiet. But when he does say something, it's worth listening to. He's a very intelligent person and also very nice. Does he still work on the weekends as a bartender at the same club?"

"Ya, so I thought I might as well work also. We can't do anything else together. So we might as work together. Sometimes when it's not so busy, I go up to the bar and talk to him. Maybe I'll come home on one of the days that I have off work during the week."

Her mother hesitated while she thought. "No, that's not a good idea. With me working during the week, I really wouldn't get to visit with you that much. Weekends are better." She didn't want Margie finding out how late she came home on weeknights. "Sorry, Margie."

"Ah, that's okay, Ma. You're right. I couldn't see Dad then either. Weekends are better. The first day Paul and I have off together, we'll be coming home."

"That would be find. Your room is always there for you and Paul can sleep in Mikie's room just like before."

"That sounds real good. Bye, Ma."

"Bye, Margie."

Pamela put the phone receiver back on its hook. Suddenly, she was full of excitement. The wedding gave her a goal, something to plan for. The place for the wedding would be the best. Yes, the banker's old house, Lyra's place. It had a fantastic stairway and an elegant dining area. She remembered the house from a Christmas party that Charles Stoner had for the local businesspeople one year. If someone like Amanda Leer could get married in such exquisiteness, surely an Aslen should. After all, Aslen's were "pillars of the community." She'd talk to Margie about having the wedding sometime in summer when the lawn around Lyra's place was a mass of blooming, colorful flowers. Oh, Margie would agree. Anything that was luxurious always met her approval. For the wedding dresses, they would go to Milwaukee or maybe even Chicago and get the most glamorous and expensive. Her daughter, Margie, would have the wedding that she never had.

KNOCK! KNOCK!

Pamela was so deep in thought. The knock startled her. Putting on her housecoat, she went to answer the door. "Well, hi, Susie, come in."

"No, I really can't stay." Susie's face revealed a troubled, saddened look. "Did you get any word on how Mikie is doing?"

"Mikie? No, I haven't heard from him for a long time. Why?"

"Well, I got this very strange package in the mail today. The package contained this deck of cards and a note from a man named John. I guess Mikie and him were friends. Mikie gave him the cards to remember him by. He said Mikie was terribly sick from the Malaria and maybe would die. John thought he'd send the cards to me as a remembrance of Mikie just in case something happened to him. I'm so worried." Her chin quivered and her eyes became filled with tears. "Did you hear anything about him being sick or--dying?"

"No, Susie, Otto and I haven't heard anything. So he must be okay."

"Do you really think so?"

"Yes, I'm sure. Can I see the deck of cards?" Pamela extended her hand to take the cards.

"Sure, but I would like them back." She handed Pamela the cards and wiped the tears from her face. "If only we would get word--one way or the other--but I guess no news is better than bad news. At least if we aren't told he's dead, we can still hope he's alive."

"Mikie's cards." Pamela examined them and handed them back to Susie. "Huh, he never could keep anything looking descent. You can have the filthy things."

"Thank you." Considering Pamela's attitude, Susie replied, "I'm sorry I bothered you." Reaching for the deck of cards, she turned and walked across the lawn into her parents' house.

Pamela watched and thought about how close Mikie and Susie's relationship had been over the years. Susie was a nice girl and she liked her. Susie was a lot like Lillian. Pamela didn't see Lillian very much anymore ever since she was working the first shift. Sometimes after church they would talk as they walked home from services. Times change--people change. People grow apart--like Otto and her. Would Tony and she also grow apart? God, she prayed not. Then she'd be alone again--really alone, especially, when Margie got married in two years. She would have no one. What about Mikie? They had not heard anything. If he had died, surely they would have been notified. Wouldn't they have been?

Pamela slowly closed the door. Her mood had made a complete turnabout. The excitement had left her; her soul felt heavy. Over to the desk she went. With serious concern, she sat on the swivel chair. As if in a trance, she pulled open a side drawer on the desk. Inside the drawer, white files were organized in alphabetical order. In the file marked with an "S," she searched with her hands. Pulling out a white piece of paper--a letter, she examined it. Looking up from it, she thought, had she been wrong to sign that letter--doing what she did to her own son? Well, she was not alone. Otto had signed it also. He was the head of the house. If there was anything done wrong, it was Otto's blame--not hers. If she told herself that enough, she could rid herself of even the smallest amount of guilt that she might have had. If it would not have been Mikie, it would have been Tony. At that point in time, she was glad Otto had decided on Tony. Tony was more important in her life. But now, what if Mikie was dead? Was Tony worth her son? Rationalizing made things right. Mikie had only given her grief from the day he was born--waking her up three to four times a night for a feeding--crying all day so she could never get her work finished--wetting his bed at night until he was five--damaging his shoes and schoolbooks that one fall--having the appendicitis and causing that expensive hospital bill--almost burning down the garage with smoking those cigarettes with Chuck and Jerry--but worst was lying and blaming Margie. Why couldn't he have been as good as Margie?

Dark clouds rolled across the sky, and it began to rain swiftly and violently. The afternoon became dusky. She turned on the kitchen light and started to make herself something to eat. By the time she had finished her meal, the violence of the storm had ended. Only a mild rain shower remained. The afternoon sun had reappeared and a brilliant rainbow stretched across the sky. She went over to the mahogany radio console and turned it on. It was almost time for the news and after that a "soap opera" she enjoyed listening to. With the house cleaned, she sat at the kitchen table with a steaming cup of coffee. Resting her elbows on the table, she held the cup and quietly blew at its hot contents to cool it off so she could drink it. The music played and her thoughts wandered. She imagined herself dancing with Tony. Sometimes on Friday night, he'd have a fish fry waiting for her and a glass of wine. After eating, he'd put some records on his phonograph, and they'd dance so close. Sometimes they'd move so slow it was as if they were standing still--holding each other in that moment of time that she never wanted to end. The hours seemed so long until she would be with him again.

The music stopped and it was time for the news. She slowly sipped her hot brew as she listened to the announcer:

"In the national news today, Americans landing on the Solomon Islands and on nearby Rendova Island on June 30 resulted in the capture of Munda today. The German's sank another ship, but in the battle lost another one of their submarines. In the local news, the torrential afternoon rain caused a chain reaction of accidents at the Milwaukee stockyards today. At this time, it appears that a truck hauling cattle from Beechwood hit a cement embankment causing other trucks, which were unable to stop, to collide with it. Rescuers are working vigorously to remove the trapped driver from the truck before the leaking gas from its ruptured gas tank explodes. We just received word. There has been an explosion. At this time, we don't know if they got the driver out before the explosion or not. We will keep you informed as this broadcast continues."

Pamela dropped the cup from her hands. As the cup hit the table, it cracked into a multitude of splinters. The hot coffee spilled onto the table and ran down onto her lap. She did not react to the scalding of her thighs. She was in a trance of dreadful shock. Oh, my God! Who was it--Otto?--Tony?

"Oh, my God, don't make it be Tony! Not Tony!" If it was Tony, what would she do? How bad was he hurt? Would he die? Was he dead? Oh, God, it may not be right but please don't let it be Tony. If you want to punish me, fine--but don't punish Tony. Please, God--please!"

Suddenly, she sprang from the table. Pain surged her thighs. Lifting her housecoat revealed her beet red thighs where the coffee had fallen. Going into the bathroom, she removed her wet clothes and carefully patted her burnt thighs dry.

Should she get dressed for work? She had to get dressed sometime. Now was as good as time as ever. When was someone going to call to inform her about what was happening? Maybe the announcer was mistaken? Maybe it wasn't a truck from Beechwood? Could he make such a mistake?

"Oh, God, make it a mistake. Don't let it be Tony." She began to cry. "Oh, why do I feel so weepy? Is something inside of me telling me it was Tony?"

Chapter 16
****
Meddling Sister

CHIRP! CHIRP!--CHIRP! CHIRP!--CHIRP! CHIRP!--

It seemed to her that those loud birds must sit right outside her open window letting her know exactly how early daylight really came. She could not close the window. The early morning air was hot already. In desperation to sleep a little longer, she wrapped the pillow around her head to cover her ears. However, it did not muffle the noise enough. It seemed the more she tried to sleep. The more she heard every noise there was to hear. Down in the basement, she heard the oscillating "hum" of her mother's wringer washer. Outside she would hear the neighbors' house doors slam shut. Their cars start. The gravel stones ping against the metal underbody of cars as they drove by on the gravel road in front of the house. She would toss and turn with the pillow tight to her head. It was of no avail. She might as well get up.

After putting on a floral sun dress, which she hoped would be cool enough for the scorching day ahead, she made her bed, topping it with a white ruffled bedspread and pillow shams. She pulled her matching curtains back and held them to the side of the window frame with tie backs. From her upstairs window, she could see him putting gas into his milk truck before he left on his daily route. The smile in her heart flowed up to her face. It was so good to have him home again--oh, so very good. She turned from the window feeling a peace within her soul. The anxiety of the time he was gone had been replaced by a tranquilness of knowing he was here and safe.

She bounced down the stairs and into the kitchen. The pleasant odor of fresh coffee filled the air. The basement door opened and into the room her mother came, carrying a wash basket full of wet clothes in her one hand and a pailful of wooden clothespins in her other hand.

"Good morning, Ma, I'll hang that out for you." She grabbed the basket and pail from her mother's hands.

"Good morning and thank you. I should be finished washing before I leave for work." Her mother walked toward the stove where a tin coffeepot was percolating.

"Why do you have to wash before you go to work, Ma? You know I'd do it when I get up." She headed toward the door.

"I know. It's just that the early morning sun bleaches the white clothes so much better, and it's so peaceful outside early in the morning." Her mother turned off the gas flame beneath the pot, took the pot from the stove, and poured herself a cup of coffee.

"Well, I don't know how you can call all that chattering of those birds peaceful?" She pushed against the screen door with her back to open it.

"I like to hear them. During the day I'm in the factory, and in the evening there is so much other noise that the birds can't be heard anymore." Her mother reached into the cookie jar and pulled out a handful of cookies.

"Thank God." She smiled and went outside, letting the spring on screen door slam the door shut.

"Good morning," she called to him as she walked up to the clotheslines, which were fastened from one tree to another in the backyard.

"Good morning." He waved to her as he opened the truck's hood, pulled out the oil stick, and checked it.

SLAM! He closed the truck's hood. Wiping his hands on an old rag, he walked toward her. "Up kinda early, aren't you?"

"I couldn't sleep. It's going to be a long day. The canning factory doesn't need its crews to work today. None of the peas are ready." She set the wash basket and clothespin pail on the green lawn, took a few clothespins into her hand, and grabbed a piece of clothes.

"You have anything planned for today?" he asked.

"Not too much, I'll probably do some cleaning in the house and maybe hoe in Ma's flower beds around the house." She pinned the piece of clothes to the clothesline.

"Why don't you come along with me on my milk route? You used to do it all the time before I left. Come on, it'll be fun!"

"Oh, I don't know." She continued to hang up the clothes.

BANG! BANG! BANG!

The noise accompanied a car that just speeded into the yard and then quickly came to a screeching stop beside the milk truck. Gravel stones flew about. The car door flung open and out stepped a man.

"What is that?" she commented on the car that seemed to be held together with rust. "And who is that? He drives like a maniac!"

"Oh, that's my friend, John. You know the guy who sent you my deck of cards. Hi, John." He waved and smiled at John.

"Hi, Mikie." The tall, red head stood outside his car looking over the roof of the car. "Am I early enough?"

"Ya, but I didn't think you'd really come. You were 'pretty plastered' last night."

"Ah, I can handle that stuff."

Mikie started to walk toward John. He stopped, turned back toward her, and motioned at her with his hand. "Come on, it's about time you meet John."

She finished hanging up the clothes that she had in her hand and walked toward Mikie.

Mikie waited. When she was near, he put his arm around her shoulder. Together they walked toward John.

"John, this is my best friend, Susie."

John extended his hand. "Susie, finally I meet the girl who made all those good cookies we devoured." John smiled.

"Nice to meet you, John." Susie smiled back.

"John's going on the route with me today. Come along, Susie. It'll be fun--the three of us."

"I don't know. I really should help Ma with the wash before she leaves."

"Hey, no problem, we'll go down to the restaurant, eat, come back, and pick you up," Mikie suggested.

"Why don't you eat here? You always used to. Remember? Before we'd leave on the route, I always made us breakfast."

"Ya, I remember." Mikie smiled about the pleasant memories he had of things that they had done as friends.

"Well, it's about time you return all those breakfasts I made for you. I think you should go into the house and make us all breakfast. Ma has coffee made." Susie took Mikie's hand and led him toward the house.

John stood still and watched.

"Come on, John, you can help Mikie make us breakfast." She stopped at the wash basket, left go of Mikie's hand, and continued to hang up the rest of the clothes. As John walked past her to join Mikie in the house, they exchanged smiles.

"Good morning, Mikie." Mrs. Benson was sitting at the table dipping a cookie into her steaming cup of coffee.

"Hi, Mrs. Benson, Susie ordered me to make everyone breakfast."

"Just like old times, huh." She got up out of her chair and hugged him. "I wanted to hug you the first time when I saw you were home, but I didn't know how your ma would feel about that. To repeat myself, 'glad to have you back home.' You're only home a short time and already you're busy working. You're a good kid, Mikie. You always were." She patted him on his back and returned to her chair.

"Ya, Dad needs the help."

"Too bad he didn't need it before, then maybe you wouldn't have had to leave us for the war." Mrs. Benson took a sip of her coffee.

The radiant glow in Mikie's eyes disappeared.

"Oh, I'm sorry. I didn't mean to upset you and bring back bad memories of the war." She touched his hand as an extension of her heartfelt apologize.

"I know, Mrs. Benson." He remembered that letter; it reopened the wound in his heart. It hurt to be stabbed again with the harsh reality of the truth--of how things really were--of how unloved he really was by the people who should love him--his family.

"Hi, I'm John, Mikie's friend." John smiled and extended his hand to her as he came through the door.

"Glad to meet another friend of Mikie's." With a smile she shook his hand and then finished her cup of coffee. "Got to take another load out of the washing machine and put it in the rinse tubs until Susie brings the basket down." She walked toward the basement steps.

"I'm making breakfast. What would you like, Mrs. Benson?" Mikie opened the cupboard and took out a frying pan.

"Oh, nothing, Mikie, thanks. I've had my cup of coffee and cookies. It doesn't matter how hot the weather may be. I've got to have that cup of coffee in the morning. Otherwise, the day doesn't seem right. You kids go ahead and make whatever you want." She disappeared down the stairs.

"John," Mikie called to get his attention. "As long as you're staring at her, why don't you ask her what she wants for breakfast?"

John blushed and then went outside by Susie.

A few minutes later they came in together. John was carrying the empty wash basket for Susie.

"Thanks, John, I'll take the basket now. Ma needs it in the basement to put the rest of the clothes in." Susie reached for the basket.

"Oh, that's okay. I'll take it down."

"Thanks, John." She smiled.

Smiling at her and walking, he almost fell down the first basement step. Catching his fall and feeling his face flush again with embarrassment, he went down the stairs.

Mikie opened the refrigerator door. "Scrambled eggs okay?"

"Ya, that's fine." Susie walked over to the counter.

"Well, what do you think of John?" Mikie took a carton of eggs out and closed the refrigerator door.

"I really don't know him that well to make a comment. He seems very nice." Susie took three cups out of the cupboard and filled them with coffee. "Whoops! I forgot you like a little coffee with your milk."

They chuckled as she poured half of the coffee out of Mikie's cup. Setting the cups on the table, she got out the milk and filled the remainder of Mikie's cup with milk.

"Just like old times--now isn't it?" Mikie grabbed a bowl out of the cupboard, broke the eggs into it, and beat them with a wooden spoon.

"We all missed you, Mikie, and worried about you." Susie took slices of bread out of the breadbox and put them into the toaster.

"Well, it's nice to know some people did." He poured the beaten eggs into the pan sizzling with hot lard.

"Mikie, your family cared about you." She wanted to make him feel good. Taking the plates out of the cupboard, she set the table.

"I know differently, Susie. Let's talk about something else." Mikie stirred the scrambled eggs in the pan. "So you got your teaching degree while I was gone. Is teaching all you thought it would be?"

"Yes, it is. I enjoy it tremendously. Working over the summer months in the canning factory really makes me appreciate my degree. I don't mind the work at the factory. However, I could never find any satisfaction working in a factory all my life. I can understand why Ma dislikes her job at the shoe factory." Susie took the pieces of toasted bread out of the toaster, buttered them, and placed a piece on each of their plates.

"I'm glad for you, Susie." Mikie took the pan off the stove and divided the eggs onto the three plates.

"Susie, you want to hang this out now?" John was standing in the kitchen holding the basket full of clothes.

"Oh, that's the last load--trousers. I'll hang them up after breakfast." Susie smiled at him and then sat at the table.

John smiled back, put the wash basket down, and joined Mikie and Susie at the table.

Mrs. Benson had followed John up the stairs. "Well, time for me to go to work. See you later." Mrs. Benson smiled to them all as she went out the door.

Finished eating, Mikie got up from the table. "I'll do the dishes. You two can hang up the clothes out on the line and then we can leave." He turned on the sink faucet and let the water run into the sink as he started to clean the table.

"John, you don't have to help me with the wash." Susie walked over to the basket and grabbed it.

"But you want to--right, John." Mikie smiled at John as he took the soiled dishes off the table.

John blushed again and smiled at Susie. He took the basket from her and carried it outside.

"John's a nice guy, Susie."

"I'm sure, Mikie." She smiled and followed John outside.

It was not long before the milk truck was roaring down the dusty gravel roads. The three of them sitting inside the cab with the hot breeze whirling about through the open windows. At farmers' places, Mikie would back the truck up to the milk house, unlatch the back doors of the truck, leaving them wide open. Inside the milk house, he would take the filled milk cans from the cool water tank. With one full milk can in each hand, he'd carry them out to the back of the truck. His biceps would bulge. At that point, he'd take one can at a time and swing it up onto the back of the truck. Then he'd crawl up onto the back of the truck, place the cans in an orderly manner, and secure them with a large, leather belt.

"Hey, Mikie you need any help?" asked John.

"No, I'm fine." Mikie would smile to himself. Who was he to interrupt the obviously interesting conversation Susie and John were having? Having the milk cans loaded and secured, off they drove to the next farmer and then the next. It wasn't that Mikie didn't want to talk. He had plenty that he would like to have said, but he didn't have a chance. How could two people who just met find so much to talk about? He didn't know, but he was glad they got along. They were his best friends. At the end of the route, he was glad to see that John had ventured to putting his arm around Susie's shoulder as they sat in the truck. With all the milk picked up from the farmers and delivered to the creamery, the empty milk truck, with its three passengers, traveled toward home.

"Oh, gees! Not her again!" Mikie commented as he drove into his parents' yard.

"I saw that car last Saturday in the yard before I went to work. Whose car is that?" asked Susie.

"Paul's." Mikie stopped the truck and sat with his hands gripped to the steering wheel. "I hope they didn't bring anyone else along."

John got out of the truck and then helped Susie down.

"Come on, Mikie, you can't stay in the truck all the while she's here. If you don't want to see her, you can stay at our house. My parents will understand. You can sleep in my brother's room."

The back door opened and out she came, all smiles and dressed in her fancy city clothes and shoes. "Hi, Mikie! Come in the house. I want you to meet someone."

"Hi, Margie." Susie waved and smiled as John and she stood beside the truck.

"Hi." Margie didn't care to recognize Susie. She was a city girl now, so much better than Susie. Who was that guy beside her?

Another "country hick"? Guys around here were so beneath her, but good enough for someone like Susie. Getting a bit impatient because Mikie didn't "jump" to her order, she put her hands on her hips. "Come on, Mikie--now!"

"Damn her!" Mikie whispered under his breath. "Ya, in a little while," he shouted out of the truck at her.

"Right now, Mikie! Right now! "

"Come on. Let's go downtown and have a couple of beers." He motioned Susie and John back into the truck. As he started the truck and backed it out of the yard, he could see Margie stomping toward the truck.

"Mikie, you get back here--now!" she shouted.

"See you later," Mikie yelled back as the truck backed out of the yard onto the road. As they proceeded down the road, Mikie put his arm out the window and waved to Margie over the truck's cab.

"Mikie, she's really mad!" John commented as he put his arm on Susie's shoulder again. He smiled at Susie and pulled her closer to him. "I take it that is your sister, Margie?"

"Ya, that's Margie. Nothing has changed. Why can't she leave you alone?" Susie responded.

"She's older. So she thinks she can run my life. She has everything in life planned, and that's the way she thinks it should be. Well, she's going to have to learn that life doesn't always turn out the way a person plans it. She should have been in the war. Maybe it would make her appreciate what she has, instead of planning for what she wants."

"You're right, Mikie. When we were in New Guinea, I swore we were in hell. When you've been in hell and back again, life has different meaning."

The truck stopped and inside the tavern the three of them went.

"To think this place used to belong to the town's banker. Bet it was elegant--just look at those crown moldings--solid oak." Mikie sat at the bar. "Give us all a beer, please," he said to the woman with the olive complexion as she approached the three of them.

"This used to be a banker's house?" John asked as he looked around. "Look at the window moldings. The hand-carved designs. Why did he ever sell it?" He pulled one of the wooden bar stools away from the bar and helped Susie sit down on it.

"He died. His only heir was his son and no one could locate him. He just left. No one knew where or why. Just one day he was gone. There was no one who could maintain the house so the lawyer for the estate, Fremont Jr., sold the house. He's been using the money from the estate's sale to try and locate the banker's son."

"What if he never finds him?" John took a drink of his beer.

"I guess if they don't find him within seven years then he will be declared legally dead." Susie drank some of her beer. "Whatever money is left will probably go to his wife. It's really too bad because his wife and daughter could use the money now. By the time the lawyer gets finished with all the legality, there probably won't be too much left. I guess there really wasn't that much of an estate, just the house. The depression was quite hard on his family."

"Bartender, could you give me another, please." Mikie pushed the empty beer glass toward her.

"My name is Lyra." She grabbed for his glass. "What's yours? I've never seen you before." She poured the yellow brew into his glass and tipped the glass slightly to get rid of some of the white, excess foam.

"Mikie Aslen." He grabbed the beer and took a few swallows. "You know, Susie, drinking won't really change anything. She'll be there when I get home. I might as well face her, and get it over with. Do you two mind if we leave?" He took another swallow and left the rest of the beer in his glass.

"I think that's a good choice, Mikie." Susie set down her beer and got off the bar stool.

"Hey, pal, you're driving. It's whatever you want to do." John finished his beer, got off the stool, and held the door open for Susie and Mikie to pass through.

"See, you again." Lyra took their glasses off the bar.

"Sure thing, Lyra." John waved and closed the door behind him.

In a few minutes they were back in Mikie's parents' backyard. He stopped the truck; they all got out. They could see Margie looking out the window--watching them. When she noticed that they saw her, she pulled the curtain back over the window.

"Want us to go in with you, Mikie?" Susie asked as John and she waited for Mikie to walk around the truck and join them.

"No, that's okay. I can handle the barracuda." Mikie walked toward the house.

"Hey, Susie! Hop in my car! We'll get something to eat." John opened the passenger's car door for her. "Mikie, we'll be back in a little while." With Susie in the car, he closed the door, walked over to the driver's side of the car, and got in.

"Ya, see you later." Mikie smiled and waved.

BANG! BANG! BANG! John revved his car's engine.

Susie smiled and waved to Mikie as John backed the car out of the driveway. Susie didn't seem to mind the car now. She moved away from the passenger's door until she was sitting beside John. He smiled at her and put his arm around her shoulder.

Susie smiled to herself. She liked John, and she felt that he liked her. That made her feel good, bubbly, excited--from her toes to her head. Oh, it had been a wonderful--truly gorgeous day! "Do you like birds?"

"Birds? Ya, I guess so." Why would she ask that, he thought?

"Ya, I do to." She smiled to herself. If they hadn't woken her, she would have missed out on today. She would have never met John. She rested her head on his shoulder and enjoyed every minute of being with him.

Up the house steps Mikie went, very slowly. He anticipated the situation he was about to encounter. Why couldn't she keep out of his life? As he opened the door, he could feel the tension that filled every inch of the room.

At the table, three people were sitting.

Margie gave him a look with eyes full of daggers, ready to carve out his heart. If only she could--he knew she would.

Paul was sitting beside her. His hands calmly folded. His eyes were empty--no hate--no anger--just silent with no emotion.

The other person he didn't know--at least not right now--but he knew Margie had her plans about that. As she smiled with her bright red lips, he noticed two little dimples in her rouge painted cheeks. She resembled a doll with her shaved eyebrows that had been painted on. Her hair seemed glued on her head and there was not a hair out of place. Her fashionable clothes looked so frivolous in this place. He wondered if Margie got a commission from his parents if she found someone who would marry him so they could get rid of him again.

"Mikie, this is Loretta." Margie motioned toward the woman.

Loretta continued her smile and held out her beautifully manicured hand for a handshake.

Mikie wasn't going to appease Margie by returning her gesture, but then he thought, it wasn't the girl's fault Margie had brought her here. He smiled and shook her hand.

"There's a dance at Lyra's tonight. I thought we could make it a foursome, Paul and me--you and Loretta."

Mikie glanced at Paul who meekly smiled at him.

"I'm sorry, Margie. I have other plans." Mikie started to go up the stairs.

"Oh, I don't think so, Mikie. I think you'll be going with us to the dance." She smiled at Loretta.

"I told you I have other plans." He disappeared up the stairs. As he entered his bedroom, he heard footsteps behind him.

It was Margie. She grabbed at his arm. "You will be going to the dance," she whispered with a furor in her voice.

Mikie pulled away. "No, I won't. I can find my own girls. Last week I was only home a few days, and you brought that girl Alice. I want to spend time with my friends that I haven't seen since I was in the service. If I want to go out with a girl, it'll be someone I want to spend time with. Not someone you think I should."

"Mikie, you'll hurt her feelings. She never did anything to you. She's a really nice person. All I'm asking is to go to a dance with her, one night out of your life. You might have fun. Come on, Mikie, you don't want to hurt her feelings, do you?" Margie would use her knowledge of his deep concern for others to her advantage.

"I told you last week not to bring any girls home for me. Can't you hear? You invited her. You take her to the dance."

"I'm only looking out for you, Mikie. I just want you to marry someone who would bring dignity to the Aslen name. I'd hate to see you marry a simpleton, like Susie."

"Susie is a fine person and my very special friend. We have never thought any other way about our relationship. In fact, I actually consider Susie the sister I never had."

"You jerk!" She raised her hand to hit him.

He grabbed her hand and held it tight. "You could hit me in the past but not anymore, Margie. Not anymore." He let go of her hand.

She put her hand down. "Well, will you go with us?" Her tone changed to all sweetness. She knew that he was getting angry. She didn't want to push him.

"I'll let you know after I talk to Susie and John."

"Why do you have to talk to Susie first and who the heck is John? Was he the guy with her? He looks like a real winner." She walked over to his dresser, looked in the mirror, and fluffed her curls with her hand.

"You don't really care, so why do you even ask?" Mikie walked out of the bedroom.

"Where are you going?" She hurriedly followed after him.

"I'm going outside to wait for Susie and John to come back." He went down the stairs.

"When are they coming back?"

"I don't know? When they get here--they get here." He walked through the kitchen on his way outside.

Passing Paul and Loretta, still sitting at the table, Margie smiled. "I'll be right back."

"Wait, Margie, if he doesn't want to go out with me that's okay," Loretta commented.

"Of course, he does. He just doesn't know how to break the date he already has." Margie was an experienced liar, but then she had years of practice. "I'll be right back." Smiling, she followed Mikie outside. She found him sitting on the running board of the milk truck.

He pulled a cigarette from his pack. "Want one, Margie?" He held the pack of cigarettes out to her.

"Of course not, 'ladies of class' don't smoke." She had a haughty gesture.

"Ah, don't act like such a goody-two-shoes. It's Mikie, the guy who took the blame for you that time when the garage almost burned down because you, Chuck, and Jerry threw your cigarette butts in the oily rag barrel." He took a drag on the cigarette. "They don't come around anymore. Why?"

"I don't know, and I really don't care." She held her hand out and straightened the ring on her finger. "Isn't it beautiful?"

"He's just right for you." He blew the cigarette smoke from his mouth. "I may just have met him last week, but I've seen enough to know what's going on. You snap your fingers, and he follows you around like a dog on a lease." He flicked his cigarette butt onto the gravel road.

"You're disgusting, Mikie." She shook her head and started to walk toward the house.

"Maybe too disgusting for Loretta?" Mikie took the cigarette pack from his shirt pocket.

"No--you will be going to the dance with us," Margie replied.

"We'll see, Margie--we'll see." He lit another cigarette.

****

RING! RING!

"Hello."

"Hi, Susie, this is Rosalia."

"Hi, Rosalia, how have you been?"

"I've been fine. I was wondering if you'd like to go to the movies with me tonight?"

"Gee, Rosalia, that would be nice. We haven't seen each other for quite sometime, but I've made plans with John. I'm sorry."

"Oh, well, maybe another time."

"Hey, I've got an idea. Why don't you come with us?"

"No, I couldn't intrude on your date."

"Oh, it's not really a date. We're just getting together at Lyra's for a surprise birthday party for one of our friends."

"No, I'd be intruding. I probably don't even know your friend."

"No, I don't think you do. So why don't you come and meet him?"

"Maybe some other time."

"Can you be over here by four o'clock?"

"If I leave now--probably. It only takes a half-hour to walk to your place."

"Good, John is picking me up. We're going to Lyra's to decorate the barroom."

"Oh, I don't know?"

"Come on, it'll be fun. There are going to be a lot of people our age there. Mikie has got so many friends. I don't know if we'll all fit in Lyra's place. I'll have to introduce you to Mikie. He's one swell guy. That's why everyone likes him so much and you will too."

"Oh, okay."

As Rosalia was walking and neared Susie's house, she heard the loudest, irritating noise ever. Looking in the direction of the noise, she saw it was a car that had just entered Susie's parents' driveway. That must be John, she thought. She hastened her walk so Susie and John wouldn't have to wait for her.

Rosalia watched John go up to the house door, knock, and wait for the door to be answered. Soon Susie came to the door and joined John outside. They walked toward the car.

"Hi, Rosalia." Susie waved and greeted her with a most enthusiastic smile.

"Hi, Susie, I hope I'm not late." Rosalia was a little out of breath.

"No, you're just in time. This is John."

John and Rosalia exchanged greetings.

After being a gentleman and escorting the girls into his car, he drove it toward Lyra's. At Lyra's they saw that quite a few of Mikie's other friends had come early to help with the decorating. They twisted streamers of multicolors and hung them from one wall to another until the ceiling was hidden. They exhausted their breath blowing up balloons, which they fastened to the backs of the bar stools, the jukebox, and coat hooks. Streamers and balloons monopolized the place.

"Hey, you have some lipstick, Susie--Rosalia?" John asked.

Rosalia opened her purse. After exploring its contents, she removed a tube of lipstick and handed it to John.

John took off the cover and rolled up the lipstick. "Perfect! Which one of you girls have good handwriting?"

"Rosalia." Susie pointed at her.

John handed the tube back to her. "Go write on the mirror."

"What? I can't write on the mirror."

"Sure, go ahead if they want you to," a woman who had been sitting quietly observing commented. "The deal was that you would clean everything up after the party, right, John--Susie?"

"That was the agreement, Lyra. We're good for it." They both nodded approvingly.

"Okay, then go ahead, girl, mark up the mirror."

Rosalia went behind the bar, and John gave her a bar stool to stand on so she could reach the mirror better. "What should I write?"

"Happy birthday, Mikie," they both said together.

She began to write in big bold letters. "How does it look? Am I writing okay?"

"That looks great, Rosalia." John helped her down from the stool.

"You finished just in time. Here come some more of Mikie's friends." Susie was looking out the door. "Maybe you should leave to get Mikie."

"Shouldn't I wait until everyone is here?" John approached her.

"Most of his friends are all here," replied Susie.

"His family isn't here," John commented.

"I didn't invite them. This is just a party for Mikie and his friends," replied Susie.

"Ya, they didn't have time to write him in the war. So they surely wouldn't have time for his party," John said.

"I didn't tell them because I was concerned they'd ruin the surprise and tell him."

"I'll see you in a while." John went out the door.

The barroom buzzed with the noise of people talking while they drank their glasses of beer and snacked on the popcorn in bowls, which Lyra had set on the bar.

The anxiousness of waiting for John to return with Mikie made the time seen so long to Susie. Rosalia brought her a beer and together they watched. Before they could see the car, they heard it.

"They're coming. Everyone be quiet now!" Susie shut the door and moved back away from the door entrance with the rest of the people. Everyone was quiet--not even a whisper was heard. They all wanted this to be a surprise for Mikie, their very good friend.

The noise of the car became louder and louder as the car came closer and closer. The car stopped and let out two extremely loud blasting sounds. Shortly thereafter, the sound of one car door slamming shut was heard, then another. A few minutes later, footsteps were heard outside on the wooden porch. The doorknob turned. The door opened.

"Happy birthday, Mikie! For he's a jolly good fellow, for he's a jolly good fellow which nobody can deny! Happy birthday, Mikie!"

They raised their glasses as their cheers bounced about the room.

"What the heck." He looked about bewilderedly. "Susie and John, you two are responsible, aren't you?"

"We wanted it to be a surprise," said Susie.

"It was. I can't believe you could keep this secret, John. We were just out drinking last night. As drunk as you were, you never let it out."

"Hey, as drunk as you were, my pal." He put his arm around Mikie's shoulder. "You probably wouldn't have remembered."

The crowd that had gathered around Mikie let out a roaring laugh. People were patting him on his back and giving him beer. The girls were kissing him on his cheeks. Everyone was talking to him.

Rosalia sat at the bar by herself. With a glass of beer in her hand, she watched how Mikie seemed to possess an allurement. People enjoyed talking to him, listening to him, just being around him. How could anyone have so many friends? Then she thought, to have a friend, a person must be a friend, he must be a very special friend to all these people. People next to her started conversing with her. Telling her about how some of them had gone to school with Mikie or knew him from the milk route, before he went into the service and after he had come home. They bragged about his good qualities as if he was their son or brother. Everyone liked him, but to her he was still a blank face hidden by crowds that still gathered about him. She'd often stretch her neck to see if she could see his face, but she was too short to see over the crowd. So as the people talked, she visualized this admired guy called Mikie.

"Come on, Rosalia." Susie grabbed her arm. "I want to introduce you to Mikie."

"No, he's to busy with all of his friends." Rosalia pulled away.

"Come on, Rosalia," Susie insisted.

Rosalia smiled. "Okay."

Through the crowd they ventured. As they squeezed between one person then another, people greeted Susie and talked to her. Susie would introduce Rosalia to the people. It was only a short distance from where she had been sitting and to where Mikie was standing and talking. Yet, it seemed like they were moving through a bed of mud.

"Hey, Mikie!" Susie called as they neared him.

"Susie, my pal." He hugged her.

"Mikie, this is Rosalia, my very good friend."

Rosalia smiled timidly.

"Hi, Rosalia, glad to meet you." Mikie gave her a friendly smile.

"Rosalia helped decorate and wrote the greeting on the mirror."

"Really nice, thanks." He looked about at the decorations and then at the mirror. "Very nice." He smiled at her again. "Susie and I are very close. I wonder why I haven't seen you before?"

"Rosalia and I met at the Teachers Normal School."

"So you're a teacher like Susie."

"No, I have to go for a while yet. Right now I'm working at the shoe factory until I have enough money saved to go back."

"My ma works at the shoe factory. Maybe you know her, Pamela Aslen?"

"Ya, I know her. She works the second shift, doesn't she?" Rosalia knew her all right. If Mikie was such a nice person, how could he have a "witch" like that for a mother? She remembered how her mother prayed for the time that she could go on the first shift to get away from Pamela Aslen. Her mother didn't care what job it was. When she finally was put on the first shift, Rosalia remembered how her mother had changed. From a sad, withdrawn person, into a woman who once again wore a smile and was actually glad that she had a job. Rosalia was lucky. When she worked part time in summer, she was hired for the first shift. Later, when she wanted to work full time to save more money for her education, Lillian had helped influence the foreman to let her stay on the first shift.

"Hey, Mikie how about a game of sheepshead!" John and some of the guys sitting at the bar shouted. "Give us a deck, Lyra." John grabbed the deck of cards and taking his beer he went to a table and sat in one of the chairs. John started sorting the cards for sheepshead as the other guys followed him and took a chair at the table.

"Be right there, guys. See you girls later." Mikie went up to the bar. "Lyra, could you also give me a pitcher of beer for the table."

"Sure thing, Mikie." She winked and filled the pitcher full of the yellow brew topped with white foam. "You guys plan on having a hot card game, huh." She smiled at Mikie and handed him the pitcher.

"Got to be prepared, thanks, Lyra." Grabbing the pitcher he joined the others at the table and filled up each of their beer glasses.

"Thanks, Mikie," they all replied.

Susie and Rosalia joined the other girls who had followed their boyfriends over to the table and were now standing about. Susie stood behind where John was sitting.

"Bring me luck, Susie." John shuffled the cards, laid the deck on the table for one of the players to "cut." Then he dealt each player an equal amount of cards.

"I'll try." She rested her hands on John's shoulders.

"That's all you guys want to do is play cards and us girls are left standing around and watching," one of the other girls complained.

"Ya, it's really getting boring," another commented.

"Here's some money. Play some music and dance. We like to play cards, and you girls like to dance," one of the guys said as he pushed some of his card playing money, which was setting on the table, toward his girlfriend.

"Thanks." The girlfriend grabbed the money into her hand. "Let's pick out some songs on the jukebox, girls."

"See you later, John." Susie turned away from him to join the girlfriend and other girls. "Come on, Rosalia."

"Ya, have a good time." John laid a card out on top of the pile. "My trump takes it." He pulled the pile toward himself.

"Nice meeting you, Rosalia." Mikie looked up from his cards and smiled at her as she walked past him to join the other girls.

"Well, what do you think of Mikie?" Susie whispered as Rosalia walked beside her.

"He seems nice, and he is rather good-looking, isn't he?" She peered over at Mikie--so deeply involved in the card game.

"Oh, he is a very nice person. He'd give a person the shirt off his back."

Rosalia continued to watch Mikie.

"Come on! Let's help them pick out some songs so we can listen to what we like also." Susie pulled Rosalia toward the other girls at the jukebox.

Music filled the room along with the cigarette smoke. The guys played cards, swore, drank--played more cards, swore more, and drank more. The girls put money into the jukebox, danced, drank beer, asked their boyfriends for more money--played the jukebox some more, danced more and drank more. Streamers fell from the ceiling. Balloons popped on the chairs--the hooks--the jukebox. More drinking--more dancing--more playing cards. Time went fast. The guys stopped playing cards and the girls stopped dancing when Lyra put out on the bar a lunch of raw ground round, sliced ham, potato chips, pickles, and raw sliced onions. The guys sat with their girlfriends--some at tables, some at the bar, and some outside on the porch. The guys devouring their favorite raw meat, ground round with raw onions. The girls enjoying a little milder ham sandwich and an occasional potato chip.

Outside under the ceiling of twinkling stars and on the green lawn, Mikie sat with his plate of food. John joined him along with Susie and Rosalia. Their eyes were glassy and sometimes a few words became slurred, but they had a good time.

"Ah, Susie, remember when we were little, how we'd clothespin a blanket to your ma's clothesline. Then we'd pull the blanket out on each side and hold the sides out in place with stones."

"Ya, I remember, Mikie, our little tent. We'd sleep in there in summer when the nights were hot like this. We'd pretend we were Indians."

"Ah, my best friend, Susie. We have a lot of memories and now this birthday party too. I had a lot of fun. It's the best birthday I ever had. Thanks, all of you."

"Hey, Mikie, you're only twenty-one once," John remarked.

Mikie's sentimentalism began to show as he wiped a tear from his eye.

As people began to leave the party, they all took time to say a few words to Mikie.

"See you later, Mikie."

"Happy birthday, Mikie."

"See you tomorrow morning."

"Take care, Mikie."

"Good seeing you again, Mikie."

"Hey Mikie, sheepshead tournament next week. Don't forget. See you then. Bring along a lot of money and leave your luck at home."

With all of the people gone home and everyone finished eating,

Meddling Sister

Susie and Rosalia took the dirty eating utensils inside the tavern.

"I'll be here early in the morning to clean up this mess," Susie said to Lyra, who was clearing the bar of the uneaten lunch.

"That's fine, Susie. I'm not opening up until ten o'clock, so you don't have to come so early. Eight o'clock would be fine."

"Thanks, Lyra, see you tomorrow."

"Good night, girls."

Coming out of the tavern, they saw John help Mikie into the back of his car. There Mikie laid his intoxicated body on the seat and slept.

Susie sat in the front seat next to John while Rosalia sat next to the passenger's door. John drove them home.

****

He didn't need an alarm clock to wake up. After some thirty years of getting up at the same time every day of the year, his old body automatically woke up for the approaching day. He was tired and how he wished--just once--he could stay in the bed and be free of the usual work that he had to do every day. The resilience of youth was gone. Sometimes every limb seemed to ache of pain. Just one day away from work would be so welcomed. Oh, well--not today--maybe one day in the future--maybe--he thought. What was today? Sunday? Oh, that would be nice. Sundays were special to him. He enjoyed going to church, sitting in the old wooden church pew, and singing. Singing seemed to relax him--renew him. Renew him for more work. His ecstasy ended. It was Saturday--time to get up for work.

Something wasn't right. He felt a deep sharp pain in his head. As he tried to raise himself from the bed, he felt a weakness on the right side of his body. It was a struggle to lift his body into a sitting position at the edge of his bed. He held his head in his hand and tried to rub away the pain. It would not leave his head. Instead, the pain became sharper and sharper. There was a swimming sensation in his head. He gripped his hands onto the edge of the bed. This feeling was a new experience to him. Would he fall off the bed onto the floor? Should he lay down? Confused! Wrapped in the fear of this unknown, he thought to call for help. He opened his mouth, but he could not remember how or what words to say. As his head swam around and around, his body fell back onto the bed. Thinking if he lay quietly, he'd feel all right in a short while. He closed his eyes and rested.

After lying there a few seconds or maybe minutes, he didn't know--he seemed to have no realization of time. Time was irrelevant. He just wanted to be feel better. He opened his eyes. Something was not right! Something terrible was happening! Was he going blind? He could only see half of the room. No, it couldn't be? Yes, he remembered seeing more before. He tried to call out again, but he could not. He had to get someone to help him. He could hardly get up! His one leg and arm did not move. Still feeling extremely lightheaded, he awkwardly pulled his body along the side of the bed. Trying to visually focus, he reached out to where he thought his highboy was. Not touching it, he continued to move his hand about slowly in the air. He knew he would eventually have to touch it. He kept trying. When he finally felt it, he clung to it and pulled his body up along its side. He clung desperately to the highboy. His body whirled in an unsteadiness--a daze--a sensation of spinning--faster and faster. His body felt so weak. Was this it? Was he dying?

THUMP!

The noise woke Lori, or had she imagined it? A glance at the clock told her it was time to get up. Maybe the noise was her father moving about the house. He was usually up before her. She got out of bed and dressed in a simple white blouse and dark pair of shorts. She looked at herself in the mirror as she brushed her long hair, braided it, and rolled it into a bun at the back of her head. She thought, how old she was getting, thirty-one already. What did she have of life? It was the same, day after day. One day of work moved into the next day of work--month after month--year after year. Lucy had her chance at her youth. She had dated, gotten married, and had a family. Of course, they didn't own as much land then, so there wasn't that much work. Now there was so much work. There was no time for anything else. She had never wanted to buy more land. Lucy was the one. Lucy did work hard but there were times when she used the boys as an excuse to get out of work--like threshing. Lucy was a good mother. She was working so her boys would have a good life. She enjoyed Lucy's boys and loved them as if they were her own children--the children she would probably never have. From generation to generation, she would be known as the family spinster. There would be nothing from her carried on. When she would die, it would be the end. There would be no one to look like her in another generation--nothing. She looked away from the mirror that had revealed more about what was inside of her than on the outside. Putting on her shoes, she left her room and walked past her father's bedroom door. She paused. Something seemed different. His door was closed. Usually he left it open when he left the room. He must still be asleep. She was about to rap on the door to wake him but then decided not to. Let him sleep, she thought, he works hard enough. She could handle the chores. He was seventy-one. He shouldn't work that hard anymore. She wished they'd sell some of the land, so he could retire and sleep late whenever he wished. It would be good for him to enjoy life, although, it would be lonely for her not to have him work beside her.

In the entry way, she reached up and took one of the manure-covered bib overalls off one of the hooks. On the other hook hung her father's barn clothes. She pulled the overalls that were stiff with the week's dirt over her other clothes. The bib overalls protected her other clothes from the cows' splashing feces and from the manure she later would clean out of the gutters. She put on her black buckle boots and went outside. Going into the pasture, she herded the cows into the barn and started milking. Each time she went into the milk house, she'd look out the open door toward the house. It was beginning to worry her that her father was still in the house. As she milked the cows, she'd often look up, hoping to see him. Should she go in and see if he was all right? Yes, she probably should, but for some reason she sensed a fear--a fear of what she might find. He was old. She stood inside the milk house debating. He might need help. She had to go. It was easy to walk into the house but not so easy to open his bedroom door. She hesitated, held her breath, knocked, and prayed he would answer. She waited to hear his voice. He did not reply.

"Pa, are you all right?" She knocked again, still no reply. Her hands trembled as she reached for the doorknob and slowly turned it. What would she find behind the door? Oh, God, make him be all right!

The open door revealed the sight that she was afraid of. With her entire body quivering, she rushed to his body sprawled on the floor. Her eyes became glazed with tears. "Pa, please don't be dead!" Possessed with an overwhelming fear, she knelt beside him and reluctantly felt his body. He was warm. What a relief! He wasn't dead! She held him in her arms. "Wake up, Pa. Wake up, please." She sobbed. What should she do? She had to get someone to help. This condition he was in was not right. She gently laid his body on the floor. She stood up. Her mind was clouded. She wrung her hands as she moved about in a nervous manner--to and fro--to and fro. What should she do? She'd have to calm down so she could think. She'd go by Lucy. Lucy had a phone. She could call the doctor there. Like lightening, she flew out of the bedroom and out of the house. Seeing the car, she rushed inside of it. Only to find in her anxiety, she had flooded the car's engine. She turned the key in the ignition again and again. It groaned and groaned but would not start. In her mazed mind, she could not remember what her father had told her to do in a situation like that. She concluded that she was wasting time trying to get the car started. Dashing out of the car, she ran across the field toward Lucy's farm. It seemed so far away. Her heart was beating rapidly. She ran with her mouth open to facilitate her breathing. The harder she ran, the more difficult it became to breathe. She felt an inability to take a full breath, and she felt faint. This anxiety fed her fear, the fear of not being able to get help for her father. She had to make it to Lucy's. She had to! His life was in her hands. Onward she ran, pushing her body to its extreme limits. Stabbing pain began to afflict her sides. Could she go on? Yes! She'd make it--for her father she would. Lucy's farm looked closer and closer.

She ran past the house and into the barn. "Lucy! Lucy!"

Lucy, who was sitting between the cows, stood up. "Lori, what are you doing here?"

"It's Pa!" She tried to gasp for breath. "Oh, please!" She sank to the barn floor. She was afraid of passing out and felt secure on the floor. She couldn't faint. She had to get help. "Call the doctor! Go help him!" She gasped again. Her face flooded with tears. "Hurry!"

Alex, who was coming out of the milk house, set down the milk pail that he had been carrying and went over to help Lori up.

"No, go to Pa--hurry!" She gasped again. She was afraid that she couldn't get her next breath, but she kept her fear silent. It was more important that they help her father. She'd be all right. She stopped breathing through her mouth and took deep, controlled breaths through her nostrils. She'd be all right. She told herself.

"Lucy, you go quick and call the doctor. I'll meet you up by the house with the truck. Will you be all right, Lori?"

She nodded her head and started to get up. "Please, wait for me."

"First, let's see what the problem is before we get the doctor. Maybe there is nothing to be concerned about." See walked out of the barn toward the truck. Why spend money on a doctor if one wasn't required, Lucy thought.

Alex extended his hand to help Lori get up. "Are you sure you're okay?"

"I'll be all right. It's Pa I'm concerned about. The way he looked I know something terrible has happened. Please, call the doctor, Alex."

"Well, Lucy doesn't think that's necessary right now." Alex helped her walk toward the truck.

"But she didn't see Pa." Lori wiped the tears from her face. "I know he needs a doctor, oh please, Alex."

"Lori, he'll be all right. It will only take a few minutes to get to him." He helped her up into the truck next to Lucy.

"Oh, Lori, you make a mountain out of a mole hill sometimes. I'm sure it's nothing serious," Lucy commented.

Alex closed the truck door and hurried to the driver's side. Within a few seconds, the dust was flying behind the truck as it speeded toward the farm.

"Oh, God! I hope Pa's okay." Lori gripped the dash as the truck spun around the corner of the road and up the driveway.

Before the truck completely stopped, Lori opened the door and sprang wildly toward the house into her father's bedroom. She rushed to his body. She could see his chest move as his otherwise motionless body lay on the floor. "Pa! Pa!" Her tears dropped onto his colorless face.

"Is he alive?" Lucy asked as she entered the room.

"Yes, I can see him breathe."

"Let's get him in bed." As Alex lifted him into his arms, Pete's eyes opened.

"There see he's all right." Lucy walked past Lori to the bed. "Right, Pa?"

Pete lay there. Helpless! He couldn't talk, couldn't move his one arm or his one leg. He had continuous pain in his head and felt a sickness in his stomach with an urge to vomit. He knew what had happened. He would be like this forever. Oh, death would have been better than to live the rest of his life like half a person, dependent on others. Oh, God, why didn't you let me die. I don't want to live like this, he prayed within the silent chambers of his mind.

"Can't you answer me, Pa?" asked Lucy.

"Of course, he can't. He can't even move his body. Oh, Alex, please help him." Lori felt so helpless. He could be dying while they stood around doing--NOTHING!

"I think we should call the doctor, Lucy," suggested Alex.

"Nonsense, Alex, what can a doctor do now? He can't make Pa talk if Pa can't. He can't make him move his body if Pa can't. The doctor can't do anything for him. Pa's body has to heal itself. He should rest in bed for a while. If he's meant to get better, he will. Why have the doctor come out here to tell us something we know? We can take care of Pa. Right, Lori!"

"I have no problems with taking care of Pa. I love him, and I'll do whatever is necessary. However, I still think we should have a doctor examine him. I don't like to see Pa that way. Maybe he's in pain. Lucy, please, get the doctor. What if he gets worst? He might die." Lori went up to the bed, touched her father's hand, and held it in hers.

"The two of you are ridiculous! Can't you understand the doctor can't help him?" She went over to the highboy and started opening one drawer after another searching about the neatly folded clothes and leaving them in a cluttered mess.

"What are you looking for, Lucy?"

"Never mind, Alex." Upset, she slammed the last drawer shut.

"Pa, would you like something to drink or eat?" Lori looked into his weary eyes.

He tried to speak but could not. He slowly shook his head.

"Would you like to rest for a while?" asked Lori.

"Of course, he would," Lucy snapped. "Come on, we all got work to do." She motioned them out of the room.

Pete watched them leave and then the door closed--leaving him alone. Unable to speak and move properly, he lay there in pain as he listened and comprehended the words that penetrated the door.

"Right now we all have work to do. Later on when the work is finished, we'll have to find Pa's will," Lucy commented.

"What?" Lori was applauded! It was so inappropriate for Lucy to think of something like that at this time.

"If Pa should die, it's important for him to have a will. If he doesn't, the State may take some of the estate. You live with him. Does he have a will?"

"I don't know. Frankly, I don't care. Pa will be all right again. I will see to that. He's not going to die. I'm not staying in here to listen to any more of such talk. I've got milking to finish." Lori shook her head as she exited the house. Lucy was unbelievable!

****

The morning after the birthday party came much too early for Mikie and John.

"Oh--don't shake my body!" Mikie moaned as he slowly and so gently touched his head.

"Hey, pal, you've got to get up. You've got a milk route to go on." John shook Mikie's shoulders again as he lay on the sofa.

Mikie slowly turned on his back and opened his eyes. "What the heck are you doing here?"

"I live here."

"No, I live here." Mikie very cautiously raised part of his body from the sofa. Sitting on the edge of the sofa, he held his head in his hands. "Oh! My head hurts so badly." He observed his environment. "Why am I here?"

"Because last night when I took Susie home, I saw Paul's car in your parents' driveway. The lights were on in the house. I figured if I took you in the house in your condition, you'd probably get a very bad welcome. I wasn't in the mood for a nasty scene, and I knew you weren't."

"Ya, good thinking, I better get home and start my route." In a very slow manner, he rose from the sofa. His head throbbed and throbbed. "I have to get out of here!"

With his back hunched and his hands over his mouth, he walked his way outside as fast as his throbbing head would let him move. Every step made his head feel like someone was hitting it with a hammer. Behind the house, he went inside the small white building with vented louvers above the door. Closing the door upon his entrance, he leaned over the cutout hole in the raised platform. Onto the pile of human feces below, he regurgitated again and again. Finally, there was nothing left in his stomach, but still his body tried to regurgitate his empty raw stomach. It felt as if his intestines were being ripped out. He had never felt so terrible. There was no one to blame except himself. He had made himself this way. At this point in time, he didn't know which was worst, the strong unpleasant smell of the outhouse, his gutted stomach, or the unmerciful pain in his head. He could control the smell and he did. Leaving the outhouse, he went to sit on the back porch steps of the house.

"You want to leave now?" John came out the door and sat next to Mikie on the step.

"I suppose, maybe if I start working, I'll feel better."

"Top of the morning to you lads." A gray-haired woman stood looking through the closed kitchen screen door. Her lilac scent floated out onto the porch.

"Good morning, Grandma."

"Good morning." The words dragged out of Mikie's mouth. It was not a good morning, not for him!

"Would you lads like some breakfast?" She opened the door and joined them outside.

"No, thanks, Grandma," replied John.

"Happy birthday, Mikie," said the grandma.

"Thanks."

"I can assume you lads had fun at the party last night."

"Ya, I think it was really nice what John and Susie did. I'm lucky to have such good friends."

"Yes, a person may have many friends as they pass through life. Some come and go, but the truly special friend is the one that is always there. If you find one friend like that in your lifetime, then you are blessed."

"Well, I think we should get going, Mikie." John rose from the step.

"Oh, before you go, John. I'm walking to the store this afternoon to do some of my grocery shopping, and I need to know if you will be bringing Susie for Sunday dinner again?" asked the grandmother.

"I would like to--if it's all right with you," John responded.

"Of course, it is. She's a very sweet girl. I actually look forward to seeing her and making dinner. It's something special for an old woman like me to plan meals for a guest again."

"I would think after working as a cook in the restaurant that you'd hate cooking," John commented.

"No, it brings back good memories. Memories of many things shared with someone who thought me everything I know about cooking. She was one fantastic lady." Grandmother's face glowed as she reminisced.

"See you later, Grandma." John waved as he and Mikie walked toward the car.

"I think I got your hangover, too," Mikie said as he got into the car.

John started his car and the noise doubled the throbbing in Mikie's head.

"I'll drive and load the milk for you, Mikie. You just tell me where to go. I've only been on the route a few times. I think I know your route, but I could be mistaken and miss someone."

"Thanks, John, I appreciate that."

"Well, that's the least I can do. I had the party for you. I feel somewhat responsible for the way you feel." He turned his car into Mikie's parents' driveway.

"Thank God! A person is only twenty-one once." With the car stopped, Mikie got out and closed the door very quietly.

"Poor, Mikie." John sat behind the milk truck's steering wheel and waited for Mikie to get in before he started the truck.

Down the rough, graveled country roads they traveled. Mikie found he felt better if he got out of the truck and moved about when they stopped by the farmers. So occasionally, he'd help lift a few milk cans into the truck for John. He wanted to help more, but his head continued to make him aware that it was still very much attached to the rest of his body. His body moved in a very low speed. However, he was not the only one in this condition. The majority of the farmers had been at his party. Therefore, in their reunion of the night before, they compared who looked and felt the worse.

Around the corner the truck went and past a farm that was set back farther in the field than most of the other farms.

"Stop. You'll have to back the truck up. You missed a farmer."

"Oh, I thought, we were done. Sorry about that." John slowed the truck as he drove it off to the side of the road. Looking in both directions for oncoming vehicles and seeing nothing but an empty road, he quickly pulled the truck back out onto the road and maneuvered a "Y" turn. Then back down the road he drove, he slowed the truck's speed as he neared the driveway that he had previously driven past.

"Is this the last one?" John asked.

"Ya, but it's got the most milk cans. This farm has got the biggest dairy herd around here." Mikie opened the passenger's door. Protruding his head through the open door, he verbally guided John as he backed the truck up to the milk house.

As he entered the milk house, Mikie was surprised to see her lifting a full pail of milk up to the strainer on the milk can. Usually, when he arrived, the milking was completed. In fact, he always entered a milk house that gleamed with cleanliness.

"Hi, Lori, I'm not used to seeing you out here this late in the day."

"I had problems this morning. Could you please wait until I've finished milking so you can take all the milk today? Otherwise, I'll be short milk cans tomorrow." She emptied the remainder of the milk that was in her pail into the strainer.

"Sure, no problem, we can help you finish. This is John." Mikie took the metal milk pail from her hand and went into the barn.

"Hi." John smiled at her then followed Mikie into the barn.

Mikie sat on the small, three-legged wooden stool, which stood between the cows, and started milking. "Where's your pa?" Mikie looked about the barn.

"Oh, Mikie, it was a terrifying experience! I found him lying on the floor in his bedroom this morning." She grabbed a metal pail which was hanging on a nail on the barn wall. Then she picked up a wooden stool identical to the one Mikie was sitting on. "He sat on this stool for as long as I can remember." Small tears began to fill her blue eyes.

"May I ask what happened?" Mikie was genuinely concerned.

"I don't know for sure. It appears as if he can't talk and move his right arm or leg."

"I'm sorry to hear that. Your pa is a really nice guy. I always enjoyed hearing him talk about how he and a man named Hans had cleared the land and built the town of Shady Lane. Also, how lucky he was that he had moved to Beechwood when he did."

"Ya, Pa always did talk about life here, but he never really ever talked about his life in Germany."

"Did the doctor say if he'll be all right again?"

"If he's not, I'll take care of him. Pa was always there for me. It's the least I can do for him." She didn't want him to know that they had not gotten the doctor. She was embarrassed to have anyone think that they didn't care enough about their own father to get a doctor. Well, she did care. She didn't want to lie either. So she evaded the question the best way she could. She had finished milking her cow and carried the pail out into the aisle.

"I can carry that for you." John smiled and took the pail from her hand.

"Thank you." She smiled at him. She went to the front of the stalls and released the cows that had already been milked. "That's the last one, Mikie. I really appreciate you and your friend helping me."

"No problem. I hope your pa gets better." Mikie rose from the stool and waited in the stall until the herd of cows had paraded past him and out into the pasture. "That's a lot of cows for you to be milking by yourself until your pa gets better."

"I've been trying to convince Pa to sell either this farm or the homestead. However, Lucy insists that in a few years her two boys will be old enough to help with the work. So we should keep everything." She walked with Mikie into the milk house.

With milking completed and the milk cans loaded, Mikie secured the latch on the back of the truck. "See you tomorrow, Lori." Mikie returned to the passenger side of the truck.

"Nice meeting you, Lori." John hopped into the truck. Within a few minutes, they had resumed traveling down the road.

"That's the homestead she was talking about. Next to it was my godfather's property. When he died, her pa bought it. That farm over there is her sister's farm."

"They must have money. They own all the property on each side of the road. Wow! It must be nice to have all that money."

"Ya, her pa has money. He worked hard all his life. He was quite old when he married, and his wife owned her farm, the homestead. When Lori's sister married, she got her farm as a wedding present. Lori was to get a farm when she married also. But when she was twenty-one and not married yet, her pa didn't think it was fair that she didn't have a farm like her sister had at that age. So on her twenty-first birthday, he gave her the farm we just came from."

"The homestead and your godfather's property her pa owns?" asked John.

"The homestead was only eighty acres. When her pa bought my godfather's property, he had those eighty acres added to the homestead." Mikie pointed out the property as they drove past it.

"She's still not married?" asked John.

"No. She probably doesn't have time to date. She works all the time. Now without her pa to help, she'll work herself into the grave also. It's too bad because she is a very nice person and quite pretty when she's dressed up. When she comes to church on Sundays, if a person didn't know her, you'd never recognize her."

"Well she must like the work; otherwise, she'd sell her farm and leave."

"I think she stayed mostly to help her pa. She wanted to sell several years ago. Instead, her sister convinced her pa to buy more land."

"Why don't you take her out, Mikie?"

"Na, she's fine as a casual friend, but I'm not attracted to her that way."

"She's got money. You'd start life out owning your own place."

"Farming ties a person down too much. Besides, money isn't that important. I want someone I can share my life with. I want my family to be filled with love. That's something money can't buy."

"Love doesn't pay the bills, Mikie."

"That's true."

John stopped the truck at the creamery. They unloaded the milk cans and dumped the milk into large holding tanks. Rinsing out the cans, they placed then upside down on the railing bars in the back of the truck. The water would run out, and the cans would be fairly dry when they would be returned to the farmers in the morning for them to use again for other milkings.

It was four o'clock when the milk truck finally pulled into Mikie's parents' backyard.

"They're still here," John commented upon seeing Paul's car still parked in the yard.

"Ya, he's still probably sleeping in my bed." What a joke, he thought. He heard Margie's bed rattle an awful lot when Paul was supposedly in his bed. Why couldn't Paul sleep downstairs on the sofa? No, instead he had to give his bed to Paul. That's the way Margie wanted it. So that's the way it was. Oh, well, such is life.

"You want to come back to my place?" asked John.

"No, thanks, I want to talk to Susie." Mikie got out of the truck and walked toward Susie's house.

"Ya, let's plan something for tonight." John walked with him.

Mikie rapped on the wooden frame that outlined the screen door.

Susie opened the door. "Well, hi you two." She held the door open while they entered the house.

"Hi, Susie. Boy, am I glad today is over." Walking into the kitchen, Mikie dropped his body onto a chair, which was setting beside the table.

"Happy birthday, Mikie!" Mrs. Benson came into the room. "Sorry, we didn't come to your party, but Bob had a baseball game last night."

"Thanks, Mrs. Benson. How was the game?"

"Bob's team won. They're one in ten. Can I get you boys anything to eat or drink?"

"No, thank you, Mrs. Benson." John walked over to Susie and put his arm around her shoulder.

"Oh, Mrs. Benson don't rub it in. Say, Susie, who was that girl you introduced me to last night?"

"Why? You forgot her name?" John and Susie looked at each other and smiled.

"I think it was Rosie--Rosa?"

"It was Rosalia." Susie laughed in a sly, partly stifled manner as she looked over at her mother.

"She's a good friend of yours?"

"Yes, she's almost as good a friend as you are, almost, but not quite. Why? Do you want me to arrange a blind date for you?"

They all chuckled, except for Mikie.

"Don't even mention 'blind date.' That's all Margie does is fix me up with all her 'high class' girlfriends. Besides, I've already seen her so this wouldn't be a blind date."

"You may have seen her, but do you remember her." Susie chuckled.

"Oh, I was in good shape when you introduced her to me. I remember enough to know I'd like to go out with her."

"Well, how do you know if she wants to go out with you?"

"I don't know. That's why I want you to ask her."

"Oh, Susie, stop teasing this poor 'love sick' boy." Mrs. Benson ruffled Mikie's hair.

"Oh, my head still hurts!"

"Oh, I'm sorry."

"It's not your fault, Mrs. Benson. Come on, Susie, what do you say?"

"Think I should call her?" She winked at her mother.

"Would you, please?"

"Why don't you ask her to go along on the milk route? It worked for John and me. That old romantic milk route." She laughed. "Maybe you should first know her whole name?"

"Why?"

"Some people might not approve of you seeing her," commented Susie.

"So what's her last name?" inquired Mikie.

"Stoner, Rosalia Stoner," Susie replied.

"So I never heard any of the guys brag about 'making it' with her. In fact, I've never heard of her."

"Of course not, she's a worst wallflower than me."

"Who's a wallflower?" Rosalia entered the room and joined John and Susie standing about the table.

"You Rosalia," Susie replied.

Mikie stood up from the chair and swallowed the very large lump in his throat. There she stood, so beautiful--her glistening blue eyes, her shiny blonde hair, her radiant smile. He had faced death a thousand times in the war, but now his body trembled at the mere thought of asking her for a date. It was the fact that he cared so much to take her on a date that the thought of her saying "no" frightened him. His hands became sweaty. He was speechless. He had wanted time to find out how she felt about him first. If he ask her on a date and she said "no"--he'd feel so devastated.

"Hi, Mikie," Rosalia greeted him with a smile. Ever since she had met him last night, she had wished for a second chance with him and here it was. She had spend the night at Susie's house and during their intimate talks, she had told Susie how she had liked Mikie. She looked at Susie and in her eyes her thoughts were revealing. Would he ask her on a date and give her a chance with him? Her body was tight with tension. Would Susie help make her wish come true?

Chapter 17
****
Terrifying Stranger

The stale, moldy scent of autumn filled the air as the carpet of yellow and red leaves crumbled beneath her small feet. Sometimes she would shuffle her feet. Sometimes she would kick the leaves about in a carefree manner as she walked along the edge of the road. What a beautiful day! She would look here and there trying to take in completely the things around her. With its gray, fluffy tail bouncing, a small squirrel scampered up the rough trunk of a tall tree and then perched itself on one of the tree's woody branches. Like a statue it stood, motionless--listening. For what?--a dog barking--a house door slamming shut--a sudden laugh from a child--someone calling someone--. It did not matter. For when the tranquillity was broken, the squirrel would leave the perch and race higher up into the tree, which was almost completely depleted of its foliage. Below the tree, children were raking the fallen leaves--small girls were making leaf houses--boys were building leaf piles and then tossing each other onto the piles. Sometimes the boys would aggravate the girls by kicking apart the leaves that they had gathered into rolls to represent the walls of their leaf house. The laughter, the shouts, the screams, all the sounds of the autumn day traveled far and clearly in the early morning air.

"Hi, Rosalia," a voice from a distance greeted her.

Rosalia looked up. There sitting on the front porch step of her parents' house was her friend. "Hi, Susie." Rosalia waved, darted off the edge of the road down into the ditch, up onto the lawn, and headed toward the porch and her friend.

"What's up, Rosalia?" Susie had her arms wrapped around her knees.

"I'm going to the store for Ma. She needs some milk. You want to come along?" She stood at the bottom of the steps.

"I'll ask Ma if she needs me to help her with anything." Susie rose from the steps and walked toward the door. "Come along, Rosalia." Susie motioned her to come inside the house as she held the door open.

Rosalia followed her into the house.

With the sound of the door opening, Susie's mother looked up from the dress that she was ironing on the ironing board. "Hi, girls." She smiled and continued with her ironing.

"Hi, Mrs. Benson." Rosalia smiled.

"Ma, if you don't need me to help you anymore, I'd like to walk to the store with Rosalia."

"Sure, go ahead. There's only the ironing to do and since we only have one iron, only one of us can do it. Go--enjoy the weather. It's not going to stay this nice much longer."

"Thanks, Ma."

"See you later, girls."

"Bye, Mrs. Benson." Rosalia followed Susie outside.

At the bottom of the porch steps, Susie stopped. "Do you want to visit Mikie?"

Rosalia thought for a moment. She would like to see him--but--. "No, she might be there. Mikie hasn't told her yet. It's better if he tells her than for her to see it."

"He hasn't told her yet? Well, she's sure to find out. News travels like a wildfire in this town."

"Well, he just gave it to me last night. I'm sure he'll tell her today."

"If he doesn't, she'll surely find out tonight."

"Why tonight?"

"My parents and Mikie's parents are invited to the wedding. In fact, they are driving together."

"If you ask your parents not to say anything, they won't, will they?"

"If I ask them not to, they won't, but be realistic, Rosalia. There are going to be a lot of people attending that wedding and odds are that someone will probably say something. Especially, when they see what you are wearing. People are sure to see something like that."

"Ya, you're probably right."

They walked across the leaf-covered lawn and onto the edge of the graveled road toward the store located several buildings down the road.

"Does it upset you that John is marrying her?" Rosalia's tone was one of loving concern.

"Well, I guess in a way. However, if I look back at our relationship, John and I were more or less just friends. We were really just thrown together because of our mutual friendship with Mikie. When John would go along on the milk route with Mikie on Saturdays and Sundays, she'd often be out in the barn cleaning the cow manure out of the gully. Sometimes in summer when I went along with Mikie, I'd see her clean out the barn in her bare feet. The cow manure would ooze between her toes and bury her feet."

"Yuk! You're kidding." Rosalia made a disgusting face.

"No, I'm not kidding. Often in summer when I went along, John would stay at the farm to help her bale hay later in the day. Mikie and I would leave him there; we'd finish the route by ourselves. I thought at first John stayed to be a nice person. With her pa being the way he is, she did need extra help. That's why she was out in the barn yet when we'd come to pick up the milk. Before, when her pa helped her, all the barn chores would be done. They'd be out in the fields working when we came for the milk. She's a hard worker, and I guess she's probably more John's type."

"Why do you say that?"

"John wants a family and a place he can call his. I don't want that yet. I just became a teacher, and I enjoy it." Was she convincing Rosalia or herself? Inwardly, she questioned her true motive behind the words.

HONK! HONK!

They both turned in the direction of the automobile horn that was blaring down the road. In the car a girl's hair was blowing about the open window. Out the window the girl waved her hand wildly. Smiling, she shouted, "Hi, Susie!"

Susie smiled and waved back. "Oh, God! It's her again. Wonder why she's so friendly today. She must want something from me.

Thank goodness, she only comes home on the weekends. Oh, boy! I bet she'll be at the wedding. That's enough to make me stay home. Poor, Mikie!"

"Who's that?"

For a second Susie was bewildered by Rosalia's question. Then after a second of thought, she understood exactly why Rosalia did not know who that girl was.

"Mikie's sister--the one and only Margie. Thank God! One is too much!" Susie said scornfully.

"Mikie doesn't talk about her much," Rosalia remarked.

"She's something else. Mikie probably doesn't talk about her because there's nothing nice to say about her. A nun we had in school once said 'if you can't say something nice about a person, don't say anything at all.' Mikie lives by that rule," Susie replied.

"Too bad a lot of other people don't live by that rule. The world would be a better place. There is so much sorrow when people viciously malign other people. The church preaches and preaches about the third commandment but doesn't preach very much on the ninth. Everyone is entitled to a good name, and no one should take that away by gossip."

"You sound like my ma. She hates it when people gossip."

Up the cement steps they walked and into the store.

"Hello, girls, what can I do for you today?" the old man, withered with age, behind the counter asked.

"A gallon of milk, please." Rosalie laid the money on the counter.

A whiff of cold air could be felt. The girls let out a shiver as the old man opened the glass doors on the cooler and pulled out four glass-necked bottles. They were filled to the brim. The cream had separated from the milk and had floated to the top revealing how much cream was in the jar.

"Here take this. You can use it to bring back the empty glass jars." He handed Rosalia a metal basket with four, individual wired sections that could hold four quarts of milk.

"Thanks." Rosalia placed the milk into the basket.

"And what's that you're wearing, Rosalia?" the old man asked.

Rosalia, feeling overpowered with joy, spontaneously smiled.

"Mikie?" The old man smiled. He knew.

Rosalia nodded as her face flushed with radiance.

"He's a good boy. Going to the wedding today?--Oh, I'm sorry, Susie."

"No need to be. I'm happy for John, and I hope they will be happy." Susie smiled. "See you later." She proceeded toward the door and held it open for Rosalia to pass through.

"Have you and Mikie talked about a day?" Susie broke the silence on their walk back home.

"Not really, I'd like to get my teaching license first. But when we're together, I think about how wonderful he makes me feel. I want to be with him all the time. Well, I guess the first thing we have to do is tell them." She motioned to Mikie's parents' house as they walked past it.

"I think someone was watching us. I saw the curtain on the window move upstairs," Susie whispered to Rosalia.

"Really?" Rosalia looked toward the house's upstairs windows, "Which one?" she asked.

"The first one." Susie motioned with her head.

"That's Mikie's room. Maybe it was Mikie," Rosalia commented.

"No, Mikie is on the milk route. The milk truck is gone. It must be his ma."

"What would she be doing in Mikie's room?" Rosalia wondered.

"She's probably cleaning it. Pamela is a very meticulous housekeeper."

"Will we see you at the wedding?" asked Rosalia.

"I told John I was coming, but I don't know if I really should?"

"Come on, please, we'll have fun. We always do." Rosalia stopped at the edge of the lawn in front of Susie's parents' house.

"Oh, I don't know Rosalia."

"Well, I've got to get home and dressed. Mass is at eleven o'clock and Mikie will be picking me up early. It's going to be strange going into that church." Rosalia looked up the road at the church--the projecting stone structure with its sharp rising, lofty roofs and its pointed arches. "Oh, here he comes already." She saw Mikie's truck coming down the road. "I've got to get going. I hope you'll come to the wedding."

"I see Roger is with him," said Susie.

"Ya, he's going to finish the route for Mikie. Bye, Susie." In a hurried stride Rosalia continued down the road, the basket swaying to and fro in her hand.

Susie sat on the step that she had been sitting on when she had first seen Rosalia coming down the road. Susie had been a good actress, but now the smile was gone and the tears came. She had dreams about John and her. She had loved him and still did. But what could she do when he stopped coming to see her less and less, and she had found out that he was seeing Lori more and more. It hurt to lose him, but she was not going to reveal those feelings. She would just make a fool of herself because it was quite obvious that he did not love her. She wiped the tears from her face. That was enough of the thinking about what she had lost. It was a waste of time. He was gone. She would move on from this and never think of it again. Her life was meant to be spent with someone else. Somehow, things always happen for the best. It was difficult to rationalize that way once and awhile. So she sat and thought away the time. Remembering the things, John and she had done. Then as Mikie drove past in his car and blew the horn at her on his way to pick up Rosalia, she began to think of all the memories that she had of her good friend, Mikie. So many things were changing--so fast--or maybe it was not so fast. Maybe she never really seen how all along things were changing a little at a time, and she never really noticed until now? This town and its people were so predictable. She never thought that she would agree with anything Margie did, but maybe getting out of this town would be a good thing. Most people in the town were related because everyone married into everyone else's family. Alex married Lucy. Now Lori was marrying John. So now Rosalia would also be related to John because Lori's sister was married to Rosalia's brother. The entire town had situations like that.

"Susie." A soft voice came from behind, and a smile greeted her when she turned in the direction of the voice.

"Just wanted to let you know we are leaving now. If you're not going to the wedding meal, there is a leftover meat loaf and scallop potatoes in the refrigerator you can get out and reheat."

"Thanks, Ma, have a good time. You look really pretty." Susie got up from the step and joined her mother in the house.

"I'm sorry, Susie." Her mother hugged her and kissed her head.
"It'll be all right, Ma. It wasn't meant to be."
"We really have to go because your pa did work with John in the foundry. I hope you don't feel betrayed."
"No, Ma, I understand. John and Pa are friends."
"Bye, Susie." Her father opened the door and escorted her mother out the door.

Susie watched out the screen door as her parents joined the Aslens in their car. What would Pamela really do when she found out about Mikie? Susie knew--Pamela would be outraged!

Meanwhile, with Mikie being the best man, he and Rosalia arrived at the church early. Mikie went into the sanctuary while Rosalia sat in the back of church. She watched as neighbors and friends filled the pews one by one. John entered the church escorting an elderly, gray-haired woman, his grandmother, who walked with pride beside him. Following them was a tall man dressed in an army uniform decorated with numerous honorary medals. She recognized the man as John's father. Who else would have such red hair? In his huge hand, he held the small, narrow hand of a petite, dark, reddish brown skinned woman. Her black, straight hair flowed along the contour of her round face. An epicanthic fold dressed her dark sparkling eyes. A smile graced her flawless, youthful face. They sat in the first church pew on the right side of church.

Within a few minutes, two small boys entered the church dressed in dark suits, white shirts, and dark bow ties. They stood with their eyes focused at the entrance, anticipating the arrival of someone. Soon Alex appeared with a chair on wheels. The taller of the two boys grabbed onto the two handles that protruded from the back of the chair. Soon Alex appeared carrying Pete whom he put into the chair. Alex whispered something to the oldest boy who nodded his head. They smiled at each other, and Alex took the hand of the smaller boy and walked down the aisle. They went into a front pew located on the left side of church.

Moments later, Lucy appeared inside the entrance. She was dressed in a light-blue dress and holding a bouquet of large, orange-bronze chrysanthemums.

At the front of the church, the priest dressed in a white cincture and a red chasuble came out of the sacristy. Immediately walking behind him were four altar boys. Each boy was dressed in a long, black vestment which was covered by a loose, white, wide-sleeved, knee-length vestment. With the four altar boys standing beside him, two on each side, the priest looked up into the choir. Seeing the priest nod his head was a signal to the organist to commence with the bridal march.

The music began. The people stood in their pews. All eyes were eagerly focused on the church's entrance to see the wedding begin.

Step with the right foot--step with the left foot--stop--step with the right foot--step with the left foot--stop--this is how, Lucy, with her solemn face, continued down the aisle.

Behind her in the doorway stood Lori. Her body, tanned from the months of summer farm work, accented the white, calf-length dress. Frills of lace decorated her neckline and a white belt garnished her slender waist. Beams of happiness radiated from Lori's eyes; her face blushed with rapture. She had never thought a day like this would ever exist for her. She felt like she was floating on air. In her white gloved hand she carried one, long-stemmed rose with big double blooms of velvety red petals. She only carried one as a reminder of the one person who was missing from this day, her mother. Within the vision of her mind, she could see her mother cut the roses from her flower garden and fill each room of the house with a vase of roses. Now that rose smell, a delicate aroma of tea, made her feel the presence of her mother. In her other hand she held her father's fragile hand as he sat in the wheelchair being pushed so carefully down the aisle by his oldest grandson, Eddy.

Nearing the front of the communion rail, which separated the sanctuary from the rest of the church, Lori stopped and so did the wheelchair. As John approached to take her hand and walk beside her up to the altar, Lori gave her father a long hug. With his left hand, the only hand he could now move, he gave her a loving squeeze. Then he gave her hand to John. She placed the single rose on her father's lap. Tears filled both their eyes. It was a day of joy but also one of sadness for the one that was not there to share this day. But things are very seldom as we want them to be, and so reality is accepted. Life goes on, and unfilled wishes are replaced by new wishes.

As she saw Lori march down the aisle, Rosalia wondered how she would go down the aisle. Alone? Where was her father? Would he be here to give her to the man she married? These were sad thoughts that made her heart heavy. Why did he leave without saying anything to her? Why had he never even made an effort to contact her at all? She had always thought he loved her, but his sudden leaving like that made her feel otherwise. She had prayed for him to return. She had prayed that whatever the reason he had left, it was not as strong as his love for her and he would return. Tears came to her eyes as she thought the worst. Maybe he was dead. Maybe she would never see him again. No! She would always hold on to that hope that he was alive, and one day he would come back home. She wiped her eyes dry.

During the ceremony, John's grandmother would occasionally glance over at Pete. She didn't mean to stare, but it was difficult for her to see him like that--tarnished with age. She had aged, what made her think he would not? How quiet he was. She thought, how terrible for someone who was so active to be unable to move on his own accord. He was younger than she, but God seemed to have blessed her in her old age. She had forgiven him for his part in the deception. She had often thought about him over the years, wondering if he was still alive. If so, what he was like now. How small the world was. She never thought their paths would ever meet, after all those years. She wondered if he'd even recognize her. She doubted it before. Now seeing him in this state of health, she did not think recognition was possible and maybe that was for the best.

Rosalia was quite inattentive about most of the ceremony. She simply adored watching Mikie being at the altar--his black velvet hair, short and naturally curly--his young, healthy rosy cheeks--his slim, masculine body shape. He was the most handsome, desirable boy that she had ever seen. She was so very lucky to have someone like him. Curiously, her eyes roamed over to where the Bensons and Aslens were sitting. She had seen them come into church earlier. However, they had not seen her. The church was quite full when they arrived, and she had been hidden behind some people. She had watched the Aslens' arrogant manner and how they observed what everyone around them was doing. They were together, yet they didn't seem to be. They never looked at each other and never seemed to acknowledge each other's existence. They would smile and display a very cordial attitude toward others, but it did not appear to be the way things really were between them. It was as if they were in a play and following a script of the way things should appear to be, but in reality were not.

Rosalia felt a gentle push of an elbow on her arm. Turning to see who it was, her face became radiant. A smile spread from cheek to cheek. It was Susie.

"I decided to come and wish him--both of them happiness," she whispered to Rosalia.

"I'm glad."

With the ceremony over, the church pews emptied one by one from the front to the back. Being in the last pew, the girls were the last to leave. Standing outside the church, being congratulated by everyone who left church, were John and Lori.

"Congratulations, Lori." Susie extended her hand and gave Lori a smile.

"Thank you, Susie--Rosalia." Lori smiled sweetly and timidly.

"Congratulation, John, I wish you both much happiness." It was hard to say, but Susie did mean every word.

John hugged her. "Thank you, Susie. The friendship we have will always hold a special place in my heart." He released his embrace and gently kissed her on the cheek.

"Take care." She smiled and quickly turned away. She struggled inside of herself and managed to keep her composure. No one knew her heart was crying. Her smile hid it all.

The girls walked to Lyra's. The rest of the wedding would take place there--the meal, the reception, and the dance. As they entered the reception hall, the smell of food tantalized their taste buds. It would be awhile before they would eat. The bridal party had gone to the studio to have their pictures taken. With Lucy having to leave around four o'clock for farm chores, they had decided to eat as soon as they came from the studio. The reception would take place while Lucy was at the farm. While waiting for the bridal party to arrive, the girls strolled outside amongst the aromatized, blooming flower gardens.

John's grandmother searched about the crowd of wedding guests looking for Pete. There, looking out one of the French doors, she saw him sit--surrounded by solitude. She walked up and positioned herself in front of him. Her face, set with deep wrinkles, probably hid the face that he once knew. She touched his hand. "Oh, my dear friend, Pete, when we were young, we never thought we'd ever get old. Now when we're old, we can't remember ever being young. It is good to see you. Yes, it is. I'm sorry for your bad health. Even in my most turbulent thoughts of you, I never wished you bad."

Pete looked away from the space that he had been staring into and focused in the direction of the voice. He felt a sense of familiarity, but he did not recognize her. Who was this woman?

She sensed his look. "I'm--"

"Grandma, they are waiting at the table for you and Pete." John took hold of the wheelchair's handles.

"Oh, you and Lori are here already." She was glad to see him, but regretted the interruption.

"Ya, the photographer didn't take long. The cooks would like to serve the meal now." John pushed the wheelchair up to the side of the table reserved for Lori's side of the family. Then he helped his grandmother sit next to his father's wife.

At the middle of the long, white table sat John and Lori. The best man, Mikie, sat to the left of John followed by the rest of John's family--his father, his father's wife, and his grandmother. Lucy, the maid of honor, sat to the right of Lori then Pete and Eddy.

"Where do you want to sit, Rosalia?" Susie looked about at the other two long tables set up in the hall for the other guests.

"Let's sit at the front of this table." Rosalia had seen the Aslens sit at the end of the second table. She wanted to sit as far away from them as possible.

"Oh, you want to be close to the bridal table. I wonder why?" Susie smiled figuring that Rosalia wanted to be as close to Mikie as she could get.

To the front of the table they went and sat. Later, they were joined by Alex, Jeffery, and Amanda. During the meal, Mikie would often look over at Rosalia and wink at her. Rosalia would smile and feel her face flush. She hoped no one else saw that.

Eddy assisted Pete at the table by cutting the food on Pete's plate into bite size pieces. Since his stroke, Lori's persistence and patience had resulted in Pete being able to function with his left hand. As Pete slowly ate, he thought of that old woman. The scent of her perfume that had lingered in the air seemed so familiar. There was only one person he had ever known who wore that scent. Was that her? Yes, it was. How foolish he had not recognized her maiden name. It was the same as John's last name. He had often wondered what had happened to her. If only he could turn his head to look at her--if only he could talk. If the grandfather was who he thought he had to be, he began to worry. Why did John marry his daughter? Was John as scheming as his grandfather? For his daughter's happiness, he hoped not. He prayed not.

"Lillian, I was quite shocked at what I saw early this morning," Pamela commented during the meal.

"What was that?" Lillian was seated across the table from Pamela.

"Well, I seem to be seeing the same thing now as well."

"Oh?" Lillian continued to eat.

"I would think you wouldn't want your daughter to get a certain kind of reputation merely because of whom she socializes with."

"I'm sorry, Pamela, but what are you talking about?"

"I see Susie is getting very friendly with that Stoner girl. I'm surprised you allow that. You know she comes from a family of whores that have illegitimate children. I'd hate to see Susie get a bad name like that girl's family has just because she talks to her."

"Oh, Pamela, you listen too much to the idle gossip in the bakery that Regina spreads around. Most people know that gossip comes from the bad feelings that Regina had about Anna and Amanda. Now she carries on her dislike to Alex and Rosalia."

"Lillian, that family has a bad name. The grandma had an illegitimate child. The mother had one. Alex is only a Stoner because of Frederick's good-heartedness. That girl will probably follow the family tradition."

"Rosalia is a fine girl and a good friend to Susie."

"Lillian, if you care about Susie you better advise her to stop being seen with that girl."

"I think you should sweep in front of your own doorstep, Pamela."

"If you're talking about Mikie dating her those couple of times, well, I ordered him to stop seeing her. If he was smart, he listened. I told him to watch out for her. I told him, 'before you know it, Mikie, she'll be calling you the father of her illegitimate child.' She's trash, pure trash!"

Lillian decided not to comment any more. It was obvious Mikie had not told her, and she was not going to be the person to say anything. Mikie was the one who should tell them.

"So when is Mikie getting married?" asked Bob who was also seating across the table next to Lillian.

Lillian almost choked on her food. She poked Bob with her elbow to keep him quiet, but it was too late.

"What are you talking about?" Pamela asked.

At that moment Bob knew, he should have never opened his mouth.

"Who is getting married?" Otto, who had been previously occupied with other thoughts, joined in the conversation.

Lillian and Bob looked at each other. Neither was about to volunteer that information.

"It's not her? Is it?" Pamela looked at Rosalia.

Silence! Bob and Lillian lowered their heads as if they were resuming eating.

"Oh, my God! It is? I told him and I told him. She'd trap him! He can never listen, never did and probably never will!" She wiped her mouth with the linen napkin that had been resting on her lap and then tossed it onto her plate. "I'm not hungry anymore. He made a fool of us. Everyone knows except us?"

"I don't think so. He just gave her the ring," Lillian replied.

"He maybe gave her the ring so he can get something from her. When he gets what he wants, he'll probably tell her to get lost. I'm not worrying about it. Let's go to the barroom." Otto got up from the table, pushed his chair back under the table, and waited for the others.

"What if he gets her pregnant?" Pamela spoke in an angry, sharp tone.

"That's his problem. He'll have to live with his mistakes, just like the rest of us live with ours."

"Boy, you're a great help." Pamela gave Otto an unapproving look for that remark as she got up from her chair.

As they all four moved from the hall into the barroom, Pamela seen Rosalia get up from her chair and proceed to the ladies' restroom.

"You go ahead, Lillian. I'll be there in a few minutes."

"Pamela, don't." Lillian lightly grabbed her arm. "Let the girl alone. She's Mikie's choice. Please, get to know her before you place judgement."

"It's my family! Stay out of this matter and let go of my arm!"

Lillian released her hand from Pamela's arm. She shook her head as she saw Pamela follow Rosalia into the restroom. She knew how "razor sharp" Pamela's words could be, especially when she did not like a person. She felt sorry for that sweet, little girl; however, Rosalia would have to face Pamela sooner or later. It was inevitable.

As Pamela entered the restroom, Rosalia turned away from the mirror where she had been touching up the bright red lipstick on her lips.

Pamela immediately eyed her finger and the ring that sparkled in the restroom light. "I heard you and my son are engaged. When is the wedding day?" Every word was full of hateful venom. Her eyes were vicious with rage.

"We haven't decided." Rosalia forced a smile as she felt herself being swallowed in a room that was engulfed with hatred.

"Well, I suggest you don't set a date. We don't want someone like you in our family." Pamela moved closer and closer toward Rosalia. Finally, she had Rosalia backed tight against the restroom wall.

"Someone like me? You don't know me." The words quivered in Rosalia's throat.

"That's right, and I don't care to know you either. For your own good, I suggest you give that ring back and tell him that you've changed your mind about marrying him." Every word was full of threatening furor.

"Why should you care whom he might marry? You never cared about him before."

"You little 'snip.' I care because it's our family reputation that will be dragged through the mud if he married you. We have a good reputation in this town, and we don't want to be associated with a family of whores and killers."

"We are neither."

"Huh! You think I'm dumb. You can tell others that but not me! Just look at your brother, Alex. He's not only illegitimate, but he killed his friend by pushing him in front of that train."

"You don't know what you're talking about. I was the only one on top of that hill, and I saw it all. I saw my brother grab for Steven to pull him off the track. That's how Alex lost his hand."

"Well, that's not how the town tells it." Pamela's eyes were piercing straight into Rosalia's eyes.

"The people from town didn't come to the hill until after it was over. None of them seen the train kill Steven, but my brother and I did." Horror filled her eyes as that tragic moment from the past flashed back so vividly, forcing her to remember.

The restroom door opened. "Rosalia are you all right?"

Pamela turned away from Rosalia to see who had entered.

"Yes, I'm fine, Susie." Rosalia smiled with relief. She was so glad to see Susie.

"Well, hi Susie." Pamela moved away from Rosalia and smiled. Then glancing in the mirror, she moved some of her hairs off her forehead. "Nice seeing you, Susie." She smiled and left the room.

"Did I come just in time?" Susie had sensed the tension as she entered the room. Seeing Rosalia tremble, she went over and hugged her.

"That woman doesn't like me." Rosalia began to cry. "I never did anything to her. Why does she hate me so?"

"I don't know, Rosalia. I don't know." Susie could not understand a woman who seemed to even hate her own son.

"I'm afraid, Susie. What kind of life will Mikie and I have if she hates me already."

"Don't let her ruin your dreams with Mikie." Susie wiped the tears from Rosalia's face. "You put your pretty smile back on your face and let's join Mikie. That's why I came in here. Mikie was looking for you. He's the only one who matters." As a gesture of her genuine, caring feelings, Susie put her arm around Rosalia's shoulder.

Out into the hall they went where they joined Mikie, John, and Lori.

"What's the matter, Rosalia?" Mikie put his arm around her waist. He had noticed the redness in her eyes and the disheartened look on her face. He could feel her body tremble as he caressed her.

"Nothing." She smiled at him then looked at Susie. She made a quiet gesture at Susie not to say anything. If Mikie found out about the incident, she was fearful that he'd confront his mother. She did not want that incident to go any farther than the restroom.

"We're going into the barroom to socialize with some of the guests. You want to join us, Susie?" Mikie started to escort Rosalia into the barroom.

Rosalia stopped, stood firm, and did not move. "I'd prefer not to go in there now." She had seen Pamela sitting at the bar and did not want to be in her eyes' view. The incident had made Rosalia feel uncomfortable. To be in the same room with Pamela's eyes staring at her, making her feel like a "piece of dirt," was more than she wanted to tolerate at this time. She had to have time to calm her emotions and take control of herself. Right now her hands were still trembling. She never had the ability to response rudely to someone else's rude remarks. Situations of intense conflict always upset her tremendously.

"Would you two mind walking me home?" Susie thought that would be a good way for Rosalia to get out of this unpleasant circumstance and regain some of her composure. Susie had seen how Rosalia's hands were trembling.

"It's beautiful outside. Would you mind, Mikie?" Rosalia looked at him with her adoring, somewhat begging eyes and sweet smile.

"Let's go. It will give us a chance to talk about our wedding. I suppose we should tell them first." Mikie had seen his parents drinking at the bar.

Rosalia and Susie just looked at each other. No words needed to be said.

"There'll be time for that later, Mikie," Susie quickly suggested.

They both grabbed each one of Mikie's hands and led him outside. The sun, a brilliant red and orange, lit up the horizon as the trees in the distance stood as silhouettes against the sky. In another hour it would start to get dark. There was a peaceful breeze that fluttered through the trees, as the leaves that had reached their prime red and yellow gently cascaded to the ground one at a time. As they would pass some residences, an occasional owner's dog would bark at them until they were out of sight. Some neighbors sitting on their porches would wave and greet them as they passed in view. There were very few cars on the road this evening, making their walk a carefree one and one they would never walk together again. They were changing. Time was changing and in the sadness of their hearts they knew that they could never capture this moment in time again. They would still all three be friends, but it would be different. Susie would no longer be Mikie's confidant or tomboy friend who went fishing and hunting with him. She would not be Rosalia's confidant anymore either. Their days of private "girl talk" were gone. Mikie and Rosalia had each other, and it was right to be that way. Susie was alone now. She had made her decision. It was because of that decision that she cherished this last time they would be together like this.

"Thanks for walking me home." She hugged Mikie and then Rosalia. "Everything will be fine," she whispered to Rosalia then released her with a kiss on her cheek. "I love you two." Tears filled her eyes.

"What's the matter, Susie?" Rosalia asked.

"Oh, I'm just a sentimental fool. You two go back to the wedding and have a good time." It was heartbreaking to realize the past was gone, and things would never be like they were.

"When we get married, I would like you to be my maid of honor." Rosalia's eyes showed the love that she had in her heart for her dearest friend.

"You know how I feel about you, Susie. If I could have you as my best man, I would." Mikie hugged her also. "We'll see you tomorrow, probably after my milk route."

Susie watched them walk down the street hand in hand. A smile soon erased those silly sentimental tears from her face. She found happiness in knowing that Mikie had finally found someone who would love him and treat him like someone--someone who had feelings, who needed and deserved love. Maybe his life would finally be filled with contentment and love. He deserved that!

Meanwhile, at Lyra's, the dining tables had been cleared away, and the chairs had been set against the walls in preparation for the customary wedding dance. The drummer was setting up his drums and cabals. The pure, full, and mellow practice tones of the horn player echoed the room while the clarinet and saxophone players sorted out their music sheets. The piano accordion player was pressing keys and buttons while pushing the bellows, which produced sounds that had people filtering from the barroom onto the dance floor awaiting the start of the polkas and waltzes.

Alex and Lucy had departed after the meal to go home and do the farm chores. They had taken Pete and the two boys with them, planning to return later in the evening for the grand march. However, until then, Amanda was alone. She did not mind that. It gave her time to remember her life in this grand house. There was the stairway that she had walked down on the day she married Frederick. The stairway that Alex and Rosalia, so full of young energy, would run up, and the shining oak railing they would slide down. It seemed a lifetime ago. A lifetime she could never get back. The parlor, where her mother had sat in the evenings knitting, was gone. It was the barroom now. Charles's library had been made into part of the dining hall. A door had been placed at the top of the stairs and their bedrooms had become living quarters for Lyra. As the simple, melodic style of the band's clear and penetrating tunes filled the hall, she walked through the crowd out onto the terrace. She stood wrapped in memories. The present world around her did not exist at that moment.

He had noticed Amanda in church. His quietness was a result of him watching her every move during the day. He stared at her breasts that were big, soft and round. He admired her shining, long hair and wanted her red moist lips. He watched her enticing body wiggling with excitement with each step that she took and he longed to touch her shapely legs. She had been like wine, improved with age and just as desirable. All these years he had gone so far to get what was so close.

"Lonely?"

Amanda turned with a smile to greet the voice. Quickly, her smile was ripped away with a fear that paralyzed her body. The demons that had been locked away in the dungeons of her mind were suddenly set free. The terror of that night now drowned her body in a sea of panic. Her heart pounded. Her breath raced on. She wanted to scream! But it did not help her then and it would not help her now. She had to get a grip of the situation. He would not do anything. There were too many people. She would just walk back into the hall.

"Where are you going? I'm not done with you." He grabbed her arm and crushed it his huge hand.

"Please, let go of me." Her body became frozen with fear. He was touching her!

"I'll let go of your arm if you promise not to leave."

She looked into the hall. People were flying about the room with the beat of the band. She did not want to make a scene and call any attention to herself. Being older and smarter now, she could handle him. She would not be afraid. He thrived on fear. She nodded her head and felt the chill of his touch leave her body as he freed her arm from his grip.

"You get lonely with your husband gone so long?" He took a drink of his beer. His eyes glistened with the connote of those words.

"That's really none of your concern." She stood fearless up to him.

"Boy, I thought you were a wild one when you were young." He felt her hair with his hand.

She moved away from him. "Leave me alone!"

"Well, I hear we're going to be related. Won't that be nice?" He grabbed her arm again, except this time he was more gentle.

"Mikie is a fine boy. I find it hard to believe Pamela and you are his parents."

"Ya, that Pamela, she's a real bitch. Isn't she? I've got to find my loving somewhere else." He stood in back of her, his hand still on her arm, and started to breathe very heavy as he visualized his erotic thoughts becoming reality.

"I think it would be best if you let go of me--now!"

"Just remember, if you get lonely with your husband gone, I'll be there to help you out. It would be my pleasure." He laughed to himself, took his hand off her arm, and backed away from her.

Amanda closed her eyes for a few seconds and felt her body surge with relief. Of all the boys Rosalia had decided to marry, why did his father have to be that man. The horrid sleeping phantoms of her mind had been awakened and as long as he was a part of her life, they would never be put to rest. How could she handle the situations that surely would arise with Rosalia and Mikie being married? She looked up at the sky full of stars and prayed within her soul. Oh, God, help! Help me! Please protect me from that man's evil ways. Then she thought, God only helps those who help themselves. So in the future, she would have to be very careful not to get in a comprising situation with Otto. She had planned to stay for the grand march, but she was still shivering from Otto's presence. The best place for her was at home, but first she would stroll about the familiar yard. She did not know when she would get this opportunity again to be so close to her memories of this place. Her stroll took her near the pond where she stopped. She thought, how ironic it was for Charles to die at the same place Eva had died.

With the moon beams dancing on the water, she recalled that day two years ago. After her mother had died, Eddy often spent the summer days with Charles. Eddy filled the lonely days for Charles, and Eddy being with Charles helped Lucy out at the farm. It made things easier for Lucy to only have one boy to take care of. Charles and Eddy's daily routine was to fish in the pond. It was a good day for fishing. The sky was filled with clouds just ready to burst with a downpour of summer rain. She was outside taking her wash off the clothesline when Eddy had come around the house. She was concerned about little Eddy being by himself and had asked Eddy where his great-grandfather was. "Great-grandpa doesn't wake up," he said as he pulled at her, "help me wake him up." A strange feeling flowed through her body. She dropped the clothes in her hand into the wash basket. Holding onto Eddy's hand, she walked as fast as she could toward this place. Her heart dreaded the worst. She forced herself to remain calm so she would not upset Eddy.

As they neared the pond, she slowed her momentum. What would she find? She stopped. Eddy pulled her on. "Please, wake up Great-grandpa," he said.

There he sat, his body leaned against the trunk of the mighty oak. His fishing pole was lying at the tip of the hand that it had been released from. His head had tilted backwards and his cold eyes were gazing upward as if he was watching himself enter the heavens. She held Eddy to herself and turned him from a sight no child should ever see. She did not want him to remember his great-grandfather that way. Quietly, he had died. He had been doing the two things that he had enjoyed most in his later years--fishing and telling stories to Eddy, who had brought him so much companionship in those years after her mother's death. He had grown to love and accept both Eddy and Jeffery as his own great-grandsons. Even though, in reality they were not. She could still see Charles ruffling Eddy's hair, hugging him, and saying, "love is where you find it. Cherish it and it will flourish. It will make all things beautiful and life worthwhile." Reflections on those words filled her eyes with tears. Charles had loved her as his daughter, and he was the father that she had been deprived of. Her heart was heavy in those last years knowing the lost that Charles felt in his heart for Frederick. She wiped away the tears and wished she could have wiped away the events of the last night that she was with Frederick.

So many good memories--so many bad memories, she would leave the bad ones here and take the good ones with her. Life should be so simple. The path home was lit by the full moon and the pole lights people had in their yards. While walking she noticed the silence around her was broken by a sound. It was after passing the last tavern that she had first noticed it--footsteps. Footsteps were following her--slowly. Should she turn to see who it was? No! She would keep on walking and listening. The footsteps were far behind her. She could hardly hear them. Maybe she was imagining them. While walking, she decided to turn her head back. Yes, someone was behind her. Maybe it was a neighbor walking home just like her? Nothing to be concerned about, or was it Otto? Oh, my God, not him, please! She passed the Benson house. She didn't have far to go now. She walked on and the footsteps followed. Three more houses and she would be home. She lived at the end of the road. Which neighbor could it be? There was her house. The footsteps still followed her. It was no neighbor! Anxiously, she ran up the front porch steps, reaching into her purse she pulled out the key for the door. In her hurried actions, she dropped the key. The footsteps were still coming. Groping about the porch floor, she finally located the key and quickly opened the door. Inside she rushed and locked the door behind her. Safe! Catching her breath and regaining her senses, she wondered who that was. Leaving the house lights off, she slowly moved to the window. Slightly pulling the curtain away from the window, she peered out. There lurking in the gathered darkness was a shadow of a man at the edge of the road. She watched him as he stared and stared at the house. Who was he? Was it Otto? Why was he there? When would he leave? Why didn't he leave? She watched and watched. She would not leave the window. She felt a minute sense of security knowing where he was. She would watch him as long as he watched the house. What if he came up to the house? Were the windows locked? Yes, she thought so. Was the back house door locked? Oh, go away, go away! It seemed like hours. Then finally, he turned and walked away from the house. She did not leave the window until his silhouette had disappeared down the street.

Inside the ballroom, Pamela sat by herself nursing a glass of beer that had gotten warm from being held in her hand for quite some time. Occasionally, if Lillian wanted to rest between dances or did not care to dance to the music, Bob would dance with Pamela. Pamela enjoyed twirling around the floor to a good polka tune. Other than that, Pamela's social evening at the dance was like any other social event. She socialized with the neighbor women while Otto moved about the crowd drinking and talking. She had seen him go out onto the terrace and socialize with Amanda. She contemplated what he would be conversing about with a woman of such ill repute. When they had moved out of view, her curiosity mounted. However, she was pleased that they were also out of view of others at the wedding. He had not been out there very long when he returned to the hall with a clever smirk spread across his face. Was she his whore now? She did not really care. The man that she desired to be with her was not here.

Then Pamela's roaming eyes seen them, Mikie and HER. Something had to be done about that situation. Mikie was not going to marry that THING! She would watch them waltz around the floor. Sometimes they would dance so close together it was as if they were one person. They were constantly smiling at each other and holding each other's hands as they walked about the crowd, talking and laughing with Mikie's acquaintances. Such "love birds"! How disgusting! The rage multiplied within her. She was so ashamed to have others see her son with HER and even more ashamed to have others find out that they were engaged. She had to break them up before that THING got herself pregnant and tricked Mikie into marrying her. She hoped that she had not done that already. Well, if she was pregnant, that was her problem. She could raise that illegitimate child herself. Pamela would make sure no one would ever consider that child Mikie's. Marrying HER would tarnish their good reputation. Mikie had to marry someone that came from a family that was held in high regard in the community, a family that had a good heritage. How could Mikie even think of marrying something like THAT? It was revolting! So revolting!

With the arrival of Lucy, the entire bridal party was now present at the wedding. It was now time for the grand march. But first, the band would take their twenty-minute intermission.

"Alex, where is your ma?" Lucy was having difficulty controlling Jeffery's anxiousness to run about the hall.

"I don't see her. She must have gone home." His eyes searched the crowd in the hall.

"How inconsiderate of her! She could have stayed and taken care of the boys so I could enjoy myself."

"You should have said something."

"I don't know why Lori had such a big wedding. At least she didn't have both dinner and supper. Two meals are too expensive."

"We had a big wedding." Alex shrugged his shoulders, as he thought, so what, if that's what Lori wanted, why not?

"Ya, well Pa was working then. He's not working now. If he keeps drawing out of his savings, there'll be nothing left. He should have never given her the farm until she was married. All those years the money made off the farm would have been Pa's, not hers."

"It was your pa's decision. He has enough money in stocks to last another lifetime. I don't think he minds."

"Well, she better pick Pa up tomorrow right after milking. I have enough to do to take care of the boys."

"Why don't we take care of Pa for a couple of days so they can be alone? I'll help you."

"No! John knew what he was getting when he decided to marry her. If he thought that he was just getting an old maid who owned a farm, well, he better think again. Pa comes with the marriage. I'm not taking care of him."

"A couple of days won't do any harm."

"I said 'no.' If we do it once, they'll think that we can always do it. Here take Jeffery. They're getting ready for the grand march." She shoved Jeffery at Alex and walked away toward John and Lori.

The night continued in much the same fashion until the dance came to an end. When the band and people left the hall, the doors were closed and the lights deadened. From the hall, Pamela, Bob, and Lillian joined Otto in the barroom. Needless to say, Otto was very incoherent. Bob helped Otto walk out to the car. There, Otto moved his inebriated body onto the passenger side of the car and passed out. Pamela drove home and left him sleep off his condition in the car. Maybe he would get a second hangover from the fumigated car. She did not care, to hell with him--the sooner the better!

Pamela made herself coffee. She was not about to sleep with that unresolved situation lingering. It would be resolved tonight, and she intended to stay awake as long as it took to get it settled, her way. In the kitchen, sitting at the table, she waited--one cup of coffee--two cups of coffee--three cups of coffee. Waiting was fermenting her already extreme agitation. Finally, she heard a car drive into the driveway. Was it Mikie or Margie? Although she was anxious to confront him, she had hoped it was Margie. Two against Mikie would be better. The car stopped. She heard one car door slam shut. Could it be Mikie? Could it be Margie getting out on the driver's side with Paul? The outside door opened.

"What are you doing up yet? You just get home?" Mikie walked toward the stairs.

"Do you think that you're cute by letting us find out about your engagement from other people? Do you know how embarrassing that was? It really makes us look like a close family! Everyone knew but us! Damn you!" Pamela shouted.

"I was going to tell you--"

"Ya, sure! When? On the wedding day!"

"We just got engaged. It's not like we were engaged for a long time."

"Well, it's usually considered proper to inform the parents of an upcoming engagement."

"I'm sorry."

"Well, sorry doesn't help or change anything. You're not marrying her. So ask for the ring back!" Pamela demanded.

"I'm not asking for the ring back. I'm marrying Rosalia," Mikie asserted. He turned away from her and started to walk up the stairs.

"You get back here! We're not finished talking!" She walked after him.

He stopped on the stairs and turned toward her. "We're finished talking if you're going to be that way."

She grabbed at his arm. "I don't want something like THAT in our family."

"What are you talking about? Rosalia is a fine person." He pulled away.

"She comes from a family of whores. How could you ruin our reputation like that? I forbid you to marry her."

"I'm marrying her!"

"She's not even Catholic. If you marry her, you can't get married in the Catholic church. My God! She's older than you! You can find someone better."

"Someone better? In comparison to whom? She's going to take instructions and become Catholic. She's only a couple years older than me. She loves me, Ma. Someone actually can love me."

"What's all the noise?" Margie and Paul entered the room.

"Oh, Margie, you're not going to believe what he did. He's engaged to Rosalia Stoner." Pamela threw her hands up in the air in despair.

"What! Rosalia Stoner! You're not degrading this family's morals by marrying into a family like that! Oh, Ma! Everyone will laugh at us! Snob us! No one will want to associate with us if we have them in our family. How can you do that to us, Mikie?" Margie stormed about the kitchen. "You can't marry her! Think of our family name! My God, Mikie, you've got to marry someone with an important name, someone with prestige in the community. Don't humiliate us like this, Mikie! Ma and Dad have worked hard to build a good name in this town."

"I can't believe this. Neither one of you knows Rosalia. Yet, you both think you can tell me not to marry her. Well, she's the girl that I want to marry. I consider myself lucky that she will marry me."

"Mikie, you better think about what you're doing. You better stay away from her kind. Before you know it, she'll tell you that she's pregnant," Pamela angrily commented.

"Well, for your information, Rosalia is too much of a lady to go to bed with someone before she's married to that person. Some other people should be so moral." Mikie stormed up the steps.

"What a 'trash mouth.' " Margie looked over at Paul. They knew whom he was talking about but pretended differently. After all, Paul and she were careful. She would never get pregnant before she was married. The dumb ones got caught and got pregnant. She had their life planned out. Nine months after she was married, she would have her first child. She did not like this idea of Mikie being engaged. She was the oldest. Therefore, she should be married first and have the first grandchild. What if Rosalia got pregnant? Maybe she already was. Mikie could not have the first grandchild. He could not get married before her. That was not the way things should be. No, she was the oldest and things should be the way she wanted them to be.

"Margie, what are we going to do? I don't want that THING in our family."

"I don't know, Ma, but we'll have to think of something."

Chapter 18
****
Attempted Murder

Over the winter months she had painted the wicker rocker a glossy white and had cushioned it with pillows so his long days of sitting in the chair would be comfortable. As spring approached, between her usual chores and field work, she had also painted the porch and the support pillars white. Around the porch, which encompassed the entire length of the front of the house, she had transplanted her mother's shrub roses from the flower garden. On each side of the porch, she had a freshly painted white trellis garnished with the climbing red roses that he had given her mother for her birthday the year before she died. She had taken extra good care of those flowers because they were her mother's. In addition, she had flower pots, filled with a profusion of color from her begonias, set at intervals on the flat railing. Her thought was to put the flowers where he could enjoy their beauty as he sat on the porch, thereby, making his confinement as pleasant as possible.

After breakfast, he would be placed outside in the wicker rocker, which faced the barn and the fields. In front of him set a small table. Within his reach, she had set a pitcher full of lemonade and ice cubes. Beside the pitcher set a dinner plate heaped full of his favorite oatmeal cookies. He had enjoyed their aroma last night as he had lain in his bed. She had stayed up late to bake them. However, the cookies were not all for him. He could never eat them all. They would mostly be eaten by the person who would play with him the game that he had just finished setting up on the table. With a natural inclination, he now moved the rocker back and forth with his one foot as he waited for his playing partner.

Across the field his aged eyes stretched. He had seen the boy's small silhouette cross the road into the field where the oats had been harvested. The silhouette in the distance became larger and larger as he walked closer across the yellow oat stubbles in the field, which were quickly being overtaken by the green foliage of this year's newly planted alfalfa. He looked forward to days spent with the boy and would not let the sadness, which he would feel when the boy's daily visits would end, ruin their time together. As the boy neared the edge of the field, the boy was greeted by "Brownie." The boy stopped to stroke the dog's thick, straight, black and white hair. Then he hugged the dog around its fluffy tan collar. The dog's feathery tail waved gracefully. He had never owned a dog, never thought of any practical reason to have one. Feeling that way, it was probably best that he never had a dog. A dog needs love and attention. Something he would have never had time to give a dog. John had gotten the dog from a farmer on Mikie's milk route the other day. John had plans of training the dog to bring the cows up to the barn for milking. It was a good idea if it worked. After greeting the dog, the boy quickened his pace and was soon clumping up the wooden porch steps with his shoes. Once on the porch, with the dog following him, the boy ran to the man sitting in the wicker rocker. The boy's smile brightened that moment for his grandfather as the sun brightens the early morning with its warming rays.

"Hi, Grandpa." The boy poured himself a glass of lemonade. "Boy, that walk made me thirsty." He quickly drank the entire contents of the glass. "You want some, Grandpa?"

His grandfather slowly moved his head to say "no."

"You ready, Grandpa?" The boy sat across the table from his grandfather. "You lost the last game so you can start first." The boy smiled. Then with a serious look, he watched the square wood board, marked with alternating small squares of red and black, for his grandfather's first move.

Grandfather chuckled inside. It was true. He had lost the last game, the game before that, and the game before that. In fact, he could count on his one hand how many games he had won all summer. However, it did not matter. He enjoyed the game whether he won or lost. So here was another day and another game--maybe two--maybe three. They never became bored with the games. Time passed without any comprehension from them or the dog that lay on the porch watching them with her almond eyes.

With another game coming to an end, the boy concentrated more intensely. All that remained on that painted square of wood were three double stacks of red and one double stack of black checkers. The black stack was the boy's. Just one mistake on the part of his grandfather and the boy could capture all three of his grandfather's kings. The boy watched his grandfather take his left hand and touch his one red king. The boy thought. Oh, yes! Go on, move it! Yes, that is the one. The boy held his breath. The excitement tensed his small body. He watched his grandfather pick up that red king and move it, move it right where he wanted it to be moved. But it wasn't a finished move until his grandfather took his hand off the king and when he did the boy burst with exuberance inside. The boy immediately took his king and jumped all three of his grandfather's kings. "I win! I win!"

His grandfather smiled and forced out the words, "Go--od ga--me."

"Do you want to play again?" His words were full of enthusiasm.

"Su--re."

"Great!" The boy gathered up the checkers that were scattered about the table and placed them on the checkerboard on top of the appropriate squares. However, there were two missing, but he knew who had them, the same person who had taken them the last time. He viewed the toddler sitting on the porch floor playing with them. The boy grabbed one of the oatmeal cookies off the plate. Getting up from his chair, he moved toward the curly-haired toddler. "Hey, Jimmy, what you doing?" he spoke softly.

The toddler looked up with his ocean-blue eyes and smiled at the boy.

"Can I have them, Jimmy?" The boy reached toward the checkers that the toddler held in his hand.

With a gleeful smile, the toddler held out the two checkers to the boy.

"Thanks, Jimmy." The boy handed the toddler the oatmeal cookie as he took the checkers from the toddler's chubby hand.

Jimmy took the cookie, got up, and followed the boy to the table. Putting the cookie on the table, he grabbed two more checkers off the checkerboard.

"Jimmy, please don't do that." The boy picked up the cookie and held it out to the toddler again.

The toddler looked at the older boy, smiled, put the checkers back on the board, grabbed the cookie, and started to munch on it.

"Jimmy giving you trouble?" A woman dressed in bib overalls and carrying a small metal container moved with fatigue up the porch steps.

"He keeps taking our checkers, Aunt Lori." The boy replaced the checker in its appropriate square.

Jimmy ran over and wrapped his arms around the woman's legs.

"I'm sorry. Next time I'll keep him in his playpen in the barn when we milk." She smiled and looked down at the toddler. "I think it's time for your bath, my little man." She took his hand and walked toward the house door. "He won't bother you two checker players any more tonight."

"He wasn't that bad. He only took a couple of our checkers. It wasn't any problem."

"Well, I do appreciate you watching him while we milked. Thanks, Eddy." Into the house she disappeared with the toddler.

"You ready to go home, Eddy?" John walked up onto the porch and over to where they were still playing.

"Can Grandpa and I play one more hour?"

"Well, you can play until Lori puts Jimmy to bed. Then we have to get Grandpa ready for bed. You'll have to quit the game then." John knelt down and lovingly stroked the dog.

"Okay, we can always finish tomorrow."

"You have to go back to school soon, huh, Eddy?" asked John.

"Ya." His reply was rather depressed. He thought for a minute. "Maybe I can come after school." His smile and voice were full of optimism.

"Don't you ever get tired of playing the same game?" asked John.

"No, I like playing with Grandpa. The more I play, the better I'll get. I'm going to be the champion checker player in school this year."

"You think so," replied John.

"Yup." He jumped several of grandfather's checkers and put them on his pile of other jumped checkers.

"Who's been winning all day?"

"I won Grandpa every game."

"Grandpa hasn't won at all today?" John chuckled. He knew Pete got more enjoyment out of seeing that smile of excitement on little Eddy's face than he could ever get out of winning. However, John did wonder if allowing Eddy to win the majority of the time was the best thing. A person does not always win in life. Nevertheless, he kept his thoughts to himself. Everyone was happy this way. John pulled up a chair and sat at the table watching them play. It was good Eddy came over to keep Pete company. He knew Pete looked forward to it, and he enjoyed watching them play when he had time.

"Sorry, Eddy, but it is time for Grandpa to get ready for bed." Lori came out, took the wheelchair that had been sitting in a distant corner of the porch, and pushed it next to the wicker rocker.

John got up and helped Pete into the wheelchair.

"Will someone please bring in Grandpa's cushions? If it rains tonight, I don't want them to get wet. The feathers inside will stink if they get wet," Lori spoke in a gentle manner.

"You take the cushions, Eddy. I'll carry in your checkerboard." John grabbed the checkerboard.

"Be careful, Uncle John, don't move any of our checkers." Eddy got up from his chair and grabbed the cushions, hugging them to his body. "They are so soft. Grandpa is lucky. I had to sit on the hard wooden chair."

"Well, if you work as hard as Grandpa did all his life, you'll deserve such a soft chair also someday." Lori pushed the wheelchair over the threshold into the house as John held the screen door open for her.

Eddy struggled walking with the cushions. Only his dark-blue eyes could be seen above the pile he carried. With those eyes, he kept a very close watch on every checker setting on the board that John still held in his hand. Once inside, he put the cushions on the floor. "Please, put the checkerboard up high so Jimmy can't get it."

"Is this okay?" John reached up and put the checkerboard on top of the kitchen hutch.

"Ya, that's great! Thanks, Uncle John."

"Bye, Grandpa." Eddy kissed Pete on the cheek. "Bye Aunt Lori and Uncle John. See you tomorrow." With the wave of his hand, he quickly headed in the direction of the porch door.

"Remember, if it's raining, you wait for Uncle John to pick you up. Okay?" Lori's voice was commanding out of loving concern for Eddy.

"Okay, but don't pick me up too late. Grandpa and I have to finish that game before dinner."

"Why before dinner?" John inquired.

"So we can start another. We got to play three of them you know."

"Oh, I'm sorry. I forgot. I'll be there right after milking." John chuckled. "Will you be ready?"

"You bet." Out the door Eddy spirited with his gleaming smile.

John helped Lori prepare Pete for bed. Lori's petite frame could never maneuver Pete's tall, husky body by herself. Pete felt so refreshed after the sponge bath and lying on the bed of fresh linen. Although he did not like his dependant condition, he had resigned himself to it. Lori and John took good care of him, and he had grown accustomed to his forced leisure life. He looked forward to seeing Eddy and to the Sunday rides that they would often take after Sunday Mass. John was not a person to work on Sundays, unless there were things that absolutely had to get done on the farm because of the weather. He was a hard worker, but he also took time to enjoy life. In hindsight, Pete wished that he had been more like John.

Sometimes the Sunday rides would take them to John's grandmother's house in Jennings. She always had such a feast of food. Although John's grandmother and he were never alone to talk about the past, Pete was positive that he was correct in his assumption as to whom she was.

Other times the Sunday rides would take them around the local countryside. He enjoyed the scenery, but he was saddened by the fact of how the countryside was changing from what he had long remembered it to be. So many of the woods were being cleared to make more land available for planting more crops. Yet other farmland was being taken to expand the city limits of Beechwood. Last year his heart broke when he saw the people chop down all the trees that had shaded the main street. All those trees destroyed so they could widen the road and make a paved street. Why? Because people were complaining about the dust of the gravel, the mud holes after rains, and the impossible driving conditions when the frost came out of the ground in spring. Well, the people got their nice paved road at the cost of trees that were hundreds of years old. Some people just don't understand that there is a cost for everything, and some things can never be brought back once they are gone. However, he was not one to judge others. He was no better. In his lifetime, he had also destroyed things in nature to get what he wanted--money. If only others could and would want to learn from his mistakes and experiences then they would have been worthwhile. Such were the things Pete often thought about; after all, he had all the time in the world to think now.

"Good night, Pa." Lori pulled the white top sheet from the back of the bed, where it had been folded neatly, and gently covered him up to his shoulders. She tucked the sides under the mattress to help keep the sheet in place while he slept. "I'll leave the window open. If the night air gets too cold, you ring the bell." She repositioned the small bell on the night stand closer to the bed, so he could easily grab it with his left hand. "See you tomorrow, Pa." She kissed his wrinkled brow.

Coming out of the bedroom, she saw John's face was shaved and he was dressed in a clean pair of "dress" slacks and shirt. "Where are you going?" she asked softly.

"I'm going to Lyra's. When Mikie picked up the milk this morning, he told me about the big sheepshead tournament tonight. Roger had signed up for it, but he can't make it. Mikie asked if I'd take his place. You don't mind, do you?"

She frowned. She was not too pleased. She knew what tomorrow morning would be like. Oh, well, he was like that every morning whether he went to bed early or stayed out late drinking. Guess some people just had that problem. After two years of marriage, she had accepted that minor flaw in his character. He did work very hard and never complained about the extra work they both had because of her father. However, of more importance was the fact that he was a good husband and father. "Go ahead and have a good time."

"Hey, the prize for the most points is a hundred dollars. If I win, I'm taking you out to eat and buying you a new dress."

"Well, I hope you are lucky, but we need more important things than a new dress for me. I don't really like to go out to eat, but it was a nice thought, thanks."

He hugged and kissed her then went out the door. She followed him outside and sat on the porch step as she watched him drive the car down the driveway and out onto the road.

The sun had set, and the sky was streaked with red and pink clouds. The air was full of the cheerful, chirping sound that the male cricket made by rubbing his wings together. An occasional fire fly, lighting the evening up with its on and off flashes trying to attract a mate, could be seen dotting the air. In the pasture, some of the black and white Holsteins were still grazing on the green grasses. While others had settled down for the night, lying about contentedly and chewing their cud. The collie, Brownie, lay in front of the open milk house door. Her narrow, wedge-shaped head, flat from her ears to her nose, rested on her out stretched, feathered legs. On the green lawn, the black cat, Lori's favorite, was catching June bugs and eating them. She often wondered why they were called June bugs because those bugs were around all summer. She hated to hear their brown, hard wings crunch in the cat's mouth as she ate them. Ugh! Oh, well, despite that it was still so wonderfully peaceful out here. Being married to John had slowed her down to enjoy times like this. In fact, she would have liked to have sat outside much longer, but she was tired. She had baked quite late last night. During the summer, she preferred to bake at night. First, it was the only time that she had available to bake because of the tremendous amount of outside work. Secondly, the house did not get as hot as it did when she baked in the afternoon. In winter she would bake right after her morning barn chores were completed. The extra warmth from baking was welcomed on those cold days but not now.

Into the house she went and made herself ready for bed. When John came home and went to bed, she did not know. She was sleeping tightly until she heard Jimmy's usual early-morning cry for his bottle and diaper change. Still partially asleep, she searched blindly for the knob to turn on the small lamp on her night stand. CLICK! The light flashed on, and she squinted her eyes from its radiance. In the corner of their bedroom, Jimmy stood in his crib with tears rolling down his fat cheeks. With his hands gripped to the crib's railing, he was rocking the crib with such power that she thought he would tip the crib over on its side. Experience told her it would be a waste of her time to try and silence him with sweet, cuddly talk. Only two things would satisfy him--a full bottle of milk and a dry diaper. Getting out of bed, she went into the kitchen. There she grabbed a baby bottle full of milk out of the refrigerator and returned to their bedroom. Seeing her approach with his bottle, he stopped rocking the crib and reached his arms out toward her.

As she gave him the bottle, he gripped it tightly in his hand. Between the few remaining sniffles, he put the bottle into his mouth. Quiet now, she took him out of bed, grabbed two neatly folded cloth diapers off the dresser, and carried him over to their bed. Laying him on her side of their bed, she changed his diaper while talking gently and lovingly to him.

She began to hear the rain beat against the house and remembered the windows that she had left open in the house. Putting Jimmy back into his crib, she quickly rushed to close their bedroom windows. The curtains flew wildly about with the rain. With their windows closed, she went through the living room on her way to her father's bedroom. Inside her father's bedroom, she tiptoed past his bed and up to the window, which she closed as quickly and quietly as she could. Her hand became wet as it touched the flooded windowsill. The furious wind had blown the curtain to one side of its metal curtain rod, and the lightning was violently flashing into the room. She reached up and pulled the rain-drenched curtain back along its rod until it once again covered the entire window. However, the closed window did not muffle the rumbling thunder that kept getting closer and louder. The storm was directly overhead now, and the sharp, sudden loud crashes of thunder were continuous. Going up to her father's bed, she replaced the part of the sheet that had moved off his body. She stood still for a second as she watched how peacefully he slept. She hoped the storm would be over when he woke up so he could sit outside. There was so much for him to see outside, and she had noticed how he seemed to have a happier glow when he was outside instead of being inside the house. Leaving his room as quietly as she had entered it, she returned to their bedroom. Going over to the crib, she observed Jimmy sleeping with the empty bottle lying beside him. He would probably sleep until she came in from the barn after milking. Looking at the alarm clock on her night stand revealed it was almost time for her to get up. Still tired, she went over to the bed and turned the alarm to allow herself another half-hour of sleep. She hoped by then the wild turbulence of the storm would have diminished because she would have to get up to get the cows into the barn for milking. Turning out the light, she crawled back into bed next to John. Putting her arm around his body, she fell asleep.

When the alarm went off, she felt more tired than she did before. She did not want to get out of bed, but what she wanted was not of importance. It was what had to be done. She shook John's body. "John, time to get up." She waited a few seconds, then shook him again. "John, time to get up."

"Ya," he mumbled and that was it for his respond.

It was nothing new. He never could get up in the morning. Not one day since they were married did he ever get up to help her get the cows into the barn or help her start milking. So she did not waste her energy trying. Sooner or later he would get up. Since he was out drinking and playing cards last night, odds were that he would not get up until she finished milking.

The weather outside had not improved. It appeared as if the storm was circling the area. Over her bib overalls, she put on a plastic raincoat and hat. She opened the door and stood in the threshold watching the torrent of rain fall off the edge of the porch's roof. In the path of the forceful wind, the resilient trees bowed to its strength. The sky was filled with huge, dark clouds, topped with anvil-shaped heads, often looking like towering mountains. Intense lightning flashed swiftly across the sky, sometimes branching out into several forks, and sometimes consisting of a single, white wiggly line. So close that she could not even count to the number one, from the time of the lightning flash till the sound of the crackling thunder.

She did not want to venture out into that storm, but she had to. It was getting later and later into the morning. If she hesitated much longer, Jimmy would wake up. It was troublesome enough at night milking with him in the barn. He was a good child, but she hated those filthy flies setting on his body and his bottle. He had to have that bottle; otherwise, he would cry. Should she try to wake John one more time? Why? She would still have to go out into the storm. The cows had to be put inside the barn for milking.

Reluctantly, she went outside. She could feel the rain beating down on her and hear the rapid pinging sound of the rain violently attacking her rain coat and hat. Running, she was inside the barn within a few minutes. In front of each stall, she placed a scoop of ground feed. The cows, knowing it was there, would go more easily into their stalls. With that finished, she opened the large barn door for the cows to enter the barn. Seeing they were still all huddled under the old, massive maple that stood alone in the pasture, she walked out into the pasture to chase them into the barn. Her black buckle boots slushed through the wet, soft sticky earth. The pasture sloped into a lowland area that was now flooded with rainwater, causing a situation of a fast-moving stream. She had to go through it to get the cows. Hesitatingly, she proceeded through the water. Quickly, the water rose above her boots. Her boots filled with water and walking became a heavy, burdensome chore. The gushing water rose to her waist. Suddenly, she lost her balance. Flying backwards, her body fell down. Rapidly water surged all about her. It invaded her nose, causing a stinging sensation. It forced itself into her mouth and down her throat, choking her. She realized that she had to get a foot hold somewhere on the unstable ground that caused her to slip and slide beneath the water. Unable to stand, she grabbed her hands into the muddy earth and pulled her body along, walking as an animal on all fours as the water rushed above her head. She had to reach a level of the flooded ground where it was not so deep. However, was she moving from one side to another or was she moving down the center of the stream, thereby, moving in the deepest section with no chance of getting into the shallow section? She could not hold her breath much longer. A hard object hit her head. With her hand, she felt the object. It was one of the boulders in the pasture. Clinging to the boulder, she felt secure and slowly stood up. Her head was now above the water. She was terrified to move from the security of the boulder. However, she had to. Cautiously, she moved one foot forward, then another. Slowly, the water became more shallow, eventually only being knee-deep. Up to the tree she went and started moving the herd of cows toward the barn. Then there came a bolt of lightning right at the tree, which had protruded high above everything else. Instantaneously, the heat of lightning boiled the sap within the tree, and the expanding steam ripped the massive tree apart.

BANG! The tree fell with such force that the ground shook.

Lori was horrified! Never had she ever been that close to anything that had ever been struck by lightning. It was an experience that grabbed her soul with an overpowering fear. She was so glad that the cows and she had been out of reach of the fallen, ancient tree. At this point, all she wanted to do was get out of that pasture and into the barn. Ahead of her waited the flood of water that she would have to tread through again. This time, however, she had grabbed a stick, which she hoped would help her keep her balance in the raging water. Lightning flashed again and again across the sky. Thunder cracked and pounded one loud explosion into the air after another. It had struck close again because there was no time between the flashes of lightning and the thunder's mighty rumble. She moved closer toward the water, dreading going through it again, but it was either going through the water or staying out in the storm. It was inevitable. She would have to cross it. The lightning continued to flash, and the thunder clap.

****

KNOCK! KNOCK!

He did not want to get out of bed. All he wanted to do was continue sleeping. The boy was still crying and wildly rocking his crib. Why wasn't she getting up to take care of the boy and answer the door? Slowly, he moved his hand to her side of the bed. She wasn't there. Surely, she would be taking care of the boy soon. So he stayed lying, waiting for the silence, so he could resume his sleep in the comfortable bed.

KNOCK! KNOCK! KNOCK! KNOCK!

"Hey, where is everyone? Is everything all right?"

That sounded like Mikie's voice. What was he doing here, waking him up with his knocking and yelling? Where was she? Why wasn't she answering the door and taking care of the crying boy? Sleepily, he raised his head, extended his arm and turned the alarm clock's face toward himself.

"Holy, shit!" John's nude body sprang out of bed. How could she have left him sleep that long? He scrambled to find his pair of undershorts. Putting them on, he then scurried out into the kitchen where he had laid his barn overalls from last night.

KNOCK! KNOCK!

"Hey, is everyone all right in there?" the voice called from outside the house again.

Hurriedly, John pulled on his overalls, zipped them up, rushed to the door, and opened it. "Has she finished milking?"

"Milking is the least of your worries." Mikie stood shaking his head. "What is going on? You both oversleep? What's the matter with the boy?"

"She's not in the house. Isn't she out in the barn?" asked John.

"There's no one in the barn except the cows, and you have got a mess out there."

"Come on in, Mikie, I've got to take care of the kid first. Where the heck is she?" John went to the refrigerator, got out a baby bottle of milk, and took it into the bedroom.

The boy's eyes, nose, ears, and face were a blazing red from his continuous crying. When John gave him the bottle, he could hardly drink from it because he had been crying so intensely. The aftermath of humongous sniffles hampered his drinking.

"It'll be all right." John soothed him by softly rubbing his forehead. When he had quieted down, John covered him and left the room. He looked into Pete's room. She was not in there either. "She has to be outside." He grabbed his shirt off the floor. Buttoning it, he went outside. The sky was still overcast with dark, rain clouds that made the day seem like the night. Drizzling down its wet gloom in a steady mist. Near the barn, drenched in rain he viewed some of his cows. The teats on their huge udders were dripping milk like a faucet of water, and the ground was covered with puddles of milk.

"You'll not like what's inside," Mikie commented as he walked the fast pace with John toward the barn.

Opening the door, John stopped. "Holy shit! What a mess!" The wheelbarrow full of ground feed had been knocked over. The ground feed was strewed about the barn and mixed with fresh cow feces. His stacked bales of hay were pulled down, ripped apart, and lying about the entire barn. Cow excrement was everywhere.

"Looks like someone left the barn door open," Mikie noted.

"I could swear that I closed it last night. Get the hell out of here!" John waved his arms in the air hoping to chase the cows out of the manager into their stalls.

Mikie helped. As they were putting the cows that were in the barn into their stalls, the other cows ventured in. Soon the stalls were full.

Inside the door opening, John stood. As his eyes surveyed the pasture, he wondered where Lori was. He saw the fallen tree.

"Looks like you got some wood to make." Mikie joined him in the doorway.

"Ya."

Mikie's eyes roamed the rest of the pasture. "Is that Brownie out in the pasture? What's lying beside her?"

"Ya, that's Brownie." He looked in the direction where the dog was standing. "I don't know, but I'm going to find out."

They both raced out into the pasture.

****

Crashing thunder woke her as the lightning flashed through the curtained window greeting her to another day. Was this the day, she wondered? They were both getting anxious as the months just seemed to go on forever. The space beside her in bed was empty. Earlier, while she was sleeping, he had gotten up as usual and quietly gone to work. It would be early evening before she saw him. Just thinking about him beamed a warm smile to her face as the tremendous love she had for him radiated from inside her heart. Lying quietly in the bed, she could feel the life within her move. Gently, she touched her raised abdomen as if she was actually touching the child, their first child, his and hers. To carry on his name, she had hoped it would be a boy. However, when she prayed it was for a healthy child. Boy or girl, they would both love it. It kicked, and she could see her abdomen move. She marveled at the sight. Life was such a miracle.

The gloominess of the day could not dampen her happy spirits. Getting out of bed, she walked over to the bassinet covered with pure, white eyelet and lace. Inside the bassinet was a white sheet, blankets, and such unbelievable small, white undershirts and sleepers. Beside the bassinet set her small suitcase. Everything was ready. It had been so very exciting getting things ready for the arrival of their baby.

They would be so happy--forever. As she imagined the baby lying in the bassinet, she felt it kick inside of her and her face flushed with jubilance.

Shuffling, she walked into the kitchen that was darkened by the storm. She looked outside the kitchen window at the rain that had made a rapid flowing stream of the ditch in front of the house. At that moment, she saw the lightning strike the large etched cross at the top of the church steeple. The tremendous heat melted the cross into a disfigured clump of metal that smashed to the ground. The thunder rumbled, the windows rattled inside the house, and the baby jumped inside of her as if it had been startled by the noise. To add some sense of security, she turned on the kitchen light. From the basement she heard the sound of water running as from an open faucet into a water-filled sink. Opening the basement door revealed to her how the ground floor had allowed the water to flood into the basement. Only the top four basement steps were not submerged in the water. Her concern was how she could stop the water from rising so high as to flood the first floor of the house. Last time, when it had risen so high, Mikie walked down through the water and opened one of the basement windows so the water could not rise above it. At that level, the water would exit the basement through the window. Every time it rained, they had that problem. She hoped Mikie would remember and come home to open that window. In her condition, she was not going to venture into the water. Also, she was too afraid to go out into the storm and try to open the window from the outside.

When this problem first occurred, Mikie had asked his parents, whom they rented the house from, if they could cement the basement and put a drain in it to alleviate some of the problems. However, Mikie's suggestion was ignored. In their words, "the basement was good the way it was." Mikie's conclusion was that if no attempt was made to fix it after the birth of the baby, they would move. Such a condition would be very dangerous once the baby started crawling and walking. Sure they could lock the door, however, it would only take one time to forget to lock it that could result in a terrible tragedy. Of course, they would have to rent again, but maybe it would be better not to rent from relatives. They could not buy a house yet because the money they had been saving would probably be used to pay hospital expenses. Nevertheless, some things were much more important than money. They could always start saving again. Maybe in the future, she could continue her education and get her teacher's license. However, at this time in her life the most important concern of hers was to be a good mother and enjoy every moment of their child's life. It was going to be fantastic to be a mother!

Closing the basement door, she sat at the kitchen table where she thought of the things that she had wanted to do today. She had wanted to wash clothes and maybe wash off the walls in the kitchen. However, with that storm still raging she was not about to put her hands in any water, especially, after seeing what lightning did to that cross. Viewing the kitchen walls, she seriously contemplated if there really was any benefit to washing them. Yes, she would get the satisfaction of knowing they were clean, but they probably would not really look any better. Washing the living room and bedroom walls off had not really improved their appearance. All the walls had peeling paint exposing the ugly paint beneath. She had volunteered to paint the walls, but as usual, "the walls were good enough the way they were." It did not take Rosalia very long to "read between the lines." She knew what it all meant, "good enough for someone like HER."

After satisfying her hunger with a bowl of cereal, she got dressed in her maternity outfit and passed the remaining morning hours cleaning the house. It was something she did out of routine, not necessity. She had to keep herself busy or the anxiety of waiting would become overbearing.

Finally, the rain ceased and the sun paraded across the sky. Opening the windows left the fresh smell of the rain glide into the house. Her nervousness about the basement disappeared as she saw the swollen ditches slowly diminish in size. Across the road, parishioners had gathered assessing the damage done to the church's cross.

Filling her white wringer washer with hot steaming water and her two metal rinse tubs with cold water, she began to wash the clothes.

While in the backyard hanging up the clothes on the clothesline, she saw Margie walk from her parents' house, across the two neighbors' backyards, into their yard, and approach her.

"How are you feeling, Rosalia?" Margie's eyes roamed about as if she was not very interested in Rosalia's response.

"Okay." Rosalia, accustomed to Margie's inattentive attitude the several times that they did talk, knew that a one worded response would be sufficient. Margie could really care less.

"How much washing you got to do?"

"One load of Mikie's trousers then I'm done." Why did Margie care?

"You want to go shopping with me?"

Rosalia was shocked. "I don't know?" She continued to hang up the clothes until the wash basket was empty.

"I thought we'd go shopping for something for the baby."

"I really--" Was Margie trying to be nice? If she was making the first move to build a good relationship with her--maybe she should try also. "Where do you want to go?"

"Milwaukee."

"Milwaukee is a long drive." Rosalia thought about how terribly "car sick" she sometimes got. Also with the baby this close to birth, would it be safe to be that far from home? Well, since Margie was taking the first step to be nice. It would not be very considerate to hurt her feelings. Maybe she wasn't such a bad person. Maybe a person just had to get to know her. After all, Paul did marry her, and Paul was an extremely nice person. Was he seeing something in Margie that everyone else was missing?

"Oh, come on Rosalia, it's not that far." Her smile was so charming. "It'll probably be the last time you'll go for a long time. Once the baby comes, you won't be able to go."

"Oh, okay." Picking up the wash basket, she walked into the house with Margie.

"That was quite a storm wasn't it?" Margie sat in a chair near the kitchen table. "Where is that water I hear running?"

"The basement is almost full of water." Rosalia put the trousers through the rollers of the wringer washer as she emptied the machine of the washed clothes.

Getting up, Margie walked to the basement door and opened it. "You've got your own built in swimming pool. How fantastic! Can you swim, Rosalia?"

"No, in fact, I'm terribly afraid of water. I hang on for dear life whenever we drive over a bridge." What a strange comment to make about the flooded basement, Rosalia thought. It was a serious matter.

"What a silly thing to be afraid of." Margie turned around and smiled.

Rosalia had finished rinsing the clothes in the first tub and was now rinsing them in the last tub.

Margie watched her for a few seconds then moved over to the cupboards, opened them, and examined the contents. "You eat a lot of cereal. I think eggs are more nutritious."

"I can't tolerate the smell or taste of an egg right now." It appeared as if nothing really had changed. She still had to be defensive with Margie.

"Oh, that's right. You get morning sickness."

"Not lately, but some foods do still upset me."

"I'm lucky. I never get it. In fact, I still can eat everything I did before."

"You are lucky." Rosalia questioned if she was trying to really be a friend or just making criticizing remarks.

"I see a blue car here quite often when Mikie is gone." She rearranged some of the items inside the cupboard in height order, largest to smallest.

"That's my brother's car." Rosalia was getting upset. What was she inferring--that she was having an affair and cheating on Mikie? Also, what right did she have to snoop in her cupboards and arrange those items!

"You and Mikie have enough saved for the hospital bill?" Finished with the rearranging, she turned to watch Rosalia work.

"Ya, I hope so." Rosalia pulled the last trouser out of the water and up through the wringer.

"You got all new furniture. That must have cost a lot." Her inquisitive eyes looked through the door into the living room.

"It was money I had saved for going back to school to get my teacher's license."

"Too bad you got pregnant. Now your plans are ruined."

"No, Margie, I'm glad about the baby. I intend to devote my time to raising the baby and being a good wife to Mikie. That's the most important job there is, being a wife and mother." With the wash basket full of the wet clothes, she lifted it and carried it outside.

Margie stayed in the house until she had investigated the rest of the house. She loathed seeing that bassinet just as much as she scorned seeing Rosalia pregnant. Mikie and Rosalia had deprived her of being the first one to marry and now they were depriving her of having the first grandchild. It was not supposed to be that way. She was the oldest and should be the first in everything. Turning from the bedroom, she put her smile back on her face and joined Rosalia outside where she took pleasure in seeing the difficulty Rosalia had in bending over her protruding abdomen to pick the clothes out of the wash basket and hang on the line.

Rosalia had done it many times before and she did not complain. It was only for a short while, and then she would be back to her old self. Nevertheless, she did think if Margie was trying to be a friend, why didn't she help her? Well, maybe it was hard for Margie to be nice and the shopping trip was all she could handle at this time.

"Would you like something to eat before we leave?" Rosalia, carrying her empty wash basket, walked back to the house.

"No."

"Well, I think I'll make myself something." Rosalia grabbed a loaf of bread from the breadbox and a can of tuna from the cupboard.

"Ah, Rosalia, we can stop at the club I used to work at to eat. That'll make shopping even more enjoyable knowing that we're going to eat there. It's such an elegant place. You'll like eating there."

Putting back the bread and can of tuna, Rosalia took a writing tablet and pencil out of one of the kitchen drawers.

"Kind of messy in there." Margie stretched her neck like an ostrich to spy inside the drawer.

Rosalia felt embarrassed, humiliated at first. Then her feeling became spiteful, "how dare she," but she held her harsh words inside and reminded herself that if Margie was trying, she should also make the effort and overlook some things. After all, they were only words, words that did offend, but maybe not meant to. Maybe she was just too sensitive. With those thoughts behind her, she wrote on the top sheet of the notebook, tore the sheet from the notebook, and placed the sheet of paper on the table. "There, now Mikie will know where

I am when he comes home and I'm not here." She smiled at Margie.

"Oh, that's not necessary, Rosalia." Margie smiled so warmly as she grabbed the sheet of paper. "We'll be home before Mikie comes home. Besides, Ma knows where we are."

"Oh, I'd feel a lot better leaving the note. If I'm not here, Mikie might become quite concerned, especially since the baby's due date is so near. Please, let's leave it." She took the sheet of paper from Margie's hand and put it back on the kitchen table.

Out the door they went.

The road zigzagged around hills, went up and down others. They would drive through small country towns, each one almost the same as the last one--a stone church--a red, clapboard schoolhouse--a garage with gas filling pumps--a grocery store--and always two taverns, one on each side of town.

Rosalia felt uneasy being in the car that close to Margie. There was a tense feeling although nothing was said or done during the drive to cause it. Rosalia was quiet. Margie was also, as she was quite involved in listening to the "soap opera" on her car radio.

With the rural areas disappearing, the skyline became filled with dark smoke from industries that outskirted the city. After passing this section of town that greeted them, it was not too long before they were driving down the streets crowded with cars. Sidewalks occupied by women dressed in the most fashionable attire and men clothe in business suits. She had never seen so many people dressed so exquisitely. Looking at her dress, she felt out of place. She looked like an old country woman and wondered if Margie would be embarrassed to be seen with her. Margie would fit right in with all these people, she thought.

Margie drove around, this way then that way. Rosalia was completely lost in the maze of all those tall buildings that all looked the same. At least in Beechwood, each place had its own individual design. Erickson's store was different from the restaurant, the restaurant different from Lyra's, and the bank different from Fremont's office. Did the same person build all these buildings or couldn't anyone think of anything different? She could never live here, and she was getting very apprehensive about shopping here. It was so big, too big. Finally, Margie drove into a flat graveled area where there were numerous other cars parked, more cars than Rosalia had ever seen.

"Well, here we are." Grabbing her purse off the seat, Margie got out of the car.

Rosalia just sat there. She was not excited about this situation that she had gotten herself into.

"Come on, Rosalia, it will be fun." The city excited Margie--revitalized her dead country soul.

The ride had made Rosalia tired, but she got out of the car. At first, they were walking side by side, but then it started to become very difficult for Rosalia to keep up. Had Margie increased her pace? Or was she just so tired that she could not keep up?

"Margie, I'm sorry, but could you please wait for me?" Rosalia was struggling with every step, but Margie kept walking. Didn't she hear her? Rosalia wished she could run to keep up with Margie, but she could not. When Margie disappeared around corners, Rosalia became driven with the fear that she would lose sight of Margie after she turned the corner and not know where she was. To her relief, Margie stopped outside a store, turned, smiled at her, and held the door open for Rosalia to pass into the store ahead of her.

"Thanks." Rosalia was panting, her legs ached with fatigue, but she kept moving. She was beginning to think Margie was deliberately walking fast to make her walk faster. However, when she saw Margie's smile and how polite she had been to hold the door open for her, the suspicions diminished. Rosalia rationalized that Margie probably did not hear her. The streets were noisy with people talking; cars and trucks driving and honking their horns.

Inside the store, Rosalia's eyes were widened with amazement. Before her stretched aisles and aisles and aisles of racks full of items --dresses, skirts, blouses, suits, coats, hats, and shoes of more colors than she had ever imagined. There were counters with glass cases displaying jewelry of earings, necklaces, brackets, and rings.

"Can I help you?" a slender woman dressed in a dark tailored suit greeted them.

"No, thank you. We're going upstairs to the baby department," Margie replied.

"Well, if you need assistance, the clerk upstairs will gladly help you anyway she can. Have a nice day." The clerk cordially smiled.

Up they walked. At the top of the stairs, Rosalia clung to the newel. Fatigued, she had to rest. Holding her hand to her chest, she gasped for breath. Suddenly, she was not feeling very good. She wished that she had stuck to her first decision of not going shopping and staying home.

"Ma'am, would you like to sit down." A kindly clerk touched her arm to provide support.

"Yes, please," Rosalia replied as she felt the baby moving around so wildly inside of her.

Gently, the clerk helped Rosalia to a cushioned chair, and she sat down.

"What's the matter, Rosalia?" Margie seemed so concerned.

"I just need to rest for a few minutes then I'll be all right." Taking several deep breaths, she reclined back into the chair and gave a deep sigh of relief.

"Here's some water." Another clerk who had seen the situation came to help also.

"Thanks." Rosalia took a few swallows of water. Abruptly looking up, she thought she detected a repugnant look on Margie's face for a split second before she smiled so lovingly at her. Again, she dismissed her nasty thoughts of Margie. Thinking maybe, she was the problem, not Margie. "I feel better now." Rosalia got up. "Thank you, all, so very much."

"The baby clothes are over here." Margie led the way walking toward counters and counters full of clothes. "You pick out what you want. I'm going over there to look at some maternity clothes. It won't be long before I lose my good shape and look like you."

"You could wear mine. I'll be done with them by the time you would need them." Rosalia looked up from the stack of clothes that she was leisurely looking through.

"No, that's all right. You never know. You might need them again." Leaving Rosalia, Margie walked toward one of the circular racks, which was crammed tight with maternity outfits.

Rosalia held up one baby outfit after another, examining it and liking it. There were so many nice outfits, too many to choose from. Not knowing what to get, she let the price decide. She would take the cheapest of the one's that she liked. It was so nice of Margie to do that. She didn't have to. Taking the chosen one in her hand, Rosalia turned to where she had last seen Margie. Rosalia could not see her. She began to walk up to the end of the aisle. At the end of the aisle, she still was unable to see Margie. She turned and walked down another aisle. She continued this with each aisle but still couldn't find Margie. Maybe she was in one of the dressing rooms. Sitting on a chair near the rooms, Rosalia waited and waited and waited. While she waited, her eyes constantly searched the racks and aisles. As her stomach began to growl of hunger, she looked at the clock. With the hunger came a headache causing her to feel nauseated. After waiting, what seemed hours, she approached the clerk who had first helped her.

"Have you seen the lady I was with?" asked Rosalia.

"Not for quite sometime." The clerk smiled with the expression that she wished she knew more and was sorry that she did not.

A cold panic flooded Rosalia's body. Did Margie leave without her? Why? How would she get home? Where could she go? She was alone in this tremendously huge concrete jungle. That's what it was a jungle compared to the one street town that she had come from. Here every street and every building looked the same. It was such an entanglement, and she was in the midst of it. Not knowing where to go or who would help her? Calm down! She told herself. Maybe Margie just left to go downstairs or upstairs. Perhaps the best thing to do was to stay here and wait. Although she did not know where Margie was, Margie did know where she was. Why didn't Margie tell her when she left the floor? Guess it did not matter. The important thing was to find Margie. However, at this moment, she did not know how to do that. It was terrifying!

Positioning herself at the top of the stairs, she surveyed the section of the downstairs that was visible to her. Should she go down there and check the area that she could not see from upstairs? What if Margie came back here?

She walked over to a clerk who had helped her earlier. "Excuse me, I'm going downstairs to try and find the lady that I was with. If she comes back here when I'm gone, could you please ask her to wait here for me. I'll be coming back."

"Sure, no problem." The clerk smiled. "Good luck."

"Thanks." Down the steps Rosalia trudged. Once on the floor, she walked down one aisle then up another. She waited at the dressing rooms to see who came out, always hoping it would be Margie, but it never was.

The question of how she would get home if she did not find Margie weighed heavy on her mind. She could not call Mikie. They had no telephone. Should she call Pamela? And tell her what? Margie had left her at the store. They probably had the whole thing planned. They would probably laugh at her. Mikie would never get the message. Whom could she call? Her mother? She was at work. The foreman would never allow her to leave until after her shift at three-thirty. Besides, her mother had no vehicle to get here with. After her father had left, her mother had sold the car deciding it was an unnecessary expense. She had often wondered why her father had not taken the car. Nevertheless, the only thing her mother could do was to stop at their house on her walk home and leave Mikie a note. Mikie would not be home that early in the day. What if he stopped in by Lyra's before he came home, which he occasionally did? He would not get the message until late.

"Excuse, me. How late is the store open?" Rosalia asked the clerk at the counter.

"Until five o'clock, ma'am." The clerk smiled and continued stamping square white cards with the bold red word, SALE.

Five o'clock! Oh, my God! Mikie will never be able to get here before five o'clock, even if he came right after work. What would she do once the store closed?

Weary, in soul and body, she gripped her hand onto the wooden banister and pulled her body up the stairs. With the energy draining chore completed, she sat in a chair. She had sat there previously, when she first came up those exhausting stairs several hours ago. Looking at the other floor above, she thought of searching there for Margie. However, fearing the total collapse of her body, she decided against climbing another flight of stairs. Resting, she would sit and wait until three o'clock. At that time, if Margie had not appeared, she would call her mother at work to give Mikie the message.

How well did Mikie know Milwaukee? Probably not very well, it had been his father who had come down to the stockyards and been familiar with this town. Where would she wait for him, outside on the street? She did not know where else to go? Her chin quivered, but she would not cry. It would not help. It would only make her feel worst than she already did. Her stomach growled and ached with a biting hunger. Her head throbbed and throbbed. The hunger and the stress were extracting a physical and mental toll from her. With her one arm resting on her abdomen and the elbow of the other arm resting on that arm's forearm, she lowered her head into the palm of that hand. Closing her eyes, she took deep, relaxing breaths. She tried to keep her mind void of her situation, hoping to alleviate some of the stress, but it was impossible.

"Oh, here you are." A hand touched her shoulder.

Startled by the touch, she quickly turned. "Oh, Margie!" Relief invigorated her body. Margie was a miracle to behold. "I'm so glad to see you."

"Where have you been?"

"Where have I been? Where were you?" Rosalia was confused by Margie's question.

"I've been here all the time looking for you."

"No, I've been here all the time. Except for when I went downstairs to look for you."

"No, you weren't. I know you weren't."

Rosalia's anxiousness of the previous problem was soon erased by a raging turbulence inside of her. How dare she say something like that, implying that she did not know what she did or did not do! Nevertheless, there was no sense in arguing. Mikie always said, "Margie is always right." Rosalia's body was beginning to shake already from Margie's verbal attack, so she kept her silence to avoid carrying the conversation any farther. Whatever, Margie--whatever --have it your way, she thought.

"I suppose it's time to go back home. I spent most of my time looking for you. I didn't get to buy everything I wanted." Margie huffed off toward the checkout counter. Putting the items on the counter, she turned back at Rosalia. "Well, come up here and put what you want on the counter. I'm buying it for you." Margie pulled a wallet out of her purse.

Rosalia put the baby item on the counter and then stood back very quietly.

"That's a very pretty baby outfit. Yellow is a safe color to get." Margie smiled at Rosalia as if nothing had happened.

Rosalia did not know how to figure Margie. Was she really trying to be nice? Or was Margie just pretending so Rosalia would leave her guard down, opening herself to another attack. Was she playing with her mind? If she was, it was working. Rosalia was getting so confused.

"Please, put this in a separate bag." Margie pointed to the yellow baby outfit. As the clerk did so, Margie grabbed it. "Here you go, Rosalia."

"Thank you." Rosalia grabbed the bag and started to walk beside Margie. However, just as before, Margie seemed to increase her stride. Rosalia found it impossible to keep up and hoped, as before, that she would not lose sight of Margie as she went around the corners.

Going around the last corner revealed the parking area full of cars, a relieving, familiar sight. As Margie sat in the car waiting, Rosalia inched her way to the car. Once inside the car, Rosalia took the shoes off her swollen feet. "Margie, could we please stop someplace to eat?"

"I had planned on taking you to the club where I used to work, but I'm afraid that's impossible now. Not enough time, I wasted more than two hours looking for you. I am really disappointed." She started the car and began driving down the streets out of the city.

As the car traveled along, Rosalia's eyelids became heavy. She tried to keep them open but the burden of the day was too much. They closed and her head jerked forward. Catching herself, she forced her eyelids open and pulled her head back into a straight sitting position. Perhaps if she looked away from the road and at the passing countryside, she could stay awake. It was only wishful thinking. Her body demanded sleep. With her eyelids closing, her head bobbed forward again. In her semi-consciousness, she raised her sleepy head only to have it flop backwards onto the car seat.

Margie looked over at Rosalia with her vicious eyes. Then a smirk covered her face. The earlier events of the day brought extreme glee to her soul that pacified her body. Looking down from the third floor of the store was the most enjoyment that she had for a long time. Watching Rosalia desperately search up and down those aisles and then seeing her struggle up those stairs--too bad she didn't fall--was so delightful to watch. In her condition, Rosalia looked like an apple with two toothpicks sticking out from underneath it. She was such an ugly, pregnant woman. She would look so much better than Rosalia. Rosalia had taken away the right of her being the first married, but she was not going to take away the right of her having the first grandchild. It troubled her at first, but now with her being pregnant four months, it troubled her more. If Rosalia lost her baby, she would have the first grandchild. Everything she had tried today so far had failed, the long ride in the car, making Rosalia almost run to keep up with her on the streets, the long climb up those stairs. If only that clerk would not have been there, she could have easily bumped into Rosalia. As fatigued as she was, she would have surely fallen. Oh, well, then she would not have had all that fun watching Rosalia look for her. Hearing Rosalia's stomach growl with hunger and not letting her satisfy it, fed Margie's ecstasy. There was one thing she could still do. How foolish she did not do it this morning. Nevertheless, she still would have a chance when they reached Rosalia's house. They would be there alone. Accidents do happen. She would have to be careful to make it appear to Rosalia it was just that. Just if by a miracle Rosalia survived--the terrible accident.

It was a sudden pain in Rosalia's lower abdomen that radiated up the front of both sides that woke her. Gently, she grabbed her abdomen and pulled her body up into a straight sitting position. The familiar countryside assured her that they were almost home. She was so nauseated from the headache, which she knew was caused by her famished condition. Around the corner Margie drove, down the road that led right to their house. So close, yet so far, this was the longest part of the drive.

Into the driveway the car drove and stopped. Although, her heart wanted to run up the steps into the house, her body moved differently. Opening the car door, she slowly moved her legs to the opened side of the car. Sitting for a few seconds, she took a deep breath, and with her one hand on the door and the other on the top of the car seat, she pulled her body up into a standing position. Waddling, she went to the house. Climbing the stairs, she felt another pain as before. Once inside the house, she leaned against the kitchen table for her body's support.

"You forgot your shoes and package in the car." Margie placed them on the table and smiled so convincingly, kindly at Rosalia. Then she looked at it, the door to the basement. Was the basement still flooded? With gleeful hope she walked toward the door and opened it. Yes, it was still flooded. The water had subsided only a few steps. There was enough in the basement to achieve what she wanted before she left today, and she would not leave until it was done. It was to her advantage that Rosalia could not swim. Margie's story would be that while she was outside getting the dry clothes off the clothesline, Rosalia must have lost her balance and fallen down the steps into the water. How sad! A smirk, applauding how clever she was, crept slowly across her face. "Oh, Rosalia, come here. There is something in the water."

"I'll be right there." Rosalia grabbed an apple out of the refrigerator. She started to eat the apple as she walked toward the open door. "I don't see anything."

"I'll move out of your way." Margie moved behind Rosalia and thought. Once and for all that "piece of trash" and the little bastard inside of her would be out of her life. As jealousy flowed into hatred, it overrode her conscious as to what was right. Planning now to put her evil thoughts into action, she watched as Rosalia approached the edge of the door opening. Rosalia had to be in the right position, and Margie watched carefully for the right moment.

****

Driving in the car today was different. She was not along. He had not seen the familiarity of her face yesterday or today. She no longer fed him or cared for him. When he awoke for his usual early-morning bottle, her side of the bed was empty. Now, the hands that cared for him, were large and crude. Those hands lacked her softness and gentle touch. As he drove in the car, it was the old man's lap that held him not hers. The old man he called, "Gapa." There was a strange feeling in the car, a quiet sadness that was absorbed with each breath. Clutching his hand to the steering wheel, his father followed the slow moving black vehicle traveling in front of him. Turning his head and looking out the car's back window, the small boy seen other cars following in a procession. They all had their headlights turned on.

The black vehicle turned into a large graveled area and in front of a huge building constructed of stone. There seemed to be no end to the large building as the small boy looked up at it through the windshield of the car. He had been here before but never without her.

The black vehicle stopped. A man came out of the driver's door and opened the large black door in the back. Soon there were several men standing there and helping the man move a large, long bronze-colored case out of the vehicle.

His father stopped the car and took him off the old man's lap and held him on his lap. The passenger's door opened. It was Alex. He helped the old man out of the car and carried him up the numerous steep cement stairs. Opening the driver's car door, his father got out holding him in his huge arms. Taking his small hand, the boy touched the wet drops of fluid on his father's cheeks. He hugged his arms around his father's neck in hopes of erasing or closing the gap of hollowness that haunted this day. Where was the woman that was his mother? He felt an eeriness lingering in the air. He felt her presence, but it was a strange kind of presence. He looked but could not see her.

The six men carried the bronzed case up the steps into the two huge, hung doors. At the entrance, they stopped and waited.

His father set him down on the ground beside him. As he stood at the bottom of the long flight of steps, his father grabbed his hand and held it in his. He could feel his father's hand tremble. With reddened eyes, flooded with tears, his father looked up at the church door entrance where they waited for him and his father. As his father stepped upward, his father's arms moved forward. However, he held his body firm resisting his father's upward movement.

The small boy looked up at the monstrous church and the steps that appeared to go on forever. He did not want to go up there. There was something in that church that caused him to fill with a heavy fear. He pulled back, away from his father. As his father pulled him forward, the boy began to cry and pull away. As his father tried to pull him up again, the boy took his freed hand and tried to use it to pull his other hand free from his father. Something terrible lurked up there. It gave him a frightful feeling that wrapped his body. When his father picked him up into his arms and began to carry him up the steps, closer and closer toward those huge doors and that bronzed case, he grabbed his tiny arms around his father's neck so tightly that the tears on his father's face mingled with his. The only thing he knew how to do, to let his father know that he did not want to go up there, was to cry. So he cried and cried, "No Dada, no Dada, no Dada."

The boy's efforts were useless, and up the steps his father went. Clinging and crying, he pushed his small body tighter against his father's. Hoping it would keep him from getting closer to those doors and that bronzed case. Then there they were, behind the bronzed case slowly walking down a long aisle. In the pews that they passed, women's eyes became more teary as he, the small boy passed in front of them crying. At the communion railing, the six men set the bronzed case on a stand and then proceeded into the left front pew. The small boy, still in his father's arms and crying, entered the right front pew. Alex pushed the wheelchair, with Pete in it, in front of the pew where the small boy, Jimmy, and his father, John, were now sitting.

In the second pew sat Lucy with her two boys. She tapped John on the shoulder and when he turned around, she motioned that she would take Jimmy. Being annoyed by his crying, she thought that being a woman she was more knowledgeable in getting him to be quiet. As John began to hand Jimmy to her, Jimmy clung desperately to his father. Jimmy had an unpleasant feeling about the woman and did not want to go with her. He persisted by crying more loudly, "Gapa, Gapa," and reaching out to Pete.

Lucy took Jimmy, squirming in her arms, and carried him in front of the pew and set him on Pete's lap.

Pete held him with his left hand and soothed him. Jimmy ceased crying and cuddled in his grandfather's arms.

Looking down at the boy, Pete realized that the small boy was all he had of his Lori now. His heart had broken. He saw no sense to this tragedy. How old he was and how his quality of life was worth nothing compared to hers. His youngest daughter, in the prime of her life, was gone. He could not even see her for the last time. The thunderbolt that had struck her had scorched her body like a burned piece of meat. The last time that he had seen her was when she had put him to bed that night. Forever, that would be his memory of her.

It was not the way that life should be. A parent should not see their child die. The empty space left in his heart now flooded with tears of great loss and then tears of regret--regret that he had not died. Oh, dear God, why didn't you take my soul instead of hers? There was no measure for the depth of his pain. The small child needed his mother whom he no longer had. The situation was one that cut his heart into a million shredded pieces. It tormented him beyond all his ability to understand. He could not understand a God that could be so cruel as to take a young mother from her child and leave the child motherless. No! It was not right! He hugged the child closer, a child that would never remember his mother, a child he could never tell things about his mother. Oh God, why didn't you take my old useless body? God, you are so cruel! Staring at the casket, he tried to imagine this was not happening. One day they had it all. The next day it was gone and things would never be the same. Who would take care of him? John could never do both. He had tried since her death, and it had been a disorderly condition.

The songs at the funeral were the most unbearable for Pete, John, Alex, and Eddy. Jeffery was too small to realize. Lucy also shed tears. However, her thoughts were dwelling on the fact that with Lori dead, she did not have to share her father's estate with Lori when he died. Looking over at John, she despised the fact that he would get that farm with Lori's death--but that would be all he would get! If there was some way she could get it away from him, she would. But she did not think that would be possible. No, there was no way. That farm was gone from her! Damn it!

The interment concluded. The flower draped casket set alone, as did their lives at that moment with no desire to continue on. Their life with her had been so short. Now it had come down to this--to only this. She would be alone in the earth and they would be without her on the earth. With only a child to verify she had ever existed.

The child was silent. He didn't know what was occurring. He only sensed things were different in a world now dampened with an enormous cloud of sadness and emptiness. Nothing could stop that hollow feeling in their stomach. The husband and father felt the same loss but for different reasons.

Being pushed in his wheelchair back into the church, where a meal was to be served in the basement, Pete could still not believe this was real. It was a nightmare, and he would soon wake up. Yes, he would wake up, and her smile would greet him as she entered his bedroom. She'd start his day off with a kiss to his wrinkled brow. Then she would help him out of his bed, get him dressed, wheel him into the kitchen, and set him before a breakfast that he sometimes thought he could never eat all of. It was Lori, John, Jimmy, and him. Oh, he could tell his old mind things would be that way again, but his mind was too strong. It knew this was a harsh reality. Why not me? Why not me?

> The sun will no longer kiss her cheek with a blush,
> The wind will no longer finger her glistening hair.
> She has been taken away, leaving them with a saddened hush,
> And all their praying will never bring her back there.
> Gone are the days that were filled with her laughter,
> Gone from the crying child is his mother's soothing touch.
> Gone from the father are the dreams he had for his daughter,
> Gone from the husband is the woman he loved so much.
> Only with memories can they try to fill that void in this life,
> As from one day to the next--alone--they must go.
> A father without his child; a husband without his wife,
> And the child without a mother he never got to know.

Inside the church basement, the people gathered and ate. The company of others made them forget, for a short time. Then as the others left, only the immediate family remained and gathered into a small crowd.

"I'm going to need help," John spoke to Alex and Lucy. "I love Pete and Jimmy, but I can't take care of them both. I've got too much work on the farm. I hate to suggest it, but maybe it would be best if we put Pete into a home. He would get excellent care in the nursing home in Jennings."

"No, my pa is not being put in a nursing home," Lucy ardently protested. Of course, it would cost too much money. "Pa, can stay with us. We'll take care of him. Eddy spends all day with him at your place anyway. Now he'll just spend time with him at our place."

"I was thinking maybe you could help me out with Jimmy."

"No way! He's your kid. I got two of my own to take care of," snapped Lucy.

"I'm sure that Jimmy won't be that much trouble, Lucy. We could take care of him. I think he would be easier to take care of than Pa. At the nursing home, Pa would be taken care of by people who are familiar with his condition and medically trained to help him. With Pa in the home, we could take care of Jimmy," suggested Alex.

"If Lori could take care of Pa, I surely can, and I will. I'm sorry, John, but we all have to make sacrifices and do the best we can. Lori's death was most unfortunate, and the living are left to live with the way things are. If you can't take care of Jimmy, why can't your dad and his wife?" Lucy commented.

"No, I didn't like that traveling when I was small, and I don't want Jimmy to go through that. Currently, my dad is stationed in Germany. He couldn't get here for the funeral. There is no way I could even get Jimmy to him if I wanted to, but I don't want to."

Quietly, the old woman stood and listened. Her eyes gazed upon the small boy now asleep on Pete's lap. How inconsiderate, she thought, for them to discuss what to do with Pete in front of him. Standing silent, she wondered if she could take care of the child. Although she was old, the child was not that small and caring for the child would fill her days. The child was so adorable, and she could smother him with the deep love that she had in her heart for him. She had struggled through worst things. After all, she had raised John's father and helped John's mother raise him. She would have an easier time raising the child than John would.

"John, I'll take Jimmy."

All eyes turned to the old woman.

"Grandma, are you sure? He's very active."

"I remember how active boys are. I'll try it. If it doesn't work out, then we'll have to discuss another plan. At this time does anyone have any other ideas?"

"No, and I think we should try it." Lucy was not going to get stuck feeding, clothing, and taking care of that child. If she had wanted the expense of another child, she would have her own. It was not her fault

Lori died, and she was not going to be inconvenienced by that child. "Why don't we all go out to Lori's? I'll get the things Pa will need for tonight, and you can take the things for Jimmy," Lucy suggested.

"Ya, let's get out of here." John gently took Jimmy off Pete's lap and hugged him to his body. Jimmy exhausted from his excess crying earlier, laid his head on his father's shoulder and slept.

John put his other arm around his grandmother's small, aged shoulders, as they walked out to his car. Inside the car, John sat and looked out into the cemetery. The bronzed casket had been lowered and two men with shovels were finishing covering up the hole where she had been laid to rest. It was final. She was gone.

As his hand gripped the steering wheel, his grandmother's hand touched it. "It was God's will, John. She's merely closed this door of life and opened another door into another kind of life." The words were easy, but they could not keep her eyes dry either.

It was a strange feeling to enter the house. To know she was not there and never would be again. Everywhere John looked, there were things to remind him of her--where she always sat at the table--her doing dishes--feeding Jimmy--her smile that always greeted him--her apron hung on the hook. What would life be without her? He did not want to find out, but he had no choice. There were no words, only silent thoughts of her.

"Help me get Pa's things," Lucy commanded as she entered the house and broke the silence.

"Everything is in his bedroom, Lucy." John motioned his hands toward the room.

"Well, help me! I've got things to do at home. The wake and funeral made me fall behind on my work," she grumbled as she walked into Pete's bedroom. "Bring me a box or something to put his things in."

John grabbed an empty wash basket and took it into the bedroom.

"I'll just pack what he'll need for tonight. Tomorrow you and Alex can move his dresser, night stand, and bed over to our place. I should have that one bedroom ready for him." She took the neatly packed things from his dresser and tossed them loosely into the wash basket. "That should do it."

"What the heck did you bring him in here for?" Lucy snarled at

Alex as she exited the bedroom and seen him push Pete into the kitchen. "We aren't visiting. I've got work to do!"

"Sorry, Lucy." Alex turned the wheelchair around toward the door. "See you tomorrow, John."

"Sounds good, Alex. Bye, Lucy." John stood in the threshold of the door and watched them drive away with Pete. John would miss Pete not being around. One day the house was full of life. The next day it was full of loneliness.

The old woman stood holding the child, not saying a word, just observing, and forming her opinion of things.

"Grandma, I appreciate you taking care of Jimmy. Would you consider maybe living here and taking care of him?"

"I'd have to think about that, John. Jennings has been my home for more than fifty years. My friends are there. I've got my church choir. I wash all the altar cloths for Father. Living across from the church allows me to go to church every day, which I love. I have my garden with my asparagus, strawberries, and raspberries. I don't think I would like to move, not at my age."

"Well, would you think about it?"

"Sure, I'll think about it, but don't rely on me moving. I ask you not to insist on it, please."

"I understand, but I think maybe tonight might be better spent here. Tomorrow I'll ask Alex to help me move the things that Jimmy will need. Will that be all right?"

"Maybe that would be best. He's sleeping. I'll take off his shoes and put him into his bed." Sitting on the kitchen chair, she very carefully took off Jimmy's shoes.

"I think it would be best if you slept in our bed tonight. If Jimmy wakes up at night, I don't know if I'll hear him. Lori would often tell me about him crying in the night, but I never heard him. I'll sleep in Pete's bed tonight." He took the sleeping child from her arms, carried him into his bedroom, and laid him very gently into his crib.

The old woman followed him into the room and stood beside the crib. Looking about the room, she wondered if maybe it would be best to raise the boy here. Everything was here. His clothes folded neatly on the dresser near his crib. His toys scattered about the room. Was she being foolish in her old age? Would it be more convenient to move her instead of the boy? Could she be happy here too?

****

"Ah!" The room echoed with her cry of pain as she grabbed the doorknob to steady her body from falling. With her body now hunched in pain, she slowly maneuvered over to the kitchen chair where she sat. After a few minutes, the pain ceased.

Margie looked with scorn upon Rosalia. Unfortunately, she had moved away from the flooded basement before she had a chance to push her. Damn it! Well, she would try again. "What's the matter?" Margie masked her face with a look of concern.

"For a moment I had such pain. I feel better now." Rosalia smiled.

"Good, come over her and see what you think is in the water?" Margie smiled so sweetly. It was part of her plan to convince Rosalia to once again stand in the threshold of that basement door. Margie desperately wanted another opportunity to push her into the water.

Rosalia did not want to get up. Actually, she really did not care what was in the water. Nevertheless, she thought her disinterest would hurt Margie's feelings. Therefore, to appease Margie and not hurt her feelings, in a fatigued state, Rosalia rose from the chair and proceeded toward the open basement door.

Margie smiled with pleasure. Yes, Rosalia, come over here and look, just a few more steps. This time she would not wait for just the right moment. As soon as Rosalia was in front of the open door, she would push her and it would all be over with.

"Look, Rosalia, there it is." Margie moved away from the open door to let Rosalia move in front of it. Oh, perfect, Rosalia! Margie moved her arms toward Rosalia's back.

KNOCK! KNOCK!

They both turned in the direction of the knock. Standing outside the screen door was Amanda.

"Oh, hi, Ma!" Rosalia moved away from the open basement door toward her mother.

"How are you feeling today, Rosalia?" Her mother entered the kitchen and walked toward her. "Hi, Margie." Amanda smiled.

"I've been having some pain."

"Where?" Amanda was deeply concerned.

"Right here." Rosalia moved her hand in the area where the pain had occurred several times during the day and just a few minutes ago.

"Looks like it won't be long now, tonight or tomorrow for sure."

"Oh, Ma, do you really think so?" Rosalia sat on a chair. Her emotions were mixed. There was excitement of finally having the baby but there was also the fear of the unknown of childbirth. What was really going to happen? Anxiousness wrapped her body! Would the baby be all right? Would Mikie get home before she had to leave? She wanted him with her.

Margie closed the basement door. Damn it! She wished Amanda had not come. "Well, I think I'll be leaving now. See you later."

"Margie, maybe you should stay just in case Rosalia has to go to the hospital before Mikie comes home. We don't have a car." Amanda followed Margie to the door.

"Oh, I'm sorry. I really should get home and start making supper for Paul. I'm sure Mikie will be home before it's time to go to the hospital. However, if you do need me, just go over and call me from Ma and Dad's place." Margie walked out the door. She would make sure that she was not around to help. Rosalia could find her own way to the hospital. Damn it! Rosalia would have the first grandchild! Margie's blood was boiling! Nevertheless, she kept herself calm and in control. Into her car she went, down the road, and out of town toward Jennings where Paul and she now lived. She would meet Paul at work, and they would go out to eat. Then she would not be home to be bothered by Rosalia and that damn baby. Oh, she could just cry! It was not supposed to be this way. Mikie was first with everything! Damn him! Damn Rosalia!

Amanda watched out the window. "I don't think she was too interested in staying and helping. Why was she here?"

"She took me shopping for the baby today."

"Margie took you shopping?" Amanda sat at the table with Rosalia.

"Ya, I was surprised. She is trying to be nice."

"What does Mikie think about that?"

"Mikie doesn't know. Oh!" Rosalia clutched her abdomen.

"Another one?"

"Ya." Rosalia nodded as her face shrouded with agony. "I'm afraid, Ma. I want Mikie here."

"Keep calm." Her mother reached across the table to hold her hand. "It's your first baby so you'll have contractions quite a long time before the baby comes. Mikie will be here to take you."

"Oh, Ma, are you sure?" Her mother's hand gave her a sense of soothing security.

"I'm sure." Amanda was reassuring. "You got your suitcase ready?"

"Ya, it's in the closet." The pain ceased and Rosalia got up from the chair.

"You stay sitting. Rest while you can. I'll get your suitcase. We'll wait together until Mikie comes home."

Amanda went into the bedroom and within a few minutes she had returned to the kitchen with the suitcase.

Rosalia was standing at the kitchen counter making herself a tuna sandwich. "I've got such a terrible headache from not eating since breakfast." She sat at the table and began to eat the sandwich.

"Why didn't you eat dinner?" Setting down the suitcase, Amanda opened the cupboard, took out a glass, filled it with milk, and set it in front of Rosalia on the table.

"Oh, Ma, it's a long story. This day was very tiring." Exhaustion could be heard in her voice. "Ma, would you mind taking my dry clothes off the clothesline for me?" Rosalia took a drink of the milk.

"Of course not, when you're finished eating, I think you should lay on the bed and rest." Grabbing a wash basket, Amanda went outside to take the dry clothes off the clothesline.

Finished eating, Rosalia went into the bedroom and rested. She would doze off only to be awakened by the pain of the drawing up and tightening of her abdominal muscles. She was getting fearful. Should she go to the hospital? She did not want to wait too long and have the baby at home. Being in the hospital would give her a sense of security. The doctor and nurses would help her. She anguished as to when Mikie would come. Then resting, she dozed off for an indefinite amount of time. Waking, she heard voices in the bedroom.

"I walked over to Ma and Dad's and called the doctor. He thinks we should take her to the hospital. He doesn't think she'll have the baby for sometime, but he wants her there. I'll have to take her to the hospital in the milk truck. I've got the engine pulled out of the car. I planned to work on it tonight in hopes of getting it fixed before the baby came. Guess that was bad planning on my part."

"It doesn't matter as long as she gets there," remarked Amanda.

Rosalia sat up in the bed. "Oh, Mikie, I'm so glad you are here."

Mikie hugged and kissed her. "How are you doing?" He held her hand in his.

"Oh--I've got another one, Mikie. I'm afraid." She grabbed his arm. Tears accompanied the pain in her eyes.

"I've got your suitcase in the truck. It's time you go." Amanda helped Mikie lift Rosalia off the bed and walk her out into the kitchen.

"Oh, Mikie, here comes another one. Please hurry. I don't want to have the baby in the truck. Oh--please, hurry! Oh, God, help me!"

"It'll be all right, Rosalia. You have plenty of time. Mikie will get you there before the baby comes." Amanda hugged her, helped her up into the truck, and sat beside her holding her hand.

"Oh--the pain is getting worst--hurry, Mikie! Go faster, please!" Rosalia did not know which way to move to alleviate the recurring pain.

The truck sped down the main street of town then along the country roads with the dust flying up behind them. As he neared the city of Jennings, he had to slow his speed. There were more vehicles and pedestrians to be concerned about.

Despite the continuous pain, Rosalia felt a relief pass through her body as the hospital passed in view. She had help now. The sight of the nurses in white, soothe her with confidence as they prepared her for the delivery of the baby.

On the bed, inside the labor room, she lay. Between the metal posts of the bed's railing, she reached for Mikie's hand. With each contraction, she squeezed his hand in hopes that somehow the pain would be lessened. As the contractions became to increase in strength and at a greater frequency, they moved her onto a moveable bed. As they pushed her down the hall to the delivery room, Mikie remained at her side holding her hand. When the nurses opened the two large swinging doors and pushed her into the room, his hand left hers. She was without him--alone.

Mikie and Amanda sat in the waiting room. Time seemed so long.

The minutes seemed like hours and hours of waiting. Mikie was so concerned about his Rosalia. His eyes cried for the pain that she was having. Amanda prayed the baby would be all right. From her own experience, she knew Rosalia would forget the pain as the child increased her joy from day to day.

Inside the labor room, Rosalia lay in a green gown on a table covered with white sheets. The lights above glared down on her as her legs were bent, parted, and strapped into metal stirrups on each side of the table.

Standing beside her was a woman who put a cover over her nose. As Rosalia inhaled the sweet smell, she would experience a slight unconsciousness and some insensibility to the contracting pain. When the mask was removed and the effect of the gas lessened, the contractions again became stronger. She would grip the sides of the table with a mighty force as she felt the urge to push.

"Come on, Rosalia, push more--push!" the doctor ordered.

"I can't! I just can't!"

"Rosalia, come on, push!" the doctor ordered again.

She would push again with all her strength, but the fatigue was overwhelming.

"The feet are first. There's the rump. The legs are bent with the knees against the baby's chest. Nurse press on the top of the uterus to help ease out the baby. I've got to do an episiotomy."

"Okay, Rosalia, the legs and torso are out. Now you've got to get out the head. Push again!" the doctor ordered again.

"I can't! I can't!" How long was this going to last? She drifted away.

"You can't stop now, Rosalia! One hard push! Once you've got the shoulders out, the rest is easy. Come on Rosalia!"

"I--can't." She pushed again.

"Rosalia, get the head out! Push again! You have to get the head out or else your baby will die!"

She pushed one more time with a low mournful sound of pain as her body was consumed with tremendous fatigue.

"Okay, Rosalia, the baby is out," said the doctor.

"Is--it--okay?" Rosalia asked.

"Yes, Rosalia, it is a beautiful little girl," said one of the nurses.

"Can--I--see--her?" Rosalia's smile was weak. "My--baby." After seeing the baby, she seemed to drift into a subconscious condition. The next thing she remembered was waking up in a different room and hearing Mikie's voice.

"Rosalia, I love you." He held her hand, and she could feel his love warm her soul.

"I love you too, Mikie." Her voice was still weak and her speech slow. "Did you see Angela?"

"Yes, I did. She's beautiful. I'm sorry you had so much pain." He kissed her hand, and she could feel it being moistened by his tears.

"How are you feeling, Rosalia?" asked another voice.

Her eyes drifted in the direction of the familiar voice. "Okay. Did you see her, Ma?"

"Of course, she is such a little cutie." Amanda bent over and kissed Rosalia's forehead.

"You did a good job, Rosalia." The doctor entered the room. "The first one is always hard but for it to be a breech, makes it harder. I'm sorry your first experience had to be that way. I had to cut you a lot so you have a lot of stitches. I'm going to recommend that you stay in the hospital five days."

Rosalia smiled tiredly. She was fighting every second to stay awake. She would go in and out of consciousness.

"I think we should leave her rest." The tall, bald doctor motioned for them to leave the room.

"No, don't leave, Mikie." She extended her weary arm out to him and then it fell to the side of the bed.

"I'll be back. You rest Rosalia. I love you." He kissed her lips, and she fell into a deep sleep.

"Wake up, Rosalia." It was a nurse holding Angela. "It's time to start nursing Angela. Let her suck frequently, but only a few minutes at a time. This will provide her with colostrum and also stimulate the breasts to produce milk." Smiling, she placed Angela into Rosalia's arms. "She is a little cutie, so much dark hair."

Rosalia was apprehensive. She was afraid she would hold Angela wrong and hurt her.

"Don't be afraid to hold her. She's not a china doll, and she won't break. Just watch her head." The nurse helped position the baby in

Rosalia's arms. "There, if you're comfortable, I'll leave you two." Smiling, the nurse excited the door.

"Thanks." Rosalia smiled then began to nurse Angela. She looked down at how tiny she was. Her body filled with ecstasy as she thought, this was her baby--her baby! A person so special from the love she and Mikie had for each other. She never would have imagined how wonderful this moment could be. This was her life now, being a mother and wife. Nothing else in the world was important. She very carefully rested Angela on her shoulder and kissed her small head.

"All finished?" The nurse's smile came around the open door.

"Yes."

"I'll take her back to the nursery." The nurse reached for Angela.

Rosalia did not like to see Angela go, but she did need her rest. It had been a long night that had brought her into this day. Into a deep sleep she went, only to be awakened to eat her meals and nurse Angela.

After dinner was visitation time, Mikie brought her mother. Margie, Paul, and Otto came together. Pamela was working at the shoe factory. Paul, Margie, and Otto stood at the back of Rosalia's bed. Amanda stood beside Mikie at the front of the bed.

"Hi, Rosalia, how are you feeling?" Mikie kissed her.

"All right. Did you see her yet?" Rosalia could not sit up. Under her bed covers, her legs were situated over a heat lamp to help hasten the healing of the stitches.

"No, I thought I would take them to the nursery now. Is that all right with you?" Mikie held her hand in his.

"That's fine. I can't walk very well yet. Besides, I have to sit with the heat lamp another thirty minutes. I just nursed her."

"Rosalia, you should not nurse. It stretches out your bust. You will look top heavy after a while," remarked Margie.

"I enjoy it, Margie. I want to experience every aspect of motherhood."

Mikie smiled at Rosalia and shook his head slightly as he thought, Margie will never change. He kissed Rosalia and said, "I love you."

"For God's sake, Mikie! There is a time and place for that. A public place like a hospital is not! Let's look at the baby." Rolling her eyes, Margie turned away from the bed and moved toward the door.

"Are you coming, Amanda?" Mikie walked toward the door with Otto and Paul.

"I'll keep Rosalia company. When you come back, I'll go." Amanda sat in the chair next to the bed and watched until Otto was out of the room. Her feelings about him would never change. The mere sight of him repulsed her.

"Ma, you don't like Otto do you?"

"Let's not waste our time talking about him. How was your day with Angela?" She touched Rosalia's hand.

"I'm worried about not having enough milk. Here they weigh her to see how much she is getting. When I get home, I won't know. I'm afraid she might starve."

"You don't have to worry about that. When she's hunger, she'll let you know." Amanda was reassuring.

Mikie tapped on the glass window of the nursery. The nurse pulled out one of the metal trays with a pink bassinet set on it. The big label on the front of it said ASLEN.

Through the window they examined the little girl wrapped in a pink receiving blanket.

Mikie's face was aglow with tremendous pride. To him she was such an unbelievable miracle. "She has Rosalia's nose. Don't you think so?"

"A girl doesn't carry on the Aslen name," Otto remarked.

"Dad's right. Only you can carry on the name, Mikie," Margie interjected.

"I think that is irrelevant at this point. I guess it was too much to expect that you people could say anything nice. I'm going back by Rosalia, and don't you dare make a remark like that to her." More hurt than angry, Mikie walked down the hospital hall.

"Are you coming, Dad?" Margie took Paul's arm and followed Mikie. She had seen enough of that damn child.

"I'm not going back to the room. I'll meet you downstairs by the car." Otto walked toward the stairs.

At Rosalia's room, Margie and Paul bid their farewells.

"Did you give Rosalia the letter?" Mikie asked.

"Oh, no, I didn't think of it. We were talking about other things."

Amanda reached inside her purse and handed Rosalia the letter. "It's from Susie. I knew you were anxious about not hearing from her for a while. So when I got the mail and seen it was from Susie, I told Mikie we're taking it to the hospital for you to read."

"Thanks, Ma." She opened the letter and began to read. "She's in Germany teaching at an army base. Well, when she said she wanted to get away from Beechwood, she really meant it. She met a German guy at a church dance, and they've been going out for several months. No wonder, I haven't heard from her for so long." She folded the letter and put it back into its envelope.

"Did she ask about John?" Mikie asked.

"No, she didn't. Guess maybe she is really over him," Rosalia replied.

"So ironical, isn't it, how things turn out? Well, I'm going to see Angela. When you're ready to leave, please, let me know." Amanda rose from the chair. She sensed their need to be alone. Besides, she was looking forward to seeing Angela.

When the hall of the maternity floor was empty of people, he came from his hidden position to view the baby. This man, dressed in tattered clothes that smelled from lack of cleanliness, smiled as he looked through the glass window at the sleeping baby. With his hand, he grabbed at the glass as if he wished he could reach through and touch her. If only he could come back and have things the way they were. But time had changed him and he did not want to be remembered as he now was. His problem was beyond his control. He had remained sober because his will to come here had overridden all his other desires. However, in time--maybe tonight--tomorrow--or next week, he knew he would weaken. He did not want them-- especially her, his little girl of so long ago--to see him like this. Her memories of him were of a different person--a person she could be proud of. In his present condition, he would bring her shame. Tears dampened his eyes as he watched the baby sleep. Why did he have to change? He had ruined his chances of having these little things that were really the most important in life. What a sad, lonely man he had become. In his sober state, he reverted to things like this. Stolen moments to watch at a distance the one's he loved, never having a chance to hold. He had it all. It seemed like such a long time ago.

Now his life was passing him by. Leaving at the completion of each day, regrets that the day was so much different from the way he had wished it to be. Too late, he realized how in her own way she had loved him. But he had desired what he knew he should not have. For what? He had given up all this. Wiping the tears from his eyes, he heard approaching footsteps in the hall. His time here had come to an end. He scurried to get out of sight.

As she came around the hallway corner, Amanda thought she saw someone disappear into the exit door for the stairs. She paused to look closer. Huh, no one! As she looked through the nursery's glass window, she felt as if eyes were watching her. She looked down the hall from where she had come and then down the hall to the stairs. Was she imaging it or did she see a gap in the door close as she turned? She walked toward the stair exit, then stopped. Everything was quiet. She had imagined it. Satisfied with her conclusion, she returned to the nursery window.

"One last look then I think we'll leave. If that is all right with you?" Mikie had come down the hall.

"That's fine with me. After being up late last night and getting up early for work this morning, I'm very tired. She is beautiful. Isn't she?" Amanda smiled to herself as the joy leaped from her heart.

"Yes, she is," Mikie agreed.

Down the stairs and out of the hospital they walked toward the milk truck.

From across the street, standing in front of an old brick building, he watched from where they couldn't see him. He watched Amanda get into the truck and be driven down the road. The truck became smaller and smaller until it disappeared completely from view. He opened the door of the brick building and went inside. Sitting at the bar, he ordered himself a beer--then another--and another. Alcohol would make his painful heart bearable. As others use alcohol as an excuse to deaden physical pain, he used it to deaden his emotional pain. This was the excuse that he had created his life around.

Chapter 19
****
Evil Brother

It was the end of another brisk autumn day, and he felt a sense of accomplishment knowing the farm chores for the day had been completed. Tomorrow would be another day for filling the large cement silo with more green corn silage. After a long summer of field work, filling the silo marked the end of such work except for corn picking. At the end of this day, he relaxed in a round, metal tub of hot water. After such a luxury, he shaved and splashed his face with a nice smelling aftershave. Then dressed in clean slacks and shirt, he would leave the farm and drive down the countryside roads that led into town toward Lyra's for supper. He was a regular, nightly customer. After all, what else was there for him? Now that she was gone.

As he entered the car-cluttered parking lot, he recognized most of the cars. They belonged to the group of farmers and factory workers who usually satisfied their thirst after a hard day's work. After parking the car, he entered the tavern where everyone greeted him with a friendly "hi." At the crowded, long mahogany bar, he sat talking about the farm work and drinking until Lyra had the "special" of the day prepared for him to eat. Today it was his favorite--meat loaf, mashed potatoes, gravy, and buttered beans.

While enjoying his meal, he watched her behind the bar--filling empty glasses with her manicured, small hands--smiling and talking to her customers. Occasionally, she would look in his direction and smile with a gleaming glow as her dimples creased her pink cheeks. He would nod his head in acknowledgment of her smile. She was a beautiful woman.

"Hi, John." Could be heard above the noisy talk of the tavern.

John turned to see who had greeted him. "Hi, Mikie. Hey, Lyra, give Mikie a drink on me!"

Smiling, Lyra grabbed a glass from under the bar and filled it with the yellow brew. "Hi, Mikie." Placing the glass of beer in front of him, she smiled.

"So how have things been going, Mikie? Don't see you much anymore now that you don't drive milk truck." He grabbed the glass of beer, which Lyra had given him earlier, and took a few swallows.

"I had to get a different job. Working for Dad wasn't paying the bills."

"How do you like factory work?"

"It pays the bills, and now we have insurance. It was tough paying the hospital bills for the last three kids. This time the insurance will pay for the kid."

"Rosalia pregnant?" John took another drink of his beer.

"Yup, about a month now."

"Gee, Mikie, you'll have a baseball team pretty soon. How old is Angela?" Setting his beer glass down on the bar, he continued to eat.

"She started first grade this fall."

"Boy, time goes fast. Jimmy is in second grade already. Grandma is looking forward to his first communion. It's better that he lives with her right now. I see him on Sundays. We all go to church together. That's the biggest reason she wouldn't move. She would miss going to Mass every day. Are you still thinking about moving?"

"Ya, Rosalia gets into a panic every time it rains and that basement fills up with water." Mikie took another drink of his beer.

"Lucy is selling the house on the homestead. It needs a lot of work. She never let Pa fix anything up on the property. Cost too much money." Finishing his meal, he pushed his empty plate toward the end of the bar. "It was good, Lyra."

"Thanks." Lyra approached to take away the plate.

"Give us another beer." John made a hand gesture indicating Mikie and himself.

"No, thanks, I'll take a rain cheek. I've got to get home. Rosalia has supper ready by now, and then I've got to go over by Dad. The long bathroom sink pipe under the crawl space is clogged. Dad can't get in there so he asks me. I told him I'd come after supper."

"That sounds like a really nice job."

"Ya, I'm not looking forward to it. See you later." Mikie gave John a friendly tap on his shoulder, turned, and left the tavern.

As Mikie was driving into the yard at his house, the house door flung open and out ran Angela and her two brothers toward the car. They hovered outside the car until Mikie opened the door and got out.

"Daddy, Daddy!" They hugged him around his legs as they looked up at him with their shining faces of happiness. Immediately, he surrendered his black metal lunchbox to the kids. Hurriedly, they opened it to view the goodies inside. He would always leave something in the lunchbox for them--cookies--chocolate stars--butterscotch candy. It was nothing that special--except to the kids. All three of them would sit on the wooden steps that led into the house and equally divide what they found among themselves. From experience, Mikie knew to always leave enough to be shared. Everyone was happy then.

As he climbed the steps, the door opened and there stood Rosalia smiling at him. His heart leaped at the sight of her.

She welcomed him with a kiss and hug. "Come on in, kids. Supper is on the table. You wait to eat those cookies until after supper." She held the door open. "Come on, scoot inside, wash your hands, and sit at the table."

"Oh, Ma." Regardless of all their complaining, they got off the steps and did what they were told.

The steam from the hot food, setting on the table, swirled about. The potatoes were from Rosalia's garden as were the other vegetables. The meat was from half a cow, which they had bought from John. Rosalia believed in the basics--meat, potatoes, and another vegetable at a meal. Dessert was not a necessity.

"I hope it doesn't take me too long at Dad's tonight. I had a hard day at work today." Mikie filled his plate with food.

"You are always helping him. This summer you shingled his house roof for him. Last year you helped them paint their house. Yet they can't even get me paint for the walls or cement that basement. It's always you. What was Paul's excuse this time?" Rosalia asked.

"It was too far to drive after he worked all day. The time that he'd spend on the road, I could have it cleaned out." Mikie began to eat.

"It's not too far to drive for Sunday dinner, is it? Your parents invite them over almost every Sunday. We're lucky they invite us for Christmas. When it comes to the dirty work, then they know you. Otherwise, you don't exist." Rosalia sat at the table.

"They are my parents. At least my conscious is clear. I've always helped them. Maybe someday they'll help us."

"Mikie, you are too good-hearted, and they take advantage of that." Rosalia began to eat her supper.

"Let's not talk about it anymore, especially, in front of the kids. Tell me about your day."

"It went good. I got some of the fall housecleaning done upstairs. Curtains and walls washed off in the boys' bedroom."

"John told me that Lucy wants to sell the house on the homestead. You want to drive out there tomorrow after supper and talk to Lucy about it."

"Sure, that's a good idea. It's Friday night. Angela doesn't have to go to bed early because of school. We can visit. I haven't seen Alex for quite some time."

"Supper was good, Rosalia." He pushed himself away from the kitchen table. After giving Rosalia and each of the children a good-bye kiss, he walked two houses down to his parents' house.

Arriving at his parents' house, he went into the garage, grabbed the big pipe wrench hanging on the wall, and took a roll of heavy gauge wire wrapped in a circle. He was very familiar with this roll. He had used it on more than one occasion. When he got married and moved into his own home, he thought that he had laid to rest the terrible job of cleaning out clogged pipes.

"Hi, Ma--Dad." He entered the kitchen. "Are you going to light my way Dad?"

"Ya, I'll get the flashlight." As his father got up from the kitchen sofa, which he had been lying on, Mikie could see from his staggered walk that he had been drinking. Beside the sofa set the evidence --several empty brown beer bottles. His father reached inside the cupboard, pulled out a small red flashlight, and turned it on to see if it still had a beam of light. Satisfied that it did, he turned it off. "Let's go." He walked out of the room into the basement.

"Do you like the first shift, Ma?"

"I had no choice. They don't need a second shift anymore." Sitting on a kitchen chair, she did not even take her eyes off the big black box, full of moving pictures and accompanying sound, to look at him.

"See you later, Ma." Toward the open basement door he headed. At the door he paused, looked at his mother. He was hurt by her lack of response, but he had experienced worse treatment from her. His eyes wandered over to the desk. There in his memory, he could still see that letter. He never told them that he knew of its existence. He wondered, after all these years, if that letter still existed. Oh, well, he had survived. God had been good to him. He had a wonderful wife and healthy children who loved him. That's all that was important.

Down into the basement, he followed his father. At the bottom of the stairs, in the foundation of the fieldstone wall, was a hole. Into the dark hole he crawled with the wrench and wire. The flash of light from his father's flashlight lit the way. He dragged his body along the ground, as a worm, inching his way farther into the darkness of the confining hole. He kept his head low to avoid hitting it on the house's floor joist. When his father first built the house, he had not put a basement under the porch section of the house, only footings. Later, when indoor plumbing became more popular, he had converted part of the porch into a bathroom. However, the only way to put in the plumbing was by going through this crawl space. Now Mikie lay there on his back, turning loose the couplings on the metal pipes, putting the wire into the clogged pipe, and slowly pulling out the black, slimy, smelly, clogged globs of sewage. Globs fell onto the ground beside him, in front of him, and on him. He smelled like a "sewage" rat. Inch by inch he cleaned out the pipe. More black globs fell on him--in his hair--on his face. It would flow from the wire onto his hand and then down his arm as he continued sticking the wire into the pipe, moving it about to loosen more globs, then pulling it out again. The process was repeated for hours. When the pipe appeared clean, he replaced the couplings. Out of the crawl space he came dragging his body over the globs of removed sewage. He was covered with it. The only visible things were the whites of his eyes. Over to his mother's washtubs he went. Letting the water run from the faucet, he washed his face, hands, and arms.

"Dad, can you go home and get me some clean clothes. I don't want to go in the house like this. I'll leave them here, and Ma could wash them. Then I don't have to carry this mess home."

"Ah, wash up and go home like that. It's just two houses away. By the time I get back, you'd be home already. I'm going to bed." He checked his watch. "It's eleven o'clock already. Make sure you shut the outside basement door when you leave." He motioned to the other basement door, which lead directly outside, as he climbed the inside stairs into the kitchen.

He watched his father walk up the stairs. He had never taken notice till now how his father had aged. His crop of hair was now white, and his large, overweight body moved in a slow gait up the stairs. Physically he had changed but not any other way. Mikie had helped him, but he could not even afford a "thank you." It was their sewer that covered his body and clothes, but Rosalia would end up cleaning up the mess. She had enough work with the three kids and being pregnant again. He thought that they could be more considerate. Guess tigers don't change their strips. With that he walked out of their basement, locked the door, and went home. Quietly, he entered the house. Rosalia had let the small light above the sink lit to guide his way through the house. Carefully, he walked through the kitchen trying to avoid getting the floor full of the black sewage dirt. Into the basement he went. There he took off the soiled clothes. If he had known how to wash, he would have done it for Rosalia. Instead, he left the pile of soiled clothes lay on the ground floor.

****

The smoke-filled bar was now empty except for her washing off the bar and him sitting on the bar stool staring into his glass of beer and thinking--thinking of her and waiting. With the bar clean, she came out from behind it. One by one, she pulled out the plugs on the neon signs that lit each window. Turning the latch on the outside door, she locked it. The tavern was closed for the night.

The sight of his broad shoulders that tapered to his thin waist and small buttocks attracted her to him like a magnet. They were good together. Slowly, she wrapped her arms around his neck and then gradually began to stroke his red hair. She would tease him with short, moist kisses on his tempting pink lips. Looking into his soft green eyes seem to float her away.

Her tenderness intensified his excitement. Aggressively, he took her into his arms and kissed her hard.

"Let's go upstairs." She could feel his heart thunder against hers.

Hand in hand they left the barroom and walked up the stairs into her bedroom. In anticipation of this time, earlier, she had started a fire in the fireplace to remove the damp chill from the night. The log now sparked as the flame slowly consumed it. In the warmth of the room, they undressed each other. In their nakedness, they lay on the bed evoking the excitement of each of their erogenous zones by caresses and kisses. Through hand touching and physical contact between their sensitive sexual organs, their excitement now became more rapid. Their movements were involuntary, twisting movements of relaxation then contraction. As their hearts raced on with excitement, their breathing turned to heavy panting. The fast heart beat coincided with the numerous, intense pulsations of their entire bodies. The sexual excitement spread throughout every cell, and their erections became simultaneous.

His need for exhalation relaxed his chest and in this sexual position--breast upon breast--he felt closer to her now at his height of excitement. His body, moving of its own accord, brought him relief as he now moved into a tranquil state. The sexual act had finished as jerkily as it had started and now vibrated within his body as an accepted fatigue. He felt a gratitude to her and expressed it with a caress of her body. "I love you." He lay beside her holding her hand. The excitement abated.

Her body felt a glow of happiness. "Good night, John." She moved closer to him, and rested her arm around his chest.

"Good, night, Lyra." He lifted her arm off his chest, kissed her hand, and laid it beside her on the bed. Then sitting at the edge of the bed, he grabbed a pack of cigarettes and a book of matches out of his shirt pocket. Lighting the cigarette, he walked toward the window. Enjoying each puff of the cigarette, he stared at the moon. What was he thinking about? Nothing in particular--the work he had to do tomorrow--on Sunday he would see Jimmy--tomorrow night with Lyra again. Being with her and the excitement she gave him is what made life worthwhile. Was he really in love with her? No, they were words to make her feel as good as she had made him feel.

Making the cigarette out in the ashtray, he dressed, and left her. Tomorrow would be another night. She was always available.

****

Under the thin blanket, his body shivered from the chill of the autumn morning. A scant layer of prune-wrinkled skin covered his skeleton. The degeneration of his skin--red, painful areas that had become purple before the skin broke down and developed open sores--plagued his bony shoulders, elbows, lower back, and heels. He turned his head, full of long greasy strands of gray hair, and his face now covered with brown aged spots, toward the window. His eyes that had lost the luster of life looked at the tree with its autumn coat. The autumn of his life had ended many years ago and now he was in the winter of his life--a life so barren and senseless. Was this even life to lay like this--to live another day just like the day before? What had he done so terrible in life to merit this hell on earth?

The house was quiet now. The clock ticked--ticked--ticked. Across the room he could see a mouse scamper about the floor. If the mouse was looking for crumbs of food, it was in the wrong house. She watched everything, even down to the last crumb of food. The mouse stood still, ears perked. As it heard the silence being broken by footsteps on the wooden porch, it ran into a gnawed hole in the woodwork--out of sight. The door creaked on its old hinges. It had to be Lucy. She always came into the house first after the milking chores. If the door slammed, she was angry. If she just closed it, she was in a good mood. He listened. She slammed it. Fear vibrated throughout his body. She would play God with his life today again-- and it would be hell.

"Get up for school!" Lucy yelled up the stairs at the boys.

In their warm and cozy bed under the blankets they wanting to stay.

"Get up now!" she yelled again.

Denoting the anger in her voice, they quickly spirited out of the bed. With their small bodies shaking and their teeth chattering, they threw their pajamas off and put their trousers and flannel school shirts over their winter undershirt and long johns. Down the stairs they ran and stood beside the cooking stove, the only heat in the house. Lucy would not use the wood burner to heat the house until she was afraid the water pipes would freeze. Until then, she considered the cold only a small discomfort and there was no need to waste wood over it.

With their breakfast set on the table, they left the warmth of the stove to sit at the table. For breakfast, Lucy rationed out one egg to each of them, one glass of milk, and a slice of her homemade bread. They could have a second piece of bread but no more milk or eggs. The eggs and milk could be sold for a price. Therefore, indulgences in them were limited. Concern for the pocketbook was priority.

After gulping down their breakfast, they hurried to the hooks on the wall where their coats hung. Putting on their coats, they went outside. The tallest boy was carrying a white-enameled bowl that he had grabbed off the kitchen shelf.

"What do you want to do this morning?" the tallest of the boys asked as they walked toward the white chicken coop.

"I'll feed the chickens." Opening the door to the coop, the smallest boy proceeded toward the bags of chicken feed.

"That's why you let me grab the bowl, huh."

"It's better if you do it. Last time when I broke one of the eggs, I didn't get an egg for breakfast the next day." The small boy filled the feeders and then filled the water containers.

"Ready?" The tallest boy had collected all the eggs and was waiting for the small boy to finish his job.

"Ya, let's go." The small boy latched the door.

They didn't walk as fast now as before. Those eggs had to be pampered.

Into the house they went. "Here are the eggs, Ma." The tallest boy handed the bowl to her.

"Well, off to school then." Lucy grabbed the bowl and counted the eggs.

"Can we say a good-bye to Grandpa?" the tallest boy asked.

"No, he's sleeping," his mother snapped.

"We never get to see him anymore. I got to see him more when he lived with Aunt Lori," Eddy, the tallest boy, complained.

"Well, things have changed. Haven't they? Are you boys sure that you didn't break an egg? It doesn't look like we got very many today."

"No, Ma, we didn't break any--honest."

"No, we didn't." The youngest boy shook his head.

"Bye, Ma." They got out of there as fast as they could.

"Why did you have to say that, Eddy? You should know from last time she doesn't like remarks like that made about Grandpa. Last time she stayed mad at you all week and neither one of us got anything for breakfast except milk and toast."

"Ya, I remember." Eddy had his own private opinion about that. She just used that as an excuse so she could sell the eggs and make more money. However, he did not share this idea with anyone. After all, she was his mother. It would not be right for him to talk badly about her. Even though he disagreed about what he knew she was doing to his grandfather.

As he lay in bed and looked out the window, he watched the boys trod across the farm field toward school. Of all the things Lucy had done to him, depriving him of the boys' company, especially Eddy's, hurt him the most. He did not want to favor Eddy over Jeffery, but something attracted him more to Eddy. It was the eyes. He could look into Eddy's eyes and see his pure soul. Jeffery's eyes were different. He could not see his soul reflected in his eyes and for some reason he did not have good feelings about the boy when he was around. Those two boys were so different, as were Lori and Lucy--as different as day and night.

HONK--HONK--HONK--HONK--HONK--HONK--HONK--

The loud sound vibrated through the walls and windows of the house. From out of their "V" formation, which had graced the sky as they flew, the geese now landed in the picked cornfield. The field became darkened with their presence as their black heads, necks, and legs set about searching for corn that might have been missed by the corn chopper. If they had no luck feeding in that field, they would move into Alex's unpicked cornfield. They would destroy the field. He had seen it happen so many times before. Especially, when there were so many of them going South to avoid the cold winter.

Lying there in such a relaxed state, he felt pressure on the walls of his rectum. It was a natural reflex of his body to expel the waste material from his body. He tired to stop it, but he could not. He felt its warmth and softness on his buttocks and genital area. The room soon filled with a strong, unpleasant smell. It was so humiliating. This bowel movement was every day at about the same time. Lori had always gotten him up and placed him on the commode. What would be so hard for Lucy to do that? How long would she let him lay like that?

Watching out the window, he saw the sun move higher into the sky. He would see Alex drive past with the tractor, corn chopper, and an empty wagon. A little later he would see Lucy return with a full wagon and he would hear the blower fill the silo with silage. He could feel the muscular wall of his stomach contract rhythmically. It was a disagreeable feeling caused by his body's need for food.

The sun rose higher in the sky. The Angelus, the ringing of the Catholic church bells at noon, echoed across the land and faintly drifted through his closed window. Still lying in his feces, his stomach continued to beg for food. The noise from the blower ceased, and he heard her working in the kitchen. After a short time, he heard the key turn in his bedroom door. Was she bringing him something to eat? Would she remove the refuse matter from him and the bed?

"My, God, does it smell in here!" Lucy entered the room carrying a tray with a glass of water and bowl of steaming soup setting upon it. Placing the tray on the dresser next to the bed, she opened the window. The air was damp; it chilled his body.

"What a mess!" She flung the blanket off his body onto the floor. Roughly, she unpinned the cloth diaper that she had wrapped around him. "All the stuff I do for you. When I ask you to do one little thing, you refuse. That's gratitude all right!" Pulling the soiled diaper off his body, she exited the room momentarily.

"All the extra work I have to do. Is it appreciated? No!" She fastened another diaper to him. Covering his legs with the blanket, she sat him up in the bed. Reaching for the glass of water, she held it up to his mouth. Tipping the glass too far into the air caused his nose to be submerged in the water. Up his nose and down his windpipe the water went. He coughed and gasped for a breath. Water flowed down onto his nightshirt and bed covers. She removed the glass from his mouth. "Until you learn how to drink, don't expect me to waste my time. Want something to drink? Do it yourself." She set the glass on the dresser. He could see it but would never be able to reach it.

After dipping the spoon into the bowl of soup, she put in up to his mouth.

Opening his mouth, she placed the soup inside. It burned his tongue, the roof of his mouth, his throat, and all the way down to his esophagus. Then came another hot spoonful, then another--then she stopped. Walking toward the highboy, he knew what she wanted again. Opening the drawer, she pulled out that same white piece of paper, placed the paper on a board to provide a hard writing surface, and grabbed a pen out of the drawer as well. She approached him, putting the pen in his left hand.

"Sign right there, Pa." She placed his hand, which held the pen, in the area where she wanted him to sign.

He let the pen fall from his hand. He could still read, and he would never sign that piece of paper. It's not how he wanted things.

"All right, Pa, how ungrateful you are to me. I took care of you longer than Lori." She picked up the pen and returned it along with the paper to the drawer. "Dinner is over, Pa. When you decide to cooperate, I'll feed you again." She took the tray with the half-eaten soup out of the room, locking the door again.

She would feed him just enough so he would not starve to death. After all, that was the last thing she wanted to happen. At least not until he signed that paper. She put the bowl into the refrigerator and would reheat it for supper for him. She would feed him just enough to give him a taste of what he could have, if he cooperated.

The rest of his day went as usual. He watched across the field for the boys to come home. Part of his punishment for not signing was to have the boys taken away from him. As he lay there, he often thought of his grandfather. Is this the kind of life he had when he lived with Oslo and his wife? Was his father like his Lori and Oslo like Lucy? Did history repeat itself even in families? Where some characteristics heredity? What made Lucy so much like Oslo? How had they raised her so differently than Lori? Jimmy was all he had of Lori; he was not going to sign that away. He would die first and maybe he would.

A weary smile forced itself across his face as he saw the boys come across the field. The light-gray breasted geese took flight at the sight of the boys. He would watch, and his heart would yearn for the companionship of Eddy.

Up the porch steps, the boys would run. Inside the house, they'd set their metal lunchboxes and cloth school bags on the kitchen table. Up the stairs into their bedrooms they would go. There they would take off their good school clothes and put on their old farm clothes, stiffened from the accumulation of grease, ground, and manure. During the day, the sun coming through the South and West windows had warmth the room. At this time of day, changing clothes was a more pleasant experience than in the early morning. Down the stairs they went and out the door into the barn to do their chores--getting the feed ready for each of the cows, setting up the milking machine, bringing the cows into the barn from the pasture, and then securing the cows inside their stalls. When this was done, they had to finish unloading the silage from the wagon for their mother while she went into the house to make supper.

"How was your day at school?" their father asked as they all sat at the table eating.

"It was okay, Dad." Jeffery was not very enthused about the supper--beef soup--again. It was mostly juice and vegetables. The meat chucks were very sparse.

"Can I use your 4-10 to shoot some of those geese, Dad?" Jeffery extended his soup by breaking bits of bread into it.

"If you shoot it, you're cleaning it!" His mother finished sipping her food. "No time for that until the silo is full."

"Can I feed Grandpa tonight?" Eddy pushed his empty bowl up to the large, deep dish, removed the lid, and filled his bowl with more soup.

"No, you milk cows until I get done in here--as usual. I don't want to hear any complaining from you either." She finished her bowl of soup, rose from her chair, put the bowl into the sink, and started to fill the sink with water.

"How is your dad?" Alex took his bowl and put it into the sink. "I haven't seen him for so long with working late into evening and getting up so early to get everything done. He doesn't go to church with us. If he's that sick, maybe we should put him in a nursing home."

"You know my opinion on that, so don't mention it again. He's fine. There is nothing a little rest won't cure." Lucy began to wash the dishes. "If you boys want to get done early, you better get at milking now," she ordered.

Within a few minutes, the humming of the milking machine could be heard. Also, the grunting sound of the tractor and corn chopper as Alex continued his field work where he had stopped when he came in for supper.

Once again, Lucy repeated the events of dinner at supper. Despite his tremendous hunger, Pete actually wished that she would not take care of him. He wished that she would just let him starve to death. Life this way was not living. It only made him pray to die. After the feeding of the soup, she left him alone in the room that was slowly filling with the darkness of the approaching night. In the distance, he could see a cloud of dust swirling up into the air. It was a car. Someone was coming up the driveway.

"Oh, what do they want now?" Lucy continued unloading the silage from the wagon. She did not have time to stop working for idle conversation.

"Who is that, Ma?" Jeffery had just finished milking the cows and was joining his mother where she was working.

"It's your Aunt Rosalia and her tribe." Lucy would not stop working to greet them. She watched them stop the car. First, Rosalia and Mikie got out of the car. Then the kids, one by one, squeezed out the two front doors of the two-door car.

"Hi, Lucy." Mikie approached her holding onto the four-year-old boy's hand. Rosalia followed carrying the two-year-old boy.

"Hi, Mikie--Rosalia. What brings you out here?" Lucy continued to work.

"We heard you were selling the house on the homestead, and we were wondering if we could go and look at it." Mikie put his arm around Rosalia's shoulder as she stood beside him holding the two-year-old boy in her arms.

"Hey, Angela, want to see the new kittens we have in the barn?" Eddy asked.

"Ya. Where are they?" Angela's eyes gleamed. She loved kittens.

"Come on." Eddy took her hand and walked her around the blower, and up the small incline into the hay barn. Hay was stacked up to the top beams of the barn.

"We have to climb the ladder." Eddy began to climb up the stationary wooden ladder that extended from the hay barn floor up to one of top support beams of the barn.

Angela looked up. It was a long way to climb. "I don't want to go up there. I'll fall."

"Ah, don't be such a chicken." Jeffery teased her. "Come on start climbing. You can't see the kittens if you don't climb up to where they are. Come on, Angela, start climbing." He pushed her toward the ladder.

"No, I'm afraid." Angela began to cry.

"Jeffery, leave her alone. We can each bring a kitten down to her." Eddy yelled down from the top of the mound of hay. Then he disappeared out of sight.

"Cry baby!" Jeffery gave her a mighty shove that made her fall backwards onto the hay barn floor. Snickering at her, up the ladder he went.

Amongst the soft hay lay the mother cat cleaning her four kittens.

Eddy picked up one of the kittens by the nape of its neck. Holding it in his arms, he stroked its soft, black fur until the kitten purred. "I'm taking this one down by Angela." He unbuttoned one of his shirt buttons and stuck the kitten inside. Buttoning his shirt again, he walked toward the ladder and climbed down. At the bottom of the ladder, he unbuttoned the shirt and gave the kitten to Angela.

Angela's bright eyes widened, and a smile graced her face. "Oh, thank you. She is so pretty." Holding the kitten, she rubbed its furry body against her cheek.

A kitten's shrill scream echoed within the walls of the hay barn.

Angela and Eddy looked at each other bewilderedly.

"What's going on up there?" Eddy called.

"Oh, nothing." Jeffery had picked a kitten up by the tail and was swinging it around in the air. Setting the kitten down, he would find great pleasure in watching the kitten stagger and fall in its dizziness. "You want another kitten?" he yelled.

"You want to see another kitten, Angela?" asked Eddy.

Angela, sitting on the hay and stroking the contented kitten that rested on her lap, smiled and nodded.

"Ya, bring down one of the gray ones," Eddy yelled up.

Jeffery grabbed another kitten, gripped it tightly in his hand, walked to the edge of the mound of hay, and stood at the ladder's edge. "Here's another!" He laughed and dropped the kitten into the air.

"No, don't--" Eddy could only watch helplessly from below as the kitten clawed into the air, hoping to stop its inevitable fall.

"Why did you have to do that?" Eddy picked up the kitten, limp with death. "Why, Jeffery? Why?"

"Will it be all right?" Angela got up, holding the other kitten, and walked toward Eddy.

Eddy wiped his watery eyes. "It's in animal heaven."

"It's just a dumb cat. You want another one?" Jeffery yelled down.

"No!" He saw Jeffery disappear into the hay mound. "Jeffery, you stay away from those kittens! Get down here!"

"Here's another one. Want it, Angela?" He held another kitten suspended in the air, ready to drop it.

"Jeffery, put the kitten back and get down here!" Eddy was frantic. Would he drop that kitten also?

"Are you sure you don't want it?" He dangled the kitten by one leg. Its cries of pain did not concern Jeffery.

Angela began to cry. "Make him stop hurting the kitten."

"Jeffery! Put it back!" Eddy yelled.

Laughing, he tossed the kitten back to its mother and started climbing down the ladder.

Relieved, Eddy started to walk toward the open barn door to go outside.

"Where are you going?" Angela followed.

"I'm going to get a shovel and bury the kitten," said Eddy.

"Can I come with you?" Angela asked.

"No, you better stay in the barn with the kitten. If she gets away from you outside, we might not be able to find her. Play with her until I come back, then I'll have to put it back up by the mother cat." Eddy left her in the barn with Jeffery.

"Let me have the kitten." Jeffery stood beside her.

"No." She knew what he had done to the other kitten, and she feared for the kitten's life. She hugged it close to her body.

"You little brat." Taking the palm of his hand, he pushed roughly against her small shoulder--again and again--harder and harder.

Falling onto the floor, the kitten fell free of her hands.

"Now I've got your precious little kitten." He reached down, picked it up, and held it in his hand.

The kitten screamed loudly as he squeezed, with extreme pleasure, its stomach tightly in the grip of his hand.

"Give me back the kitten!" Angela cried frantically, in fear of him killing the kitten. Spontaneously, she sprang to her feet and pulled at his body for him to release the kitten.

He pushed her down again and threw the kitten at her. She felt the sting of the kitten's claws as they ripped the soft flesh on her face. As she struggled to get up, he took her fragile head in his strong hand and pushed her face into the pile of loose hay. The hay stubbles pricked and scratched at her face. She found it very difficult to breathe. With her tiny arms, she pushed down on the hay trying to push herself up and away from the dusty, moldy hay. The more she tried, the harder he pushed on her head. Deeper and deeper into the pile of hay her head went until it seemed completely covered. Into the air she wildly kicked her legs. Then she felt her legs being restrained by the sharpness of his knee digging into her calves. Her chest was being crushed by the weight of his body lying on hers. She could not move. She could not breathe.

****

Below the trees, which had been ripped of their red and yellow leaves by the damp, blustery wind of the autumn day, she raked the leaves in the calmness of the evening hours up onto her flower beds to provide cover for her chrysanthemums over the long winter months. To keep the leaves secured on top of the plants, which she had pruned to ground level, she ventured into the garage. There on the workbench set a bolt of white cheesecloth, which the men used to clean their hands of grease while they performed mechanical work on the trucks. Taking the bolt of cheesecloth, she unwrapped the amount that she thought she needed to cover the leaves. With a screwdriver in her hand, she made a rip in the cloth. At that point, she ripped the cloth free from the bolt. Taking the cloth outside, she placed it over the leaves. She secured the cloth at intervals with stones to prevent the wind from blowing off the cloth and dispersing the leaves all over the yard, thereby, exposing her chrysanthemums to winter damage.

With the chrysanthemums covered on one side of the house, she ventured to the front of the house following the same procedure. As she worked, people would drive past and blow their car horns or wave to her as she looked up from her work. It made her feel good about how well-liked she was in the community.

Hearing another car horn honk, she looked up to see the car's red flashing blinker. The car was going to turn into their driveway. It was Margie and Paul. As they turned into the yard and drove past her, she waved. Setting the rake against the tree, she walked to the back of the house where she knew they would park the car. Coming around the house, see seen Paul and Margie standing beside their car, waiting for her.

"Grandma, Grandma!" Two girls ran out of the back seat of the car and clung to her.

"My, don't you two girls look so nice." Holding their hands, she examined their frilly dresses. "Come on, Grandma's got something for you." Hand in hand, they walked to where Margie and Paul were still standing. "Hi, Margie--Paul, this is a nice visit."

"We've got to talk to you and Dad about something." Margie spoke in a troublesome tone.

"Well, your dad's in the house. Let's go in there." Hand in hand with the girls, she walked into the house.

"Hi, Grandpa." The girls, viewing the candy dish on the kitchen table, dashed toward it. Removing the glass lid, their small hands searched for the pieces of candy they wanted.

"Oh--hi, girls." The old man's body sat up from his slumbered position. A tuft of white hair stuck on his head. "Margie--Paul--what brings you here on a weeknight?"

"Oh, good! Lassie is on television! Can we watch it, Grandpa?" Sucking their candy, the two girls crowded onto the kitchen sofa with Otto.

"Ya, go ahead." He rose from the sofa and joined Margie and Paul at the kitchen table.

"Paul and I have a little problem."

"How serious is the problem?" Pamela sat at the table.

"You know the new television that we bought a couple of months ago on credit from Erickson's store," said Margie.

"Ya, what about it?" Otto asked.

"Well, we've been unable to make the payments and Erickson is sending us notes about repossession."

"For God's sake, Margie, we have a good reputation in this town. How could you not make the payments?" Otto shook his head disapprovingly.

"We're sorry, Dad. We just borrowed more than we can handle." Margie's eyes became watery.

"How much do you owe?" Otto inquired.

Paul reached into the back pocket of his trousers, pulled out his wallet, and handed Otto a piece of paper that had been stuffed inside the wallet.

After examining the paper, Otto went into the bedroom. Inside the closet was a gray, floor safe. Otto opened it and pulled out a stack of dollar bills held together with a rubber band. He counted through the stack then removed several of the dollar bills. Replacing the rubber banded stack inside the safe, he closed its door and locked the safe again. Lying on the floor, a small white piece of paper caught his eye. Upon picking it up and examining it, he placed it into his shirt pocket and rejoined the others at the kitchen table.

"You pay Erickson tomorrow," Otto ordered Margie as he handed her the money.

"Oh, thank you, Dad--and you too, Ma." The eyes that had been clouded with tears now gleamed like the rays of the sun. "Well, we have to be going." Margie rose from the chair. "Come on, girls. It's time to go home."

"Oh, Ma, can't we finish watching to see what happens," the girls complained.

"No! Let's go--now!"

With that order, the girls sprung off the sofa.

"Here, take a piece of candy before you go." Pamela took the glass container off the table, removed the lid, and held the jar out to the girls.

"Thanks, Grandma." Putting the candy into their mouths, out the door they ran. Letting the screen door slam behind them.

"Kids!" The loud bang of the door annoyed Pamela.

Otto and Pamela walked out to the car with Margie and Paul. Waving, they watched the car leave their driveway.

The two girls, kneeling on the back seat of the car, waved back at them through the window.

Pamela proceeded to walk around to the front of the house to resume the raking of the leaves.

"Pam, wait," Otto called after her. Reaching into his pocket, he pulled out the piece of paper that he had found on the floor. "To make sure this isn't accidentally found, I'm destroying it. So if you can't find it, that's why." He showed her the paper as he approached her.

"It's the note for the down payment on Margie and Paul's house. Don't you want them to pay it back?"

"They know they owe us. If they pay it back--fine. If not, we'll live without it. I just don't want anyone else to know about this. Taking a book of matches out of his pocket, he lit the paper. Tossing it onto the ground, he watched it transform into black, crumbled pieces of ash. Into the house he walked, nothing more needed to be said, in his opinion.

She watched Otto disappear into the house. It was part of her money also, but she had no say. She didn't mind giving things to Margie. It just would be nice if after all their years of marriage he would just include her. Oh well, she was no longer going to let that annoy her. She went to the front of the house and continued raking the lawn and covering her plants.

****

A soft, white blanket had covered the earth during the night, and everything was white as far as a person could see. The wet snow had clung to the deciduous trees' barren branches and flocked the greenery of the spruce. No school today. Yesterday had been Thanksgiving. The snow would be great for tracking the deer. However, first the farm chores would have to be done. He shook his older brother's shoulder. "Wake up, Eddy! We got to do chores! Hurry, so we can go hunting before the snow disappears." Hurriedly, he got dressed.

Eddy peeked his head out from under the covers. He wasn't enthusiastic about going hunting. It was his thought that a deer was too beautiful to shoot for the minute amount of meat a person actually got from it to eat. Nevertheless, it was time to get up for chores.

With chores finished, the rest of the day was theirs to do with as they wanted until it was time for the night chores.

"Come along with me, Eddy." Jeffery grabbed into the closet and pulled out his dad's 4-10 by the steel-rifled barrel mounted on its wooden stock. Reaching up onto the shelf, he pulled down a box of cartridges. "Get your coat! Let's go!" He headed toward the door.

"Where are you going with your dad's gun?" Lucy entered the house.

"We're going hunting. If I get a deer, it'll save us on meat. We don't have to butcher a cow so soon," Jeffery commented.

"Ya, that's a good idea. Eddy, go along. Help save this family some money," Lucy remarked.

"But I don't have a license," replied Eddy.

"So what! Be smart enough not to get caught. You get caught. You pay the fine yourself." Lucy held the door open for them to go outside.

"I don't like shooting the deer," said Eddy.

"There are a lot of things I don't like either, but I have to do them. Now get going," Lucy commanded.

Across the fields they walked, following a fresh set of deer tracks that led toward their Uncle John's farm. From the field, they could see John leave the farm in his truck.

"Let's go and play with Brownie for a while." Jeffery had seen the dog follow John's truck down the driveway.

"John's not home, I don't think it would be right of us to snoop around his property. Let's go home." Eddy stopped.

"Come on, we're just going to play with the dog." He pulled on Eddy's sleeve.

As they neared the farm buildings, Brownie began to bark.

"Hey, Brownie, it's just us," Jeffery yelled.

Recognizing the boys, Brownie ceased barking and came toward the boys waging her tail.

Eddy bent over and stroked the dog.

Up to the house the boys and Brownie walked.

Jeffery broke a branch off one of the trees and broke it into several small pieces about a foot long. "Go get it, Brownie." Jeffery flung one of the small pieces of the broken branch out into the field.

In a wildly, playful manner, Brownie ran into the field where the stick had landed, picked up the stick with her mouth, and returned it to Jeffery.

Removing the stick from Brownie's mouth, Jeffery flung the stick out into the field again.

Brownie once again retrieved it.

"You throw it, Eddy." Taking the stick out of Brownie's mouth, Jeffery handed it to Eddy.

Eddy stroked Brownie then also flung the stick into the field. "Go get it, girl." After ruffling her fluffy collar with his hand, he released her from his touch.

Meanwhile, standing in back of Eddy, Jeffery inserted a cartridge into the firing chamber. By means of steel-bladed front sight, he aimed the 4-10. With his finger, he exerted a squeezing action on the metal trigger. His target was in sight.

The squeezing action disengaged a catch that held the hammer against its spring. In return, the spring hurled the hammer against the cartridge, which struck the primer in the cartridge case. The powder then ignited, and the explosion of the powder sent the bullet out the 4-10's muzzle. The 4-10 forced itself back against Jeffery's shoulder.

BANG!

The loud sound startled Eddy. His ears rung from the explosion so close to his body. He stood shocked in disbelief as he saw Brownie fall quick in her tracks as she was running toward him with the stick in her mouth. Around her fallen, deadened body, the red liquid of life oozed out onto the white snow.

"My, God! What have you done? Why? Why, Jeffery?" A hand grabbed at Eddy as he started to run out into the field.

"She's dead. There is no sense going out there. We have to get out of here before John comes back," said Jeffery.

"You shot her. I think you should tell John," said Eddy.

"Are you crazy?" Jeffery held his grip on Eddy's arm. "You better keep your mouth shut. Maybe this incident is just a sample of what could accidentally happen to you if you don't keep this secret and the one about Angela."

Eddy shivered from the cold look in Jeffery's eyes. The coldness of his devilish eyes pierced Eddy's soul like cold slivers of ice.

What kind of a brother did he have? They had the same parents. How could he be so evil? Yes, it was evil what Jeffery was becoming. What he had done to Angela was terrible and now this to Brownie. Had he killed Brownie as an example of things to happen if he revealed the two secrets he now kept about his brother? Hideous secrets--too hard to believe! To say anything would be foolish. Jeffery had an excuse for everything. He stood in awe as Jeffery had lied away what had really happened to Angela. He knew the truth because he had seen what Jeffery had done to her.

"Let's go home." Eddy pulled away from Jeffery.

"We're going down the driveway and then out onto the road. They can't follow our tracks there because almost all of the snow is melted on road, and its full of vehicle tracks. They'll never know who did it." Down the driveway he went.

Eddy followed, afraid to walk in front of his brother. It was terrible to have such a fear of one's own brother. Although he would still have to share the same bedroom with his brother, he would not sleep in the same bed. The floor would be fine. He could not let anyone know things had changed--for fear of his life. Silence and a withdrawing inward of himself would be the safest, and so it would be from that moment on.

It seemed like the long walk home would never end. Finally, there they were walking into the house.

"Come on, Pa. Eat this." They heard their mother's voice.

Eddy walked toward his grandfather's bedroom door that was ajar. She must have forgot to lock it as she usually did. Slowly, he pushed against the door. His eyes widened at the sight of the man lying in the bed. Was he even alive? Was he even a man? Surely, this could not be his grandfather! His eyes were sunk deep within his skull. His wrinkles of age hung in flabby folds on his gray, skeletal face. His straggly, thin, gray hair draped over his bony shoulder joints that protruded from under a blanket, a blanket that outlined every inch of his skeleton.

"What are you doing here?" asked his mother.

Caught in a trance of unreality, he did not hear or even see her.

"Now you know why I didn't want anyone to come in here," said his mother defensively as she saw the shocked look on Eddy's face.

Hearing her this time, he looked at her. What should he think? Had she done this to him or was this deterioration of the body from the advancement of age? The vision in his mind of his grandfather had suddenly changed and was replaced with this one. This was not how he wanted to remember him, but he would. He could not change what he had seen.

His grandfather turned his eyes in the direction that Lucy had been looking and talking. Oh, my God! It was Eddy. The corners of his mouth turned up into a mere smile. Oh, my Eddy--my Eddy. His mind knew these words that he could not utter.

"I'll take care of Grandpa. I'm old enough."

"Yes, that you are." She handed him the bowl of soup and the spoon. "In fact, I think you are old enough to have full responsibility of taking care of Grandpa in addition to the same farm chores you have now." To her relief, her father had finally signed the paper. Therefore, there was no need to continue the control she exercised over him earlier. In addition, she was sick of taking care of him. Whatever happened now would be on Eddy's shoulder. She left the room.

Inside his soul, Eddy cried at the sight of his grandfather as he slowly fed him. He was not going to let him die. He would get him back to what he was before. Could he? Maybe all he could do was watch him die? Nevertheless, he would try. He would ask his mother for the key. When he was not around, he would keep his grandfather's bedroom door locked. He feared what Jeffery was capable of doing. Caring for grandfather would keep him busy and it was a good excuse for not being around Jeffery. However, that was not his reason--he loved his grandfather.

Chapter 20
****
Last Wish Before Death

Red buds were developing into foliage on the branches of the massive silver maples that graced the new, bright green grass of spring. On the grass, a robin was struggling to pull a worm out of the ground--food for her young? Herself? Spring--a time of new beginnings--life. She finished watering the indoor plant that set on the wooden flower stand in front of her viewing window.

She was in a nostalgic mood that had started at the beginning of the week and had lingered until today, Sunday. It was a good name for today. The sun's rays already brighten these early hours. She would be out of character today and do something that she had not done for such a long time. Something she had always done in her youth. Maybe it was her feeling of going back in time for a little while, yet knowing she really wasn't going back at all. She wanted to see it and be there one more time. Why? To do it before she could not anymore, which was a future possibility. She had lived beyond the years that God had noted in the Bible that a person should live. She had lived fourscore and ten. As such, she had lived on borrowed time for the last twenty years. The boy was eight. He did not really need her anymore and isn't that when it is time to leave--when one is not needed anymore. Of course, if God gave her more years, she would take them. She had more than she had ever planned on; every day she thanked her special friend--her only true friend--for that. How could she have tried to do something like that? There would have been less people in the world to love others. Enough of such thoughts, if she wanted to do that today, she would have to start her work now. She had to be done before they went to ten o'clock Mass.

The crackling sound of the lard and chicken frying in the pan on her gas stove filled the kitchen. Out of the refrigerator she took a bowl of cold potatoes that she had boiled yesterday. At the sink, she removed their soft brown jackets and sliced the white potatoes into a bowl. Finished with that, she cooked up a dressing for the potatoes and garnished them with it. Onto a piece of clean cloth, which she had placed on the counter, she placed the fried chicken to cool and soak up some of the grease.

"Great-grandma, that smells good. Why are you making it before church?" The small boy, wearing flannel pajamas, walked up to the counter and viewed the chicken.

"Because after church we are going to do what I used to always do after church--but only when the weather was nice." She smiled at him as she turned the pieces of chicken in the frying pan.

"What did you used to do?" The boy quickly removed his finger from the hot piece of chicken, which was lying on the cloth and that he had just touched.

"It will be a surprise. I'm the only one who will know."

"Not even Daddy?"

"No, he doesn't know either. Last year he promised me that he would take me there the first day the weather was nice in spring." She put another piece of fried chicken on the cloth. Finished frying the chicken, she made the small boy breakfast and then walked up the flight of stairs to the second floor. Clutching her hand to the newel, she rested her tired legs before proceeding up the other staircase into the walk-in attic. Her climb was slow, as she felt her heart pounding against her ribs and her lungs gasping for her next breath. While resting in the attic, she surveyed the attic for what she wanted and knew was there. Seeing it, she slowly walked over to the item and picked it up--a brown wickerwork basket. Rubbing her hands over it removed years and years of accumulated dust. She handled it with care. It held so many memories. It was one of the few things her true friend had taken when she left that place. A vision of her father making the basket floated in her mind. He was a very precious man to her and to her true friend. Wiping the tears of reminiscence from her aged cheeks, she very carefully guarded her every step down the stairs into the kitchen.

"What you got there, Great-grandma?" asked the boy as he cleaned the soft, yellow yoke of the egg off his plate with a buttered piece of toast.

"A picnic basket. Your great-great-grandpa made it. Someday when I die, I want you to have it. Today when we come back from that place, I'm putting it in your closet so you don't forget."

"Oh, Great-grandma, you won't die." He finished his glass of milk.

"There comes a time when God's angels come to get us all. The angels take us into heaven to be with God and the others that his angels have taken." She touched the soft, young skin of his cheek.

"Is that what happened to Mommy?"

"Yes, the angels came and now she watches you from heaven every day."

"Great-grandma, you won't leave me too, will you?" He clutched her hand. He did not want her to die and leave him alone.

"Don't be afraid if the angels come. Be happy for me. I'm old and this life is getting hard for me. Oh, heaven is such a nice place, and I would always be with you--every minute of the day and night. Your mom and I would be watching you--enough of such talk! We better get dressed for church or for a change we will be the late ones, not your dad." After clearing the table of the dirty dishes and wiping it with a damp cloth, she packed the picnic basket, washed the dishes, took off her bib apron, hung it on a hook behind the kitchen door, and went into her bedroom to get dressed in her Sunday dress. The pink of the dress seemed to illuminate her face with a tinge of color. Using a big hat pin, she secured a wide-rimmed pink hat to her white hair that was set in soft, flowing waves. With white gloves adorning her small hands, she grabbed a white leather purse out of her closet, and put the loose change that was lying on her dresser into the purse. Wearing white pumps, she walked into the living room, sat in her rocker, and watched out her viewing window for the sight of John's truck.

A few minutes later, the small boy was standing in front of her, with his usual Sunday morning problem. She smiled to herself as she reached for the tie that dangled around his neck. With her old hands she performed magic and tied his tie for him. "You are a handsome one." Hugging him close to her, she kissed his freckled cheek.

"Daddy's here." He turned in the direction of the loud BANG, which came from the truck, lacking a muffler, that had just turned into her driveway.

"Yes, he is." Rising from the rocker, she took the boy's hand and walked outside onto the porch.

"Good morning, Grandma--Jimmy, I didn't hear the church bells ring yet, so I must be early." Getting out of the truck, he walked up to them.

They laughed at the joke between them. Then they proceeded toward the church located at the end of the block. Jimmy walked between them, each of them holding onto one of his hands.

"Great-grandma has a surprise for us, Daddy." His face gleamed with a smile as he looked up at his father.

"She does?" John smiled at his grandmother.

"After church could you please take me to the place we had talked about last year?"

"I promised you the first nice day, and I will keep my promise."

"Oh, thank you. Thank you so much, John." Her eyes glimmered with gratitude.

"It's no problem, Grandma. Now what's this surprise?"

"I'll tell you after church."

"Oh, Great-grandma, please tell us--please. I won't be able to think of God in church. I'll be thinking about the surprise. Please, tell us, please!"

"All right." She couldn't resist Jimmy's ocean-blue eyes.

"We're going on a picnic."

"Where--where?" Jimmy's eyes lit with excitement.

"Where I used to go--many--many years ago." She wondered what the place looked like now. Would the memories of that time bring her only sadness now? Maybe--maybe not? There were good memories there also. Nothing is ever always bad. To dwell on only the bad was to poison a person's body with bitterness and such bitterness only makes a person think that their life isn't worth living. She was lucky to learn such a lesson when she did. Life has no room for bitterness.

Anticipating the picnic and the visit to that place, made church seem so long. Finally, Mass came to a conclusion, and they joined the other parishioners in departing the church. Outside the church, at the bottom of the numerous cement church steps, the priest greeted them and the other parishioners with a friendly "hi" and a gentle handshake.

John, holding Jimmy's hand, socialized with the priest while his grandmother walked behind the church into the cemetery.

"Why does Great-grandma go there every Sunday after church?"

"She visits a very special person," John replied.

"Who--Great-grandpa?"

"No, her special--true friend."

"Why can't I ever go with her?"

"She likes that time alone."

"Did you ever go with her?"

"Yes, when I was very small."

"Why could you go and I can't?"

"When Grandma wants you to go with her, she'll let you know."

"Who is her special friend?"

"My goodness, Jimmy, you do ask a lot of questions?" The priest ruffled Jimmy's bronze-colored hair.

At the grave she knelt and bowed her head. There she talked as she had always done, telling her true friend of the week's happenings and of today's plans. "One more time before I leave this world I want to go back. I don't know what I will feel, but I want to see it. Time has been so long and lonely without you. Oh, I have the boy, but he fills another part of my life. The part you filled is so empty--so very empty. Good-bye, my friend, until next time--maybe next time I'll be seeing you."

"Great-grandma, Great-grandma, can we go on the picnic now? Can we?" Getting a glimpse of her coming around the back corner of the church, Jimmy quickly freed himself of John's hand and ran toward her.

"We sure can." She hugged him close to her. "You are my little sweetheart. Let's go to the house and get our picnic basket."

"Oh, boy, this is going to be fun. Come on, Daddy." He tugged at John's brown suit trousers.

"See you next Sunday, Father." With a smile and a wave John was pulled down the street by Jimmy.

"We'll get the basket, Grandma. You wait in the truck for us."

By the time Grandmother reached the truck, John and Jimmy were coming out of the house and down the porch steps with the basket.

John helped her up onto the running board and onto the truck seat.

"I want to hold the basket." Jimmy commented as his father lifted him onto the seat next to his great-grandmother.

So it was. Jimmy held the basket, while John drove following his grandmother's directions.

The last time she had been on this road, she was lying in the back of a wagon. Her body was being tumbled around by the crude country road. The bright sun was glowing down on her as she turned to see the driver of the wagon. It was her friend, of course, who else would have interfered with her attempt. She remembered how at first she cried that she had been prevented from succeeding. However, time and her friend had deterred her from any more destructive ideas. In fact, with the passing of time, she thanked her truly special friend for what she had done. And time went on--giving her all these years. Her only regret was that her friend had not been allowed to share all these years with her.

The road across the open farm fields passed over a railroad track and then a wooden bridge over a stream. They took a fork in the road that traveled away from Beechwood into an area of young woods, driving parallel with the railroad track.

"I think this is the place." She tried to find something recognizable but there was nothing except the track and the rumbling, thunderous sound of a rapid, flowing stream. An inward sense, so unexplainable, made her feel as if this was the place. Then, in the distance, she could see the ruins of a fieldstone foundation. Trees and more trees crowded into the deteriorated foundation. Yes, this was the place! A feeling of coming home tranquilized her body. "Come, let's go!"

"Grandma, are you sure? There is a lot of underbrush. It's not going to be easy walking through it." John got out of the truck and went around to the passenger side to help her.

"I've done a lot harder things than this. I came here for a reason. I'm not leaving until I do what I came here for." Under the towers of green maple and oaks, over the black, humus soil, just sprouting with new seedling growth, she walked. Stopping every now and then to relive a scene from the past. Amongst the intertwined overgrowth, the charred foundation told of the event that had caused this place to disappear. She could not keep her eyes from the place where the other building--the barn--had stood. Instinctively, her hands went to her neck where they felt the lumpy growth of a scar that was a constant reminder of that night. Then she grabbed Jimmy's hand and caressed it in hers. "Thank you, God! Oh, thank you so much!"

"Are you all right, Grandma?"

"Oh, yes, I'm very much all right." Hovering over Jimmy, she clasped him closely within her arms.

"Great-grandma, can we eat your chicken soon." Jimmy rubbed his growling stomach.

"Yes, follow me. I know a very nice place for a picnic." Holding his hand, she led them to the edge of a stream. The old oak was gone but another tree had taken its place--and so it was with life.

She spent the afternoon telling them the stories that were associated with the area and her life. Only the last days of her life here did she omit, the days of deception, betrayal, and the complete draining of her soul that had led her to attempt the most unforgettable event of her life. She had dealt with that and there was no need for anyone to know. It had been their secret--from the time her true friend, Molly, had found her and cut the rope from the rafter.

"Your great-grandpa was one of the people killed in the fire that destroyed this town and the surrounding area."

"Were you here also, Great-grandma?"

"No. By the grace of God, Molly and I were in Jennings."

"Why weren't you here? Who is Molly?" Jimmy asked.

"Because God didn't want us here, he knew you were supposed to be born. If I had been here with Great-grandpa, there would be no Jimmy. Molly was my true friend."

"Why did God let Great-grandpa die?"

"God has a purpose for everything. He always does what's best."

"Where did you live? Wasn't it hard without Grandpa?" asked John.

"Molly had sold some property that she had owned. With that money, she bought a big Victorian house. We converted the enormous parlor and dining room into an eating area. Molly was the best cook. She taught me everything I know. Together we raised your dad. I wish you could have known her. She was such a wonderful person, an angel--my guardian angel from God." A smile graced her face.

"What happened to her, Great-grandma?"

"Every morning Molly would get up early and make the coffee for the restaurant. The aroma would fill the entire downstairs and upstairs. I would wake up, and the aroma always made me feel so good. One morning I woke up, and she wasn't awake yet. When she didn't answer my knocks on her bedroom door, I ventured inside and found that she had passed away in her sleep. That's how I want to die. I just want to go to sleep and wake up in heaven."

With those words there was silence. She had faced her immortality and would not fight the inevitable. Quietly, she absorbed all the sights of nature that still flourished in this area--a brown deer, with its white tufted tail, serenely grazing on young, tender grass--a swift, flying swallow, with its long, graceful, blue-pointed wings and forked tail, swooping low to caught insects in midair--the sound of the small, gray-breasted, white-cheeked sparrows chirping in the trees--a brown, furry muskrat nipping on a green plant at the muddy edge of the sparkling blue stream. Away it swam as Jimmy waded barefoot into the water with his Sunday trousers rolled up to his knees. She enjoyed watching him play in the water as all boy's like to do. To her those were the best things in life and to think she almost lost it all because of her ridiculous concern about other people's deception. It took almost that tragedy for her to realize that other people's words and deeds are not important. Instead, it was how she lived her life that really mattered. Contentment caressed her soul. She found great happiness in knowing that she would leave the world a better place because of the three extra people the world was blessed with because she had lived.

****

Quietly, he sat at the table, deep in thought. What was he going to do? How was he going to provide for his family? He watched her remove the soiled supper dishes from the table. She moved in a slow, tired manner. She'd smile, but her eyes lacked their usual luster. Another month and then it would be over for her. The baby would be born. How would he pay for the hospital bill if he couldn't even make this month's insurance premium payment? Before the strike the factory, where he worked, had taken care of that. Damn it! Why did they have to go on strike? Just one more month and the insurance wouldn't matter so much. Damn it! Reaching into the pack of cigarettes in his shirt pocket, he took out a cigarette and lit it. Puffing on the cigarette, he watched the children sitting on the wooden floor beside the tall, reddish-brown floor radio. Attentively, they listened to their favorite show, *The Lone Ranger*.

"My, you're quiet tonight." She wiped the table clean.

"Oh, just thinking." There was no need to bother her. There was nothing she could do. She was in the same situation. If he told her, she would upset herself worrying.

"What time are we going to the wake?" With her hands submerged in a sink full of white bubbles, she began to wash the dishes.

"I don't know. I was thinking of asking Ma if maybe she could watch the kids for a little while so we could go to the wake together. I really don't like to take the kids to see a dead person." He took another puff of his cigarette.

"I agree, but you know your parents." She placed the washed ashtray on the table in front of him.

"After all the times I've helped them out, she surely could watch the kids for an hour. I'm going over there now." Finishing his cigarette, he smothered it out in the ashtray and rose from the table. "You kids want to come along with me?"

"Where are you going?" Angela asked.

"Grandpa and Grandma."

"Ya, I'll go along," one of the boys replied.

"What about you two?"

"No." They sat with their ears perked for the next spoken word on the radio.

"Good luck. Somehow I don't think I'll be going to the wake, or the kids will be coming with us."

After hugging her and giving her a short kiss, he left the house. With the boy's small hand in his, they walked over to the car. Setting the small boy beside him on the car's front seat, he traveled the country road into town. Passing the place Rosalia and he used to live, he turned into his parents' driveway.

"Hi, Mrs. Benson." Mikie lifted the small boy out of the car.

"Hi, Mikie." Looking up from the flower bed she had been hoeing in, she waved. "How is Rosalia? I don't see her very much anymore."

"She's got one more month left." Mikie carried the small boy up to the house and knocked on the door.

"Say 'hi' to her for me. It was nice seeing you, Mikie." Finished with hoeing, she went into the garage to put the hoe away.

Following his knock, the door opened.

"Mikie, what do you want?" Although she seemed annoyed at his visit, she did motion him inside.

"How do you like your new television?" Mikie sat on a kitchen chair and set the blonde, curly haired boy on the floor.

Climbing onto a kitchen chair, the small boy stretched his short arm toward the candy dish, centering the table.

"No, you don't." Pamela grabbed the jar away from him and set it on top of the white refrigerator out of the small boy's reach. The candy was for others, not for him.

Mikie was hurt, especially since Margie's children were allowed to eat as much as they desired. "Come sit on my lap, Thomas." Mikie reached his arms out to Thomas and held him on his lap. Should he ask her or not? It would be either a "yes" or "no." What had he to lose? "Are you and Dad going to the wake, tomorrow night?"

"Of course, John is a customer. We didn't really know Kate O'Leary, but she was his grandma." She walked up to the television.

"What time are you going?"

"As soon as your dad comes home from his cattle route." She began to turn the station channel.

"Do you think you could watch the kids for a while so Rosalia and I can go? We'd go at three o'clock. We would be back here before Dad came home."

"You can take care of your own kids like everyone else does." Having found the station she desired, she moved away from the television.

Like everyone else! Except Margie! Ya--sure--mother--whatever! How many times did she have to say "no" before he would really believe that she didn't care about him? Should he ask her for help in paying the insurance premium? The answer would probably be "no," but maybe he should ask. No, he had too much pride to ask. It was his family, and he could support them. No, to be realistic, he could not and would have to swallow his pride. His family came before pride.

"I hate to ask, but I need a few dollars to make the monthly insurance payment before Rosalia has the baby. Otherwise, the insurance will not pay the hospital bill. Do you think you and Dad could borrow me the money? I'll pay you back a little every month."

"What do you do with your money? Thought working in the factory was going to make you rich." She sat in the chair at the desk.

"The strike was something unexpected. I didn't vote for it but the majority did. I have to go along with the rest of the union employees. Strike pay isn't very much, but we can survive without any extras. It's just that I can't pay this month's premium. After the baby is born, it doesn't matter. We can go without insurance. We did before. Just one more payment to keep Rosalia and the baby's expenses covered by the insurance--just one more month."

"Well, if it's that important, then I suggest you better learn to handle the money you do get better. Maybe you should stay out of the taverns then you would have more money."

"I don't go in the taverns when I'm not working. When I was working, I'd only stop for a beer or two maybe one or two nights after work. I haven't stopped since the strike began. I'm not--" Mikie stopped--"like Dad"--words like that were best left unsaid.

Huh! She thought! Men are all alike--fathers--husbands--sons--all alike! Women--sex--booze--all they think about--all they do. She looked over at the kitchen sofa where Otto lay asleep. Empty brown bottles lined the floor beside the sofa. He was probably having a sexually exciting dream. Even when they're asleep, that's probably all they still think--dream about.

"We don't have any money to give you," she snapped back.

"Thanks for all the help."

"Don't get sarcastic with me. You made your bed with Rosalia. Now you lay in it. Margie had plenty of girls for you from influential families, but you wouldn't think of going out with them. Well, you picked her. Now you live with her."

"I guess we'll be going now." He set Thomas on the floor and rose from the chair. "See you later, Ma." Taking Thomas's hand, they walked out of the house. She had said enough about Rosalia. He hoped that the boy was too small to notice or remember the overtones of dislike in the conversation. With his mother's negative feelings about Rosalia, probably it was best that she did not take care of the children. His concern was that she would malign Rosalia in the children's presence. In his opinion, it was not good for children to hear bad things about their mother. The children loved their mother and to hear others talk badly about her may make the children think badly about themselves. After all, they were a part of her. If there was something bad about their mother, they may think there was also something bad about them.

What would he do? As he drove past John's farm, he thought maybe John could use some help on the farm. Farmers are always busy from spring until fall. He could work before he had to walk in the strike line and after he had his daily walking hours in. However, it would not be appropriate to ask now. It was a time of grieving for John--the wake--the funeral. Something would come up. God always took care of them in the past and he would now also. As long as Rosalia and the baby would be all right that was all that was important.

Arriving back home, Mikie parked the car, lifted Thomas out of the car, and sat on the porch steps. Lighting a cigarette, Mikie watched Thomas join the other two children at the edge of last year's vegetable garden. There they played amongst the soft ground. It saddened him that he had no extra money to get them a load of sand. In the ground they played with cars Rosalia had made from empty matchboxes. With crayons, she had designed each car differently, so each of the children knew which one was theirs. It was her hope that would eliminate fighting amongst the children. Using small gravel stones from the driveway, they each set the boundaries of their property. As they played in their world of imagination, he thought about what he had done. Had he made a terrible mistake buying this place? He knew it needed fixing, and he had planned to do some repairs every year. Now those plans, without a job--without money --were useless. What had he done to Rosalia and the children? The weathered house needed paint on the peeling clapboards. The rotten windows, which allowed the snow to blow inside the house, needed to be replaced. However, for this winter, he would have to put plastic on the windows and secure the plastic to the house with wooden laths.

Rosalia would have to continue to heat her own hot water. They would have to continue using the outhouse for bathroom facilities in the rain, snow, hail--whatever the weather. If only this would not have happened--if only he had his job. His plans were now just hopeless dreams.

****

Driving into the yard, he recognized the car parked in front of the house. It was Alex's.

"Hi, there, Jimmy," Mikie greeted the boy, who was sitting on the porch steps, as he got out of the car. As he approached the porch, he noticed how the place had changed over the years. The roses, which had flourished under Lori's care, were all brown with death. Weeds had overgrown every inch of the flower beds. Pete's wicker rocker had turned brown with decay from years of weather exposure. Shriveled leaves and blown dust from the fields had accumulated on the unswept porch.

"Hi." The boy's face was dressed in a scowl.

"Your dad in the house?" Mikie stopped at the bottom of the steps.

"Yup."

"You can't take care of the boy properly. He needs a motherly person around at such a young age." A voice radiated through the walls of the house to the outside, within their hearing distance.

"I can take care of him just fine. He is my son, and I'll decide what's best for him."

"You don't know the first thing about raising a child."

"And you do?"

"Yes, I do. I've raised two fine boys."

"You can talk all you want. You're not going to change my mind. He's not going to live with you."

"It would be best for the boy."

"The only reason you want him is for the work he can do."

"John, that is a terrible thing to say. It's not true."

"Who are you trying to convince? Yourself? You didn't want him when he was small."

"I never said I didn't want him. It's just that I had Pa to take care of also."

"That's not the way I remember things. Nothing has changed

except that the boy is bigger and old enough to work now."

"Eddy takes care of Pa now. So I would have time for the boy."

"No, you would work him to death. Jimmy is staying with me!"

"You shouldn't judge me by yourself."

"What are you talking about?"

"You're the one who wants him for the work."

"Get out of here, Lucy."

"We'll see who gets the boy."

"What are you going to do? Get your lawyer friend, Fremont's son, to help you. I heard people talk in the tavern that you've been to see him lately. What have you been scheming? How to get the boy if and when my grandma died. Well, Grandma is dead and there's nothing your young sleazy lawyer can do to get him. No matter how much money you slip him 'under the table.' Now get out of here!"

"Very well, you'll see how nice it will be." How dare he order her out of a house that should--by all rights--be hers. Storming out the door, Lucy slammed it behind her. "Oh, hi, Mikie." Startled by his presence for a second, she quickly smiled. She had hoped that he had not heard the conversation and hoped her smile would cover the guilty look on her face. It was true. She did want the boy only for work. As she walked toward the car, she couldn't help but snicker inside her soul as she thought of his remark about her visits to the lawyer. If he only knew what those visits were really about. He was such a fool. Did he actually think she would spend money to get that boy? She had spent her money on something worth a lot more. What she had paid Fremont for his "dirty tricks" was nothing compared to what she would reap--all in good time--all in good time.

"Hi, Mikie, good to see you. How long have you been here?" John asked.

"Just got here." He didn't want John to know that he had overheard such a personal conversation.

Turning the key in the ignition, Lucy again snickered as she spoke to herself, "You fool, John, you stupid fool." With that she sped out of the driveway.

"I don't like her, Daddy. I don't want to live with her." Jimmy's face was so sad.

"You're not living with anyone but me." John sat on the step next to Jimmy and patted his knee in reassurance. "So how is Rosalia and the new baby?"

"They're doing fine." Mikie joined them on the steps.

"Four kids and three are boys. What are you trying to do overpopulate the town with Aslens?"

They both chuckled.

"So how have things been going with you?" Mikie inquired.

"Well, to tell you the truth, Mikie, I could use some help baling hay and later combining the oats. Do you think maybe you could help me out once and awhile?" John had guessed that was why Mikie had come. He had heard people talk in the tavern about how Mikie had been inquiring at some of the Beechwood businesses for part-time work. John suggested the need for help to alleviate any embarrassment Mikie would feel in asking.

"You tell me when, and I'll help." Mikie was enthusiastic.

"Whenever you don't have to walk the strike line is fine with me."

"Thanks, John."

"How long do you think the strike will last?"

"The company doesn't want to give on any of the factory employees' request. It doesn't look very good for the strike to end for quite sometime. The worst thing is that most other businesses don't want to hire someone out on strike. They figure, as soon as the strike is settled, you'll be leaving. I really can't blame them. However, if I would get so lucky as to be offered a full-time job, I'm quitting that factory--the hell with the strike pay."

"Ya, I don't blame you. Hey, you want to come with us?"

"Where you going?"

"To Lyra's for supper. Come along we haven't been out together for a long time." He took a pack of cigarettes out of his shirt pocket and offered Mikie a cigarette.

"No, I better be getting home. Thomas is asleep in the car." Mikie grabbed a cigarette. "Thanks." Taking a book of matches out of his worn shirt pocket, he lit both their cigarettes.

Silence filled the evening air as they puffed on their cigarettes. How opposite their lives were now. Mikie had a wife and children but no money. John had money but no wife and only one child. Mikie was glad he had the children and Rosalia, but somehow a little money would also be nice. John was pleased with his money and the farm, but he wished he had a wife to help him and love him. Nevertheless, they each took the days as they came and never regretted how life had treated them. After all, a person can't have it all--can they?

"Well, I'll be leaving now." Mikie snuffed out his finished cigarette with his foot as he rose from the step. "I'll come after my strike walk tomorrow to help you."

"That'll be fine with me. See you then." John rose from the step. "Ready to go, Jimmy?"

Jimmy rose from the step.

Together they walked toward the truck. As John drove the truck with Jimmy sitting beside him, they followed Mikie in his car down to the end of John's driveway. Once again their paths took different turns. John going toward town to Lyra's. Mikie going away from town to his house.

As he drove, Mikie would look back at Thomas sleeping on the back seat. He tried to treat all his children the same, and he did. He never wanted to show favoritism toward any of his children. From experience, he knew how such a thing could hurt a child. In his heart, he loved all his children.

However, he had a closer relationship with Thomas. Thomas was the one who always went along with him when he went to the store, to his parents' place, to John's place. Thomas was the one who constantly climbed onto his lap after a meal as he listened to the radio or just sat outside on the steps. Thomas was the one who followed him when he took a walk into the garden or along the country road to the asparagus or the wild berry patch. Sometimes Thomas seemed like a shadow--a good shadow. Tender thoughts of the boy caused a smile to grace his face as he drove into his driveway.

How long could he keep the house? Mikie wondered as he stopped the car and gazed around. The mortgage was hard to pay. Especially since he had the additional monthly installments to the hospital for bills that had incurred because he had no health insurance. If things got too bad financially, he had contemplated putting the house up for sale. However, that would be his last resort. Deep in his heart, he wouldn't like to do that.

Stopping the car, Mikie got out of it, pushed the top of the front car seat ahead, and reached back to lift sleeping Thomas into his arms. Just then Thomas awoke. Rubbing his eyes, he sat up on the back seat. "Where are we?"

"We're home." Mikie reached to help sleepy Thomas out of the car.

"Hi, Daddy," the other children yelled from the smooth ground they were playing in.

"Hi, kids!" He waved and smiled at them as he went into the house. He still regretted not being able to buy them sand to play in.

Thomas followed his father into the house and reposed on the sofa.

"How did things go?" Rosalia was rocking in her chair as she nursed Frankie.

"I can work for John. He said any time I want to work is fine with him."

"That'll help." Rosalia smiled. "If only Frankie wouldn't be so small, I could get a job." She gently rubbed his small fingers in her hand.

"No, Rosalia, the kids need a full-time mother. Besides, there is no one to take care of the kids. It's better this way. We'll be fine. Things will be all right." He sat next to Thomas on the sofa. "Right, Thomas." He gently rubbed Thomas's shoulder blades.

"Right, Dad." Thomas smiled and then went to sleep.

While smoking his cigarette, Mikie watched Thomas sleep, Rosalia nurse Frankie, and through the window his other children playing. He worried. The words were easy to say. Easier than it was to make them reality.

****

At Lyra's, Jimmy and John sat at a table eating their supper. Jimmy didn't eat much of the meat, potatoes, or corn. He was saving room in his stomach for other things a little later in the evening. After supper, John would sit at the bar, drink, and socialize with Lyra and some of his acquaintance that stopped frequently at Lyra's.

Little Jimmy spent his time using a wooden, long, tapering rod to strike the colored, numbered, hard balls on an oblong, green table with raised, cushioned edges. Occasionally, he'd interrupt his father and ask for a glass of soda or a bag of treats--potato chips, pretzels, popcorn. Sometimes, if some of the men needed an extra card player, they'd ask Jimmy to play. He was quite a good player. Of course, he had a lot of practice. Ever since he lived with his father, he had spent every night in the tavern. Needless to say, he was also a very good billiard player.

Most of Lyra's patrons left early because of work the next day. However, John and Jimmy stayed until closing. By this time, Jimmy had fallen asleep at a table. His legs dangled from the seat of a chair; his head rested on his folded arms that set on the table.

With the tavern closed, the lights out, and Jimmy still sleeping, Lyra and John disappeared upstairs as usual. Awhile later, John reappeared in the barroom with Lyra, dressed in her lingerie. John shook Jimmy's small shoulders until he woke up. Then John guided Jimmy's sleepy body out the door. Before Lyra shut the door, John would give her a kiss and feel between her legs. "Keep it warm for me until tonight."

"Anything for you, John." She returned the kiss, shut the door, and locked it. Inside the dark barroom, she wondered when he would marry her. He always said he loved her. They had been together so long. However, she couldn't ask him. No, she did have some pride. She would wait for him to ask. But when? Her deep desire to marry him caused her heart to bleed.

During the drive home, Jimmy stayed awake. He thought how his life with his great-grandmother had been so different. When he was tired, he'd go to bed. She would tuck him in, sit at the side of the bed, read him a story, kiss him good night, turn out his light, and leave his room. During the summer, he'd help her cut her small lawn, hoe in her garden, and help her harvest her garden vegetables. Great-grandmother's house had a lot of memories--memories--that's all he had now. His grandfather had sold her house, and he could never go back.

Jimmy's childhood was gone. Early every morning he had to help with the milking of the cows. He carried the milk and poured it into the milk cans. When he was finished, he had to clean out the manure in the gutters and the stalls. When they baled hay, he was in the hay mow dragging and stacking the bales. As he got older, he was the person who had to stand on the moving hay wagon and stack the bales of hay onto the wagon as they came out of the hay baler. The hot sun would beat down unmercifully on him, but he had to keep working and keep up to the hay baler. During the harvesting of the oats, he was inside the barn unloading the oats into the granary. The sweat of his body attracted the dust that clouded the hot, humid air. The dust would make him itch, sneeze, and clog his sinuses. In winter, he had to climb up into the tall cement silo. With a pick, he'd loosen the frozen silage from the sides of the cement silo. Then using a barn fork, he'd pitch enough silage down into the barn to feed the cows twice a day. School days were no excuse for not doing the farm chores. He had to do them before and after school--every day. Sometimes he did wonder if his Aunt Lucy was right, "all his dad wanted him for was to do the work." But then, that was probably true of Lucy also.

Chapter 21
****
Sinister Memories

The rays of warm, summer sunlight beamed into the sparsely furnished room--a bed, dresser, and night stand. He didn't need much to live, if his existence could even be called living. He looked out the window where he used to watch two small boys walk across the field from school. The small boys didn't exist anymore. They were grown men now. The oldest boy was getting married after all the outside farm work of filling silos and picking corn was done. His fiancé had brought into his bedroom the glass vase full of brilliant flowers that now set on the dresser near the window. She was a good girl. He was glad when she stopped dating the younger of the two boys and began dating the oldest boy. She'd have a better life with the oldest. Was it terrible to think so badly of one grandson and wish only the best for the other? He had tried over the years not to. Nevertheless, he couldn't dismiss some of the things that he had seen. However, worst than that was his feeling that there was a lot he had not seen.

His eyes gazed long at the old tree that stood outside his window. It brought back a sinister memory: On one of the branches, there sat a nest of young birds. Their necks extending above the nest; their small yellow beaks open and uttering continuously short, shrill tones waiting to be fed. Up into the tree he had seen the youngest boy climb. After getting himself comfortable on the branch, he grabbed one of the noisy, little birds. In the palm of his hand, he held the featherless, black-skinned bird. Then the old man seen a sight that made his stomach turn and twist as if to regurgitate. The boy took a small twig and shoved it into the small bird's open mouth. The boy continued to push the twig down into the bird until the small bird was dead. Returning the dead bird to the nest, he grabbed another chirping bird out of the nest. The boy repeated his actions until all four birds lay dead in the nest.

"Good morning, Grandpa." A young man walked into the bedroom carrying a washbowl in his hands and a towel slung over his broad shoulders.

Grandfather smiled. He was always glad to see that young man.

After setting the washbowl on the night stand near the bed, the young man gently washed his grandfather's face, hands, and arms.

Grandfather felt so refreshed.

Shortly after departing from the bedroom, taking along the washbowl and towel, the young man returned with his grandfather's breakfast--an egg, toast, and a glass of milk. When he finished feeding his grandfather, the young man dressed him, put him into his wheelchair, and set him outside on the porch.

There grandfather sat, passing the time watching others work about the yard and in the fields. Often he'd watch--the milking cows graze; the milk truck come and leave; the vehicles travel the country road near the farm; the cats come home with their dead prey dangling from their mouths; the kittens romp and play; the chickens move about the barnyard with their scratching and pecking at the ground. The morning would go and the Angelus wound ring across the farm fields. It was twelve o'clock--noon. They'd all come home for dinner. The young man would feed his grandfather dinner. After dinner, he'd lay his grandfather on his bed for his usual afternoon nap.

KNOCK! KNOCK!

The door opened. Grandfather woke from his nap.

"Hi, Grandpa, you got some visitors." The young man held the door open.

"Thanks, Eddy." A young male voice outside the room could be heard.

A young girl, dressed in a bright pink dress, entered the room. She had a petite, shapely figure with cascading dark-brown hair, slender nose, and glimmering blue eyes.

Grandfather's eyes were glued to her. Had he died and gone to heaven? He must have! She was dead! He knew that she was dead! He had seen her gravestone. No, he had not died. Had he gone back to that time in his life? Was he a young man again? Was he given a second chance to do things differently? Looking down at his wrinkled hands covered with large, brown age spots, he knew he was here in this room. The same time--place--person he was a moment ago. Confused! What was going on? It was her! He knew it was her! Yet, it couldn't be her! Could it?

"Hi, Grandpa." He heard another voice, but it seemed so far away. The sight of her still entranced him.

"Hi, Grandpa," the voice repeated the greeting. He felt a warm hand touch his.

Looking up, grandfather smiled. It was Jimmy, his Lori's boy, grown into a young man. He was pleased to see him; however, his eyes continued to fix themselves on the young girl.

"Grandpa, this is my girlfriend, Angela Aslen. You know her dad, Mikie Aslen." Jimmy reached over and held her hand as he pulled her closer to the bed and himself.

Angela smiled.

She even has her smile, grandfather thought. Angela's smile brought back the memory of her and all those years that his days had been filled with constant thoughts of her. Finally, he could no longer live with just the thoughts. He had to see her one more time to see if her feelings and his feelings were still as they were that year--so long ago--when it all happened. The year he had let her go and gave her to another. As he went looking for her, he found out the kind of life she had with him, how she had died, and he had also found out about Pamela. He had seen a young woman crying at her grave that day. Later, he had seen the same woman with Otto at his new house in Beechwood when he had delivered roofing supplies for Ewerdt. He had put together the pieces. It wasn't hard. Pamela resembled Todd in some ways. This girl was Betsy's great-granddaughter. It was unbelievable. She resembled Betsy in every way. His grandson and Betsy's great-granddaughter! Was life repeating itself in another generation? Are there certain things that attract people to one another generation after generation? Would his grandson have the chance he never let himself and Betsy have? Would his grandson even want such a chance? How different would both his and Betsy's lives have been if he had left his heart rule instead of his pride and desire for money and for things to be perfect? How foolish youth can be, for nothing in this life is ever perfect. So he learnt as life went on.

He had a feeling about this young girl and Jimmy. It was right for them to be together. He gently squeezed Jimmy's hand as he looked into his eyes. Jimmy please read my eyes, "marry this girl--it's right --I feel it--marry her--don't let her get away. Have the chance I passed by." If only he could talk. Would Jimmy really understand or would he let her go also?

They left, and grandfather wondered if he'd ever see them get married and if they would even consider marriage. Days passed-- months passed and he began to recall so vividly the things from his past. Sometimes, he'd remember the past more clearly than the things that happened an hour ago--a day ago. He remembered how he had told Hans that someday he would go back to Germany and show them all how rich he had become, especially Oslo. Well, Oslo, by now, was a long time dead. No one would even know who Pete Hof was. All the work, for what? He had money in stocks and farms, but yet he lived no better than a pauper. There was only so much he could eat-- drink--wear. At this point it was all irrelevant. He lived from day to day with one thought. What would happen to him when Eddy married? Would Eddy still care for him? Would Jeffery? That thought frightened Pete as much as the thought of Lucy once again taking care of him--or rather--not taking care of him.

The sky became dark and overcast. A storm was coming. The snow soon fell, and the wind began to whirl itself around the barren trees and howl around the house. The cows huddled near the barn door waiting to get in from the storm. The cats would scurry into the barn as soon as a door opened. The empty birds' nests blew from their summer perches on the branches. The wind whistled through the old misfit windows, and the cold crept into the room.

His feet became cold and the coldness graduated up his entire body. The winter of his life had come--and gone.

****

"He maketh me lie down in green pastures . . . ." The clergyman, dressed in black, began reading the twenty-third psalm over the coffin that set above a hole dug for its later containment.

Being his daughter, she stood near his coffin. The words fell upon deaf ears. Her thoughts were too involved with looking at John and the woman who stood beside him. So you're married again, John. Why did your German bride really marry you? For the same reason you married my sister? Turn around is fair play! You reap what you sow! She looked at the small child that stood between them. So you and your German bride have a son now. Which one will get the farm someday, Lori's boy or Bertha's? A farm that should have never been yours but mine instead. She then looked at Jimmy who was holding Angela's hand. Why was she here? They weren't engaged. They were only dating. After what Jeffery told her he had seen last weekend, Jimmy couldn't be too serious about her--Angela, a girl from a large, poor family. Mikie had to sell the homestead back to her because he couldn't afford the mortgage payments. Well, that was all right. She had made money on the deal, and now her son Eddy and his wife lived there. Is Angela pushing herself on Jimmy thinking that he'll inherit some of his grandfather's estate? Well, think again, Angela! She was never about to let that happen--never! In fact, she had taken care of that a long time ago. When her father finally signed that paper, Fremont made everything legal--disinheriting Jimmy.

Jeffery watched Eddy shed tears of grief, then he focused his eyes on Eddy's wife, Sheila. He stared knowing that eventually she'd feel his eyes upon her and look at him. When Sheila did, Jeffery's eyes gave her the most piercing evil look. His eyes glared at her, "you were mine, and you'll be sorry that you ever left me for Eddy."

Sheila trembled, turned from Jeffery, and clung closely to Eddy. How could she have ever gone with Jeffery so long? Why had she thought so little of herself as to think she deserved such treatment?

Eddy, thinking she was shivering from the cold, held her close to his warm body. However, when he looked over at Jeffery, he knew the real reason. Eddy had never had a mean thought in his body or soul, but he vowed to himself that if Jeffery ever touched Sheila--he'd kill him! No one deserved to be treated the way he had treated her--not even an animal.

Jeffery, seeing Eddy look at him, smiled in a complacent manner.

Pamela stared at him for the longest time. In all those years, she had never seen the similarity in appearance until now. Could it be because she had just finished sorting through a box in the attic containing photos? The photo taken the day Otto and she had been married was in the box. The fact that he resembled Otto at about the same age was undeniable. He must have been with her at the same time. He had climbed from her bed into Amanda's. There was no way to deny it. Alex was Otto's son. She looked at Otto--you son of a bitch--I could kill you. Her thoughts were full of rage. She wished her thoughts were daggers that could cut his heart out!

Pamela wished that more now than ever, as she saw Otto stare at Amanda lasciviously. After all these years, was he still climbing into bed with her? Was that why Amanda's husband had disappeared? Had he known about Otto and her? Well, it was a well-kept secret. She had never heard any gossip. But then, no one had ever found out about her and Tony either. The thought of him--Tony--made her smile. That was a happy time in her life.

As Pamela turned from Otto's sight, she saw Angela standing there. Why was she dating Jimmy? He wasn't good enough for her. Jimmy had grown up in a tavern around the vulgar words and drunken stupor of men with low morals who frequent such places. Men like Jimmy's father. The entire town had whispered about his father's lewd relationship with Lyra. Growing up under such circumstances, the boy would probably amount to nothing. Already Jimmy and his friends had been given warnings by the constable because of their excess drinking. Angela--Angela--get rid of him. Date someone who doesn't drink so much, and someone who has a better reputation. Thoughts--thoughts--that's all she could have, she could never say anything to Angela. As her grandmother, she was not very close to Angela, the reason being, her relationship with Mikie. Her reminiscence thoughts made her realize that she had taken her hateful feelings toward Otto out on Mikie. Why on Mikie? Because as his mother, she had a control over him. Something she could never have over Otto. It frustrated her that Otto dominated her. The only way she could retaliate was to dominate Mikie. In addition, she had never allowed herself to get close to Mikie. Why? Was it a defense mechanism? She had loved her father and lost him. She had loved Otto and then lost his love. Was she maybe afraid to love Mikie for fear of losing his love? If she didn't love, she couldn't lose. It had been a safe world that way. It also had been a sad one except for Tony. She had taken a chance loving him. She had not seen him since the accident. His sister from Indiana had taken him to live with her so she could care for him in his disabling condition. Was he still alive? If he was, would he still want her after all these years? Was she too old to find that same happiness they had so long ago? Had he found someone else? Should she find out? Could she get away to see him? Would she want to travel that distance herself? If she went, she had to go alone. If the feelings were still there, what would she do? As usual, she couldn't divorce Otto. She would become an outcast in the church. The church and being involved in its activities were sometimes the only things that kept her motivated. Also, Otto would never share their assets with her if she wasn't his wife. Divorced, she would be left with nothing. Should she even dare to pursue her thoughts any farther? If she decided to, and the feelings were still there, she'd think about solving her problem with Otto then.

"May he rest in peace." The clergyman sprinkled the coffin with holy water.

"Amen," the women dressed in black dresses and veils, the men dressed in black suits and ties, responded as they all started to depart from the area and leave the coffin.

Silence filled the air as Jimmy and Angela walked hand in hand. Jimmy thought about the last time he had seen his grandfather. What was his grandfather trying to tell him when he had caressed his hand? His grandfather's eyes seemed to talk to him. What was he saying? He could only guess now. He'd never know for sure.

Angela worried about Jimmy as they walked. She liked him very much. What about the war? The selective service was drafting young men. Would Jimmy get drafted and be sent over there? How could he get out of the draft and get out of going over there? Such a small country that no one had ever given a second thought to now terrified a whole nation. She recalled one neighbor boy that had come back from there. He no longer had his legs. Another neighbor boy had lost an arm. Yet another, who was married, was sent to Germany. Was that the only other alternative? If he married, would he be sent to Germany when he was drafted? If so, that would be safer than the other place--Vietnam. However, she was only a senior, and marriage before she had graduated from high school was not in her plans. She'd have to answer the question. How much did she want Jimmy?

Tonight, in the quiet of her room, once again she would pray. She would pray that the war would end and that her Jimmy wouldn't be drafted. Time would tell the future, but time tried patience and could be such an adversary.

As Amanda followed the others, walking by herself away from the grave sight, she noticed a small gravestone protruding above the ground. It set in solitude along a fieldstone fence tangled with wild grape vines. She stopped as she recognized the names engraved on the gray granite. She recalled unpleasant thoughts of the persons that now rested below her feet. They both had spent their lives finding pleasure in hurting others--her with her vicious tongue and him with his drunkenness. Now here they both lay--dead--no better than anyone else. They would be remembered for a long time in this town. Not for the way they lived, but for the way one had died. It surely was not the way that woman would like to have been remembered. Perhaps that was justice. She spent her life maligning others. Now it was her turn. The town would never forget how the neighbors recalled her throwing the scalding potato water in his face as he opened the kitchen door. Then, with his red, scalded face, how he angrily charged into the house after her as she fearfully fled from him. The sounds inside the house echoed through the quiet neighborhood--the screams --the shouting--the breaking glass--the smashing of furniture--and then--the explosive shot from a gun--followed by another explosive shot--then silence. Sprawled in a pool of red blood his lifeless body lay. She had killed him. Although she didn't spend one day in jail, her life was filled with the knowledge of the townspeople's whispers-- behind every door--every corner. In her later years, she had reaped the harvest of the many seeds of gossip that she had thrown into the wind. There was little sympathy for her. There were to many people in town whose good name had been destroyed by her maligning tongue over the years. "Justice Regina--justice to you both," she thought aloud and then turned to walk away.

Once again he watched her from a distance as he performed his gardening duties on the church premises. She would never see him trimming the evergreen shrubs. Even if she did, she would never recognize him. He didn't even recognize the man that he once was. No one would ever guess who the man was that did the varies "odd" jobs around the town and was only known as the gardener.

Although she walked through the cemetery alone, a man appeared to deliberately fall behind the rest of the crowd and wait for her at the edge of the cemetery. Curiously, the gardener stopped his work and watched. Why was the man waiting for her? As she ignored the man and walked past him, the man grabbed her arm. Sharply, she pulled away and increased her stride down the road toward her house.

The man stood still, snickered at the fact that he had annoyed her, and then walked in the direction of Lyra's. As the man passed more in view, the gardener recognized the man as Otto. Why did Otto do that to Amanda? When the gardener turned to watch Amanda, he found that she had vanished down the street.

Through the remainder of the day, Amanda monopolized the gardener's every thought. This situation had gone far enough, he thought. So much time had already been wasted. Why waste the little time there was left?

With his job completed and the gardening tools put in there proper place, he went to the clergyman's office to get his pay for the day. Rolling the money up, he stuffed it inside the pocket of his trousers and left the church premises. Down the street he walked, what should he do--stop in at Lyra's and drink himself into a drunken stupor--or? He looked over at Erickson's. Should he buy himself some new clothes, get himself shaved and go to see her? He would never know how she really felt about him if he didn't at least try to see her. Grabbing into his pocket, he pulled out the rolled up money. Straightening it as best he could, he walked toward the door. Before he entered, he turned and took another look at Lyra's. Was he sure he wanted to spend those few dollars at Erickson's?

Standing in front of the mirror in his room, he now held a razor in his hand. The unkept beard--the long hair--it was the style of the time, especially among the young. Guess it was a sign of revolt against an establishment they didn't understand or didn't care to understand. For him it was a way to hide himself from others and from himself. As he stared in the mirror, his image began to disappear and the mirror became a vision of what was to happen or what he wanted to happen:

Dressed in his new clothes, his shaved face, and trimmed hair he began the walk to her (their) house. His body felt refreshed and the scent of the soap, which had washed away the accumulated salty sweat from his pores, lingered on. He felt good about himself and the old feeling of self-worth began to fill his soul. He would be better than the foolish husband that had left her. Yes, he was that fool.

Then there it stood before him, the house where she lived. At the edge of the sidewalk, he stood and paused. Was she inside the house? Would he have the courage to find out--to knock on the door? He would never know if she still cared for him if he didn't walk up that sidewalk and onto the porch. It was a slow walk. Each step seemed to take forever. The house came closer. One by one, he climbed up the porch steps. The door came closer and closer. Standing in front of the door, he took his fingers and closed them tightly into the palm of his hand. Raising his hand to the door, he rapped on it. The door opened. His heart stopped. He looked at her. She stood silent --motionless. What would she do? The mirror wouldn't tell him. He would have to take his mirrored image into reality. Once again he asked himself if he possessed that courage? Courage by itself, with no help from the six-pack of beer that set on the dresser near his bed. Oh--just one drink would do no harm--would it? But could he stop after one? How determined was he really to have her again? But maybe she didn't want him anymore? Would he show his desire only to be turned away? She had every right to do that. After all, he was the one who had left. The new clothes lay on the bed. The razor was in his hand. The choice was his.

Alone at night, she would often sit and still think of him. Sometimes she felt as though she could feel him near her. Was he alive or dead? A rug covered the area of the floor where his blood had stained the boards that night. She was so relieved when she heard him moan and knew he was alive. She had begged him to stay. But that was not his choice--she was not his choice. Why would he ever come back? He had never really wanted her. Nevertheless, something inside still desired that he wanted her. Sometimes even an old woman can have fantasies. Although he did leave her, she was glad he hadn't taken Rosalia. With her thoughts, Amanda sat in the quiet of the room--surrounded by years of loneliness--always alone--forever alone.

****

The clock ticks away the time--darkness creeps into the night--sunshine leads the day--the earth turns from hour to hour--day to night--month to year. Time is ours to do with what we want. We can waste it worrying about petty things--or we can love and enjoy the ones we love and who love us as long as life allows us to. To late, we realize how short time really is. To often, more value is placed on material things. The value of love is not placed that high. Foolishly, we think we can always find it. It will always be there. So we say, "wait until the time is right," or we wait for a person who we think may be better. Love is often set aside until it is convenient for us. But to wait--is to lose. Love has no demands--no conditions--only value beyond compare. For to find someone who truly loves you is a once in a lifetime treasure--if you are lucky--and some are not that lucky. So if you have love--treasure it every moment. For moments have a tendency to disappear--and true love very seldom knocks twice in a lifetime and for some it never knocks at all.

Without love, the seeds of hatred, jealousy, greed, and lust thrive. Eventually, these seeds produce--one by one--the skeletons in the closet. Sometimes the skeletons torment there creator, sometimes others. For there is no justice--only life--and sometimes the sins of the past become the sins of today.

BUTLER PUBLIC LIBRARY
BUTLER, PENNSYLVANIA 16001

F STE
Sterr, Barbara Ann.
Skeletons in the closet /
Barbara Ann Sterr.